THEY
CALLED HIM
PREACHER

WILLIAM W. JOHNSTONE

THE FIRST MOUNTAIN MAN:
Cheyenne Challenge
and
Preacher and the Mountain Caesar

THEY CALLED HIM PREACHER

P

PINNACLE BOOKS
Kensington Publishing Corp.

www.kensingtonbooks.com

PINNACLE BOOKS are published by

Kensington Publishing Corp.
119 West 40th Street
New York, NY 10018

All Kensington titles, imprints, and distributed lines are available at
special quantity discounts for bulk purchases for sales promotions, pre-
miums, fund-raising, educational, or institutional use. Special book
excerpts or customized printings can also be created to fit specific needs.
For details, write or phone the office of the Kensington sales manager:
Kensington Publishing Corp., 119 West 40th Street, New York, NY 10018,
attn: Sales Department; phone 1-800-221-2647.

PINNACLE BOOKS, the Pinnacle logo, and the WWJ steer head logo are
Reg. U.S. Pat. & TM Off.

ISBN-13: 978-0-7860-4321-7
ISBN-10: 0-7860-4321-0

First printing of *Cheyenne Challenge*: August 1995
First printing of *Preacher and the Mountain Caesar*: October 1995
First printing of omnibus edition: May 2019

10 9 8 7 6 5 4 3 2 1

Printed in the United States of America

Electronic edition:

ISBN-13: 978-0-7860-4461-0 (e-book)
ISBN-10: 0-7860-4461-6 (e-book)

Also available as separate e-books:

Cheyenne Challenge
ISBN-13: 978-0-7860-3903-6
ISBN-10: 0-7860-3903-5

Preacher and the Mountain Messiah
ISBN-13: 978-0-7860-3904-3
ISBN-10: 0-7860-3904-3

CONTENTS

CHEYENNE CHALLENGE

BOOK ONE

1

Nothing much moves in the High Lonesome when Old Man Winter holds the land in his frigid grasp. The mountain man known simply as Preacher— though to many, the name held far more meaning than its simplicity implied—settled in at the cabin of an old friend, in a steep-walled valley that shielded it from the violent blasts of Canadian northers. He hunted for meat, smoked and jerked it, gathered other provisions, and watched the sky for signs of snow.

When the white powder lay hip-high, he had enough wood split and stacked to last the winter. By the time it grew to belly-high on a seventeen-hand horse, he had every small crack chinked, the chimney brushed clean, and a neat little corral set up with a four-sided shelter backed against one stern granite wall. Heavy yield in that winter of 1840–41 soon brought the snow level to roof-ridge height. Preacher had a tunnel out to the livestock, and kept the corral clear by some energetic, body-warming shoveling. Through it all, his cuts, scrapes, and bullet wounds healed.

Altogether, Preacher reckoned, when the buds began to swell on the willows, the cabin had been snug enough, nearly warm enough, and he had been almost amply fed. Lean and fit, although a little gaunt from his limited diet, Preacher began to itch to move along. He figured it was getting on toward late March and his only complaint came from a rhumaticky knee that resulted from too many hours in cold streams tending his traps in days gone by. Time to stretch like a cream-filled tomcat on the hearth and look for new places. The sun felt warm on Preacher's back as he breathed in the heady, leathery aroma of freshly saddle-soaped tack.

Looking up from tightening the last rope that secured the load on his packsaddle, he took in another chest-swelling breath tinged with the tang of pine resin and needles. Suddenly, his ebullient mood collapsed as he sensed the presence of another person. Preacher hadn't seen a single human since last October, when he went to the trading post at Trout Creek Pass for supplies. And he for certain didn't recall inviting anyone to drop in for a visit.

Thunder, his spotted-rump Appaloosa stud, had become aware of the intrusion, Preacher saw, as he cut his eyes to the suddenly tense animal. Thunder had gone wall-eyed, his ears pointed toward the front of the cabin beyond the corral. No doubt in his mind now, Preacher stepped away from the pack-horse and walked past the brush-and-pole shelter. With what quiet he could muster, he mucked his way through the March mud toward the stout log dwelling. His right hand rested on the butt of one awesome four-barrel pistol.

Behind Preacher, the horses snuffled and whickered, having caught human scent and that of at least one of their own kind. Preacher tensed slightly. One did not survive more than twenty years in the wilds without being constantly alert. Preacher had come to the Shining Mountains as a wet-behind-the-ears lad of twelve or so and had so far kept his hair. He sure didn't hanker to lose any of it now.

So, Preacher had the big four-shooter halfway out from behind the broad, red sash at his waist when he rounded the cabin. He came face-to-face with a small, rat-faced individual who exhibited considerable surprise.

"Uh! You be the mountain man name of Preacher?" a fittingly squeaky rodent voice asked.

Right off, Preacher took in the long, narrow head, over-sized nose, and small, deep-set black eyes. Buck teeth and slicked-back ebony hair completed the likeness to a weasel.

In fact, though Preacher didn't know it, the man before him went by the handle "Weasel" Carter. Preacher saw, too, that his unexpected visitor exhibited all the nervousness of a tomcat in a room full of rocking chairs. It all served to set Preacher's internal alarms to clanging.

"I be," Preacher allowed as he cut his eyes for a careful glance around the treeline.

That glance revealed to him some furtive movement among the aspen saplings and underbrush. His alarm system instantly primed Preacher for whatever might happen next.

Weasel Carter forced a fleeting, sickly, lipless smile, removed his hat and mopped his brow with a grimy kerchief. A fraction of a second later, Preacher's keen eyesight picked out a thin spurt of smoke from the priming pan of a flintlock rifle, an instant before he whipped out his four-shot and blasted a ball into the gut of his Judas goat.

At the same time, Preacher lashed out with his free hand, closed on a big fistful of shirt, and yanked his betrayer in front of himself. He did it in time for misfortune to strike the man in the form of the bullet meant for Preacher. A second later, three men rushed out of the concealment of the trees and fired at Preacher.

One ball moaned past, close to Preacher's left ear. The other two delivered more punishment to the runty piece of sorry trash Preacher held before himself like a shield. By then, Preacher had his four-barrel back in action. The hammer dropped on a brass cap and the big .54 caliber ball spat out in a cloud of smoke and frame.

It struck the nearest would-be assassin in the breastbone and tore out a fist-sized chunk of spine on the way out of his body. Preacher worked the complicated action, lining up another barrel, and fired again. Double-shotted, it had considerably more recoil, yet the charge went true and gut-shot a scruffy, bearded man whom Preacher reckoned deserved to be called "Dirt."

With his final load, Preacher blew away the left side of the head of the last killer trash. The flattened ball left a glittering brown eye dangling on a sallow, hollow cheek. Bleeding horribly, the thug managed to draw a pistol from his waistband and bang off a round in Preacher's direction.

Preacher dodged it as though it represented nothing more than a snowball. While he did, he switched for the other fully charged four-barrel and let fly. "I didn't ask for this," he yelled at the miraculously upright man, whose skull had been shot away in a wide trough above his left ear.

This time the ball entered the empty eye socket and blinked out the lights for the verminous gunman. That barrel always had shot a little high and right, Preacher recalled as he surveyed his littered dooryard.

"But I ain't disinclined to jine the dance to someone else's tune," he muttered a moment before Dirt moaned pitifully. Preacher crossed to the fallen ambusher. "You ain't got long. Speak," he commanded roughly.

"Th-tha's a fact. You done got me through the liver."

"Good riddance to trash like you, I say," Preacher growled as he knelt beside the dying man.

"You—you gonna jist leave me out here? Ain't gonna give me no Christian burial?"

"Weren't no Christian thing you done, sendin' that weasel-faced punk in to set me up, neither."

"Jeez, you really are Preacher."

"I be. Who sent you four after me?"

Dirt eyed Preacher a long moment. Then he swallowed hard. "Thirsty."

"You're gut-shot right enough. Shouldn't be givin' you nothin' liquidy." Then Preacher grunted, shrugged and came to his moccasins from one knee. "Seein' as you're dyin' anyhow, I don't find no harm in it. I'll be back . . . and I'll be wantin' the name of whoever it was sent you."

Preacher returned to Dirt's side after what the back-shooter thought to be an eternity. Preacher carried a small stoneware jug in one hand and a gourd ladle in the other. He eased down beside Dirt and put the ladle to the dying man's lips.

Dirt spluttered and tried to push it away. "That's not whiskey," he gasped out. "That—that's water."

"You got the right of it. The whiskey is for me, water for you. Last time, then I give you a whole world of more hurt. Who . . . sent . . . you?"

"Ez-Ezra Pease," Dirt gulped out, along with a bright crimson spew.

"Damn!" Preacher exploded. "I knewed that man were no good, first time I laid eyes on him. Ezra Pease," and Preacher pronounced the name to rhyme with peas. "Knew he was crooked, cheated the Injuns and whites alike, sold guns and whiskey to the Injuns. That finally riled me enough I beat the hell out of him and runned him out of the High Lonesome. He was tough, right enough, and I'd never have figgered him for a coward, that'd hire someone else to do his killing for him."

"Ain't no coward in Ez," Dirt retorted in a raspy whisper.

Preacher took a swig of whiskey. "That depends on whether you're on the receiving end or not. Where can I find him?"

Dirt forced a wan smile. "Ain't tellin' you that, Preacher."

Preacher shrugged, indifferently. "Then you'll take it to hell with you."

"I'll see you there," Dirt snarled, then he shivered violently and died.

"Maybe . . . maybe not," Preacher observed idly, took another swallow of whiskey and set the jug aside.

He roused himself and dragged the four corpses to a deep wash, rolled them down to the bottom and collapsed a wide section of dirt and rocks from the lip on top of them. That would at least keep the critters away from them. He gathered up their weapons and located their horses. These he freed from bridle and saddle and sent them off on their own.

"Time to get goin', Thunder," he announced when he returned to the corral.

Preacher swung into the saddle and caught up the lead rope to the pack animal, then gigged them into motion. Ezra Pease had returned, Preacher mused as the miles slowly rolled by in an endless stream of aspen, hemlock, and pines. It had all begun some ten years ago at Rendezvous. . . .

"New trader in camp," Jim Bridger confided to Preacher when he rode into the wide, gentle valley that housed Rendezvous for those in the fur trade that year. "I'll point him out. Like to see what you make of the cut of him."

Right then, Preacher suspected there might be something not quite right about the man. Bridger didn't often take to the judgments of other men, lessen he thought himself a mite too harsh in his own. Not that Jim Bridger was given to an overwhelming flow of the milk of human kindness. Most of his decisions were harsh. That's what kept him, or any man, alive out here in the Big Empty. All the same, Preacher ambled on into the growing gathering of white canvas tents, buffalo-hide tipis, brush lean-tos, and other mobile dwellings of the hard, adventurous men who worked the mountains for the valuable furs that fed a hungry eastern market.

He came upon the new man only a quarter mile into the swarm of white men, Indians, and breeds. A big canvas awning had been stretched from the side of a small, mountain-type wagon. In its shade, behind the upright brass rods that held the outer edge, piles of boxes and crates, and stacks of barrels had been laid out to make what their owner hoped would be an attractive display. Several of the barrels bore the black double-X mark that had already become a common symbol for the contents: whiskey.

Well and good, Preacher thought to himself. Wasn't a man jack among them who didn't plan on some powerful likkerin' up while there. That's a lot of what Rendezvous was all about. For his own taste, though, Preacher opted to push on until he found the stout, pink-faced German fellow from Pennsylvania who dispensed the finest Monongahela rye this side of heaven.

A couple of hours later, his campsite staked out and shelter erected, somewhat mellowed by some of that smooth whiskey, Preacher had his warm attitude of contentment shattered by an uproar. It reached his ears from the direction of the new trader's layout he had passed on the way in. Always curious, and always eager to view or get involved in a good brawl, buckskin-clad streams of mountain men flowed past Preacher's haven.

Smacking his lips, Preacher put aside the jug of Mononga-hela rye, pushed upright to his moccasins and trotted off to witness the excitement. He elbowed his way between Slippery Jim and Broken Jaw Sloane to get a better view. The new trader, with the help of a pair of louts who turned out to be his swampers, was whipping up on a slender, youthful Nez Perce brave. The white man looked to be in his mid to late thirties, which put him a good ten to twelve years older than Preacher at that time. While the louts held down the teenaged Nez Perce, the factor smashed vicious, painful blows to the Indian's face.

"You were gonna steal that knife, gawdamnit, I saw you," he roared.

"No, no," the brave protested in his own language, which Preacher had just put in six long months of winter learning. "I give two hands sable skins. Poor pelts you say," he added in heavily accented English. "Two hands sable skins for one knife. That too much but I take."

His watery blue eyes narrowed, the trader sneered back at the bleeding Indian. He hit the boy twice more and growled. "You don't have any way to prove that, buck. So, give up that knife and get out of here before I finish you off."

"I got it right here, Ez," one thick-lipped lout blurted, reaching under the securing thong of the Nez Perce's loin-cloth and pulling free a scabbarded Green River black iron butcher knife.

"Good. Toss it on the table over there." He bunched the youngster's hunting shirt in both fists and yanked the bruised and blood-smeared Indian upright. Ez spun him and gave the groggy youth a powerful boot to his posterior.

Propelled forward off balance, the Nez Perce rebounded off the shoulders of laughing mountain men. Some offered him a swig from a jug of liquor, others gave him friendly claps on the shoulders, or pitying looks. Two more rocky steps and he came up against the broad chest of Preacher.

"Blue Heron," Preacher said softly, recognizing the youth.

"White Wolf. That man cheats. He lies. He steals from us." It wasn't a self-pitying whine, or an excuse, it was said with the hot fire of anger burning brightly.

"You are sure?"

"I am sure," Blue Heron responded.

For a moment, Preacher looked beyond the shoulder of the young Indian and his eyes grew to slits. "It will be taken care of."

"White Wolf does not lie. I will be satisfied. Come visit us again. My sister misses you awfully." The last was delivered with as much as a mischievous expression as his bruised features could produce.

Preacher chose to ignore this reference to his amorous proclivities of the past winter. "Go with the wind, Blue Heron."

Despite his pain and discomfort, Blue Heron's eyes twinkled. "Find sleep in a warm lodge, White Wolf."

Their exchange had been observed by Ez, who came at Preacher in a rush. "What'd that thievin' Hole-in-Nose say to you?"

Preacher gave him a cool, appraising gaze. "Nothin' that's any of your business, feller."

"B'God it is my business."

"Nope. Not by half," Preacher assured him. Then, his eyes the color of glare-ice, he added. "But I can make it a whole lot of mine."

Ez glowered as he studied the young man before him. Lean-hipped and rawhide tough, Ez could see this stranger had tremendous power in his upper body. He figured him to be smart, too, since he had learned that heathen savage's turkey-gobble lingo. Something about the casual way he wore those two .50 caliber pistols in his sash warned Ez that this stranger could be panther quick and deadly accurate with them. That, most of all, gave him pause. With a snort of impatience, Ez broke their locked gaze first.

He turned on one boot heel and stomped off. Slippery Jim

and several others swarmed around Preacher in the next instant to welcome him and press invitations on him to visit firesides for a friendly round of "cussin', discussin', and drinkin'." Preacher said yes to all, though many knew full well he would not make it to their camp that night. Preacher spent the rest of the day asking questions about the new trader, Ez, and sharing jugs.

First off, he got a last name for the surly man. Pease. "He says it like them little green vegables," Beckworth informed Preacher. Coupled with what he had witnessed, Preacher soon developed an image of the man which far from pleased him. Yet, Ez Pease had done nothing directly to Preacher and he, like most of his fellow trappers, strongly believed in a man tending his own trapline.

As a result, Preacher decided to leave well enough alone. Yet, if the shadow of Pease ever fell across his path, Preacher would be more than happy to do something about it. The opportunity had come sooner than Preacher expected.

Three days went by in the usual boozy, raucous *bonhomie* of Rendezvous. Preacher had all but forgotten the incident with his young Nez Perce friend. He had traded with the boy's father for Thunder. Now, horse trading was serious business to the Nez Perce. If a feller entered into the spirit of it, and they believed he had treated them fairly, although shrewdly, they respected that man for it. If he was generous with his sugar and coffee in the bargain, that man could have friends for life. Not forgetting, of course, that Injuns have notions. The day that recalled all of this to Preacher began normally enough.

Around noon, he and Big Foot Joe got into an eating contest. The man who could consume just one more than half of the small lumps of force meat, onions, and wild rice in a chain of pit-roasted intestine, in this case from an elk, was the winner. He split half of the gold, pelts, or other items bet on the outcome. Preacher's stout, youthful teeth gave him an advantage, which put him well on the way to the mid-point in the chain when an uproar rose from the southern end of the string of camps.

Preacher ignored them and munched on. More voices joined the clamor of support for opposing sides. They ended abruptly in a shout of alarm.

"Look out!" Followed by the flat report of a pistol shot.

Ah, hell. Just when I had this thing won, Preacher silently lamented. He had no doubt as to the source of the disturbance, or who had fired his weapon. He bit off the tasty rope and set out at a trot for the gathering crowd of men and haze of dust that rose in the still air of the valley.

Although independent, tough, and wild, several men gave way when they saw the hard expression on the face of Preacher as he approached the center of the dispute. A mountain man lay, writhing, on the ground, shot through the meaty place above one hip bone. Two others held onto the trader, Ezra Pease, who still waved a smoking pistol in one hand.

One old-timer nodded a curt greeting to Preacher and brought the young mountain man up to date. "Liver Eatin' Davis caught that one sellin' a gun to an Injun.'

"Ain't nobody's business who I sell to or what," Pease growled.

"It is in this neck o' the woods," a burly mountain man with a flaming beard snapped.

Considered quite young, especially by mountain man standards, Preacher had already accumulated a considerable reputation. Enough so that when he stepped forward, the others fell silent to hear what he had to say about the situation. Preacher approached Pease and got right up close and personal in his face.

"Pease, you've out-lived your welcome at this Rendezvous. Hell, in all the Big Empty for that matter." Preacher paused and cut his eyes from face to face in the crowd. "I reckon these fellers will go along with me when I say we want you out of camp before nightfall."

A sneer broke out on the face of Pease. "Why, hell, you ain't even dry behind the ears as yet. Who are you to tell me that?"

"I'm the man who's an inch from slittin' yer gizzard, which is reason enough."

Pease cut his eyes to the men holding him. "Turn me loose. I'll show this whippersnapper where the bear crapped in the buckwheat."

Knowing grins passed between his captors. "Oh, we'd be mighty pleased if you did," Yellowstone Frank Parks, a close friend of Preacher's, responded, releasing the arm he held.

Ezra Pease had only time to realize his challenge had been accepted when one of Preacher's big fists smashed into his thin, bloodless lips. Strands of his carroty mustache bit into split flesh and those lips turned right neigh bloody all at once. Preacher followed up with a looping left to the side of Peas's head. It staggered the corrupt trader and set his legs wobbly. Dimly he saw an opening and drove the muzzle of his empty pistol into Preacher's exposed belly.

Hard muscle absorbed most of the shock, yet the blow doubled Preacher over and part of the air in his lungs whooshed out. He raised both arms to block the attack he expected to come at his head. He had reckoned rightly. Still grasping the pistol, Pease slashed downward intent on breaking Preacher's wrist. The wooden forestock landed on a thick, wiry forearm instead. It would leave a nasty bruise, but at the time, Preacher hardly felt it.

Without pause, he raised a knee between the wide-spread legs of Pease and rammed it solidly into the cheat's left thigh. That brought Pease to his knees. He dropped the empty pistol and groped for another. Preacher kicked him in the face. Pease flopped over backward and Preacher was on him in a flash.

Instantly they began to roll over and grapple for an advantage. Pease gradually worked his arms down into position around Preacher's ribs. Slowly he raised one leg to get his knee into position to thrust violently upward on Preacher's stomach and snap downward with his arms. The result would be to break the back of the younger man. Preacher would have none of it, however.

He wooled his head around until the crown fitted under the chin of Pease. Then he set his moccasin toes and rammed upward. Pease's yellowed teeth clopped closed with a violent snap. A howl followed as stressed nerves signaled that the crooked trader had bitten through his tongue. Blood quickly followed in a gush and his grip slackened.

It proved enough for Preacher, who broke the bear hug and came up to batter the exposed face of Pease with a series of rights and lefts. Pease swung from the side and hard knuckles put a cut on Preacher's right cheek. A strong right rocked back the young mountain man's head. Preacher punched Pease's mushed mouth again and sprang to his moccasins. Pease slowly followed.

Dazed, yet undefeated, Pease tried to carry the fight to Preacher. A sizzling left and right met his charge. Preacher danced away and pounded Pease in the middle. Then he worked on the chest, at last he directed his violent onslaught to the sagging head of Pease. For the second time, Pease went to his knees. Preacher squared up facing him, measured the angle, and popped hard knuckles into Pease's forehead. The lights went out and Pease crumpled in the dirt, jerked spasmodically for a few seconds and went still. A faint snore blubbered through his smashed lips.

Preacher stumbled away to wash off the blood, slobber, and dirt that clung to him, oblivious of the man he had defeated. Behind him, the other mountain men gathered up the stock in trade Pease had brought with him, loaded his wagons and provided an escort out of the valley.

And now Pease was back . . .

Preacher shook off the dark recollection as he topped the crest of a low saddle and found himself facing four hard, coppery faces, topped by black, braided hair, with eagle feathers slanted downward from the back, past the left ear. Preacher also noted that the four Indians held their bows casually, low over their saddle pads, and that arrows had already been nocked.

2

Preacher's hand automatically dropped to the smooth butt-grip of one four-barrel pistol at sight of the warriors. Then he recognized the older man in the middle. Talks To Clouds could be considered an old friend. Particularly since he had been the man Preacher traded with for Thunder. Now a fleeting smile curled the Nez Perce's full lips.

"Ghost Wolf. I am pleased to see you," Talks To Clouds broke the silence in his own tongue.

"And I, you. It has been a long time," Preacher acknowledged.

"Too long for friends who have shared meat and salt," the expert horse breeder responded.

Preacher studied the men with Talks To Clouds. They were not painted for war and appeared well enough at ease. "What brings you so far from your green valley?"

"We trade horses with the Cheyenne. My son remembers you. I heard of what you did. An old man is grateful."

Preacher grunted; that had been ten years ago. He had traded for Thunder only four years past. No accounting for the depth of an Injun's gratitude. "You are not an old man."

"I am if I must rely on others to protect my own." Talks To Clouds paused, then gestured behind him. "Come, Young Joseph is watching our spotted ponies." He paused, chuckled. "Only he is not so young anymore. He is a father. A boy named In-Mut-Too-Yah-Lat-Lat* was born to him this past winter. Already, he is being called Young Joseph. We will eat, drink coffee, talk of the times since we last saw one another."

An agreeable nod preceded Preacher's answer. "It would be my pleasure."

The Nez Perce had located their camp over the next rise. The camp's appearance completely relaxed Preacher's innate caution. Women and children accompanied the group of half a dozen warriors and their sub-chief, Talks To Clouds. The youngsters swarmed out to surround Preacher when he was recognized. Laughing, he dismounted to bend and chuck the girls under their chubby chins, eliciting giggles all around.

Then he turned and hoisted the four boys to the back of Thunder and let them walk the Appaloosa stallion into the encampment. The boys had the big horse cooled out by gentle walking in just under a half hour. By then, the women had completed preparations and served up a meal of thick, rich venison stew, fry-bread, and cattail slips. Preacher made a generous offer of salt, coffee, and sugar that complemented the feast to the satisfaction of all.

When everything was in readiness, the men filled bowls and settled in to enjoy. Talk centered around the weather, the unusually early spring in particular. Forked Tail gestured to the east and made the sign for the Sioux.

"That is why we decide to go afar in our trading of horses. Talks To Clouds wants to reach the Dakota. They are said to be hungry for our spotted ponies. And not to eat them," he added with an expression of disgust.

"There was no snow left in the valley of Wil-Ah-Met by the first of the Moon of Returning Buds," Talks To Clouds verified. "I see many warm buffalo robes for next winter if we can start early."

"Good idea," Preacher contributed. "How are things between here and your valley?"

*This is the Nez Perce name of Chief Joseph, who later led his people in resisting white encroachment of their reservation and on a desperate flight to reach Canada. He was captured by Nelson Miles.

Talks To Clouds and the others considered it. "Peaceful. Except for the Blackfeet. There is much green showing and it will be a fat spring. That should keep peace."

Always the Blackfeet, Preacher ruminated. He'd get into that after the eating was done. He asked of men among the Nez Perce he had known, of babies born, and the talk slid away the time until their bowls had been emptied. As a man, those around the small fire in the lodge of Talks To Clouds wiped grease from their chins, rubbed full bellies, and belched loudly. At once the women and children fell to their eats. Once more, and more appropriately according to Indian etiquette, the man-talk turned to the world around them.

"Is there anything that would cause you to say the Blackfeet are more troublesome than usual?" Preacher cautiously prompted.

Talks To Clouds broke out a pipe, a habit obtained from the plains tribes, and tamped it full of kinnikinnick and wild tobacco. He lighted it with a coal and drew a long, satisfying puff before answering. "Yes, White Wolf. They are already making for war. They have many guns, provided by white men in trade for pelts and horses. It is not a good thing."

Preacher nodded and Forked Tail reached for the pipe, took a drag, then put in, "The word on the wind is that the Northern Cheyenne are also fixing to make war medicine when spring opens up a little more."

That's odd, Preacher thought, and frowned. Although known as fierce fighters and highly territorial, most skirmishes with the Cheyenne in the past had been between small bands of warriors and some enemy tribe, to settle a score or to raid for horses. That, or in reaction to what must appear to be an avalanche of whites pressing westward.

Talks To Clouds spoke again. "The Cheyenne will be making war on the Blackfeet, that is certain. They must do so to protect the western villages. It is said they know of the white men arming the Blackfeet." He spat, to show his contempt for such an action.

"It looks bad, then?" Preacher pressed.

"Yes. We may spend the summer in trading with the Dakota and even the Omaha. Let the fighting wear itself out, and then we can go home with our robes."

"Will they come south?" Preacher asked.

Talks To Clouds considered this. "I think so. One or the other. Whoever gets the worst of their fight together."

Preacher sighed and cleared his throat. "I would be sorry to see that."

A fleeting smile lifted the corners of the mouth of Talks To Clouds. "So would I. Yet, we must accept what we get."

Preacher ruminated on all he had heard through the evening. When the night's chill reminded him, he broke out his bedroll and settled down for the night. When morning came, he would head on toward Trout Creek Pass.

Preacher left for the trading post before daylight. Talks To Clouds stood silently in the open door flap of his lodge and waved a dimly seen salute to his friend. Preacher rode with the warmth of that friendship. He also rode with the awareness of the return of Ezra Pease. Constantly on the lookout for any more low-grade trash who might be working for Pease, he kept well below the ridge lines and frequently circled on his back-trail.

Ezra Pease removed the floppy felt hat from his head and ran a hand over the balding dome with its fringe of carroty hair. His fractured smile was hidden from the men with him, though they caught his high spirits from the tone of his voice.

"There it is, fellers. Just like them wanderin' Injuns told us. Black Hand's village. I reckon they've had time to hear about the Blackfeet. Should be glad to see us."

"We break out the whiskey first, huh, boss?" a not-too-bright thug named Bartholamue Haskel gulped out between chuckles. "Likker up them bucks right good, huh—huh—huh?"

"Awh, hell, Haz," Ezra complained, embarrassed by the low state of the henchmen he had been able to attract.

In truth, Ezra had to admit, times had not been good for

him. His fortunes had plummeted, rather than soaring as he always envisioned. After his ignominious expulsion from these mountains some ten years past, Pease had wandered his way back to St. Louis. Down on his luck, he had been forced to lower himself to the most basic of scams; for half a year he rolled drunks for whatever they had on their bodies.

He had nearly been caught by the law several times. And he had been caught once by a riverboat man who appeared a whole lot more drunk than he turned out to be. The brawny riverboater thoroughly and soundly beat the living hell out of Pease. He'd done a job to rival that handed out by Preacher. Ezra Pease lay in a bed for three weeks recovering, and thought of both those shaming incidents.

When he could once again face his fellow man on the streets of St. Louis, he visited a dockside swill house that he had frequented when first in town. There he bought whiskey and many beers for furtive men who inveterately glanced nervously over their shoulders at the doorway. They drank his whiskey and chased it with the beer and nodded in silent agreement.

After three days of this, Ezra Pease and his gathering of bullyboys set out one night to find a certain loudmouthed rafter. They located him, all right. What resulted was that Ezra again got the tom-turkey crap stomped out of himself. He wound up in the hospital this time. When he regained consciousness, he learned the identity of his assailant. Mike Fink.

By damn, that was worser than Preacher, Pease reasoned. Because Preacher was near to a thousand miles away and no immediate threat. Ezra Pease would learn the error of his judgment when he finally worked up nerve enough to return to the High Lonesome.

Meanwhile, he had to recover from his broken bones, mashed face, one chewed ear, and an eye that no longer saw clearly. Mike Fink had missed by only a fraction of an inch from gouging the orb from its socket. While he mended, Pease went about rebuilding his minute criminal empire. He left the infirmary with seven men solidly behind him. They drifted into Illinois and tried stagecoach robberies.

Three of them died in the process and the survivors did five to nine years in prison. Ezra Pease proved to be a model prisoner and was released after only four years and seven months for good behavior. He thanked the warden with almost fawning gratitude and immediately set out to organize a new, better, and definitely stronger gang.

At last, it seemed, his fortunes had taken a turn for the better. Ezra Pease met Titus Vickers inside prison, and when the opportunity presented itself, Pease broke Vickers free from the chain gang on which he labored in a granite quarry in southeastern Illinois. Together they attracted a dozen hard men, who knew how to fight with tooth, nail, knife, and gun.

Some scattered successes drew more of those disinclined to exert any honest effort or sweat to earn a living. Before long, he had thirty heavily armed, morally bankrupt representatives of the worst dregs of border trash, scoff-laws, back-shooters, rapists, and sadists ever assembled in one place at one time. It offered a splendid promise for the future.

They spilled over into Missouri. Pickings were slim there. All the while, Ezra Pease had his dreams disturbed by a slowly awakening vision. There was vast wealth just waiting for the picking out beyond the prairie. Even though the fur trade had all but dried up, an enormous fortune waited only for an enterprising man to seize it. When the image became full formed, Ezra and Titus conferred with a shadowy group from New York, and announced to their men that they would outfit an expedition to the far off Shining Mountains.

Buffalo robes and hides were beginning to bring high prices back East. Those could be traded for, if one had the right things to offer the Indians. And Ezra knew what they wanted: guns, powder and shot, and whiskey. Better still, he knew that gold just waited out there. He had seen plenty evidence of it during his short, disastrous year as a trader. Mining it would be easy.

More people moved west every year. They left St. Louis

and Independence by the hundreds from March to June. Before long it would be in the thousands. Some of them never made it. Those not killed by accident, disease, or Indians sometimes went mad from the emptiness, or got lost, and wandered off to simply disappear. They could be found by someone intent and with the time to look for them. And they would make excellent slaves to produce that precious yellow metal.

Another snicker from Bartholamue Haskel jerked Ezra Pease out of his reverie. He blinked and refocused his eyes on the thin smoke trails rising from cook fires before the Cheyenne red-topped lodges.

"We'll go on down now, and get all we can get," he declared.

Black Hand knew of the white men long before they came into view on the downslope toward the camp. He had known of them for three days. That would have surprised Ezra Pease. He had not seen any sign of Indians since leaving the last Blackfoot village, where they had traded munitions for high quality beadwork buckskins, bearskin robes and other items. He had not spent enough time among the trappers and ridge runners of the High Lonesome to be familiar with the statement that had become almost their credo.

"Just because you don't see any Injuns, don't mean they ain't there."

Often, those who lived in ignorance of that didn't live long. But the day would prove beneficent to Ezra Pease and his worthless followers, if barely. Black Hand had heard of the rifles, powder, shot, and bar lead these men brought with them. He badly wanted them, along with bullet molds and replacement ramrods for the older weapons in the Cheyenne camp. So, he made ready to welcome the white men.

To do that, he paid them the infrequent compliment of meeting them at the edge of the village, instead of waiting in his lodge until they made their presence known. Behind him ranged a dozen warriors, one for each of the whites, weapons to hand but not held at the ready. A ring of women, children, and camp dogs formed behind them. Cheyenne ponies neighed greetings to their iron-shod brothers from the meadow to the left. The one who looked to be the whites' leader reined up in front of Black Hand and made the universal sign for peace.

"I am called Pease," he announced.

Better he spoke the language of the people, Black Hand thought as he answered in fair English. "I am Black Hand."

"Good," Pease responded, then went on to diminish their welcome. "I'm glad someone around here speaks a sensible language. We've come to trade."

"What do you have to trade with us?"

Grinning, Pease turned in the saddle and gestured to one of the heavily laden packhorses. "Well, now, I was just fixin' to show you. I think your bucks are gonna like what we have."

"Come in among our lodges then. We will eat, smoke, then make trade." A slight frown furrowed the high, smooth brow of Black Hand. He wanted the rifles this man brought, but he didn't like the insulting way the one called Pease spoke.

"Mighty generous of you, Chief, but we ain't got the time. Need to be pushin' on. We'll just break out our goods right here."

"Too close to the ponies," Black Hand protested.

Meanin' you know we've got rifles, you old fox, Pease thought as he gave in with a shrug and led the way behind the chief to the center of the village. All considered, the white men received a warm welcome. Black Hand did give in to their time concerns by offering the bare minimum of food, a quantity any decent Cheyenne would consider insultingly small. While the women brought it, Pease directed his henchmen to unload the whiskey and open one crate of rifles.

Black Hand's eyes narrowed when he recognized the XX marking on the barrels taken from the gray horse. For all he wanted the rifles, he had no use of the spirit-stealing water.

Even so, convention required him to wait, with mounting anger, until Pease had finished rambling on about the excellence of the rifles he had brought.

"You may stay and trade, but the headache water must go," Black Hand stated with a noticeable lack of diplomacy.

Pease took on an expression as though he had just been struck. "Well, now, I don't see any reason for that. 'Never trust a man who won't take a drink,' my poppa always said. Won't do no harm. C'mon, Chief, I'll fill you the first cup."

"Take it out of my village," Black Hand demanded hotly.

Angry mutters rose among the warriors surrounding the white men, and Pease noted that they apparently shared their chief's dislike of liquor. There appeared to be nearly twenty-five of them, all armed. Although only a few had pistols or old trade muskets, Pease knew that a good man could get off six arrows in the time it took to recharge a rifle or pistol. At this range it would be slaughter.

He also considered their usual practice of getting the savages drunk and then trading for inferior rifles and even smooth-bores instead of the fine weapons displayed beforehand. They got more valuable trade items that way, too. Pease noticed the reaction of his men. They were spoiling to do something rash. If they wanted to come out of this with their hair, he had to act fast.

"Uh—sure. Anything you say, Chief. You boys put that whiskey back on the packsaddle, hear?"

Two hours went by haggling over the rifles. Shrewd barterers, the Cheyenne gave precious little of value and wound up with the good weapons to boot. All in all, Ezra Pease considered they had gotten the better of the deal in that they got out of the camp with scalps in place.

From the top of the ridge, he looked back on the village. "We're coming back to this place," he declared ominously.

3

Three of the scruffiest louse-infested louts Preacher had ever seen in the Big Empty hunkered down around a hastily constructed ring of stones at the bottom of the slope. They warmed their hands over the coals that roasted hunks of fresh-killed venison and slopped down coffee from steaming tin cups. He took that in with his first glance. Then his eyes narrowed and his lips turned down as he viewed the rest of the scene.

A trio of men lay sprawled in death, two of them clearly back-shot. A fourth, whom Preacher recognized at once, lay with his back against an aspen sapling, several turns of rope binding him in place. He had also been shot, although in the leg. John Luscomb, Preacher named the captive as he studied the grayed face behind a brush of beard.

That would make the others Quail Egg Walker, Trent Luddy, and 'Possum Smith. The four had been partnered up for a number of years, trying to make up for low prices with volume. They had also scouted for a couple of the pestiferous wagon trains making the westward push, shot meat for the soldier boys, and done other odd jobs available to men who preferred to live the solitary, free life of the High Lonesome. Well, they had been done dirt, for certain sure.

One of the many things no mountain man could abide was treachery. The ruined campsite showed no indication of a pro-longed struggle. No doubt, Preacher read the signs, the three piles of buzzard puke had come on friendly, gotten in among Luscomb and the others and done their foul deed. It seemed to Preacher that a little lesson in right and wrong was in need.

With that in mind, he withdrew from the screening line of pines and walked Thunder down in the clear. At about a hundred yards, he howdied the camp and asked to ride in. Their bellies full of pilfered supplies and fresh meat, the three killers tended to be friendly. And, after all, it was only one man. They could easily jump him, rob him, and kill him once his suspicions cooled down.

Preacher approached with caution and dismounted still some distance from the scuzzy trash. He cut his eyes around the clearing. "Looks like you had some ruckus."

"That we did, friend," said a gap-toothed brute with a brow so low it left no room to hang a hat on his forehead. "This bunch of driftin' trash came up on us and tried to give us what for. We tooken care of them, didn' we, boys?"

"Sure enough. That's what we did, all right," a sawed-off, shallow-faced punk with dirty yellow hair joined in.

"Don't reckon anyone will miss them," Preacher drawled.

"No. Not likely. It's gettin' so a man don't know who to trust out here anymore."

Preacher fought to keep the disgust from showing on his face. "I'd say that's mighty keen figgerin'." He'd heard enough of their lies. So he cut his eyes to Luscomb. "What do you figger ought to be done now, John?"

"Kill 'em all, Preacher." John Luscomb gave the obvious answer.

"Preacher!" the acne-ravaged punk squealed.

"Ohmygod!" gulped the smooth liar.

"Mother Mary, help me!" an Irish-looking dirtbag wailed.

In all their reactions, every one of them forgot to draw iron. Preacher's big, right-hand pistol spoke with final authority. The first barrel, double-shotted, discharged its burden into the chest and gut of the gap-toothed braggard. He promptly sat down, spraddle legged, and lost his supper. Preacher ignored him to turn another barrel into position.

He banged off another twin load at about the same time as the remaining pair concluded that they had a fight on their hands. The black-haired son of Erin actually got to one of a trio of pistols shoved behind his wide leather belt. He had it out and the hammer back when Preacher's second shot took him through the throat and his open, cursing mouth.

His legs jerked reflexively and he flopped over on his back as the rear of his skull exploded in the late afternoon air. By then, Preacher had worked the complicated trigger mechanism to put the next barrel in line.

"It flat irritates me," he lectured the dough-faced fugitive from someone's secondary school, "when I come across four men I count as friends, one shot up an' the others murdered in cold blood by buzzard punks like you three."

"I didn' have anythin' to do with it," the juvenile trash whined as he wet his trousers.

"You don't lie any better than these other horses' patoots. Now, you gonna use one of those pistols you're totin' or do you want to settle it another way?"

Such an option had not occurred to the trashy brat. "Like what?"

Preacher's lips quirked rapidly up and down. "There's always knives. Or how about war hawks? I'm sure John here would lend you his."

The young punk blanched even whiter. "I won't do nothin' like this ever again, I swear it," he pleaded.

"Oh, I know you won't. 'Cause you'd best face it, you murderin' scum. One way or the other, you're gonna die this very day."

"But I don't want to die! I'm—I'm too young to die."

"You're old enough to pack those shooters, you're old enough to die with one of them in your hand. Now, pull iron, or I'll just up and kill you with my bare hands," Preacher growled ferociously.

Quaking with fear, desperation decided the boy's actions. He clamped palsied fingers around the butt-stock of a Hopkins & Allen .64 caliber single-barrel pistol, and yanked it free from his waistband. As he raised it to eye level, he was surprised to see the black hole of the awesome four-barrel pistol in Preacher's hand centered steadily on his forehead. Flame spurted from the muzzle and became the last thing that piece of human vermin ever saw.

Preacher watched him twitch awhile, then walked over to the aspen. He bent low and cut John Luscomb free. A second length bound the mountain man's hands behind him. Preacher sliced through it and Luscomb remained in place, flexed his wrists, rubbed them to revive circulation and beamed a wide smile up at his rescuer.

"You done good, Preacher."

"I'm only sorry I didn't happen along sooner. Might have saved your partners." He knelt beside Luscomb and cut away the buckskin trouser leg to reveal the wound.

"We all got our time to be called," John Luscomb responded philosophically.

Preacher nodded agreement. "Though it don't seem fittin' to be at the hands of maggoty trash like these. I got some Who-Shot-John. Take a few knocks and hang on."

"I'll wait till it's over," a white-lipped John Luscomb said. Preacher nodded, then probed the through-and-through hole with a peeled willow stick. Luscomb gasped, gritted his teeth and nearly passed out. When Preacher finished his exploration, he rocked back on moccasin heels.

"It went plum through."

"Good. Didn't hit no bleeder either, or I'd be a goner by now. We gonna bury them?" Luscomb asked.

"Hell no. Let the buzzards claim their own. Where you headin', John?"

"With this bullet through my leg, I reckon I'll mosey up toward the trading post."

"I'm for Trout Crick Pass myself," Preacher advised him, as he bandaged Luscomb's wound. "Don't reckon you'll fork a horse too well. I'll rig a travois an' come mornin' we can go on in together."

"Mighty nice of you, Preacher. I'll be obliged."

"Naw, you won't." He offered the whiskey jug. "Not after givin' me such a prime opportunity to rid the earth of some of its filth. Can you do for some eats and coffee while I cut saplin's and tend my horseflesh?"

"Sure enough. If they didn't eat it all."

"I can see to that, if needs be," Preacher added as he headed to picket out and unsaddle Thunder and the pack-horse. First, though, he saw to reloading his pistol. Never could tell what else might happen by.

Ezra Pease sat on a folding camp stool and glowered into the embers of the fire in front of his gray canvas tent. The more he thought of the loss of high-quality rifles and plenty of powder, lead, and molds to those stinking savages, the madder he got. Forced to knuckle under to a man whose people had not even managed to invent the wheel rubbed him in a sore spot. He had been smarting over it for several days.

Morale had fallen among the men as a result. He knew that, though would have been hard-pressed to articulate it that way. The men he sent for supplies had not been in camp as yet to hear of the humiliation. Perhaps when they returned their enthusiasm would fire up the others. Pease came to his boots and crossed to a small trestle table, where he poured half a cup of good Tennessee sour mash from a barrel of his private stock. None of that snake-head rotgut he provided for the Indians for as refined a taste as his. After the second sip, sudden inspiration illuminated him.

"Vic," he summoned his second in command. "Come here." When the lean, hard six-footer arrived, worry lines furrowed his brow. It gave his gaunt face more of a human aspect, rather than the likeness of a skull, its usual appearance. "It's bound to be another three, four days before Ham and the boys get back from the pass. I want to round up everyone in camp at first light tomorrow. We're going back to teach those savages a lesson."

"You think that's wise, Ez?" Titus Vickers asked.

"I think it's necessary, which counts for more. You've seen how the men go around all hang-dog. Give them a little blood to let and they'll snap right out of it."

Preacher's keen hearing, enhanced by years of having little or nothing to dull it, picked up the clamor long before they scaled the long, muddy slope to the clearing at the summit of Trout Creek Pass. He screwed his features into an expression of distaste, halted Thunder and went back to check on John Luscomb. Hands on hips, Preacher tilted his head in the direction of the clearing ahead.

"Can ya hear that carryin' on?"

"Don't, I reckon. Sounds like a passel more of them brain-numb pilgrims."

"Perzactly," Preacher snapped with a sharp snort. "Now what in tarnation could have brought them clear up here? Ain't no clear trail to the Oregon Trail this-a-way."

"No accountin' for pilgrims' whims, Preacher. Say, you got a bit more of that Who Flung Chuck? My leg's givin' me a mite of a twinge."

A gross understatement. Mountain men were known for many things, a high pain threshold one of the more notable. Any lesser man than John Luscomb would have been a screaming wretch long before this. Preacher dug into the smaller of two parfleche envelopes on the right side of the packsaddle and pulled out his rapidly dwindling supply of whiskey.

"Swill down your fill, John. We'll be resupplyin' right soon."

"How much longer?"

"Quarter hour, tops," Preacher estimated.

"That long? From the beller that's rollin' down on us, I'd have judged we be no more than a long rifle shot from the place."

"Waugh! When I think of all them East Coast idjits swarmin' out here, ruinin' our clean, purty-smellin' country, I just just want to bawl." Preacher did a double-take, blinked, and nodded. "I do. I done said it an' I mean it, too. Makes a feller plu-perfect sick to see it all happenin'."

"Won't argue with you," Luscomb said by way of agreement. "First thing you know, they'll be puttin' them iron rails out here with those steam cars runnin' on 'em."

Preacher wore a rueful expression. "Pilgrim type told me about them near a year ago. Didn't believe him at the time. Then I flung myself back East way for a spell and seen them with my own eyes. Still don't know if I believe in them. Somethin' that'd go that fast would plain suck the air out of a body."

"Seems likely." Luscomb took another long pull, smacked sallow lips. "Might as well be on our way." He offered the jug. "Best you take a little to keep off the chill."

Preacher accepted the ceramic jug and put it to his lips. His Adam's apple rose once, sank, then rose again, and went still. "A little is all there was, John." He peered closely at the container. "You know, I think this thing's got a hole in it."

Glassy-eyed, John slurred his words. "Sure does. Right up there at the top . . . for whiss I'm e-ternal grateful." Gently, he slumped into a boozy daze.

Preacher got the horses moving again and his scowl deepened with each hoof fall as he gradually made out the antlike crawl of humanity between buildings and white-capped wagon boxes. "Damn," he muttered over and over. "Damn pilgrims."

"Stars and garters!" the big, burly man in the doorway to the trading post bellowed when he recognized the rider approaching. "It's Preacher. How'd you winter out in that place?"

"Just fine, Walt," Preacher answered.

Then Walt Hayward saw the bundle on the travois. "Who you got here?"

"John Luscomb. He ran afoul of some cowardly trash."

Hayward bustled to the travois. His belly swelled out as far as his barrel chest, but consisted of a slab of solid muscle. He frowned as he looked down on the wounded man.

"We'll have to get you in a good bed for a while," he commiserated.

Luscomb roused enough to respond. "I'd rather it were a lean-to, if you don't mind, Walt."

"Good. He can reckanize folks he's seen before."

"Well, hell, Walt, he's shot in the leg, not in the head," Preacher drawled.

The bearlike Hayward chose to ignore the sarcasm. He tugged on his shaggy salt-and-pepper beard. "I'll get Lone Deer to fix up one of those little cabins we built last fall. Now, c'mon, Preacher, I've got something important to talk to you about."

"I'd favor a drink of your good rye, first, Walt. I'm right on the edge of bein' parched."

"Fair enough," the trader allowed and led the way inside.

After the first tin cup of whiskey went down Preacher's throat with the speed of one of those steam cars, Walt poured another and launched into his appeal. "What we've got here is somewhat of a problem. I'm sure you saw the pilgrims out there. They wintered at Bent's an' now they're up here all full of piss and vinegar. Well, they're real pilgrims, if you catch my drift? It's a flock of missionaries on their way, so they say, to bring the Word to the heathen Injuns."

"Why, that's a damn-fool notion if ever I heard one," Preacher erupted.

"Sure it is. At least if they are left on their own. What they need is someone with experience to see them through to wherever they want to settle."

Preacher quickly took in the meaning behind Walt's bright blue eyes. "No sir! Not this chile. I've had all I want of gospel-shouters and Bible-thumpers. You of all people ought to know that, Walt."

"Oh, I know you've had your encounters with the—ah—type. But . . ."

"But nothin'," Preacher all but shouted. "The thought of any of these pilgrims an' tenderfeet westernin' plain sours my stomach. You got yourself the wrong boy this time, Walt. I plum ain't gonna do it."

In the awed silence that followed Preacher's outburst, a snotty, sneering voice rose from the direction of the bar. "My, my, I always knew you was yellow clear through, Preacher. A lazy, shiftless no-account Injun lover who hates every white man on God's green earth." The speaker turned from his hunch-shouldered stance at the plank bar.

Preacher recognized him at once. That nerve-rasping voice, like sawteeth on a nail, pegged him as Bull Ransom, a failed trapper who hung around in the High Lonesome doing odd jobs from time to time, stealing what he wanted the rest. Preacher's eyes narrowed.

"Where I come from, we never stack bullshit that high, Ransom," Preacher said in a deceptively mild voice.

Bull Ransom went livid. "You callin' me bullshit, Preacher?"

Preacher cut his eyes around the nearly empty saloon portion of the trading post. "Seein' as how there's nobody else here but me an' Walt . . . yeah, I say you're nothin' but a great big over-sized pile of shit."

Raging inwardly, Ransom nearly choked on his hot words. "I'll stopper that smart-aleck mouth of yourn. I'll fix you good." Bull changed his tone, became taunting and oily "I can take you, you know that, Preacher? I can shoot you where you sit before you can touch a gun. I could slice your lily-livered throat with my Green River. Or I might turn your face into ground dog meat with my bare hands."

Preacher shook his head and sighed sadly. "Either you're stupid enough to believe that, or you're the worst, bald-faced liar I ever met, Bull."

That tipped the scales for Bull Ransom. With a roar, he came at Preacher, who rose to his moccasins with the fluid grace of a panther. Preacher didn't wait. He met Ransom halfway. At least the big, balled fist at the end of a rapidly snapped right arm met Bull there with full force. White knuckle marks stood out on the florid skin of Bull's forehead. He grunted and his eyes crossed. Then Preacher began to seriously whip up on Ransom.

Swift, powerful one-two combinations hammered the rib cage of Bull Ransom. Each blow threatened to break ribs. The fat on Ransom's belly jiggled and his jowls wobbled from the tremendous force. Preacher remained squared off with him, which proved to be a mistake the moment Bull recovered from the shock of the sudden, ferocious attack. Grunting with the effort, Bull brought a knee up into Preacher's crotch.

Bent double from the flare of pain, Preacher left himself wide open. Bull moved in and seized the advantage. His fat, though whang-leather-tough, hands pummeled Preacher's head. A scarlet haze settled over Preacher's vision. Bull had stepped in so close Preacher had no target for his own punishing fists. Then he recalled an old trick he learned from a Pawnee. Having been on the receiving end might account for his undiminished dislike for the Pawnee, he thought giddily before he flexed his knees and rammed the top of his head into the point of Bull's chin.

Teeth clicked together as Bull's jaw snapped shut. Instantly, Preacher sprang backward and went to work on the face of his adversary. Callused knuckles bit and tore into fleshy lips. The upper one split and Bull bellowed his burning rage. Before he could recover, Preacher finished the job of mashing Bull's mouth into a crimson smear. Then he took on Bull's nose. He landed a solid right, then a left and another right. Preacher heard cartilage pop like the hinge-gate stopper of a bottle of beer.

Bull Ransom back-pedaled from the violence of Preacher's assault. Desperately he made a swipe at the bar. His fingers closed around the neck of a blown-glass whiskey bottle, with which he took a swing at Preacher's head. Preacher ducked as the container whistled past. Then he planted a ringing left on Bull's right ear.

Nearly dropping the bottle, Ransom readjusted his grip,

broke the bottle against the raw plank of the bar top and lunged at Preacher's face. "Enough's enough, goddamnit," Preacher did his thinking out loud.

Then he sidestepped and let the jagged glass whiz past. In a flash, he snatched the wrist and upper arm of Bull Ransom and swung down hard. At the same time he shot his right leg upward, the top of his thigh forming a hard crossbar. Both bones of Ransom's forearm snapped with a loud, sickening sound. The bottle fell from instantly numbed fingers. Howling, Ransom went to his knees. Preacher gauged his enemy and delivered a sturdy kick to Ransom's ruined face. When he turned back to Walt Hayward, the trader noted that Preacher wasn't even breathing hard.

"He certain sure had that comin', Preacher. Let me get another bottle and we'll wet our whistles some more." Walt started across the floor to the bar when he noticed weak, furtive movement from the fallen Ransom. Almost before it could register, Walt watched the battered trash come to his feet, a long, sharp Green River knife in his left hand.

"Preacher, look out," Walt shouted. "He's got a knife!"

4

It happened so fast that afterward the hastily gathered witnesses had difficulty recalling if they had, indeed, seen the lithe, lanky mountain man draw and fire. The sharp report of the pistol in Preacher's hand did make its impression clearly. The force slammed painfully into their ears, causing squawks of alarm. This remarkable display of speed and accuracy came as a result of Preacher's strict adherence to the basics of staying alive on the frontier.

Not long after possessing himself of these remarkable firearms and making custom holsters for them, Preacher had experimented with means of getting them into action the easiest and quickest way.

Unknown to him, and to history, Preacher had invented the style that was to become known in later years as the fast draw. It saved his life again this day. His bullets arrested Bull Ransom's lunge in mid-stride. The back stabber rocked back on boot heels from the impact of the double-shotted load that pierced his sloppy-fat belly. Slowly, a forest giant yielding to the lumberjack's saw, Bull Ransom toppled backward to strike the unfinished planks of the floor with a resounding, drumlike thud.

"I'm dyin', Preacher," Bull said weakly.

"I reckon you are, Bull. You want to make yer peace with God?"

Black-hearted hate distorted Bull's last words. "Damn

Him and damn you, too, Preacher." Then his boot heels made a brief, rapid tattoo on the floorboards, he uttered a gurgling rattle and left to meet the Supreme Judge.

"I'd say it's you should be most worried about bein' damned," Preacher observed. A certifiably feminine shriek sounded from beside the inner doorway immediately after.

Preacher cut his eyes that direction and saw three women, overdressed in the current Eastern style. They had entered during the ruckus caused by his fight with the dead Bull Ransom. One, her gray hair protruding from the fringe of a bonnet, had a hand to her mouth, her face pale and waxen. She appeared about ready to swoon. With her other hand, she clung to the arm of another lady about her own age. The third had uttered the scream. She was much younger, Preacher took in at a glance, and really quite pretty. At least until she screwed her smooth-complexioned face into a mask of moral outrage and advanced on Preacher, small fists flailing the air.

"You barbarian! You savage brute! Why, you—you murdered that poor man for no earthly reason"

Preacher caught both flailing arms by the wrists, in one hand, and stilled her furious assault. He gazed down into deep, cobalt eyes, like hidden mountain pools. "I consider him tryin' to knife me in the back more'n enough reason."

She rounded on Walt Hayward then. "Where's the law around here? This cold-blooded killer must be arrested."

Walt produced a smile that parted the hair around his mouth. "If by that you mean an honest, God-fearin' man who rights wrongs, I'd have to say it's Preacher, Miss Cora."

"'Preacher?' You mean you have a minister nearby, Mr. Hayward?"

"Nope. Preacher's been called a lot of things, but a minister ain't one of them. He's—ah—he's the one's got you caught up by the hand."

A startled squeak emanated from the throat of Cora Ames. Her eyes got an even darker blue and went wide and round. "Oh, Lord have mercy! Spare us from the madness of this wilderness," she prattled.

"The best way for Him to have done that is to have seen that you stayed where you belong," Preacher offered his opinion.

That proved too much for Cora. Not that she backed down. Rather, she stamped her tiny foot, clad in a black, high-button shoe, and jerked free of Preacher's relaxed grasp. "I'm not finished with you. You must be judged for the awful thing you did."

"Oh, I figger as how that's all taken care of. I asked the Man Above to weigh the soul of the departed Bull Ransom and decide where's best to put it. And not to look too harshly on my havin' to send him off so unexpected like. Thing is I can't abide a snake who'd stab a man in the back."

Cora realized what was going on and spoke her mind. "You're making fun of me, aren't you?"

"I wouldn't say that, miss. You're much too pretty to be made fun of."

"Uh—Preacher," Walt began tentatively. "I reckon as how you'll have to act as guide now. Seein' as how you've just done for these mission folks' wagonmaster, that is."

Shock registered on the face of Cora Agnes. "No! Absolutely not! Why, the very idea of allowing this—this—this monster in the company of gentle souls and God-loving people like our family of missionaries is out of the question."

Grinning, Preacher agreed. "Oh, you've got the right of it, miss. Couldn't have said it better myself."

Walt gave Preacher a "You've got to get me out of this" look. "Really, it's the best solution. There's no one who knows these parts better than Preacher, Miss Cora."

"Bu—bu—but he—he just killed a man right before our eyes."

"And considering conditions out here, is likely to do so again if the situation calls for it," Walt advised her.

"I would not permit it," Cora announced bravely. "I would stand between this wretched beast and his intended victim and defy him to shoot me first."

That, said with such a tone of serious intent, brought a

laugh from Preacher. "That's all fuss and feathers, miss, if you don't mind me sayin' so. There's wild Injuns, renegade whites, border trash, and all sorts out there. Bunches of them deserve killin'. They'd not be kind to you and, when they'd had their way, they'd like to kill you for good measure."

Icily, Cora defied his advice. "I don't believe you."

"Suit yourself. But it don't cut no jerky strips, 'cause I ain't gonna take you folks anywhere."

Suddenly realizing her plight, Cora changed her stand. "Oh, but you must. We simply have to reach our mission site in time to build lodgings and a meeting house. We have to plant crops and care for our livestock. And . . . that—that lout didn't impress me with his ability to carry out his duties. We need someone reliable."

The more this fiery damsel spluttered, the more beguiled Preacher became. She had plenty else to say and at great length. Eyes twinkling, Preacher bantered right back. Her passion at their goal made her even more attractive in Preacher's eyes. At last, he relented enough to ask the key question.

"Jist whereabouts are you headed, miss?"

"We are going to bring the Word of God to the heathen Cheyenne up north of here," a portly man, done up all in black, complete with dickie and Roman collar, announced as he pushed through the Hudson's Bay blanket that served as a divider between the saloon and the trading sides.

Knowing what he did from Talks To Clouds made it imperative for Preacher to see that these folks understood. "No. No, you're not," he told them, all humor erased from his voice. "There's war talk flyin' around the Cheyenne lodges. From what I hear, they're fixin' to take the war trail against their old enemies, the Blackfeet. That means someone's gonna get their hair lifted." Preacher paused a moment and then went on earnestly. "I'd be the worst sort of some of those names the young lady called me if I was to take you into that. And, besides, I ain't eager to get my scalp picked off by any Injun, Cheyenne or Blackfoot."

"We have no fear, sir," the minister blithely told Preacher. "We have the protection of God, who sent us to the Cheyenne."

Preacher pulled a droll face. "Now, isn't that right comfortin'? Must let a feller lay down to sleep with an easy mind. Pardon my bein' so pushy, but I ain't never met a man on such close personal terms with the Almighty before this. Might I have your name?"

The minister drew up his short, portly figure and spoke with the ringing tones of the pulpit. "I am the Reverend Thornton Bookworthy, sir. It is my privilege to serve the United Mission Conference to the heathen."

Bookworthy? Preacher nearly stumbled over the name. "Well, Reverend Bookworthy, the 'heathen' are fixin' to make war this whole summer. All the signs say that's so, an' my ol' friend Talks To Clouds says so, an' he's one mighty savvy Nez Perce, so I expect he's right. So, there's no way you're goin' up in Cheyenne country this year an' settle down. Unless to settle on the ground and let your bones bleach in the sun. If you're smart, you'll take that as the last word on the subject."

"You astound me, sir! Surely a man of such prowess with fist and gun can have no fear of any mere ignorant savages," Reverend Bookworthy blustered.

"Now, there's where you missed the point entire, Reverend. From personal experience, I allow as how those 'ignorant savages,' as you put it, are ever' bit as smart as you or me. They don't want your God, ain't got no need for Him. They got their own. Hear me good, Mister Minister, they ain't heathens, an' they might do savage things by our lights, but they're kind to their youngins, provide for their old folks, love their wives, and are loyal to their friends. They are only different. They have their own ways, but if you ask me, so long as they're livin' by their own lights, they're doin' the exact things our God wants of us to do."

During what to Preacher constituted a windy speech, Cora listened with a growing expression of understanding and enchantment. With his conclusion, she inserted her now gentle voice between the two men. Her tone alerted Preacher to the fact that she sought to try some modestly Christian forms of feminine wiles on him.

"That was most eloquent, er—ah . . ."

"Preacher, miss."

"Cora Ames, Mr. Preacher. Quite stirring indeed."

"Just, Preacher."

"Ah—Preacher. It gives remarkable insight into the sav—er—Indians to those of us who are woefully ignorant of their ways. But, our dilemma remains the same. Even were we to want to go back where we came from—"

"A capital idea," Preacher broke in to say.

"If we were, we could not get there without a guide. We would, in fact, be stranded here, at this remote place, forced to spend another dreary winter."

"I thought you wintered at Bent's Fort?" Preacher asked, astonished.

"They did. Came in week ago, more's a pity, Preacher," Walt Hayward contributed. "Lost their guide on the way up from Bent's Fort. Hired Bull Ransom first thing he showed up after the thaw, in mid-March."

Preacher eyed the Reverend Bookworthy. "You could have hired any one of the woolly-backs hereabouts and done better for it."

"They were in a hurry," Walt advised Preacher with a wink. "I told them it was a mistake."

Preacher muttered softly to himself for a while, then pulled the weather-beaten hat from his head. "I reckon I could take you as far as down to Bent's Fort. From there you can find an escort back East. But, there ain't no way anyone will take you north into Cheyenne country. By now the word's out all through the Big Empty about the Blackfeet and the Red Top Lodges mixin' it up come summer."

"I must protest," Reverend Bookworthy gobbled in agitation. "We've been directed by God to carry salvation to the savages. Nothing can turn us from our course."

"God didn't direct you to get these lovely ladies killed, did He?" Preacher snapped back. "Listen close, Mr. Reverend

Bookworthy, youd be smart to take what you've been offered and be grateful for it. I've got no time for more of your insistin', an' I jist might change my mind if you keep that jabber up."

Running Bear, Stone Drum, Wind Rider, and Falling Horse stood in the midst of the charred lodge poles and ashes that had been the village of Black Hand. They found the body of their fellow chief, along with four warriors, where they had fallen. Behind their corpses lay a mound of dead women and children, whom they had been protecting. The ruins of the village, in its once beautiful, peaceful valley sweltered under the stench of so much death.

"It was white men, I'm certain of it," Running Bear stated flatly. "Who else would waste the food and burn the lodges?"

Falling Horse nodded thoughtfully. "I agree."

"It might have been the Absaroka. Those Crow dogs have rubbed up against the whites so long that they even think like them. We must gather a large war party and send it against our old enemy."

"And have the Blackfeet at our backs?" objected Wind Rider.

"What do you know about it, Breaks Wind?" Stone Drum asked in jest, using the irreverent form of his fellow chief's name.

"I know that the Blackfeet have been buying guns from some white men, that they have many of the latest kind. I know, too, that these white traders had visited Black Hand's village."

"Too much talk about whites." Falling Horse grunted. "I say we take the war trail against all whites, run them out. They have no reason to be here. They kill the game and leave most to waste, or run it off. They foul the ground with their waste, muddy the water, and cut deep gashes in the breast of Earth Mother. It is for us to stop their coming."

"You would stop the flow of the Great Water to the east?"

Wind Rider countered. "The whites number like the drops of that mighty river. These are different days. We must learn to be tolerant of our enemies, the Crow and the whites."

All three of his companions looked at him as though he had confessed some unspeakable vice. Running Bear spoke first. "That is not for us to decide. We must take this to the grand council and gain agreement of a plan that will work."

Nodding their approval of this idea, Stone Drum and Falling Horse walked with Running Bear to their ponies. Wind Rider hesitated a moment, then followed.

Arapaho Basin had long been a gathering place for the Indians who roamed the fringes of the Rocky Mountains. The hot sulfur springs that bubbled up from the depths of the earth were considered good for the bones of the old. The current occupants of the basin had little consideration for that. Ezra Pease had established his base camp there because of the shelter provided by the high peaks that surrounded the lush valley.

He was taking his ease outside his tent and sipping on his fifth cup of coffee, laced with rum, when two of his disreputable gang rode into camp. They had barely dismounted from their lathered horses when the older of the two blurted out his bad news.

"Weasel Carter an' those you sent with him to do in Preacher? He done kilt them all."

Ezra Pease came to his boots in a jerky motion. "What! I sent Weasel because not even Preacher could figure out that he was a danger, until it was too late."

"Well, Preacher sure must have learned mighty fast," the shaggy-haired brute with a waxen scar from his left ear to the corner of his mouth opined.

"Damnit! Our whole operation hinges on getting rid of him. Preacher is all too friendly with most of the Indians, and he's known by every white man in this country. If he gets word of what we're up to, he can make the world a mighty mean place for us."

"What should we do about it?" the knife-cut thug asked bluntly.

"Get the job done right," Pease snapped. "Get Bart Haskel, Two Thumbs Buehler and about ten more over here right now."

When the reluctant volunteers assembled, they wasted no time making it clear they were none too happy about the reason for their summons. Ezra Pease eyed them coldly, then reminded himself that these were the best he had, better than most in the past. Too bad most of them came out of the prairie lands of Missouri and Illinois. He'd be glad to trade the lot for half a dozen wild and woolly mountain men. Nevertheless, they were loyal to him to the man.

He could at least count on them not to shirk in their duty and eventually succeed or die in the process. Pease preferred not to think of dying. Every day Preacher remained alive increased the risk for him and his bully-boys. He took a deep breath and launched his effort to spell finis to Preacher.

"I can see by the looks on your faces that you know what happened to Weasel and the men with him. I never said Preacher was going to be easy to stop. He's smart, mean, and knows these mountains better than any man living. He'll be wary now, and a whole lot harder to run to ground. That's why I'm sending a dozen of you. Preacher is a legend, out here as well as in those silly penny dreadfuls you may have seen back East.

"It's going to be your job to track him down and finish him. But . . ." Pease let the word hang. "I don't simply want him dead. I want him dragged around from place to place so folks know for certain sure that he's a goner. With him out of the way, our path is clear to fortune and power. Provision yourselves and ride out within the hour. The sooner you go, the sooner Preacher dies."

5

Preacher slouched in the saddle of his spotted horse, Thunder, at the crest of the notch that led south out of Trout Creek Pass. He had replaced his battered, floppy hat with a crisp new one, though he had to allow as how it didn't shade his face the way the old one had. It made him look a little less disreputable, Cora Ames thought as her wagon rolled by the immobile mountain man.

"You all keep rollin'," Preacher advised to the drivers. "I'll catch up and scout ahead in awhile."

Complaints still came from the missionaries about being turned back, yet Preacher noted that most of the women accepted it with relief evident in the less pinched expressions they wore. Not all of them, he reminded himself as he gazed on the ash-blond hair that escaped in wisps around the bonnet on the head of Cora Ames. Drat it, it somehow didn't seem right to him that someone who looked so pretty should be wrapped up in saving the souls of folks who didn't want 'em saved. She belonged in a nice white clapboard farmhouse, like the ones he'd seen back East, with a gaggle of kids running around her knees and clinging to her skirt.

Could she have made up her mind to the spinster's life so young? There were plenty of married couples among the twenty wagons in the missionary train. Youngsters, too, blast the luck. Preacher firmly believed that brat-kids had no business out in the Big Empty, leastwise not those too young to take care of themselves. Grownups had their hands full keeping themselves alive and their possessions intact. They had no time to give to doing for a batch of babies and infants.

Yet, they persisted in coming, more each year, damn their stars. He recalled the year he took a train of tenderfeet clear to the Big Water in Oregon country. Three women had birthed on the trail. Only one of the infants survived the trip. Fools. Preacher dismissed his gloomy contemplation to mentally review for the hundredth time the trail south and eastward to Bent's Fort. It would be rough, but these pilgrims had been over it once. Maybe they had learned something.

At least, the fort was out on the flats and these folks would have easy going from there. They could take the Santa Fe Trail as far as Independence, for that matter, and then on down to St. Louis. They'd just have to look out for the Southern Cheyenne, the Kiowa, Pawnee, Kaw, and the Osage. No mean feat, but with the right men to guide them, it could be done, was done day in and day out for that matter. There was some talk of building some military forts along the Trail, but Preacher doubted he'd live to see the day.

He pushed that out of his mind and gigged Thunder into a lazy trot. In a short time he caught up with the wagon that carried Cora Ames. She greeted him with more cordiality than he might have expected. Enough to encourage him to rein in to the slow walk of the mules pulling the lumbering vehicle. Preacher might prefer only his own company in the High Lonesome, but the lure of a pretty young woman could be resisted by just a few.

"I suppose you know we're terribly curious, Mr.—er—Preacher," the good looker offered without preamble.

"Curious about what?" Preacher asked, genuinely unaware.

"About you, of course. Surely you have a Christian name, unless, like some of those scallywags at the trading post tried to get us to believe, you were mothered by a she-wolf."

Preacher couldn't figure out if she was teasing him or not.

"Yes, Miss Cora. I do. Name's Arthur." He said it so softly she barely heard it.

"That's a perfectly lovely name, Arthur."

Pink touched Preacher's cheeks. "Maybe that's why I don't cotton much to usin' it."

"I would think your mother would be disappointed you did not," Cora tossed at him without being censorious. "Where were you born, Arthur?"

Preacher winced. "Please, jist Preacher." Then he went on to answer her. "On a farm in Ohio. Long enough ago that it was the frontier at the time. The Sauk and Fox were still there in great number."

"Do you have living kin? Brothers or sisters?"

"I do," Preacher answered curtly. "If you don't mind, it's downright uncomfortable talkin' so much about myself. Don't think me bold, but what about you? What sort of life has brought you out into all this emptiness?"

Cora gave a moment's thought before answering. "My family are all Green Mountain folks from Vermont. I am the fifth of seven children my mother bore. In addition to dairy cattle and harvesting maple syrup, my father was a circuit-riding preacher." She let go a brief trill of laughter. "No pun intended."

Preacher shared her amusement. "Then your family all grew up God-fearin' and full of rectitude?"

A fleeting frown darkened Cora's forehead. "Not . . . all of them. But, that's another story. I don't mean to offend, but I've noticed that you don't talk like an uncouth, unlettered dolt all the time. You seem to pick and choose."

Preacher shot her a quick grin. "You're not the first to make that observation. I had acquired some six years of book learnin' before I made tracks for the Shinin' Mountains. After that it was mostly self-taught, but I did learn some proper grammar. Some of the men I associated with helped me on that."

"How was that? No, please, I really am interested," Cora urged.

"A number of years back, I don't remember exactly when, some of us who could read and write and do our sums took to sharing our knowledge amongst ourselves an' those who could not read for themselves. I even learned some Shakespeare, and about the heroes of long ago, Horatio and Odysseus, Julius Caesar."

Cora Ames clapped her hands in delight. "I'm so glad you called him by his proper name. Ever since those terrible translations of the *Illiad* and the *Odyssey*, people have taken to calling him Ulysses."

Preacher nodded his thanks for her compliment. "You're a learned woman, then?"

"My, yes. More, I'm sure, than a lot of people think I should be. Most girls back East still finish school with the eighth form. Then it's off to a home and children, or to one of the sweatshops to labor until death."

"Don't reckon a sprightly filly —er, pardon— a spirited lady like yourself would be content with either of those," Preacher stumbled out.

"A few go on to the young ladies' seminary—that's where I matriculated." She paused, frowned, then made a surprising revelation. "I'd not turn down a husband, family, and a stout home." Then Cora confided with vigor, "As for the other alternative, it is, as they say, 'a man's world.' They have all the positions on the top of the heap. For a woman who undertakes to support herself or her family, the workplace offers little more than it does for slaves down in the South. Drudgery and dehumanization are the watchwords of the few factories and sewing shops, or even teaching positions open to women in the East."

"But you chose missionary work," Preacher brought her back to speed. "What influenced that decision?"

Cora flushed and diverted her cobalt gaze from Preacher's

slate eyes. "As you said, there are some things I am 'downright uncomfortable' talking about."

"Sorry I brought it up. Well, I'd best get along up the string and see what's ahead. We'll be makin' camp in about two hours."

"So early?" Cora responded. "There are still hours of daylight."

"First day on the trail. There'll be need to fix what broke and shake down the way the wagons are loaded. That all takes time. Good day to you, Miss Cora."

Preacher rode off along the line of wagons. Behind him he left Cora Ames with a vague sense of being unfulfilled.

Cook fires had been lighted and the pilgrims settled in. Three wagons needed to replace wheels with loose iron tires. Preacher had to admit that was one fancy Eastern idea that had a practical use out here. Shod wheels made sense. The rough trails, mostly only enlarged animal tracks, punished wheeled vehicles mercilessly. The recent advent of iron-tired wheels had its downside as well. It made it easier for these pestiferous greenhorns to travel far beyond any hope of help from civilization when they got in trouble.

"Will you take supper with us, Preacher?" Lidia Pettibone asked sweetly from where she bent over a tripod that held a bubbling pot of stew.

Preacher drew a deep breath of the rich aroma and identified fresh venison. "Don't mind if I do. I want to make a round of camp first, if that's not makin' it too late for you folks."

"Not at all. It will be a while, at least."

Her husband, Asa, had the strangest occupation Preacher had ever heard of. He was an organist. The freight wagon that accompanied their living quarters held a large bellows-pumped pipe organ, complete with brass tubes to produce the majestic, imperial sounds of that instrument.

"Good dang thing they ain't headed clear to Or-e-gon,"

Preacher muttered aloud to himself. "The tribes twixt here an' there would be supplied with arrow and lance points for the next century." Brass, he knew, was mighty precious to the Indians.

For a people who had never learned to smelt metals, or forge them, or even invented the wheel, they were right adaptable. They appreciated the value of forged or cast metal almost at once. Which meant they were right smart. Which made them damned dangerous. All of a sudden Preacher came upon an impression that was so far-reaching and prescient that it all but staggered him. Given enough time, like the white man had with this new science, the Indians could easily push folks whose families came from Europe back into the sea.

"Good evening—ah—Brother Preacher," the Reverend Thornton Bookworthy rumbled as he passed by where Preacher stood staring into space over the concept of industrialized Indians.

"Evenin', Reverend Bookworthy." Suddenly he had a burning desire to share his revelation with someone. "I just had me a startlin' thought."

Although he looked pained, Reverend Bookworthy responded with enthusiasm. "I'd be delighted to hear it."

"It just come to me, thinkin' about Pettibone's pipe organ. What if, when our ancestors came here, the Injuns had been smelting and forming metal objects for as many hundreds of years as the white man had?"

"But, they're ignorant savages," Bookworthy protested with typical white blindness.

"Yeah. Only what I said was, 'what if?' You may not believe it, but what I said at the trading post is true. They're smart, they're crafty, they's absolutely fearless, and they know better than to line up and march off to shoot at each other and stab away at one another with bayonets in the heat of the day. I tell you, Reverend, it's downright frightening to consider."

Bookworthy still wasn't sold. "You've been out here, among

them, for longer than any of us. I suppose you could be right. If so, let us be thankful it wasn't that way."

Preacher grunted and went on his rounds, inspecting the fringes of the camp. He didn't expect any hostiles to swarm down on them, not so close to the trading post in Trout Creek Pass. Nor had he seen any sign throughout the day of any drifting bands of white trash. Yet, an uneasiness gnawed at him.

Maybe it was his stomach, Preacher considered a half hour later when he returned to the Pettibone wagons. The aromas rising from the cook fire made him growly as a grizzly on the first day after hibernation. His mouth watered when his nose made out the distinct scent of apple pie. Guiding these folks would have a few advantages after all, he decided.

Over a week's time, Preacher learned a lot more about the gospel-shouters. Enough, indeed, to make him uncomfortable. Some, he knew, had joined this crazy expedition as a last-chance opportunity. They considered themselves to be losers, talked and acted like it, too. They wouldn't last a year out here.

Some would go around the bend, wander off, and get killed by any number of roving predators, human as well as animal. That would be their problem, he supposed. Others, like the Bookworthys, had the wild fire of the zealot in their eyes. They could be trouble. Good thing they were all going back. If they got there, he reminded himself.

Since early that morning, which Preacher reckoned put them a short three days' travel from Bent's Fort, he had been seeing signs of others out there. Indians, and a lot of them, with no indication of women or children along. Of course, they could be a hunting party. Not likely, Preacher reasoned. Accordingly, he rode back to the lead wagon and spoke with one of the several drivers hired by those unable to handle their own teams.

"When we make camp for the night, Buck, I want you to circle the wagons. Make it nice and tight. After the teams are unhitched, make it box to box. No spaces between. And leave the animals inside the circle."

Having grown wise on the way out, the burly driver frowned at this. "You expectin' trouble?"

"Might be. There appears to be Injuns out there. I've seen signs. That means they know we're here."

"I'll see to it, Preacher," Buck Dempsey agreed.

Preacher studied the stout, dark-complexioned Buck Dempsey. He gauged a steadiness in the hickory nut eyes and smooth brow, the set of a square chin. Yeah, he'd do to lead the other drivers. "I see you've got a good Hawken along. Were I you, I'd see to it being loaded and at hand from now on. I'm gonna drift along the line and tell the others."

Preacher's efforts met with somewhat less than enthusiastic results. Reverend Bookworthy was quite vocal in his objections. "We will do no such thing. I am a man of God, and these are the children of God. Besides, we'll only be inviting trouble," he pontificated. "If the savages see us all bristling with arms and in a defensive position, it will alienate them."

"Reverend, they don't need us to alienate them. If it's some what's got it in for whites, they'll already be as sore as a boil on your behind. What's going to happen is that if they see us all ready to take them on, if they're not already cooked up for war, they will decide to ride on and leave us in peace."

"That doesn't make sense," Bookworthy protested. "A belligerent posture invokes a belligerent response."

"It might be so back where you come from. But, Injuns think different from us. If they believe their medicine is strong, that the light is just right, and specially if we're afeared of them, they'll attack. On the other hand, if they ain't too sure about their medicine, or that we are able to knock too many of them off their ponies, they won't. Injuns ain't stupid. Numbers are real important to them. Gotta have men to protect the village, to hunt meat for everyone. Get too many killed off in battle and everybody suffers. Some might starve, or the village get wiped out by an enemy tribe."

"Why, that's preposterous, Preacher. I've been informed by knowledgeable men at Harvard and other colleges that the Indians are peaceful among themselves, at least until the white man came. Only the white man represents a threat to their way of life."

Preacher wanted to laugh in the fool's face. He held it back, though. "An' that's just so much heifer dust, Reverend, if you'll pardon my language. Their lives are as precarious as I've said, but war's a part of their way of life, they're used to it. Over thousands of years they have become expert survivors. Now I'd advise you to make some arrangements to be armed through the next day or so, like I'm tellin' everyone else."

Preacher found the attitudes divided along the lines of the nature of those he advised. The hired drivers, there were six, all loaded up and spent the nooning hour twisting cartridges out of paper, powder, and shot. The soul-savers were uniformly horrified by the prospect of violence, except, surprisingly, Cora Ames.

"My father sent along his fine Purdy English rifle and a pair of horse pistols. He may be a man of the cloth, but he's practical, too. We have our share of highwaymen in Vermont."

"Ummmm—yes," Preacher muttered through his dismay. He also revised his estimate of Cora upward by several notches.

Later, once camp had been established, Cora came to where Preacher peered beyond the circled wagons. "We were fortunate in not having trouble with the Indians on the way out. Maybe it would have been better if we had. Reverend Bookworthy is expending great effort to talk our people into having nothing to do with guns. He wants us all to stay close to the fire . . . and to build it up even more."

Preacher turned to her. "That danged fool. He'd make perfect targets out of all of you."

"He pointed out that night has fallen and we've not been attacked. And everyone knows that Indians don't attack in the dark."

Preacher made a rude sound. "What 'everyone knows' ain't necessarily true. Injuns will attack at night. Like I tried to make him understand, if the Injuns think their medicine is good and their numbers big enough, they'll attack day or night. Now, I'd better go do something about gettin' that fire down to coals, so's we can see them when they come."

"You're . . . that sure?" Cora asked uncertainly.

"I feel it in my bones. I can smell 'em out there. I reckon they'll pick a time closer to the middle of the night. When they do, you'd best be ready to bang away with that rifle and the pistols you brung."

Preacher excused himself and went to get something done about the fire, which he insisted be put out entirely. He got a windy objection from Reverend Bookworthy and several missionaries, which he addressed by simply shouting them down. Cora looked on and shook her head in dismay. With that accomplished, Preacher retrieved his two rifles and checked the loads in them and a brace of pistols from saddle-boxes Thunder carried.

Then he went around the circled wagons until he found a place where, if he were an Indian, he would figure as a prime one to launch an attack against. There he settled in to wait. It turned out not to be as long as he had expected.

A mixed band of Kiowa and Pawnee hit about ten o'clock, in the dark of the moon. Preacher first saw blacker shapes flitting from one bit of sparse cover to another. It didn't take long to figure out that it wasn't a pack of coyotes or wolves. One of them reared up abruptly and drew taut a bowstring.

Preacher let one of the big .70 caliber horse pistols bang away. A brief, shrill cry of pain answered and the bowman disappeared from sight. Another quickly took his place.

Preacher put a fat .70 caliber ball in the Kiowa's breastbone, showering both lungs with bone and lead fragments. The hostiles were in too close for rifle work, so Preacher ignored them to get one of his four-barreled blitzers into action.

By then, the drivers, led by Buck Dempsey, had opened up on the invading Indians. Preacher took his eyes off the assault to cut a quick look around the compound. He turned back in time to all but stuff the muzzle of his four-barrel in the screaming mouth of a Pawnee warrior. The double-shotted load took off the entire back of the hostile's head.

Showered by brain tissue, a youthful brave behind him gagged and mopped at his eyes. That reflex bought him a quick trip to the Happy Hunting Ground. Preacher had barely turned the next barrel into line when the young Pawnee rushed at him. He gut-shot the teenage brave and quickly cranked the last load into position.

"Pour it on, boys!" he shouted encouragement as he took a quick, inaccurate shot at a Kiowa who had leaped onto the tailgate of the wagon belonging to Cora Ames.

Preacher's ball cut a thin line across the bare back of the warrior, who disappeared into the wagon's interior. A pistol barked and flame lighted the canvas cover from inside. Preacher had moved within reach of Cora's wagon when the warrior appeared again, a look of disbelief that a woman had mortally wounded him clear on his face.

"Good shootin', missy," Preacher called to Cora. He would have liked to do more, but right then he had his hands full of two Pawnee braves. One bore down on him with a lance, the other brandished a tomahawk. Preacher promptly drew his second fearsome pistol and plunked a double load into the lancer's chest and belly.

The Pawnee went rubber-legged and wobbled off toward the side. Preacher turned back toward the one with the war hawk. Lightning quick, the man had closed in on Preacher so fast it prevented revolving the barrels of his four-shot. He used it to parry the overhand blow instead.

While he did, he drew his own tomahawk and planted it deep in the base of the Pawnee's neck. Numbed by massive shock and sudden, profuse blood loss, the man sagged against Preacher, who wrenched his hawk free and stepped back. From behind him he heard a shrill scream and cut his eyes over his shoulder in time to see Cora Ames disappear over the outer side of her wagon, in the arms of a howling Kiowa.

"One of them Kiowa got Miss Cora," Preacher shouted. "Buck, Luke, come over here and hold 'em off. I'm goin' after her."

6

Preacher leaped to the top of a wagon wheel and vaulted the driver's seat. He swung his legs over and dropped free. His moccasined feet came down on the back of a Pawnee who sought to crawl under the vehicle and enter the defensive circle. With a stout flex of his knees, Preacher put an end to that plan. The audible crack of the hostile's spine was music to Preacher's ears. He bounded across the ground in the faces of the astonished Indians.

Only vaguely could he make out his goal. Two darker blobs in the faint, frosty starlight wavered unsteadily. Cora Ames fought her captor with tenacity. Preacher closed gradually. He managed to draw his second four-barrel pistol and held it ready. A sharp howl came from the mouth of the Kiowa who carried Cora upright with an arm around her waist. Improving night vision gave Preacher a sight he would marvel over for years to come.

Cora had not worn her bonnet in her bedroll and her ash-blond hair, done in thick sausage curls, star-frosted, flailed about as she violently shook her head. Then he realized the reason for the scream of anguish and her actions. Cora had the Kiowa's right ear in her teeth and was worrying it like a terrier with a rat.

Good girl, Preacher thought as he drew close enough to think about firing a shot. Not a good idea, he rejected, recalling he had double-shotted this one, too. He shoved the gun back into its holster and brought out his tomahawk instead. He had come close enough to hear the hostile grunting and grinding his teeth in pain. His breath came in harsh, short gasps. Incredibly, Cora was growling like the terrier to which Preacher had compared her.

Then he was where he wanted to be. Preacher raised his arm and brought the hawk down swiftly on the crown of the Kiowa's head. It buried its flange blade to the haft in the Indian's skull. With a final grunt the warrior let go of Cora and sank to the ground. Without breaking stride, Preacher yanked his war hawk free, caught up Cora, and reversed course. They started back at once.

"My Lord, what did you do?" Cora gasped.

"I got you away from that Kiowa brave," Preacher said simply.

Speechless, Cora stared in shock at Preacher. His face was grimed with powder residue and spattered with Kiowa blood. He looked every bit as savage as the hostiles who had attacked them. Then she amended that when she realized where she had been only moments before. No, Preacher didn't look like a savage . . . he was absolutely gorgeous. Preacher's stride faltered to a stop.

He had been keeping unconscious track of the battle's progress and now noted a sudden increase in the volume of fire. Either the pilgrims had taken up arms or at least realized the sense of reloading for those who were fighting back.

"I can walk perfectly well, Preacher," Cora advised him.

"Uh—sure—sure." He released her and they started off again. Preacher had his charged pistol in hand, the hammer back on the ready barrel. The sound of moccasined feet crashing through the grass ahead came to his ears. In a second two figures in fringed buckskin shirts came rushing at them. Preacher spotted a low sage bush and gave Cora a light shove toward it.

"Get down," he commanded.

"What . . ."

"Just do it." He crouched low in accord with his words.

The two Pawnees rushed on past them without even a glance. Behind them came five more. Gradually the firing slackened from the circled wagons. To left and right, hostiles fled past where Preacher and Cora huddled. They all seemed intent on but one thing. They wanted to get as far away from that deadly fusillade as they could.

In what seemed no time at all, Preacher and Cora found themselves alone in the meadow where the wagons had stopped. Cautiously, Preacher raised upright. Without moonlight to help, he found himself unable to verify that the hostiles had all departed. Slowly he turned a full circle. Faintly in the distance he heard the rumble of departing hooves. Holding back a smile, Preacher bent and helped Cora to her feet, which he noted by starlight to be narrow, pale white, and nicely formed.

"If you're determined to get cactus spines and sand burrs in those dainty feet of yours, it's all right with me. But I do think I should carry you in from here."

"Oh! Oh, dear!" she blurted in realization. "I never thought of that."

Preacher reholstered his pistol and extended his arms invitingly. Cora settled herself with an arm around Preacher's neck. Preacher strode across the uneven ground as though completely unincumbered. To her consternation, Cora released a contented sigh.

"I hope you know this does not constitute a proposal of marriage, Miss Cora," Preacher said quietly.

Cora tittered in delight. "The thought hadn't entered my mind. But it is a pleasant way to travel."

When Preacher could make out the shapes of the caravan, he paused and called out loudly. "Hello, the wagons. It's Preacher. I'm comin' in with Miss Cora. Don't nobody get trigger happy."

"Come on in, Preacher," Buck Dempsey called back. "I got all the guns grounded."

Preacher started off again, only to detour around the body of a Pawnee. He would be gone before morning, Preacher knew. With that he dismissed the dead Indian . . . a little too soon.

The Pawnee, who had been shot through the arm, had been playing possum. Preacher had taken only three steps beyond him when he came up off the ground, a wicked knife in the hand of his good arm. Cora looked over Preacher's shoulder in time to see him lunge.

"Preacher!" she hissed in his ear. "Indian," she added. In the next instant she found herself roughly dumped on the ground, Preacher turned around and standing over her, one of those terrible-looking pistols already in his hand. The sound of its detonation pained her ears. In the flame from the barrel, she saw two dark spots appear on the chest of the Pawnee. Then it went dark again.

She heard the body fall and gasped. Then Preacher said something that struck her as remarkably odd. "Never could abide the Pawnee. Maybe it's because they're sneaky."

Back inside the ring of wagons, Cora Ames gratefully wrapped herself in a woolly house robe, offered by Patience Bookworthy, and shuddered. The females among the missionaries made over her and showered her with questions about her ordeal. When she had quieted them, Cora shivered again and faced their avid, curious faces with a wide-eyed expression.

"It was terrible. He—he just jumped in while I was reloading, grabbed me and dragged me off. My skin was crawling. I—I feel sullied and shamed forever."

Preacher snorted and turned away. He thought of telling her about some of the women he'd come upon, victims of hostile action; brutally raped, tortured, their heads bashed in. Then he decided not to. There were other things to take care of first.

"I want every gun in camp loaded, double-shotted. We'll take turns keeping watch. No fires at all. We have to be able to see without being seen."

"Surely you don't think they will come back," Reverend Bookworthy blustered.

"As certain as Old Nick, I'd say. Somethin' just scared them off. Injuns are notionable, don't you know?"

"But, we soundly defeated those savages," the reverend persisted.

"Nope. Nothin' of the sort." He cut his eyes to the jubilant faces of the unaware missionaries. They may have just won a battle, but they hadn't won the war. Exasperation colored his words. "I don't think it's possible for you lint-brained Eastern folk to learn anything out here. Them hostiles have just gone off to whup up some better medicine. They'll sneak back for their dead and any wounded they missed, then pound the drums and dance until they drop. Come mornin', they'll be back."

At dawn, the hostiles came again. This time they charged on horseback, howling their fierce war cries and brandishing lances. Some reined in and nocked cumbersome-looking arrows to their bowstrings. Preacher took it in and quickly issued his commands.

"Get them water barrels ready. We're gonna get fire arrows." Several women squeaked in fright. "Water'll put 'em out. Have some kettles ready for throwin' it on where they hit. We're backed against this ledge, so they can't circle us. You drivers spread out anyway."

That made sense, Buck Dempsey reasoned. The savages would hit more than one place at the same time. He settled in under a wagon and patted the barrels of his two rifles and a shotgun provided by one of the missionaries. Strange fellow, he called it a "fowling piece." Buck sure hoped the nipples didn't foul when he needed to use it. Preacher stopped by where Buck lay and patted the man on one shoulder.

"That Hawken's got good range. See if you can knock that big, handsome brute out of the saddle." By then the warriors had spread out, ready to close on the wagons and swarm over them.

Buck took aim and fired at the same time the first volley

of fire arrows took flight. "Here they come," Preacher shouted. The ball from Buck's .54 Hawken smacked flesh in the shoulder of the muscular Pawnee that Preacher had indicated and the brave dropped his lance, though he remained in place. Preacher moved off to his own position.

He crouched in the space between the dashboard and seat of the wagon behind Cora's. From there he had a good view of the attacking force. Too bad that shot of Buck's went high and left, he mused. That buck had the look of a leader. Might have been able to end it without any damage done. He took aim with one of his rifles and let it bang away.

One of the warriors who had shot the fire arrows uttered a brief scream and pitched backward out of the saddle, shot through the chest. Preacher immediately set that rifle aside and took up the other. This was the finely made sporting rifle he had taken off one of those fancy-pants, titled dudes who had chased him and the boy Eddy across most of Indian Territory and into the mountains of the High Lonesome.

Weren't many of them went home, except in boxes, Preacher recalled. He'd not liked the feel of being a wanted man, with a bounty on his head. Preacher sincerely hoped that the last of those flyers had been disposed of. For now, though, he had other things to worry about.

Beyond the Kiowa and Pawnee renegades rushing the wagons, he had seen the colorful feathers of a war bonnet. Might be the real leader, and this rifle had the legs to reach him. Preacher rested the forestock of the long-barreled weapon on the side of the wagon and took aim.

Right then the defenders opened up. Six rifles spoke almost as one, with a seventh a moment later from nearby. That would be Cora Ames. The very real danger of the hostiles had sure changed her outlook on turning the other cheek. Or maybe she figured she'd turned all the cheeks she had and it was time for a little "eye for an eye." Preacher fined down his sight picture and squeezed off a round.

After a short pause, feathers flew from the war bonnet and the head beneath disappeared as its owner sought communion with the earth. He wouldn't be giving orders for a while, Preacher thought with satisfaction. No time to reload. He pulled free one of his pistols as he sensed a hand move past him and take the Hawken. Preacher cut his eyes in a backward glance to see Mrs. Pettibone.

"My husband has a shotgun. He has joined the defenders. I'll load for you," she said, as pleasantly as welcoming worshipers to their little New England church.

"You folks have got some sand, I'll say that," Preacher returned in high praise.

Less than fifty feet separated the laagered wagons from the hostiles when Preacher returned his gaze to the front. At once he cocked and fired. The double-shotted load cleaned a Kiowa off his pony and sent him sprawling in the grass. A quick turn, hammer back, another pair of .50 caliber balls on their way. A howling Pawnee leaped from his horse to the side of the wagon Preacher occupied. He took the third barrel point-blank in the face.

Sizzling lead and hot gases blew off the back of his head. Preacher cranked the barrel again. Another shower of fire arrows made weird sounds overhead. One punched into the rump of a draft mule, which promptly went mad with pain and fright. It broke away from the picket line and crow-hopped toward a wagon side.

Mrs. Landry appeared at its side to soak its rump with a kettle full of water. Her husband, Art, caught up the animal, snatched the barb from its haunch and worked to calm the beast. "They also serve who stand and wait," Preacher said to himself.

Then he unloaded the last barrel into the chest of a lance-wielder who loomed large in his vision. Quickly reholstering the pistol, Preacher reached out in time to take the Hawken from Mrs. Pettibone. "Obliged," he muttered as he shouldered the rifle and took quick aim.

Another hostile died and Preacher traded for his other big pistol. If this kept up much longer, he'd be down to his brace of horse pistols. Fully a dozen hostiles lay writhing on the ground, or still in death. So far the drivers had kept the pace with the assault. Preacher picked a target and let fly. Shot through the throat, the Kiowa hastily departed the earth for the Happy Hunting Ground. Motion from beyond the swarm of Indians around the wagons caught Preacher's attention. Their war chief must have gotten over his scare.

Preacher gathered up the cartridge box for the rifle and then blasted another hostile off his horse with a ball that shattered the hapless Indian's collarbone and lodged in his shoulder blade. Preacher turned away.

"Miz Pettibone, I'd be obliged if you'd load this one for me right away," he asked, handing her the long-range weapon.

When he had the rifle back in hand, Preacher stood and took careful aim at the war leader. When the chest of the Pawnee centered in the sights, Preacher squeezed off with care and rode the mild recoil as the weapon discharged. At that range, it took the bullet a hair over two seconds to reach the target, the sound of the shot a second longer.

Preacher couldn't see the surprised look on the war chief's face when the heavy lead ball smacked into his chest and burst his heart. He did see the buckskin-clad Indian rise in the stirrups and then fling forward along the neck of his mount. At once a loud wailing came from those near to the dead leader. That proved too much for the warriors assaulting the wagon train.

With yips and howls, they pulled off out of rifle range and sat their ponies wondering aloud what could be done. Preacher seized the moment to try a little medicine of his own. He remained standing in the wagon in full view, raised his rifle over his head and let go a loud whoop.

"I am White Wolf! Man Who Kills Silently! White Ghost to the Arapaho, who fear me," he shouted in Pawnee. "You have lost one of every three. Your war chief is dead. This fight is over. Go now, or you will all meet Corpse Eater before the day ends."

The older and wiser among the hostiles now knew only too well who they faced. Badly shaken, they cut worried eyes to the fallen war chief and back to Preacher. A few words were exchanged, then they turned their ponies and withdrew. Many rode with lances reversed, points to the ground, to signify the battle had truly ended.

"Well, we got out of it that time," Preacher announced into the stunned silence that followed. "Next point of call, Bent's Fort."

Ezra Pease stood spread-legged over the man he had just punched in the mouth and knocked to the ground. "What are you skulking around, spying on us for?" he demanded again.

"I weren't spyin', mister. I heared you was lookin' for some men with a gun."

"And you are, I suppose," Pease sneered. Anger tended to banish his carefully cultured, rough-hewed, frontier persona. His excellent Eastern upbringing and education seeped out readily. "If you're such an excellent specimen, how in hell do you explain why my men were able to sneak up on you so easily?"

"I was—I . . . I don't know," the lean, rugged man admitted.

"Where do you call home?" Pease snapped.

"Mis-Missouri. Really, mister, I ain't got any bone to pick with you. If you feel I'm not fit for your outfit, jist let me up and I'll go on my way."

Pease looked pleased with himself. "Well, now, we can't do that, can we? You've been watching our camp for the past two days, made a count of how many I have riding for me without a doubt. You have an idea of how many firearms we possess. And, most likely, seen us trading guns and whiskey to the Indians who have dropped in. What's to keep you from dropping off at the closest settlement and passing all that on to whatever passes there for the law?"

The man looked blank. "Why, I'd never do that. Didn' I just say I wanted to get in on it with you?"

"There's no room for amateurs in this organization," Pease stated bluntly. "I suppose we could take you in, but that would be too much like running a charity ward." So saying, Pease drew one of the fancily engraved, double-barrel pistols from his waistband and eared back the hammer.

Instantly the drifter's face washed white. His lower lip trembled and he raised a hand in pleading. "Say now, mister, I don't even know your name. I'd sure not spread word on you, if you were to let me go, mister, please!"

Ezra Pease shot him in the chest. The man jerked and raised on one elbow. Eyes wide and showing a lot of white, he again tried to plead for his life. Only a gush of blood came from his mouth. Pease cocked the second hammer and fired again. This time the ball entered the center of the drifter's forehead and pulped a mass of brain tissue.

He jerked and twitched for a while, then lay still. "Drag that trash out of camp," Pease commanded. "Vic, when are you expecting those men who went after Preacher to report back?"

Titus Vickers contemplated a second. "Most any time now, Ez."

"They had better, and soon. I want that black-hearted jackal dead, dead, dead."

7

Cora Ames stood on a low knoll overlooking Bent's Fort with one of Preacher's big hands in both of hers. "I shall never forget the experiences we shared, Preacher. Before now, I never considered myself capable of taking a human life. Not that I'm proud of myself for having done so."

"You did what you had to, missy. And I'm sure these folks with you are grateful . . . if only they could get it past their gospel-spoutin' ways an' admit it. Asa Pettibone turned out to be a mighty cool shot, too. Though I doubt any of you will need those skills back home."

Cora sighed. "I really wish we didn't have to leave here, Preacher. It's so lovely, so clean and sweet-smelling. I'll miss it, awfully. Why, when we were up in the mountains north of here, it felt as though I could reach out and touch the hand of God."

"You're not the first to think that, Missy. I said those very words myself for the first time back when I was thirteen. Or was it the year I turned fourteen? No matter." Preacher flushed slightly, made the more evident by his meticulous shaving which had left only a full, brushy mustache. "I'll admit, the Big Empty will seem a little more empty with you gone. But, you'll be safe where you're headed. Maybe, some day when the Shinin' Mountains fills up with people—God forbid—it'll be all right for you to journey here again."

He saw the pained expression on her lovely face and

hastened to stammer an explanation. "No—not that I mean to ask God to forbid you return. It's . . . jist all those people fillin' up space out here that rubs wrong."

"I understand, Preacher. Well, I had better be getting back to the wagons."

"I'll be leavin' shortly, so I reckon this is goodbye, Miss Cora Ames.'

"Not 'goodbye,' Preacher. Just farewell . . . Arthur." She turned on one neat heel and walked back to her wagon, gathered with the others outside the front wall of the fort.

Preacher crossed to Thunder and his packhorse. He had resupplied upon their arrival the previous afternoon. Nothing held him back now. He felt good about that. He would head north. Curiosity about the Cheyenne directed that decision. What could be stirring them up so much? No one at Bent's trading post had an idea. Well, at least he'd seen the last of the Bible-thumpers.

Or so he thought.

With a violent cast of one arm, Ezra Pease hurled the tin cup of coffee at a thick old oak. He showered those near him with the hot, brown liquid. "Goddamn that man! How could he do that? Not a one of them got away?" he asked of the messenger sent from the dozen he had dispatched to bring an end to Preacher.

"No, sir. All five were done for when we came upon them. It had to be Preacher. There was sign of only one horse and rider and a pack animal."

"Five good men lost and we have to send someone else for supplies. Is Preacher headed this way?"

"More or less. Vickers wanted you to get the word so I rode back while they followed the trail. Looks to me like he's cuttin' due north toward Trout Crick Pass."

"They'll get him then." He turned to those around him. "Time's running short. We'll break camp and get on the trail. We need to move further north into Cheyenne country."

"Do you think that wise? I mean, considering the slaughter at Black Hand's village, they might be laying for us," Two Thumbs Buehler prompted.

Pease dismissed it contemptuously. "Those savages have the minds of children. By now they've forgotten all about that. Besides, the only thing they understand is force. Any who might still remember will have learned their lesson and be on their good behavior. After all, they'll want the rifles we have so they can make war on the Blackfeet."

Activity grew to a bustle then, and Pease took the final cupful from the coffeepot. He laced that with a spoon of sugar and a dollop of whiskey from a silver flask he carried in his full-cut Eastern coat. Privately he considered the impact of that fit of temper over Black Hand's village on the men who had employed him to create a war between the Blackfeet and Cheyenne. What attitude might they take over it?

They shouldn't get too upset. After all, it all went to the ends they desired. The gold was there, waiting, he knew that. And slavery was totally legal everywhere in the country. All that had been outlawed was a man importing fresh slaves from Africa. And Pease held personally that those woolly buggers would not do well at mining and sluicing gold anyway. Didn't do well in mountains and cold country either. A man could lose his whole investment that way.

The only investment in obtaining their slaves would be in a little powder and ball. Let all these starry-eyed idiots strike out in droves from the East. He'd soon have them broken and cowed and bending their backs to dig the yellow metal out of the ground. And he, Ezra Pease would be rich, rich, rich!

A week's journey to the east of Bent's Fort, on the old portion of the Santa Fe Trail, which had long been known as "the hard way," just west of Indian Territory, two wagons had stopped for the night. Silas Phipps, the owner, was being royally catered to by a scruffy band of eight children, aged eight to fifteen.

They were not kin. Rather, they were orphans, gathered by Phipps from Eastern cities teeming with castaways. The boys had built a fire ring, kindled a fire, and got it burning well, two hours before sundown. The oldest girl, Ruth, worked with Helen and Gertha to make corn bread, heat a pot of beans from the previous morning, and cut slices from a slab of bacon that had long ago gone green around the edges. They would be needing fresh supplies soon, but Ruth dreaded bringing that up to Phipps.

When the coffee had boiled long enough, Ruth took a cup to Phipps, who sat in a large, thronelike chair under the spreading branches of a solitary cottonwood. He grunted acknowledgment of it and smacked his lips over the first taste.

"Tastes peaked," he grumbled.

"We—we're running low on coffee beans," Ruth responded in a quavery voice.

"There's supposed to be someplace up ahead where we can get supplies."

"Yes. Bent's Fort. Will we —will we be staying there?" Ruth asked eagerly.

"Nope. We're gonna go amongst them New Mexicans," Phipps expanded. "Santa Fe, that's the place. Nothin' but miles and miles of miles and miles around there. We can settle in an' no one will ever know we're there."

Ruth's eyes narrowed. "That's what you want, isn't it? For us to disappear off the face of the earth." Her bold confrontation shocked her.

Phipps squinted his close-set, mean, black eyes and taunted her. "Seems like a good idea, now you mention it. Git along now and tend to supper."

Back at the fire, Ruth cut her eyes to Helen. With a nod of her head, Ruth indicated that they should get off to somewhere that offered a bit of privacy. They rounded the wagons and walked a way onto the prairie. Certain they were out of earshot, Ruth still talked in a low, whispery voice.

"He says we're going to New Mexico and just . . . disappear."

"Oh, Ruth, that's awful. What will happen to us? How can we keep on like . . . this?" Tears sprang to Helen's eyes.

"I noticed earlier that you'd been cryin', Helen."

"It's nothin', Ruthie. I—I just felt bad. It's so empty out here."

"I know, believe me, I do. But, I want you to answer me honestly now. Has Silas been pesterin' you, too, now?"

Helen lowered long lashes over her blue eyes and gave a shake of her head, which disturbed the long, auburn sausage curls. "Not—not before this. He—he's asked me to come to the rear wagon after the younger ones have been put down for the night. I—I'm afraid. I've heard . . . things, and imagined what he must be doing with you."

"It's not your fault, and it's not mine. We can't help what he does and we can't get away."

"I feel so awful, Ruthie. The way he looks at me and licks those fat, ugly lips of his makes me seem so *dirty*."

"It's not you who's dirty. He's the only filth around here." Ruth planned to say more to comfort Helen, but an only too familiar roar of furious impatience interrupted her.

"Where'n hell are you lazy girls? Git back to your work."

Summoned thusly into the presence of Silas Phipps, the girls stood next to Peter, their faces alight with trepidation. Phipps studied them a while, then pushed out his fleshy lower lip in purple imitation of a small boy's pout.

"I got something to tell you," Phipps began, his voice a raspy taunt. "I been thinkin' on it, an' there's too much law in that Mezkin country around Santa Fe. I've decided we will continue west to Bent's Fort and then figure out where to go next while we're there."

Ruth, Helen, and the twelve-year-old Peter shared stricken expressions. Only minutes ago he had been talking of settling around Santa Fe. Now Phipps had come up with another vague idea of their destination. It flooded them with despair. They knew that if they were ever to get away from this foul, evil old man it would have to be somewhere with people around. But all realized that the law never gave a damn about orphans. They would most likely be shoved into some cold, grimy institution, like the ones they had escaped so recently, and forgotten. They would have to come upon folks who cared a lot for children. And Ruth had read in a book at the orphanage where she had last been held that the Mexicans thought the world of their children and treated all children kindly.

Ruth thought fast for a defense of the original destination. "Oh, but you made Santa Fe sound so wonderful, so grand an adventure."

"You can forget all about it now. We're goin' somewhere else. Now, git back to your cookin' before you feel my switch. An' you, little miss," he directed to Helen. "Don't forget our little talk a while back. I'll be lookin' for you."

Three of them. Preacher studied the faint sign left by the men ahead of him on the trail and made note of the distinctive marks that separated the trio. They had left no more tracks than he did.

"Mountain men for sure," he said aloud. "Wonder if I know them?"

An hour later he came upon the three, stopped to give their horses a blow. A wide, white smile split Preacher's face. He knew them for sure. That big, house of a man in the bearskin vest could be no one but Beartooth. The slender, hawk-nosed feller to his right had to be Nighthawk. Which made the last the dapper Frenchman, Dupre. Preacher skirted the trail and circled behind his old friends.

He dismounted and made a cautious approach. They would jump right out of their britches when he walked in among them, he reckoned. When he reached a spot some ten yards from the trio, Nighthawk spoke up loudly.

"Did anyone ever tell you that you made too much noise, Preacher?"

Laughing, Preacher stepped out from among the aspen.

"Ain't lost your hearin' yet, I see, Nighthawk. How long have you knowed I was behind you and that it was me?"

"Better part of half an hour, Preacher," Beartooth boomed. He gave Preacher a mighty hug and all three danced around a while, slapping one another on the back.

"Still ugly as always," Dupre gleefully insulted Preacher. "When are you going to learn that clothes make the man?"

Preacher studied Dupre's store-bought coat, shirt, vest, and trousers and waggled his head in dismay. "You look like that Prince Albert, I swear, Dupre. Don't you think you are a mite overdressed for where you are?"

Dupre sniffed. For all his fine attire, his full mane of black hair was incongruously hidden under a fox-skin cap. "We are wearing our finest because we are on our way to visit Beartooth's in-laws."

Preacher removed his still stiffly new felt hat and scratched his head. "Last I heard, you was hitched up with a Cheyenne gal, Beartooth. That still right?"

"Right as rain, Preacher. She's a good cook," he added with a slap to his hard slab belly.

Preacher cocked an eyebrow. "Might not be the best time to visit with the Cheyenne," he suggested.

"We heard about the Cheyenne bein' stirred up," Nighthawk responded, his flawless English belying his Delaware origins.

"Yep," Beartooth contributed. "Figgered it would be better I went an' took a look, so's my wife wouldn't wear me to a nub with her curiosity. So I latched onto my old friends and partners and brung them along. Where you bound, Preacher?"

"Same place."

"You are welcome to ride with us, *mon ami,*" Dupre offered.

"Obliged. Four sets of eyes are better than one," Preacher accepted.

That decided, the four men mounted up and took the trail northward. Late afternoon found them about halfway to Trout Crick Pass. Nighthawk located a small meadow for their night camp. The three rugged mountain men deferred to

Preacher's skill with bean pot and skillet and all enjoyed a good meal, cooked over a hat-sized fire laid under a thick pine to disperse the smoke. Preacher finished the last of the coffee and came to his moccasins.

"I'm gonna turn in. No telling what tomorrow will bring," he announced as he headed for his bedroll.

Kid Ralston had almost ridden up on the four men camped in the meadow shortly before nightfall. Kid had been fortunate in that he had remained inside the treeline and quickly bent to cover the muzzle of his horse. He dismounted and studied the quartet through what remained of daylight. From the description they had been given, the tall, lean, broad-shouldered one had to be Preacher. But who were the others? They sure knew how to handle themselves, though.

Their fire had been put out before twilight settled on the grassy clearing. Preacher had rolled up first, his muscular form a mound under his blankets. Wisely, Kid Ralston waited until the others turned in before walking his mount out of the area. Once far enough away that the sound of hoofbeats would not carry to the unsuspecting men, he swung into the saddle and made tracks through the night to the rendezvous point given by Two Thumbs Buehler. Kid gave a shiver. That hand with two thumbs on it always got to him. Someone had told him once that those sort of oddities came from brother and sister getting married. Or even first cousins. Could that be? he wondered at the time.

Now the novel idea returned to fire his imagination. Suppose he and his cousin, Hilly, had done somethin' really bad when they had been fussin' around out behind the barn that day. Not that the Kid looked like anyone capable of something bad. He stood only an inch over five feet, and that in his boots. A remarkably slow developer, he had the bone structure and features of a twelve-year-old, although six years older. His blue eyes, cottony hair, and cherub's mouth artfully hid a hot, vicious temper and sadistic personality. He fantasized about that steamy afternoon with Hilly all the way to the meeting place.

Five of the dozen men sent to get Preacher waited at the isolated bald knob that stood out in the middle of a wide valley. Kid Ralston withheld his big news, choosing not to share it with them out of profound dislike. They, along with others in the gang, tormented him mercilessly about his small stature. Two of them, in fact, had hung the handle "Kid" around his neck. He overrode his discomfort over the two thumbs to ride apart from the others to meet Buehler when he arrived.

"I found him, Two Thumbs. I know where Preacher is. It's jist like we heard, he done went south of Trout Crick Pass. He's got three other fellers with him."

"You done good, Kid," Buehler praised and reached out to pat the youthful trash on one shoulder with the two-thumbed hand.

Kid Ransom nearly lost the supper he hadn't gotten to eat. He gritted his teeth and endured. "They're about four miles from here, to the south."

Two Thumbs grinned. "We'll move in on 'em durin' the night, hit them at dawn."

Preacher roused out first. A peach-blush band of soft light lay along the eastern horizon. With nothing to hurry him along the way, Preacher saw nothing to be gained by rising in total darkness to do everything by feel. He stretched and stood like a stork to shake some small pebbles from one moccasin, then stretched again and headed for the fire ring.

He blew some kindling to flame from the buried coals of the previous night, added some wrist-sized sticks and warmed himself out of the lingering March chill. Then he set the coffeepot to boil. He had just bent over his kitchen parfleche to retrieve coffee beans when a ball moaned over his bowed back and smacked into the trunk of the pine. Preacher dropped as though he had been shot.

But not before he freed one of his fearsome pistols from its cured-and-stiffened hide holster. His companions, wise in the ways of attacks by Indians and whites alike, remained outwardly motionless. After a long, tense minute, voices came faintly to Preacher's ears.

"I done it! I done kilt ol' Preacher."

"I wouldn't be too eager to go down and take his hair, Kid," came sage advice.

"Why not?" Kid Ralston asked.

"You figger those other fellers up an' died of fright?" Two Thumbs Buehler taunted.

"Huh! I never thought about that. They ain't moved. You reckon they're layin' for us?" Blushing furiously at his *faux pas*, the Kid reloaded hastily.

"I figger you did a fool thing in not waitin' until we all opened up. You've put us betwixt a rock an' a hard spot. Nothin' for it, though. We'd best get it on."

So saying, Two Thumbs and the other ten opened up on the reclining figures. Only the blankets of Beartooth, Nighthawk, and Dupre took the punishment. The moment smoke spurted from the muzzles of the assassins' weapons, the trio rolled violently to the side away from their attackers. Their answering fire roared across the meadow.

The volley was followed by a charge. As the bushwhacking trash came into sight, rifle balls tore into their irregular rank. Two men went down, one with a shrill cry and a shattered kneecap. Eager to claim a trophy from his victim, Kid Ralston charged ahead of the line. He had his knife out, ready to take Preacher's hair, when the wily mountain man came up with a roar and let fly with the deadly four-barrel pistol in his right hand.

Hot lead stopped the Kid in mid-stride. The first ball of the double load clipped the lobe from his left ear. The second punched through a rib and tore a path from front to rear of his left lung. Kid's vision got all blurry and he dropped his skinning knife. It didn't matter at all to him that Preacher had apparently risen from the dead to take retribution.

Kid Ralston only knew that his chest burned with the fires of hell and he had gotten awfully weak. He thought of his Ma, of Pa and the hickory switch he'd used to try to make Kid walk the straight and narrow. How he wished now that it had taken effect. He thought of his brothers, all three younger than his eighteen years, yet every one bigger, taller, and stronger. He didn't think of his cousin Hilly. Or anything else for that matter, as his lung filled with blood and he passed into unconsciousness that would swiftly lead to death.

Preacher ignored the dying youth. He immediately turned his attention to the motley band of unwashed whites who streamed out of the trees toward them. "Don't cotton to your invite, you pond scum," Preacher hollered at them. "But I sure favor to join the dance."

With that he shot another of the dregs of the criminal brotherhood. To his right he saw Dupre dump a fat, red-faced specimen of depravity in a shower of buckshot with which he had charged a .70 caliber Flobert horse pistol. Beyond him, Nighthawk ducked a blow from a rifle butt and buried his knife in the belly of a similar dirtbag. Beartooth discharged a pistol in each hand and brought down a pair of vipers who had carelessly gotten too close together.

We work well as a team, Preacher thought, although we haven't been together for several years. He dodged to one side to avoid a shot from the thinning ranks of killer trash and ended the man's life with the last load.

"*Sacre bleu!*" Dupre cursed in French. "You have ruined my jacket and this shirt."

Preacher cut his eyes to Dupre, to see where a ball along his ribs had released a torrent of blood. While he studied his friend, Preacher exchanged his pistols.

"*Dormez vous avec le Diable,*" Dupre spat in his assailant's face a moment before he shot him with another

Flobert .70 caliber. The shot pellets wiped away all of the man's face above his lower jaw.

"What d'you call him, Dupre?" Preacher asked. Only four of the louse-infested thugs remained on their feet. Preacher took aim at one.

"I told him to go sleep with the devil."

"I reckon he will, partner." Preacher shot his target in the small notch between the collarbones. His head snapped to an odd angle when the .50 caliber ball shattered a vertebra. The field of battle fell suddenly silent.

"Say, fellers, I think we finished them all," Preacher called out.

Right then, to make a liar of Preacher, Two Thumbs forced himself up on his elbows and winged a shot at the mountain man that missed. Preacher put a round in the center of the balding spot on the top of Two Thumbs' head.

"We have now," Beartooth said through a powder-grimed grin.

After they inspected the dead, Preacher stood beside the last man he had killed, a deep frown on his forehead. "This one I'd know anywhere. He ran with Ezra Pease back ten years ago, when I drove Pease outta these mountains. He sent a lot of men to do a job on us. What's he done? Bring an army out here? If so, maybe we'd best split up. I've got a feeling there's a heap of trouble up ahead."

8

Reverend Thornton Bookworthy gazed at the tall ramparts that grew with each hour on the trail. They had been on the road for three days, but not headed east. Bookworthy removed his wide-brimmed, black hat and mopped at his sweaty brow with a snowy kerchief. Then he slapped his meaty palm on the leather cover of the Bible that rested on his black-clothed thigh.

"Yes, Patience, my dear. We have God's work to do, and no buckskin-bedecked near-savage is going to prevent us."

"What if that Preacher man was right about the Cheyenne going to war?" Prudence a bit more sharply than her usual submissive tone.

"Not even the Cheyenne can stop us, for I am certain they are thirsting for the Word. We're doing the right thing, mark my words, Prudence."

"Yes, dear." Prudence kept her composure although her mind swarmed with images of the painted, screaming faces of the Kiowa and Pawnee who had attacked them so recently. The mules in front of her shifted their rumps and complained with grunts as they labored up the incline.

Since leaving Bent's Fort, the grade had increased steadily. Now, with the foothills of the Rockies towering over them, their progress had decreased by three miles each day. They would be in those mountains tomorrow, Prudence reminded herself. And within two weeks, they would reach the land where the Cheyenne lived. Her husband's singing put her gloomy thoughts to flight.

"*Bringing in the sheaves . . . bringing in the sheaves, we shall come . . .* Yes, my dear, that's the first song we shall teach the benighted heathen. Don't you see the symbolism of it? We will be the harvesters of their souls."

Prudence winced and wanted to groan like the mules. A tiny echo of her own question haunted the back of her mind. What if Preacher was right?

A tall column of smoke rose from behind the nearest ridge. Preacher and his companions reined in to study it a moment. Preacher raised an arm and pointed a long finger at the wide base of the dark cloud.

"That's comin' from more than one thing burnin'. Now, as best as I can tell there ain't any cabins up there, unless they be built in the last two weeks. And that ain't no fire in the woods."

Nighthawk nodded agreement. "That's elementary. The animals would be acting strange if it was a conflagration in the forest," he stated the obvious.

Preacher caught him with a cocked eyebrow, mischief glinting in his blue-gray orbs. "Do I have to remind you how gawdawful those fancy words sound comin' outta the mouth of an Injun?" he teased.

Nighthawk gave him a straight face. "Heap good idea, white-eyes. Many smokes mean many fires."

"Awh, git off that, 'Hawk," Beartooth grumbled. "You sound worser playin' dumb Injun than you do playin' edji-cated Injun."

"The question remains, what is burning?" Nighthawk returned to his usual cultured tones.

"I've got me an idea, an' I don't think any of us is gonna like it," Preacher announced.

He gigged Thunder in the direction of the fires. The others quickly joined him. They rode through saddle notch between two peaks and looked down on the tragedy below. It proved to be exactly what Preacher expected. A small wagon train of some twenty vehicles had been raided, the people slaughtered, their possessions rifled, and valuables stolen. Preacher grunted and walked Thunder forward. His Hawken out and ready, rested across the saddle horn.

"Right like I expected. More damn-fool pilgrims. We'll have to find some way to cover 'em up. Pease and his vermin can wait."

Dismounted, the mountain men took turns standing guard, two-and-two, while the other pair gathered bodies. Slowly something became clear. The men had been killed outright, the women and older girls raped and then killed, some of the boys under about the age of ten had been misused also and then killed. All of the adults had been scalped.

"There's a few arrows over here, Preacher," Beartooth announced. "Got red markin's on 'em."

Preacher didn't like that at all. He had been on friendly terms with the Cheyenne for a number of years. "I saw them. Given that all the horses were shod, I'd call it a clumsy attempt at puttin' blame on the Cheyenne. Did you notice something else? Like most of their kind, these poor fools brought along enough youngin's to fill a good-sized school. Only the balance is off.

"We got boys up to the age of—oh, maybe ten or so, an' older boys, about sixteen an' up. None others." Preacher paused to fix his thoughts into words. "Now, Injuns is known to take right small kids to replace some of their own lost to sickness or stolen by enemy tribes. It's rare for them to take off only boy kids from eleven to fifteen. Which says again that it must have been whites. And I've a good idea who is behind it"

"That Pease feller you mentioned?" Dupre asked.

"None other. Only thing I can't work out is why. What would a gang of no-accounts like that want with boys of that age?"

"Maybe for the same things these little nippers got done to 'em," Beartooth suggested.

"I doubt that. They'd have had their way an' left 'em dead, too," Preacher responded, brow wrinkled in concentration. "But I reckon we're gonna find out right soon. All we gotta do is run them down. Now, let's get these folks buried."

Beartooth kicked his mount in the ribs and trotted up beside Preacher. "We've got company over in there." He pointed with his chin to a thicket of chokecherry bushes.

They had cut signs that some of the folks from the doomed train had managed to slip away. Following the faint trail westward had brought them here. Preacher nodded his understanding to Beartooth.

"I wanted to ride on past them a ways. Give them a chance to relax a little. Wouldn't do to ride into a ball o' hot lead, now would it?"

"Sure nuff," the older mountain man agreed.

Preacher pointed ahead. "We'll cut back and approach on foot from where they don't expect us."

While they rode off, Preacher made light conversation to add a further cloak of innocence to their passing by. "What you reckon to do, Beartooth, once you find out the Cheyenne's intentions?"

"I figger to find me a place that's still got plenty deer an' elk and settle in with my woman. We've got a good start these past three years with two youngin's, an' I hanker for more. Trappin's all but done for. Ain't seen a bone-i-fied buyer out this way in two years."

Preacher grunted. "I sold my traps last year. Ain't like the good days. Rendezvous was wild and hairy, but it shore were fun. Now, a man alone, goin' to Trout Crick or Bent's to sell his pelts—an' dang few of them anymore. Jist ain't the same."

They had ridden out of sight of the hiding survivors and Preacher signaled a halt. The four mountain men dismounted, tied their horses off to aspen saplings and slid silently into the woods. Years of this life had conditioned them all to move as quietly as possible. As a result, they reached their objective without giving any sign of their presence.

Even so, Preacher and his companions hunkered down low and studied the motley collection of women and a few youngsters for a long five minutes before making their presence known. The count came to eleven grown women, five girls a tad under marrying age, and seven boys, five of which were in their early teens. Preacher ghosted upright and stepped to the protection of a large pine behind the pilgrims.

"Howdy, folks. We're friendly, so don't go puttin' any holes in us," he called out. Two teenaged boys started and spun to train rifle muzzles in the direction from which he had spoken. "Now, now, jist lower them things, boys. If we had it in mind to do you harm, you'd been done for already. They's four of us. We need to come down amongst you an' figger out how to get you safely out of here."

"Oh, praise the Lord!" one female cried out, her face lifted to the sky. "We're delivered."

"I'm not so sure, Miz Kenny," one lad, still in the cracking voice stage, questioned the situation. "We'd better take some time on this."

"What you'd best do is lower them rifles an' let us come out before someone gets bad hurt," Preacher insisted. "'Sides, much as I like 'em, I don't cotton to huggin' a tree all day."

That broke the ice with some of the women. "Yes, boys, do put down those awful things," one matronly voice demanded. "This gentleman is right. If they meant us harm, they could have gotten to it a long time ago."

"Uh—well—all right," the adenoidal youth relented. "Chris, put your rifle down. I'm going to."

"Me, too, Bobby?" a voice asked from the far side of the cluster of women.

"Yeah, Nick," Bobby Gresham, the obvious leader, if such label could be applied to a boy not more than fifteen, answered.

The dowager quickly revised her appellation of gentleman

when first Preacher, then Beartooth, Dupre, and Nighthawk drifted out of the trees and came down among them. Preacher looked around and then addressed himself to Bobby.

"You picked a good place. Only thing is you left too much sign."

Bobby looked chagrined. "I never thought of that. Are those men coming after us?"

"The ones who hit your train, boy?" Preacher asked.

"Yeah. Er—I'm Bobby Gresham. Are they after us?" Bobby asked again, uncertainty in his eyes.

Preacher reassured him. "Not that we saw any sign of them. Pulled off to the north from the looks of it." He cut his eyes to the dowager and removed his hat like one would in polite society. "My name's Preacher, ma'am."

"Y-you're a minister?" she asked with inevitable doubt.

"No, ma'am. I'm on speakin' terms with the Almighty, but I ain't one of his servants. I—all of us—used to trap beaver before the demand dried up. These mountains," Preacher made a sweeping gesture to encompass their surroundings, "is sort of our home stompin' grounds."

"I'm Flora Sanders, this is Mrs. Grace Kenny, and this is Mrs. Falicity Jones. You've met Bobby, the other boys are Chris and Nick Walker."

"Did . . . anyone else . . . get away?" Nick, the youngest, asked with trepidation.

Preacher pulled an uncomfortable expression. Telling folks, and young ones in particular, that near everyone they held dear had died was a hard task. "I'm afraid not, son. You folk must be the only ones got away."

"Th-then I'm a widow. We all are," Falicity Jones cried in a tiny voice.

Preacher cut his eyes to Falicity for his first good look. What he saw was a devastatingly beautiful young woman. Robust and busty, and quite obviously pregnant. She spoke on, stammering now. "My—my ba-baby wi-will be born an—an orphan!"

Preacher knew a great deal about a lot of things. He didn't

know much about women. Particularly women in such a state. All he could do was answer, haltingly, "I—I'm afraid so, Mrs. Jones."

Wise in the mood shifts of her gender, Mrs. Sanders stepped into the breech. "I'm sorry to say we are all widows now, Falicity. But life does go on. What are we to do about that, Mr.—ah—Preacher?"

"There's a couple of wagon boxes didn't get burned clear down. And I reckon we can find enough stock to pull them. Gather what you brought with you and we'll start back to where you was ambushed." He paused and thought on it. "After that, it's closer to go on to Trout Crick Pass than back to Bent's. What is a puzzlement to me is what you folks were doin' wanderin' up into this country in the first place?"

"We were told it was a shortcut to the Immigrant Trail," Flora Sanders told him.

"It's that, right enough, but not for tenderfeet and wagons. You headed to Oregon?"

"Well, sort of. We were told back East that prime land abounded in the Snake River country."

"Oh, it's fine land," Preacher told her dryly. "Only thing is it's swarmin' with Nez Perce, Bannock, and Shoshoni. And they all feel mighty touchy about people settlin'in there."

"Then we were lied to?" Mrs. Sanders asked indignantly.

"Not exactly. There is fine country thereabouts. Let's say whoever told you about it and left out the Injuns sort of misrepresented the facts."

"Then what shall we do?" three of the women chorused.

"You can rest up at the trading post in Trout Crick Pass, and resupply. Then I'd advise you get a good guide, turn back and head for Bent's Fort."

"But we have no desire to turn back," Flora Sanders blurted.

"Suit yourselves," Preacher said pleasantly. "But don't expect us to burden ourselves with your protection any further than Trout Crick Pass."

Relief at their rescue turned to a smattering of grumpiness after this pronouncement. Ignoring it, the four mountain men helped gather the refugees and herd them off toward the damaged wagons. Half an hour along the trail, Preacher spoke up to Falicity Jones.

"Miz Jones, you happen to get a look at the ones who attacked your wagons?"

"Oh, yes. I'll never forget their faces."

Preacher squinted and cocked his head to one side. "Were they Injuns?"

"No!" Falicity barked with certainty. "They were all white men. The lowest, crawling, filthy trash on the face of the earth. I shudder to think about . . . what happened to those who didn't get away."

"You wouldn't want to know, ma'am. We'll make camp just short of the place they hit you. Those big boys, my friends an' I will go rig up some wagons. Tomorrow we start for Trout Crick Pass."

Their journey so far had toughened these women and the teenaged boys who had volunteered to protect them. Preacher noted that with satisfaction as the two creaky wagons, assembled from salvaged parts of several, groaned along the narrow trail toward the trading post. At this rate, Preacher figured about five days to reach there. Several of the women had minor injuries, and a child had a cut on one foot. That slowed them considerably.

At least, Preacher thought, they were under way. The older two boys drove the wagons, while those children who could, walked. Nick had appealed with big, dark blue eyes until Preacher, embarrassed in front of his friends, let the lad ride behind him on Thunder. He would, Nick promised, trade off with the other boys at driving. The peace of their sojourn lasted two days.

Quentin "Squint" Flowers pulled the sodden poultice from the bullet wound in his left bicep and replaced it with a fresh one. Buster Chase helped him bind the bandana around the injured appendage and stiffened and came to his boots.

"Hush, y'all," he harshly whispered to the others of the human vermin who had attacked the wagon train for Ezra Pease. "I hear somethin'."

"Sounds like wagons rollin'," Frank Clower opined.

"Couldn't be none of them folks got up from the dead," Rubber Nose Jaspar declared flatly.

"I wished we'd stayed with the rest," Squint Flowers of fered mournfully.

Frank Clower, the nominal leader, eyed him coldly. Squint's smallpox-scarred face rivaled the surface of the moon, Frank considered. Those eyes so close together and always scrunched near shut so's not to be able to tell the color. He made about the ugliest thing a man could look at and not run away. "It was you who whined about them brat boys always sobbin' an' takin' on. Wanted to get away from the li'l snot-noses, you said. Well, you're away now an' there's someone comin' our way. Rubber Nose, you an' Buster go take a look."

Within ten minutes the two devil's disciples returned with disturbing news. "They's some of them wimmin, must have got away when we hit the train, they's comin' on in two broke-down wagons. Got four tough-looking fellers with them. Also some kids."

Frank pulled a face. "Well, we sure's hell can't leave no livin' witnesses, now can we?"

"I say we set up a little ambush and finish them off," Buster Chase suggested. "They ain't much, jist some soft-in-the-head leftovers from the trappin' days, an' there's seven of us."

Frank considered that a while. Seven, with two of them wounded, their mounts tired and the wagons they had along with booty in them to slow them down. "What we ought to do is let them get on by us, then hit them in the rear. Complete surprise and we can take out those trappers, the rest'll be easy."

That decided upon, the human offal melted into the trees and Frank sent Squint Flowers back to obliterate the obvious sign of their presence. It wouldn't pass muster if anyone took time to study the ground, but folks like these, on the move, would miss the traces. It seemed to take no time for the first outrider to round a bend in the trail and come into view.

He looked tough, right enough, Frank Clower considered. Especially those pistols in the boxy-looking holsters slung around his hips. No nevermind, though. This would be easy. He hunkered down, like the rest of his men, and held his mount's nose. Slowly, then, the two-wagon cavalcade rolled past.

Frank gave them time to cover some three hundred yards and round another bend in the track, then motioned his corrupted followers out of concealment. They mounted quickly and left the wagons of loot behind. At a gallop, weapons at the ready, they streaked for the curve ahead. Tubby Slocum took the lead as they rounded the bend.

He let out a whoop when he saw the wagons, then a strangled cry as he ran into a powerful blast from the Hawken rifle in the hands of Beartooth. The burly mountain man lowered his rifle and got another of the riff-raff with the pistol that quickly filled his hand.

9

"Looks like the surprise is on you, buzzard breath," Beartooth shouted gleefully as he turned aside to avoid an answering volley from men slowed by astonishment.

Two more rifles cracked and Buster Chase flew from his saddle. One boot hung up in the stirrup and Buster flopped and sprayed the underbrush with his blood as the charging animal ran, unchecked, toward the wagons they had coveted so recently. Nighthawk watched him bound past and chose a pistol to replace his expended trap-door Olin-Hayes. Time later to slide in a paper cartridge and fit a cap in place.

Preacher gave Nighthawk a cheerful wave as he drew one of his deadly four-shooters and galloped back from the head of the column. The lean mountain man, with the smooth forehead and bright blue eyes, cackled as he drew near.

"Hee-hee, looks like it worked perfect. Damned amateurs, can't do anything right," Preacher chortled.

He filled his sights with the shocked face of Rubber Nose Jasper and shot away the pliable appendage that had earned Jasper his sobriquet. Jasper howled and clapped a hand over the blood-spouting stump. It brought him no mercy, though, as Preacher put another ball through Jasper's brisket.

Preacher bent forward to work the trigger mechanism and revolve the barrels again when a ball cracked through the space his head had occupied a moment before. That was downright unfriendly, he judged it. Such goin's-on would have to be brung to an end, and damn fast.

Preacher let his gaze rove over the remaining thugs and spotted the likely shooter. His big pistol banged out and the scowl of anger at missing changed to an expression of horror as Preacher's ball set off a bright flash in the brain pan of the lowly rubbish that illuminated his on-rushing afterlife.

Squint Flowers made an error in judgment. He continued his fatally determined charge against the men around the wagon instead of diving for cover among the boulders strewn along the road. He ran right into a pair of speeding balls fired by Dupre and Preacher. Flowers rose above his saddle and hung suspended a moment, before plopping into the churned-up turf to kick and jerk until death stilled his jammed reflexes.

Seeing this, Frank Clower managed to slow his horse and turn about. With balls chasing him, and Hashknife close at his side, he beat a hasty retreat. Preacher went to his second pistol and downed another lump of Pease slime. Through the fury of battle, Preacher faintly sensed a reduction in the volume of fire. A cross-eyed lout in a paisley shirt slid from his mount, caught himself at the last minute, and staggered toward the shelter of a boulder.

He didn't make it. Preacher fired a double-shotted load that put the first ball across the outer surface of the hard case's thigh and the second through its meaty portion. He went down in a graceless sprawl. Preacher gigged Thunder and approached the wounded man.

Two of the vermin who had taken shelter opened up in desperation then, intent on fixing Preacher's wagon once and for all. They both shot wide of the target and received a vengeful response from Dupre and Nighthawk. Lead balls howled off the convex faces of the granite lumps and showered each killer scum with fragments.

One of them, blinded by rock chips and slivers of lead, stumbled out into the open, one hand pawing at his blood-streaming eyes, the other holding a pistol, which he discharged wildly. Not all that wild, Preacher discovered when he felt the wind of the ball's passage by his cheek. Once more he gave thanks to the All Wise Above for guiding him to pause long enough to let little Nick jump from Thunder's rump onto the seat of the lead wagon before answering the call of the attack. That ball would have finished the little lad right smartly.

A pang of sorrowful remembrance of young Eddie,* so like the saucy image of Nick, came to Preacher as he let go the final load in his pistol and split the breastbone of the trashy thug. Dupre's rifle banged loudly close at hand and the last skulker in the rocks gave up his hold on life.

"C'est fini," Dupre declared.

"Yeah, it's done, all right," Preacher agreed. "Let's check out the bodies."

They found one man still with breath in him. "Buster Chase," he gasped out his name. "You boys done kilt me good. H-how'd you know we was back there?"

"A blind ten-year-old could tell where you left the trail and tried to cover it up," Preacher said with sincere contempt.

"Who be you men?" Chase spoke in a whisper.

"I'm called Preacher. This here's Beartooth, Dupre, and Nighthawk."

Chase's lips curled into a sneer. "Back-shooters all, I've been told. Damn you into hell, Preacher, and all your kind." He went on cursing the mountain men while pink froth gathered around the hole in his chest and a huge bubble formed. With a rapidly fading voice he hurled his last brag.

"There's thirty more just like us up ahead, Preacher. You an' your lice-infested friends won't find them so easy to take." With that said, he shivered, convulsed mightily, and went still.

"Don't bury that one," Nighthawk demanded. "He said I had lice."

"He's one to talk," Beartooth put in. "Look, there's a big gray one crawlin' out of his hair right now."

*See *The First Mountain Man*. Published by Pinnacle Books.

"Unpardonable manners," Dupre agreed. "I've never had a louse on me in my life."

Preacher peered at him studiously. Dupre's impeccable clothes bore not a wrinkle nor a smudge from their violent encounter. "You know somethin', Dupre? I believe you. Let's gather up what all we can. Those boys can put the guns to good use."

Cora Ames wore a worried frown as she approached the rotund figure of the Reverend Thornton Bookworthy. They had stopped for the nooning in a small swale only miles short of the ramparts of the Rocky Mountains.

"We should have come upon Bent's Fort before nightfall three days ago," she stated flatly. Then worry colored her words. "We've strayed from the trail somewhere along the line. We—we could be anywhere."

In fact, they had taken a trail much used by Indians in the area, that swung roughly northwest off the old Santa Fe Trail. With the decline in the fur trade, Bent's Fort also suffered a loss of activity. Few journeyed there from the east and the main trail had fallen into disrepair. The many horses' hooves and travois of the natives marked a clearer, rutted path for such novices as Bookworthy and his hired drivers. Totally convinced of his ability, the reverend could not accept criticism from a mere woman.

"I assure you, Sister Ames, that we are on the right path." Truth to tell, Thornton Bookworthy would have been hard pressed to point out which way was west at sunset.

"Beggin' yer pardon, Reverend, but I'm sure the lady is right," Buck Dempsey offered. "We're way north of Bent's Fort. Way I figger it, we'll come upon the trail to Trout Creek Pass by sometime tomorrow mornin'."

Reverend Bookworthy brightened. "Why, splendid! That puts us ahead of schedule. Let's push on, perhaps we'll find it yet today."

"I—ah—don't think so," Buck stated softly, looking beyond the portly minister.

"Why not?" Bookworthy demanded.

"We've got company."

Reverend Bookworthy turned abruptly to face three Arapaho women, with twice that number of small children at their feet, and a lithe, smooth-limbed youth of perhaps sixteen years. Bookworthy's jaw dropped and he felt faint. The oldest boy made the sign for peace and spoke in lilting-accented English.

"We are friendly. Not . . . make you harm."

"Why, you speak English," Bookworthy blurted in his surprise. "Are you Christian? Do you know Jesus?"

"I am called Little Raven. I not know that man. But I know . . . you lost. I know man who can help you."

"You do?" In his eagerness to find aid, Bookworthy dropped all pretense of being comfortable with their situation. "Who is that?"

"He is called White Wolf. You round eyes know him as Preacher."

Astonishment washed over Bookworthy's face. "He's nearby? How far? Come, my good boy, tell us."

A faint smile flickered on the young Arapaho's face. "You are going the right way. Preacher is two, three days ahead of you. He has three friends with him. They are with people in rolling lodges, like yours."

"That's simply marvelous," Bookworthy babbled, forgetting entirely that it was Preacher who had expelled them from these mountains. "We must make contact. He'll absolutely have to guide us now," he appealed to his fellow missionaries. "Buck," he called to the driver. "Take another teamster and push on ahead until you contact Preacher. Use my big Walker, Brutus, and make all speed. I shall drive your wagon."

"And I the other," Cora offered. Then, remembering what Preacher had told her about manners among the Indians, she turned to the youth. "Will you take food with us?"

Smiling broadly now, he told his companions of the invitation. The oldest of the three women said something in Arapaho, which he translated. "She asks do you have the sweet sand. She means sugar."

"Why, yes, of course," Cora responded with a light laugh. "We have plenty. Come, there's coffee and beans and corned beef."

Looking back on it later, Cora realized that a good time was had by all.

Peter looked around in wonder and awe. "These are the biggest mountains in the whole world," he declared after closing his sagging jaw. "Bigger than those in Pennsylvania or Missouri."

"It's the Rocky Mountains," Helen, the reader in the group of orphans, informed him. "The fur trappers called them the 'Shining Mountains' or the 'High Lonesome.'"

"Are we goin' up there?" Peter asked of Silas Phipps, his thin arm extended, small finger pointing.

"Most likely," Phipps grunted. He regretted not resupplying on whiskey at Bent's Fort.

Things cost so dang much out here, he had soon discovered. It had taken all the rest of his cash money to get two wagon wheels repaired, buy food and some warm blankets. The latter were for him, of course, not the brats. They could make do with what they had.

Nightfall had them well enfolded in the ramparts of the Rockies. Silas Phipps sat in his usual, somewhat frumpy regal splendor in the large chair for which he had traded off a six-year-old boy to a childless couple in Missouri. Well and good. The kid had a constantly runny nose anyway. Ruth and Helen cooked supper, their regular chore. While they toiled over the fire pit, Helen shot nervous glances in the direction of Silas.

It made him smile, while he sipped sparingly at the whiskey jug. There was supposed to be a single other trading post up further north, at a place called Trout Creek Pass. Surely he could knock down something worth trading for, or the boys—who he had put to setting out snares—could trap some furry animals. The odor of cooking meat made his belly rumble.

Peter returned first from putting snares in the grass beside a stream. He had noted small footprints and calculated where the animal who had made them would be likely to walk. Proud of his accomplishment, he went to the fire to share his woodsman's wisdom with Ruth and Helen.

"I found an animal path. Put my snares along it by the creek," he informed the girls.

"What good will that do?" Helen asked, distracted, at least for the moment, from her contemplation of what awaited her later that night.

"It's been used more than once. I figger whatever made the prints will use it again: And . . . zap! One nice pelt for that ol' bassard to trade for booze."

"I wish he'd drown in the stuff," Ruth said hotly.

"Yes. And before tonight," Helen choked out.

"Again, honey?" Ruth asked with warm compassion.

Helen nodded jerkily and big, hot tears ran down her cheeks.

"You three shut up and tend to yer cookin'," Silas Phipps growled from his throne. "Ain't that grub about ready?"

"Yes, Mr. Phipps," Ruth replied, subdued. "Peter will bring you your plate." She gave Peter a "this will get even for Helen" look.

Ruth had no idea how terrible a form her attempt at revenge would take. Peter started apprehensively across the clearing to where Phipps slumped in his chair. He dreaded being around the filthy old man who held them captive. Why didn't they just run away? Peter had wondered that a hundred times. In his anxiety at not riling Silas Phipps, Peter missed seeing the wrist-thick bowed branch that had fallen from a big old cottonwood.

As a result, the boy tripped over it and went sprawling. The plate flew from his hand and the gravy-covered food took off from there. Some of it splattered on the boots of Silas Phipps. With a roar the thick-shouldered brute came to his feet and charged down on the terrified Peter.

"Goddamn you!" Phipps bellowed. "Can't any of you do

anything right? I'll teach you to be so clumsy. Waste all that food, will you?"

He bent and yanked the petrified child upright. One big, hairy fist closed around the leather suspenders that held up Peter's trousers. Phipps pulled them off, then ripped the shirt from Peter's back. Peter lost it then and began to sob wretchedly. Long, dry, sharp wails came painfully from deep inside. Phipps dragged the boy into the light from the fire.

There he jerked down Peter's linsey-woolsey trousers and exposed the lad's bare behind. He snatched up a willow rod, thick as one of his muscular fingers, and yelled at the astonished orphans. "C'mere, all of you. You're gonna witness what happens for a show of defiance."

"I didn'—didn' defy you, sir," Peter pleaded.

Phipps shoved Peter roughly forward. "Bend over that wagon wheel."

Then he began to apply the willow switch. He started at Peter's shoulders, and worked downward. His arm rose and fell rhythmically. The wooden shaft made a wet, meaty smack with each blow. The more Phipps lashed the boy, the greater his fury grew. By the time he reached the small of Peter's back, each strike split the skin and blood ran in thin, red sheets.

Phipps had entered such a frenzy that he breathed in great, gusty bellows blasts when he reached Peter's buttocks. He spent the least time there, though, delivering only four sound, stinging stripes. Phipps desisted then, stood looking at the horrified expressions on the faces of the other children.

"Bring me some of that axle grease and some cotton waste," he commanded Ruth.

Through all his ministrations, Peter continued to whimper softly. When the clean-up had ended, the boy drew up his trousers, his face crimson with embarrassment and humiliation. Then he went to find another shirt.

His whole body throbbed with agony, stung and burned, an hour later, as Peter curled up near the fire pit, under a thin blanket. He bit his tongue to keep from making any outcry, and lay in icy fear as he listened to the whispered pleading, whimpers and cries of agony that Helen made from some distance beyond in the back of the second wagon. Mind awhirl in misery, Peter vowed that he would kill Phipps before anything like that happened again.

"He's a ring-tailed whoo-doo, ain't he?" Rupe Killian said proudly to the man who rode beside him.

"Who?" Delphus Plunkett asked.

Rupe rolled his eyes. "Who else? Mr. Pease, ya ninny. He's got more smarts than any man I know. Talks like a real gent'man, too."

"So's Hashknife, only he don't put on no airs," Delphus revealed his opinion of Ezra Pease.

Killian and Plunkett rode in a column of twos, along with the rest of Ezra Pease's gang of cutthroats, headed cross-country in the wide, fertile valley ringed by the Laramie and Medicine Bow Mountains. They had reached the heart of the Cheyenne country. Unlike many of the men, Rupert Killian did not experience any unease. Nearly 5,000 Indians called this land home. Most of those were warriors. The nearest help, in the form of white men in sufficient numbers, lay 800 miles to the west, nearly a thousand to the east. Yet, Rupe Killian had no fear.

Infused with his hero worship of Ezra Pease, Rupe Killian waxed expansive on his favorite subject. "Take this little jaunt. Ol' Rough-house Pease gets word there's a big pow-wow goin' on about the Cheyenne makin' war with the Blackfeet. So what's he do? He saddles us all up and heads out. We're gonna ride right up to that confabulation an' offer to sell 'em guns to use against their enemy. Now, that's right smart thinkin', I tell you."

Delphus Plunkett cut his eyes around the flat terrain that surrounded their exposed position. "I ain't so sure of that. Those Injuns could find us out here quick as a wink."

"Why, hell, boy, we'd whup 'em easy. We's white men, ain't we?"

Delphus twisted his head to peer behind, just in case. "But there's a whole lot more of them than there is of us, Rupe."

"That don't matter none, nohow," Rupe dismissed with sublime contempt. "Besides we're comin' as friends. They'll welcome them guns, I tell you."

The sound of drumming hooves from ahead of the column reached Rupe's ears. He perked up and rose in the stirrups to look forward. One of the scouts sent forward by Pease came fogging down on the outlaw band on a foam-sheeted horse. He started shouting something while still out of earshot.

"My God, they're right behind me! Hunnerds of 'em!"

Ezra Pease and Titus Vickers spurred their mounts forward to meet the excited man. "Who are, my man?" Pease demanded.

"They be Cheyenne, Mr. Pease. Gobs of 'em. There's a village jist beyond this ridge. We showed up on the back slope an' thcy come boilin' out at us."

Shots cracked out before he could say more. Some twenty bare-headed warriors came into view on the crest of the ridge. They reined in and sat their ponies, took aim and fired another ragged volley. Rifle balls plowed dirt a hundred yards from the column of white men.

"What are we gonna do now?" Titus Vickers asked, his throat tight with fear.

10

Ezra Pease recovered rapidly. "Why, my good man, we're going to charge them."

Those around the well-dressed leader blinked in incomprehension. The number of Indians on the ridge continued to grow. Eyes widened as the count of the angry Cheyenne increased to overwhelming odds. Several of the hard-bitten thugs with Pease cut their eyes to Titus Vickers in appeal. He gave them a curt nod, though not a word had been spoken. Titus Vickers *knew*.

"Not likely, Mr. Pease," he responded with more formality than usual. "At least not by this chile. I think we'd best make a run for it while the gettin's good."

Pease studied the ranks above, war lances aflutter with feather decorations, bows and rifles ready. He sighed gustily and gave a reluctant nod. "Your calm evaluation of the situation may have saved our lives again, Vic. Under the prevailing conditions, I have no choice but to defer to your wisdom." He paused and then sucked in wind. "Let's get the hell out of here!" he bellowed.

None of the men needed encouragement. They reversed their mounts on the narrow trickle of a trail and put spurs to flanks. In an eye-blink, only a column of roiling dust remained where the invading white men had been. A smug smile bloomed on the face of Falling Horse. He pointed to the retreating backs of their enemy.

"We will follow them, punish them some. It will be for the honor of Black Hand, not our own."

At once, the Cheyenne warriors streamed down the slope from the saddle notch in the ridge. Hooting and whooping, they set up rapid pursuit. Those at the rear of Pease's disorganized column heard them even over the rumble of the hooves of their galloping horses. They cast apprehensive glances behind them.

When the swift Cheyenne ponies closed enough, those in the forefront loosed rounds from their rifles and trade muskets. Balls whined overhead and one took a chunk from the fat rump of Vern Beevis. His wail blended with the war cries of the Indians.

"You know, I think we've got ourselves in some deep cow plop," Rupe Killian shouted over the pounding hooves.

"I don't 'think' no such thing," Delphus returned the shout. "I damn well know it."

"How we gonna get outta this?" Rupe wanted to know.

"You acquainted with foldin' yer hands together an' lookin' up at the Almighty?"

"You mean *pray?*" Rupe asked, astounded.

Delphus answered soberly. "Seems the only thing might work."

Tension so thick she could almost taste it, Falicity Jones thought as she heard the call from the rear of the column. "Riders comin'!" Whatever did that mean? Would they be attacked again? She cut nervous eyes to the broad-shouldered figure of the man called Preacher.

"Dismount the wagons," he ordered. "Up in them rocks until we know who it is."

Quickly the refugees from the ill-fated wagon train halted the patched-up wagons and scrambled into the tumble of boulders at the uphill side of the trail they followed. While they did, Falicity observed Preacher checking the caps on his multitude of weapons and sighed with relief.

What a competent man he was. Had she not been so recently widowed, she might look upon him as handsome and dashing. Silly goose! she chastened herself. Preacher worked by feel, she noticed, while his eyes remained set on their back-trail. With that accomplished, he trotted his horse to the rearmost wagon and lowered the long-barreled Hawken rifle to his saddle bow. From a pocket sewn into the saddle skirt, Preacher withdrew a compact brass tube. He drew it out to form a spyglass and peered through the single lens.

White men, Preacher detected at once. Only two of them, so far, his thinking progressed. Might be more of Pease's trash and again, might not. Then he, too, left the trail, secured his horse and disappeared into the rocks.

A flight of arrows sailed their way overhead. Ezra Pease winced at the moaning sound and instinctively ducked his head. Three of the projectiles found sticking points in horse-flesh. The animals turned frantic. They uttered nearly human squeals and groans. The men atop them flung about like stuffed rag bags. The Cheyenne fired their rifles in irregular order. Fortunately for Pease and his gang it was as equally hard for a Cheyenne to hit a moving target from a moving mount as for a white man.

In the lull to reload, following the discharge, the desperate white men put more distance between them and their pursuers. All form of order had disappeared. Their flight had become a matter of staying alive. Titus Vickers hung back, urging the men to get control of themselves. At last a few overcame their panic enough to offer some resistance. They reined in among some rocks and took careful aim.

Rifles cracked and two Cheyenne fell from their saddles. Hastily the empty weapons got reloaded while a handful of others took up positions and opened up on the charging Indians. Vickers looked forward to see the scattered riders disappear around a bend he did not recall from their approach. He had to find out what had happened.

"Hold them off as long as you can, then pull back," Titus Vickers told Bart Haskel.

He spurred ahead to discover a terrible blunder. In their eagerness to evade their enemy, those in the lead had turned into a blind canyon. Sheer granite walls rose along a narrow stream, through which the unwitting men splashed, silver sheets of icy water spraying nose-high on their mounts. They could not be left behind, Vickers realized and held in place to direct those beyond to join the others. Their only chance remained with superior firepower.

When Bart Haskel and the last two thundered down the main trail, Titus Vickers waved his hat at them and drew them into the box canyon. "We didn' come this way," Bart observed.

"I know. Ride on to the others. I'll be right with you."

Vickers dismounted and led his mount away from the entrance to a place of safety. There he tied off the lathered roan and pulled a short-handled spade from his saddle gear. He rushed back to the mouth of the canyon and up a talus-strewn slope to the base of a large boulder. Working cautiously at one side of the huge stone, he began to sling away shovel-loads of dirt. It didn't matter to him why the Cheyenne had held back. While he labored on, an idea came to him.

This was their home country and they probably knew it better than anyone. They would figure out that the gang had trapped itself. No need to hurry. Take time, reload. Bind up any slight wounds, and come on at their convenience. Meanwhile, he had plenty to do. The dirt and decomposed granite flew faster. Finally the boulder rocked precariously with each solid chunk of the spade.

Carefully, Vickers worked his way to the upper inside edge of the big rock and put his shoulder to it. Flexing his legs, he pushed with all his strength. At first it seemed as though nothing would happen. Then, with a loud, grating groan, the ponderous rock canted out over the excavation Vickers had made. He bunched his legs and shoved again. The top of the boulder rocked past the center point and the whole mass let go. Loudly it crashed down into the notch that defined the mouth of the box canyon. That would slow the Indians one hell of a lot, Vickers thought with satisfaction as he walked back to his horse. In minutes he joined the milling stew of misfits and high country trash.

"I've got the entrance partly closed off," Vickers announced to a pale-faced Pease. "We can get out, single file, but the Injuns will have to come at us the same way. A few good shots can hold them off for long enough for them to lose interest."

"Good thinking, Vic. You hear that, men?" he challenged. "All it takes is a little cool thinking and some determination and we'll get out of this without any harm done. I want ten of you to go back with Vic and take up positions where you can keep the entrance under fire. Make every shot count. The rest of you settle down your mounts and someone, for God's sake, start a pot of coffee."

That last brought a grudging ripple of laughter from the thoroughly demoralized outlaws. By the time the dust settled and the horses had been wiped down and cooled out, a fire crackled in a stone pit, a coffeepot of chill stream water put in place and a tripod erected to hold a pot for beans. Noting this last, Pease nodded toward it with satisfaction.

"Good idea. We may be here awhile."

His prediction proved all too true. The coffee water had yet to boil before sporadic gunfire came from the mouth of the canyon. Light and irregular at first, the output quickly increased in volume. Many of the hard cases in camp wore worried frowns. A wounded man straggled back into camp.

"Them damn Cheyenne must know another way into this place. They're swarmin' all over us out there."

"We had all better get down there," Ezra Pease decided aloud. "Check your powder and shot. If we hit them hard, they should pull back."

With twenty guns roaring in action, the gang fought the Cheyenne to a standstill. Then, as the muzzle-loading rifles and pistols ran dry, the bows and arrows of the warriors made up the difference. Ezra Pease was shocked to discover that less than a dozen braves had penetrated into the box canyon. Their bows had devastating effect, wounding men more often than fatal shots. Half a dozen rifles cracked again, soon followed by more, and stalemate returned. Fatigue must be playing with him, Pease thought as visibility seemed to lower in a gray haze. A quick count showed his men to be less than fifteen still on their feet. More Cheyenne had slithered up through the rocks and fitted shafts to bowstrings. What he needed, Ezra Pease concluded, was a miracle.

A crash of gunfire set them to ducking before the warriors could release their arrows. Ezra Pease blinked rapidly. It had grown noticeably darker. A new sound intruded on the intermittent battle. A seething hiss grew in volume as it raced down the canyon. Suddenly visibility dropped to less than a hundred yards. Icy rain began to pelt Ezra Pease in the face. Titus Vickers appeared on his left.

"Rain, by God! That'll play hob with their bowstrings. I think we've got this-un won."

Wiping streams of chill droplets from his face, Ezra Pease made short reply. "Call it a draw and be damn grateful for that."

Another look through the spyglass revealed the riders to be Buck Dempsey and Kent Foster. They had been with those Bible-thumpers. What the hell were they doing up here? Preacher wondered to himself. Oh, no. That couldn't be By the Almighty, ain't no way any proper guide could have been talked into something that stupid. No.

"Yes," Buck assured Preacher ten minutes later when they reached the spot where he waited for them with growing unease. "They never engaged a guide. Took the wagons east out of sight of the fort, then cut back north. That Reverend Bookworthy's a determined man, even if he's a fool."

"I'll agree with all you've said. He's sure a fool. They must have taken that Injun trace to catch up so soon."

Relieved that the blame would not fall on him, Buck relaxed enough to produce an admiring smile. "Right you are.

Me an' Kent, here, tried to talk them out of it. They weren't hearin' none of that. 'We've been sent from Gawd to minister to the heathen and nothing or no one is going to stop us,' ol' Bookworthy spouted when he ordered us to turn off. None of the other drivers is too happy about it, either. But the pay is good and the food even better. Them mission women sure know how to handle a skillet."

Preacher snorted through his nose. "I'll allow as how that's sure right. A feller could put on a few pounds right fast eatin' with them folks. Now, how far back would you say they were?"

Buck's brow furrowed. "Three days by horseback, but that don't mean much. They's plum lost and not on the right trail. Wagons won't make eight miles a day in this country. So I'd say five to eight days."

"Damnit!" Preacher slapped a thumb-thick aspen branch against his left thigh. "It's plumb ignorant. Any man'd know that. Well, me an' my friends ain't got time to lead them pilgrims outta here. You go on back for them, get 'em out of whatever pickle they got themselves into, 'cause they sure ain't up to doin' it on their own. I reckon the good Reverend Bookworthy knows as much about readin' trail sign as he does about real sinnin'. We'll wait for you here, then it's on to Trout Crick Pass. They'll just damn well have to spend the summer an' winter there."

Buck's eyes twinkled. "You know dang well they won't, Preacher. They'll just hire on some no-count guide like that Bull Ransom and head off into the wilds."

"An' get themselves kilt. Serves them right if they do," Preacher snapped as he turned away. "I've got these dang refugees to tend to. Might as well grain your horses out of their supplies an' rest 'em good. Then hit the road back after them idjit flatlanders."

By nightfall, Preacher almost had a mutiny on his hands. The refugees had grumbled among themselves about waiting at this spot for more lost souls to join the cavalcade. Their supplies were dangerously low, thanks to the raid on their wagon train. They wanted to push on to where they could make connections with the Immigrant Trail and join another train. Most of all, they felt put upon that these strangers were missionaries and thus considered by Preacher to be even more addle-pated than he thought his present charges to be. Finally, while magenta, gold, and purple painted the western sky, a delegation made up of Mrs. Kenny, Flora Sanders, and Falicity Jones came to where Preacher bent to put a cover over the cookfire.

Wise in the ways of handling their men, and aware of the covert admiring glances Preacher had been giving Falicity, the older women appointed her as spokeswoman. They approached with self-generated confidence. Preacher's stony expression quickly cooled some of that. "Preacher," Falicity began with firmness. "We have some say in what goes on. At least we should have," she hastily amended.

"Not in this, you don't," Preacher countered.

Falicity had still not been put in full retreat. "Back at the beginning, we elected for the train to be run as a democracy."

"Damn-fool word, you ask me. Means 'mob rule' in Greek," Preacher snapped.

Falicity's jaw sagged slightly. How could she reach this man? "What I'm saying is that we need to press on northward, to find a train to the west as soon as possible. We have nothing to return to. This delay might cost us any chance we have."

"Be a good thing if it did. Now, you take any of these men here. Ain't a one couldn't guide you to the trail. Not Nighthawk, not Dupre, nor Beartooth. Especially since they're headed that way anyhow. Ain't a one of them will do it, though. None of them's crazy enough to. Miz Jones, you jist don't get it, do you? There ain't a one of you suited to be out here. This country is pretty civilized, compared to up north. Even so, we got to watch you like a mother hen does her chicks. Beyond the Medicine Bows, way up on the Platte, there plain ain't nobody to help you."

"We would have you—ah—gentlemen to protect us . . . if you'd agree to guide us that far," Falicity offered, less sure of herself.

"Nope. All's out there is high-country meadows and mountains. And, of course, Injuns. Whole lots of Injuns, none of who take kindly to white folk invadin' their territory. What you propose, to sit out there an' wait for a wagon train to roll along, would only serve to get all our hair lifted."

"You're . . . serious about this, aren't you?" Falicity said wonderingly, reality at last dawning on her.

Preacher came to his moccasins, dusted off his hands as he spoke. "Dang straight I am. You ain't crossin' the Ohio River Valley, Miz Jones. Up there . . ." he pointed north, "there's the flats, the Platte, and Injuns."

"But, we're determined to live in the West." Falicity's tone had turned apologetic, pleading for understanding.

Now, Preacher had been thinking on that very thing for some time, since first encountering these displaced pilgrims. An idea had been toying with his brain for the past two days. Might be now was the time to trot it out and see if these female frontiersmen liked its shiny coat.

"Like I said, you can always summer at Trout Crick Pass. If you've all your minds set on livin' in God's Country, you could scout around, with someone local to guide you, locate a nice valley somewhere an' settle in. You could hire enough men from amongst the driftin' boys to build right smart cabins before the leaves turned. Anything more I can't guarantee. Hell, I can't even offer it. Plumb too dangerous."

Falicity's eyes came alight with bright new hope. She clapped her hands in enthusiasm and turned to the rest of the delegation. "You see? I told you Preacher would solve this dilemma for us. We're going to settle in the West after all."

"An' God he'p us all," Preacher grumbled as he turned away to wonder what new outrage would befall them next.

11

Scavengers had been at work on the hurried graves of the ambushed wagon train. When they arrived, after five hard days of travel, Reverend Thornton Bookworthy took one look at the gnawed limbs and eviscerated torsos and promptly lost his breakfast. The burned wagons presented a grim sight. Shaken to her core, Patience Bookworthy put a hand on her husband's arm.

"Why, we came through here not long ago. This . . . could have happened to us."

Himself badly unnerved, Reverend Bookworthy still relied on his main assurance. "We had God's protection, Patience. On the way up we had five capable, armed men to guide us. Coming—ah— coming back, we had that Preacher fellow to scout for us. This is an oddity, something rare if the accounts we saw back East are to be believed." He looked around, and back at the crude mass grave. "We should give these poor people proper Christian burial."

"We haven't time, Reverend," Buck Dempsey advised. "Preacher's waitin' for you all to catch up. An' I've a mind his patience runs on the thin side."

"Surely we can take the time to cover them up better," Bookworthy blustered. "It's the least we can do."

Some of Preacher's sass had rubbed off on Buck. "It's the most, you ask me. If we take our noonin' here, it might be all right."

Reverend Bookworthy made a face. "Our Deacons and the other brethren can be put to the task, naturally. Also myself, of course," Bookworthy hastened to add.

With that agreed, the wagons pulled on up the trail a short distance to avoid the grisly scene, and the women set about preparing a meal. Rocks, fallen branches, and dirt were used to enlarge and deepen the mound that served as a final resting place for the unknown adventurers. All of the missionaries kept the possibility of an attack on the surface of their thoughts as they went about the effort of entombing the less fortunate pioneers.

A warm sun soon put large, wet stains in the armpits of the white shirts worn by the Holy Joes. They labored until blisters and hot red spots covered the palms of their hands. The summons to the noon meal put their faces aglow with relief. After Reverend Bookworthy offered thanks for the food and called on God's blessing for their enterprise, they fell to.

For all its quantity, the food rapidly disappeared. Afterward, the good reverend made the hoped-for announcement. "We have completed the monument over our departed, unknown brothers and sisters. I think we can spare the time for a prayer and song over their earthly remains."

Buck Dempsey started to rise and object, but a stern look from Cora Ames, with whom he had become smitten of late, stilled him. He joined the others as they trooped back to the mass grave. Reverend Bookworthy stepped out in front of the semicircle of immigrants.

"Shall we all raise our voices in two verses of that comforting hymn, 'Rock of Ages.'"

Asa Pettibone produced a mouth harp, and Tom Ashton put bow to his fiddle. The women and other men among the mission group sang beautifully. When they had concluded, Bookworthy offered a long-winded prayer and they sang another hymn. As the last notes of that died away, Buck Dempsey stepped forward.

"Now, let's get the hell an' gone away from here before the renegade whites who did this decide to come back."

"How did you know it was white men who did this awful thing, Buck?" Cora asked.

"Preacher told me," Buck answered. Cora's expression of raw admiration cut him.

"Yes, he would know about such things," she replied in worshipful tones.

Ah, hell, there goes any chance I ever had, Buck thought miserably as the holy pioneers took their places in the column and he gave the command to move out.

He had been known only as Hashknife since he signed on with Ezra Pease back in St. Louis. Hashknife had a hard, cruel face, with a frozen expression of suppressed anger, small, glittery, close-set eyes and a beak of nose that had been broken several times. None of the second-rate hard cases would mess with Hashknife. They steered clear of him, even during the rare drinking bouts in the semi-civilized surroundings of Missouri and along the Santa Fe Trail. Even the few, quality frontiersman types among the forty-man contingent walked softly around Hashknife. Ezra Pease did not miss this.

When the man came up the trail with a dozen hard-bitten drifters from the trading post at Trout Crick Pass, Pease summoned him to his tent. He waved a hand at the small keg of bourbon that rested on a folding stand, and nodded to a camp stool.

"Help yourself to the bourbon. Or, if you prefer, there's rum."

"Bourbon will do fine," Hashknife rumbled in that deep, Eastern-accented voice of his.

"Take a seat. I have a proposition I wish to discuss with you."

Hashknife downed half of the brass goblet of whiskey while Pease trimmed the end of a fine cigar. "What sort of proposition do you have in mind?"

Well-spoken bugger, Ezra Pease acknowledged silently.

He mused on how to present his case before answering. "You seem to be a cut above most of the men who follow me, Hashknife. I'd put your frontier skills on a par with those of Titus Vickers. Your ability to handle those men you brought in speaks well for your initiative in recruiting them, and your leadership abilities." The blank look Pease received prompted him to inquire, "Am I speaking over your head?"

"Not at all, Mr. Pease. I was only surprised that you had taken note of me in the least."

"Quality shows, my good man," Pease answered flatteringly, to cover his misstep. "I'm in the process of making some changes in the organization. I feel we need more flexibility. You can do a lot for me in that direction. A lot for yourself, for that matter."

Hashknife looked interested, at least as much as his stone face would reveal. "Go on, you have me curious."

"As you know, each man receives a share in our enterprise, with a quarter share bonus for a successful completion. Titus Vickers receives ten times that. I want to split the group into two wings, to operate independently, but with the same common goal. I would like for you to command that second wing. With an equal share to Vic's."

Hashknife swallowed hard and nearly choked on the whiskey. "You amaze me, Mr. Pease."

"That's all? I 'amaze' you?"

"I'm grateful, of course. But, why me?"

"To put it crudely, Hashknife, like the men you'll be commanding would, you've got the balls for the job." Ezra Pease cleared his throat on that one.

Savoring another swallow of the fine Tennessee sour mash, Hashknife considered the possibilities this opened to him. "It's an honor. One I appreciate more than I can say. Of how many men would I be in charge?"

"After that unfortunate run-in with the Cheyenne, but considering the twelve you've brought in, you would have twenty guns to direct. All will be of my choosing, though not all will be top quality. I have to spread around the inferior ones so that neither wing will be unduly weakened."

"I understand. When will this go into effect?" Hashknife asked.

"By tomorrow. I'll make the selections today."

Hashknife rose to his boots and extended his hand. "You have your man, Mr. Pease. You've got my word on it."

A twinkle blossomed in the eyes of Ezra Pease. "I suspect it's the word of a gentleman, in spite of that curious name you have," he stated flatly, taking the hand of Hashknife and giving his new lieutenant a conspiratorial wink.

Falling Horse was ready to give up the chase. He had brought his men far from their village, deep into the White Top mountains. They had punished the white men, though he would have liked to have done more. Falling Horse strongly suspected that these were the same men who had destroyed the village of Black Hand. If that turned out to be true, he would regret not taking the risk of hunting them down, even in this place where so many whites had settled. Although the white population of the Rocky Mountains at that time averaged around one per five hundred square miles, that constituted far too many for the Cheyenne, Arapaho, and Ute who had lived there for ages.

"It is wise to return to our village," old Red Hawk remarked to his nephew, Falling Horse.

"I am not so sure. I believe those to be the men who killed Black Hand."

Red Hawk nodded at the younger man. "I knew you would be thinking that. We are not strong enough to challenge them for now." The graying counselor produced a wisp of a smile. "Let them grow confident once more and come into our valleys and along our waters. Then is time enough to show them who is master of the high plains."

Falling Horse clasped his uncle on one shoulder. "My father told me that you were born wise beyond your years. Now I know it is so. Yes, Uncle, we shall return to our village . . . after one more day on this trail. There we can replenish our arrows, cast many balls for our rifles. And always the young boys will keep a watch for the return of the white men. They will not like what they find when they come."

All grumbling about the course northward, and the possible results of rejoining Preacher, ceased when the mission wagon train rolled into the camp set up by Preacher, Nighthawk, Beartooth, and Dupre. Brimming with compassion, sympathy, and understanding, Cora and the women descended on the refugee women with eyes spilling over.

"Oh, you poor, poor dears," Patience Bookworthy cooed to Mrs. Kenny. "Your menfolk are safe in the arms of Jesus. We prayed for them and sang three lovely hymns."

"Covered them up better, too," Buck Dempsey muttered behind her, which brought a hot scowl from the minister's wife.

"Covered? I don't understand," Mrs. Kenny began in confusion.

"Don't pay him any mind, my dear. We—ah—we understand the necessity for haste that drove you when you—ah— laid them to rest," Patience quickly injected. "We put more stones and earth on the grave is all."

"I think I see," Mrs. Kenny said vacantly.

Cora added a brightening bit of news. "We'll be traveling together now, so all will be safe. You can distribute what you saved among our wagons and get rid of those wretched vehicles."

"But we can't," Flora Sanders protested. "It—it's all we have of our past." She nodded to the jury-rigged wagons. "They've made it this far, they'll do for the rest of the way."

Accustomed to being the strongest woman in any group, Patience Bookworthy took careful note of Flora Sanders. Then she dismissed this show of obstinacy. Given time, she would be fully in charge, the stout, determined Patience assured herself. Preacher, who had been out hunting game for the hungry refugees, walked up then, a frown furrowing his brow.

"I can't say I'm glad to see you folks," came his first words. Then he addressed the Reverend Bookworthy. "Of all the tom-fool dangerous things for anyone to do, you've done the worst. Only thing for it is to take you all in to the tradin' post at Trout Crick Pass. Then us four," he indicated his companions, "are headed north to see how serious this Cheyenne trouble is gonna get."

"Good," Bookworthy boomed. "We shall accompany you. Our mission is to the Cheyenne."

Big fists on hips, eyes glacial gray, Preacher examined Reverend Bookworthy with a glance he might give to an insect on a pin. "We've been over this before, Reverend. 'Pears you've got a hearin' problem. So, I'll say it again. *Not this year.* Not any year if I have the say-so. Now, let's just let it rest. Trundle them wagons along best you can and do like these folks have decided."

Reverend Bookworthy's full lower lip formed a pink pout. He tried to copy Preacher's belligerent stance . . . and failed. "What, exactly, is that?"

"They are goin' to put up around the tradin' post, and scout for some nice little place where they'll be secure for next winter. After that, they're on their own. You'd be smart to join 'em, then all of you head back come next spring." Bookworthy started to voice more protest and Preacher raised a hand, palm out to halt him. "I'll not hear any more on the subject. It's plumb closed."

Preacher turned on one moccasin heel and took in the cluster of wagons, the scampering children and grazing stock. "It's plain we ain't movin' anywhere today. Ever'one rest up, stock plenty of water and check yer wagons. We head out at first light tomorrow."

To Preacher's great surprise, the caravan made good time. Buck and Eric offered to drive the makeshift wagons of the refugees, and led the way, the pace set to the ability of their vehicles. Behind them stretched the missionary wagons. Preacher and Nighthawk ranged ahead, to keep constant watch. Not that they seriously expected to encounter any trouble. At least none that could not be handled by the weapons and fighting men at hand.

It came as a considerable turn, then, when Preacher's senses began to tingle with a faint edge of alarm. He had never been able to put a proper word to what he considered as his "notions," until a learned man Preacher had encountered on his first, and only, return visit to his father's house had put words to it. The gentleman visiting had labeled it as Preacher's "sixth sense."

Preacher preferred "notions," as in, "Injuns is notionable." What his notions told him now was that there were a whole lot of Indians around. It didn't surprise him that he and Nighthawk had not seen a single brave. Nor any sign left by unshod hooves. The air just . . . smelled different. The birds didn't sing as brightly as usual. A small, black-bellied cloud high up in the azure sky passed over the sun and sent a tingle up Preacher's spine. All in all, he summed up, things had gotten out of kilter.

"You sense it too," Nighthawk remarked, his once handsome, Delaware face curving into smile lines.

"Yeah. But, I don't *know* it. If I didn't know better, I'd swear there was half a hundred Cheyenne around us. Only the southern Cheyenne stay mostly out on the flats, an' the northern ones don't often come south of the Big Horn Mountains."

Nighthawk sucked a deep breath into his barrel chest. "The air . . . tastes different from an hour back."

"'Zactly," Preacher pounced on the observation. "An' listen to them birds. Slightly off key, wouldn't you say, Nighthawk?"

Nighthawk grunted and shifted his narrow-hipped rear in the saddle. Idly his right hand eased to the curved butt of a large .64 caliber horse pistol in a saddle holster in front of himself.

"Somethin' tells me we ought to mosey back to the pilgrims and make them ready for what might be comin'," Preacher speculated aloud. "Yet, we ought to scout it out complete so's we *know* what to expect."

"You can do that well enough on your own, old friend. While I can carry the news to our charges."

"Right enough, but somethin' else tells me that because there's two of us is why whoever is out there ain't takin' any potshots."

"You might have something there. Or, maybe they already know about the wagons and want us to get clear through them and long gone before they hit."

Instantly, a light glowed in Preacher's eyes. "I'll buy into that, 'Hawk. Sneaky things like that is usual amongst the Dog Soldiers. B'god, I swear I can smell me Cheyennes now."

In tense situations, Preacher had often noticed, Nighthawk tended to employ the best of his English vocabulary. "How do you propose we proceed?"

"I say we turn back and get the hell an' gone to them wagons. There'll be enough of those boneheads what won't have their guns loaded as it is."

Except for Beartooth—who had his familiar "itch" behind his eyeballs for the past hour—and Dupre—who could not recall the words to a well-known *voyageur* song for the same amount of time—it came as quite a shock to those in the column of wagons when shrill war whoops announced that they had come under attack by some forty-five Cheyenne warriors.

Led by Falling Horse, the Dog Soldiers took the forefront of the crescent sweep of braves who pounded down the slope ahead of the wagon train. They numbered only eleven, and rode in a straight line at the deepest part of the semi-circle, but made up for their number by the ferocity of their fighting skills. The Cheyennes first appeared well out of rifle range and made as swift a progress as the terrain would allow. Their surroundings also dictated that they had to use this tactic if they wanted to ride their horses. It didn't matter to Beartooth.

Rising in his stirrups, he bellowed, "Circle the wagons! Be quick about it. Git them guns ready."

Under a growing cloud of dust, a tight enclosure rapidly formed. The wagon box ahead served as shelter to the team from behind. The hired drivers had their weapons ready and close at hand. The pilgrims had to find and load theirs. Would they never learn? Beartooth wondered.

"Steady! Hold steady. No one fires until I say so. Watch them horns. They mean to close around us," Beartooth cautioned. "Take aim on them fellers first. Knock 'em outta their saddles an' we got a chance." He cut his eyes around the stockade. "You boys on this side, pick targets amongst them bucks in the center. Whang enough of them an' the whole pack will pull back to regroup."

"Who are they?" Bobby Gresham asked, clutching a .36 caliber squirrel rifle in a competent manner. "Chiefs or something?"

"They be your worst nightmare, sonny. Them's Dog Soldiers unless I miss my guess," Beartooth told him. "Wonder where Preacher is?" he took time to puzzle aloud.

A few eager beavers among the warriors opened fire the moment they came into extreme range. It bothered Falling Horse that the gunfire failed to draw out a response. Someone had taught these white men well. Only a few heartbeats remained before they clashed with the wagons. Abruptly, the wagon sides facing Falling Horse and his Dog Soldiers erupted in a wall of white powder smoke.

A meaty smack and soft grunt came from the Dog Soldier on the right of Falling Horse and the young chief saw the man sag in his saddle, a bullet hole clear through the meaty part of his shoulder. Two more of the elite warrior society went down in sprays of blood. Falling Horse cut his eyes to the points of the crescent and saw more braves go down at each end. Without a spoken word, the cream of Cheyenne fighting men cut to left and right and raced to reinforce the edges of the formation.

Suddenly, from behind came the loud, flat reports of heavy-caliber horse pistols discharging. Falling Horse nearly upset his pony as he wheeled it to see two buckskin-clad, wide-eyed creatures charging the Cheyenne from the rear.

12

"We got here too late," Preacher stated with chagrin.

"What are we going to do about that?" Nighthawk inquired.

"Simplest thing in the world, ol' hoss," Preacher appraised him. "We're gonna get down in among 'em and raise a little hell."

Nighthawk studied that over a while. "I can see that is the only way to get to the wagons. But is being there worth losing our hair over?"

"You've got too much anyway," Preacher bantered, his hand drawing a saddle gun and cocking it. "Well, like your friends the Dakota say, *hokka hey,* it's a good day to die."

He and Nighthawk charged as one. Their thundering hoofbeats could not be heard above the tumult of all those Cheyenne ponies. It allowed them to get right up behind the center of the crescent formation undetected. By then both men had their reins in their teeth, both hands filled with powerful .64 caliber horse pistols. They fired point-blank into the backs of the nearest warriors and reholstered.

Preacher drew one of his awe-inspiring four-barrels and fired away at any bronze figure that caught his attention. Working the complicated trigger mechanism to revolve the barrels with what speed he could accomplish, Preacher broke free of the double rank half a length ahead of Nighthawk, who had pulled a pair of .50 Hayes double-barrel pistols.

Muzzles flashing fire, Nighthawk caught up to Preacher a moment after the Dog Soldiers broke away to either side.

"Nice of them to open the gate for us," Nighthawk shouted around the leather straps in his mouth.

"Now if those folks below will open the door, we'll be just fine," Preacher responded, eyes fixed on the circled wagons, while the Cheyenne wheeled away to regroup.

Slowly, one of the gathered smaller, lighter cousins of the Conestoga wagons began to roll backward. A warm glow filled Preacher's heart when he recognized it as Cora Ames's wagon. Bless her heart, that gal had all her gear in her possibles bag. He heeled Thunder that way and streaked for the small opening. Nighthawk matched him stride for stride, then reined sharply to let Preacher dash through the narrow opening first.

Cora's wagon had barely heeled into position again when the Cheyenne attacked for the second time. A torrent of arrows made a black cloud against the sky. Most thudded into the wooden sides of the wagons, but a handful reached the inside to clatter on the hard ground. Now that he had time for it, Preacher studied the warrior he'd marked as the leader. Under the hastily applied paint, his face looked familiar.

"Naw, it couldn't be," Preacher opined aloud. "He's never stood against the whites before."

"Who is that?" Cora Ames took time away from aiming her rifle to ask.

"Falling Horse. I wintered in his camp a couple of times. He made it clear to me then that he held nothing against us whites, long as we didn't take up permanent space in their hunting grounds or such like."

"Do you really think you know the man leading these savages?" Cora pressed.

Preacher took another look. "That I do, Miss Cora. And I aim to do somethin' about it." Preacher levered himself up on the driver's stand of the wagon behind Cora's and waved his hat over his head. "Falling Horse!" he called out in Cheyenne.

"It's me, White Wolf. I have shared your lodge before. I gave my protection to these people."

It worked so far, Preacher noted thankfully as the man he addressed raised his lance in the signal to halt. "Hold your fire, now," he cautioned the pilgrims. Then to Falling Horse, he challenged, "Is this how you honor an old guest?"

Tension did not whisk away at this impugning of the Cheyenne war chief's honor. Rather, Falling Horse rode forward alone, peering through the dust at the tall figure silhouetted on the wagon seat.

"Is that truly you, White Wolf?"

"In the flesh, Falling Horse."

"I see you now, White Wolf."

"I see you, too, Falling Horse. Sorta outta your usual range, ain't ya?"

"We seek some white men who wronged us."

"Well, this ain't them, Falling Horse." Thoughts of Ezra Pease and the sale of guns to the Blackfeet trickled across Preacher's mind. "These folks has got a message from their Great Spirit. They sure ain't sellin' whiskey and rifles to the Cheyenne, nor the Blackfeet for that matter."

Falling Horse lost his mask of impassivity. His eyes widened, eyebrows shoved up his high forehead, his mouth formed a black circle. "You know of them, then?"

"Sure do. We're takin' these folks to Trout Crick Pass an' then goin' on to look into what is carried on the wind about those bad men."

"It is said that Preacher never lies," Falling Horse responded. "We want to punish those men, but if you are hunting them I almost feel sorry for them."

"You'll put aside the war trail against these people and join us for coffee? We have lots of sugar."

Red and black streaks of war paint wriggled like snakes as Falling Horse split his face with a white smile. "Getting ready for war makes a man hungry, White Wolf."

Preacher laughed heartily and glanced over his shoulder

at the anxious faces of the greenhorns inside the circle. Quickly he explained the gist of their exchange. Then, without waiting for a reply from the flatlanders, he turned back to Falling Horse.

"I think we can manage to fill your bellies. You lost a couple of ponies. I'd say six or more wounded. We have spare horses. They are yours to make right between us."

"You are generous, White Wolf. We accept," Falling Horse called back without consulting his followers either.

"It might take a while to fix for all of you, but these women are darn fine cooks. You'll see, they make a feller shine."

Weapons lowered, the Cheyenne warriors rode together and formed a double file. Much to the uneasy doubts of the missionaries, they walked their mounts like peaceful lambs to an opening that Preacher directed be made in the side of the ring of wagons. When half of the wagons had been drawn to the sides and the first Indians left their bows and rifles with their ponies, several of the women showed their relief with audible sighs.

"All righty, folks," Preacher announced with arms raised over his head to command attention. "It's time to cook up the best feast you've ever whomped together. An' remember, these are our honored guests. Keepin' our hair depends on it."

Ezra Pease beamed his pleasure at the three men who had returned to report success. "That is exceptional news, gentlemen," he praised. "Rest yourselves and your horses and then you may have the honor of leading us to this paradise you have discovered."

"Wha'd he say?" one hard-faced, yellow-toothed ruffian asked his companions as they led their horses to the edge of a creek.

"I think he liked it, Blane," a hawk-nosed individual guessed correctly.

The third scout snickered. "Said we'd have the honor of

leadin' 'em. You damn betcha. Ain't a one of them flatlanders he brung with him could find his butt with both hands in broad daylight. 'Course, that means we've got to ride right through Trout Crick Pass with all them like on pee-rade."

Blane studied on that while his horse took a long drink of the cold mountain water. "Say, couldn't us three jist mosey through there an' howdy any fellers we knew, then wait for the rest of them to come on?"

Hawk nose pointed to the sky, a smile bloomed on the face of the brightest of the trio. "They could go by the tradin' post a few at a time, attract less attention that way."

Blane nodded his head, his eyes vacuous. "That shines. I reckon they're lucky havin' three boys smart as us workin' for 'em."

Big slabs of teeth, like yellow tombstones, showed in a crooked grin on the second man's face. "Sure enough. An' I don't reckon any Cheyenne will be pokin' into that li'l valley, all tucked away amongst those high peaks. Uh-oh," he added a second later as the familiar, if irritating, sound of a triangle sounded the summons for a general conference. "Pease's dog-robber's bangin' that tinker bell again. Best go see what he wants."

When he saw the three scouts standing at the edge of the gathering, Ezra Pease made it short and sweet. "These three gentlemen have found us a likely place to establish camp and wait for the humor of the Indians to change. I have been assured we will be safe there, and more important, out of sight." The weight lifted from his shoulders, Pease allowed his thoughts to blossom on an old, sore subject.

"It will also allow us time to complete the destruction of Preacher and whoever is riding with him. That damned half-wild mountain man could ruin all of our plans. Make sure everything is secured, the wagon wheels well greased and the horses rested. We start out after the noon meal."

Later, at the head of the column that had turned northwest again for Trout Crick Pass, Ezra Pease had time to reflect on the plans to which he had referred. Indeed, it was paramount that they eliminate any threat, he admitted as he recalled his last conversation with the men who had brought him into this grand scheme . . .

"This must not fail," the stout, balding New York City banker stated vehemently. "We will hold you personally responsible, Ezra, for the success or failure of our enterprise. Reports our engineers have sent indicate a phenomenal quantity of high-grade ore and nuggets. I don't care what these Army engineers say—gold is out there. And not in small quantities either. All one need do is scratch the ground and gold appears. The land on which the finds are located is ours for the taking.

"Provided, of course, that you can bring about a situation that will force the Army to occupy the territory, drive the Indians out, or perhaps down into the Nations, and leave all that empty land for us to claim." The banker paused a moment. "The only fly in our ointment, according to all information at hand, is a tempestuous mountain man named Preacher. It is said he can keep peace between the Indians and whites, and even between the tribes."

Cheeks flared red with the remembered humiliation handed him by Preacher, Ezra Pease chose his words carefully. "Yes. Yet, he may no longer be there. The fur trade is moribund. Those shiftless men who prowled the mountains are scattered to the four winds. Or he may be dead, killed by Indians or some other half-animal like himself." Pease drew himself up in the big, leather chair. "But if Preacher is there, I have my own axe to grind with him. I'll bring him down and open the gateway to riches for us all."

"Umm, yes," the pinch-faced banker on Ezra's left offered acidly. "And using slave labor to do the mining, we will be on the way to cornering the gold market entirely."

Stunned, Ezra Pease fought to keep his expression unreadable. By an unguarded word, the frail, money-hungry little banker had revealed something to Ezra the likes of which he had never dreamed of before. And he stood in line to share in it. What a lovely proposition . . .

With a start, Ezra Pease brought his awareness back to the present. He had learned that Preacher was very much alive. And recently, with the help of his friends, had accounted for the demise of more than fifteen of the men Ezra had brought with him. That would end, Pease vowed, and soon.

With their guests—and former enemies—relaxed by many tin cups of coffee, laced with sugar to a syrupy consistency, the promised feast began an hour before nightfall. Through Preacher's interpretation, Falling Horse had offered some story dances for afterward by bonfire. Always the zealots, Reverend Thornton Bookworthy, along with the other male missionaries, spent the eating time trying to sell their God to the Cheyenne. It taxed the vocabularies of all four mountain men to explain the esoteric concepts of faith. Especially one with which they held little familiarity.

"Therefore, God is the Father of us all," Bookworthy summed up his recitation of the Creation. Bookworthy paused to allow this to be translated. To his great delight, Falling Horse nodded sagely, then spoke with what sounded like deep feeling. His first convert! Reverend Bookworthy rejoiced in this marvel . . . at least until the war chief's words were translated.

"I am puzzled by your words," Preacher took silent pleasure in interpreting, adding a few colorful turns of his own. "Falling Horse allows as how everyone, not touched in the head, knows about the One Above Us All, the Shaper of Men. That he formed man from clay is a true thing. We, he tells me, have always known that. Only now, why should we have to call Him by another name?"

Bookworthy's face went blank, then he drew a deep breath and launched into an explanation. "Because of the revelation of the Savior. When man began to wallow in sin and degradation, He sent His only Son to redeem us. He did this through the power of the Holy Ghost. And here's the good news. We have come to lead you to His salvation."

"Oh, sure," Preacher offered the response. "White Buffalo Boy, who brought the bison and taught us to hunt in the time before the horse. He also taught us the rules of how to live with one another in peace."

All the while he had been translating, Preacher and his mountain man friends had been fighting the desire to roll on the ground and howl with laughter. Preacher watched the parson carefully while he recited this last bit of wisdom from Falling Horse. Reverend Thornton Bookworthy gaped, gasped, and snapped his jaw closed. His theology in full retreat, the good reverend spun on one boot heel and went off to sulk in the privacy of his wagon.

"Tomorrow is a Sunday, I have determined," he tossed over one shoulder as he walked off. "If you will excuse me, I have a sermon to prepare."

Beartooth ambled over and nudged an elbow into Preacher's ribs. "I think we've seen the last of that one for awhile."

"I reckon so." Then Preacher put a sly look on his face and cut his eyes to Falling Horse. "Why'd you choose them particular words to address to the sky chief?"

Falling Horse shrugged, eyes alight with mischief, a fleeting smile curled his full lips. "It seemed the right thing to say at the time. In my father's days, the Black Robes came to our people from the place you call Canada. They told of the same Almighty Father and his Son. Also they spoke of the good Mother."

"I know," Preacher said quietly, thinking of the French missionary priests who had come among the plains tribes.

"Their Blessed Mother could easily have been our Earth Mother. Or, so my father told me as a boy," Falling Horse went on. "We had no need then for new names for the creating spirits we had always revered. We don't now. Why is it that a man, and usually a white man, thinks his ways are always better?"

"That I can't answer you. Now, to this other thing. Why is it that you come so far south wearing war paint?"

"I have told you before, White Wolf. It is the white men

who sell whiskey and guns to the Blackfeet and try to sell to us. Fifteen suns ago, they attacked the village of Black Hand. But, all of this you know. It is decided by the great council that they must be stopped."

"My friends and I are hunting the same men," Preacher told him. "Does the council have names for these white men?"

"The one who leads them, he is called Pease."

"By dang it!" Preacher flared. "I've known that no-account buzzard-puke was behind all this trouble in the north. You have my word on it, Falling Horse, if we come upon these men, we'll leave them wandering in darkness, unable to enter the Spirit World."

Another rare smile lighted the face of Falling Horse. "And if we find them first, the same will be true, my friend White Wolf."

Beartooth scratched in his full, ruddy brush of beard. "I hate to mention this, Preacher," he addressed to his companion where they sat their mounts in a deep pool of shade under an ancient fir tree. "But I think someone among them pilgrims we're babyin' along has got theyselfes some louses."

Preacher laid his head at an angle and cut his eyes to his friend. "What makes you say that?"

"Because I itch, that's what," Beartooth said hotly. "It feels like there's critters crawlin' around in my hair an' beard."

"Dust 'em with some sulphur."

Beartooth didn't think much of Preacher's suggestion. "What? An' smell of hell-fire an' brimstone for a month?"

"If you'd take a bath more'n oncest in three months, you wouldn't have to stink of sulphur."

"Don't get off on that now, Preacher. Least I don't smell as bad as Polecat Parker. You gotta admit that."

Preacher pursed his lips, canted his head left and right, cast a long gaze at the azure sky, and hummed a brief snatch of tune. "If you say so, Beartooth."

Beartooth's eyes went wide. "You sayin' I do stink as bad as Polecat?"

"Nooo," Preacher drawled. "Sometimes you got you a' aroma about you far worse than Polecat."

Spluttering, Beartooth flung his hat at Preacher, who ducked, laughed and set heels to Thunder's flanks. Beartooth was obliged to dismount to retrieve his floppy head cover, which made him late riding into the ambush laid among rocks at a narrow spot on the trail.

He saw Preacher, bellied down in the dirt, banging away with one of those awful four-barrel pistols. A ball moaned past Beartooth's head. He saw the puff of smoke and caught a hint of motion when the shooter drew back to reload. Hugging his Hawken to his cheek, Beartooth saw to it the man didn't need to charge his weapon.

Preacher's pistol made a flat crack almost upon the discharge of Beartooth's rifle and a scream came from the low scrub brush in the boulders. One of those new conical balls cracked past Beartooth's head and reminded him he made a good target sitting high in the saddle. He came down, cussing and squalling. He brought his second rifle with him.

It went into action at once as a buckskin-clad figure bolted from a spot made uncomfortably hot for him by Preacher. Beartooth put a ball through his left thigh and the would-be assassin went down with a shrill cry. His rifle clattered in the rocks as it slithered away from his grasp. Preacher emptied his first four-shot and went to the other as Beartooth pulled a .60 caliber pistol free and busted a cap. A healthy growl came from a dark puddle of shadow and Beartooth cut his eyes that way.

He focused in time to see Preacher stand upright and run toward the mysterious noise, firing his multi-barrel with all the speed possible. The growl turned to a scream of terror. The brush thrashed and waved while the thud of pounding boot soles faded into the distance.

Preacher stopped firing and went to the rocks to gather

weapons and powder. Beartooth joined him there. "You arrived in the nick o' time, friend," Preacher remarked dryly.

"Had to get my hat," Beartooth responded without any sign of contrition.

"If you'd been here, you'd likely taken a ball."

Beartooth squinted at his old sometimes partner. "You sayin' I done good comin' in behind like that?"

"Plum upset their plans, I'd say. Now, let's get these guns back to the folks on them wagons."

Remounted, Preacher scanned the scene of the ambush. "There's somethin' not quite right about this, Beartooth. I've got the feelin' we're missin' the most important part."

Beartooth sniffed the air and started to agree with Preacher when a slug cracked through the trees, releasing a shower of leaves, and smacked into the head of Beartooth's horse, killing it under him.

13

"That's what I didn't like about this set-up!" Preacher shouted to Beartooth as he finished reloading his second four-shooter.

Beartooth had rolled free of his dead horse, and used the animal for a barricade to protect him from the incoming balls of the rest of the frontier trash that came swarming down on them from among the jumble of boulders above. He looked around him and saw that Preacher had disappeared. Never mind. He leveled his reloaded Hawken on a target and let her bang. "Looks like there's an ambush within an ambush," the older mountain man remarked as he poured powder down the barrel of the Hawken, added patch and ball and rammed home.

"Stars an' garters, my good man, however did you figure that out?" Preacher unleashed his tension in jocular sarcasm.

"No call to get pouty with me, Preacher," Beartooth bantered back.

Another thug attempted a dash from the cover of one boulder to another. He never made it as Preacher clipped his legs out from under him with a through-and-through shot from his own Hawken. The man yelped in pain and flopped on the ground. Thinly his voice came to the beleagured mountain men.

"He shot me through both legs, Quint. What do I do?"

"Good enough for you, ya sneaky polecat," Beartooth roared back.

Quint answered his wounded man. "Stay low. We'll get you out."

"But I'm in th' wide open," the wounded one protested.

"Not for long," Preacher muttered as he fined his sight picture and let go another ball. The ambushing scum died before Quint could offer more advice.

"Does seem we found the wrong place to be in," Beartooth quipped as he reloaded.

The downhill charge continued and the riff-raff swarmed into the meadow where Beartooth lay. They had a hundred yards of open ground to cross to reach the redoubtable mountain man. They got only a few feet into the clearing when Preacher opened up with his two rifles once more, then leaped into the open to charge their flank.

"They're gettin' in pistol range," Preacher advised as he abandoned his Hawken for a four-barrel terror. Two shaggy-haired louts reared up among the lupine and both went off to meet their Maker in a twinkling as Preacher closed on their attackers and worked his complex shooter with a speed that surprised even him.

"How many more of them?" Beartooth asked as he sighted in on a burly ruffian in homespun who zigzagged toward him.

"Been too busy to count," Preacher answered.

"I make it six," Beartooth advised as he triggered his .60 Hayes and grunted in satisfaction when the broken field runner tripped over his feet and went down with a hole in his chest.

"Before or after that one?" Preacher asked lightly.

"You're enjoyin' this, ain'tcha?"

"Ain't my favorite mess to be caught up in," Preacher allowed. "Still, there's somethin' to be said for it. It sure keeps the blood pumpin' through your veins right smartly."

Beartooth groped for another pistol. "We'd best put an end to this right sudden. There might be more of these rag bags out there."

Preacher changed his empty pistol for the second one. "I was thinkin' the same thing."

The one called Quint showed himself then, along with four others. "You ain't got a chance, Preacher We got you cold," he taunted.

A ball from his rifle put a plume of dust up inches from Preacher's face. "Now that's plumb unfriendly," Preacher growled. He sighted in and fired the first barrel.

Bark sprayed from the trunk of a big old silver-tipped fir and gouged half a dozen bloody cuts in Quint's face. He yelped and jerked back behind the tree for protection. Preacher took aim on another of the misbegotten brethren and watched dust puff off the jackal's leather vest as the .54 caliber ball smacked home.

His numbers cut down to three now, Quint decided that he had been sent on a fool's errand by Ezra Pease. Why, there was just two of them down there and they done killed off eleven men. Pease had been right about one thing, though. Preacher had been easy to find, right about where Pease and Vickers said he'd be. South of Trout Crick Pass, only moving slower than expected. They had laid out a good ambush.

If only young Lukins had not fired too soon. A lot of good it did, Quint decided. Time for him to get out of this. But how? he asked himself as another man went down, screaming, his neck ripped open on one side, and gushing blood. Keep the tree between him and those deadly shooters down there. That was the way.

"See him, Preacher?" Beartooth asked as he nodded toward the moving shadow of Quint.

"Shore enough. We'll give him a little time. He'll show in the open in a bit," Preacher answered calmly.

That prediction proved true some two minutes later as Quint gained more altitude up the slope of boulders. Preacher had readied himself with the fancy sporting rifle and popped the cap when the whole of Quint's left shoulder filled his sights. The smaller caliber ball moved with incredible velocity and drilled through the shoulder blade of Quint, then collapsed his lung. Quint fell face-first through a spray of his own blood.

Both of the survivors had had enough. They fled in wild disorder, gaining ground in long bounds. To add to their panic, the sound of laughter followed them uphill from the men they had sought to kill. When they reached the safety of the beeline where their horses had been tied off, they silently thanked all they held sacred for being spared. From below, Preacher and Beartooth continued to hoot and guffaw in derision.

When their merriment subsided, Preacher spoke for them both. "It had to be Pease. Something's going to have to be done."

"Yep. An' iffin I know you, it ain't gonna be pleasant for our Mr. Pease."

Silas Phipps cocked his head and cupped a grimy hand around one ear. From far off, he faintly heard a booming sound, like thunder. There, it came again. Too fast and too many for lightning strikes, he guessed correctly. A sudden image came to him and he licked newly nervous lips. Once, long ago, a year or two before Silas had reached his teens, he had heard a sound like that. Gunfire!

Yes, it had to be. Long-buried images resurrected themselves in his mind and he saw again, with the same horror as the first time, the gang of ruffians swarming down on the isolated cabin in the western part of Virginia that his parents called home. Located on a rocky slope in the Appalachian Mountains, the thin, sickly farmland claimed by the senior Phipps stood in the middle of a clearing hacked out of the tall, thick trees that surrounded it. Most of what it grew was rocks. The desperadoes were upon them before anyone knew it.

His father and two older brothers died in the first hail of gunfire. After that, the unshaven, unwashed hill bandits made sport of rounding up the younger children. They had their way with his Ma and the girls, down to seven-year-old Betsy.

He never forgot. He had been adopted by a kindly family in neighboring Pennsylvania, raised and educated through the secondary school. When he grew older, he hunted down some of those men and killed them, albeit they were shot in the back. That gave him moments of satisfaction, though he failed to find all of those responsible. Yet, his mind seemed filled with strange and terrible cravings. So, he had sought out some orphans, and street waifs, using his inheritance from his adoptive parents to put on a show as a philanthropist and gaining the trust of overburdened police, and operators of orphanages.

Through those first children, he had relived the childhood he had lost. He entered into games with all the enthusiasm they generated. He dressed them well and saw they received proper schooling. Later, a darker side emerged. He became cruel and harshly demanding of the youngsters. At last he could not contain the fiercely hot flares of outright lust that sent him into fits of agony. He gave in . . . and indulged.

None of which mattered in their present situation. The distant gunfire had engendered frightful memories to haunt him. Silas could not face yet another encounter with violent men. Peter, riding one of the saddle mounts beside the lead wagon, stared at Phipps in surprise and puzzlement when he began to mutter to himself.

"I think we should turn off about here," Phipps mumbled darkly. "Maybe even go back."

Encouraged to boldness, despite his frequent bouts with the switch, Peter answered sharply. "Why? It's only thunder. I hear it too."

"That's not thunder, boy. It's something far more fearsome than a thunderstorm."

Beside him on the driver's seat, Ruth gave him a startled glance. Knowing that to get away from any source of whiskey would be their only hope, Ruth struggled with her thoughts to come up with some reason to keep going. A careful study of their surroundings gave her a direction.

Fearful of a stinging blow to her face with every word, she

hesitantly stated her case. "We must go on, Mr. Phipps. There are no trails to follow otherwise. We would have to cut our way through this wilderness. At least we have to go on as far as that trading post we heard of."

Phipps swiveled his over-sized head and stared at her as though she was a stranger. He blinked and licked his dry lips again. Then he delved behind him for a half-full stoneware jug of whiskey he had placed there that morning. He removed the stopper and put the mouth to his lips. His Adam's apple bobbed up and down three times before he set the container aside. Then he wiped whiskey off and courage back on his face. Ruth's blood turned icy in her veins as he produced a lewd grin, eyes twinkling, though badly bloodshot. He nodded to acknowledge her comments.

"You've got a good point there, missy, an' tonight I'll have to reward you for comin' up with it," Phipps stated as he patted Ruth's thigh through the thin cotton dress she wore. "Yep. We'll surely have to continue."

Neither Silas Phipps nor anyone else in the High Lonesome needed to worry about a spring thunderstorm. No, the signs Preacher noticed as the rag-tag wagon train set off again indicated something potentially far worse. It began as a gray haze on the horizon. The sky turned to slate, while the overcast extended downward until wisps brushed the mountain peaks. While the wagons creaked and groaned along the rutted trace that led to Trout Crick Pass, the front swept in with teasing slowness.

Within an hour visibility had been cut to below a mile. In the next half hour the temperature dropped into the uncomfortable range. Silvery plumes came from the nostrils of the mules that hauled the rickety wagons up the steep incline. The men and women of the train had clouds of white before their faces at all times. Preacher first noticed the dampness that formed on every metal object. He raised a hand to signal a halt and turned Thunder to face the oncoming pilgrims.

"We'd best make camp right now. Circle the wagons and send the youngsters out to fetch all the firewood they can find."

"Why should we do that, sir?" Reverend Bookworthy demanded. "It's barely mid-afternoon."

Preacher gave him a pained expression. "You greenhorns never learn, do you? When I say to do something, you do it an' be damn quick about it. That way you have a chance of stayin' alive. There's a snow comin', an' unless I'm addle-pated, it could be a big one. Now, you folks what's got 'em, pitch yer tents on the lee side of the wagon boxes." The first wide-spaced flakes began to trickle down while Preacher spoke.

Reverend Bookworthy waved at them disdainfully. "What harm can a few light flurries like these do us?"

Preacher eyed him with stony gray disgust. "They can bury you nose deep in a couple of hours is what. Now, do as I say or me an' the boys is pullin' out to make camp where we have a chance of weatherin' the storm. We'll come back for yer bodies."

"My word, I think he means it," Bookworthy blurted, entirely flustered.

Buck Dempsey, in the lead wagon with Patience Bookworthy, clucked to the team and began the circle. Visibility had been reduced to a couple of hundred yards. Heavier snowfall began to cut that even more. Preacher noted it and called out advice.

"Have a rope guide strung from the wagons to the edge of them trees. The youngin's will get lost without it."

The children had already become dark, indistinct figures in the swirl of lacy flakes. They bounded about with youthful energy and began to form an antlike double file to and from the windfall that littered the treeline. When the wagons halted in place and the menfolk had unharnessed the draft animals, Preacher and his friends hastily constructed a corral from sapling poles carried under the vehicles for the purpose.

They erected it snug against the northwest wall of the cut they followed, a scant three paces from the wagons on that side. Twilight dimness descended on the encampment.

Women set to making fires while shelters were rigged for the occupants of the train. Preacher stood with Dupre, eyeing the preparations.

"I reckon we got us a heller on the way," Preacher opined.

"I see it like you, *mon ami.* Mother Nature will have one last trick on her children, *mais non?*"

"She al'ays does, Dupre. She al'ays does." Preacher sighed. "Thing is, can these tenderfeet survive it iffin it comes on real deep?"

"They are learning, Preacher. Most of them, at least. I cannot say the same for the good *Pere* Bookworthy."

Preacher chuckled softly. "Like most of his sort, his mind's made up, don't want nobody confusin' him with unpleasant facts."

"You are unusually harsh on this man of the cloth. Why is that?"

"You know as well as I, Dupre, Nature's got her own rules out here. She don't abide fools lightly. Truth is, I'm hard on him because I want him to survive. I want him to go back East an' tell the rest of that passel of fools to stay clear the hell an' gone away from here."

Dupre chuckled. "You are soft as a cream horn inside, Preacher. And transparent as isinglass."

Preacher put on an expression of mock resentment. "Am I now? Well, we'll just see about that." He bent and scooped up the first of the sticking snow and fashioned a ball of it, with which he pelted his old friend solidly in the center of Dupre's chest. Dupre did likewise and soon the white stuff clung to the front of both men. Laughing uproariously, they grappled, fell over and rolled joyfully in the growing layer of snow.

Puzzled and shocked, Cora Ames and the other missionary women looked on at them as though they had lost their minds.

Yellow lantern light formed a fuzzy halo around the head of Martha Yates. Bundled up in the warmest clothing they could unpack in the short time at hand, she went frantically from wagon to wagon, calling out for her eleven-year-old son.

"Johnny, are you in there? Johnny, you must come to our wagon right now. Johnny, are you there?"

"That's darn foolishness," Nighthawk grumbled from his warm nest in thick buffalo robes, piled high on pine boughs on the floor of his small, war-trail tipi.

A hat-sized fire flickered in its central ring of stones. Preacher and Dupre had crowded in with him and also looked out the raised flap of the doorway cover at the antics of the pilgrim woman. Beartooth stood first watch outside. It had not stopped snowing in four hours. Three feet of white fluff had piled up on the ground, insulating the sides of the skin lodge as effectively as thick cotton padding. Thankfully the wind had not whipped up with the usual force down the canyon walls.

That made for a slow, steady snowfall, rather than a howling blizzard. Yet the Eastern missionary had no business outside in this. Preacher said as much. "If she dropped that lantern, turned around a couple of times, and blinked, she'd be as lost as the damned souls in Perdition."

"I know it," Nighthawk agreed. "Maybe we should do something about it."

"You want to go out there? It must be nigh onto rock-crackin' cold outside," Preacher proposed.

"Uh-oh, where did that light go, *mes amis?*" Dupre asked uneasily.

"Where? Hell, I don't know," Preacher grumped.

Beartooth appeared at the door flap. "Did that fool woman climb into a wagon? She's done disappeared."

Grumbling, Preacher roused himself. He belted a thick buffalo capote around his middle, pulled on his rabbit-fur-lined moccasins and the sheepskin leggings, then covered his ears and face with wool scarves. His hat went on top of it all.

"Reckon I'd better go see. Beartooth, come along and show me where you saw her last."

"Dang-fool pilgrims. They gonna be the death of us yet," Beartooth predicted.

"Thing is not for them to be the death of theyselves," Preacher jibed back.

"Over here, you cantankerous galoot," Beartooth rumbled.

Beartooth led the way to a space between two wagons. Faint tracks showed in the disturbed snow. For all the darkness looming over them, Preacher and his old friend clearly marked the path between the high wooden walls. Preacher peered beyond. Then whipped back to Beartooth.

"How in hell did these wagons git separated?"

"I dunno. They's supposed to be tight closed. Someone made a bad mistake."

"That ain't the half of it." Far off, toward the treeline, Preacher saw a faint splash of yellow ambling in a circle. "Nothin' for it, I've gotta go after her. See over there?"

Beartooth strained his eyes, blinked, gazed a long, quiet moment more, then shook his head. "I don't see nothin'."

Preacher stared into the distance. "Dang. She musta dropped it. I'm gonna have to find her and fast."

A harsh wind swept over them and blew the snowflakes into whirling clouds that confused all direction. It brought a fierce chill to both mountain men. "You can't do that, Preacher. You'll get lost out there."

"No talkin' me out of it. Leastsomewise, we'll find that woman all friz up."

"More likely, we'll find *you* out there tomorrow, friz like a block of ice."

14

Preacher searched the ground near the tall, moaning fir trees with a sense of helplessness. He saw nothing. He had to work by feel in the billows of blowing snow. At last he admitted the worst possible case. The woman had wandered off among the trees. He returned to the wagons bent nearly double against the wind.

"That fool woman didn't drop her lantern. She took it off with her into that stand of fir," Preacher announced. Beartooth cursed hotly. "Yeah," Preacher agreed. "You could say that, and in spades, too. I'll have to get Thunder and go after her. Get me a lantern from one of the pilgrims, Beartooth."

"Sure enough. And a couple of extra buffalo robes."

Their activities awakened Cora Ames and the Reverend Bookworthy. Preacher explained that Mrs. Yates had misplaced her son, Johnny, and had blundered outside the wagons searching for him. "I'm goin' after her before she freezes solid."

"That woman never was wrapped too tightly," Reverend Bookworthy observed, coming as close as he ever had to using the mountain man vernacular.

Cora caught it and, despite the seriousness of the situation, responded amusedly "Why, Reverend, I do think Preacher and his friends have had an influence on you."

Reverend Bookworthy garrumphed and huffed and stalked off to his wagon to take shelter from the increased storm. A small figure shuffled up, to reveal himself as a shame-faced Johnny Yates. Tears welled in the boy's eyes as he admitted his harmless prank that had suddenly turned dangerous.

"I—I'm sorry. I just wanted to get away from her for a while. I was gonna sleep in the little tent with Chris and Nick. They're so much more fun than the kids in the Missionary Alliance."

Preacher took the boy's thin, bony shoulder in one big, hard hand. "I know what you're gettin' at, boy. But you should have told your ma."

Johnny's eyes went wide and the tears spilled at last. "She wouldn'a let me. She says they ain't one of us, ain't been saved. That they're not washed in the Blood an' so not fit company. B-but, I like them."

"For now, then, you'd best go back with them. I'll find yer mother, son," Preacher advised.

Mounted on a protesting Thunder, Preacher left the circle of wagons to search for Martha Yates. Before he departed, he left a charge with his companions. "Find out who th' hell left that gap betwixt wagons."

Unlike the inexperienced woman, who had held the lantern high and blinded herself to her surroundings, Preacher kept the dim yellow glow down close to his mount's legs. The candle cast enough light for him to pick up the prints left in the snow by Mrs. Yates. Those, he noted, were rapidly filling with new fall and drift. Thunder snorted and threw long plumes of steam into the night.

Preacher rode on for half an hour. By careful note of the characteristics of rock formations and tree shapes, he came to the conclusion that the Yates woman wandered in a wide circle. He drew his big knife and put a blaze on a tree to check his assumption. Ten of Thunder's strides further on, he cut bark on another. He repeated it as he followed the tracks.

Sure enough, about an hour later, when he came to a spot where he felt certain he had passed before, he checked for any blaze marks, and found one. The tree was some sixty feet to his right, the yellow-white of the bared cambium layer a pale smear in the darkness. The befuddled woman had to be walking an inward spiral, Preacher decided. Should he cut across and intercept her?

A sudden increase in the force of the wind decided him against it. Stinging particles of snow, mixed with sleet, lashed at his exposed face. Himself confused for a moment, Preacher sat still on Thunder's broad back. After a hundred heartbeats, an imperceptible change in pressure occurred. Preacher didn't notice at first. Not until the snowflakes ceased to whirl and filtered straight down. Preacher was stiff with cold. His fingers and toes tingled and ached with the threat of frostbite. He longed to turn back, seek warmth and continue the search in the morning.

He couldn't do that. The face of that frightened little boy hovered before him. He couldn't let Johnny Yates down. But, more than that, his own honor goaded him on. He had given his word. Besides, the sky seemed to be lighter above. The black bellies of the larger snow clouds had moved on. Preacher blinked and then roused himself when his eyes picked out the tiny, pale pinpricks of starlight.

Preacher waited with legendary patience while the sky cleared. Slowly the banked and drifted snow took on an internal glow, frosty white, from the celestial rays, augmented by the fat presence of a three-quarter moon. Now the advantage had shifted to Preacher. He set out at a faster pace, for the moon's position told him it had to be around two in the morning. Thunder nodded and snorted his approval.

Time had grown short. No doubt the Yates woman would have done something foolish. Something else, Preacher corrected himself. The tracks he followed grew fresher, deeper. After another hour, up ahead, Preacher made out the soft glow of a lantern, its candle nearly burned down. It began to sputter and flicker fitfully as he drew near. With a start, Preacher realized that the light was unmoving. Had she fallen?

A dozen strides brought Thunder up to the lantern. It rested on the top of the snow, which had mounded up against a low ridge with squiggles across its surface like waves in a sea. Preacher dismounted and went forward. No sign of the woman. He took another step . . . and sank out of sight below the snow. He rolled, arse over ears, to the bottom of a dry wash. Floundering in a suffocating miasma of powdery snow, Preacher knew at once what had happened. The early, heavy, wet snow had bent limber aspen branches over the wash and the later sleet had covered that so that it had frozen in place, forming a fragile platform. Later snowfall had covered this trap. First, Mrs. Yates had blundered into it, then he followed. He knew also that he had to save himself before he could look for the missing woman.

Preacher found himself on the rocky bottom of the draw. He moved his arms with great effort and began to work the compacted snow away from his face. He needed room to breathe. Ice crystals, from sleet that had fallen earlier, made his eyes sting. The desperate need for open spaces threatened to overwhelm Preacher as he forced the oppressive weight of snow away from his head.

He rested only a second when he had finished that, then started to free his torso. Preacher knew that he had to tunnel out before the flakes that had fallen in after him had time to compact. Then there was the woman. She might not have as much time left as he did. He would have to get to the top of this mess, find where Mrs. Yates had fallen through the crust, and then burrow back down to pull her free of the thick, white blanket.

Preacher began a swimming motion, thrusting upward. The compacted snow clung stubbornly to his legs. He thought a moment, began to scissor-kick, pointed the toes of his moccasins, and tried again. He moved. Hardly a foot, yet it was progress. Another sweeping, pulling maneuver . . . another foot gained. Now he could shove against the snow below his feet.

He gained two feet the next time. On the fourth try, his fingers broke free into open air. One last effort and his head popped out. His brows, lashes and mustache wore a crust of frozen crystals. Sputtering, Preacher worked his way clear of his icy trap. For a long minute, he sat, spread-legged, bent over, heaving for breath. Slowly he became aware of a growing yellow glow to the east.

"Not possible," he dismissed aloud. He could not have been down there for what remained of the night.

Still the light grew. Preacher looked around him for some sign of where Mrs. Yates had fallen through the crust. He could see no dimple or disturbance of any sort. Only the now extinguished lantern on the edge of the drop-off. The grating crunch of a footfall on the crust came to his ears. He looked up, toward the dim light. His jaw sagged in disbelief.

"Whatever are you doing out here, Mr. Preacher?" Martha Yates asked as she approached, lantern held high overhead.

"Look—lookin' for you, ma'am. You wandered out of the corral," he stated the obvious dumbly.

"I'm looking for my boy. Johnny is lost out here."

"No, ma'am, he's not. He's safe an' sound inside the wagons. He wanted to bunk down with two of them refugee boys, Chris an' Nick."

Martha's lips pursed in disapproval in the dim lantern glow. "I do not approve. They are not . . . like us."

Preacher didn't see it that way. "They're no different than your Johnny. Jist boys."

Her lips compressed in a hard line of stubbornness. "That may be from your point of view. But then, you are not one of us either."

An' glad of it, Preacher thought, then nodded toward the dead lantern. "Your lamp, ma'am. I fell through the snow into that wash. Thought you might have also."

"No. I left that here to guide me back. I had brought a spare along. I thought the search might be a long one."

Preacher grunted acknowledgment of that and roused himself gingerly. He worked his way back toward solid ground. While he did, it came to him why she had not fallen into the wash. Her slight build wouldn't carry enough weight to cause her to break through the icy crust like he had. When he reached the place where Thunder waited, he turned back to Martha Yates.

"I've some spare buffalo robes. There's not much sense in us tryin' to get back to the wagons in what's left of the night. I came upon a sort of overhang back a ways. We can go there, I'll build a fire and we'll wait it out."

She agreed with a nod and they started off, Preacher leading Thunder by the reins. He found the shelter from the still-sharp north wind and set about locating dry branches. Preacher's fingers moved with practiced skill over tinder, flint, and steel. The first sparks were whirled away in the wind. On the third try, they landed in the wad of milkweed down and Preacher nursed them to life.

When a tiny flame bloomed, he edged the white strands under a tent of kindling, which caught rapidly. Martha Yates had been watching him intently in the dim light of her lantern. Now she clapped her hands delightedly.

"You have amazing abilities, Mr. Preacher. And you make them seem so easy."

"It is easy, once you get the hang of it. An' the name's Preacher, ain't no 'Mister' about it."

"Uh—yes, of course—ah—Preacher. Will we be safe here?"

"Safer than many places in the High Lonesome. Now, you just hunker down, put that buffalo robe over you, head and all, hair side in, and turn your back to the wind. Nothin' to it. Come mornin', we'll be back with the wagons right an' proper."

A scandalized expression darkened Martha Yates's face. "Won't people talk? I mean, our being out here alone, all night?"

"Ain't much night left," Preacher observed indifferently. "An' I can guarantee a good hard look from me'll discourage any of that sort of talk."

"Umm—yes, I can see that," Mrs. Yates said a moment before her head drooped and she fell into a deep, exhausted sleep.

* * *

Nighthawk saw them approaching first. He and Dupre had heard two, widely spaced gunshots near daybreak and judged that Preacher was taking advantage of his successful search to bring in a little fresh meat. Beartooth agreed.

"Reckon he found her right enough. Likely too far off to make it back durin' the night. Jist like Preacher to take the chance to bring in a couple of deer or such."

Preacher proved his friends right half an hour later when Nighthawk saw him and the woman emerge from the trees, walking ahead of Thunder, who had two young bull elk draped over his rump and saddle. That amount of meat would feed the lot of them through a couple of days.

"Plenty of good eating in those elk," Dupre remarked. "And sweet as the langouste the fisherfolk along the Gulf bring from the depths."

Beartooth removed his fox skin hat and scratched his head. "What's a *langouste*?"

"A saltwater-dwelling shellfish," Dupre explained. "In the same general family with shrimp and crayfish, only much larger."

"Crawdaddies?" Beartooth squalled. "Lord, that's disgustin'. They's fishbait."

"Your English progeny call *langoustes* lobsters, Beartooth," Nighthawk informed the huge mountain man. "And they are all the rage back East."

"Not to this chile, they ain't. Giant crawdads. Ugh!"

Nighthawk rolled his eyes. "So much for trying to enlighten the great unwashed."

Dupre joined the funning. "Right to the point, Nighthawk. This one is indeed the unwashed."

"There you go badgerin' me about my takin' baths. Well, I won't do it, won't, won't, won't."

"Won't what?" Preacher asked as he reached his companions.

"Take a bath," Beartooth replied in a wounded tone. "I'm not gonna do it. At leastwise, not until come blossom time in May an' I can cut myself outta these longhandle drawers."

Preacher treated Beartooth to a thousand-mile stare. "You amaze me, Beartooth. I was jist thinkin' that a nice, steamin' hot tub would feel right relaxin' after all this snow." Martha Yates had gone on past the mountain men to where her son stood with contrite expression, expecting at the least a stinging bottom for this escapade. That gave Preacher free rein to speak his mind.

"Fool woman took two lanterns out there with her. Left one of them on the edge of a dry wash that was filled up with drifted snow. Like to kilt myself searching for her on the bottom."

"How'd you get on the bottom?" Dupre asked shrewdly.

"You would have to ask. 'Cause I fell in, idjit." Then Preacher went on to describe his ordeal. He concluded with, "Then to add insult to injury, that fool woman comes walkin' up to me right as rain and nowhere near buried in snow."

Cora Ames wandered over from her wagon about that time, arms crossed over the thick, blanket-material coat she wore against the cold. "I thought it was spring out here?" she remarked, making a question of it.

Preacher touched thick fingers to the brim of his hat. "It is, Miss Cora. That'll probably be the last heller we see until, oh . . . late October."

"We'll be leaving soon, then?" Her eagerness was obvious.

Preacher studied on that for a while, as though for the first time. "Not for a while, Miss Cora. Not today, nor prob'ly tomorrow."

"And why not?" she asked with a tiny stamp of a shapely foot.

"There'll be some bodacious drifts in the narrow parts of the pass. Wouldn't do to hitch up to go only a mile or so and be stuck by the snow."

"But, isn't there something that can be done about it?" Cora's impatience grew more agitated.

"Yes, there is. We can sit tight right here and let 'er melt."

"We have our mission to the Cheyenne to fulfill," she countered.

"No, you don't. I've done told you an' told you. That's

completely out. Too dangerous. And now we have these leftovers from that other train. You all have to be settled somewhere safe."

Cora gave Preacher a melting look of her own before she turned away with a predictable retort. "Oh, you men are all impossible."

Preacher's ears burned as his companions chuckled at his discomfort. "I can certain sure say the same thing about womenfolk," he grumbled. Then he put a big hand to his chin, worrying the bare skin where his beard had been, as he did when he sought to bring forth a great idea.

"'Hawk, Dupre, Beartooth, we gotta do something to take these folks minds off the delay. I think I have the an-swear."

"Do tell. What's that?" Nighthawk quipped.

"I'm gonna give them what they want . . . in a way, that is. I'm gonna call 'em all together and describe to them their paradise."

"Where you gonna find them that, Preacher?" Beartooth demanded.

Preacher got a sly look, and waggled a finger under Beartooth's nose. "You jist hide an' watch an' you'll hear all about it."

Twenty minutes later, all of the misguided pilgrims Preacher had taken under his wing gathered in the center of the circled wagons. They chattered among themselves, asking the reason for the summons. That ended abruptly when Preacher stepped up onto the top of a flour barrel and raised his arms above his head.

"Folks, I've been studyin' on something for the last few days, since we all joined up. I know of a perfect place, to the north and west of Trout Crick Pass. A lush valley, with plenty of grass for graze, trees to build cabins, a good water supply, even some flats that can be put to the plow," Preacher made a persimmon pucker at the flavor of that word, "to put in gardens an' even some grain. It's well sheltered for winters."

That sounded like what they'd been told about Oregon, so Flora Sanders burbled happily, "Why, that's exactly what we have been looking for."

Falicity Jones, Bobby Gresham, and the others from that train nodded agreement. Even some among the missionaries began to show interest. Then the pulpit voice of the Reverend Thornton Bookworthy boomed out.

"Where, exactly, is this place, my good sir?"

"I wintered there. It's far off the beaten path, where you'll be safe from Indians and anyone else wanderin' the High Lonesome. I told you I'd be leaving you off at the tradin' post. Well, if you accept this valley, I will agree to lead the way and my friends an' I will help you all get set up."

"What are you going to do after that, Preacher?" Cora Ames asked suspiciously.

"I'll be goin' after Ezra Pease, to make certain ever'one out in these mountains can have a safe time of it."

Spatters of conversation broke out over that. Asa Pettibone stepped forward. "What if we accept this offer, Preacher?"

Preacher clapped his hands and shot a wide-eyed gaze at the organist. "Why, exactly what I told you. Now, you folks talk it over amongst you an' I want your answer by the time the snows melt."

After the wondering pilgrims had wandered off, Dupre stepped close to Preacher. "I noticed that you neglected to mention that this splendid place of yours is also miles away from any large Indian camp, *mon ami*."

Preacher pulled a droll expression. "Come to think of it, I might have left that out . . . accidental-like, so's to speak."

It took three days to clear the route through the mountains to Trout Crick Pass. When the wagons left, Preacher had his answer. They would "allow" him to lead them to his chosen refuge. Only Reverend Thornton Bookworthy showed an uncharitable reluctance, for a man of the cloth, to accept the refugees from the plundered wagon train, according to Preacher's lights.

15

Forty miles south of Preacher and his band of greenhorns, it did not snow. Silas Phipps and his orphans made good time as a result. Unbeknownst to Silas or Preacher, only a day's travel separated them. When both parties stopped for their nooning, less than that divided them from a fateful encounter. It was then that Gertha, the ten-year-old, came to Helen and Ruth while they went about preparing the meal. The child told a frightful tale of abuse by Silas.

Ruth remained silently furious. Slowly she regained her composure enough to speak in a tight, angry tone. "This is too much. We have to make Phipps stop."

Peter had overheard part of the conversation and his high, smooth brow furrowed. "You're right. Someone is gonna get bad hurt."

Helen, the compassionate, studious one, brushed at a lock of auburn hair. "Your back, Peter. Isn't that hurt enough?"

The slender boy shrugged. "It's nothing, not along side what I mean. One of you . . . one of us, is gonna get hurt awful bad if someone doesn't stop him."

"You're right, Peter," Ruth said coldly. "Only what can we do?"

Peter thought on it a while. "We're bound to find someone who believes us. Some grownups *do* listen to kids."

Helen considered that. "That's true. Only what if they go and ask Phipps and believe him and don't do anything else?"

Gertha offered her solution. "We could tie him up sometime when he is drunk. All of us could run away."

"To where?" Ruth asked. Gertha only shrugged.

They offered several more suggestions on how to achieve their goal. None of them seemed entirely satisfactory. In conclusion, Ruth pinched her brow in determination and her lips became a firm, straight line as she offered a final solution. "If nothing we can come up with works, then I'll . . . I'll take a butcher knife to him."

Ezra Pease and his gang of cutthroats set up business in the small valley in the core of the Mummy Range. For hardened criminals, more accustomed to town life, they did a fair job of building some roomy, brush-covered lean-tos and frame a cabin. By that time, men sent out under Hashknife to spread word of their enterprise had made contact and Indians from miles around came to trade for guns and whiskey.

Business grew brisk. Plumes of smoke from the outlaws' cookfires mingled with those of their visiting customers. A friendly atmosphere prevailed, though that did not prevent Pease from assigning men to keep a constant vigil over the Indians in the valley and those who left with new weapons.

"You can never be too careful," he reminded those he dispatched on these duties. "An Indian's mood can change in an instant. They're like children. I learned that much my first trip out here." Pease refrained from mentioning that it was his only trip into the High Lonesome.

Ezra Pease brightened considerably on the morning that the first Cheyenne rode into the valley. He had worried lest the savages' unfriendly greeting of them constituted a unified position. Apparently not, he decided as a feather-bedecked sub-chief and some fifteen warriors trotted their ponies down into the camp area and made a friendly sign.

"I am called Little Knife," the sub-chief announced in sing-song English. "Do you have coffee?"

"That we do, Chief," Titus Vickers responded, giving out

a dazzling salesman's smile. "Y' all dismount and tether your ponies. We keep a pot hot and ready all the time."

Little Knife gestured with his chin to the tarpaulin-covered mounds. "We drink coffee, make talk, trade for guns."

Vickers did not like the sound of that "make talk." He worried it around his head a while, then elected to grab the wildcat by its tail. "What'd you have in mind to talk about, Chief?"

Curved lines deepened around the mouth of Little Knife, and frown furrows gullied his forehead. "It is said that you also trade for the burning water. Is this so?"

Even Titus Vickers could clearly hear the disapproval in the voice of Little Knife. "Oh, sure, Chief Little Knife, we keep a little around. To seal trades when we make them, just a token, you see?"

Little Knife, dismounted now, produced a scowl. "Running Fox took from here a small barrel of whiskey."

"Only a keg. A small keg," Vickers hastened to reassure the displeased chief. "That's seven and a half gallons."

Little Knife had no idea how much a gallon might be, but he knew one thing. "It is enough to make every man with Running Fox sick. They go crazy. Shoot at each other. Two men stab each other. It is not good." He drew himself up to his full six feet, Hudson's Bay blanket wrapped tightly around his shoulders. "You will stop giving whiskey to my people. No more. Stop."

"Sorry. Can't do that, Chief Little Knife. It's part of the deal. You trade for guns, you trade for whiskey. Not one without the other."

Little Knife might not have heard him. He turned to order his men to search out the whiskey and destroy it. Titus Vickers had been on the frontier long enough to have learned the rudiments of the Cheyenne language. Vickers let his gut think for him. Swiftly he reached to the sash around his waist and drew a double-barrel pistol.

Vickers's first ball punched through the right forearm of Little Knife before it burst his heart. At once sidearms appeared in the hands of the gang members who surrounded the Cheyenne warriors. When the gunfire echoed away to silence, not an Indian lived.

His face ashen, Ezra Pease rushed up to the scene of slaughter. "You acted precipitously, my friend. And I fear that to be a mistake. We must dispose of the bodies and any sign they came in here."

They would find out later exactly how big a mistake it had been.

Preacher thought he had seen it all. Yet, what he saw through his spyglass beat hell out of anything past or present. "What the Betsy-be-damned are Dakota warriors of the Raven Owners' Society doing this far south?" he asked himself in a whisper. "An' so deep in the high country?"

Settled down for a long spell, Preacher continued to observe the warriors, who rode along with the casual air of men well-pleased with themselves. When they drew nearer, he could make out more detail. All of them were armed with brand-spanking-new rifles. Here and there, suspended from thongs around the necks of the owners, he saw untempered bullet molds. Several among the band passed a stoneware jug around.

Pease and his damned guns for sale. Preacher had seen enough. Carefully he edged his way back to where he had left Thunder to crop fresh spring grass. There, he confided his discontent to the patient animal. "Set out to do a good turn for someone, an' sure's there's heat in July, there's some ol' bull buffalo ready to dump a big patty on yer head. We got our work staked out right dandy for us, Thunder."

In the saddle, Preacher ruminated on what he could do. First off, he had to make good and sure those pilgrims he an' the others were escorting stayed clear and hell far away from those proddy Dakota. Quietly he walked Thunder in the opposite direction from the Sioux braves. After a good two miles, to allow for the travel of sound, he put heels to Thunder's flanks and headed back for the wagon train at a fast trot.

Preacher would have gotten along well with ol' Bobby Burns regarding the best laid plans thing. At least that's what he thought when late in the afternoon there came a sudden *ki-yi* yell from behind the wagons on the trail and Dakota braves popped up among the surrounding trees.

"How'd they do it?" he asked of no one in particular. "I plumb left them behind."

"Must have had some braves following their back-trail," Dupre suggested.

"That or jist recovered from being passed out drunk, and cut my sign," Preacher grumbled as the wagons began to circle.

Arrows flew around them. Preacher cursed the foul luck that had delivered them into the hands of the Dakotas. For all the precautions he and his friends had taken, the hostiles had found the wagons and gave every appearance of hankering for a passel of scalps. More arrows showered on the wagons, then the Dakota opened up with their new rifles.

"Keep yer heads down, folks," Preacher called out urgently. "We're in for one whale of a fight."

Sits Tall let a broad, white smile split his coppery face as he gazed down on the approaching wagons. He had been wise to send men to observe their back-trail. They had seen sign left by a white man, not many, and those hard to find. A man who knew the mountains. Like the sort who had taken to leading more of their white brothers into where they did not belong. Perhaps this one did the same.

It would pay to find out, Sits Tall decided. He knew a way to quickly reach the main trail to the pass. He and his warriors could be in position to cut off the wagons, maybe even before the clever guide returned to them. His gamble had paid off. Although they had given too much for the rifles and ammunition five sleeps ago, now they had come upon enough whites in their rolling lodges to provide a quantity of loot that would get them even more of the precious firearms. The time to strike had come, he gauged, as the wagons drew closer.

Sits Tall raised his ceremonial lance over his head and turned his gaze from side to side, assured by the way his warriors made their weapons ready. When the last bowstring had been drawn and the last rifle cocked, Sits Tall looked front again and swiftly slashed his lance downward. At once, his Raven Owners charged.

"Ki-yi! Ky-ky-ky-ky!" Broken Feather yipped beside his old friend Sits Tall.

"Huka-hey!" Sits Tall joined the growing volume of war cries.

This would be a very good day . . . and one where the whites would do the dying.

"Here they come," Ernie, one of the hired drivers, observed unnecessarily as the Dakota braves plunged down the hill toward them.

The wagons had no time to circle when the Dakotas hit them the first sweep. The Indians rode along the sides of the wagons, firing into them, albeit wildly. None of the pilgrims took a hit, Preacher noticed, as he urged greater speed from the team driven by Buck Dempsey. Gradually the circle closed. The Dakota pulled up in the meadow below them.

"They'll be comin' back," Preacher warned.

After a short palaver, the Sioux advanced in a line abreast to barely inside rifle range. Preacher and his fellow mountain men easily picked out the leader; the one with the fancy lance. This one put moccasin heels into the ribs of his pony and walked it forward a few paces, another lean, handsome brave at his side. Beartooth, who spoke excellent Dakota, elected to open with an offer of peace.

"We are not in your land. We mean you no harm. Let us go in peace and we'll let you go in peace."

This seemed to anger Sits Tall. He barked out a harsh string of Dakota. "I am called Sits Tall. You are few, to our many. We will hurt you badly."

Beartooth stood his ground, arms across his chest. "Maybe so, maybe not, Sits Tall. I am called Beartooth. So far you ain't hurt any of us, not even women and children. If you try to harm us now, you'll find out how few we really are . . . to your regret."

Beartooth discovered he had gone too far when Sits Tall's expression changed to one of pure rage. His voice rang with his fury. *"Hu ihpeya wicayapo!"*

Preacher knew enough Dakota to understand the meaning of the obscene Dakota war challenge. He took Beartooth's place as he made a cleaned-up translation to those around him. "He's callin' on his warriors for a total defeat of us."

"Why, that black-hearted bastard," Buck Dempsey growled.

Preacher had his own way of answering. *"Maka kin le* (I own the earth)! *Huka hey! Huka he!"* he added as he drew one of his four-barrel pistols.

"Huka he!" Preacher repeated.

It's a good day to die! echoed in Nighthawk's head. "Speak for yourself, white man," he tossed jokingly to Preacher.

The double load in Preacher's first barrel cleared Broken Feather from his saddle, shot through the heart and liver. Sits Tall whirled his pony and sought to gain ground. Without need to be told, the other Sioux made ready to charge.

They came the instant Sits Tall reached them and reversed his pony. This time they formed a deadly ring around the stalled wagons and opened up with accuracy little better than before.

"We're in for it now," Beartooth grumbled to Preacher. "Why in hell did you have to use that particular challenge?"

"Seemed like the thing to do. Look to your powder and shot, Beartooth, these fellers ain't givin' up easy."

* * *

"Hell no, they ain't givin' up easy," Beartooth said an hour later after two attacks had been repulsed. "What we need is a reg'lar goose drowner. Wet up that powder and soften bow-strings right smart."

"Hold that good thought, Beartooth," Dupre responded as he took careful aim on a charging Dakota.

With whirlwind swiftness, the warriors threw themselves at the wagons a third time. Around they circled, firing with little hope of hitting a target, so long as the flatlanders kept their heads down. Or so Preacher saw it. Sue Landry loaded for him and Cora Ames. In spite of the confusion created by the dust-billowing swirl of the hostiles, he had to take time to admire Cora's marksmanship.

So far she had hit two of the Dakota warriors, one seriously. When each shot went home she had muttered something under her breath, a prayer for her target, Preacher supposed. Then, when a third brave who had played possum to sneak up on the wagons reared up at close quarters and Cora blew off the top of his head, her words came louder.

"Take that, you heathen bastard."

Preacher couldn't help blurting through his laughter, "Why, Miss Cora."

Cheeks flamed scarlet, Cora Ames made a face. "Can't a girl have any privacy?"

She handed the rifle to Sue Landry, who said feelingly, "Atta girl, Cora."

Preacher fired again and spun a pudgy Dakota off his saddle pad. A hoot from Sits Tall and the warriors streamed away. Quickly as it had begun, the fighting ended. Slowly people peeped out of their wagons, or rose from firing positions under the boxes. A frightened mule had kicked forearm-sized billets of burning wood from the cookfire and Patience Bookworthy hurried to spill a bucket of water over two of them.

"Yer learnin', folks. Yer doin' jist fine," Preacher praised. "I think we've got 'em fit to a standstill." He studied the retreating backs of the Dakotas. "Don't reckon they'll be back until sometime in the night, maybe not until dawn."

"Why's that, Preacher?" Asa Landry asked.

"Like I done tole you a hunnard times, Mr. Landry. Injuns is notionable. They ran us down the line, an' then attacked three times in a row. Didn't get anythin' accomplished. That smacks of weak medicine to an Injun. They'll draw off to cook up some grub, dance and drum some and sing up some more good medicine. Speakin' of which, if you ladies don't mind? I think all that fightin's whipped up an appetite for everyone."

Shortly after the last of the Dakotas disappeared beyond the notches at the upper and lower end of the trail through the valley meadow, the faint, rhythmic, heartbeat thump of a drum invaded the consciousness of everyone in the train. Nighthawk began to tap a finger in time with it on the buttstock of the rifle he cleaned. Preacher soon noticed that even Beartooth, who was rumored to have a touch of Cherokee or Chickasaw in him, began to rock his moccasined right toe with the tempo.

Funny how most white folk either heard them with dread, or didn't react in any manner to the drums. Yet, given the lest smidgen of Injun blood and the rhythm got to a feller right fast, Preacher mused. He saw to cleaning his own weapons, as he had advised the greenhorns to do, and thought on the meaning of this unprovoked attack by Indians far from their usual stomping grounds.

About the time a plate of thick stew came into Preacher's hands, he had the beginnings of a wild idea. One that involved a lot of risk, but one he saw as bearing a great deal more promise for their future. Provided he could carry it off without being killed.

16

Dupre thought Preacher's idea to be a crazy scheme. He minced no words in telling the mountain man so when he came upon Preacher as he worked on some gourds he had found in a narrow gulley. Preacher chuckled and patted his older friend on one shoulder.

"B'god, it's worked before, ain't it? Remember that time those Blackfeet had you an' me an' Lame Jack Riley cornered up in the Blue Smokes country? You an' Lame Jack slipped out an' done it whilst I kept the fire stoked up and talked to two bedrolls stuffed inside blankets. Skeert the livin' hell outta them Blackfeet. An' they knows the mountains. These Dakota don't. Likely to have 'em mussin' up their pretty beaded breech cloths iffin I do it right."

"I agree," Nighthawk put in his penny's worth. "They hadn't the opportunity to make an accurate count of how many we number. Come deep darkness, they'll not see one man slip away. If anyone can accomplish this, Preacher can."

Beartooth clinched it with his offer. "Sure you don't want anyone along for company?"

Preacher cut his eyes around the group and smiled broadly at Dupre. "There you are. It's settled. I'll be leavin' around ten o' the clock. The Dakota will be drummin' an' singin' up a storm about then. Any watchers they put out will be gettin' bored and droopy eyed. I'll catch the ones behind us first, that should start some confusion when they go rushin' in among their brothers. Then another dose ought to get the whole batch on the run."

True to his word, Preacher slipped unnoticed out of camp at ten that night. The Dakota had not the slightest idea what awaited them.

Preacher glided through the chest-high grass in a whisper of near silence. He had with him the gourds he had found near the circled wagons, left from last summer. He had spent a long, careful time preparing them in a special way. They would play a big part in his plan to break the spirit of the hostiles. The grade increased steadily as he advanced toward the beeline to the south of the meadow.

With all the skill he possessed, Preacher wormed his way through the stand of alder saplings and over the crest of the low hill. Once more he went over his plan. Ordinarily, his repertoire of animal and bird sounds would not fool any Indian over the age of ten or eleven. But, added to some special tricks he had prepared, he figured he might get these Dakota thinking something else was afoot besides a nasty mountain man. It all centered on those gourds.

Half of them had rags stuffed down hard around the fuse and cap stuck in them. The others did not. That way, he knew, some would go off with a big, loud bang, while the rest would produce a flash, a whumph, and a whole lot of smoke. Preacher made his way to where the watchers had set up a small camp. Only a handful of the braves had remained on this end of the trail. They had a fire and a small drum. Half their number must be keeping an eye on the wagons.

This would make it easy. He'd use the smoke bombs on these braves. Chuckling silently over the anticipated results, Preacher aimed for the rear of the Sioux camp. There he found the horses and made ready for his presentation. First, though, he had to find the pony guard.

Preacher located him after a patient fifteen minutes' wait. A slender young man in his late teens, he squatted with his back against the bole of a large fir, head constantly turning, eyes alert to any hint of movement. Preacher watched longer, to determine any pattern. Slowly it emerged. The youth rose from his position after a quarter hour and moved to a rock, where he could cover the angle previously overlooked. This would be a tough one, Preacher decided.

It tasked all of Preacher's skills to sneak up on the competent, though youthful, warrior. In the last two minutes he held his breath as he closed the distance in a rush. His angle of attack put him atop the boulder against which the boy leaned. Preacher's moccasin made a small scraping sound as he slithered down the lichen-frosted stone face to land feet-first on the top of the Dakota's head.

A soft grunt came from the boy's mouth. Preacher continued on down, driving his knees into the exposed chest. Air rushed from a contorted mouth, the lad stiffened, convulsed, and went slack in unconsciousness. At once, Preacher set to work.

Bent low, he freed the ponies from their grazing tethers. Then, from a tinder box he extracted a live coal, touched it to the fuses in the gourds he held, then hurled them into the general area of the crude camp. At once he moved away from where he stood, burrowed into the underbrush, and made ready. When the first whumph came, he loosed a deep, soulful cough, followed by the hiss and roar of a cougar. The second projectile went off. Shouts of alarm rose from the resting warriors. Again, Preacher did his cougar act. The third bomb exploded. The ponies panicked. With a grunt of amusement, Preacher decided to throw in a little grizzly bear.

"Wahanksica!" a warrior shouted. *"Wahanksica!"*

With a single mind, the hostile Dakotas set off after their horses. Chuckling to himself, Preacher retraced his steps to where he had ground-reined Thunder. In a matter of minutes, he trotted toward the camp ahead, where the larger fire burned, the bigger drum throbbed, and more Dakota waited to be an audience for his next performance.

* * *

Preacher found his quarry easily enough. He screwed a ground anchor into the turf and tied off Thunder, then equipped himself with an armload of homemade bombs. As he had done before, he headed for where the ponies had been picketed. To his surprise, he found a boy of about fourteen guarding them. On his first war party, no doubt, Preacher reckoned. He set his deadly gourds aside and slipped up on the lad easily. With the butt of a pistol, he knocked the youth unconscious with a single blow to the head. He eased the body to the ground and went back for his explosives.

The Dakota sang a war song as Preacher laid out his bombs. These had longer fuses than the first set, and he lighted them as he went around the camp. He saved two to hurl in among the warriors. The drum stopped suddenly as Sits Tall rose from his cross-legged position on a blanket.

"Enough," he told his followers. "We must rest and be fresh to fight when the sun comes."

Not likely, Preacher thought to himself as he made his way back to the horses. A harsh panther cough and snarl set the ponies off in a restless trot. Wolf howls followed and then the first of the bombs went off. The Dakota's mounts stampeded. Around the fire, pandemonium erupted. The explosions shook the ground. Preacher turned back then, lighted the remaining pair of fuses and hurled the gourds into the camp.

They erupted seconds later and set off a wilder scramble. In the midst of it, he threw back his head and shouted his earlier challenge. "I own the earth!"

Preacher gave another panther cough and raced back to where he had left Thunder. A swift ride though the moonlit night brought him to the circle of wagons. Several of their out-facing sides still bristled with arrows. The folks would be able to get rid of them come morning, Preacher thought with satisfaction.

* * *

Early morning light showed evidence that the Dakota had given up any idea of an attack. No warriors lined the ridges, Preacher noted as he poured a second round of coffee into a tin cup. He cut his gray eyes left and right, seeking any hint of concealed braves in the tall meadow grass. He saw not the slightest presence.

"Well an' good," he rumbled as he sought the last of his Catlin clay pipes and a small pouch of tobacco.

Now was a good time for a smoke. Not even the powerful medicine of the Raven Owners' Society could prevail against the ghostly events of the night gone by, he reasoned with a touch of smugness. Best take advantage of it, before they got their nerves reined in and their wind up again. To that end, he turned to the late awakeners who crawled muzzily from their bedrolls.

"You'd all best make it a quick breakfast. Menfolk set to harnessin' the mules. Dupre, 'Hawk an' Beartooth will git you lined out on the trail. I'm goin' ahead to sniff the ground."

Cora Ames had a newfound friend in Falicity Jones. They came forward to where Preacher stood by the fire. "We heard the awfulest sounds last night," Cora began. "We thought the Indians must have gotten drunk and set fire to their ammunition when the explosions started."

Preacher gave her a small, secret smile. "Dakota don't take much to drink, leastwise not so far. I'd say they ran up against some medicine too big for them to handle."

Falicity caught the twinkle in Preacher's eyes. "You're not going to tell us, are you?"

"Nothin' to tell, Miz Jones."

"Are they going to attack?" Cora inquired.

"Nope. I reckon whatever spirits troubled them last night got 'em headed back toward their sacred Black Hills. We be makin' the tradin' post come midday tomorrow."

Preacher put a slab of fried fatback between the halves of two biscuits and wrapped them in a square of neatly worked buckskin. He stuffed that in a coat pocket and headed for

Thunder. Saddled up, he rode out of the bustling camp. Flora Sanders called after him with words sweet to his ears.

"I'll have a dried apple pie waiting for you tonight, Preacher."

Immediately when he crossed the forward ridge, Preacher saw confirmation that he had read the mood of the Dakotas correctly. Or rather, he saw not a sign of any of them. Scuffed ground and wide-spaced moccasin prints indicated that the Indians had left, and in some considerable disarray. Preacher chortled softly. Must have taken them most of the night to round up their ponies. No doubt the rest of it packing up to get out of there. Be a lot of drooping eyes among them bucks on the trail today. He touched boot heels to Thunder and continued his scout.

Beartooth and Nighthawk remained behind to do what they could to wipe out any sign of their passage once the wagons left the narrow trace through the soaring mountains. While they worked, Beartooth spoke of past events.

"Preacher was smart to pick this side approach to the pass. Only thing, none of us could have expected them Dakota. If Pease has men lookin' for us, it'd be on the main trail."

"That's a mouthful for you, Beartooth," Nighthawk observed. "Although I suspect you are right. Bad fortune. We will be out of it before long, though."

"Yep. Only I don't reckon those wagons will make it as soon as Preacher expects. A couple of them look to be on the edge of breakin' down."

Nighthawk made a face. "All we need."

"So true. I was lookin' forward to findin' my woman's people and settlin' in for a summer of buffalo huntin'."

Nighthawk rubbed his lean, hard belly. "I can taste a plate full of roasted hump. Did you know that the forest bison were all but hunted out before the white man came? It was rare that any of our people ever tasted that sweet, rich meat."

"That's bein' deprived some, I'd say."

"You know it, friend."

With their task completed in early afternoon, Nighthawk and Beartooth came unexpectedly upon the wagons. They had halted due to a broken wheel on one of the vehicles salvaged from the raid by Pease and his men. Also, Asa Pettibone's wagon had a cracked connecting bar in the running gear.

"Might have known it," Beartooth sighed in resignation. "We'll be stuck here a day at best."

Four large, sacred drums throbbed in the central clearing of the Cheyenne village. A huge fire burned, although it was midday. Cooking went on at other, smaller fires among the concentric circles of lodges. Boys ran foot races in imitation of the more serious adult contests to come after the Grand Council concluded its business. Others played at mock hunting or war. The little girls helped their mothers by washing vegetables, cutting strips of meat into cubes for stew, and stirring bubbling cauldrons. A number of the older female population, those in their teens, looked on with admiring glances at the youthful warriors, excluded from the council hearing that had gone on for the past three days.

Everyone said it would end sometime before the sun went to sleep in the west. No one knew for sure. Occasionally, angry voices raised from behind the brush walls of the ceremonial lodge, its top open to the sky. When the messenger, bowed with fatigue, wended his way among the lodges toward the entrance to the council lodge, most of the boys gave off their games to follow along. The camp crier preceded him. The lathered pony stopped outside the brush arbor and snorted. His rider stared stupidly, as though dazed and unaware of where he had reached. Two young civil chiefs came out to confront him.

Slowly he slipped from his mount and staggered forward. He had ridden hard for three days and nights without sleep.

When he entered, his message roused new shouts of outrage and anger.

"Little Knife killed by whites!" Stone Drum blurted. "I say we know who they are. Where is this?"

Blinking, the messenger recited all he knew. "Some white men made a large camp in a valley on the slopes of the White Top Mountains that face the Medicine Bows. They are many in number. It is said they come to trade guns with our people. Little Knife heard they had whiskey. He went to make them spill it on the ground. A man I know, who died later, rode with Little Knife. He was much wounded and escaped the whites that way. He saw Little Knife fall."

Mutters ran among the gathered chiefs. Heads nodded, an agreement formed. Stone Drum spoke for the council. "We are agreed, brothers? We must hunt down these white men and fight them until all die." He looked around and noted three chiefs who had club lodges of Dog Soldiers in their camps. He nodded to them. "You will gather your best men, have criers sent out at once. Let the Dog Soldiers deal with these evil men."

"I will go also," Falling Horse announced from near the entrance.

Stone Drum turned, looked hard at Falling Horse. "Yes. You will take up the war pipe and lead them, Falling Horse. Let not a white man escape."

In a flurry of activity, nearly a hundred Cheyenne Dog Soldiers and others who wanted to avenge Little Knife had gathered food, weapons, and equipment. The feast would be delayed, though the women showed not a sign of disappointment that all their hard work had gone for nothing. They knew that this day it would be they who ate until their bellies swelled like that of a woman with child.

Silas Phipps came upon a narrow, winding pathway that led off the sorry trace he had been following shortly after their nooning. He called for Peter to halt the front wagon and hold fast. Phipps, a poor excuse for a frontiersman, still had a good sense of direction. He studied the lay of the land and forced his whiskey-dulled mind into activity.

Best he could judge, this could be a shortcut to the pass and that trading post he had heard of. Maybe they should turn off into it? On the other hand, he ruminated, the trail he followed was supposed to be the main fork that led to Trout Crick Pass. Further careful scrutiny revealed what appeared to be recent wheel marks. Someone had taken this way. That decided him, almost more so than the crying need to replenish his whiskey supply.

"We gonna be taking this trail," he commanded his orphan entourage.

"Aren't we on the right one?" Ruth asked from beside Peter.

"Leave questions like that to your betters, missy," Phipps snapped. "I say we go on this one, then this is the trail we take."

Inadvertently, Silas Phipps put his two wagons behind Preacher and the larger train. The youngsters' spirits rose at the awesome beauty of the steep canyon walls. Thickly wooded at the lower levels, a silvery stream, alive with jumping trout, beckoned. Peter dreamed idly of better days, long gone by, when he fished from the banks of the Taunton River in Massachusetts. On hot summer days, he and his friends would strip off their clothes and jump into a cool, deep pool formed by a bend in the river. Life had been good then, before his ma and pa had died in a boat wreck during a storm.

Even acidic Silas Phipps mellowed a bit, lulled out of his bad humor by the beauty of their surroundings. Gradually, though, the peacefulness awakened his darkest urges. At day's end, unbeknownst to him, they had come within a morning's journey behind Preacher's pilgrims. Phipps had the itch something powerful after he had eaten and given up his tin plate to be washed by the girls. His watery black eyes searched out the object of his desire and fixed on her. Grunting, he pushed himself to his boots and walked over to Gertha.

He draped an arm around her slender shoulder and spoke disarmingly. "I've sort of taken a fancy to you, Gertha. You know that?" Gertha did not reply, only looked up at Phipps with big, solemn, frightened eyes. "Oh, my, yes. We have those skins the boys trapped to sell at the trading post, and I'm going to buy you something pretty. How about that?" Again, Gertha did not reply. "Yes, well. I want to show you how much I've come to favor you, so I'll expect you at my wagon after the others have been settled down for the night. You won't disappoint me, will you?"

She could but shake her head and dread the night.

17

With the wagons overhauled, the last leg to the trading post went without event. At Preacher's insistence, they resupplied and pushed on. That didn't happen without loud objections from the missionaries. Preacher and Nighthawk traveled ahead. Preacher wanted to get a close look at the valley where he had wintered, to make certain no one else had settled in.

No one had, only the early blossoms in the April warmth. Preacher and Nighthawk split up and went out to hunt for game. He wanted to give the gospel-shouters a headstart on laying in supplies. Plenty of smoked meat would be a sizable contribution. Well he did, for the wagons rolled in four days later.

Dupre, still nursing his shoulder wound, and Beartooth organized the missionary men and supervised while they felled trees to build cabins. Domestic tranquility settled over the valley. It made Preacher uncomfortable. He set off to hunt for more game.

Preacher leveled the sights of his Hawken on the big bull elk that stood spraddle-legged, its head lowered into the silvery spring to drink. That's it, he thought, right behind the left leg. A gentle squeeze. The big .54 caliber rifle slammed into Preacher's shoulder with a familiar impact. The elk stiffened, all four legs splayed now, then went down. The hooves dug into the ground beneath the dying animal while Preacher approached.

It shuddered its last and went still. A perfect heart shot. Hardly any blood had spilled onto the ground. Preacher's sharp knife opened the veins of the neck and he wiped the blade clean before resheathing it. Then he went for Thunder. It would take the powerful Appaloosa horse to raise the animal for skinning and field dressing.

With that task completed, Preacher buried the offal to keep away scavengers and washed his bloodied arms and hands in the stream. He brought his packhorse and loaded the quarters of elk, wrapped in sections of the hide. Weary from four days of hunting, Preacher decided to head for home, visiting each of his earlier caches along the way, to retrieve the meat waiting there. If Nighthawk had equal luck, he speculated, the pilgrims would not need to hunt again before fall. Plenty of time to build cabins, to shut themselves in from the spectacular summer nights.

"Fool folks," Preacher grunted to himself. "Winter's the time to be closed in, out of the cold. Anyone knows that."

Sundown would not be near for another three hours when Preacher rode down a slope into a tiny vale where a camp had been set up. His keen vision picked out five disreputable-looking ruffians lounging around a low fire. Two of them looked up incuriously when Preacher had covered about half of the distance to them.

"Hello the camp," Preacher called to them.

"Howdy, yerself. You be friendly?"

"That I am. Mind if I ride in and set a spell?"

"C'mon. We got coffee."

"Good. An' I could sure use a sup of Who-Shot-John, if you've got any," Preacher suggested, curious as to the nature of these strangers.

"Nope. Don't bring whiskey in where there's Injuns about. Makes 'em plumb crazy if they git their hands on it."

Tight lines around Preacher's eyes relaxed some. Didn't

sound like they were tied up with Ezra Pease. He walked
Thunder down close to the fire and dismounted. His sweat and
blood-stiffened buckskins rustled as he walked to the fire.

Coffee in hand, Preacher cut his eyes from man to man,
studying their features. None seemed tensed to spring. The
one who had spoken first opened the conversation.

"Name's Clower. Ya been huntin' I see."

"Yup. Name's Arthur." For some reason, Preacher's inner
caution warned him to use his given name. "Never too early
to put away meat for winter."

"Then yer not jist passin' through?" Frank Clower prompted.

"Tired of roamin'," Preacher kept up the fiction. "Got me
a little cabin tucked away a piece from here. I usually go far
afield like this so's to keep the game close to home in case
of need."

"Good idee, Art," Clower said with irritating familiarity.
"You boys trappin'?"

Clower shook his head. "Nope. Jist driftin' through."

"Picked some pretty country for it," Preacher observed.

"Right you are."

Preacher finished his coffee, it tasted like sour mud, and
cleaned the cup. Then he turned to walk to Thunder. "Nice
jawin' with you gents," he said over his shoulder before he
put his attention to tightening Thunder's cinch strap, which
he had loosened when he dismounted.

That's the moment three of them chose to jump him. He
caught the movement from the corner of his eye. Preacher
swung in time to plant a hard fist flush in the mouth of a
small, pinch-faced thug that dumped Preacher's attacker flat
on the ground. He put an elbow in the gut of another. Raw
whiskey fumes gushed out of a corded throat. Preacher
popped him on the side of the head and he dropped like a log.
He advanced on the last one. By then the third hard case had
his knife out.

"Hey, stupid!" Preacher shouted in the man's suddenly
astonished face.

"I ain't stupid," the riff-raff protested.

"Yes, you are," Preacher teased.

"Why?"

"You brought a knife . . . to a gunfight," Preacher concluded as he yanked one of his four-shooters and let bang with a double-shotted load.

Cut down like a thin sapling, the vermin fell away in time to reveal Clower and the last man groping for their guns. Preacher waited for the faster of the pair to clear his waistband. Then he sent the ugly sucker off to meet his Maker.

Howling, Frank Clower dived off to one side, rolled and came up shooting. A ball whizzed past Preacher's right ear. Preacher replied. His ball also missed. By then one of the buzzards he had punched out roused enough to reach for his pistol. Preacher had stepped away from his animals in the opening round to save the lives of Thunder and the packhorse.

Still groggy, the filth bag fired hastily. It popped through the loose portion of Preacher's coat on the left side. Two holes. Damn, Preacher thought. He quickly educated the lout with a ball to the chest. Then he turned back to Clower in time to see the black hole of a .60 caliber muzzle pointed directly at his face.

Triumphant, Clower pulled the trigger. The big Hayes misfired. Preacher's four-shooter didn't. One of the balls caught Clower at the base of his throat. The other broke a collarbone and punched through the shoulder blade behind. Clower gurgled as he went slack-kneed and sagged to the ground. His free hand twitched and clawed at his wounds. Then, his eyes glazing, he tried to focus on the big man standing over him.

"Y-you be Preacher, ain't ye?" Clower asked.

"I be."

"That Arthur thing had me fooled for a moment. Smart, thinkin' it up so quick."

"Didn't think it up. My ma did."

"No foolin'?" Clower said through a froth of pink foam.

"Nope."

"I'll be danged. I'm dyin', right Preacher?"

"You are."

"Bury me?"

"You work for Pease?"

"Yeah. Though I'm regrettin' it right about now."

"Then I won't bury you. Not fit for proper puttin' away."

"You're a hard man, Preacher."

"I know it. Goodbye, Clower."

"Oh, God—God, it hurts so much."

Preacher watched silently until Clower gave up his spirit. Then he collected the weapons, loosely tied the surviving vagabond, and took their horses with him. He'd use them to carry meat back to the valley.

Preacher sensed their disapproval the moment he rode up to the busy center of activity. All it had taken was for the missionary folk to count the number of horses he led. They didn't give a hoot about the meat he had brought in. They could count, and they knew he had taken only one packhorse with him. As expected, Reverend Thornton Bookworthy expressed their disapproval.

"What happened to the men who owned these horses?" the rotund cleric demanded.

"They sort of suddenly got dead. An' they pro'lly didn't own them. More likely they stole 'em," Preacher answered him.

Reverend Bookworthy chose not to listen and believe. "That doesn't bother you at all?"

Preacher pulled out his coat to illustrate his point. "Yes, it does. One of them put a couple of holes in a perfectly good coat. They worked for Pease, who—unless you've forgot—is tryin' mighty hard to kill me."

That registered on the good reverend. "Do . . . his men know about this valley?"

"Not likely," Preacher answered lightly, coming off his prod. "I left one alive and afoot, to carry a message back to Pease. Told him I was comin' after him. Then I rode out, headin' north. By the time that feller gets to the pass and finds another horse, all sign of where I really went will be wiped out."

Bookworthy looked at the string of heavy-laden animals. "We're—ah—appreciative of the meat. The—er—smokehouse was completed in your absence and is already working."

"Humm," Preacher responded. "Smoked venison or elk haunch is right tasty. But I'd eat the thinner parts fresh, and right fast."

Reverend Bookworthy seemed bemused. "Yes—yes. I'll see to it right away." He wandered off, leaving Preacher with his load of meat.

Only scant minutes passed before men from among the missionaries came to relieve him of his burden. Preacher put Thunder in his private corral, the one he had built for the previous winter, and placed the others in the common pen. A barn had been laid out next to that, and framing for one wall already stood tall, raw and proud. *Civilization,* Preacher thought uncharitably.

His mood improved an hour later when Nighthawk came in with both of his horses complaining under enormous loads. The news the Delaware brought quickly restored Preacher's dark outlook.

"There is a large party of white men to the west. I cut their sign three days ago." He did not need to mention that as the reason he had come in late.

Preacher spoke through his scowl. "The bunch jumped me worked for Pease."

Nighthawk raised an eyebrow. "Oh? I won't ask why it is you have a whole skin."

"Thank you, Nighthawk. But my coat didn't fare near so good. Five of 'em. An' one told me before he expired, that they worked for Pease. Things, they is a heatin' up, ol' hoss."

"I'm inclined to agree. What do we do about it?" Nighthawk prompted.

"Nothin' for the time bein'. We got these pilgrims to edjicate," Preacher said with a snort.

Preacher heard more about his treatment of his would-be

murderers after Reverend Bookworthy spread the story through his congregation. Cora Ames and several of the good women of the mission flock came to him to demand if he had provided proper Christian burial.

"What for?" he asked, clearly not understanding the reason for the question.

"I would assume that after brutally murdering five men . . . ," Patience Bookworthy ranted at him.

"Four. It was four men. I left one alive," Preacher defended himself.

"Four men, then. The least you could have done was to give them proper Christian burial."

Preacher could not believe what he had heard. "Waall, hell, ma'am, if you'll pardon the language, them fellers had just tried to kill me. Jumped me when my back was turned. Now, do you think that's a proper Christian thing to do? D'you think they had even a speakin' acquaintance with the moral way of doing things? Or that I owed them anything for their efforts?"

Patience must have bitten down on something sour from the look that came on her face. "Oooh, you're an abomination," she forced out. "You have a way of twisting everything a person says."

"Not at all, ma'am. Just pointin' out which way the wind blows."

To his astonishment, Cora Ames backed his stand. "He's right, you know. This isn't Philadelphia, or Boston, or New York. Life is harsh out here. Didn't those Indian attacks teach you anything?" A sudden, stricken expression washed over her. "Oh, I am so sorry. I shouldn't have spoken so harshly. I . . ."

Preacher found himself defending her. "No, you didn't, Miss Cora. Right to the point, I'd say."

"You would," Patience Bookworthy snapped, then stalked off.

With a more contrite tone, Preacher offered his amends. "I'm afraid my bullheadedness has gotten you on her bad side. Only thing is I didn't have a choice in how I handled them fellers. I did have with how I used my mouth."

Mischief lighted Cora's eyes. "If I'm in Patience's book of bad girls I think I'm in good company, Preacher. I'm glad you weren't injured."

Dumbstruck, Preacher watched, with mouth agape, as she walked to where the other women worked to prepare a meal for the laboring men of the new community.

With a week of construction and meat curing behind them, half of the missionary men and all of the boys over ten were attending a special school. It would be learning that could mean life or death in the isolated village that sprang up faster each day. The instructor was Preacher. His classroom the meadow and forested hills that surrounded the valley. He held a yellowish-white bulb in his hand and waved it under the noses of the more curious youths.

"This here is wild onion. An' no, it don't taste 'zactly like a regular one. But it'll do in a pinch. Some of you who've et with me an' the boys have tasted it in stew. They grow in clumps like you see here. Notice that the tops are flat, rather than round. There's another plant like 'em only with round tops an' whiter bulbs. Stay shy of those. They'll poison ya right terrible. Now, let's move on. There's wild turnips growin' here, along the bank of that crick. We'll look at them next."

An attentive audience accompanied Preacher to his next stop. He took the blade of his knife and dug up a round, flattened tuber with lacy green fronds above ground. "Is that a turnip?" young Nick chirped.

"Sure is. They's stronger flavored than the ones you can grow from seed next year. When you boil 'em up with a slab of that smoked elk and some onions an' yucca' root they'll make you full an' warm."

"What's yucca?" Nick asked, a frown creasing his forehead and button nose.

"That's them spiky, dark green leaves you see stickin' up

in the sandy places. Later on they'll have waxy white blossoms on a stalk. They grow big, fat roots to store water for dry spells. Sweet as a yam," Preacher unveiled, pleased with his role as teacher. He pointed to a shadowed gulley across the creek.

"Them long vines with the stickers are wild blackberries. They'll bloom in early May, put on dark fruit and be ready to eat in mid-August an' all September. That is if the bears don't get at 'em first."

"Bears?" a mousey missionary squeaked.

"Oh, sure. An' if you see any out here, don't dispute their claim to the blackberries."

"I'd shoot him an' put him in the smokehouse," young Chris declared.

Preacher made a face. "Bear meat's sorta strong, and greasy. Sometimes tastes of fish, only fish that's gone bad. And you got to cook bear meat through and through."

"Ugh!" several of the missionary boys chorused.

"That's about it for now. We'll look into pine nuts and woodsy things tomorrow. Now I've got to help the ladies learn to jerk venison."

A loner all of his life, Preacher often felt ill at ease around groups of people. Yet, he had a high old time when he spent hours with the women of the camp in the task of preserving food. He worked at their side, and took them through each step in the process of cutting, seasoning, and drying strips of venison and elk. The only thing that kept it from being a total delight was that they chattered all the time. About woman things, at that.

His cheeks flamed frequently when the subject of corsets and petticoats came up. At such times, he retreated into conjecture on the problem that kept gnawing on him. Ezra Pease and his dealings with the Indians always came to the forefront of Preacher's thoughts. At last he had to take his gleanings to his companions.

Preacher sat aside his plate and licked his lips in satisfaction. "Elk ham makes a man's day, it rightly do," he declared.

"Now, I've got something eatin' at me that we need to worry over together."

"Pease," Nighthawk said simply.

"That's right. What do you reckon we ought to do about it?"

"We've been tied down here for better than a week," Beartooth stated the obvious. "Who knows where Pease is now?"

"That's the point," Preacher seized on it. "He could be lookin' right down on us this minute. And who knows what mischief he's up to. We got this here little town off to a good start. I think it's time to go out and hunt down Pease and settle his hash once and for all."

"These gospel-shouters have ten thumbs when it comes to any real work," Beartooth complained, contradicting his earlier statement. "Someone has to stay with them to make sure their houses don't fall down when they finish 'em."

Preacher cocked a brow. "You ain't the world's greatest carpenter either, Beartooth."

"But I can hit the pegs with the hammer, not my thumb."

"Then yer elected," Preacher said simply. "Fact is, if there's no objection, I think you all should stay on to get the job done right, whilst I go hunt down Pease. I can clear out in two days' time, find him, then come back for the rest of you. Then we can clean out that nest of rattlers."

BOOK TWO

18

Ten of Stone Drum's Dog Soldiers crouched in the chokecherry bushes at the crest of the rim that surrounded the hidden valley occupied by the hated whites. The oldest among them, a smooth-muscled man in his mid-thirties, father of three boys and two girls, nodded, his hawk-beak nose pointing out the crude shelters erected by Pease's men. Although a quarter-mile away, he spoke softly.

"We must find Falling Horse. One of you go to the camp of Stone Drum. Our chief must know of this also."

"They have moved close to the land of the Blackfeet," a younger brave observed.

Good Sky nodded again and a flicker of smile lighted his face. "That is why when we attack we must do it swiftly, with all our warriors. None must escape to tell their friends the Blackfeet." He looked around at the men with him. "Young Bear, you are lightest, can move fast without tiring your pony. Go to Stone Drum. Otter, you go to Falling Horse. The rest will stay here, keep watch, guide our Dog Soldier brothers to this valley."

Young Bear's chest swelled. "We are strong enough to take them now."

"I think not. It is better that we wait," Good Sky ruled.

That wait lasted three days. Young Bear and Otter rounded up all of the roving Dog Soldiers who had been searching for the whites and brought them to the valley. There, Falling

Horse laid his plans for the attack. He saw at once that some of the whites would no doubt break free of their initial charge and escape the camp that had been established. Yet, he wanted to cause what damage they could.

"We are not enough in numbers to close off both ends of the valley," he instructed the eager warriors. "We can come from both sides, to increase their confusion. It is best after that to ride to where we can join forces and fight our way back through one side."

Wiser heads nodded agreement. "To be quiet and surprise them is important," Falling Horse cautioned.

Without further discussion, the Cheyenne set out to make ready for war. Many of the Dog Soldiers painted themselves and their ponies for the event. Others made up in soft tones of brown and green, in order to sneak up close on the unsuspecting whites before the signal was given to charge. When everyone had reached his proper place, a warbler call advised Falling Horse of this. The time had come.

Suddenly the peaceful atmosphere of the camp shattered at the sharp-edged war cries of the hundred Cheyenne. Arrows rained from the sky and made a pin cushion of one hard case. His wails and shrieks of agony joined the battle sounds of the Dog Soldiers. Ponies at a gallop, they thundered toward the assortment of tents and brush shelters from upstream and down.

"B'god it's Injuns!" Two Thumbs Buehler shouted in astonishment. His hands darted toward his rifle.

Ezra Pease jolted from his folding camp stool and rushed to the open flap of his tent. Spurts of smoke jetted skyward as the Cheyenne opened up. Belatedly, some of his own men returned fire.

"Hold tight," Pease shouted. "We out-gun them."

"How do you know?" came a nervous challenge. "There could be hunnerds of them."

"You dolt! *We're* the ones selling the guns," Ezra Pease

snapped, wondering how he had come to have so many lamebrains in the gang.

It soon became clear that the Indians advanced in a two-pronged attack. With them they brought firebrands, which they threw into the brush shelters. Flames licked high in scant seconds. A screaming man staggered out of one, his body engulfed by fire. Terrified by this, several of the thugs made a run for the brushy slope of the basin. Fire from London-made fusils erupted in their faces. One man caught two arrows from so short a range that only the fletchings protruded from his shirtfront. The captive boys still with Pease wailed in confusion, uncertain as to where their safety lay. For all their superiority in firepower, Ezra Pease soon saw they had no choice but to make a run for it.

"Harness the teams," he bellowed, regretting the inevitable loss of his stout tent.

Then, totally unexpected, when the two wings of the charge met near the middle of camp, the hostiles turned in one direction and dashed out of the encircling white men. Although not before they had snatched up a case of rifles, two kegs of powder and one crate of bullets packed in layers of sawdust. Three, who had been able to understand the pleas of the captive white boys, had youngsters behind them on their ponies. Pease roared his anger after them.

"Damn them! Damn them all. They think they can come in here and take what they want, eh? Then run like whipped dogs. They'll not get away with it." Still contemptuous of Indians in general, Ezra Pease made yet another mistake. "There can't be more than forty of them. Everyone mount up. I want them hunted down and killed, every last one."

Two wagons ambled into the missionaries' valley late the next afternoon. They presented a sorry sight. Both wagons had broken down repeatedly on the rough trail north of Trout Crick Pass. Silas Phipps suffered from withdrawal from alcohol and his orphans all appeared sickly. They stumbled around like walking corpses and all of the missionaries agreed that they needed considerable care.

"Our supplies ran out two days ago," Helen informed the concerned mission folk. "We haven't had anything to eat since then. Peter has a fever. Please, can you help us?" she appealed to a compassionate committee of women.

"Oh, you poor dears. We'll get you fed right away. Where is the sick boy?"

"In the front wagon," Helen told Patience Bookworthy.

"Now, you keep yer hands off that boy," Silas Phipps growled. "He's just faking being sick to get out of work."

Preacher didn't like the cut of the man at first sight. He had a meanness about his mouth and little, squinty eyes, that darted from place to place, as though assessing the value of everything in sight. His lack of concern for the children didn't sit right, either. It was this that made Preacher decide to step in.

"Are you a doctor?" the mountain man demanded.

"No, I ain't. An' it's none of your concern," Phipps snapped.

Preacher produced a grim smile, a sure warning sign to any who knew him. "Since you're not a doctor, you don't know any more about how sick that boy is than I do. Let the women take care of him."

Phipps had time by then to gauge the size and mettle of the man confronting him. Coward that he was, he backed down a little. "They can ply him with some soup, and maybe some medicine. We could all use something to eat. But mind, they're not to touch him or take him out of those clothes."

Preacher wondered on that throughout the day and into the next. Peter responded to the ministrations of the missionary women and roused out of his fevered state by mid-afternoon. Once the affliction had left him, he ate ravenously. Talk went around the new settlement about asking the wanderers to remain in the valley. Preacher objected to that, but withheld comment.

On their second full day in the valley, the children had lost some of their listlessness and befriended children among the missionaries and refugees, in spite of the efforts of Silas

Phipps to prevent that. When several of the boys, including young Peter, went downstream to take a bath, Preacher went along to stand guard.

When the lads had undressed, little Nick stared at Peter, eyes wide with wonder. "Jehoshephat! What happened to you?" he blurted.

"It's . . . nothin'," Peter responded quietly, his face aflame with humiliation.

"Don't tell me that," Nick persisted. "Someone whomped on you real fierce."

"NO! No one did it. I—I . . . fell. Fell off the wagon," Peter invented in desperation.

Made curious by the anxious tone in Peter's voice, Preacher cut his eyes to where the boys stood naked and knee-deep in the chill creek. His eyes widened and turned as hard as high-quality flint when he saw all the scars on Peter's back. Fresh purple welts criss-crossed the boy's shoulders, the small of his back and his skinny buttocks. It brought a flash of fury.

Then Preacher recovered his go-easy, mountain man outlook. Not his business, he decided. Some kids needed more rough handling to be brought up right. Might be that Phipps feller told the truth. Then he recalled that the Indians raised some mighty fine youngsters without ever laying a hand on them. Small wonder Phipps didn't want the women to see Peter's back.

Preacher dismissed his immediate concern. They'd spend only another day and a night in the valley, resupply what they could and then Phipps would be told to move on. He'd point the way back to Trout Crick Pass to Phipps and bid him good luck. These youngin's weren't his to be worrying over, Preacher allowed. He turned back to his guard duties.

With Preacher keeping watch for predators of the two and four-legged varieties, the boys splashed and played with the lye soap bar until they turned a bit blue around the lips and shivered violently. Only then would they admit that the water might be a bit chilly. They climbed from the stream and toweled dry. Then Nick, who was small for his age, and of a size with Peter, presented the latter boy with a fresh change of clothes. Tears of gratitude and affection filled Peter's' eyes and he turned away to hide them from the other lads. When they had all dressed, Preacher marched them back to the settlement.

There he found Cora Ames all a-tither over the condition of the older girls. "There's something very wrong in the lives of these children," she announced sternly.

"Such as?" Preacher prodded, the knowledge of Peter's frequent beatings clear in his mind.

"They won't say anything, in fact they deny that something . . . unpleasant has been going on."

"Only you don't think that's the truth?"

Cora cut her big, blue, troubled eyes to him. "Oh, Preacher, all I have are suspicions. But they seem to be in absolute terror of that Mr. Phipps."

"We'll have to keep an eye on Phipps, for as long as they're here with us then," Preacher offered.

"Will you, Preacher? It's all I can ask, I suppose. And, tell the others, too. Beartooth, Dupre, and Nighthawk?"

"Sure, Miss Cora. Done without sayin'. Ain't none of us cottons to the man. I reckon it was him who gave Peter a powerful beatin'. More than one, at that."

Cora's hand flew to her mouth to cover her astonishment. "How badly was the boy injured?"

"I reckon it's what gave him that fever. Some of them stripes was deep, could have festered."

"Why, that's monstrous."

"May seem so to you an' me, Miss Cora. But if they belong to him, it ain't again' the law. He can do whatever he wants with 'em, short of actual killin' one."

Stubborn anger colored Cora's next words. "Not if he's doing what I think he's done to those girls."

Preacher lost any doubt about her concerns. His lips thinned into a hard line. "So, it's that way, huh? Might be I should have a little talk with Phipps."

"I'm afraid that might make things worse for them all," Cora pleaded for restraint.

"Not until he got off his back and outta the splints I'd be puttin' him in," Preacher rumbled.

Preacher thought at first he was dreaming of a wounded rabbit. Yet, the pitiful cries had more volume than the squeak of a hurt animal. He came fully awake when they changed to outright screams.

"No! Please, no! I won't let you. It hurts. I won't!" a child's voice penetrated the haze in Preacher's head.

A short distance away, Nighthawk roused from sleep also. "That's a child," the Delaware stated thickly.

"Yep. An' I got an idee where it's comin' from." Preacher slipped into moccasins, drew up his buckskin trousers and padded off into the darkness. Nighthawk followed him to the source of the sounds of anguish and humiliation.

Preacher sprang up onto the lip at the base of the tailgate to the second wagon that belonged to Silas Phipps. He had been guided there by the soft, dim glow of a candle burning inside. He was the first among the occupants of the valley to see Silas at his evil pleasure.

Phipps had pulled the thin dress off the skinny, naked form of little Gertha, the ten-year-old. Gertha wretchedly struggled, hot trails of tears coursing down her cheeks. Feebly she batted at the pawing hands of Phipps.

With a roar, Preacher bent inward and grabbed the perverted vermin by the back of his collarless shirt and scruff of his neck. With no more seeming effort than jerking a fly clear off a square of sticky paper, Preacher yanked Silas Phipps out of his wagon and hurled him onto the ground. Nighthawk stood over the astonished Phipps.

"Not even the filthy buzzard-puke that rides for Dirty Dan Frazier would do a low-down thing like that, you bastard!" Preacher roared.

"Them orphans are mine. I can do with them what I want,"

Phipps wailed in his defense. "Besides, she likes it. Purrs like a li'l kitten, she does."

That set Preacher's control boiling over. "Move over, Nighthawk. This'uns got him a powerful whuppin' comin'. Git up, you sick son of a bitch."

Phipps cowered, arms up and curled around his head for protection. "Don't you touch me. I didn't do no harm."

Fire burned in Preacher's eyes as he reached down and dragged Phipps to his boots. "How many o' them little girls have you pestered?" he grated through his fury.

"Only the older ones. Them that's nine or over," came a whimpered reply.

"What about what you done to Peter?" Preacher prodded, his vision filled with the purple welts on the skin of the boy's pale back.

"Yeah—yeah, him, too, a couple of times. An' Billy, too."

Shocked to stupefication by this disgusting revelation, Preacher responded with his fists. His big knuckles mashed into Phipps' lips, pulped his nose, split the skin under one eye. Phipps bleated in terror, twisted and pulled in an attempt to escape this terrible punishment. Preacher gave him no slack.

When Phipps wilted in Preacher's grip, the mountain man brought up one knee smartly and smashed into the pervert's crotch. Then he went to work on the soft belly and vulnerable ribs. The disturbance awakened everyone in the settlement. Lamps bloomed with light and people began to gather. In the forefront, black frock coat draped over nightshirt, came the Reverend Thornton Bookworthy.

"Enough!" he thundered. "Desist at once. You'll kill that man."

Preacher ceased his pounding and looked at the minister from his anger. "You're right. I allow as how any man forcing himself on a woman, and in particular a child, has committed a hanging offense. I say that's what we do with this rotten trash."

Despite the closeness of their earlier conversation, Cora Ames flared at Preacher also. "You can't do that without a trial. This man is entitled to the protection of the law. Everyone is presumed innocent until proven guilty."

Preacher noted the fervor with which she had made her statements and it only fanned the flames higher. "Well, hell, Miss Cora, if you'll pardon my sayin' it, I caught him in the act, with his britches down around his knees like they are now. That ain't no sportin'-house girl in there, that's a ten-year-old child."

Gertha's small, pale face appeared over the tailgate. "Hit him again, Mr. Preacher. Hit him for me."

Reverend Bookworthy had gathered more steam. "We can't hang him. Why, it's— it's *uncivilized.*"

"That's right," Patience Bookworthy rallied behind her husband. "Everyone knows that hanging people is no deterrent to crime."

Preacher eyed her like a creature from another planet. "I beg to point out that hangin' is a sure-fire way to deter the feller from doin' it. Any rapist, once hung, sure as ol' Nick himself, won't ever rape another."

Asa Pettibone stepped forward. "I agree with Preacher. If we are establishing a community here, then we're responsible for enforcing the laws. As I recall, rape is a capital crime. I say we select a jury, from among our drivers and ourselves. Did you see what went on?" he asked Nighthawk.

"I only saw Preacher drag this wretch out of his wagon."

"Good. Then you can be prosecutor, Nighthawk. Beartooth can be bailiff, Dupre can be judge. And, Thornton, if you feel so strongly against the death penalty for such scum as Phipps, you can damn well defend the low-life trash."

More lanterns were brought, the fire built up, and everyone gathered around. Only the children were barred from witnessing the events that transpired. When summoned, Beartooth escorted each of the orphans forward to testify.

Each one sobbed out their face-reddening, humiliating evidence. Through it all, Silas Phipps grew more surly.

"Yer a lyin' whelp," he snarled at Billy when the boy told between gulps of fear and loathing what Phipps had done to him.

"It—it's the truth, an' you know it," the eight-year-old boy accused. "I swore to myself I'd never tell a soul. The shame would kill me. But if it will free us all of you, I'm glad to answer what they want to know."

Peter told of the many beatings, and of the dark, degrading, secret things Phipps had compelled him to do. Several of the missionary women swooned dead away, others erupted in fits of tears and hysteria.

"Yer a liar, same as the others, you miserable brat. Next time, I'll whip the life out of you."

Preacher could no longer restrain himself. "I don't reckon yer gonna get a 'next time.'"

Dupre rapped a pistol butt on the barrel head that served as his bench. "Let's not get out of line, *mon ami.* You'll have your chance to give testimony in a little while."

"What's wrong with now?" Preacher growled.

"I seem to recall something about establishing a link between the accused and his crimes. Mr. Pettibone was kind enough to instruct me in this custom of law. So we need to start in the past and bring it up to the events of this evening. Then we can hang this *batard* right legal and proper," he added, a cold fire in his black eyes. "Proceed, Mr. Prosecutor."

"What happened after the last beating, Peter?"

"He—uh—he smeared me with axle grease. He was real tender about it, especially my ba-backside. I just knew what he wanted."

Phipps came to his feet, hands fisted, eyes wild. "Shut up, you dirty little liar."

Dupre cut his eyes to Beartooth. "Bailiff, please restrain the defendant."

Beartooth gave a curt nod, walked to where he faced Phipps,

at a little less than arm's length, and biffed the blustering pervert in the mouth. "That good enough, Judge Dupre?"

"Fine as frog fur, Beartooth. Once again, please continue."

Peter did. Then Preacher was called, he related being awakened, recognizing the cries to be those of a child and following the sound to the second wagon of Phipps. At that point he became ill at ease, shrugged and shuffled his feet, until he at last turned to Dupre.

"Frenchy, uh, Judge, can we ask the ladies be excused before I say what it is I found inside that wagon?"

"Considering the circumstances, I find that a reasonable request," Nighthawk supported Preacher's position.

Realizing that if Preacher revealed all the gruesome details, the client forced upon him would surely hang, Reverend Bookworthy protested. "The Constitution guarantees a speedy and public trial. The Lord knows this is speedy enough. If the womenfolk are excused it will not be entirely public."

"Now, hold on a minute there, *Pere* Bookworthy. I've never been in a real court but once," Dupre challenged. "But the one I was in didn't allow women to witness the trial. I'm going to rule that the women be excused."

After they had gone, Preacher described what he had seen. When he concluded with the pounding he had given Phipps, rumbles of angry discontent swept through the long gap in testimony. Dupre rapped again and brought silence.

"Do you wish to call anyone else?" he asked Nighthawk.

"Yes. The victim, little Gertha."

After her account of what had gone on, several among the jury had to be restrained by Beartooth. Dupre turned to Reverend Bookworthy. "Do you have anything to offer in defense?"

"I call Silas Phipps."

Phipps took the oath, then slumped on the barrel used as a witness chair. "I might have done some bad things in my life. But it weren't my fault. I had an awful childhood. My parents beat me, they didn't love me. I had an uncle, my pa's brother, who pestered me when I was little," he recited his list of imaginary woes. "I was shunned by the other children because we were poor. I went hungry most every day . . ." He went on and on with the usual puerile snivel about his past life.

When he finished, the jury took only one minute to reach a verdict. "Guilty," Buck the foreman announced.

"But it ain't my fault. I can't help myself," Silas Phipps whined, squealed, and sobbed out.

"Having been found guilty as charged, I sentence you to be hanged by your neck until you are dead, dead, dead. And may *le bon dieu* have mercy on your soul," Dupre pronounced in a sepulchral voice.

Phipps squealed like a pig. He struggled and fought with the four men who wrestled to restrain him. He thrashed and howled all the way to the tall fir tree with long, thick lower branches. There his hands and feet were tied and a hastily fashioned rope fitted around his neck.

He was still shrieking when the rope went suddenly taut and hauled him off his feet. No one wanted to break the silence that followed that.

19

War talk resumed among the Cheyenne. Many of the younger warriors and war chiefs had grown highly discontented with the failure to settle decisively with Pease. Their representatives on the council made their position known. The debate turned even more serious.

"It is foolish to make war on the whites. Unless we kill all of these men, others will come to avenge them. Think of our women, our children," Running Bear appealed to reason.

"While we spend our days chasing after them, the Blackfeet are making up for war," Wind Rider reminded the assembled chiefs. "We cannot fight them, and all the whites, too."

"No. It is the white men who sell guns and whiskey we must kill," Gray Cloud rose to speak his thoughts. "When we do, the Blackfeet will have to take counsel again about fighting us."

Falling Horse rose next, a brief smile flickering on his wide, handsome face. "I do not think the whites think well of these men who sell guns and whiskey to our people. I have met with the one they call Preacher. He and three friends are hunting this man called Pease. They mean to stop him."

"What can four men do against all those who ride with Pease?" Gray Cloud demanded scornfully.

"That is not the point, old friend. What we must do is find Pease first and finish off his fighting men. With Preacher opposed to what Pease is doing, he will speak in our favor to his kind. I believe that no other white men will seek to punish us if we kill Pease."

Little Mountain rose to add his sentiments. "Falling Horse is right. This Pease rides like a mighty chief across our lands. He and his warriors are crowding up our open spaces, selling rotten whiskey to those who would drink it, and being troublesome in many ways."

"Yes. The white boy-child I took from their camp told how the men with Pease killed his parents, and many other whites in a rolling lodge train and took them captive," Falling Horse informed them. "This is also why I say the whites will not care who it is that ends the days for Pease."

"It is known that they are the ones who sold guns to the Blackfeet," White Bow added in mounting anger. "We are agreed to fight the Blackfeet if they come into our land. I say we take the battle to them. Attack their villages. Punish them for trading guns with the whites."

"But first we must make Pease pay for what he has done," Falling Horse urged.

Running Bear sighed and shook his graying head. "Your words are good, Falling Horse. Yet, we must take counsel in what is true, and not give in to being guided by what we wish could be done. I say it is to be moon-struck to decide for a general uprising. Look at the power of the Blackfeet, their great numbers. And the endless stream of whites. Do you forget their Tall Hats who keep the log wall villages?"

Falling Horse had to admit the wisdom of that argument. Although few in number, and widely spread over the high plains, the forts provided a constant thorn to irritate the Cheyenne. After much wrangling, the council decided not to change their initial decision. They would first hunt the whites who had killed Little Knife and his warriors and destroyed the village of Black Hand. More than half the number of braves able to fight would be needed to protect their villages from any surprise attack by the Blackfeet, while the rest went in pursuit of Pease. They would discuss widening the fight later. Falling Horse had the last word.

"I will lead the Dog Soldiers, if you approve," he told the council. None objected.

Cora Ames was not speaking to Preacher after the drumhead trial and hanging of Silas Phipps. That pleased Preacher mightily. He decided to set off on another hunting sweep, then see to finding Pease. To his surprise, young Peter and Billy overcame their ordeal enough to share their skill in setting snares for smaller game with the boys of the village. Before Preacher departed, the youngsters were out in the woods to trap rabbits, squirrels, and other edible, fur-bearing critters. Preacher used a big hand to cover his satisfied smile.

"You will be back when?" Nighthawk asked.

"Before the first game I shoot spoils," Preacher answered.

"The one who has her eyes set for you is angry, I gather."

Preacher sighed, more in relief than regret. "That she is. I'll never understand wimmin. Cool as ol' Jim Beckworth, she was when it came to shootin' Injuns. Wouldn't abide hangin' that rotten trash. Oh, well, I reckon the Almighty will sort out whatever, if any, was good about Silas Phipps. Be seein' you, Nighthawk."

Preacher took similar leave from the other pair, along with some ribald advice about how to rewarm the cockles of Cora's heart. That, he told himself, he didn't need. In the meanwhile, Cora had found herself a new distraction. Over coffee and sweet cakes, she conferred with Lidia Pettibone, Sue Landry and, of course, Patience Bookworthy.

"These orphans are truly alone now," she began her campaign.

Lidia Pettibone gave a shudder. "Better that than the life they had."

Cora sipped from her cup and eyed Lidia over the rim.

"What I'm getting at is they can hardly strike out from here all alone."

"Certainly not," Patience Bookworthy gave her opinion. "Yet, they have been so degraded, so shamed, that they are hardly fit for ordinary society, let alone to live among the righteous."

"I would expect that, comin' from you," Flora Sanders said as she bustled up, fists on hips. "I am so tired of hearing how righteous you folk are. Wasn't it the Pharisees and Suddusees who were considered the most righteous among the Jews? And didn't Jesus tell them that he was of his father and they were of theirs, 'who was a liar and a murderer and a thief from the beginning of time?'"

In a huff, Patience sprang from her rocking chair. "Why, I never . . ."

"Nope. Don't reckon you ever did think about that. You been too busy being righteous. Now, dear," Flora directed to Cora, "what was it you had in mind?"

Pleased and inwardly warmed by this show of support, Cora carefully framed her reply. "These children need homes, and parents to love and care for them. Surely there are those among our group who could open their hearts to these waifs?"

"I'd say so. I'm not too old to be a mother hen," Flora volunteered. "I'd be right pleased to take in that little girl, Gertha, and perhaps Billy."

Cora turned to the others. "There you are. That leaves only ten more to be comforted. And, another thing, we should start thinking toward a school. Our own children are running wild, without the education they need. Twelve more only add to the importance of schooling."

"I agree," Lidia Pettibone offered. "Our Jason is becoming more like those mountain men every day. He even wants a set of buckskins to wear."

Patience Bookworthy recovered from her snit enough to be scandalized. "That goes to show you. We must be shut of those uncouth hooligans as quickly as possible. They are a bad influence on the children."

Cora had another view of the issue. "I think buckskins make a lot of sense . . . out here. We have no ready supply of cloth, and tailor-made clothing costs dearly, if any is available. With animals in ample supply, we can have an endless quantity of clothing. Preacher . . ." She stumbled over the name, then recovered her composure. "Preacher says we can even trade with the friendly Indians for ready-made buckskin clothes."

Sue Landry joined Patience in her objections. "Just the thought of that animal skin against my—my person, makes me cringe."

"And rightly so, dear," Patience supported in prim disapproval.

Not to be put off, Cora made a sweeping gesture with one arm to the stacks of hump-backed trunks outside each nearly completed cabin. "Judging from what we brought along, we women would not be subjected to that for a long time. Perhaps never, if the land is settled as quickly as our mountain men guides seem to think. Yet, it would certainly stretch our husbands' and sons' meeting-house clothes a lot longer. It does no harm for boys and men to wear clothing made from animal skins. Not if they are decorated as attractively as those of Pre—er—that man."

Patience would not let it go. She felt her control of the women slipping away. "Well enough for you to say, with neither man nor child to care for."

That struck home, though Cora vowed not to let it show. "Yes," she said sweetly. "But that's of my choosing, not for any lack of suitors."

Squelched, Patience let it go without challenge. Talk returned to the proposed school while the level in the coffeepot lowered steadily. Lidia Pettibone offered to teach the lower grades, and her husband would provide instruction in music. Martha Yates, recovered from her fright over Johnny, offered to teach the older children. Patience Bookworthy, naturally, stated that she would teach religion.

"But not all of us are of your persuasion," Falicity Jones reminded the officious minister's wife.

To her surprise, Cora found herself on the side of Patience. "True enough, yet we all worship the same God. The moral truths of religious belief are the best guidelines children can have when growing up. Take the Ten Commandments out of the schools and we'll raise up a nation of heathen savages more benighted than the Indians."

Patience Bookworthy shot Cora Ames a gimlet eye before accepting the reality of what the younger woman had said. "I heartily agree. The Ten Commandments were not the Ten Suggestions or Hints. They represent the absolute distillation of moral law. Without them, where would civilization be?"

Their talk went on until the women realized with a start that they would have to scurry to prepare the noon meal for their laboring men. They set off in a flutter of skirts and hair in disarray. It would have pleased Preacher mightily, Cora Ames thought.

Cord Dickson cut his eyes to the ugly features of Grant Ferris. The bucktoothed Ferris had the unsightly habit of picking his nose in the presence of others. Had Cord Dickson not been a knife artist, who gloried in gutting his victims, it would have turned his stomach. He and Seth Branson had been partnered with Grant Ferris for nine days now, searching for any sign of Preacher.

They had gone to the trading post at Trout Crick Pass three times in those days. All with negative results. If anyone knew anything, they sure didn't share it with the scruffy trio of hard cases. Now Dickson, the nominal leader, wanted a unanimous decision from his companions. His hard look made Ferris uncomfortable.

"Whaddayasay, Ferris? I'm for trailin' north an' west of here. Odds are, that's where Preacher went. He sure'n hell ain't to the south of the pass."

"Right you are, Cord," Grant Ferris agreed readily. "Only I for one ain't all that eager to catch up to him."

"Why not?" Cord Dickson need not have asked. He had

his own doubts about the advisability of confronting the legendary mountain man.

"You know what's happened to all them others what ran afoul of Preacher," Ferris clarified his response. "Well, I don't aim to become the next."

Dickson tried to reason with his man. "All we have to do is find him. See where he's holed up, an' then go get the rest to finish him off."

"Sounds simple enough," Seth Branson agreed. "Only we've seen enough to know Preacher is a sudden man. He might not let us just walk away."

"He will if he don't know we've seen him," Dickson let his overconfidence say for him.

"It might be easier to let an Injun not know we've seen him," Ferris offered.

Dickson's eyes narrowed. "Sometimes, Ferris, I think you've got a yeller streak wide as my hand runnin' clear down your spine."

"No I ain't!" Ferris barked at the insult. "Only, I think through somethin' before I act on it."

Ferris turned away in his saddle to gaze behind them at the steep trail they had just descended. "I'm hongry. What say we stop here and chew on something?"

"Good enough," Dickson agreed. "So long as we head northwest when we leave."

Preacher had been following Dickson, Ferris, and Branson for half a day when he made his decision. He had been in close enough to learn their names, and their business, from their careless conversation on the trail. These flatlander highwaymen who had come so recently to the High Lonesome had yet to learn the value of noise control in the mountains.

Soft breezes and the deadening of hoof falls on mats of pine needles gave the false impression that voices would not carry far. In truth, the high granite walls of the canyons, valleys, and hills became natural channels to convey sound a long ways. Too bad these three would not live long enough to learn that lesson, Preacher mused as he edged Thunder down the sharp decline, through thickly growing fir, beech, and aspen.

He had judged that they had come entirely too close to the protected valley where his ration of pilgrims worked to build a home. His hunting would have to wait. Already he had four plump stags tied high in trees to keep away hungry scavengers. He would take care of these three, then round up his kills and head back. His sharp ears picked up the whiny voice of the one called Ferris.

"I say we've gone far enough. Not a sign of Preacher anywhere."

There had been, Preacher thought with contempt. They had cut his trail three times, only they were too stupid to know that.

"Look at it this way," Branson, the calculating one of the trio, suggested. "When we get done with this, we'll know more about this country than near anybody."

Not likely by a damn far shot, Preacher refuted. "What good's that?" Ferris asked.

"Well, if we ever decide to break off with Mr. Pease, we can lead folks in here and collect good, hard gold for it. We'll be the best guides around."

"You will like hell," Preacher muttered aloud as he came down out of the trees and onto the trail ahead of the three louts.

Dickson, Ferris, and Branson rounded a bend in the trail and came face-to-face with Preacher. Dickson and Branson filled their hands. Ferris gaped . . . and filled his drawers. Dragged along by their momentum, Ferris charged with the other two. It did them little good. Preacher had both of his four-shot pistols out and ready.

He let one bang when less than fifty feet separated him from the trio of lowlife trash. One of the balls from the double-shotted load went over the left shoulder of Ferris. The second smacked meatily into his shoulder. He kicked free of his mount with a yowl and hit hard on the granite surface of the trail.

Rolling to one side, Ferris careened down the bank and into the icy little stream that cut through the canyon. At least that washed away the foulness his fear had created. Above him, Dickson fired wildly with a .60 caliber pistol. His ball didn't hit the target, Ferris noted when a loud, flat blast followed the discharge of Dickson's gun.

Dickson's ball put another pair of holes in Preacher's coat. "That's about enough," Preacher roared and fired another barrel.

He took the hat from Dickson's head. By then Grant Ferris had scrambled to the lip of the bank and looked on as both of his friends fired again. That emptied their supply of pistols. They rode on past Preacher, giving him a wide berth, and he held his fire, loath to shoot them in the back. That gave them time to reload one pistol each.

Preacher waited for them when they turned about. He had dismissed any threat from the downed Ferris. That slip nearly cost him his life. Grant Ferris found one of his pistols sound, and the powder dry, when he triggered a load at Preacher's back. Hastily fired, the ball went low and struck the cantle of Preacher's saddle. The stout, fibrous oak of the saddle tree absorbed the energy of the ball, so that it burst through much slower and with far less force. It still punched through the wide leather belt beneath the sash Preacher wore and gave him a painful, stinging bruise in the small of his back.

He repaid Ferris's kindness by swiveling in his seat and plunking a ball between the cowardly thug's eyes. That still left the other two to deal with. Preacher faced front again, in time to see both their weapons discharge. This time he went to the ground, to avoid a fatal collision with hot lead.

"I got him! I got him!" Seth Branson shouted gleefully.

"No you ain't, he's jist duckin'," Cord Dickson corrected his overjoyed companion.

Preacher proved him right a moment later when he put

a ball in Branson's belly. A mournful howl came from the bearded throat of the St. Louis grifter and he wavered in the saddle. Seth Dickson grabbed for the rifle scabbarded behind his stirrup fender. Preacher shot Dickson through the back of his hand. The ball also wounded Dickson's horse, which stumbled at the impact and threw its rider face-first in the sharp-edged sand. Skin shredded in dozens of places by the decomposed granite, Cord Dickson shrieked as he rolled over and over along the trail. He ended up near Thunder's forehooves.

Gasping, Dickson raised his head to Preacher. "You— you've gotta be out of loads by now." His good hand slid toward the big butcher knife at his left side.

"You think you're lucky? Did you count right while the shooting went on? Ready to try it? It'd really please me. I don't cotton to killing an unarmed man."

"Jist let me go. I'll not do you any harm."

Preacher chuckled. "Oh, I'm sure you wouldn't. It's for what you've already done that I'm gonna send you off to see yer Maker. Go on, try it," Preacher taunted again.

Cord Dickson did. Which made it three-for-three for Preacher when the four-shot in his left hand blammed again and sent two balls into the chest of Cord Dickson. While he looked down on the dying man, Preacher reflected on what he had learned from them before this encounter. He had become a marked man. No doubt of how serious Pease was about having Preacher killed.

"Things are gettin' right interesting," he spoke aloud to Dickson. "If I had a scrap of paper and a stub of lead, I'd leave a note for ol' Ezra Pease. But, chances are it would never be found." He frowned down at the foamy, red ooze that billowed from Dickson's chest. "I done shot yer lights out, Dickson. If you're so inclined, I'd say you best make your peace with your Maker."

"Go . . . to . . . hell, Preacher."

"Most likely, it's you's headed that way, and right sudden, I'd say."

With that, Preacher turned away and picked up the arms of the other two, returning to Dickson after the man expired. The folks in the valley were getting right well outfitted with weapons, courtesy of Ezra Pease, Preacher considered as he led away the dead men's horses.

20

Preacher soon found out that a message would have been received. Not three miles along the trail that led to the quartered deer waiting him, a dozen more of Pease's hard cases thundered along in pursuit and struck from the rear. Preacher had wisely reloaded, and took the first three out of their saddles with fast work on the trigger mechanism. Quickly he exchanged the pistol with only a single shot for the second one. Then he turned to face the others.

They had wisely taken cover in the boulders along the side of the road and poured heavy fire toward Preacher. He let go of the captured horses, which ran off in the direction their noses pointed. In a smooth motion he slid from Thunder's saddle and snagged up his pair of rifles. He laid the pistol aside and nuzzled the Hawken to his shoulder, after he had hunkered down behind a large boulder before any of the rattled gunhawks could recover enough to take careful aim.

At once he saw motion beyond a fallen pine, the thick trunk of which provided protection for Preacher on his right flank. Some fool was charging him. He gave a .54 caliber ball from his Hawken to the ignorant lout and reached for the rifle. Only the crown of a head and an eyeball showed above the curving surface of a boulder at extreme range behind the dying outlaw. Preacher steadied his own breathing enough to take careful aim.

Finely engraved, the barrel heated up as the conical bullet

sped down its length. It emerged at tremendous velocity, speeding true to the target. A chunk of the exposed head exploded in a shower of scarlet. Preacher grunted in satisfaction. A lull came as all who were left ran out of loaded weapons.

Preacher took the time to reload while his enemies did the same. One of the swifter of Pease's men opened the dance again with a ball that screamed off the top of the boulder that sheltered Preacher. Preacher responded with another kill and the nasty vermin grew more cautious. Muttered words reached Preacher where he waited out their plan of attack, while he reloaded his first pistol.

"You, Trump, make a careful count of how many shots he's popped off. That was the fifth. You saw those funny-lookin' pistols. Four shots each, so keep that in mind."

"Gotcha, boss," Trump replied louder than necessary.

More than good, Preacher thought as he methodically reloaded the Hawken. A rattle of gunfire got his head down low. Two more made a rush along the trail. Preacher put the Hawken aside, the ramrod still down the barrel, and drew a pistol. His first round set one target to dancing a jittery death waltz.

Preacher turned from the fallen tree to engage the second thug, who charged the blind side of the boulder. A head and shoulder appeared around the mound of granite, followed by the barrel of a pistol. Preacher triggered his four-barrel and fanned his free arm at the cloud of smoke that quickly filled the space between him and his attacker.

When he could see again, Preacher noted a splash of blood on the gray surface of the boulder. A low groan came from the ground beyond the rock. Three mounted bits of trash spurred forward. Preacher moved to the open side of his stone fortress and downed two of them with the last pair of loads.

Switching pistols, he emptied the third saddle and rotated the barrels. From the screen of brush beyond the downed pine, he heard the voice of the man named Trump.

"That's five more shots. He can't have had time to reload his rifles and he sure can't carry more than those two pistols."

The boss apparently agreed with that, because Preacher heard some indistinct mutters in the chokecherry and the rustle of inexperienced booted feet moving through fallen leaves. Four men came at him at once, from three directions. Preacher sighted in on the nearest one and doubled the thug over with a double-shotted load to the gut.

Quickly he picked another target while the first gunrunner sagged to his knees and fell forward to remain in a folded position, his head against the ground. Preacher's next round shattered the right shoulder joint of a pasty-faced lout with a mouthful of crooked teeth. Howling, the wounded man tripped over his feet and rolled to the bottom of the slope.

By then, the other two had gotten dangerously close. Both fired at once and showers of lead fragments and granite went flying around Preacher's head. Blood trickled from several cuts on his face. Preacher fired and missed. He worked the tricky trigger again and scored with both balls high in the chest and neck. It knocked the hapless vermin over onto his back.

Preacher didn't slow down as he stuffed the empty pistol into its holster and reached for his Hawken. A cap went into place on the nipple and he eared back the hammer. As he brought the weapon up he started to turn toward the fourth gunman. Hot pain burst in the under side of his left upper arm. The trashy whiskey peddler had shot him.

Without thinking about the ramrod, Preacher blazed away. He received a tremendous recoil as the brass-tipped hickory rammer retarded the expansion of gas in the barrel. It shot out, however, ahead of the ball it had seated. It struck the target and, like a slender lance, drove three quarters of its length through the chest of the boss a fraction of an inch above his heart. In seconds the attacker bled to death internally from a punctured aorta.

"D'ja see that?" Trump blurted from his concealed position.

Someone made a gagging sound and began to run downhill toward the horses. "I'm gettin' outta here," he wailed.

Preacher tied a paisley kerchief around the bullet hole through his arm and hastily reloaded the rifle. He stepped from his cover and easily downed the nervous one as the latter stepped into his stirrup. Only Trump remained and he took a hasty shot at Preacher before bolting for his mount. Preacher grabbed a .60 caliber Hayes pistol from the brace of holsters on Thunder's saddle and took a deep, steadying breath.

Trump died a second later with a look of total horror on his face. Preacher winced at the various pains that racked his body and lowered the smoking Hayes. "Gonna be one hell of a bruise," he muttered over the throbbing in his shoulder.

Businesslike, Preacher gathered up the weapons and other possessions of the outlaw scum who had jumped him. Then he located the proper type of moss and stuffed his wound with it. That accomplished, he rounded up the horses and started off for camp.

Those among the denizens of the High Lonesome who had chosen to spend at least part of the spring around Bent's Fort didn't know what to make of him. He dressed much like an Easterner, in tight black britches and a distinctly military tunic, sort of like the Dragoons, only without all the fancy colored piping and brass. He wore a fine, store-made white linen shirt, with a plain black stock that fluttered in the constant breeze.

A hard-faced man, with close-set eyes, and a brace of pistols in his waistband, he arrived at the Fort in early April. After tending to his horse, he went directly to the trading post and began showing around sketches. Without any explanation, he asked if anyone had seen the children, or the man who might be with them.

"What business might that be of yours?" Jake Talltrees asked pugnaciously.

"I'm a United States Marshal. Ruben Talbot is my name. This man," he lifted the sketch, "is Silas Phipps. He is supposed to be in the company of a band of orphans who have raped, murdered, and robbed all the way across the country from Pennsylvania."

His disbelieving onlookers held a different opinion. Black Powder Harris put it to words. "No, sir. I don't believe those youngsters to be capable of any sort of mischief. I runned into them on the Injun trail north of here. That one dickered with me for a jug of whiskey. He's a drunk, an' poison mean, I'd wager. But those youngin's looked too skeert to do evil."

Marshal Talbot ran the back of one hand across his brow. "We all have our opinions, stranger. I allow as how you're entitled to yours. But, these warrants I have say different. How long ago did you encounter them?"

"Oh, better than a week." He meant more than two.

Talbot thought on that a moment. "I'd be obliged to stay the night. Then I'll be headin' north after them."

Ezra Pease stomped across the bare ground of the campsite. He stopped on the far side of the fire to confer with Titus Vickers and Hashknife. "We should be headed north, not southwest."

"Not if we want to stay shut of the Cheyenne," Vickers opined.

"Titus is correct, Mr. Pease. The men I sent out to search for Preacher haven't returned as yet. Perhaps when they do, they will have useful information."

Pease considered that a while. "That leaves us with no option but to poke along their trail."

"The easier to consolidate our force when the time comes," Hashknife suggested.

Pease nodded curtly. "You're right, both of you. Now, when we run Preacher to ground, and we are going to, I guarantee you that, I want to deal with him myself. I've been thinking on this and nothing else will give as much satisfaction as seeing genuine fear on that ugly face of his."

"Might be he won't be so easy to contain," Vickers offered. "He could force us to kill him from long range."

Pease's face got a testy look. "Well, you'll just have to see to it that he does not. I want to feel my fingers around his throat, crushing the life out of him. Oh, yes, Preacher is going to be mine, all mine. And you two are going to see that it happens that way."

John Dancer came to knowing that he had been bad hurt. Shot through the side and bled a lot. He could remember how it happened and falling from his horse. Then, everything had gone blank. Who and how many had jumped them? He had a flash of a tall, broad-chested man, clad in buckskins, who held a strange-looking pistol that spouted flame four times before being empty. Surely not one man.

Pain knifed through his side, an inch or two above his hip bone. Dancer wanted very much to survive. He also wanted a drink of water in the worst way. His mouth felt like a sawdust box. Slowly he roused himself and inched his way through his agony toward the sound of a rippling stream. He saw no sign of his horse, or any others. All his eyes took in were the bodies of the men who had ridden with him.

Again he saw the flickering image of the wild-looking man with the odd gun. Preacher? The name taunted Dancer as he eased his way down the embankment to touch a feverish hand to icy water. They had been sent out to find Preacher. The three men he had ordered forward to scout had been gunned down, they had all heard the shouts and came on fast. Yeah, that was it. They rounded a bend and there he was, bigger than life and twice as deadly.

From there on everything went to hell in a handbasket. Preacher fought like a cornered wildcat. In no time he had the upper hand. And he showed no mercy. That young pup,

Trump, must have miscounted the shots, Dancer reasoned. Because at the exact moment he thought they had regained the initiative, Preacher opened up with another hail of lead. Shooting the boss with that ramrod had been the final bit needed to spook those who remained.

Even he had been shot trying to flee from the demon in buckskin, Dancer thought ruefully. He lowered his head and drank deeply. After that he wiped at his wound and took stock. At least he didn't have any guts pokin' out. If he took care of himself, he might survive after all. But miles from nowhere, without a horse or eats?

The prospect of it gave him a fit of the cold shudders.

Back at the settlement in the valley, Cora Ames ignored the welcome addition of more meat in her excitement over Preacher's wound. Over his objections, she led him by one hand to her recently completed cabin.

"I'm tending to that personally," she insisted.

Preacher grumbled and complained, then had to admit that these Eastern feather-heads had toughened up as he watched Cora remove his makeshift bandage and the poultice of moss, then clean and dress the through-and-through bullet holes. She made the new binding as neat as any school-taught doctor, the mountain man saw with satisfaction.

"There, all done. I will want to see it again tomorrow. And the day after. We don't want it to fester."

"Dang right, that's why I'm gonna fix me some willer bark an' some other stuff to pack in the holes," Preacher told her with a straight face.

Quickly fading, the glow of accomplishment left Cora's face. "Don't you dare. Why, who knows what that would cause?"

"It'll cause it to heal, that's what," Preacher's stubbornness dictated. "Besides, I ain't got three days. I'm takin' Nighthawk an' Buck and startin' out tomorrow mornin' while the trail of the men who jumped me is still fresh. We can track 'em right back to Ezra Pease."

Horrified by this, Cora clapped both hands to her cheeks and spluttered her objections in rapid fire. "Why, you can't. You would be risking the loss of that arm. I won't allow it. I'll talk to your friends."

"There's nothin' you can do. An' the boys'll tell you that these Injun cures work right good on gunshot wounds."

Cora tried another tack. "You lost a lot of blood. You're too weak for such goings-on."

Preacher nodded thoughtfully. "Fact is, I do feel a bit peaked. Nothin' a big chunk of elk steak won't fix."

Cora Ames blinked in dismay. "Preacher, Preacher, you are impossible," she gave in, albeit with only a slight return of good humor.

Early the next day, Preacher set out with Nighthawk and the driver, Buck. They rode in companionable silence for long hours. After crossing the spine of the Sierra Madre by way of Rabbit Ear Pass, they entered a wide, sweeping highland prairie. As the hours and miles went by, Preacher began to notice something that mightily displeased him.

"Lookit over there," he addressed to Nighthawk and Buck. "See them smoke trails on the horizon? Over the past fifty miles, I've seen more than a dozen of them, scattered out where none existed last year a-tall."

"It's called progress, Preacher," Buck said lightly. "Folks are moving West."

"I call it a disaster. This keeps up, 'fore long there'll be so many that the cabins will be cluttered up near to every couple of miles. Now, we're right close to where I took my last deer. Over in those mountains to the east. If we move out at a little smarter pace we can make it there first thing in the morning."

"That suits me fine," Buck commented.

"You weren't far from there when you had your run-in with Pease's hooligans?" Nighthawk probed.

"Right you are. That's when the work begins."

* * *

Mid-morning found them well past the large tree where Preacher had hung his last kill. In fact, they had been on the trail of the men sent by Pease for better than an hour. It led constantly north and east. Preacher topped a small saddle draw that marked the access to yet another mountain highland valley. A string of dark objects, moving determinedly westward caught his eye.

"I got me a bad feelin' about this," he told his companions as he took the spyglass from his saddlebag.

With the brass tubes pulled to full length, Preacher focused in on the far-off blobs. One by one he counted thirty of them. His mouth twisted in a grimace of dislike.

"Wagh! They's comin' like flies to a dung heap," he spat his disgust.

"They're what I think they are?" Nighthawk asked.

"Sure enough. More greenhorn pilgrims headed west. Odds say they don't have the least idea where they are or where they're going. I tell you, boys, I've had more than my fill of 'em. I'd like to run this bunch clear the hell outta these mountains."

"But you won't do that," Nighthawk tweaked Preacher.

"Nope. Onliest thing we can do is ignore them an' hope they don't see us. Well, let's ride. This trail ain't gettin' any newer."

"What are we going to do when we find this Pease?" Buck asked.

"Go back for the rest of the boys an' wipe Pease out lock, stock, and barrel," Preacher pronounced carefully. The hot glow in his eyes verified that his annoyance with the corrupt trader had changed into implacable anger.

21

Falling Horse and Little Mountain still led their Dog Soldiers south and west toward the suspected location of Ezra Pease. One of the advance guards sent out by Falling Horse came back to the column of warriors with exciting news shortly after midday.

"We think we have found them. Six of the rolling lodges, some men, women, a few children."

"Yes. Pease took children from a white man's traveling lodges," Little Mountain declared.

"I know this to be true, we took three of them from the camp when we raided it," Falling Horse verified. "Even if they are not with Pease, it will be good to eliminate some of these wiggling white worms that invade us."

"We ride there now?" Little Mountain asked eagerly.

Falling Horse nodded to the scout. "Show us the way."

What the Cheyenne found were six stragglers who had become separated from the wagon train spotted by Preacher and his companions. Quickly the Dog Soldiers spread out to launch their attack on the unwanted visitors. Cries of alarm from the whites soon reached their ears and the wagons began to circle. Little Mountain led his braves to the south to close around the lumbering vehicles, while Falling Horse took his warriors above the hastily formed laager. They opened fire at a range of fifty yards.

Two pilgrims exchanged frightened glances. "My God,

where'd those Injuns come from? I never saw a one," the burly one with a gray-streaked beard blurted.

"We made a mistake in stopping to fix that harness on the Kilmer wagon, Caleb."

"Now you know we couldn't have left them there all alone, Stub. They'd of been sitting ducks."

"Now all six of us are sitting ducks, Caleb. Watch yerself, they're gettin' close." Stub discharged both barrels of his shotgun in his nervous excitement. The recoil of the ten-gauge nearly dislocated his shoulder. Pellets struck several braves and their ponies. It didn't put them out of the fight. They came on, whooping and howling.

Three small tow-headed youngsters in Caleb's wagon added to their war cries. In a flash it seemed to be over. The Cheyenne broke off their charge and began to circle the wagons. An arrow thudded into one thick, oak side. Bullets moaned and cracked overhead. It soon became clear that the settlers would be going nowhere and the Indians had no intention of breaking off.

"We're all going to die out here," Caleb's frantic wife screamed from the rear of the wagon.

"Hush up, woman, and get to loading."

A flurry of shots blasted the hot, dry afternoon air. Dust rose in smothering clouds from the skiddery livestock. Once again, the Cheyenne wheeled their mounts a quarter way around and charged the wagons. Rifles and shotguns in the hands of men and women alike roared in defiance. When the heavy curtain of powder smoke cleared, the Indians were seen to have ridden a short ways off.

"There seems to be some sort of palaver goin' on," Caleb observed.

"Figgerin' who gets whose scalp most likely," Stub complained. He had reloaded his shotgun and now worked on the second of three rifles close at hand. What he disliked most was not that possibility, but that only three Indians lay on the ground beyond the circled wagons. While the whites recharged their weapons, even that changed as six warriors broke from the Indian position and rode out to recover their fallen friends.

When they returned to the lines, another charge began. They were doing well this time, when Preacher, Nighthawk, and Buck showed up over the rise to the west. The increased volume of fire startled the Cheyenne. They broke off the circle on the west side and turned to confront the men who rode to the relief of the settlers.

When the three white men drew nearer, Falling Horse identified Preacher. These two had sworn repeatedly not to make war on one another and, knowing that, Falling Horse called off the assault on the wagons. He came forward, making his identity clear to Preacher. Tension held for a while, during which the men from two worlds talked. Then Preacher walked Thunder toward the huddled immigrants.

"Git them wagons straightened out and set the mules off lickety-split. Don't spare 'em none, either. I can't hold these braves here for very long. Your other folks is about two hours ahead of you on the trail."

"You saved our lives," Caleb stated wonderingly. "We're eternally grateful."

"If you was smart as well as grateful, you wouldn't be here in the first place," Preacher growled back. "I don't know where you think yer goin', an' I don't care. But, sure's Hades is hot, you are in the wrong place now. Tell your wagon boss to cut north beyond the Bighorn Mountains if he's bound for Oregon. Now, step it up or you'll be the guests of honor at a scalpin' party."

After the last wagon trundled over the ridge to the west, Falling Horse came to where Preacher stood beside Thunder. "Where do you go that you are this far away from where we met you last?" the Cheyenne chief asked.

"Like I told you then, Falling Horse, we're out to get that no-account scoundrel, Pease."

"Then, once again we seek the same man, Preacher.

This time it might not be wise for you to get to the whiskey peddler first."

Preacher cocked an eyebrow at his Cheyenne friend and grunted. He ignored the implied threat when he made reply. "Ride with the wind, Falling Horse."

"May the rain not take the strength from your bow, Preacher," the Cheyenne chief replied politely.

Then the two parties turned their separate ways and headed off on the trails they had been following.

Walt Hayward peered over the top of his half-spectacles at the sheets of vellum art paper. Yes, he'd seen these faces before. One big, callused hand stroked his beard in characteristic fashion. Them woeful-looking kids and that sneak-thief-looking feller with them. After they had left, he'd discovered his storehouse to be shy of three gallon jugs of whiskey, a small keg of powder, and a gunnysack of potatoes.

"Yep. They passed through here better than a week ago. This one," Walt hefted the drawing of Phipps, "was a shifty-eyed little rat. Sticky-fingered, too, I'm thinkin'."

"How's that?" Marshal Talbot asked, alert to any news of the wanted band.

"Right after they took off up north, I came up short three jugs of whiskey. The good stuff, too," Walt added grumpily.

"I gather they haven't been back?" the lawman inquired.

"Nope. Nary hide nor hair. And good riddance to them. Though I feel sorry for those youngins, headed the way they are. The Blackfeet an' Cheyenne are cookin' up a war."

"Might be I'll catch up to them before that."

Curiosity put a light in the eyes of Walt Hayward. He'd never heard of anything important enough for a man to walk directly into an Injun war. "You plannin' on keepin' company with them?"

"No. They are wanted for a scad of crimes all the way back East. I'm here to arrest them."

Hayward didn't like the sound of that. "The kids, too?"

"That's what the warrants say."

"Well, Marshal, I'm right sorry to hear that. Those youngsters all seemed too scared of this-here Phipps to do anything lest he yelled at 'em to do it."

"That may be true, but it's not mitigating circumstances under the law," Talbot replied stiffly.

Walt Hayward reared his head back and eyed the marshal with obvious distaste. "You know, you're the first real lawman we've seen out here. They might do it that way back where you come from, but out here we take more store in fairness and justice than in whatever the law says. Find them good homes, with folks who'll love them, and they'll never give you another minute's trouble."

Marshal Talbot cleared his throat, emptied his tin cup of raw whiskey, and licked his lips. "I'll certainly take that under consideration, innkeeper. Now, I would appreciate a room for the night."

"A *room!*" Walt Hayward bellowed through a stout guffaw. "Marshal, I got *a* room, out back, with twelve rope-strung beds in it. He'p yerself."

For the past hour, as they rode on northeast, Preacher had grown uneasy over the weather. There had been that freak snowstorm three weeks back, and now clouds had started to pile up to the west. Already the highest peaks were lost in dirty gray mantles. Fat white bellies spilled down the wrinkles of the slopes. The air remained mild, almost balmy, so Preacher shrugged off his premonition and kept a wary eye on the buildup.

After an hour more, the impending change could no longer be ignored. "We've got us a storm brewin', Nighthawk."

"I can feel it in my bones, Preacher," the Delaware replied.

"What? No scientific double-talk to tell us what's happenin'?"

"It's the rhumatiz, Preacher, from those long days in the cold water. Don't tell me that's not what tipped you off."

Preacher snorted in merriment. When he recovered, he made a swift decision. "We'd best be lookin' for someplace to shelter. It could be a bad one."

"I've spotted several places already," Nighthawk answered smugly.

"Why, you ol' coot," Preacher barked.

"It's him, all right," Titus Vickers remarked as he lowered the spyglass. "Preacher, in the flesh."

Delphus Plunkett, one of the eight men with Titus Vickers, crawled up beside him and spoke softly into the outlaw leader's ear. "Think we could take him right here an' now?"

"There's two more with him," Vickers pointed out the obvious.

"Yeah, but there's nine of us. That means we outnumber them—uh—uh—three—or is it four?—to one."

"Haven't you learned as yet that three to one means nothing to Preacher?" Vickers snapped. "We'll wait a while longer. There's a storm brewing. What we'll do is move in on Preacher's back-trail and then close on them when the storm reduces visibility."

Ahead of them, the air split open with eye-searing light and a calamitous roar. Tremendous peals of thunder shook the ground and startled a flock of pigeons out of the trees. The pungent scent of ozone surrounded Preacher as he reached behind him for his poncho-like capote. The first drops of an icy rain fell around them as he whipped his hat from his head and draped the garment over his shoulders. At either side, Nighthawk and Buck sought similar protection from the elements.

With a seething hiss, the downpour increased, sped along in nearly horizontal sheets by a lashing wind that bent the tops of the fir and pine trees and wildly whipped the limber aspens.

"D'you have one of those places you saw in mind now?" Preacher drolly asked Nighthawk.

"I cannot see the nose of my horse, how can I be expected to find shelter?" the Delaware answered calmly.

"Well, I got a spot in mind," Preacher answered. "We're gonna get wet aplenty before we reach it."

"Then don't sit here jawing about it in this deluge," Nighthawk ripped out.

Preacher took the lead. He kept to the trail, that led up a steep incline. Water quickly gathered and ran in freshets along the sides of the course they followed. The constant booming of celestial artillery prevented conversation and each man retreated into his private thoughts.

Unaware of the crusade by Cora Ames to find homes among the missionary families, Preacher mulled over what to do with the orphans. Clearly, they had been handed some of life's rougher portions. From what they revealed at the trial of Silas Phipps, he had made every day, or at least the nights, pure hell for them. Considering the holier-than-thou attitude of most people, Preacher reflected, who would ever take to their hearts children who had suffered such perversions?

A grunt silenced Preacher's ruminations. He had more important things to think about. The way his mind wandered, he sounded as maudlin as those schoolmarms and gospel-shouters that kept insisting on moving out here. Take, for instance, Ezra Pease. Preacher had heard nothing more about Pease after running the renegade out of the High Lonesome. Yet, Pease obviously kept him in mind. He'd spent enough time trying to bring an end to Preacher. Somehow that didn't add up. Not with the youngins Pease's men had taken from that wagon train. The trash riding for him might use kids in a bad way, but Pease didn't strike Preacher as being the Silas Phipps type. So, what were they for?

When Preacher saw the overhang, a blacker smudge against the darkness of the storm, he forgot about everything else, save getting out of the wet and cold. He touched Nighthawk on one shoulder.

"Over there, across the crick."

"I see it. A good place," Nighthawk answered.

Buck, with his flatlander's perceptions, stared right at it and had to have the arch of soil and boulders pointed out to him. "Oh, yeah. What'er we waitin' for?"

They found branches and twigs enough for a small fire under the lip that shielded them from the tempest. Preacher built it and then all three tended diligently to their horses, wiping them down and slipping nosebags on to feed the tired animals. "Coffee next," Preacher announced, producing a small, battered tin pot.

Along toward nightfall, with the rain still in blinding sheets, Preacher spoke the obvious. "We'll not be havin' any trail to follow when this is over."

"Only too true," Nighthawk agreed.

"Even I'm smart enough to know that," Buck added. "What do we do next?"

Preacher didn't even blink. "We figger out some other way to get to where Pease is holed up."

Beyond the other two, who hunkered with Preacher around the small fire that gave scant warmth, he saw flickers of movement against the grayish walls of water that dropped from the sky. Dark figures cut through the tortured aspens and moaning pines. Preacher had one of his four-shot pistols yanked free even before he spoke again.

"By gum, we've been jumped by more of them carrion-eaters."

Decent, law-abiding men didn't sneak up on a camp. They let everyone know of their presence loud and clear. Not these fellows. Preacher saw that right off and made the wisest move. Those with him flattened themselves on the rock shelf and he fired one .50 caliber barrel through the space previously occupied by Buck.

None too soon, because answering fire had already started on the way. Not as accurate as the ball sent by Preacher, the incoming lead smacked into and moaned off the back wall of the open-sided cave. Preacher's round found meat in the chest of one charging hard case. He flipped onto his back and gave up his life in a terrible groan.

Preacher now occupied a prone position beside his friends and they sent a heavy volume of fire toward the dimly seen figures. A horrendous flash of lightning illuminated the scene long enough for aim to be adjusted. Preacher sent another pile of trash off on the long trail of eternity with a double-shotted load to chest and gut.

Nighthawk winged a man who screamed his agony to the weeping sky. Buck gave a soft grunt and clapped his free hand to his upper arm. "Damn, got me in the shoulder."

"You all right?" Preacher asked.

"Burns like the fires of Hades, but I'll manage." To prove it, Buck downed a third of the craven bushwhackers.

Preacher put out such a volume of fire for a single man that the reports of his companions' weapons got lost in the repeated blasts. The next crash of lightning and thunder revealed the cowardly vermin in full flight.

"They're gone," Buck pronounced with relief.

"For now, maybe. An' maybe they've runned off to bring more of their kind," Preacher opined. "Might be that ray of hope we were lookin' for. Saddle up, we'll follow them."

"Jehosephat, that man has eyes like an eagle," Delphus Plunkett gulped after he steadied his heaving chest enough to speak.

"Weren't by accident," Titus Vickers allowed. "I'm beginin' to believe that Preacher ain't human."

"Whatever that means, what do we do now?" Plunkett bleated.

"Head back. They won't get far as long as this storm continues. We can lead Mr. Pease and all the gang right to their camp. That way, Preacher won't be pullin' any irons out of the fire so easily."

22

Preacher and his companions made poor headway, faced into the brunt of the storm. The heavenly outrage continued into a second day. Soaked until the pads of their fingers turned white and wrinkled, they pressed on. Preacher caught a fleeting glance of their quarry, only to lose them in a thick cloud that lowered to fill the canyon through which he, Nighthawk, and Buck walked their horses. Buck's wound had given him a lot of pain, yet Preacher knew that it would be certain death to send the man back alone.

Instead, he treated it frequently with moss and a few drops of whiskey from a small, gourd flask tied to Thunder's saddle. Preacher's own arm throbbed from the earlier gunshot and made any quick movement of his left side out of the question. They all held up well, confident the fleeing outlaws would lead them to Pease. Their expectations were nearly dashed when they made camp for the night.

A hastily constructed lean-to, covered with pine boughs, provided relief from the constant rain well enough to allow a hat-sized fire. While they dried themselves as best they could, another wave of the stalled-out front swung into place overhead. The first enormous clap of thunder shook them until their teeth rattled.

"This one ain't gonna be fun, fellers," Preacher advised.

"Have any of them been?" Nighthawk asked tartly.

"Not so's you'd notice, no," Preacher agreed dryly.

Jerky and stale, now soggy biscuits provided supper. The men munched in silence while nature raged around them. Preacher chewed purposefully, his senses tuned to the elements. A palpable intensity built within the disturbed air as Preacher opened his mouth to speak.

"I think . . ." He got no further.

A cascade of sound ripped at them. A man asleep under the mouth of a twenty-pounder cannon could not have been punished more. The world washed stark, actinic white, the air sizzled and crackled and stung their nostrils with ammonia, as a bolt of lightning struck a tall pine close to where they had secured the horses by ground anchor.

Nighthawk's mount, Sundance, and Buck's ex-outlaw plug panicked. Already weakened by the thorough soaking, the ground gave way around the corkscrew-shaped anchors and the beasts bolted into the night. Only Thunder remained behind a second later. The sturdy animal had picked up his head, whinnied as though in pain, shook his big head and then trotted about nervously at the far extent of his tether. Preacher pulled on moccasins, draped himself with his capote and ran to comfort the nervous stallion.

"Easy there, Thunder. Easy, boy. I'm gonna bring you closer to us," Preacher crooned.

When he released the anchor and led Thunder up beside the lean-to, the anxious faces of Nighthawk and Buck popped out of the low shelter. "What about our horses?" Buck asked, shaken.

"Doubt they'll go far," Preacher opined, water dripping from the brim of his hat and the fringed hem of the capote. "An' this can't last forever. Come mornin', I'll set out after them. Now'd be a good time to grab some sleep."

"After that?" Buck asked with a nod toward the blazing pine. "I got jarred hard enough to loosen every tooth in my jaw."

"You chew on enough jerky an' they'll tighten up again," Preacher teased.

Buck threw his hands in the air. "Lord spare me from such humor."

* * *

By first light, the maelstrom had subsided to a drizzle. Preacher downed coffee, another stale biscuit, and saddled Thunder for the search. Nighthawk and Buck wished him good luck and set about drying everything they could put over their stingy fire.

At noon the sky showed patches of blue, large enough, as Preacher's father had used to put it, to make a Dutchman a pair of pants. It meant a clearing trend for certain. He also found smudged hoofprints that soon led him to Sundance. The Delaware's pony wickered a greeting to Thunder and allowed itself to be led peacefully along on the continuing search.

It seemed the odds had turned against him, Preacher reasoned as the trail remained elusive. Here and there he caught the marks of a riderless horse, yet never near enough to see the missing animal. He pushed on through the afternoon. Along toward what Preacher reckoned to be five o'clock, he developed a tightness and itch between his shoulder blades. He could swear someone had put eyes on him.

Then the sensation went away. The birds warbled their usual sweet music and insects hummed accompaniment as they recovered from the past two liquidy days. Preacher shrugged off the premonition, yet remained watchfully alert.

From the moment he heard hoof falls on the trail below, Delphus Plunkett knew his stock would surely rise in the outfit. His eyes narrowed to cold slits, when the man came into view, then widened when he recognized it to be Preacher. Thoroughly disabused of any ideas of bravado by past experience, Delphus wisely selected to keep watch and then report back to Vickers. It soon became obvious to Delphus Plunkett why Preacher was alone.

From his vantage point in a thick stand of fir, Delphus

kept Preacher in sight until the wily mountain man made a solitary camp and settled in for the night. Then Delphus took the reins of his horse and led it quietly away. Excitement charged his pale, watery blue eyes when he reported to Titus Vickers.

"It's Preacher, shore enough, alone, and not an hour's ride from here. He's got another horse with him, that gold one the Injun was ridin'."

"The storm must have driven off their mounts, scattered them through the mountains," Vickers surmised aloud.

"That's how I figgered it," Delphus prompted. "What do we do now? We gonna go back for Mr. Pease?"

"I don't think so. It's six to one now," Vickers savored his expected triumph. "Besides, he don't know we know where he is."

"He didn't the last time," Delphus reminded Vickers. It earned him a hard scowl.

"We'll wait until just before dark, then move in on him," Vickers planned the attack in low, heated tones. "We take him from three sides. But, you boys be careful to not overshoot the target. No sense in killin' each other."

Delphus Plunkett didn't think he liked the sound of that, though Vickers was boss of this search party. He went off to talk with some of the others.

Titus Vickers called them together. He reviewed his plan again and they mounted up. A mile short of the camp, with the eastern horizon turning dark purple, they halted and muffled the hooves of their horses with strips of gunnysack. Satisfied after a quick inspection, Vickers spread his men out and they made straight for where Preacher had bedded down for the night.

They came out of the stuff of his dreams. Mind still foggy from sleep and visions of the lovely movement of the back-side of Miss Cora Ames, Preacher's body took over at the first sound of a boot sole scuffing ground. He rolled free of his blankets with a big four-shot in each hand. Muzzle flashes came from left and right so he swung his arms wide, wincing at the stab of pain in his left one, and triggered each of the big guns.

He had no expectation of hitting flesh, only sought to confuse and jangle his enemies. One of them, partly blinded by the boom of his own and Preacher's pistol, stumbled into the fire ring. Sparks from the hot ashes and buried coals swarmed up his trouser leg. The stench of smoldering hair and burned flesh formed a cloud around him. Howling, he hobbled away from the resurrected blaze and directly into the flight path of a bullet fired by Titus Vickers.

"Son of a bitch!" Vickers blurted when he saw the fatal collision.

Preacher cycled the barrels of his right-hand pistol and took aim this time. Before the glow from burning gases dimmed, he had moved, cat quick, to a low boulder that protruded like a giant potato from a mound of earth. Not a hell of a lot in the way of protection, but it would have to do, Preacher decided.

"Where'd he go?"

"What happened?"

Preacher had gotten his way about the confusion. Already one of the attackers had been shot by another. Maybe he could improve the score, the crafty mountain man decided as he tried to recover his night vision enough to find a target. It proved easier than it would have an hour later.

Darkness lay in shadow pools in the meadow where Preacher had camped, yet above, long bars of magenta and crimson still streaked the western sky. It intruded enough, though weakly, for Preacher to take stock of his enemy. One man stood dumbstruck at the side of the fire, his attention riveted on the fallen thug. Preacher used that one's lack of motion to sight in a perfect shot.

Trailing sparks of partly burned powder, the conical ball

in that barrel sped to the chest of the hapless man. The soft lead ball, thirty-eight to the pound, opened out to over .75 caliber on impact with the breastbone of the vicious lout, who made not a sound as he fell face-first into the fire pit. Two down, how many to go? Preacher wondered as he rapidly shifted his gaze in order not to miss any opportunity for another shot. In the darkness, the best way to lose an object, Preacher knew, was to stare directly at it.

A flicker of something darker, moving against the night shadows, drew his attention. He fired the fourth and final load in that pistol, only to discover that it missed. Three yellow-white bursts in the blackness revealed as many opponents. They fired high and wide of the intended target. Preacher patted his buckskin-clad chest in search of the powder horn and ball pouch he had come away with.

Once located, rather than go to his second pistol, he set about reloading the first. Patches came from a recess behind the hinged butt-plate, and caps from the wooden capblock at his waist. He had three barrels reloaded before his assailants recovered enough of their wits to determine the location of one another. He rammed the fourth home a moment before they tried a concerted rush on his position.

They came at a rush, bent low, as Preacher raised his unwieldy pistol and fired at the nearest. A high, thin cry advised him of success. Like nearly everyone, Preacher knew that night shooting presented some tricky problems. Not the least of which was being able to see your target. Preacher relied on a simple technique. His first shot drew their fire, which positioned them for him. He dumped two more with the next three rounds, then changed for the loaded pistol.

"Get in there, get going," a harsh voice prodded from the darkness.

Preacher tried to find that voice with a bullet. He missed and counted muzzle flashes from three weapons. Taking care to aim slightly to the left and an inch lower than one muzzle bloom, he triggered another round. A sobbing voice followed thrashing in the underbrush.

"Oh, Lordy, Lordy, I'm hit bad."

The gravel voice came again. "Where are you shot, Delphus?"

"Through my right lung, Mr. Vickers. I ain't long for this world."

Vickers didn't bother to answer. Instead, he directed his last man forward. He could not believe Preacher could be so lucky. Lucky, because no man could be that good. He and John Dancer stepped into the open at the same time. Preacher's pistol banged again and Dancer grunted softly before he fell face-first on the ground. Vickers fired at the muzzle flash. Then he bent and retrieved Dancer's pair of pistols.

No time to reload, Preacher realized. He drifted off to one side in the thicket of hemlock, eyes at work to locate the enemy still out there. The crackle of a dry twig pointed Preacher the right way. He could take the risk of reloading in the dark, yet discarded that idea for something a lot surer. Ears searching for him, Preacher continued to edge closer to where Vickers likewise stalked him. A hidden depression in the ground caused Preacher to stumble and set the brush to rattling to his left side.

At once, Vickers fired. Muzzle bloom illuminated his face, a mask of rage, which quickly faded out. Preacher moved away.

"Preacher, you hear me?" Vickers called out. "I'm supposed to bring you in alive. Ezra Pease wants to deal with you up close and personal. For my own part, I'd as soon kill you quick and leave you for the scavengers."

Preacher refrained from making any reply. Instead, he wormed his way between two stunted fir trees and glided downslope toward the sound of the voice. Gradually, the last scudding clouds cleared away and pale starlight spread downward. Preacher saw his man then.

Down on one knee, Titus Vickers swung the muzzle of his

second pistol in an arc. He didn't see Preacher, who advanced. Emboldened by the silence, some night creature that had hunkered down at the outbreak of gunfire bolted through the underbrush. Vickers fired wildly in its direction. Realization struck Vickers that he had fired his last weapon. At once his hand went to his powder horn. He worked desperately to load a pistol, as Preacher advanced to a spot within arm's reach behind the outlaw leader.

"Vickers, is it?" Preacher spoke softly. "I'm right behind you."

In panicked reaction, Vickers whirled and fired the reloaded pistol. The ball passed within an inch of Preacher's head. Vickers reversed the smoking weapon and came up at Preacher. The butt whizzed through the air, a wicked sound, and missed the mark. Preacher sidestepped and swung at Vickers's head with his tomahawk. At the last instant, Vickers blocked the blow with his improvised club. Both men grappled for a moment and Vickers reached his free hand for the knife in his belt sheath.

With a grunt, they broke away. Vickers flailed with the clubbed pistol and Preacher blocked it. This time, when the tomahawk checked the momentum, Preacher rolled the shaft of his war hawk and swung in a horizontal slash. The keen edge cut through the clothing Vickers wore and made a shallow cut on his upper chest. It burned like hot coals and Vickers bit his lip to keep from crying out. He whipped the pistol across in front of him, and aimed at Preacher's temple.

Preacher ducked away from the deadly blow and gave an overhand swing with the 'hawk. It buried deep in the meaty portion of Vickers's right shoulder. The pistol fell from his grip. His knife flashed in the starlight and Preacher decided to end it right there. Another hefty swat with the tomahawk and the skull of Vickers gave off a ripe-melon *thock!* as steel sank deeply through bone into the brain.

Eyes already glazed, Vickers went down, nearly dragging Preacher with him. His mouth worked, yet no sound came out. Short-circuited, his brain no longer commanded his body. Preacher looked down on Vickers without any show of emotion.

"Yer the best Pease has sent so far," Preacher provided an epitaph for the dead man.

With ten horses in tow, Preacher set out the next morning to locate the last missing mount. For all the rain, he was surprised to see how clear a trail had been left. A sore stiffness in his left arm reminded him of the previous night's activity. No matter how he figured it, he could not be more than thirty-five or thirty-seven years old at most. Yet, he sensed a slowing down. Wounds took longer to heal, prolonged hard activity left tight, aching muscles where none had lingered before. He had known of fellers in the High Lonesome who had not seen their fortieth birthday, and not from carelessness. The energy just seemed to drain out of them and they were found along the trail or in their cabin, frozen like a block of ice.

Taking stock, Preacher vowed that it would not happen to him. So far he had managed to keep on going. So long as he didn't give in to the increased twinges and aches, he reckoned he could continue that way. He'd let time decide for how long. His ruminations over the state of his health brought him to near midday. Dismounting, he set the horses to graze and retrieved the last of his biscuits and brewed coffee. He would soften the rock-hard bread in a cup and have it with jerky. He looked up from his tasks to see his Appaloosa horse watching him.

"It's jist you an' me, Thunder. With a good hoss like you, a man can do anything." The big, gray, spotted-rump animal raised its massive head and twitched ears inquisitively. A moment later it whinnied in greeting.

"What you pickin' up out there, Thunder?" Preacher asked.

For an answer, the Appaloosa whinnied again and snorted a horselaugh as Buck's strayed mount ambled into the meadow and lined out for Thunder. Preacher shook his head in mystified amusement. "Ain't that somethin'. Go out to find these critters an' one of them winds up findin' me."

Thunder nickered softly beside Preacher's ear. Quickly the mountain man gathered in the stray horse, rigged the string, and headed back for the overhang where Nighthawk and Buck waited. His thoughts turned right away to the lovely Miss Cora Ames. A woman like that could just about domesticate an old tomcat like him, Preacher decided after due reflection.

Nice turn of ankle—he'd caught a flash during the first encounter with Indians—good-lookin' legs, too. Good bone structure—as though he evaluated a horse for purchase. A heart-melting smile. If only—if only she weren't one of those gospel-spouting mission folk. Got on a feller's nerves, rightly enough. Enough so that he didn't harbor any romantic notions . . . or so he told himself. His mind turned to other matters.

Get these horses back. Distribute them and the guns. Then get on after Ezra Pease. He had spent enough time thinking about it. Buck had taken a ball in his shoulder. Maybe send him back alone with the animals. Sure. That shined. The days left to Ezra Pease would be that much shorter.

23

Nighthawk and Buck greeted Preacher upon his return. Buck expressed his disapproval of the plan Preacher outlined even before the mountain man had the last words out of his mouth.

"I don't like the sound of that, Preacher. I don't mean I'm worried about makin' it back by myself. I'm thinkin' of what might happen if you run across the whole body of those scum."

"I did in a dozen of them jist yesterday, didn't I?" Preacher challenged, an eyebrow cocked.

"And I still don't know how," Buck shot back. "This wound smarts some, but I can carry my load."

"Don't doubt you can, ol' son. But we'd be slowed down with all these horses, the guns, and powder. This way everyone can keep in touch."

That ended the argument. With a good six hours of daylight left, they set off at once. Preacher easily picked up the back-trail of Vickers and his gunmen. It led northwestward, which set off a tingle of premonition along Preacher's spine. He knew the mountains well in this area. If pushed by the Cheyenne, Pease and his band would no doubt flee southward. Following the most accessible route, it would take them, eventually, to the valley where the helpless pilgrims had settled. He expressed his concern to Nighthawk while the sun slanted well down on their shirtfronts.

"We'd best turn west some. I've an idee where they went. We want to be able to cut them off from runnin' south if the Injuns hit them again."

Nighthawk frowned. "We're getting close to Rabbit Ear Pass. If Pease has moved camp beyond there, going south would put them right in among our nest of pilgrims."

"Just so," Preacher allowed. "Dang if I shouldn't have thought of that before Buck took off. He could have carried a warnin' to those folks."

Nighthawk scowled and shook his head. "They wouldn't listen. You know that."

A snort came from Preacher's nostrils, fluttering the long, soft hairs of his mustache. "Damned if I don't think you're right. Those gospel-shouters can be the most one-way critters I've ever done seen. We'd best be findin' a place to stop. We'll hit the pass tomorrow."

Hashknife rode into camp at twilight. A worried frown creased his brow. He left his mount with young Vern Beevis and strode to where a pole and brush hut had been outfitted for Ezra Pease. He found the land grabber downing a stiff shot of bourbon.

"No sign of Preacher anywhere," he reported.

Pease produced an ugly expression. "Where is he? Worse, Titus Vickers has not returned. I'm relying on you to come up with some answers." With that, he gestured to the small keg of good Tennessee sour mash.

Their talk went long into the night. A pug-nosed thug brought them food, which they consumed untasted. Hashknife felt relieved to get away at last. He headed for his own lean-to, intending to clean the brace of brand-new .44 Walker Colts he wore around his lean hips. Those six-shooters were the envy of everyone in camp.

An improvement to the Colt Patent Firearms Co. revolver Model of 1838, designed by Colonel Walker of the Texas Rangers, the new sidearms featured a trigger guard and fixed trigger, instead of the open, folding trigger that made the original revolver so dangerous to carry in heavy brush. It also had a lighter cylinder and an improved barrel wedge. Six nipples, protected by a recoil plate, allowed the weapon to be carried fully loaded and ready for business. Although a smart man wore it with the hammer down on an empty chamber. A hinged rammer, affixed under the barrel, allowed for reloading while on a moving horse. Hashknife knew full well that about half of the lowlife scum in camp would have gladly killed to possess the pair he owned.

Except, of course, that he was so much more accurate a shot, and could deliver such devastating firepower so much faster than any of them that they didn't have a chance. Hashknife truly believed the astonishing weapons had saved his life several times before, and felt confident they would again.

His head a bit muzzy from all the liquor, Hashknife swung by the central campfire for a cup of coffee. He arrived in the midst of an ongoing conversation.

Vern Beevis steadily whanged the ear of Two Thumbs Buehler with his whiny voice. "Now, I tell you, an' I've seen him up close, that Preacher ain't human. He's part wolf, I swear it. No human man can sneak up so close to a body without bein' heard. An' another thing . . ."

Two Thumbs raised his disfigured hand to silence the stream. "You don't think I've seen him in action? Well, hell, boy, he's human enough. Jist good. Damn' good. Way I hear it, he's been in these mountains since he was a little tad. Growed up knowin' ever' nook an' cranny, the twist an' turn of ever' canyon an' trail."

"Well, don't that sound like a lobo-wolf to you?" Beevis persisted.

"No it don't," Two Thumbs snapped. "All that has to be done to get rid of Preacher is to catch him out in the open an' . . . *Whang!* blast him with a rifle." He gave Beevis a "so there" look.

Hashknife could not resist. "The problem is getting him in the open."

Both of the Missouri trash looked up at the tall, slender outlaw with the powerful six-guns. Beevis started to speak, then thought better of it. Two Thumbs Buehler gave him a lopsided grin.

"I suppose you've got the way to do that?"

Hashknife produced a grim smile. "I might. And if what I suspect is right and Titus Vickers doesn't return, I'll have a chance to prove it."

"Why ain't Vickers comin' back?" Beevis blurted.

"I think Preacher has gotten them all."

"That ain't possible, Hashknife. Vickers had a dozen men with him."

"Fifteen actually," the cultured voice of Hashknife corrected. "Our poor Titus insisted on searching the area where we know Preacher to have been roaming. Given his unusual properties, it takes little imagination to envision Titus running afoul of the mountain man. We know he's not alone," Hashknife went on, repeating the substance of his talk with Ezra Pease. "He has at least three of his scruffy type with him. And, even when we've found bodies, they have been stripped of weapons and ammunition. Their horses taken. Preacher is taking those for someone to use. What I don't know is who."

"Does Mr. Pease know all this?"

"We talked about it. Half the night, in fact." Hashknife yawned and stretched. "If Preacher found Vickers, he can backtrack him to us. Were I you, I'd get all the rest I could. Things are going to get rather hot around here, quite soon."

Preacher wanted to ride ahead and see what lay beyond a big bend in the trail they followed. So, he was alone when five of the fresh ruffians jumped him. The first shot caught him by surprise. For some reason his notions weren't prodding him like usual. The ball cracked past his head and he spotted a puff of smoke in some gorse at the base of the tree-line on his left.

His Hawken came to his shoulder in a smooth, swift

motion and he had the hammer back before another round could be fired. He sent the double ball load a bit to the left of the white puff, then lowered his weapon and slid the rifle from its saddle scabbard. Another of the lowlifes fired an instant before the Lefever roared.

By then, a yell told him his first shot had counted. Sitting atop a horse, like a thumb poked up from a fist, made too good a target, Preacher realized and slid from the saddle. He ground-reined Thunder and moved away toward a rotting tree that lay at an odd angle to the slope.

"Those fellers up there ain't got the good sense to give it up and make a run," Preacher surmised aloud. And they wouldn't give him time to reload, he reasoned as he lay the rifle aside.

"Right on both counts," Preacher congratulated himself a moment later when the remaining four thugs broke clear of the underbrush and ran downhill toward him, firing as they came.

Preacher eased one of his big pistols from its holster and cocked the hammer. A little bit closer, he estimated. Hold it. That's the way. One of them critters runs a bit faster than the rest. He'll get his reward for it. The four-barrel cracked. Dust and cloth formed a plume at the center of the chest of the man nearest to Preacher. He went over backward. The others suddenly discovered they had emptied their rifles.

One brought forth a pistol as they scrambled for whatever scant cover they could find. He fired wildly behind Preacher. His bullet passed over the tree trunk. Preacher didn't even blink. Instead, he rotated the barrels and fired again.

"My leg!" a bucktoothed bit of slime shrieked. "Oh, God, he done shot me through the leg."

"Crawl over here, you idiot," snarled another of the trash.

The third lout raised up from behind a rock and popped a round in Preacher's direction. The ball thudded into the wood of the deadfall. Preacher readied the third barrel. Blood, hair, and a slouchy black felt hat flew into the air and the ambusher slumped over the small boulder. That left two;

the wounded man and the one with the bad attitude, Preacher kept score.

"C'mon, Hank, help me," the leg-shot villain whined.

"Think I'm gonna show myself, yer crazy," grumbled his companion.

Preacher tried a new gambit. "Hey, Hank, don't you reckon you bit off more'n you can chew?"

"Go to hell, Preacher," Hank shouted back.

His answer came in the form of rock chips in the face and dust in his eyes. Cursing, Hank moved to one side and exposed a wedge of his thick back. Preacher changed pistols and fired at that slim target. He missed, but sent Hank scurrying on hands and knees for a more secure position.

"Ain't neither of you leavin' here alive," Preacher taunted.

"I'm bad hurt. You wouldn't kill a helpless man, would you?" the whiner bleated.

"Damn betcha. At least one o' your kind."

"Jesus, you're a hard man, Preacher."

"Got to be." Preacher sensed movement off to his right and turned that direction.

Hank came at him with a pistol in both hands. Preacher snapped off a round and fought the complexity of his weapon's mechanism. Hank closed ground swiftly. He fired blindly and showered Preacher with decomposing bark. Preacher shot back. Another miss. With a triumphant grin on his face, Hank loomed over his intended victim and fired his second pistol.

His ball burned a hot line across the top of Preacher's left shoulder. Preacher loosed his last round. It grazed Hank's rib cage. Undeterred, Preacher came to his feet, his tomahawk in his left hand. He swung at the astonished Hank and received a yelp of surprise as reward. Hank stepped back and holstered one pistol. The other he used, clublike, to batter at Preacher's head while he drew a long, slender knife.

Their action had not gone unnoticed by the wounded slime. "Kill 'im, Hank, kill him for me."

"You'd best be thinkin' about yourself, Hank, not him,"

Preacher advised, as he and his adversary circled. "Turn tail now and we'll be even."

"Not a chance. I ain't never turned tail in my life," Hank growled, still in his black mood.

"It's your funeral," Preacher observed dispassionately.

Then he struck. Swift as lightning, the tomahawk whuffled through the air, and sank into the extended left forearm of Hank. Howling, Hank released the knife and backed up. Preacher wrenched his 'hawk free and swung it backhand. The pointed knob on the rear smacked into Hank's ribs. He grunted and whipped the clubbed pistol toward Preacher's head.

Preacher ducked and brought his own knife from the sheath. It glinted in the high altitude sunlight, the edge a wicked blue fire. Hank cut his eyes to it; a bird fascinated by the snake. Too late he realized his mistake. The tomahawk descended in a whistling arc that ended with the blade buried to the heft in the top of his skull.

"Unnngh." The soft sound came from blood-frothed lips as Hank sank to his knees.

Preacher forced the axe head free and bent to wipe it on the shirt Hank wore. That's when he discovered that the wounded man had taken the interim to reload. A .60 caliber pistol ball moaned past Preacher's right ear. A second one was due to follow from another pistol, only Preacher acted too soon. He leaped to one side and did a shoulder roll.

Coming up on one knee, he raised his arm in a saluting gesture and let the 'hawk fly. It struck true and split the breastbone of the injured trash. Reflexively, his pistol discharged into the ground. Preacher came to his moccasins.

"Wouldn't leave it alone, would you? Jist wouldn't leave it alone."

He walked over and retrieved his bloodied tomahawk from the dying man's chest. Lips worked into a grimace of pain as the ruffian struggled to speak.

"B'God, ya killed me, Preacher."

"I know that. Didn't have to be."

"No," the swiftly expiring drifter corrected. "Weren't

no other way. You or us. Th-there's more. They be comin' any time."

Preacher pursed his lips. "I reckoned that. But, thank you for doin' the decent thing. When it's over, I'll see that you're buried proper like."

"Won't be time for that."

"I mean after I'm done with them," Preacher explained grimly.

"Oh . . . yes . . . I see." Then he gave a shudder and died. Quickly, Preacher began to reload. His own weapons first, then those of the dead men. Almost with no time to spare, eight more of the two-legged beasts rushed through the twi-light effect of the tree-shaded glen on foam-flecked horses. Preacher reasoned that his first pick had been a good one, and returned to the dead pine to take up position. Only two of the outlaw weapons had not been loaded. He could stand them off for a while.

He had heard the very first shots. No reason not to, they hadn't been that far away. At once Bart Haskel shouted to the men with him and put spurs to the flanks of his mount. The horses reached for distance as one. A long, uphill grade sweated their skins in no time. Over in the next valley, Bart told himself. The boys he had sent ahead had run onto something. He had a good idea what. They crested the ridgeline and reined in.

Far below in the meadow they saw dark, crumpled figures sprawled in the grass. A single man stood over them, working to load a rifle. "Gawdamn, it's Preacher," Bart bellowed. No one else, he knew, could have taken out five able gunmen like that.

"We've got him now," King Skuyler boasted.

"Only if we keep our heads," Haskel responded "Spread out as we go downhill. We have to hit him from different places and all at once."

It didn't work that way, and in less than three minutes Bart

Haskel regretted it bitterly. Preacher heard them coming and skittered behind a fallen tree. With the terrain a blur from the movement of their horses, the outlaws could not see a trace of the buckskin-clad Preacher when he melted from sight behind the deadfall. Preacher could see them, though, and in a moment, proved it.

A puff of white smoke spurted from the tree and, a second later, the ball made a meaty smack as it struck flesh. One of Haskel's men cried out sharply and fell across the neck of his mount as blood flowed freely from one shoulder.

"Awh, crap," Haskel spat. Then the fight was on in earnest.

Preacher waited long enough to ensure that any failings of the strange weapons did not affect his marksmanship, then he opened up. A hit on the first shot smacked of good medicine. He had made a quick count and knew he faced eight men alone. Oh, well, he'd had worse, and against some fighting mad Blackfeet, too. He exchanged rifles and popped another cap.

He winced with regret as the ball shot low and struck a horse full in the breast. The animal shrieked and its front legs collapsed. That vaulted the rider over the neck and head and landed him on the crown of his balding pate. Even at that distance, Preacher could hear the crisp snap of bone in spine and skull. Time for another rifle.

Preacher selected his Lefever. Some of the enemy began to hold back in the face of his deadly accurate fusillade. The hammer fell and a thin, blue spurt of smoke came from the cap. The rifle recoiled solidly and projected the conical ball into the grinning face of a lout with a brow so low Preacher swore the man could wrap his lower lip over it. Now the odds looked a little better. Back to five on one.

"What say, Thunder?" he called out as he selected another long gun. "This is turnin' out to be one hell of a day, ain't it?"

Bart Haskel wisely decided on a change of tactics. He waved an arm over his head and signaled for the rest to follow him. With a hard pressure on the right rein, and a tug on the left, he sent his horse diagonally across Preacher's field of fire. Without realizing it, he lined out directly toward the trees where the five dead men had begun. Preacher sent two more balls after them, then turned his attention to the ridge-line above.

Four more scruffy derelicts had shown up. With only a slight pause to take in the situation, they angled downhill to join up with the rest of their misbegotten kind. Preacher slapped the stock of his Hawken.

"Be damned if I ain't worser off than before," he spat.

Time dragged after the fighting dwindled to an occasional shot. That suited Preacher right fine. He used the lull to reload. Then he started taking potshots at those who wanted his head so badly. One of the vermin climbed a tree to try to get a clear angle on Preacher. His first shot gave away his position. Preacher drew a fine bead.

An ongoing shriek of pain and terror answered his efforts. When the wounded man could make himself coherent, the reason became clear. "He s-s-shot me low!" he screamed.

Pitiful wails and sobs of despair continued for a while. But no one came to help the groin-shot brigand.

"Miserable bastards, they won't even help their own," Preacher grumbled aloud. Then he stiffened. He had seen ghostlike movements from the corner of one eye.

Preacher turned his head slightly and cut a hard look at the spot where he had noticed the rustle of a sumac branch. Nighthawk, sure's God made green apples, Preacher reckoned. Darkness had begun to fall and it appeared as though the opponents had stalemated. Well, things would start to heat up a mite once Nighthawk managed to drift in beside him. Together they could cook up a real nasty stew. Might be fun after all, Preacher decided, a grin cutting his face.

24

Moonset came at a few minutes after eleven o'clock that night. Preacher slipped away from his friend to circle around the remaining outlaws. They had discussed the matter and concluded that it would be best for Preacher to go alone. If any of the human garbage made a break in that direction, Nighthawk's gunfire would serve to confuse them even more, convincing them that Preacher remained where last they had seen him.

A heady aroma rose from the dew-damp sage and lupine through which Preacher forged on foot. His moccasins made such slight whispers they could not be heard more than a couple of feet away. Each tread, he planted the edge of his foot first, tested the ground, then rolled inward to the ball, his heel never touching the ground unless he came to a full halt. Bent low, he avoided low-hanging branches which would brush noisily against his buckskins. After a half hour of circling approach, Preacher came in close enough to hear low, murmured conversation around a tiny fire. All of the men, strangers to this country, sat with their backs to the outside world, he noticed when he edged in close enough to see.

"Dang it, this sure'n hell ain't my idea of how to track a feller down," Goose Parker complained.

"How you propose to go about it?" Rupe Killian challenged. "You figger to go out there in the dark and jump on Preacher whilst he sleeps?"

Goose defended his stance. "It could be done."

"Sure, by a ghost," Killian scoffed.

Delphus Plunkett blanched. "Don't go talkin' about ghosts," he pleaded. "You ask me, that Preacher acts 'nuff like one to give us all nightmares."

Preacher smiled in the darkness. From the sound of it, they were doing half his work for him. He moved silently on to another vantage point. He wanted to find their horses before the fun began.

When Preacher reached the horses, he found with them a little pug-faced lout, barely out of his teens, if that much. Preacher sidled up behind him without giving a modicum of warning. His big, steely arm snaked around the punk's neck and tightened to the hardness of a vise. Preacher put his lips close to the ear of the bug-eyed youth and whispered softly.

"You fancy meetin' your Maker tonight?" He released his grip enough for the kid to make a reply.

"N-no—ooooh, noooo," came a soft, sincere reply.

"Then I suggest you cut your losses right fast. Pick your horse and walk him real quiet out of here and ride for the main trail, then head south."

"M-my—my saddle an' gear?" came a plaintive appeal.

"You got the things you need most; your bridle, your gun, your horse, and . . . your life. Was I you, I'd be grateful for that and haul outta here."

That didn't take much thinking on, especially when the young ruffian felt the cold edge of Preacher's knife against his throat. "Yes—yessir, I surely will."

"That's a good boy. I reckon your momma will be glad to see you back home and safe. Now get along and do it."

With the guard out of the way, Preacher swiftly arranged for the second act of his little drama. He released three of the horses and left the rest. Then he worked his way back in close to the collection of scum that hunkered around the fire. Using the advantage of the steep mountainsides that surrounded their campsite, he gave off a series of wolf howls.

He could almost feel the chills that gathered along the

spines of the tenderfoot brigands. Their conversation died off at the first mournful yowl. Then, breathless, barely more than a whisper, the questions began.

"What's that?"

"What's going on?"

"Ned, you out there with the horses?" A pause, then, "Ned? You hear me?"

Another wolf howl, longer this time and sounding closer. *"Ned! Answer me!"* came a frightened demand.

Preacher gave them the cough and hiss of a puma. Low, soft moans followed, like the tortured soul of a damned man. Then Preacher threw back his head to take advantage of the natural sound chamber.

"He's comin' to get you, too. He'll carve out your hearts and eat your livers," he drawled out in ghostly voice.

"Awh, Lordy—Lord, it ain't human. Somethin's done got Ned and it's comin' for us."

"Shut up, you idjit!" Rupe Killian snapped.

Another panther caterwaul and the loose horses broke into shrill whinnies as they thundered away from the picket line. "B'God, the horses!" Rupe shouted.

"I'm gettin' outta here," Goose wailed.

"Yeah, yeah, we'll do that, right after we get them horses," Killian agreed, his own spine having a spell of icy shivers. "Goddamn you, Preacher!" he bellowed, certain the mountain man was behind this, but unable to quell his own terror.

Preacher spooked off through the underbrush, his lips pulled back in a pleased smile, a chuckle only partly repressed as his chest heaved. That bunch would live to fight another day, but it didn't really matter. In their fright, they'd lead him right to Ezra Pease. And about time.

Rosy morning light showed a clear trail left by men in a total panic. Nighthawk nodded to the scuffed ground.

"Looks like they left in a hurry."

"Somethin' must have upset 'em durin' the night, 'Hawk. What you reckon?"

"Ghosts, perhaps? It's said these mountains are haunted by the spirits of the Arapaho ancestors. Funny, I thought I heard a cougar not far off last night."

"Mayhaps you did," Preacher replied with a twinkle in his eyes. "Reckon we just oughtta follow these fellers an' see where they've gone."

"I don't imagine it will be a long trail," Nighthawk opined.

"How's that?"

"The way they are running those horses," the Delaware went on as they rode along the clearly marked escape route, "they won't last long."

Preacher gave a dry chuckle. "You're learnin' right fast, Nighthawk."

Nighthawk put on a show of affront. "'Learnin', is it? Why, I forgot more than you know about the High Lonesome before you were out of knee-britches."

Preacher joined in with his own barb. "You ain't that old. I ain't either, for that matter. We're headed for some right interestin' valley over Elk Crick way. If Pease is anywhere around, we should be cuttin' more sign any time now."

Within an hour, Preacher's prediction came true. The tracks they followed became swallowed up in a heavily traveled stretch of trail. That decided them to press on a little faster. Preacher admitted he had developed a considerable itch to come face-to-face with Ezra Pease.

Back in his not-so-secure valley, harmony and tranquility fled for Ezra Pease the moment the survivors returned. "This can't be happening!" he railed. "I send out twenty of you and you fourteen come back, your tails between your legs, whining about wild animals working in concert with Preacher."

Hat in hand, Rupe Killian tried to explain. "It's true, Mr. Pease. There was wolves an' some sort of lion, we all heard its chillin' cry. Somethin' done et young Ned Morton. Not a sign of him anywhere."

"No blood? No intestines on the ground?" Pease asked sarcastically. "All of you," he assailed the gathered trash, the possibility that his planning was flawed never occurring to him. "You disappoint me terribly. At every turn you fail. I thought I had brought along men of intelligence, of perspicuity, instead, it seems I have recruited a company of poltroons."

His eyes narrowed as his mood changed again. "This is all Preacher's fault. His doing, and his alone." Then he deflated, realizing that it was indeed his men who had failed. For a moment he cast his eyes heavenward. "Why am I surrounded by incompetents, fools, and cowards?" he pleaded. Then his own cunning provided a solution. "You are all cut one third of what you've been promised. It will be divided equally among any of the rest of you who can stand up to Preacher and bring him to me. That is, if any of you think you're man enough to face an army of wild animals to get to him." His contempt vibrated in the mocking words.

Hashknife stepped forward. "I'd like a chance at that."

Pease beamed and clapped the Easterner on one shoulder. "Good. Now, here's a man who knows how to seize the advantage. Hashknife, select the men you want and make ready to go back with whichever of these cowards will guide you to where they ran into Preacher. Trail him, track him to his lair, and then send back someone to guide the rest of us there. He's overplayed his hand this time. There will have to be some signs left to lead you to him. This time, Preacher will be surrounded and cut down like the dog he is."

Unknown to Ezra Pease, Preacher and Nighthawk lay behind a low screen of young spruce, low on the slope of the mountainside overlooking the camp. They had worked their way into hearing range, at least of the shouted tirade of the outlaw leader.

Preacher had to cover his mouth to stifle a chuckle when

Pease laid the blame at the mountain man's feet. The way Preacher saw it, Pease refused to see his own weaknesses. He probably couldn't plan a trip to an outhouse without mishap. When the camp grew busy with activity as men made ready to go with the man named Hashknife, Preacher and Nighthawk silently withdrew.

Far enough away that their voices would not carry, Preacher rubbed his jaw and expressed a niggling curiosity about the new manhunter sent after him. "That feller Pease called Hashknife. There's somethin' mighty familiar about him. The cut of his jaw, his hair . . . somethin' says I should know him."

"You have seen him before?" asked Nighthawk.

"No. Not that I recall. More like I've seen his pappy, or someone in the family. There's . . . jist a touch of something."

Nighthawk clapped him on the shoulder. "It will come to you. Now do we go back for enough men to finish this?"

"You do, I'm gonna stay, make sure they don't all get out of here and disappear again."

Nighthawk frowned. "Even for you, that could be quite a job."

"I know, ol' hoss. Don't reckon on takin' 'em on all alone. If they move, I go along an' leave a trail."

Nighthawk nodded. "Then good luck. I should be back in three days. Near as I can judge, you were right about this location is due north of the new settlement. Should be easy."

Preacher struck Nighthawk gently on the shoulder. "Ride with the wind, Nighthawk."

"Be sure of it."

Preacher saw his friend off, then settled in to keep track of the outlaw band. Then he set about preparing some unpleasant surprises for anyone who wished to get out of the valley. He started on the trail to the south.

There he located some springy aspen saplings and bent half a dozen on each side in arcs away from the trail. These he secured while he fashioned some pencil-sized twigs into sharp-pointed spikes, which he secured with rawhide thongs along the saplings, pointed toward the trail. Then he rigged trip lines that crossed the roadway at the proper distance from the deadly traps and eased the tension of the deadly flails into their strain. Satisfied, Preacher moved on.

Silently he wished he had a dozen men with sharp spades to dig some pits. Then, thought of injury to innocent horses changed his mind. With spare ropes and thongs left with him by Nighthawk, he rigged a spike-bristling deadfall to swing out of concealment among low branches and knock at least two men off their mounts. Some tough vines and a smoothly grooved rock provided a huge snare that could yank yet another piece of vermin from the saddle.

Preacher kept up his work throughout the day and most of the next. When he finished, he had some most unpleasant surprises rigged for any of Pease's men who tried to ride out. The only way into or out of the valley he left untouched was one he felt certain the bunglers with Pease knew nothing about. Then all he had to do was settle in on the south end of the valley and wait for reinforcements to arrive. Chuckling over the expected reaction of the walking filth, he rode off in that direction, tired and sore, but hugely pleased with himself. He decided on a little snooze to help pass the time.

While Preacher waited for his volunteer force of fighting men to arrive, Falling Horse and his Cheyenne Dog Soldiers came on from the northeast, following the sign of some of the less skilled among Pease's fighters. When the Cheyenne chief realized where those tracks led them, he called for a halt.

"I know of where these men go. It is a nice, wide valley, much grass, good water. Many ways in and out. But there is one that the white men would never find. It is narrow and dark, and we must move slowly. We can use it and not be found. Our surprise will be total."

Several older, wiser heads nodded in agreement. The more

restless among the younger warriors offered their opinion in the form of questions. "Why don't we take the faster way?"

"Yes," another agreed. "They may escape."

"The known paths will be watched. We would lose our surprise," Falling Horse explained. A cold smile lifted his lips. "And I want them to be surprised."

Without further discussion, the Cheyenne war party turned away and followed Falling Horse's lead toward the hidden entrance. They soon found the progress slower than expected. Trees attacked by insects and others struck by lightning littered the way, reducing forward movement to a dragging walk. At points they had to stop and drag limbs clear of the narrow, meandering trail that followed a tiny stream.

It took the Cheyenne the rest of the day to make it halfway through the steep canyon. They made camp and talked quietly among themselves. Some of the more enterprising among them produced small buffalo paunch pots, into which they put jerked bison meat and water. When the meat softened, they shredded it with fingernails then added cornmeal, ground nuts, and salt. It made a nourishing, if not savory, stew, which they shared with the others, then all rolled into blankets and slept soundly.

Up before dawn, they advanced on their enemy. At midday, Falling Horse halted the column and pointed to the south. A wedge of blue sky showed ahead. They had little distance to go. Each warrior muffled the muzzle of his mount, to quiet any whinny of recognition when the animals scented the presence of the white men's horses. An hour later, the Cheyenne came into the clear. Falling Horse used silent signals to direct his war party into line for an attack.

Every Dog Soldier mounted and readied his weapons. Many smiled broadly, the prospect of scalps and plenty of coups energizing them. Falling Horse let his ebony eyes cut along the double line of warriors and knew satisfaction. Every man had at least two weapons at the ready. Their first sweep would be a bloody one. He nodded his approval and raised his feather-decorated rifle over his head.

When it came down, the Cheyenne charged into the valley. They had covered more than half the distance to the white camp before the first shouts of alarm rose from their enemy.

Preacher came out of a light doze with a jerk. His eyes focused on a distant haze of dust. "Waugh! It's the danged Cheyenne," he grunted aloud.

White plumes rose and the reports of discharging rifles reached Preacher's ears. He didn't expect the reinforcements much before mid-afternoon. That crafty devil, Falling Horse, had followed the careless flatlanders right to their nest and now he was bringing them a whole world of grief. Preacher longed to be in there, mixing it up with Ezra Pease and his rabble. He crawled, crablike, to his saddle and reached into one of the leather bags for his spyglass. When the brass tubes had been extended, he focused in on a wild scramble of outlaw trash, as they sought to form up to give resistance.

The bright circle of light steadied on a knot of a half-dozen vermin who stood back-to-back and poured out a steady stream of fire into the milling ranks of Cheyenne. The Dog Soldiers rallied around this strong point, hooted and yipped, and swarmed over them in a single rush. Only writhing, blood-smeared forms remained when they rode on. Preacher heard some angry shouts off to the left and swung the glass to pin the action in place.

Seven harried bits of human slime raced their horses toward the southern outlet to the valley. Ten Dog Soldiers pursued them. Both parties exchanged shots, which went wild, and the race continued. A tight smirk formed on Preacher's face. Those fellers would soon find out what losers they were. The first one disappeared into the open mouth of the passage and Preacher sighed with satisfaction over his forethought.

Two long minutes passed and then a hideous scream,

magnified by the echo effect, rose from beyond where the thugs had disappeared. The one in the lead must have found the first of his unpleasant gifts. More shrieks followed rapidly. Then a spatter of gunfire. Silence returned to the cut through the hills. After a short pause, the Cheyenne warriors trotted back to the area of the main battle. Preacher could hardly contain himself. He wanted so badly to be a part of this. He had a deep, burning need to get his hands on the throat of Ezra Pease and slowly squeeze the life out of him. That might not happen, he realized.

A lull came in the fighting as both sides exhausted their loaded weapons. Typically, the Cheyenne pulled off to prepare for another charge. That gave Pease time to rally his men. Faintly, a commanding voice drifted to Preacher's ears.

"Load up everything you can. Forget the wagons. We've got to save ourselves."

"What about the powder and guns?" a frightened voice demanded.

"Blow them up. Set a long fuse and let's ride for our lives."

Typical yellow-belly, Preacher thought. Pease showed his yellow streak more than ten years ago, and now he did it again. Let them go, he decided. That would give him another swing at them. Which way would they head? Preacher pondered that until the panicked horses had been calmed enough to saddle and the men mounted. With the Cheyenne whooping it up for a second charge, Preacher focused his glass on his nemesis at last.

Pease sat before a roughly formed column of twos. He seemed to be haranguing them with some inspiring words, unheard over the drum of galloping hooves as the Cheyenne bore down on them again. Preacher's lips curled in disgust and contempt as he gazed at the bushy brows and matching carroty hair on a balding head, the thin, bloodless lips, and snaggled, yellowed teeth of Ezra Pease. Watery, pale blue eyes glittered with malevolence even at this distance, enlarged by the spyglass. At the last possible moment, Pease gave the command and whirled his mount, and the outlaw trash sprinted away to the south.

"Well, damn," Preacher cursed aloud, then had a different view of circumstances. "Maybe we can catch them between us," he speculated.

He looked back at the battlefield to find only men too badly wounded to sit a horse receive the attentions of the blood-lusting Cheyenne. Those who had been trapped offered no resistance. Even so, Preacher noted grimly, most of them died very slowly.

25

Whiskey splashed high in the air, as a barrel head shattered under the powerful blows of three Cheyenne warriors. Flames crackled among the abandoned tents of the white trash that had fled from the valley. When a river of rotgut washed into these, a great whoosh resulted that sent a ball of fire high in the air. When the fuse set by the minions of Ezra Pease reached the powder magazine, the resulting explosion had put most of the Dog Soldiers on the ground from the shock wave, knocking several unconscious, Preacher noted.

He still fumed impatiently from his lookout on the steep slope of the eastern side of the valley. The orgy of destruction went on into the afternoon. So involved were the Cheyenne that they failed to notice when Nighthawk, Buck Dempsey, and Kent Foster slipped into place next to Preacher. Awed by the destructiveness of the Indians, Buck and Kent gaped at the smoldering ruin. Preacher nudged Buck in the ribs.

"Now you got an idee what Falling Horse meant when he said it would be better if we did not get to Pease and his nest of vipers first. Wouldn't want them Dog Soldiers takin' out their mad on us, now would ya?"

Sobered by the display of ruthlessness, Buck answered softly. "No. It's not the sort of thing Mrs. Dempsey's little boy would like to get mixed up in."

Preacher stirred himself. "I reckon it would be a mistake

to wait until things quiet down. How far off did you say the rest were waitin'?"

"Two hours' ride from here," Nighthawk informed him.

"To the south?" Preacher asked with a grimace. "Chances are that Pease an' his buzzard-pukes rode right through them."

Nighthawk sighed. "They are reluctant to fight. At least without direction. I doubt that Beartooth is enough to inspire them to great effort."

"So do I," Preacher acknowledged. "Well, we're wastin' daylight. Either the Cheyenne will chase after Pease, or more likely head for home with their fresh scalps to do some celebratin'. Whichever, it should keep them busy long enough for us and what help we've got to round up that pack of reprobates."

Preacher's uneasiness increased during the day it took for the small company to rest men and horses and make repairs on equipment. He wore an outright scowl by evening. Lookouts he had posted came in to report that the Cheyenne had pulled out to the northwest.

"That's good news," Preacher answered. The prospect of being between Pease and the Cheyenne had troubled him greatly. "We can move out in the morning. Best chance is to split up and follow the scattered trails. They will have to meet up somewhere. From then on it should be easy."

Early morning light saw the expedition on its various ways. Preacher and Buck rode together with nine men. At first the trail was easy to follow. Frightened by the prospect of Indian justice, those they sought made no effort to cover their tracks. Preacher pointed that out to his contingent of greenhorns and took the lead.

After a while the signs grew scarcer. Preacher took to dismounting and studying what scant evidence they came upon. At one such point, he poked a finger into a green and brown road apple and a hopeful expression brightened his face.

"Can't be more'n two, three hours old. Still warm. And lookie there. Ain't seen that spade shoe print before. Some others joinin' up, I'd say."

"How do you know that?" one of the more militant among the missionary group asked.

Preacher cocked his head and gave the young man a quizzical glance. "Don't nobody keep a spade shoe on a horse that's not got a tender frog. If that horse had been with the ones we been followin', we'd have seen sign of it before now."

Chagrinned, the husband of one of the gospel-shouters swallowed hard. "Oh, yes. I see now."

"We keep goin', we'll catch sight of them 'fore long," Preacher advised.

"Is that wise?" a nervous carpenter asked.

"Hell, they's eleven of us. Way these boys been rode hard and put up wet, we should be able to handle however many there are. Won't be the whole bunch, I can guarantee that."

Reassured, though not possessed of Preacher's confidence, the young man nodded and they rode on.

Night brought little rest to Ezra Pease. From the height of his success he had plummeted to an all-time low. Almost as low as when he had been savagely beaten by Preacher and run out of the Rocky Mountains. He lay on the ground, sheltered by the crudest of lean-tos, uncomfortable in blankets, every pebble, twig, or irregularity in the ground a source of fiery discomfort. He groaned and rolled onto another side for the hundredth time.

Images of war-painted Cheyennes haunted him. They screamed literally right in his face and awakened thoughts of how close he had come to death. Where would they go? Where could they hide? Bathed in sweat, Ezra Pease cried out in the darkness and sat bolt upright. Forgotten was the compact he had made with the Eastern businessmen. Vanished, the visions of mountains of gold. Only the enraged, contorted, coppery faces of the savages who had attacked them without warning remained.

"They drove us out. Drove me out," he whispered to himself. "Drove me out." Humiliation burned hotly on his face.

In those long hours of the moonless night, his resolve weakened. Groggily, Pease recognized the figure of Hashknife squatting beside the fire, where he sipped from a tin cup of coffee. Pease shrugged on his trousers and slid long, narrow, unnaturally white feet into boots and walked to join his only remaining subordinate leader.

"I couldn't sleep, either," Pease remarked with a tone he hoped would sound casual.

"I've been thinking about . . ." Hashknife gestured behind them, toward the valley of their defeat.

"So have I." Pease agonized over taking this mysterious gunman into his complete confidence. Reluctantly he admitted he needed someone to confide in, to solicit for advice. "There is something you should know."

Hashknife tilted his head, cocked a brow. "Before deciding to cut and run?"

"Uh—yes. Or something very like that. What I wanted to tell you is that I'm not alone in this. I have . . . partners. Influential men back East. For a while today, I have debated throwing over the whole thing. I could head for California, or somewhere I'm not known. Leave the whole land grab up to my partners."

Hashknife's brow furrowed. "That might prove quite unwise," he prompted.

"I know that. But then I think, what the hell have they done to help?" His expression changed to chagrin. "Of course, the answer is, they have bankrolled the whole enterprise. I am obligated to them for that."

Hashknife relaxed somewhat. "I'm glad to hear you consider that. You see, I was steered to your organization by the very men you are discussing." Ezra Pease felt a cold chill run up his spine at the words Hashknife spoke. "Obviously you wanted a second opinion before you decided what to do."

"Yes, I did. What do you feel we should do next?" Pease appealed.

"Certainly we cannot stay here. We would be better off closer to the Blackfeet."

"I can see that," Pease allowed. "So we move northwest. And first thing tomorrow, I would say."

"Not . . . quite so soon," Hashknife cautioned. "It would be wiser to go south a ways further. To—ah—throw off pursuers. Also to let the men regain some of their composure."

Ezra Pease considered this, coming as it did from an underling he considered only another passable gunman, albeit a failed gentleman. "You have a strong grasp of strategy, sir. And, you couch your words in the phrases of a military man."

"I—ah—was. Until an unfortunate incident separated me from the Army. But, speculation on my past is a waste of time under the circumstances. What we need is a sound plan. One that takes advantage of the terrain, our own condition, and the enemy's situation."

A new light shone in the eyes of Ezra Pease. "Yes, yes, I was right in promoting you in this enterprise. Go ahead. At this point, I am open to any reasonable suggestion."

Hashknife gave him a wintry smile. "I would be glad to, for . . . shall we say a fifty-fifty split?"

Anger and greed flashed across the face of Ezra Pease. "Rather ambitious, aren't you?" he fired hotly. Then recognition of their perilous status modified his outlook. "Although I must say that a successful outcome would be worth it and then some. I'll stand by my original request."

Hashknife quickly outlined what he had in mind. It met with the full approval of Ezra Pease. The cashiered officer, for that's what Pease was certain Hashknife was, concluded with a summary of their end goal. "We managed to bring away enough of the boys and youths to conduct the initial mining operation as you outlined it. Once we reach the

Blackfeet, they will welcome us, especially if we give them a few more rifles and ammunition to ensure their goodwill. Yet, the most important thing is to forget about Preacher and to get far away from the Cheyenne. After that, raids on passing wagon trains will ensure a steady supply of labor."

Beaming now, Ezra Pease rose and clapped Hashknife on one shoulder. "I like it. We'll do it that way. Make sure the men are informed of all they need to know and are ready to move out first thing in the morning."

Preacher went ahead on a lone scout. He felt certain that Pease and his remaining outlaw band could not be far ahead of them. Sign of their presence had decreased, yet remained enough to lead the way. His steady, watchful pace put him far ahead of the remaining force of volunteers by the time the sun began to slant rapidly toward the western horizon.

The whinny of a startled horse, borne faintly on the breeze, alerted Preacher of his nearness to those he sought. This was almost too easy, he reasoned. Not too much so, he amended when he had dismounted from Thunder and wormed his way to the crest of a low ridge. Beyond he picked out some twenty of Pease's hard cases, settled into a scattered camp by a stream.

"Fools," Preacher muttered to himself. "Anybody worth his salt knows enough not to camp right beside a body of moving water. The noise it makes muffles any sounds of someone tryin' to sneak up on the camp." A short distance away, Thunder nodded his big, gray, Appaloosa head as though in agreement. It brought a fleeting smile to Preacher's lips. "Even m'horse knows that."

Preacher continued to watch until three hours after nightfall. Then he slipped away to a safe distance, mounted Thunder and headed back for the small company of avengers. He reached there shortly after midnight.

"There's nigh onto twenty-two of 'em there," he told Nighthawk, Dupre, and Beartooth. "I rec'nized Pease amongst them. What I want you to do is lay low for a day and a night. On the way back here, I got some plans I want to put to use on this group up ahead. It ain't all of them, but we got to start somewhere."

Preacher picked his positions well, and in advance. As he had expected the cavalcade of carrion eaters continued south through the next day. That, he definitely wanted to put a stop to. So he picked a likely campsite and settled in to wait for them to come to him.

Now he slithered on his belly, the Lefever rifle cradled in the crook of his elbows, headed into the first of his several sniping locations. He reached it undetected, a "V" notch slightly off-center in a split boulder, and settled in. Easing the muzzle and first six inches of barrel on the rifle through the opening, he adjusted his position and sighted in. The first thing he lined up on was a coffeepot.

His imagination supplied the heady aroma of boiling grounds, the anticipation of men tired from hard travel and residual fear. Gently, he squeezed the trigger. The recoil had hardly ceased when he went into motion again, crawling toward his second spot. It took fifty of Preacher's slow, un-labored heartbeats before the flatlander trash below reacted. At that extreme range, their bullets struck ground a hundred yards short of the rock he had used as cover. Preacher made a note of that; he'd come back later for another go-around.

At rest, in an easy position behind a tall pine, he let its shade mask his presence while he reloaded and took a look at the camp. The coffeepot, holed through-and-through, lay on its side, the former contents forming a puddle around the blue-gray granite utensil. Coldly amused by this, he glanced around for the inevitable one or two louts with duller minds who would not have taken proper precautions.

He found them almost at once. "Yep," he muttered. "This is gettin' to be entirely too easy."

Preacher shot the heel of one boot, and the human one

inside it, off of a thug who had thoughtlessly sprawled behind a saddle. A yell of agony reached him a second after the report of his Lefever rolled across the camp. Then a voice that rang with authority rose above the disorganized encampment.

"Some of you get out there and stop that."

"Naw, sir, Hashknife. Ain't gonna do it. We're sittin' ducks as it is."

"You'll do it or I'll shoot you where you lay," Hashknife barked.

"Pease is gettin' smarter," Preacher mused aloud. "He's makin' use of someone who knows how to deal with the scum of the earth. Might make this job a tad more difficult."

He refrained from moving this time. Preacher wanted to encourage those beneath him to waste their advance on a place he would soon abandon. Reloaded again, he took aim on an exposed shoulder near the single wagon that had been whisked out of the fight with the Cheyenne. The Lefever barked and bucked and when the smoke blew away, a man writhed on the ground, right hand clutching his left shoulder. Only then did Preacher eel his way to his third chosen spot.

From there he watched the cautious movement of three men, who came on foot out of the camp, rifles at the ready. They spread out and swung wide of the ancient pine, so as to put the brow of the hillside between them and their intended target. Grinning, Preacher made a half-turn and waited. The first one to show himself over the rise took a ball smack between his eyes. He went down like a stone and his two companions scurried back toward safety.

"Keep going, goddamnit!" Hashknife bellowed.

Preacher noticed a blur of brightly colored cloth from the corner of one eye as a heavy-set thug darted for the back of the wagon. Preacher left the ramrod for the Lefever on the ground as he took quick aim. The conical ball smashed the big bone in the fatty's right thigh and he plowed ground with his nose and chin.

"It's the Cheyenne. They've caught up with us." Preacher recognized the voice of Ezra Pease, for all its quaver of fear.

"If it was Indians, they would be attacking us by now," Hashknife differed.

"No—no, it's them. No one else was anywhere close to us," Pease insisted.

Preacher returned his attention to the two men flanking him. At once he caught sight of the braver of the pair. He ran flat out toward the screen of wild blackberry bushes, behind which Preacher crouched. Too close for a rifle shot, Preacher quickly laid aside the Lefever and drew one of his brace of .60 caliber Hayes, single-barrels.

"A little more," he coaxed. "That's right, come to poppa."

The Hayes discharged and smeared the sky with smoke. Preacher peered beyond it and saw his target drop onto wobbly knees. Both hands clasped over his belly, the worthless scum looked first at his wound, then cut his eyes upward in a final appeal to his Maker for mercy.

Appeal denied, Preacher thought as the hulking brute toppled face-first into the grass. All but too late, Preacher exchanged the empty pistol for the Lefever and brought it to bear on the chest of the more reluctant enemy. Loping along, bent low as though that would protect him from a frontal shot, the Boston rag bag took the ball in the top of his bald pate, which released a shower of blood and tissue. Impact stunned him to a momentary stop. Then his booted feet drummed frantically in place until his body drained of impulses and he flopped on his side in silent death.

"Not bad for an afternoon's work," Preacher congratulated himself in a hoarse whisper. Then he faded away, at an angle uphill. He'd come back later and reopen the dance.

Preacher had no need of his vocal tricks that night. From a mountaintop overlooking the nervous camp of wastrels and slime, came the haunting yowl of a prairie wolf. The amorous coyote sought a mate in the waning moonlight. In another turn of the earth, it would be the dark of the moon. Far off, an answer wavered toward the frosting of stars. Preacher had worked in close enough to hear the quavery voices of the men he stalked.

"Lordy, is that thing for real? Or is it . . . Preacher?" a crack-voiced youth asked.

"Best pray it's for real," came a growl from the far side of the fire.

Preacher grinned over that so hard it became a smirk. Like a wraith he crept in closer. All at once he overstepped his bounds.

"Who's that over there?" a tense voice challenged.

"It's nothin', jist me," Preacher responded. A new, wild, impossible idea had entered his head and it tickled him like a certain peacock feather in the hands of a buxom bawd he had sported with one time as a youngster of tender years.

"Well, then, come on over an' have some coffee," the gravel-voiced one rumbled.

With a shrug, Preacher removed his tell-tale four-shot pistols and laid them aside, then stepped into the light. He settled in between two of the younger hard cases and accepted a cup of steaming brew. He sipped while they talked. Time passed in a dumb lull. They talked of the fight with the Cheyenne. Preacher allowed as how it had plum upset him a lot. He refrained from saying why. While they rambled on, Preacher eased a hand into the possibles bag hung at his waist and removed a paper twist filled with pale yellowish crystals. The ease generated by the moment vanished when a loud rustling came from the brush close at hand.

Preacher seized his chance. Widening his eyes, he pointed into the darkness and blurted an alarming, if false, discovery. "B'God, it's a bear!"

Everyone looked where he pointed, while Preacher deftly emptied the salts of epecac into the coffeepot. He was in a crouch, half-standing when the first of the scum looked back. Preacher gave a nervous grin and waggled an empty hand at the man.

"At least I thought it was a bear. Musta been a deer, frightened by all us people around."

"Yeah. Could be."

"Yep. Well, best be gettin' back where I belong. Gonna be a short night," Preacher excused himself as he drifted toward the darkness again.

No one thought to stop him. He had retrieved his favorite pistols, snugged them in place and covered about fifty yards when the first sounds of vomiting reached his ears. Suppressing a chuckle, he glided on through the frosty starlight to do more mischief.

26

Early the next morning brush flew from the leading edge of the lean-to roof that sheltered Ezra Pease. He came up with a start and a yelp that chilled the already unsettled hard cases. "It's the Cheyenne!" he bellowed.

Preacher's gunshot echoed over the ground. By the time the sound reached the camp he had the Lefever nearly reloaded. His second round split the breastbone of an incautious gawker who had foolishly remained at the fire, sipping coffee. He dropped his cup a moment before his face hit the coals.

"See, I told you it was Indians," Pease shouted, the words tumbling over one another.

"No, it's not," Hashknife growled from where he hugged the ground. "It's Preacher. He snuck in here last night and put something in the coffee that made several men seriously ill."

"I want proof of that," a terribly agitated Pease demanded.

Hashknife glanced up at the sound of approaching hoof-beats. Two of his men came toward the center of camp, a captive tied to a horse between them. "I think I can provide that in a short while. By the way, have you noticed the shooting has stopped? If it were the Cheyenne, they would be whooping down on us by now."

Hashknife went to the prisoner and roughly yanked him to the ground. He stood over him, legs widespread, and bent until his face hovered inches from the hapless man.

"Who are you?"

"I—I'm a hired d-driver."

"A driver? For whom?"

"There's—ah—there's a band of psalm-singers not far from here. I went off yesterday to hunt for meat. Got lost."

"How far are these missionaries?" Hashknife demanded.

"T-two valleys over, to the south," the gutless driver readily offered.

"Hummmm." It came from the chest of Hashknife as a sound of contentment, rather than a sign of resignation.

"We have to break camp at once," Ezra Pease broke into the interrogation. "Head west at once. We can outdistance Preacher or the Cheyenne. I know we can."

"Be quiet a minute," Hashknife snapped, then changed his command into a request, "If you please, sir." To the driver, "Does the name Preacher mean anything to you?"

"Yes—yes, he's the one who led us to the valley."

Purring like a cream-stuffed cat, Hashknife turned to Ezra Pease. "I think we have solved both of our problems. This man can lead us to some people who are enjoying the protection of Preacher. He'll have to come after us and we'll have his proteges as hostages. Preacher will have to surrender or see them all killed one by one."

Terror fled from Ezra Pease and he beamed at Hashknife. "I like your dirty, devious little mind, Hashknife. That's a splendid idea. Damn the black heart of Preacher into the hottest corner of hell. We've got him now."

Starting shortly after the impassioned speech of Ezra Pease, more of the disorganized vermin began to drift into camp. Observed in secret by Preacher, their presence did nothing to lighten the mood of the mountain man. He had managed to reduce their number to some fifteen, now twenty more gathered around cookfires and talked out their nervousness.

Preacher chafed as he accepted that he must stay longer, to determine how many men Pease would have.

He took careful note when five of the thugs, cleaner in appearance and better dressed than most, rode out of the meadow where Pease had made camp. Preacher longed to follow them, learn their destination. Yet, he had to know the enemy strength. He would wait overnight and see what the morning brought, then set out to advise the others, and to follow the mysterious quintet that had parted with the rest.

Morning brought a crushing blow for Preacher. Twenty-three Blackfoot warriors rode into camp. From what Preacher could make out through his spyglass, their war leader spoke only his own tongue, while another made sign talk and translated into English. The signs revealed that they had come to help their old friends and to get fresh Cheyenne scalps. Pease replied that they had surely come to the right place. Nothing could be worse, Preacher reckoned. Quietly, he crawled from his observation place and, mounted on Thunder, rode off to bring the latest to his band of volunteers.

The mountain men among the small company received his news with grim expressions. Yet, they agreed among themselves, they still had to destroy Pease or a summer of intertribal fighting could turn into a long campaign, with white against Indian.

"They are not making it easy for us," Nighthawk observed.

"You are even more correct than usual, *mon ami,*" Dupre admitted.

"It ain't impossible," Preacher insisted. "Thing is we can no longer take the fight to them. We must make them come to us and be ready with every nasty trick we know. If only I could stir up some trouble between them Blackfeet and Pease . . ." Preacher mused into silence.

Late the next afternoon, five presentably dressed strangers rode into the hidden valley and stopped before the largest structure in the new settlement, the church. Their leader was well-spoken and Reverend Bookworthy greeted them effusively.

"You are welcome, brothers, so long as your intentions are peaceful. If you haven't provisions or shelter, we can accommodate you. Would you—ah—be staying long?"

"No, not for long, sir. I must say I am heartened to find a house of God in this benighted wilderness," Hashknife purred softly.

A gaggle of children had swarmed forward and followed them through the meadow and into the clearing. They frolicked now around the legs of the horses and their shrill voices rose in a deafening chorus. Reverend Bookworthy rounded on them with a hint of heat in his voice.

"Here, now, that's enough. Shouldn't you be in school?"

"No, Reverend," Nick chirped. "It's Saturday."

"Then you should be working for your parents. Go along now. Make yourselves busy at something useful." He turned to the visitors. "Children. You understand, I'm sure."

"Of course." Like his men, Hashknife's eyes had picked out the abundance of young women among the settlers and he appraised them with a hungry gaze.

One among them who had drawn closer darted a hand to her face to conceal her shock. Although many years had passed, enough that Cora Ames could not be certain, yet she felt almost sure, that the one speaking to Reverend Bookworthy was Quincey. She spoke the name softly, giving it the New England pronunciation of Quinzie. And she knew it was so.

After several minutes more of conversation between the missionary minister and Quincey, it became apparent that recognition had not gone both ways. Cora Ames turned away thoughtfully and hurried from the presence of the enigmatic young man. Her mind was awhirl with conflicting emotions. Whatever could he be doing here? How had he come to find them? Had he—had he . . . changed?

Part of her didn't want the answers to those questions, while another yearned to know. Perhaps to be able to . . . to give an alarm? Foolishness, her practical side mocked her. It couldn't possibly be him.

Cora spent a troubled night and nearly swooned with relief the next morning after breakfast when she saw two of the men with Quincey making preparations to saddle up and presumably ride out. Bony fingers of ice clutched her heart a few minutes later when it became clear that Quincey and two of his companions would remain behind. What might that signify? Cora Ames dreaded the answer.

Only, having kept silent so long, she knew she had to keep her terrible secret to herself. It tormented her throughout the day as she kept a respectable distance between herself and the visitors.

Two more days had gone by while Preacher waited with his small force of dedicated fighters. During that time he made plans and prepared weapons to try his mischief and break the alliance with the Blackfeet. To further that, he was watching the camp when two of the dandies who rode out three days earlier returned. They held a brief conference with Ezra Pease. At once orders were bellowed to break camp and make ready to move out.

"What the hell now?" Preacher grumbled to himself.

He returned quickly to the waiting company of amateur fighters and advised them of the changed situation. "All we can do is follow along and see where they lead," he concluded.

They, too, broke camp at once.

By mid-morning the next day, Preacher had a haunting, uneasy feeling that he knew exactly where Pease's vultures were headed. Also why five of them had ridden out dressed to the nines. The High Lonesome held only one attraction for the foul scavengers of Ezra Pease that lay due south. His little settlement of pilgrims.

A cold blast of arctic air seemed to wash over Preacher and down his back. They would be totally helpless. And not even Pease and whatever men would stand with him could hold back the Blackfeet when they rushed in among the white women and children. Sickened by memories of past such slaughters, Preacher gnawed at the inside of his cheek to try to shake loose an idea. It took him until nightfall to decide what to do.

Preacher took Nighthawk along. Together they moved in on the night camp of Ezra Pease. A hundred yards short of the lookouts posted to secure the area, they separated and went their various ways. Preacher scouted his sector before making a move.

Fixed in his mind was the location of the Blackfeet. He intended to end up there. But first, the sentries had to be taken out. After placing each of them, he closed on the first. The chinless lout had time to utter a sharp "Huuh!" before Preacher's tomahawk split his skull and he crumpled to the ground.

Silently, without a backward look, Preacher moved on. He found that one of the guards had moved, out of loneliness and inexperience. Young, dreadfully young, Preacher noted as his intended target talked in a low murmur to the one who had left his post. Preacher gave it a moment's consideration and decided on a risky course of action. With ease, he crept up to within arm's reach, then spoke softly.

"If both of you want to keep on living, don't make a sound."

"Preacher?" the younger thug gasped.

"None other. Now, what you are going to do is ease them pistols and your belts and lay 'em on the ground. Put your rifles alongside them. Then back up to me."

Without protest, they complied. When they stood inches from Preacher's chest, he tapped each youth on a shoulder. "Now, we can do this two ways. I can knock you out and tie you up. That way, maybe you'll be found an' maybe not. Or . . ."

"Or what? Don't torment us, Preacher," the older lad whispered harshly.

"Or you can give me your word that you are going to take off walkin' and get clear the hell an' gone from anywhere near Ezra Pease. I won't hurt you and I won't come after you. But if I ever see either of you in the High Lonesome again, I'll kill you on sight."

"I believe you," they chorused.

"Well, then, which will it be?"

"We're gone," the younger blurted. "We ain't ever been here."

Preacher smiled in the dark. "Now that's fine. That's sensible, boys. Whenever you're ready, jist start walkin'."

"Can we—can we go back an' change our drawers first?" the older lad bleated.

Preacher could have fallen down and rolled around laughing if he hadn't kept a tight rein on himself. "No. Jist scoot."

They scooted. Preacher moved on. Another sentry died, which cleared his sector and gave him access to the Blackfeet. Ready in position, Preacher lighted fuses on some of his gourd bombs and hurled them in among the small war trail lodges of the Blackfeet. Almost at once they began to go off with tremendous roars. Smoke, dust, and rock chips filled the air. Preacher heard the wild whinnies of horses from the far side of the camp. Nighthawk had reached his objective also.

Preacher found the Blackfeet ponies too well guarded to risk stampeding them, so he glided away into the night. What they had done might not bring a complete break, but from now on the Blackfeet would look with distrust at their white allies. It had been a good night's work.

* * *

"They are moving on to the south," Nighthawk informed Preacher when he awakened him from a light snooze an hour after sunrise.

"Dang it. That's the very thing I wanted to discourage." The crafty mountain man considered the implications of this. He had to accept that no way existed for his small force to get around the larger band of trash and slime led by Ezra Pease. Without being able to pose themselves between the brigands and the helpless folk in the valley, all they could do was snip away at the rear and flanks of the column. He quickly outlined his ideas to that effect.

This harassment got under way almost at once. Some stragglers remained in the camp Pease had established, still loading packsaddles and gathering their personal gear. From the concealment of trees and brush, Preacher and his men opened up with a withering fire. Hot lead scythed down seven of the human dregs in an instant. The others panicked and abandoned their supplies to race off on loudly protesting horses.

"That's doin' it, boys!" Preacher shouted his approval. "Now, split up in your groups. Nighthawk, Dupre, an' Beartooth will lead you. You know what to do."

And they proved it within less than an hour. The dull thud of rifle fire drifted back northward as the small bands struck at Pease and his trash. Preacher took his group, including Buck and Kent, the most capable of the driver volunteers, and set off along the eastern flank. His goal was to get close to the head of the column before engaging the enemy. With luck he might even get a shot at Ezra Pease.

Their torment of Pease and his vermin continued throughout the day. Then, shortly before Preacher estimated Pease would make camp for the night, the other three well-dressed outlaws rode up the trail from the south. With them they brought four captives. A cold knot formed in Preacher's stomach when he recognized young Chris from the ravaged wagon train, the boy Peter who had come with Silas Phipps and with him the girl, Helen. Worst of all, he had no trouble recognizing Cora Ames. The apparent leader of this group met briefly with Ezra Pease and summoned more men.

These, along with Pease, rode a short ways off from the column of vandals. Pease rose in his saddle and bellowed his demands loudly, turning all ways and repeating them, to be certain he was understood.

"Preacher! Do you hear me? We've found your precious garbage. I have men already in that valley of yours. Back off or these will be only the first to die." Pease paused, then began to rant again. "Make no mistake. If you and those with you do not give us free rein, I will not hesitate to kill every one of those helpless grubs. I'll start with these and believe me, their deaths will be slow and painful. Now, back off, and let me hear you agree to it."

Preacher chewed at his lower lip. He had never given his word falsely and didn't intend to now. Yet, too many lives depended upon what he did. Even his hesitation proved to be the wrong thing to do. Pease made a gesture and two of his sub-human fiends yanked young Peter from the horse he rode.

They ripped the clothes from the boy's body and began to make small, shallow cuts on his chest and belly. His screams slashed through Preacher as though he were under the knife instead. Sudden fury washed away his indecision. He had had enough. Taking his Lefever rifle, Preacher rode out into the open, still well out of ordinary rifle range.

"Pease! You back-end of a polecat, hear me! We can end this without harm to any more. Face me, man to man, we'll fight it out. Winner goes his own way. You have my word on it."

Pease made a show of considering this offer, while his henchmen continued to slice into Peter's body and the boy screamed in agony. "What about the others with you?" Pease asked tauntingly, toying with Preacher. "Will they abide by what you say?"

"They will."

"I don't think so," Pease mocked him. "To give you time to secure their promises to leave us in peace, I'm going to let these gentlemen finish with this boy here, and then we are going to ride on into your little paradise. If any more shots are fired while we do, I will have the other children killed, one by one, and then the woman. I'll allow my men to have their way with the females before they dispatch them, naturally."

That did it for Preacher. He snapped the rifle to his shoulder and shot at Pease. A nervous twitch from Thunder sent the ball off course and put it through the meaty part of Pease's left shoulder.

"That's the last shot fired, Pease," Preacher roared. "We will abide by your terms. No one will fire on the column while you ride to the valley. When you get there, we'll face off man to man. And . . . I'll see you put in hell."

27

Terror-stricken, the residents of the valley ran before the onslaught of the advancing human debris led by Ezra Pease. A few of the remaining missionary men tried to resist and were cut down in a storm of lead. Pease had pushed his company of worthless trash on through the night, which caught Preacher by surprise. Now he pressed his advantage as the much smaller force with Preacher closed in from behind. Once they had driven all the way to the center of the settlement, Ezra Pease called a halt in front of the raw planks that walled the church. Again, he turned back to harangue Preacher with threats.

"Leave off! There is nothing you can do to stop us. If you persist, we will start killing the residents."

With the mutilated body of Peter, which they had recovered and brought along, fresh in his mind, Preacher had no doubt that Pease meant what he said. Reluctantly he gave the signal to break off and draw back. He had never felt so low in his life. Preacher blamed no one else for what had happened. He was the one who had led these innocents to this terrible end. His face hidden from the others, he led the way out of the valley.

Once inside the screening trees, Preacher called a halt. "There is nothing we can do tonight, but come nightfall, it's another story."

"What can we do then?" one of the drivers asked.

"We're gonna raise hob with 'em, hoss," Preacher assured him. Quickly he outlined his idea. It had everything to do with their familiarity of the valley and Pease's lack of it.

During the long, difficult day, Preacher came to a grudging admission that so far Ezra Pease had kept his word. Outside of being frightened, no harm had come to the residents of the valley. When twilight purpled the sky, Preacher called his stalwart band together.

"They'll be edgy tonight, so we'll wait until it gets near to mornin'. That's the best time to hit. I've heard say it's the last hours before dawn that a man sleeps soundest. Even the ones on guard will begin to droop. That's what gives us a chance."

"What if we get caught by daylight?" an uncertain evangelist asked.

"Then we keep on fightin'," Preacher explained. "Now, ever'body get somethin' to eat and rest up. You'll be told when it's time."

"You have sunken to a new low, Quincey," Cora Ames spat. "When you first arrived in the valley, I had the misapprehension that perhaps you had reformed your ways. I regret that I could be so mistaken."

"You should be pleased for me. I have found the way to a vast fortune, to power and respect and a good life," Hashknife responded, disconcerted to see that Cora gazed past his shoulder and out the window of her small cabin toward the distant trees where those infernal fighting men with Preacher had disappeared.

"What you've found," Cora snapped, "is a cold, shallow grave once Preacher gets done with you." Her anger rose to choke off further threats. "I'm ashamed that I ever knew you, let alone . . ."

A smirk lifted the lips of Hashknife. "Aha! That of which we never speak, eh, my dear? Never mind. I have grown quite used to rejection. The years have not been kind to me, but no matter. Ezra Pease has made me an equal partner in his enterprise. There are literally millions to be made."

Cora produced her own, knowing, self-satisfied expression. "Provided he doesn't dispose of you once your usefulness to him is at an end. Oh, Quincey, Quincey, it could have been so different, so much better. If only . . ."

Hashknife raised a hand to stem the flood of her words. "Enough. I have no need of a lecture from you, let alone another sermon from that self-righteous hypocrite. I see you are in no mood for cordial conversation, so I will leave you now. Have no fear, none of these smelly louts dares to touch you." He patted the holster that contained his right-hand Colt Walker. Turning on one boot heel, he stomped out before Cora Ames could make another caustic reply.

Preacher gave his neophyte warriors more than enough time to get into position. Then he slowly advanced. Spread around with the fumbling, stumbling missionaries, he had positioned the drivers, and his mountain man friends, to lead. To his surprise, shortly after darkness fell, a number of the more peace-loving among the male gospel-shouters had risked sure death to sneak out of the cordon set up by Ezra Pease. They begged for the chance to take up arms and defend their families.

"Those aren't men, they're animals. The lewd looks they cast on our wives and daughters. It's unspeakable," Art Landry spoke for them all. "If I can shoot Indians in self-defense, I can strike out at savage filth like those."

A chorus of "Me, too" ran through the men with him.

Their number increased the thin ranks to forty strong. Preacher knew gratitude for their offer, though he doubted how useful the newcomers would be. He would soon find out, Preacher acknowledged as he came within fifty feet of the picket line set out by Pease and his able lieutenant.

That man who called himself Hashknife still troubled Preacher. Why did his features seem so familiar? Obviously he had intelligence. Most likely far beyond that of Ezra Pease. He remained cool during the worst of the fighting. And his auburn hair haunted Preacher's memory as much as his close resemblance to . . . someone. His study ended at the sound of a foot tread on a fallen twig, only three yards ahead. Preacher tensed himself.

The blamed fool came directly toward him. Preacher couldn't understand it until the man spoke in a harsh whisper. "You come to relieve me? I can sure use it. M'eyelids is droopin' somethin' awful."

Darkness had confused the man, Preacher realized. He thought he walked toward the settlement, not away from it. Preacher didn't give him time to learn of his error. A swift swing of the billet of wood in his hand sent the lookout off to a different starfield than the one that twinkled above. The wrist-sized stick made a hollow sound when it struck the side of the man's head. Preacher leaped forward and eased the sentry to the ground. Then he turned to his right, as he had instructed all of the men to do, and set off to roll up the others close at hand.

Two more out of the way left a pie-shaped sector open in which Preacher could work his mischief. Bent low, he covered ground rapidly. The hunk of wood he held had been frazzled at one end and dipped in tallow to serve as a torch when the situation called for it. Preacher paused within pistol shot of the settlement's cabins and fished out his tinder box. He was about to strike a spark and ignite his makeshift flambeau when all hell broke loose.

Jolted out of their deepest slumber by a ragged fusillade, the sub-human detritus with Ezra Pease had little chance of organizing a resistance. Firing as they came, their shrill yells electrifying the night, the men of the settlement charged in among the cabins. Torches aflame, they set fire to tents and bedrolls. Hard cases who still remained in some of the latter began to scream as the flames licked at their bodies.

Preacher struck flint to steel and blew to life his milkweed down, which lighted a sulphur-tipped sliver. It blazed and ignited his torch. Then he joined the others. He dodged around a drowsy man who had only come to his feet and smacked him in the ribs with the firebrand. Howling, the thug spun away and fell to roll in the dirt. Preacher changed hands and drew one of his big four-barrel pistols. Two thick-chested, reckless louts reared up to block his path. Preacher coolly shot one, the other ran. In fact, Preacher noticed a whole lot of the buzzard-pukes deserting their cause.

Initially it seemed a stunning victory. Worn down by endless days on the trail, the fierce fighting, first against the Cheyenne, then Preacher and his band, nerves jangled by the harassing fire on their column, many had no heart for more battle. Even as they hunted for their horses, Ezra Pease and Hashknife sought desperately to organize some resistance.

"Stand fast. Hold on, there. We outnumber them, you fools," Pease bellowed.

"Alone you can be picked off and left for buzzard bait," Hashknife assured the men.

Gradually their words took effect. The panic fled. Scum and filth they may be, but they saw the wisdom of strength in unity. Here and there knots gathered and began to return fire. A couple of the psalm-singers went down. One of the drivers threw hands in the air and fell, shot through the head. Preacher watched the effect as the initial shock wore off and muttered a curse. Without a means of direct control, he could not coordinate a sustained attack against these strong points.

Within no time, the contenders had pulled back from one another. Firing slackened and Preacher knew he had to do something to prevent Pease from carrying out his revenge against the helpless women and children. He tossed his torch into the midst of a group of Pease's vicious swine and began a swift, long run around the perimeter of the besiegers. When he came to the individual clusters, he paused long enough to give new orders. After leaving each group, he heard his new plan being carried out as men fired alternately, keeping up a steady stream of lead into the defensive positions taken by the outlaws.

That way, he knew, it might be possible to prevent them from moving from the small parcels of ground they presently held. If it worked, it would keep them away from the residents. He reached the last batch and Beartooth greeted him with a big hug.

"We got them out in the open now," the burly mountain man brayed.

"Thing is to keep them there," Preacher replied and explained the purpose he had in mind.

Beartooth put his charges to it at once. Then he turned to Preacher. "What do you reckon on doin' now?"

"I want to move in on that big cluster out there where Pease has taken command. Cut the head off a snake and the body dies."

Beartooth nodded solemnly. Preacher glided off from shadow to shadow to avoid the bright areas created by flickering fires. He had no way of knowing it, but his plan would work exceedingly well.

It came to him when the first pale band of gray appeared in the east. Pease and his cohorts had been fought to a standstill. With improved light, the marksmanship of Preacher's volunteers would improve. So, too, would that of the tenacious gunmen with Ezra Pease. A quick count through the round field of his spyglass told Preacher that numbers no longer counted that much. Maybe the time for a charge had come. Pick one cluster of scum at a time and roll over them?

It appealed until Preacher heard the distant rumble of pounding hooves. One thing he knew for certain. It could not possibly be reinforcements for his side.

Several times during the long, pre-dawn hours, most of the underlings committed to the cause of Ezra Pease lost heart and thought of making a break. The hail of bullets from their invisible opponents convinced them otherwise. Now they congratulated themselves on standing fast. New hope came bearing down on them out of the sunrise.

"Lookie over there," Vern Beevis shouted, a grubby finger pointing at the shapes resolving out of the low ground mist.

Bart Haskel came thundering through the thin line of besiegers with a dozen hard-faced, gun-bristling men in his wake. They made for the largest cluster of their comrades, some who still crouched behind hastily dug breastworks. Relief at the eleventh hour! A ragged cheer rose.

"Well, I'll be damned," Beartooth drawled.

"We may well all be, Beartooth," Preacher answered sadly.

The words hardly out of his mouth, Preacher put hand to one of his revolving four-barrel pistols as the enemy swirled out of their defensive positions and launched a wild, screaming attack. Only a steady rate of fire slowed them at last. The final man to fall lay only ten feet from where Preacher crouched behind the stump of a fir that had been logged out for housing.

While the renegade whites regrouped, Preacher marked furtive movement to one side of the main enemy force. The man called Hashknife broke clear of the men around him and started off at a lope toward one of the cabins. The one that belonged to Cora Ames, Preacher noted with a sudden flash of anger and apprehension.

With a roar, Pease's scum charged again. Preacher had to put away his concern for Cora. This time the fighting became clouded in dust and powder smoke, men determined to triumph at whatever cost pushed on with empty weapons, to club and smash with their rifles and stab with knives. The fighting degenerated into a wild hand-to-hand melee. Preacher saw his amateur fighters waver and then begin to give ground. A sense of helplessness washed over him. How could he have been so blind, so proud as to believe they had a chance? Then, with all lost, another, distant sound blew new hope through the momentary fog of defeat. He cast off his dejection and turned to verify what his ears told him.

"Ki-ki-ki-yi-yi-yiiiiii!"

Hoofbeats pounding, the Cheyenne Dog Soldiers of Falling Horse thundered into the valley. Preacher broke away from those around him and hopped up and down, waving both arms over his head to attract the attention of his old friend. Falling Horse cut his pony to the left and rushed down on Preacher.

"We thought they had finished them," the Cheyenne chief said through a smile. "It is good we did not go home."

"That it is. Now have your braves give some new spine to those gospel-shouters of mine," Preacher replied, his voice thick with emotion. Preacher had his own agenda.

Falling Horse spun away and directed his men toward the Blackfeet, who had so far not partaken in the battle. White men fighting white men was a novelty to them. Now, in the presence of their traditional enemy, they had a sudden change of heart about allegiance to Ezra Pease. Beartooth and Dupre led their men against the Indians also, hurling explosive gourds as they advanced.

Loud blasts and whizzing pieces of scrap metal and gourd shards shattered their nerve entirely. Howling in consternation, convinced their medicine had deserted them, the Blackfeet broke from their separate camp and streamed wildly across the meadow toward an opening in the valley walls.

Dog Soldiers hooted and shouted vulgar insults at the Blackfeet. They also pursued them with wild abandon. Thirsty for Blackfoot blood, hungry for their scalps, the Cheyenne ignored what went on among the warring whites to settle old scores with the fleeing warriors.

"Now that shines," Preacher exclaimed. "I was plum worried about what those Blackfeet would take it in mind to do."

"So was I," Nighthawk admitted at Preacher's side. He cut his eyes to a struggle that went on on a small rise, outside one of the cabins. "Oh-ho, my friend. It appears the woman who hungers after you is in need of assistance."

Preacher had seen it, also. He already started that way. He had to batter two brawny hard cases out of his way, shoot another and kick a fourth between the legs before a clear path lay between him and Hashknife, who held Cora Ames roughly by one arm, half-dragging her toward where Ezra Pease had taken his last stand.

By that time, Hashknife had closed the distance between Cora's cabin and his leader. He shoved Cora into the arms of Ezra Pease. All around, the fighting dwindled to an end as men stopped to stare at the bizarre scene going on atop the little knoll. Hashknife turned to face the cause of their downfall. For Hashknife had not the least shred of doubt that their end had come. Yet, he determined to take the cause of their failure with him. He pointed a long, spatulate finger at Preacher and roared his despair.

"I'm going to kill you, Preacher!"

"No, you're not," Preacher answered calmly.

"I am, I swear it. You have single-handedly undone us. For that you must pay."

Preacher kept a wary eye on the desperate man while he canted his head to the side and thumped with his left palm above the ear. "Am I hearing right?" he asked. "Them's fancy words for a man about to die."

"Don't toy with me!" Hashknife shrieked, on the edge of losing his grasp on sanity. "Fill a hand with one of those fancy pistols of yours. Before you can fire twice, I'll pump six bullets into you," he raved on, oblivious to the silence that hung around him.

"You'd best get started then," Preacher invited as he whipped out one of the four-shooters and eared back the hammer in one smooth move.

Hashknife had hardly touched the butt grip of his Walker Colt when the hammer fell and the pistol bucked in Preacher's hand. The .56 caliber ball took Hashknife square in the middle of his forehead. His back arched in a spasm and he slowly leaned further back, until he toppled over and landed on his shoulders and heels.

Astonished gasps rose from the witnesses. Before anyone could react, the voice of Ezra Pease cut raspingly through the murmurs of surprise. "It ends here, Preacher. I've got the girl. One wrong move and I spread her brains all over the ground. Get me a horse and I'll be gone. Don't come after me, or the girl dies."

He had to get Cora clear enough for a clean shot, Preacher knew. Without it he would have a tragedy on his hands. Warily, he shifted to one side. Pease moved to keep Cora between himself and Preacher. Blocked again. Preacher sought another diversion and found he did not need it. Cora Ames took care of clearing the target for him. When Pease shifted his weight to one leg, she gave a sharp, swift upraise of her boot heel into her captor's crotch.

At once, Ezra Pease let out a howl, his face turned a beet-red, and he released his grip enough for Cora Ames to break away. His face ashen now, Pease fought to suck in the air he had so rapidly wheezed away. Much to Preacher's surprise, rather than scurry to safety, Cora dashed to the fallen body of Hashknife.

"Don't make it too quick for him," she called over one shoulder to Preacher.

Preacher obliged her. He took time and fined his aim so that his next ball shattered the left kneecap of Ezra Pease. Pease shot wild as he went to one knee, and put a ball across Preacher's shoulder close to his ear. Preacher fired again. He put a hole in the unwounded shoulder of Pease. Pease groaned and dropped his Herrison Arsenel .50, double-barrel pistol. With his previously injured arm, he reached for the second two-shot handgun. Preacher waited.

Pease cocked both barrels and took slow, painful aim. Standing spread-legged, arms akimbo, Preacher still waited. When the black holes of the muzzle came level with his eyes, Preacher fired again. His hammer fell on an empty nipple. At once, Pease emptied his last barrel. The slug tore a hot, ragged trough across the top of Preacher's right shoulder. By only a fraction of an inch it missed his collarbone. Preacher winced, but covered it quickly.

Then he holstered his empty pistol and advanced steadily on the kneeling Pease. "It don't have to be this way, Pease," Preacher offered the olive branch again.

"Goddamn you, Preacher," the renegade wailed. "I . . . want . . . you . . . dead." With that, he gingerly fished a knife from its belt scabbard.

Preacher marched up to him, kicked the knife from the hand of Ezra Pease and punched him solidly in the mouth. "I want this one to hang," he announced, then turned and walked away.

28

Preacher stopped beside the prostrate figure of Cora Ames. She lay across the chest of the dead man named Hashknife. Gently Preacher bent down and raised her. Tears streaked her face. Preacher's puzzled expression asked the question for him.

"Th-they called him Hashknife," Cora gulped. "Hi-his-his real name was Quincey Ames. He is—was—my oldest brother."

That took Preacher like a sucker punch. He had words of scorn for any man who would mistreat a woman, yet her revelation sucked them out of his mouth. How could he tell her to dry her eyes and not grieve over such a lowlife, when it was her own brother? Well, by dang, all considered, she shouldn't waste tears over him, Preacher bristled at last. He bucked up and tried another approach.

"From the first time I saw him, I was thinkin' there was somethin' familiar about his looks. His face that is. I never imagined. Can you tell me what brought him here with Ezra Pease?"

"I—don't know all of it. He was my idol when I was little. Then, when he was around fifteen . . . something . . . went wrong. He changed. Grew rebellious against Father. He held religion to scorn, despised every decent emotion. He started running with some rowdy boys from the other side of town.

Then one day, the bank was robbed and Quincey disappeared along with several of his hooligan friends. Father saw him once or twice after that, but it always upset him so, he never talked about their meetings. His name appeared in the Boston newspapers several times and then . . . he seemed to have disappeared off the face of the earth. Now, he is here . . . and he is dead."

"And I killed him. I won't say that I am sorry. He made that choice, not I. I'll leave you now, Miss Cora. Only I'm gonna leave a bit of good advice. Don't grieve for him too much. He weren't worth it."

A week passed in the valley, the missionaries busy burying the dead, the drivers nursing their wounds. Cora Ames remained distant from Preacher throughout the long days of ripe spring. Then, late on Friday afternoon, a stranger ambled his mount down into the settlement. Preacher and his friends slouched over to inspect the newcomer.

"Howdy, folks," the stranger greeted. "I didn't know there was a settlement here."

"Well, now you know," Preacher challenged, his wounds making him testy. Cora's avoidance had something to do with it too, Dupre suspected.

"So I do." The stranger cut narrowed eyes to Preacher. After a long moment of inspection, he gave a small negative shake of his head. "You're not the one, but I am looking for a man. I am U.S. Marshal Ruben Talbot." For the hundredth time, he produced the sketches of Silas Phipps and the orphan children. "They are wanted for robbery, murder, and flim-flam games all over the East."

When the likeness of Phipps reached Preacher he wrinkled his nose and gave a short. "Yup. We seen this one. Hanged him for the unnatural things he done to them kids."

"You've seen the children, then? I have warrants for their arrest. Tell me where they are, if you please."

Cora Ames pushed her way through the crowd that had gathered as Preacher spoke out forcefully. "An' if I don't please?"

"What's all of this about?" Cora demanded before an explosion could erupt between Preacher and this menacing-looking man.

"This uppity twerp of a You-nited States Marshal says those youngins with Phipps are wanted for a whole lot of crimes," Preacher summarized.

"That's not possible," Cora blurted. Then she went on to describe Silas Phipps and how he treated the youngsters. After a breathless pause, following her passionate defense of the children, she concluded a bit defensively, "If they did participate in any crimes, you can be sure they were forced into it. I've told you how Phipps beat them, nearly starved them. Here they will have good, Christian homes and lives.

"Several couples are childless and will, no doubt, make the effort, once they have settled in, to adopt them," she concluded.

Marshal Talbot muttered to himself, garrumphed and grumbled somewhat. "The law's the law; ma'am. I ain't judge and jury. All I do is bring 'em in."

"We have a judge, and enough men to make a jury. We've used them already," Cora came back perkily.

Marshal Talbot looked startled, recalling what he had been told happened to Phipps. He took a long, good look at Preacher, saw the coiled, barely restrained power and fury there, and made his decision. "I suppose what you would do is convene this court and dismiss the charges on the children and designate them as wards of the court, in the custody of those who have presently taken them in?"

"If we had to," Cora responded, her chin thrust defiantly forward.

"An' me an' my friends would back it up," Preacher announced. Beartooth, Dupre, and Nighthawk pushed through to the front of the onlookers.

Talbot took them in, swallowed hard. "I've no doubt that you would. Well, then, I see no solution but to allow them to stay." With that, the marshal extracted the warrants from an inner coat pocket and made a show of tearing them in half across the middle. "I'd be obliged if one of you would show me a place where I can take the night, then I'll be on my way."

"No problem," Art Pettibone piped up. "We have a spare room in our cabin. Mrs. Pettibone is expecting our first child."

"Obliged, indeed," the marshal responded, relaxing in this fresh, cordial atmosphere.

After he had departed, taken in tow by Art Pettibone, Cora turned to Preacher and spoke to him for the first time since he had killed her brother. "Thank you for standing up for the children."

"Weren't nothin', Miss Cora. They ain't bad, considerin' they're still kids."

"Oh, Preacher, you are still impossible," she replied, the wry twinkle back in her eyes. "I hear that you are planning to leave soon."

"Yep."

"Well, then, with Pease dead and the Cheyenne at peace again, I see no reason why you can't lead us on to the villages of the Indians."

"Oh, yes, there is."

Cora pouted a moment, then changed her tack. "At least there's no reason why you cannot stay in the valley for the summer. Perhaps take winter here and then lead us to our golden land of promise."

All at once, Preacher could hear wedding bells ringing inside his head, and see a vine-covered cottage in Cora's eyes. He had to think fast. "But there is. I have to go weltering a bit to visit the soldier-boys at the small fort on the Yellowstone. They need to know about the guns on the loose and see to gettin' them all back from the Blackfoot and Cheyenne. Otherwise, there won't be any place safe in the High Lonesome for years to come."

Beartooth slapped a big hand against a hamlike thigh. "Whoo-boy, Preacher, that's the biggest mouthful of words I done ever heard out of you."

"Hush up, dang you, Beartooth. Just hush up," Preacher protested.

Disappointment decorated Cora's face. She considered the lives of these rough and ready men and the tales she had heard, sighed and took one of Preacher's hands in both of hers. "Well, if I can't prevail on you to do what's reasonable, the least I can do is part without hard feelings between us. I've never thanked you for saving my life. I want to do so now. Also, there is something I want to give to you before you leave."

"No call for that, ma' . . . er, Miss Cora."

"Yes, there is. I'm sure you are the one who would most appreciate this gift."

"I'll be heading out early tomorrow morning."

"I will rise promptly and see you off," Cora promised.

A thin, silver band, tinged with pink hung over the mountains to the east when Preacher completed his preparation. He had been right sprightly in packing his gear and loading his packhorse. While he had worked the evening before, Beartooth and Nighthawk came to him.

"Now, we've been talkin' this over, an' we allow as how we might just stay the summer and help these good folks over the next winter," Beartooth offered.

Preacher made no effort to hide his amusement. "I reckon as how it might be a good idea, at least for Dupre and Nighthawk here, seein' as how there's some of those gospel-spouter gals that are single. But, you, Beartooth, you're a married man."

"Only in the Cheyenne way. Besides, I wouldn't be untrue to my woman nohow. It's only . . . these folks are so darn thick-headed about so many things. Like be they'd wind up croaked come spring without help. An' you gotta get the

Army to settle down the tribes before it's safe to venture that way."

"Promise me one thing?" Preacher prodded, eyes glittering a zealous fire.

"What's that?" Nighthawk asked.

"That under no conditions, no way, no how, you guide them soul-savers north to the Cheyenne. It could mean the ruination of ever'thing that's good about this country."

Laughing, they struck a bond on that. Now, Preacher tightened the cinch strap on the packsaddle a second time as a soft footfall came to his ear. He turned to see Cora. She held her hands behind him.

"I've come to say goodbye," she offered simply. "I brought you these. As I said, I'm sure you'd be the one to most appreciate them."

She brought from behind her the two cartridge belts and holsters that held the .44 Colt Walker revolvers owned by her brother, whom Preacher had known as Hashknife. His eyes went wide and he blinked to conceal the moisture that formed in them.

"Why, that's mighty nice of you, Miss Cora. It's too fine a gift for the likes of me."

"No it isn't. You explained to me why you adapted yourself to those outlandish four-barreled contraptions. I figure you'd be glad to have the convenience of these."

"Darned if I wouldn't." He reached hesitantly for them, then unbuckled the jury-rigged outfit he had for his multibarrels pistols. "They are fine as frogs' hair. I heard about them for some time now, never seen one before . . . until I faced one. I'll just fit these big ol' things across the pommel of my saddle and wear the Walkers. I can't find words grand enough to thank you, Miss Cora."

"No need to, Preacher." With that, she took three quick steps forward and was in his arms. On tiptoe she pressed her sweet lips to his weathered ones, and kissed him long, deep, and passionately.

When their lengthy embrace ended, Preacher coughed to cover his embarrassment, then gruffly said, "Goodbye, Miss Cora," and swung into the saddle. Twenty minutes later, he still smelled hearts and flowers as he rode swiftly out of the valley and off to add more exploits into the pages of history—a lot of it as yet unwritten.

PREACHER
AND THE
MOUNTAIN CAESAR

1

There's a limit to everything, by dang it, the mountain man known as Preacher fumed to himself. At least that's how he saw it. Birds twittered musically overhead; a fat, white-tailed deer bounded across the meadow in this lush, deep basin. Water burbled, clear and pure, in the narrow stream that cut diagonally through the upper end of the valley and left by way of the entrance gorge to the south. Only marginally on the east side of the Continental Divide, watercourses often did not follow the rule of the land. Tangy pine scented the clear, crisp air, while small puffball clouds floated by overhead.

So, why in tarnation would a body come along and spoil a perfectly relaxful fall? Yet, here they were, five of the most vile, stomach-churning, unwashed, buzzard-pukes Preacher had ever laid eyes upon. Worse, they looked to be fixin' to ruin his peaceful layin' up for winter by settling down in the selfsame valley he had staked out for its high mountain walls to the north, east, and west. Preacher found himself jealous of sharing the sure, swift stream that ran through the middle, and the ample tall, slender fir trees which abounded on the slopes, from which he could make a stout little cabin and enjoy a source of plentiful wood for heat and cooking. No, it wouldn't do, not at all. But despite that, Preacher decided to drop down and invite these hog-dirty, walking, talking slop jars to depart.

* * *

Preacher meandered down to where the scruffy frontier trash had put up a disreputable lean-to, and hashed together a pine bough lodge which would not shed water or keep out the cold. Stupid flatlanders, no doubt, he reasoned as he neared. Preacher halted a goodly distance from the men, who had to be bone-stupid to have not noted his approach, and hollered up at the camp.

"Hello, the camp!"

"Howdy, mister. C'mon in an' fetch up a cup of coffee."

"Thank'e. I'll come in right enough." Preacher came to within three long paces of the rude camp, then screwed a ground anchor and tied his horse to it.

Preacher entered the camp, his posture one of complete dominance. This was his valley, by damn. One of the un-shaven quintet studied their visitor with open curiosity. Only a bit over what passed for average height in these days, the man had an air of power about him. From his broad shoulders and thick chest to his narrow waist, he radiated strength. The man Preacher viewed as an intruder raised a hand in a greeting. "Rest yourself, stranger. There's coffee over yon."

"I'll not be stayin' for coffee, thank you all the same. M'name's Preacher." He noted how their eyes widened at this news. "I come to offer you an invitation."

"That's mighty nice. What's the invite for?"

"I'm askin' you fellers to pack up your gear and be outta my valley before sundown." His gray eyes, they noted, were cold and hard.

Surprised looks came from the five men. Lomax and Phelps grew angry at once. Windy Creek produced a snarl that came off more like a sneer, while Rush and Thumper separated from the others slightly, to get an advantage. Preacher noted all of that and accepted the fact that his invi-tation could be a bit more difficult to deliver than he had anticipated. They showed other obvious signs of how unkindly they took his words.

"Lomax, Windy," barked the only one who had spoken so far. "Looks to me we have to learn this boy some manners."

"You got that right, Phelps," Rusk growled from nearly behind Preacher.

From a similar position at Preacher's left rear, Thumper uttered the wheezing gasp that served him for laughter. "This is gonna be easy, Rusk. All we gotta do is jump on him and hol' him down while Phelps and Lomax work him over a bit."

A low chuckle came from the one Preacher identified as Windy. "Then we take him off with us like we was told. He—he—heee." The sound of his laughter came out even worse than that of Thumper. Preacher raised his big hands, palms up and open. He took a deep breath and sighed aloud as he spoke.

"Well, hell, fellers, if you're set on joinin' the dance, I suppose I have to accommodate."

While they took time to digest the meaning of Preacher's fancy words, he exploded into instant, furious action. He whipped out with one big hand and popped Lomax along the jaw. The contact sounded like a rifle shot. Preacher kept his momentum and spun to snap a hard right fist into the bony chest of Windy Creek. The skinny border rat grunted, and his eyes crossed momentarily.

Preacher followed up with a left to Windy's unguarded cheek. Blood sprayed at the contact. A right cross produced a screeching sound from Windy's mouth that set Preacher's teeth on edge. The spry, if momentarily befuddled, Windy began to spit out teeth as he danced backward. Rusk and Thumper grabbed Preacher from behind the next instant. Preacher raised a heel into Thumper's crotch and got a satisfying squeal of pain in return. Then the punches began to smack into Preacher's middle and face.

Phelps and Lomax closed in, working with the efficiency of steam engines. Lomax, an ugly brute of short stature, pistoned his arms forward and back, pounding Preacher in the belly with hard-knuckled regularity. Phelps, tall and skinny, worked over his crime partner's head, driving cutting, jarring lefts and rights to the planes of Preacher's face. Blood began to flow from a cut high on one cheekbone. A ringing filled Preacher's head as Phelps lopped him one in an ear. Pain exploded in his left eye, and the tissue began to swell immediately. He'd have a good mouse out of that one, Preacher reckoned.

He chose to ignore the efforts of Lomax. The short, pudgy hard case furiously drove his fists into slabs of work-hardened muscle to no effect, save to sap his own energy. Lomax tagged Preacher on the point of his chin, and stars blazed behind the mountain man's eyes. Preacher sucked in a deep breath and shifted position.

"Well, hell," he drawled, "that's about enough of this."

Preacher stomped a high instep on a foot that belonged to Rusk, yanked himself free, and boxed the ears off Lomax. Howling, the squat piece of human debris clapped hands to both ears and spun away from Preacher, to receive a solid kick in the rear as further reward. Eyes widening, Phelps took a step backward and tripped over a snub piece of granite protruding from the grassy turf. He caught a solid punch under the heart that knocked the air from his lungs and momentarily froze his diaphragm. He hit the ground seeing stars and listening to the birdies sing.

Ignoring that pair, Preacher turned his attention toward the remaining three. Rusk, Thumper and Windy Creek stared in confused disbelief. No one man had ever stood up to them like this. Not even just two alone. They had not been told something about this Preacher, the trio immediately suspected. Most of all, how goddamned mean he could be. Rusk, Thumper and Windy Creek exchanged worried glances. Windy was known as a champion free-for-all wrestler. It seemed his responsibility to take care of Preacher. The expressions of the other two said as much.

Windy shrugged his shoulders until they hunched to protect his neck, snuffled, and shifted his feet on the ground. When his partners in crime feinted to distract Preacher, he jumped forward, spread his arms and sought to clasp the wiry mountain man in a ferocious bear hug. Only Preacher was not there.

"Huh?" Windy grunted, then let out a howl as pain exploded in the side of his head.

How had Preacher gotten over there without him seeing it? Windy turned to face the threat, feeling ready now. No time for finesse, he reckoned. He'd just plow right in and throw his man with one massive twist of his shoulders. Or would he get clobbered in the head again?

Much to his surprise, Windy got a good hold on Preacher. He put the point of his shoulder in deep against Preacher's ribs and set his powerful, tree-stump legs. Arms locked at the wrist, he heaved and felt the sudden give as Preacher left the ground. Elation filled Windy as he slammed his opponent down hard on the ground.

Preacher grunted, shook his head and let his mind absorb the pain that radiated from his ribs. It took him only a moment to realize that his assailant lacked the polish and skill of a true grappler. The ancient Greek art of wrestling was better understood by the Cheyenne and the Sioux than by most white men. That gave Preacher a decided advantage as he saw it. He had learned his wrestling from the Cheyenne. While Windy scrabbled to find new purchase, Preacher drew his legs up in front of him.

When his knees reached the middle of his chest, he had Windy humped up like a bison bull mounting a heifer. The illusion lasted only a second, as Preacher put all his effort into violently thrusting his legs outward. A moment's resistance, and then Windy went flying.

Preacher bounded to his feet in time to meet Rusk and Thumper. Rusk caught the brunt of Preacher's fury. Hard fists pounded his chest and gut until Rusk dropped his guard; then Preacher went to work on the youthful, if dirty, face of the junior thug. Rusk's grunts and groans changed to yips of pain. Preacher spread the nose all over Rusk's face a second before Thumper grabbed him.

Thumper had only begun to pull Preacher around when he

got hit low and painfully, an inch above his wide trouser belt. The power in Preacher's punch lifted Thumper off the ground. Before he even had time to wonder where the blow had come from, Preacher sent him into a hazy twilight land. The big, thick-legged mountain man spun around to see what opposition remained.

In that instant, he discovered that the fight had turned serious. Off to one side, Windy Creek held a .70 caliber horse pistol. To Preacher's front, Lomax stood hunched over, breathing hard, and he had a knife out, held low, the edge up in a ripping position. From behind Preacher, Rusk, coughing and retching, pulled a short, ground-down sword. That made the day look a little darker, Preacher reasoned.

"We . . . gonna . . . fix ya . . . for this, ya . . . bastid. You boys," a panting Phelps grunted, "throw down on him. We'll . . . hold him . . . while Lomax . . . carves out his liver." Then he, too, drew a big .70 caliber horse pistol.

Faced with this opposition, Preacher did a quick reappraisal. Confronting the .70 caliber muzzles, and wickedly sharp edges, he found their attitude decidedly hostile. Cranky enough, he reckoned, that he'd best do something about it. He twisted his face into a semblance of amiability and raised a distracting left hand.

"Well, heck, fellers, why'in't you tell me this was supposed to be a gunfight?" With that he dropped his other hand to the smooth walnut butt-grips of one of his marvelous .44 Walker Colt six-shooters and whipped it out with a suddenness that left the others still thinking about what they should do next.

With cold precision, he blasted two of the woolly-eared men into the arms of their Maker. His first two slugs punched into Phelps's chest. He rocked back and sat abruptly on his skinny butt. Preacher ducked and spun, to send two more rounds into the surprised face of Windy Creek. Belatedly, Windy's .70 caliber horse pistol discharged into the ground with a solid thud. Preacher ignored it to turn and menace the remaining simpleton trash.

Rusk and Thumper fired as one. A fat ball moaned past Preacher's ear, low enough to the shoulder that he could feel its wind. He gave the shooter, Thumper, a .44 slug in the hollow of his throat. It landed the thug backward in a heap beside the dying Phelps. Rusk's eyes went wide. He had fired his only barrel and had no time to reload. He gained precious seconds, in which to go for a second pistol in his belt, when Lomax charged with a bellow, his knife at the ready.

"Some of us just never get the word," Preacher said with tired sadness as he shot Lomax squarely in the chest. "A feller never takes only a knife to a gunfight," he explained to the dying man at his feet. Then Rusk fired again.

His bullet cut a thin line along the outside of Preacher's left shoulder. With an empty six-gun in his hand, Preacher dived and rolled for cover behind a fallen tree trunk while he drew a second magnificent .44 Walker Colt, which he had taken off the outlaw named Hashknife a couple of years earlier, and answered Rusk with fatal authority.

Rusk dropped his suddenly heavy pistol and staggered backward. Preacher took the precaution of cocking the Colt again. Then he looked around himself. None of the enemy moved, except the gut-shot Rusk, who moaned and curled up on himself, his legs trembling feebly. Preacher crossed to him. He knelt beside the dirty-faced low-life and spoke with urgency in his voice.

"What brought all that on?"

"Come to get . . . you, Preacher," Rusk panted.

"Why? What got into your heads to do a fool thing like that?"

"We . . ." The dying man's voice took on a cold, haunting note as he gasped out his last words. *"We was sent."* For a short while convulsions wracked the body; then Rusk went stiff, his death rattle sounded and he relaxed into the hands of the Grim Reaper.

Preacher rose slowly, his mind awhirl with puzzlement. "*'We was sent,'*" he repeated. "Now who in tarnation would have a mad-on at me big enough to send five worthless trash bags like that to even a score?" He let the question hang in the warm, late-August air while he went about rounding up the tools needed for grave digging.

No stranger to the process of burial for his fellow man, Preacher much preferred that the task be left to others. For his own part, when he ever gave it thought, Preacher much preferred a Cheyenne or Sioux burial platform when it came time to give up the ghost. Let them deck him out in his finest, lay him on a bed of sweet pine boughs, on a platform made of lodgepole pine saplings and rawhide strips, exposing him before God and man, to let the elements do their best with him.

Preacher had neither wife nor, as far as he knew, living child to mourn him, or to quarrel over any possessions he might leave behind—although he wasn't real certain about the children bit. That's what Preacher hated most about the white man's way of caring for the dead. If a feller had anything to amount to a hill of beans, and had so-called loved ones left behind, getting possession of that hill of beans always made enemies of those who professed to most love the departed. Instead of supporting each other in their mutual loss, they quarreled like greedy children to divide even the clothes the poor feller left behind.

Preacher stopped in his task of digging holes for the hard cases he had fought. Why couldn't they do like the Injuns, and gather to lend support to one another? And in the process, leave a feller in peace? Let him take his most prized belongings with him to *Nah'ah Tishna*—the Happy Hunting Ground? Preacher sighed, wiped a trickle of sweat from his brow and returned to the chore he had given himself.

They came upon him shortly before twilight. An old man, his gray hair hanging to his shoulders, unkempt and stiff from being a long time unwashed. He was brewing coffee at his small camp in a mountain valley when the skinny pair of urchins drifted silently out of the woods and stood staring gauntly at the cooking fire. It took a moment for the old man to notice their presence. When he did, he gave a start and grasped at the left side of his chest.

"Land o' Goshen, youngins. You gave me a real start. Don't you know better than to slip up on a camp like that?" His eyes narrowed with suspicion and unacknowledged alarm. There could be others out there, lurking, to attack when he became distracted.

"We—we got lost," stammered the skinny, yellow-haired boy with the biggest cornflower-blue eyes old Hatch had ever seen.

"Where you from?"

"We—uh—we don't know, 'cause we don't know where we are now," the boy answered evasively.

"Now that ain't any sort of answer. Whereabouts is your home?"

Together they looked at the ground. "Other side of the high mountains. We got took off by some bad folks."

Hatch doubted that. Even so, he pressed for something by which to identify them. "You got names put on you?"

"Yes—yes, we do. I'm Terry, an' this is my sister, Vickie."

Hatch canted his head to one side and made a smile. "Vickie—Victoria, eh? Like the English Queen, huh?"

"I—I suppose so, sir," her sweet young voice responded.

"What's your end handle?" Hatch demanded.

"We—uh—do you mean our last name?" Terry asked.

Hatch studied them closer then. Both were barefoot and in threadbare clothes that were hardly more than rags. They had missed a good many meals; bones stuck out everywhere. Their eyes were a bit too bright, feverish mayhap. The boy had a ferret quality to him, his face narrow, hollow-cheeked, eyes close together; and he was somewhat bucktoothed. He wouldn't look a person directly in the eye, either.

The girl, Victoria, if that was her name, had a precious quality about her. For all her grime and stringy yellow hair, she could smile enough to charm the demons outta perdition. Her figure, although still undeveloped and boyish, held a certain promise. She stood before him now, toes turned in and touching, the hem of her skirt swaying around her knees as she twisted and turned, hands behind her back. Her attitude convinced Hatch.

"There's some extra grub. Welcome to it. But first, you gotta go to the crick and clean up a mite."

"Oh, thank you, sir," Vickie chirped. They started off to the creek hand in hand.

"Hold on there," Hatch called after them. "You can't go in there nekid together. One at a time."

"At home we never have . . . ," Terry blurted, then paused, an expression of nervous wariness flickering across his face. "I mean—er—we never had to do it that way when we had a home."

"Well, you're gettin' too old to jump in bare together. Just do as I say."

They took their turns, looking unhappy about it, then returned to the warmth beside the fire. Hatch handed them plates piled high with stew and fresh, flakey biscuits.

"Go on. Eat hearty. You could use a little meat on those bones."

Eloy Hatch glowed with an unusual contentment when he rolled up in his blankets that night. It made him feel good to do something kind for others. Especially youngsters cut off from hearth and home. Tomorrow he'd see about trimming the lad's hair. Maybe scare up a button or two so's to cover more of their bodies. He might even take them along with him to the trading post, where Ol' Rube would know, if anyone did, where to find them a home.

He drifted off to sleep with these good thoughts. They held him in such deep slumber, until near midnight, that Eloy Hatch never felt a thing when Terry slid the slender knife blade between Eloy's ribs and pierced his heart. When Hatch's death throes ceased, Terry and Vickie quickly stripped the corpse and campsite of all valuables, took the prospector's horses and stole off into the night. Half a mile from the scene of their latest murder and robbery, they paused to embrace. Vickie shivered with the excitement of their bloody handiwork, and her skin was cold to the touch.

Terry quickly warmed her in the shelter of his strong arms. Their eyes got lost in one another's, and they sighed heavily. "But he was *nice*, Terry."

"If we hadn't done it, we'd get a powerful beatin' when we got home, Vic, you know that."

A sigh. "Yes, you're right, Terry." She raised on tiptoe and kissed him on one cheek. It would be all right now, she knew; it would be like always.

2

Face hidden entirely behind the slouch brim of a disreputable, soft, old felt hat, the man moved with exaggerated caution between the lodgepole pines on the northern slope. To his left, another buckskin-clad figure paused, brown eyes searching the terrain from under a skunk-skin cap, a long-barreled Hawken rifle at the ready, until his partner halted behind a large fir tree. Then he went into motion, downhill, for a short distance. He pulled up sharply behind the protruding bulb of a gigantic granite boulder.

The first man advanced again. The loose coat he wore opened in the slight breeze to reveal a barrel chest and a narrow waist, which put a lie to the salt-and-pepper hair that protruded from under the dirty old hat. With practiced ease, they continued to leapfrog to the valley floor. They glanced back up the steep slope. Each tried to figure out how to get the other to offer to make the long climb back to get their horses and pack animals. A voice spoke to them from the cover of the treeline.

"One-Eye, Bart, you boys coulda saved yourselves a passel of extra walking if you'd just rid straight in."

One-Eye Avery Tookes cocked his head to one side. "Preacher? B'God's bones, it is you, ain't it?"

"Alive an' in one piece," Preacher allowed. "An' I saved you the trouble of bringin' those mangy critters down here."

That set well with both visitors. They let out satisfied

bellows when Preacher came into the open, leading their livestock. Then the one Preacher called Bart pursed his thick lips and appraised his old friend with soft, brown eyes.

"We been lookin' for you," Bart Weller advised. He cut his eyes to the fresh mounds of earth and stones close by. The turning of his head caused the tail of his disreputable cap to sway as though alive. "Looks sorta like trouble found you first."

Preacher sighed heavily and rubbed his hands together. "That it did, an' puzzlesome at that. But the tellin' will go better over a pot of coffee an' a bit o' rye." He led the way to his partially constructed cabin and added fuel to the fire in an Indian-style beehive oven-stove combination. He told his old friends about the five men and their actions in the valley. While he talked, the water in the pot came to a boil. Preacher added coffee and an egg shell. One-Eye noted that the shell had considerable size to it and was of a bluish tint. Preacher spotted his curiosity.

"Duck eggs. When I first come into this hole, I found some ducks that liked it rightly enough that they made it a year-round home. Every couple of days, I'd nick an egg from each of the six nests. Et the eggs, saved the shells for coffee. Nothin' settles grounds quite so good. Now, as I was tellin' ya," Preacher said launching back into his account of the scruffy intruders.

While he talked, he paid close attention to his visitors. He had known Bart Weller longer. Why, from way back at the Rendezvous in '27, he thought. Didn't seem that his hair had a strand more of gray in it than the day they'd met. A quiet fellow, he had already partnered up with One-Eye Avery Tookes before the Rendezvous. Been together ever since. One-Eye Avery was a legend all to himself.

Of an age with Preacher and, like that venerable mountain man, one of the last of the breed, he had not sacrificed an eye to obtain his High Lonesome moniker. Indeed, he still had the clear, light blue orbs with which he had been born. The first white man who, in a drunken rage, had attacked a then much younger Avery Tookes had been bent on snuffing out the life of the adventurous, youthful trapper. Avery had defended himself admirably, until the huge brute got him in a bear hug. Not eager to kill the man, Avery had resorted to his only other line of offense. He had gouged out the man's eye with a long, thick thumbnail. Howling, the lout had given up, and Avery answered the questions as to why he had not finished the job with the remark that he reckoned one eye was enough. His newfound friend, Preacher, had promptly dubbed him Ol' One-Eye.

That had been years ago, yet both men had maintained their health and strength. If you saw them from behind, it would be difficult to distinguish one man from the other. From the front, One-Eye's big, bulbous red nose was a sure giveaway. Tookes had invited Preacher to spend the season trapping with him and his partner. Preacher knew Bart Weller to be a man with plenty of sand, and more knowledge about beaver than any human should possess. He had readily agreed, and they had spent the next three seasons together. Like it so often happened, they'd drifted apart at one Rendezvous, only to make infrequent contact over the years. Now, here they were in his valley. He decided to ask them why.

Bart studied that for a while, then made a reply. "Well, we come across several collections of similar trash. Most been headin' northwest, into Wyoming country."

"Wonder what this batch meant by being sent?" One-Eye asked.

"That sort of has me in a hassle, too," Preacher admitted. "Just who an' why would someone send such unclean riffraff into the High Lonesome?"

Bart swept the skunk-skin cap off his head and ran fingers through his thick mane of hair. "Lord knows the place is too crowded as it is." He paused, thought a moment. "You did say these unsavory lads had been sent to get you, right?"

"Right as rain, Bart. I'm flattered someone thought it necessary to send five fellers, but I'm damned if I can put a name to who it might be. Why don't you two light a spell, get rested. Maybe in a day or two we can figger out what this is all about."

One-Eye patted his belly. "Suits. You bein' such a good cook an' all. An' we got some other tall tales to tell. Just for an instance, Bart an' me done heard of some place in the far off; supposed to have a bunch of shiny white buildings. A right colorful sight, I'd say."

Preacher shot him a frown. "You got it all wrong, One-Eye. White is the absence of all color." That set them all to guffawing, and Preacher set out the Monongahela.

Three mangy, woolly-eared drifters crested a rise in the Ferris Mountains of Wyoming. They had barely raised their heads to the horizon when they halted abruptly, thunderstruck by what they saw. The one in the center mopped his thick, gaping lips and smacked his mouth closed noisily. He shook his head in an attempt to clear his vision. He saw the seven hills, with their buildings in various stages of construction.

"All them purty buildin's," the sallow-faced lout on his left said in an awed tone.

"What you reckon they's here for, Hank?"

Henry Claypool, the one in the middle, wiped his mouth again and stared across the wide, deep basin. "Don't rightly know, Jase. There's one thing I do know. They don't rightly belong here."

"But we was *told* . . . ," the shallow-faced Jason Grantling bleated.

"I know what we was told, idjit. I didn't expect nothin' like this, though. But, yep, this is the place all right, the one we was told to find."

"Who ever saw a place like this?" the flatland trash on Hank's right asked.

"Ain't got a clue, have you, Turnip Head? I'd say we done took a step back in time."

Turnip Head, whose real name was Alvin Wooks, and

Jason Grantling stared at Hank Claypool as though he had lost his mind.

"H-how you come to mean that?" the slightly dumber Alvin Wooks asked.

Impatient, Hank gigged his horse forward. "I say we ride down and find out for ourselves."

Negotiating the inner slope of the basin proved easier than had the ascent. The smell of rich, fresh grass made their mounts frisky, their tails up and flying in the stout breeze that blew from the far-off structures. It brought with it the tangy scent of raw pine boards. At the foot of the incline, Hank and his companions were forced to rein in abruptly once more.

This time, a group of burly, hard-faced men confronted them. They all carried long poles that looked like spears and had funny round, knobby leather hats fastened on their heads by thick straps with cheek pieces that had been shaped like large leaves.

"Oh-oh, what kind of clothes is them?" Jason asked in a worried whisper.

Silas Tucker peered nearsightedly at the trembling pair before him. Tobacco juice stained his full, pouting lips and discolored the scraggly beard that surrounded the ugly hole of his mouth. He cut his shoe-button black eyes from one child to the other, despising their pale complexions, fair hair and cornflower blue eyes. Didn't look like any kids of his at all—at all. His gaze went over their shoulders to where Faith stood in the doorway of the tumble-down cabin he and his women had labored to erect three summers past.

He'd managed sure enough to stamp every one of the brats he'd given her. How had that peaked Purity managed to override his dark, hill people's blood? Course what with Faith bein' his younger sister, the blood held true, didn't it? Then there were these two. Cotton tops, with their mother's coloring and eyes. But, she sure was a good romp in bed. Li'l Faith hadn't had that much energy since she had given birth to their oldest at thirteen. That was when Pop had run him and Faith off, clean out of the Appalachian country.

"Cousins is fine and good, but yer sisters are jist for practicin' yer plowin', not plantin' a crop," the old man had bellowed when he shooed the shame-faced pair off the rocky hillside that constituted their farm. Well, hell, this place wasn't any better. Biggest crop each year was rocks. Now he had to make sure these ghost-pale kids of his an' Purity didn' leave anything behind at the old man's campsite that could be traced to him. His expression grew stony, and he pinned the boy with those obsidian orbs.

"Tell it again, Terry. You sure this pilgrim ain't gonna go to Trout Crick Pass an' yap to the law?"

"Ye—yes, sir. I done slid that pig-sticker in betwixt his ribs like you showed me."

"D'ya thrash it around like I said?" Silas asked from the depths of his shrewdness.

Silas knew himself to be a dimwit, due to the inbreeding in his family, or at least that was what that circuit-ridin' doctor had said about the whole passel of Tuckers in the hills back home. But he also knew he was as shrewd as the next feller. More so than a lot. Now he watched with a growing dread as the boy blanched even whiter with guilty knowledge.

"I—ah—I—er . . . forgot."

Rough and horny from hard work, the right hand of Silas Tucker popped loudly off the downy cheek of the frightened cherub in front of him. Tears sprang to Terry's eyes.

"Dangit, boy! How's we's supposed to stay safe if you keep forgetting the most important part?"

Long hours, days, even weeks alone in the wilderness had given Terry a new sense of self-worth, of independence. It prompted him to an unwise decision at this point. "Maybe . . . maybe if you'd come along and do some of the dirty work for a change, we'd be a whole lot safer."

Silas Tucker had the boy's trousers down and the child

bent over his knee in one swift move. His belt hissed out of its loops, and he used it expertly to flail at Terry's exposed bottom. Bravely, the lad resisted the impulse to scream out his pain and humiliation. Not so, his sister. Vickie shrieked, stamped her small feet on the hard ground, and pounded ineffectual little fists on the back of Silas Tucker.

"Stop it! Stop it! You're hurting him," she wailed.

"That's what I.damn well intend to do, Missy. An' if you don't shut up, you'll git yours next." He did stop, after seven strokes that left angry red welts on the pale flesh of Terry's posterior. "All right. Here's how it's gonna be. You'll both go to bed without any supper for the next week. Bread and water twicest a day is all you see otherwise. The next time you go out, you make sure you stick those fellers good an' proper. Wouldn't do for word to go around that Silas Tucker's brood is doin' sloppy robberies. Now, go. Get out of my sight. An' you best yank up them britches before you give your sister bad ideas," Silas added with a lewd wink.

Hurt and shamed, Terry did as he had been bade. He and Vickie knew all about what Silas had so nastily hinted at. They knew it went on among their half brothers and sisters. For them it had never held an appeal. Each loved the other and had had to look out for one another for as long as they remembered. They didn't have time for that sort of foolishness. Besides, the Good Book said it was evil. Oh, they had read the Bible all right, only in secret.

None of the rest of the Tuckers could string three letters together to make a word, let alone read. And Silas—Poppa—hotly cursed the Bible and preachers in general all the time. He claimed that man had been put on the earth to take his pleasures where he wished, and that book-learnin' an' religion got in the way of that something fierce. Only went to show, Silas didn't know everything about anything. Terry had wiped away the last of his tears by the time they got to the cabin. Their momma, Purity, stopped them and asked what had happened and what Silas had decided.

"We got punished for not makin' sure of that last pilgrim we robbed. Sila—Poppa says we get no supper for a week, an' we have bread and water only for our other meals," Terry reluctantly revealed.

Inwardly, he was thinking: *If only there were some way we could leave here and not come back. If we could just he free forever.* Terry had no way to know that his sister shared her version of the same desire, or that the opportunity to escape lay just beyond the next couple of ranges.

One-Eye Tookes and Bart Weller bent over the large cast-iron skillet, biscuit halves in hand, to mop up the last of the pan drippings left from the fresh venison steaks Preacher had fried for their breakfast. The tender meat had gone well with cornmeal mush and fried potatoes and onions. Avery Tookes glanced up from his efforts and eyed the surroundings.

"Mighty larrupin', Preacher. Course it woulda been better iffin we had some aiggs. Why don't you get you some chickens and keep a store of aiggs'?"

For a brief moment, Preacher eyed One-Eye, uncertain if he was funnin' or not. "I ain't no farmer, One-Eye. Ain't made to chase after some old Dominickers or Rhode Island Reds. Let nature provide, I alus say."

Orneriness twinkled in the pale blue orbs of One-Eye Tookes. "Couldn't be that you're too lazy to tend to some measly chickens, could it?"

Preacher popped upright, spluttered, cussed and slammed his hat on the ground. "Lazy, is it? Who cooked that breakfast to feed your worthless hide and bottomless belly?"

One-Eye patted the slight mound at his middle and produced a fond smile. "And right good it was, Preacher. I'm obliged I didn't have to wrassel you for it, like I hear some visitors got to do."

Steam escaped from Preacher. "That ain't true. Not a word of it. I've never begrudged a man a bite to eat, iffin he be friendly." He drew up suddenly. "Say, who was it told you I made a body fight for his meal?"

Tookes looked him straight in the eyes. "Bloody Hand Kreuger, that's who."

"That Kraut is a liar, plain and simple. An' I'd say it to his face if he was present to hear it. There's a bit of—ah—bad blood betwixt us. Has been for a few years now. I ride my trails, an' he rides his. We both like it that way."

One-Eye wouldn't let it go. "Might be he knows something about these strange doin's in the High Lonesome. Story is he's been up north the last couple of years. That bein' where all this riffraff is headed, he could be the key to what's goin' on."

Preacher made a face. "I'd as soon kiss a wolverine as be beholdin' to Karl Kreuger by askin' him about it."

Both guests came to their boots and ankled it over to their already loaded packhorses. They adjusted the cinch straps while speculating further on the meaning behind the recent intrusions. Tookes summed it up for the three of them.

"You ask me, it's gonna mean trouble. Too many of those light-in-the-saddle types driftin' up outta Texas ain't good for man nor beast. They all think they're good with a gun and proddy as Billy-be-damned. If we run across Bloody Hand, you don't mind if we ask him what he knows, do ya, Preacher?"

"Nope. Go right ahead. You ask me, though, I say we'll learn what is going on soon enough anyhow."

Bart Weller, the worrier of the partners, agreed, then added, "We should hope we don't learn of it to our regret."

Arms tightly around each other, Terry and Vickie clung close together. Each could feel the warmth of the other through their thin nightshirts. There was nothing arousing about it, only comforting. They were too bony; Terry knew that for certain. Far too little to eat. He and Vickie were always treated like outcasts. As though they did not belong to the family. When he had been littler, they had both cried about that. Now he was too old for things like that.

He had to find a way for them to get something more out of life than stealing and lying and sneaking around. He refused to think about the killing. He hugged his sister tightly and whispered in her ear. "Are you awake?"

"Yep. So are you," Vickie observed with the logic of a ten-year-old.

"I hate it here," Terry muttered softly.

"So do I," Vickie agreed.

Terry gathered courage. "Sometimes I think the thing we best do is to run away for real."

Vickie stiffened, her eyes suddenly bright in the starlight that seeped through the tiny window in their loft room. "Do you mean it, Terry? Really mean it?"

"Y-yes, I do. D-do you want to?"

"We . . . could try. When? Oh, when, Terry?"

Terry gave that considerable thought. "Why not the next time Poppa sends us out? We could go and just keep going."

"To where?"

"Somewhere. Anywhere. We could find something."

Vickie had become quite agitated. Her slender form trembled against that of her brother. "Let's do it. *Please*, let's do it."

After a long moment, Terry answered in a hollow whisper. "All right, we will."

Chance decided it in the end. Philadelphia Braddock had been of several minds as to where to go for the approaching winter. He had a standing invite from two old friends who had a tidy cabin on the Snake River. They put out a good table, what with smoked salmon, plenty of elk and venison, a root cellar full of camas bulbs, wild onions, yucca root, some grown turnips and other eatables. Yet, they also kept a pouch of juniper berries to flavor the raw, white liquor they distilled each summer for the following cold time.

When they drank that awful stuff, they got snake-pissin' mean. Philadelphia could not count the number of times he had been caught up in one of their brawls. The two of them spent most of each winter covered with lumps and bruises. And Lord help the outsider who strayed within range of their fists. Naw, he concluded. He'd best avoid that situation.

He also had a standing welcome from the Crow to visit them in Montana Territory. They had always been friendly to the whites exploring in their land. He even knew he would have a nice, tractable bed warmer to occupy his lodge. Only Philadelphia reckoned as how he had more than his share of half-Crow youngsters runnin' around the High Plains already. No need to build another.

That left him with the long journey to Bent's Fort. In this late year of eighteen and forty-eight, the place was but a pale shadow of its past glory. Only two factors remained, neither of them related to the Bent brothers. There'd be whiskey. Good, clean whiskey, aged in barrels and filtered through charcoal. But a winter there would cost him an arm and a leg. The soft, deerskin pouch around his neck still hung with respectable weight, but the gold would be soon gone at Bent's. Better pass that up for another day.

Which brought him to his final choice. He could head southeast and check out the Ferris Mountains in Wyoming. If that didn't suit, and the weather held, he could go on south to Trout Creek Pass. There, he had heard, some of the good old boys had taken to hanging out over the cold months. He could jaw a little, play cards and checkers, and have a warm bunk to roll up in at night. No pliable Crow girl, nor any hard floosie, for that matter, but a comfort to a man getting on in his years.

By jing! That's just what he would do. Check out the rumors about a man willing to pay out real gold for fighting men in the Ferris Range; then, if it didn't pan out, he'd go on to Colorado country and the High Lonesome. He might even run into his old sometime partner, Preacher. What with the fur trade all but moribund, Preacher and some of the old boys had taken to hanging a mite closer to civilized living. Might be he could benefit by that, too.

Philadelphia Braddock clucked to his packhorse and yanked on the rope around its neck. Long ride to Trout Creek, but only a day or two now to this outfit in the Ferris Mountains. He'd give them a took-see—that's what he'd do.

3

Three days later, in a wide valley, set off by seven low hills, Philadelphia Braddock stumbled upon a sight he could not believe. Alabaster buildings shined from the crests of several of the seven hills that clustered in the upland vale. It became obvious to Philadelphia that some serious construction work was going on along the slopes of the three still vacant hills. Flat, layered plane trees had replaced the usual aspen, and tall, slender pines, of a blue-gray color Philadelphia had never seen before, lined a wide white cobblestone roadway that led from the south end of the basin to tall gates in what looked like a plastered stone wall that surrounded a portion of the four occupied hills. From his angle, Philadelphia could not tell if the rampart ran all the way around. This was one whing-ding of a puzzler.

He had never heard of any settlement sprouting up in the Ferris Mountains. Certainly nothing like this. Why, it was a regular city. "I'll be blessed," he said aloud to his horse.

The animal replied with a snort and shake of its massive head. A spray of slobber put diamonds in the air. A peremptory stomp of a hoof drew Philadelphia's attention to a knot of men who broke off from the workers, one of them pointing in his direction. Too far off to see details, the former trapper decided to wait them out. When they drew nearer, he noted that the men wore bright red capotes—no, he corrected himself, longer than the ubiquitous mountain man garb, more like cloaks. A horseman joined them.

"Odd-looking fellers," Braddock advised his mount, while he patted the visibly nervous beast with one hand to calm it.

When they came even closer, he saw that they wore over-skirts of leather strips studded with brass knobs. Below that, they wore short skirts. For a giddy moment, Philadelphia wondered if they might be sissies. On their heads they had brown, leather-covered pots of some sort. Odder still, he noted, they carried lances and shields, like Injuns. He changed his examination of the approaching men to the one on horseback.

Wasn't he a sight! He had an even longer capote, scarlet in color, with shiny brass coverings on his legs, chest and helmet—for that's what it was, bright red roach of horsehair and all. The polished cheek pieces were shaped something like oak leaves. Then Philadelphia made out another feller, who jogged along behind the horse. He held some sort of long pole with a big metal banner on top. On closer examination, Braddock saw that it was an eagle, with spread wings, head turned in profile, and something written under it.

Now, old Philadelphia wasn't too strong on reading, but he could make out his letters as good as any man. These read: *S.P.Q.R.*

Within seconds, the rider reined up right close to Philadelphia, rudely crowding his space. He pulled a short, leaf-bladed sword and pointed it somewhere above Braddock's head. "Hold, there, barbarian!" the man bellowed with all the officiousness of a government man in a swallowtail coat. "What business have you in Nova Roma?"

From habit, Philadelphia made the plains sign for coming in peace as he spoke. "I was only lookin' for a place to hole up for winter. An' I ain't no barbarian."

Glowering, the challenger proved arrogant enough to not need to consult anyone about his opinion. *"This* is not the place. Unless you bear a scroll of safe passage, you are trespassing on the territory of Nova Roma."

Philadelphia's forehead furrowed. "I ain't got no paper on me."

His interrogator motioned two men forward with his sword as he spoke. "Then you are under arrest. You will be put to work with the rest of the slaves, to build our magnificent city."

Philadelphia Braddock did not like that one bit. His eyes narrowed. "Is that so? How long do you reckon I'll be doin' that?"

"Until you prove your worth to be a citizen of Nova Roma."

"That long, huh?" Philadelphia followed his first instinct.

His reins given a turn around the saddle horn, Braddock moved swiftly, hands closing around the handstocks of a brace of .64 caliber Chambers horse pistols. He yanked them free before any of the startled soldiers could react. The muzzles centered on the two closest to him, and he blazed away.

Loud, flat reports shattered the bird-twittering silence, and twin smoke clouds obscured everything for a moment. His actions served his purpose, Philadelphia observed as the greasy gray mass whipped away on a light breeze. The two who were to arrest him lay on the ground, writhing, shot X-wise through their right shoulders. The footmen had scattered, and the snarling leader had been put to flight.

"Appears to me you need a lesson in manners, fellers," Braddock told them.

Satisfied with the results, Philadelphia reholstered the discharged pistols and slid his Hawken rifle free of its scabbard. With a final, careful appraisal of his would-be foe, he turned the head of his mount to the south and started off, away from this inhospitable place. By then, one of the footmen had recovered himself enough to spring up on his sandals and cock his arm, the hand holding his pilum behind his right ear. He let the spear fly with deadly accuracy.

Sharp pain radiated through Braddock's right shoulder as the smooth point penetrated flesh and bone and pinned his shoulder blade to his ribs. Stunned by the sudden, enormous pain, Philadelphia nevertheless managed to swivel at the hips and bring up his Hawken. Leveled on his assailant's chest, Braddock cocked and triggered the weapon. The big, fat .56 caliber conical bullet smashed through the soldier's sternum and ripped a big hole in his aorta.

His sandals left the ground, and he crashed backward head over heels, to sprawl in the dirt. His valiant heart rapidly pumped the life from his body. Philadelphia Braddock did not wait to check his results, though. He put boot heels to the heaving flanks of his mount and sprinted for the distant pass that opened on the white cobblestone roadway.

With each thud of a hoof, new agony shot through Philadelphia's body. The lance flopped wildly up and down, caught in his muscular back. He did not stop, though, until safely beyond the crest of the ridge. Then he scabbarded his Hawken and painfully wrenched the pilum from the wound it had made. His last thought was, *What the hell did I stumble into?* Only then did he allow himself to pass out.

Preacher began his morning with the usual grumping about, slurping coffee too hot and strong to bear for normal persons, and a lot of scratching. He interspersed these activities with a lick of a brown wooden lead pencil and careful application of it to a scrap of precious paper.

He preferred the newfangled gypsum plaster for chinking logs in his cabin walls. Clay mud did all right, he allowed, but often came with an unwelcome harvest of bugs. He also needed some nails to hold door and window frames together and to build furniture for his digs. When he saw the size of his list, he decided to call it a day for the work in progress and head off for Trout Creek Pass and the trading post.

He could also pick up flour, cornmeal, beans, sugar and more coffee beans. With the meat he had already killed, dressed out and smoked, he figured to be set for the long, cold months just around the corner. But he would also have to get a bag of salt. He had not as yet built a corral, so he had to chase down his hobbled mount, the big roan, Cougar, and the sorrel gelding packhorse. That accomplished, he carefully stored all his supplies safely out of the way of raccoons, bears, and wolves alike, and departed. He didn't even cast a casual glance over the graves of those who had so recently come to kill him.

Slowly, the late-summer, pale blue sky frosted over with a thin skein of high cirrus clouds. At first, Preacher paid it no mind. The weather often did this in late August. An hour later, the leaden overcast had blotted out the sun and brought a single worry that furrowed Preacher's brow. What the heck. It was too early to snow, he felt certain of that.

Fat, black bellies slid low over the highest peaks an hour and a half later, the temperature had dropped twenty degrees, and Preacher began to worry about how close winter really was with this harbinger of a late-August snowstorm. Odd, he considered. Even a tenderfoot counted on snow not beginning in the High Lonesome before September.

Had his mental calendar slipped a cog? No, not likely. Shoot, the big, gray Canadian honkers had not yet put in their annual appearance far below and beyond the eastern slopes of the Shining Mountains. What a joy they were to observe from on high, their heavily populated vee formations winging their way south for the winter. With the same regularity they used to hail the approach of the cold, each spring they were also the first heralds of warm weather returning. Yet, it seemed that this time nature had outsmarted even them.

Tiny flakes, invisible to the eye, began to land on Preacher's face and the backs of his hands. Cold and wet, they did not remain for long. Their bigger brothers and sisters would be along soon enough for that, Preacher reasoned. He began to take closer note of his surroundings. One of these northers could blow up in a matter of minutes, and a man caught in the open would soon be buzzard meat. Temperatures could, and often did, drop forty degrees in less than ten minutes.

Given that this late in August, the high for the day hovered

around forty-eight to fifty, that could have fatal results.
Memory played its map pages in his mind. A ways farther
south, he knew, there was an old cabin, part of a failed mining
attempt. Beyond that, in a rocky gorge, another small cabin
fronted a natural cave. Preacher had often wanted to poke
around in there, only to have circumstances get in the way. He
would put his trust in his own instincts and see how far he got.

For, no matter what he hoped for, he knew dang well it was
going to snow. "Best eat some ground, Cougar," he advised
his trustworthy mount.

The invisible flakes changed to freezing rain half a mile
along the trail toward Trout Creek Pass. Preacher broke out a
sheepskin jacket and bundled up, the collar pulled high. His
breath came in frosty plumes. Cougar snorted regular clouds
of white. No question, this one would be a heller.

Fat, wet flakes drifted downward, twirled by the flukey
breeze that sent them skyward again, or into spirals that
danced vertically across the ground. Little cold pinpricks
where they lighted on the exposed skin of Preacher, they
grew steadily in number. Before he could account the time,
Preacher observed that the horizon ahead of him had been
curtained off by a swirling wall of gray-white.

In a place where visibility usually stretched on forever,
unless impeded by a mountain peak, Preacher could not see
even half a mile off. And, dang it, he'd been caught out away
from any of the shelters he knew of. Better than two miles to
the cave, about three-quarters of a mile to the mine. He took
time to wrap a bandana around his head, tied it under the
chin, to protect his ears, plopped his hat on his head again and
turned up his collar.

"Cougar," he advised his roan horse, "we're deep in the
buffalo chips if we don't find shelter. Just keep a-movin', boy."

Over the next half hour, the snowstorm turned into a regular, full-blown blizzard. Preacher remained silent through
the ordeal, batting his eyelashes rapidly to blink away the

clinging flakes that settled after icily caressing his face. Only the largest tree trunks stood out as black slashes in the thick, wild gyration of white. So dense was the downfall that he almost missed the cabin over the mineshaft when he at last came to it.

Preacher saw the reason for that soon enough. Over the years, the abandoned place had sagged to a ruin that more resembled a raw outcrop of rock than a man-made structure. No relief from the storm here, right enough, Preacher regretfully realized. He must push on for the cave, and hope that last year's thunderstorms and resulting fires had not destroyed the cabin there.

Numbness had crept into Preacher's fingers and toes a quarter hour later when he stopped to pull a thick pair of wool socks over his feet and return them to the suddenly chilled boots. Fool, he chided himself. He should have thought to bring along gloves. Or those rabbit-fur mittens, a leftover from the previous winter.

His world had become a wall of white now. To rely on dead reckoning to navigate from one place to another was to lead oneself astray, Preacher reminded himself. And to stay where he was invited a slow death by freezing. He had heard most of his life that it was peaceful, going that way. Then he snorted with derision. Who in hell had ever come back to tell about how easy it was?

Just keep Mount Elbert on my right shoulder, Preacher repeated over and over in a sort of chant. For all its size, the mountain loomed a dark gray, rather than the usual green-shrouded black. In fits and starts it disappeared entirely in the whirl of dancing snow. Preacher rode on, the comforting tug of the lead rope of his packhorse against his left thigh. In that blind world, all sense of time abandoned him.

Whenever he opened his heavy coat to check his timepiece, the resultant small movement of his hands jolted him. The numbness began again in his feet. *Frostbite!* The terribly real possibility of it ate at his vitals. His ears alternately burned and tingled with awful cold. They would be affected first. Preacher ground his teeth and urged Cougar onward. At last his fat old Hambleton registered the passage of an hour. His goal had to be near. Each breath of man and beast brought forth clouds of white. The wind increased steadily.

Preacher found himself leaning into it and realized with a start that he must have somehow circled, for the wind had been at his back from the beginning of the storm. How long had he ridden away from the safety of the cave? Accustomed, over long years in the High Lonesome, to suppressing desperation, he fought back the welling of panic from deep in his gut. Turn around, find Mount Elbert, and carry on.

It sounded so easy. Something a man could do in a fraction of a minute. But not in this raging blizzard. Preacher reversed himself easily enough. Then, try as he might, he could not find the nearby peak. Lowering clouds scudded through the snow now and blanked out everything. All he could think of was to keep going.

Another half hour crawled by, and Preacher began to note a lessening in the density of the snowfall. To his right the dark gray mass of Elbert swam out of the maelstrom. Reoriented once more, Preacher struck off a couple of points to the west of due south. At least by his reckoning, that's what he did. Within a hundred heartbeats, a darker, regular shape showed itself intermittently through the gyrating clots of flakes. Preacher's eyes stung and burned, and he blinked away more snow that assailed his face. Was that it?

Had he made it to his objective? A dark smear resolved into a straight, black line. A few labored paces farther, another smooth slash joined the other at a steep angle. A roofline, by God! Reserves of strength sent a warm flush through the cold body of Preacher. He could not contain the anxiety of his tormented flesh. He leaned forward in the saddle and peered intently.

Yes! There she stood, the tiny cabin perched on a shelf above the floor of the gorge. He had found his refuge. Straining his eyes, Preacher picked out the start of the ledge that led to the eroded cutback and the so welcome sight of the tiny cabin. He kneed Cougar toward it, hardly feeling the touch of his legs against the ribs of the horse. They made five small paces forward; then Cougar floundered in a snowbank.

With a frightened whinny, the animal sank to its neck in a hidden wash that paralleled the hillside. Preacher nearly pitched out of the saddle. He held on though and bent forward to scoop away enough of the powder to free Cougar's shoulders. Next he worked a space that would allow him to apply a touch of spur. Cougar responded with a burst of nervous energy that sent a plume of snow above his rider's head. The roan's rear haunches bunched, and he plowed forward in a succession of sheets of white.

Gradually Cougar gained a purchase and surged onto the narrow ledge. Squealing in confused fright, the packhorse followed. In what seemed no time at all to Preacher, he reined up in front of the low, crudely made hut. Painfully, he dismounted. First, he eased an icy .44 Colt Walker from the holster and tried the small people's door. He found it unlatched and it opened easily.

The whole front of the cabin swung outward, Preacher recalled, to give access to horses. He pulled the wooden pegs that held the structure together and eased the facing wall out enough to allow his animals to enter. Out of the direct wind, it felt a lot warmer. He used a lucifer to light a torch, and took note of signs of recent occupancy.

Dry wood had been stacked by a stone stove, which showed a residue of burned-out coals. The cobwebs had been cleared above a double bunk on one wall, and over the single one opposite. He led his animals farther back, where he found evidence of more ancient residents. Petroglyphs carved and painted into the walls of the cave spoke of visits by early man, hunt stories, and some sort of ritual. They made the hairs rise at the nape of Preacher's neck.

After he had secured Cougar and the packhorse, unsaddled them and rubbed them down, he returned to the cabin portion. He quickly kindled a fire, retrieved his cooking gear from one of the parfleches on the pack frame and set to boiling coffee, made from snow scooped up outside. Real warmth flooded the secure little shelter.

When the first cup of strong, black brew had become a thing of the past, Preacher shredded thin strips from a dry-cured venison ham into a skillet and brought out a scrupulously clean bandana, into which he had tied half a dozen biscuits. He chose two and set them to warm on the rock beside the gridiron over the stove. A little grease from a crock, some dried hominy from a bag he soaked in a small clutch oven, and Preacher considered himself to be in hog heaven.

He poured another cup of coffee and settled back to enjoy it. Exhausted from his fight to resist the cold and battle the storm, Preacher's head began to droop. His chin had all but touched his chest when he jerked upright suddenly. What was that he had heard?

He thought chirping birds had disturbed his sleep. Yet, the storm still raged outside, and night was fast coming on. Birds did not twitter in such conditions. There. He heard it again. Preacher came to his boots and edged closer to the front of the cabin.

A more careful listen and the chirpings resolved into human voices. *Small* human voices. Little kidlet voices. Preacher reached up to wipe the astonishment off his face. What in Billy-be-damned would brat-kids be doing wandering around in such a blizzard?

Taking a covered, kerosene lantern from his pack rig, Preacher lighted it and bundled up before stepping out into the storm. He found it greatly reduced, the wind down and the snow light streaks in the twilight gloom. The voices came from below him. He could make out the words now.

"Help! Someone help us!"

"We're gonna freeze out here, I just know it."

"Oh, please, help. Hello! Someone, anyone, help us!"

Preacher investigated the ledge and found it still passable. He raised his lantern on high and called to the youngsters below. "Hello. Stay where you are. I'll come to you."

"Oh, thank you. Thank you, thank you, thank you," a squeaky voice babbled.

Within five minutes, Preacher had descended and located the children. They shivered and shook, and hugged him, fighting back tears. They stiffened, though, when Preacher asked their identity.

"I-I'm Terrance," the slightly built boy replied in a gulp.

"I'm Victoria."

Preacher forced a scolding frown. "What are a couple of babies like you doing out here in this storm?"

Terrance shoved out a thin lip in a pink pout. "I'm not a baby. I'm twelve."

"Well, loo-di-doo. What about you, girlie?"

"I'm ten. Terrance is my brother. We're cold, mister."

"You can call me Preacher. C'mon, I've a warm place up yonder, and some victuals if you're hungry."

Terrance's eyes widened, and he put a hand to his stomach. "Are we? We're starved."

Preacher led them back, moving as swiftly as he could in the drifted snow. He had taken note, in the lantern light, of their pale skin and blue-tinged lips. Both children shivered so violently, they appeared to be caught in some sort of seizure. Once secure inside the cabin, he poured them cups of coffee and urged them to drink. Their coats were threadbare, hardly more than rags. Terrance had strips of cloth wrapped around his feet instead of boots or shoes.

Recalling a pair of moccasins in his kit, Preacher rose and turned to both shaking youngsters. "Now, you strip outta them clothes, down to your long johns, and get close to the fire."

Victoria flushed a deep red. "We ain't got no long johns, not any kind of underclothes."

"Well, then, wrap up in blankets and skin outta your

clothes. They need to be warmed and dried. For you, boy, I got a pair of moccasins. They's a tad mite too small for me, an' I figger you'll be able to swim in 'em. But, they're rabbit-fur-lined and a lot warmer than those rags."

Terrance lowered long, blond lashes over wide, pale blue eyes. "I'd be obliged, mister."

"Call me Preacher. Ev'ryone else does."

Terrance snapped his head upward at that. For all his furtive, rodentlike manner, he stared wide-eyed now at Preacher. "Gosh. You're famous."

It became Preacher's turn to blush. "Some fool folks try to make it that way. But, I was alus just tryin' to do my job as I saw fit. Let me git them moccasins, an' then I'll rustle you up some grub."

He turned away to do as he had promised. The fire's warmth, the food, and hot coffee did their job. The children became more animated. When Preacher considered them past the point of desperation, and relaxed enough to answer sensibly, he opened a little inquiry into their background.

"I know you said you were Terrance and Victoria. Only, what's your last name?"

Terrance gave him that now-familiar ferret stare. "Are you a real preacher? A Bible-thumper?"

"Nope. I reckon I'm about as far away from that sort as a man can get. Though I do consider myself on good speakin' terms with the Almighty."

"What's your name, then?" Terrance challenged.

Preacher hesitated a moment. "Arthur's m'given name."

"What's your family name?" the boy persisted.

The mountain man puzzled over that a while. "Well, by dang, if I don't think I've plumb forgot it. Folks have called me Preacher for so long, it's sort of stuck."

Terrance brightened. "Then, I reckon that's the case with us. We don't know what our family name is . . . or even if we've got one." He gave Preacher a "so there" look.

"I'll buy that. Now, tell me, how come you were out in that tempest?"

"That what?" Victoria asked, puzzlement on her wide, clear face.

"How'd you come to be out in that blizzard?'

Terrance took up the answers. "We've been wandering around for days—weeks now. Those we were travelin' with got lost in the woods. They stumbled around, and the food got real short," the boy continued, his expression one of far-off construction. "When they runned clean out, they abandoned us. Just dropped us off in a canyon one day."

Preacher scowled. That didn't ring true. "Who were these folks?"

Terrance scrunched his high, smooth brow. "Some real mean fellers. They—they stole us from our home far, far away."

This had begun to sound to Preacher like one of those melodramas in one of the penny dreadfuls. "An' I suppose they made you do all sorts of awful things?"

"Ye—yes, sir," Terrance acknowledged.

Preacher's flinty eyes bored into the boy. "Like what?"

Terrance flinched. "No—nothin' below the belt. Me an' Vickie wouldn't allow that."

"If they were that mean, what choice would you have?" Preacher taunted, having not the least interest in pursuing the salacious topic he had introduced. He merely wanted a means of verifying the boy's truthfulness.

"They—they really weren't that mean until they got lost and ran short on food. One time they made us rob a cabin that the folks were away from. Another, they offered to sell us to some Injuns." Preacher noted that Terrance would not look him directly in the eye. The boy's own pale blue orbs shifted nervously as he related his tales of horror.

After half an hour of what Preacher considered the largest collection of fibs he had heard in a long time, during which Terrance continued to stuff himself with venison ham, the lad's eyelids began to droop. Preacher took advantage of that to hustle them off to bed.

"Time to turn in, I'd say. Snow'll be down enough by midday, so we can head out. You'd best roll up an' get some sleep."

Yawning, they agreed. Preacher saw them settle in, then curled up in his blankets, a thick buffalo robe over the top. After the day's ordeal, sleep came quickly and went deep. Well into the night, when everyone should have been sound asleep, Preacher heard some creaking from the twin bunks across the room. He breathed deeply and turned his head that way in time to see two small, naked forms rushing swiftly toward him. It quickly became obvious they intended to subdue and rob him. The larger of the pair competently held a long, thin-bladed knife.

4

Although loath to harm children, Preacher had to fight for his life. For all her frail build and small size, Vickie turned out to be a wildcat. Scratching and biting were her game. She raked Preacher's left cheek with bitten nails, hardly long enough to break the skin. She bit him in the shoulder when he attempted to throw her off him. Screaming a blue string of obscenities Preacher doubted she knew the meaning of, she kicked him in the ribs with a bare toe.

For all of Vickie's ferocity, Terry proved the greater danger. The knife he wielded flicked through the air an inch from Preacher's eyes, then whipped downward, a hairbreadth from the skin over his ribs.

"Dammit!" Preacher roared. "What's got into you? Leave be. I ain't gonna hurt you."

"We want it all, everything you've got," Terry shrieked.

Preacher grabbed his wrist behind the hilt of the knife and bent the arm away with ease. Vickie kicked Preacher in the groin. Hot pain exploded through Preacher's body He gave a shake to Terry and flung the boy across the cabin. The kid cried out when he struck the rickety table and sent it crashing to the floor. He quickly followed while Preacher came to his feet.

Small pebbles bit into the bare soles, and Preacher was thankful that he wore moccasins most of the summer and spent time barefoot. Vickie came at him again. She bit him on the belly, just above the drawstring top of his long john bottoms.

"Ouch! Don't do that, dammit," he barked.

Preacher's thumb and forefinger found the nerves at the hinge of Vickie's jaw and pressed firmly Her mouth flew open, and he yanked her off her feet. She instantly began to kick. Sighing away the last fragment of any regret, Preacher began to administer to her a solid, tooth-rattling shaking.

It reduced the slender girl to hysterical tears in a matter of seconds. He gave her a single, hard swat on her bare bottom and hurled her onto the upper bunk across the room. "Now, you stay there, hear?" he growled.

Preacher turned in time to see Terry lunge at him. He sidestepped and smacked the youngster alongside the head. Stunned, Terry lost his grip on the knife. Preacher yanked Terry high in the air and shook him until sobs nearly choked the boy. With them both relatively calmed, Preacher lighted his lantern and sat them, draped in blankets, at the table.

"Someone goin' to tell me what that was all about?"

Terry and Vickie exchanged silent glances. Preacher leaned close to their faces.

"You'd best one of you open up. I don't abide sneak-thieves. Nor those who abuse a body's hospitality. Turns out you're guilty of both. I promise it will go easier if you do. You"--he nodded to Terry--"you said I was famous. Then you must know that if I am who I said I was, an' you crossed me, I would squeeze the life out of both of you and never blink an eye. I could skin you alive, an' not feel a pang." He loomed over Vickie. "I could eat your liver."

Vickie turned deathly pale, and her lips trembled. "Oh, no—no. *Please!*"

"Then you'd best be tellin' me what's true and what's not."

Terry mopped at the single tear that ran down his soft cheek. "We—we were abandoned by our parents more'n a year ago. They hated us, said we were even more violence prone and bloodthirsty than they themselves. There weren't no other mean fellers. We been out here ever since. We've lived since by takin' things from unsuspecting travelers we come upon who were dumb enough to take us in."

"Like me." Preacher prodded, his anger not entirely quenched.

"No, not like you," Terry hastened to correct. "You're different altogether. Not like them at all. I—I kinda like you, an' I'm sorry we tried to rob you."

"If I hadn't whupped you, would you be sayin' that?"

Terry looked at Preacher in naked horror, and his face dissolved. "You—you're right. We're both awful, ugly kids." He buried his face in his hands and sobbed wretchedly, no longer a would-be killer, only a small boy alone and frightened.

Uncertain as to what to do, Preacher decided to hog-tie them for the rest of the night and take them along with him to Trout Creek Pass. Surely someone at the trading post would be able and willing to take charge of them.

Pacing the polished granite floor caused the purple stripe on the hem of the tall man's toga to ripple like a following sea. Through the window, beyond his broad shoulders, the western peaks of the Ferris Range gave off a rose glow from the rising sun opposite them. The newborn orb struck highlights from the rings that adorned six of his eight fingers and the gold and silver ornaments on his bare forearms. Anger gave his long, narrow face a scarlet hue that clashed with his sandy blond hair. He reached the limit of the large, airy room and turned back. Before he spoke he drove a fist into an open palm.

"Five men have failed to return and no one says anything about it? Why was I not told of this at once?" he demanded of the other man in the atrium.

"The centurion of the guard did not consider it an important event, First Citizen."

The sandy-haired man shook his head sadly as he examined

the other. He saw a burly man, with wide-set legs, thick and muscular, protected by shiny brass greaves. A barrel chest, encased in the brass cuirass of a Roman officer, rode above a trim waist and was topped by a full neck and large, broad-faced head. The horsehair-crested helmet tucked under one huge arm seemed a part of him. His white and red kilt was skirted by brass-studded leather strips. On his feet, the plain, brown leather marching sandals. Taken together these factors made him every inch the mighty general of the Legions of Nova Roma that he was. Yet, he allowed laxness and mistakes to weaken those powerful forces.

Any newly made corporal would have known to see that such vital information be relayed upward. The First Citizen sighed before he spoke. "Gaius Septimus, I chose you as my constant companion and commander of my legions because you are awfully good at what you do. The years you spent with the barbarian army before leaving their ranks for—ah— a freer life are invaluable to Nova Roma. You must maintain the proper attitude among your subordinates. Is that not possible?"

Gaius Septimus Glaubiae, whose real name was Yancy Taggart, responded with such vehemence that it shook the pleats of his kilt and rippled his long, scarlet cloak. "Not when all I have to work with is border trash and frontier riffraff, Marcus Quintus." They had been speaking in the classical Latin as taught at Harvard and other schools in the East. Gaius/Yancy now changed to English for the benefit of the three men standing behind him as he went on. "Speaking of which, I have brought the new men along this morning to introduce them to you. Then there is some rather bad news to relate."

Marcus Quintus raised a hand imperiously. "Spare me that for now. Bring these newcomers forward."

Gaius gestured to the trio standing a respectful three paces behind the general. They came forward and made a half-hearted effort at the proper salute: clenched right fist brought upward to strike the left breast. Gaius winced. Then he took on the formalities.

"First Citizen, let me introduce our newest recruits for the legions. This is Claypool, Grantling, and Wooks. Men, the First Citizen of Nova Roma, Marcus Quintus Americus."

They saluted again, and Marcus Quintus smiled at them, rather like a shark contemplating an unguarded baby dolphin. "You could not have come at a better time. You will be given proper Roman names once you have proven yourselves in the ranks and learn Latin. Until then, your barbarian names will have to do. Gauls, aren't you? The names sound like it. Never mind," he hurried on. "I am entrusting to you an important mission, outside the realm of Nova Roma. Recently, five of your fellows were sent out to capture a notorious individual who might be a threat to Nova Roma. I have learned only this morning that they have failed to return, with or without their captive, the legendary mountain man, Preacher. It is his destiny to fight gloriously in the coliseum," Marcus Quintus continued.

While he rambled on, Gaius Septimus let his thoughts roam over what he knew of the man who called himself Marcus Quintus Americus and had the audacity to take the title First Citizen. Glaubiae/Taggart considered Quintus to be more than a few flapjacks shy of a stack. Born Alexander Reardon, into the fantastically wealthy Reardon family of Burnt Tree Plantation, Duke of York County, Virginia. He'd had the best education affordable. Only, somewhere around the end of his primary school, Yancy Taggart recalled, Alexander had begun to fixate on Ancient Rome. As little Alexander grew, so did his mental disorder.

By the time he had graduated from Harvard, he was, as the rough-and-tumble mountain men would put it, "nutty as Hector's pet coon." When his father died in a riding accident, Alexander inherited. Alex quickly converted everything into gold and set out to establish his dream, Nova Roma, the New Rome. Yancy saw Alexander as some sort of combination of Caesar Augustus and Caligula. For, oh, yes, Alexander had a vicious, sadistic streak. And his sexual appetite would have shocked even the emperor Tiberius.

In addition to a number of slaves he had brought from the old plantation, Marcus Quintus had enslaved many Indians, and the hapless victims of raids on cabins or wagon trains. These he had put in the charge of Able Wade, now named Justinius Bulbus, master of games and owner of the new Rome's gladiator school. Over the years, Quintus had constructed a replica of the Circus Maximus and the Coliseum of Trajan. And he had revived the practice of throwing Christians to the lions. In this case, cougars, Septimus corrected himself.

The physical appearance of Quintus lent to his persona as a Roman emperor. Although tall and broad shouldered, Quintus was built close-coupled, with a bit of a potbelly, and a balding pate, fringed with yellow-brown hair. In a toga, with his gold-strapped sandals and golden circlet of laurel leaves, he looked every inch the emperor. Gaius Glaubiae reflected bitterly that he had deserted from the United States Army for something far better than this madman. Yet, he never sought to put it all aside. He wielded far greater power, and enjoyed far more comfort and luxury now, than even the product of his wildest dreams. He jerked slightly to free his mind as he realized that Marcus Quintus had been addressing him.

"Yes?" he asked coolly.

"I want you to see that these men have everything they will need for a long journey in the wilderness and send them on their way."

"Right away, of course." Septimus gestured for the three scruffy drifters to leave the room. "Now, I have something else. I regret to say it is also the doing of Centurion Lepidus."

"Go on," came Quintus' icy invitation.

Quickly, Septimus outlined the situation in which two legionnaires had been wounded and a third killed, and how the mountain man who had done it had managed to escape. He concluded lamely with the familiar remark: "The centurion saw nothing in that threatening enough to report it until this morning. It happened two days ago."

Rage boiled in the face of Quintus. "He is *Legionnaire* Lepidus as of now. I'd have him in the arena if he weren't a citizen. By Jupiter, this is outrageous. I want you to put out cavalry patrols at once to find the trespasser. He must not be allowed to carry his story to the outside world.

"It is far too early, as you must know, for New Rome to begin a war of conquest among the Celts and Germanic tribes. They, and the barbarian Gauls, must remain in ignorance for a while longer. There are still more of them than there are of us," he cautioned. Then a twinkle came to his eyes. "Although I have a way to make each of our legionnaires the match of any ten of the savages. It will be revealed at the auspicious time."

"And when will that be, Quintus?"

A crafty look stole over the face of the First Citizen. "Mars will make it known to me."

Mars! My God, he has gone totally mad. Septimus shook such thoughts from himself and made to answer. "It shall be as you will, First Citizen. I will not fail you. And Lepidus shall be dealt with. *Ave Caesar!*"

Once Septimus departed, Quintus left his audience chamber and passed down a narrow, dimly lighted corridor into the bowels of the palace. Two turns and down an incline, he came to what appeared to be a solid, wooden plank wall. Behind a hanging tapestry, his hand found a lever and pulled it away from its recessed niche.

A hidden panel swung outward, and Quintus swept the tapestry aside and entered. Flint and steel provided the spark to ignite a pine-resin torch. The flames danced through the room, banished shadows and revealed a soft, metallic glow from the long racks of carefully maintained weapons.

Several makes of the finest, most modern rifles lined the walls. It always calmed Quintus, gave him renewed confidence, to view his magnificent arsenal. Now he crossed to a rack of Winchester .45-70-500 Express Rifles and caressed the butt-stock of one while he purred aloud his sense of impending triumph.

"Soon now, my beauties. Very soon now, I will call in all of this border trash my good Septimus has recruited and enlisted in the ranks of our legions. Their testing will be done before long. When my legions are welded into ranks, they will be trained and honed into a fine-edged fighting machine. Then we will march to the north against the red savages, acquiring new colonies for Nova Roma." He paused to stroll over to where a rank of six twelve-pound Napoleons rested on their high-wheeled carriages. He patted the muzzle of one affectionately.

"That will test the mettle of my men for the time when they will conquer the true, Gallic enemy to the east. We shall claim every scrap of land from Canada to Mexico and east to the Mississippi. Oh, how mighty shall be the name of Rome!"

Preacher spent an uneasy night. It just weren't natural, but them two brat-kids insisted on sleepin' all huddled together like peas in a pod. Swore they didn't do anything naughty, only that they couldn't sleep any other way. Weren't right at their age. Though from his observations, they seemed a good mite younger actin' than their ages would account for. Boys of twelve were usually on the edge of being *serious.*

This Terrance, or Terry as his sister called him, seemed no more grown up than an eight-year-old. It worried Preacher. Was they both touched in the head a little? Could be, what with all their talk of violence, robbin' an' killin'. Huh! What was he doin' wastin' his time frettin' over the lives of a couple of woods waifs? It didn't sit right. He had set out for Trout Creek Pass to jaw with others about strangers comin' into the High Lonesome. Couldn't take time to stew over a couple of candidates for an institution for wayward children. Take what they had done just this afternoon.

It wasn't warm enough for a man to take a decent bath, what with this late snowfall and the coming of fall. Yet, when they had stopped for their nooning, those two scamps had flung off their clothes and jumped into the creek buck naked. For a swim! Not a hurried bath, mind, just to play. Enough to drive a man to the crazy house. Preacher had yanked them out, one by one, and wiped them dry with an old flannel shirt. Gave them a good talking-to, he thought. At least until he heard their giggles behind his back. *What was a body to do?*

Hunkered down in the brush, Philadelphia Braddock hid on the edge of a stand of golden aspen and watched the strange men from the valley search for him. He was good, one of the best, and he knew it. Braddock had left a confusing trail that should keep these amateurs meandering through the Big Empty country for a good long time. And they would never catch a glimpse of him.

A good thing, too. His shoulder hurt like the fires of hell. In a fight he would have to rely on pistols. He remembered the spear cast that had wounded him. It had been from a distance that made a pistol shot an iffy matter. It made him shiver to think about it. Ah! There they went. Hounding off on another false scent. Must be light-headed from all this blood loss. And maybe infection, though he didn't want to think of that. Thing was, those fellers all seemed to be in some sort of uniform.

And they acted like soldiers. But whose? He'd never seen the likes in all his born days. Not live ones, anyhow. He had to get back to Bent's Fort and tell someone what he had stumbled onto.

Through the haze of fatigue and weakness, Philadelphia Braddock recalled that Trout Creek Pass lay a lot closer. That would have to do, he decided. He couldn't hold out much longer than that. Quietly he eased back into the aspens, their brittle yellow leaves giving off a dry-bone rattle as they quaked in the slight breeze.

With a maze of zigzags over the next hour, Philadelphia Braddock left the last of the thoroughly confused soldiers far behind. When he lined out on the trail south out of Wyoming Territory, headed for Trout Creek Pass, he had time to reflect on the men he had seen. *Funny,* he mused, *they looked like them fellers I seen in paintings of the Crucifixion of Christ.*

He held that thought until he made night camp and refreshed himself on broiled rabbit. He could sure use some bison. Man feeds himself regular on bison heals right fast.

5

Thin ribbons of white smoke rose above the saddle that separated Preacher and his young charges from the trading post in Trout Creek Pass. Preacher had never been so weary of a self-imposed duty as this one. Had this pair been grown up, their bones would be picked clean by buzzards and coyotes by now. Being as how they were children, he felt obliged to spare them and bring them to folks who would see to their proper upbringing.

Although, he had to admit, it might be too late. It was written in the Bible that a child must be made straight in his ways by the age of seven or he was lost to righteousness. It was a hard thing to think of little nippers of eight, nine, ten or eleven roasting forever in hell because they had not been brought up right the first seven years of their lives. That was deeper theology than Preacher had delved into for a long while. He shook the images from his mind and plodded on. Terry and Vickie sat astride the packsaddle frame on a not-too-willing horse.

"When we gonna get there?" Terry asked.

"Yeah. We've never beened there before," Vickie chirped.

"You've never *been* there," Preacher corrected the girl.

She made a face. "That's what I said."

Preacher calculated the angle of the sun. "We'll be there by mid-afternoon. Those are the noonin' cook fires, an' ol' Kevin Murphy's smokehouse you see beyond the rise. He makes the bestest smoked hams. An' his bacon will melt in your mouth."

"Ugh!" Terry blurted. "I wouldn't like that. I like to *chew* mine. Is it spoilt or something?"

"Just a figger of speech. Means that his bacon is delicious. Now, you two quit pullin' my leg. I've got a sudden, bodacious thirst a-buildin', an' I figger to tend to it soon as I get you all settled in."

"Where are we gonna stay?" Vickie demanded.

"I been over all that before. You'll go to whoever will take you in."

Fear showed in both their faces. "You won't split us up, will you?" Terry asked nervously.

It was the first time Preacher had seen such emotions displayed by either, except for when he'd broken up their attack on his person. "I'll try not. No tellin'."

"We won't go to different folks." Terry grew stubborn.

"If you send us, we'll run away." Vickie cut her eyes to her brother for confirmation. He nodded solemnly.

Preacher lost hold of it for a moment. "Dang, can't you blessit tadpoles ever make things easy for a feller? I can't guarantee anythin' because I don't know what situation we're gonna come into. Put a rein on them jaws until we get there."

Terry and Vickie resumed a sullen, sulking silence. Terry's pink underlip protruded in a pout. Preacher snorted in disgust.

Preacher reached the trading post at a quarter past two that afternoon. "Tall" Johnson, as opposed to his cousin and partner, "Shorty" Johnson, greeted Preacher from the roofed-over porch of the saloon half of the frontier general store.

"Preacher, you old dog. I heard that you were holed up for the winter." His eyes widened when he took in the children. "You a fambly man now, Preach?"

"Not for any longer than I can help it, Tall," Preacher grumbled. "You wouldn't happen to be in the mood to play father, would you?"

Tall Johnson wheezed out his laughter. "Shorty would never hear of it. He sees kids as somethin' like warts. A feller needs to cut them off his hide as soon as possible. Besides, brats needs wimmin. An' we ain't got no wimmin. Decent ones, that is. Just a couple of Utes."

Preacher faked a disapproving glower. "Utes is ugly, Tall."

"Not this pair. Now, you just take that back, Preacher, or you buy the first drink."

Preacher's eyes sparkled with mischief. "I'll not take it back, an' I'll be proud to buy you the first drink. Soon's I get shut of these youngins."

Tall Johnson made his point markedly clear. "A feller could die of thirst before that happened."

Preacher chuckled. "Chew a pebble, Tall."

He dismounted and helped the children down. He took them with him into the trading post side of the large, stout log building, which had been built like the corner tower of a fort, the windows narrow, with thick shutters into which firing loops had been cut.

Ruben Duffey, the bartender, greeted him warmly. "Hograw, if it ain't Preacher. What you got there?" he asked. "Sure, it's a couple of partners you left out in the rain to shrink?"

"Nope. They's kid-chillins right enough."

"Seems I might know them, don't I? Lemme get a closer look?" Duffey studied Terry and Vickie a moment, and his full lips turned down in distaste. "I was right, Preacher. Ye've got yourself a pair of genuine juvenile criminals on your hands, don't ye know? Sure an' it's a better thing if ye bring them with me. I've got the right place for them. Come along then, won't ye?"

Preacher led the youngsters in Ruben's path, out through the back hallway, past a storeroom. Outside, the smiling Irishman directed them to a small storage building with a low door and no windows. He opened up and made a grand gesture with a sweeping arm to usher them inside.

"Faith now, an' we'll just lock those heathen devils'

spawn in here for a while. Could be we might get enough men together later on to decide their fate, don't ye know?"

"They are that bad, Ruben?"

"Aye, every bit of it an' more, I'm sayin'."

They walked back inside, and were joined by Tall Johnson. Ruben poured whiskey for the three of them; then he told Preacher the real story behind Terrance and Victoria. His tale, in his lilting Irish brogue, took the listening men back three years.

"There was this family, there was. Name of Tucker. Sure an' they was dressed like rag-a-muffins. Don't ye know, I, like most folks, saw somethin' strange about them right off, we did. A whole passel of kids they had, an' nerry a whole brain among 'em, there wasn't. There was something even more strange about them, wouldn't ye know? This Tucker and his mizus looked enough alike to be brother and sister. Sure an' they could be, for all I know. They squatted around the post for a few days; then they hauled out to a canyon some thirty miles northeast of here.

"That's when things started happenin'." Ruben leaned close and spoke in a confidential manner. "Sure an' things started disappearin'. A man would lose his shovel, or a pig, or maybe a couple pair of long johns a-dryin' on a bush. Then a prospector turned up dead. One day, ol' Looney Ashton come in for a nip of the dew. He swore an' be damned that two nights before, out around his digs, he saw that two-headed pair sneakin' off with a brace of mules that belonged to Hiram Bittner. It was the full moon an' he saw them right clear."

"Stranger things have happened," Preacher said dryly.

"No stranger than this tale gets. Ya see, the two little nippers were stark naked."

Silence held for a moment. Then a cherry-checked Preacher added verification to Ruben's story. "They do like to get out of their clothes a lot. I found that out on the way here."

Ruben raised both hands. "So there it is, isn't it?" He took note of the empty pewter mugs and poured more whiskey. "Who's payin' for these?"

Preacher and Tall turned to each other. "Preacher." "Tall."

"Ah, saints preserve us, I'll buy, 'cause it's good to see you again, Preacher, it is."

Ruben dropped coins into the wooden till under the bar and went on to tell how the little depredations, and an occasional killing, went on right up to the present. He concluded with a suggestion. "So, if ye'll tell me what dastardly act you caught this pair performing, maybe it is we can drag the whole family in and dispatch them."

Silence lengthened while Preacher thought over all he had heard. Try as he might, he could not visualize these two as so profoundly evil as Ruben painted them. He had brought the children here to find them a good home, with stepparents who would raise them properlike. He could not turn his back on that promise in good conscience.

"I dunno, Ruben. I'm thinkin' they can be shown the error of their ways and, given a good home, turn out all right."

"Don'cha tell me ye've turned soft-hearted, Preacher, don't ye?"

"Ruben, if you weren't such a little-bitty feller, an' all frail-like, I'd break you in half for sayin' that. I'm the same man I've always been. It's only that I've got to know them over the past two, nearly three days. They can be sweet-tempered enough and obey right smartly, if a firm hand is applied."

"To their bottoms, I presume, I do." Ruben poured another drink. For all of Preacher's disparagement, Ruben stood six-two in his stocking feet and had the body of a double beer barrel.

"I have yet to do that. Though when they come at me to rob me, I shook 'em until their teeth rattled. That seemed to get their attention."

"I wonder why?" Tall Johnson spoke for the first time. "You were serious, then, when you asked me about bein' a poppa?"

"Not really. I know how you and Shorty live. Not a place for kids. No offense intended."

"None taken. There's a feller over a couple of valleys, runs horses. I hear he's been wantin' to take in a couple of yonkers to help work on the place. If that's any help."

"He have a woman to wife?"

"Sure does. And three kids of his own."

"Sounds fine. I might look into it, failing I find any closer."

A sudden shout and curse in French from the cook at the hostelry brought the old drinking friends out of their cups and onto their boots. Preacher, wise in the ways of his captives, reached the back door first. He got there in time to see the cook on his rump, legs splayed and upraised, a pot of as-yet unheated potato soup soaking him from floppy stocking cap to the toes of his moccasins. Beyond him was the open door to the store shed—and the rapidly disappearing backs of Terry and Vickie.

"You had the right of it, Ruben. They's nothin' but trouble," he shouted as he set off afoot in swift pursuit.

Being no stranger to running—Preacher had engaged in many a foot race against Arapaho and Shoshoni braves—the rugged mountain man soon managed to close ground on his quarry. Terry lost more precious space with frequent, worried glances over his shoulder. With longer, stronger legs and more endurance, Preacher far outpaced the youngsters. Then providence gave the children a much-needed break in the form of several habitués of the trading post.

"Hoo-haa! Lookie there. Ain't that ol' Preacher playin' the nursemaid?"

"Shore be. Don't he look cute a-high-steppin' it like that?"

"Shut them yaps, Ty Beecham, an' you, Hoss Furgison. Them kids is my responsibility."

"Strike me dead. Preacher's done become plumb domesticated." Tyrone Beecham rubbed salt in Preacher's wounded pride. "Nextest thing we know, he'll take to wearin' an apron and skirts."

That did it. Preacher slammed to a stop and whirled to confront his detractors. No man, unless he was a tad light in the upstairs, ever suggested that a denizen of the High Lonesome might have sissy inclinations. To question a fellow's manhood most often called for a shooting. Preacher did not want to kill these old friends, and sometime partners, but Beecham had stepped over the bounds. The least that would satisfy now was a good knuckle drubbing.

And Preacher was just the man to deliver it. He stepped in without a word and popped Beecham flush in the mouth. Surprise registered in the dark, nearly black eyes of Tyrone Beecham as he rocked back on his boot heels. He swung a wild, looping left at Preacher's head, which, much to Beecham's regret, missed.

Because Preacher did not. He followed his lip-mashing punch with a right-left-right combination to Beecham's exposed rib cage. Each blow brought an accompanying grunt, expelled by the rapidly depleting air in Beecham's lungs. Droplets of red foam flew from Beecham's mangled mouth. His head wobbled with each blow. Right about then, his friend, Hoss Furgison, decided to join in.

He came at Preacher from the mountain man's blind side. Raw knuckles rapped against Preacher's skull, behind his left ear. Sound and sparkles erupted inside, and Preacher stumbled before he delivered a final right directly over Beecham's heart. Then he spun, his left arm already in motion, and drove his back fist into Hoss Furgison's nose.

Blood spurted, although nothing had been broken. Preacher continued his punishment with a right uppercut that cropped Furgison's surprised jaw closed. Furgison stomped on Preacher's right instep. Preacher gritted his teeth and ignored the pain. He still didn't want to hurt these two badly, only drive home the lesson that there was still a lot of spit and vinegar in this old coon. Everyone witnessing their battle had seen two-on-one plenty of times, sometimes even four or five. Most had seen Preacher handle those odds with ease. It didn't take long for the betting to begin.

"I got a cartwheel says Preacher pounds them both onto their boots," Tall Johnson declared.

An old-timer next to him elbowed Tall in the ribs. "I got me a nugget that assays as one and a quarter ounce pure says those younger fellers will plain bust his bum for him."

Thirty-five dollars, Tall thought. A reg'lar fortune. Temptation, and his confidence in Preacher, overcame his usual prudence and his near-empty purse. "You're on, old man."

Preacher made to dodge between his opponents, then stopped abruptly and reached out to snag the fronts of their shirts. He thrust himself backward on powerful legs and slammed his arms together at the same time. A coonskin cap went flying from the top of Ty Beecham's head as the two noggins clocked together. It was time for them to see stars and hear birds sing.

Preacher did not let up. He shook both combatants like small children and then threw them away. Ty Beecham bounced off the ground and started to get back on his boots. Preacher reached him in two swift strides and towered over the fallen man.

"Don't."

All at once, Beecham saw the wisdom in this and remained down. Not so Hoss Furgison. He came at Preacher with a yodeling growl. Preacher mimicked it and danced around like an Injun, flapping a hand over his mouth in time with the sound that came out. Somehow that further enraged Furgison, who, blinded by the taunts, abandoned all semblance of a plan.

He walked into a short, hard right to the chest, which he had left unprotected in order to grapple for a bear hug. Unkindness followed unkindness for Hoss. Preacher stepped in and pistoned his arms into a soft belly, until Hoss hung over the arms that punished him. Preacher disengaged his arms and stepped away. Hoss fell to his knees.

"You'd do yourself a favor if you stayed there, Hoss. I wasn't fixin' to do any real harm. Push it, an' by dang, I surely will."

"You win, Preacher. You win," Hoss panted.

Tall Johnson looked to the old man. Grudgingly, the gray-beard dug under his grimy buckskin shirt and pulled out a small pouch. From it he took a large gold nugget, crusted in quartz. Tall reckoned it to be worth what the old feller said.

"You got enough in yer pocketbook to have paid, had yer man lost?" the ancient demanded with ill grace.

Tall puckered his lips and threw the sore loser a wry look. "Well, now, we'll never know, will we?"

"Don't get another hidey-ho goin', Tall," Preacher admonished. "I still have to go after those brats."

"So you do," Tall answered cheerily. "And I wish you the joy of it."

"Dang it, Tall, if my knuckles weren't so sore, I'd knock some of the dust off 'em on that ugly puss of yours." So saying, Preacher stomped off for the front of the trading post and his trusty Cougar.

Preacher reined in and dismounted. The troublesome pair had found a stretch of slab rock that made it impossible to track them. Instead of crossing directly over, Preacher skirted around the edge counterclockwise, leading Cougar. He had gone only a quarter of the way when he found traces. Something about them bothered him.

Then he saw it clearly. These prints had been made by moccasins, right enough, and Terry had been wearing the pair Preacher had given him. But these were of a different pattern than those the boy had. These marks had been put down by an Arapaho. Preacher continued his search, and found no sign of where the children had left the wide stretch of exposed granite. Had the Indians taken the boy and girl?

One way to find out. He set out to follow the trace left by the Arapahos. An hour later, he encountered their evening camp. Among them he soon found old friends. Bold Pony was an age with Preacher, and in fact they had spent several summers together as boys in their late teens. Now the Arapaho settled Preacher down to a ritual sharing of meat and salt.

Bold Pony had held his age well, Preacher noted. He still

made a strapping figure, his limbs smooth and corded with muscle. He wore the hair pipe chest plate of a war chief and proudly reintroduced Preacher to his wife and three children. His boy was eleven, with a shy, shoe-button-eyed little girl of eight next, followed by a small boy, a toddler of three.

"Makes a feller know how many summers have gone by," Preacher confided. "Last I saw of you, that biggest of yours was still peekin' at me from behind his momma's skirts."

"You have weathered the seasons well, old friend," Bold Pony complimented.

"Yep. Well . . . beauty is as beauty does." Preacher's observation didn't mean a damned thing, but Bold Pony nodded sagely, arms crossed over his chest.

"What brings you into the hunting place of the Arapaho?" Bold Pony got right to the point as he pushed aside his empty stew bowl.

Preacher described in detail his encounter with Terry and Victoria, described them and recounted how they had managed to bowl over Frenchie Pirot and make an escape from the trading post. Bold Pony nodded several times during the explanation, then sat in silence as he lighted his pipe.

After the required puffs sent to the four corners of the world, and the two to the Sky Father and Earth Mother, Bold Pony drew one more for pleasure and passed it to Preacher. "We know of these children," he said with a scowl.

Preacher repeated the ritual gesture and sucked in a powerful lungful of pungent smoke. "Do you now? Any idea where they might be right now?"

Bold Pony accepted the pipe back, puffed and spoke. "I may know that. My son and his friends"—he nodded to the other lodges in the small encampment—"range far on their boyish hunts. It is possible they saw these young white people not long ago. It is possible that they are with their no-account family in a canyon not far off. One that is hidden from the unskilled eye."

"Is it also possible," Preacher asked after another drag on

the pipe, "that you can give me directions on how to find that canyon?"

A hint of a smile lighted the face of Bold Pony. "It is possible, old friend. I could tell you simply to follow your nose. They are dirty, an unwashed lot. You can smell them from far off. Or I could tell you to follow your ears. There are many children there, and they seem to squabble all the while—very noisy. Or I could tell you to journey half a day to the east until you come to a big tree blasted by the Thunder Bird. There you would find a small stream that comes from a narrow opening to the north. Follow that and you will find them."

"I am grateful, old friend."

"It is good. Now we must eat more or my woman will be unhappy."

"I'd rather to be off right away. But—" he looked up at the stout, round-faced, beaming woman and waggled one hand in acceptance—"I reckon another bowl of that stew wouldn't do no harm. Half a day will put me there a mite after the middle of the night. I can hardly wait," he said to himself with sarcasm.

6

Eight men, who were dressed in traditional diaperlike loincloths and spike-studded sandals, marched out of a stone archway after the clarion had sounded and the portcullis had been raised. Four of them looked entirely unwilling. They had every reason to be, considering that they were captives from an ill-fated wagon train, not professionals, as were their opponents. When the eight reached the lavish, curtained box, they halted and raised their weapons to salute the imperator in the sanctioned words.

"Ave Caesar! Morituri te salutamus!"

And, right here on the sands of the Coliseum of Nova Roma, they really were about to die. At least the four pilgrims were, who possessed a woeful unfamiliarity with the odd weapons they had been given. One had a small, round, Thracian shield and a short sword. The second had the spike-knuckled caestus of a pugilist—a fistfighter. The third had the net and trident of a *retiarius*. The fourth bore a pair of long daggers, with small shields strapped just below each elbow, in the style of the Midianite horsemen. The professionals bore the appropriate opposing arms. They looked expectantly beyond their soon-to-be victims of the *imperator.*

Marcus Quintus Americus rose eagerly and gave the signal to begin with his gold-capped, ivory wand. At once, the gladiators ended their salute, each squared off against his primary opponent, and the fight commenced. Shouts of encouragement and derision rose from the stone benches filled with spectators. Many of these people, the "citizens" of New Rome, had been here for years. Not a few had formerly been the inmates of prisons and asylums for the insane. Whatever their origins, they had acquired a taste for this bloodiest of sports. That pleased Quintus, who resumed his seat on the low-back, X-shaped chair beside his wife, Titiana Pulcra, the former Flossie Horton of Perth Amboy, New Jersey.

"Rather a good lot, this time, eh?" Quintus asked the striking blonde beside him.

Pulcra/Flossie tossed her diadem of golden curls and answered in a lazy drawl. "Come, Quintus, you know the games bore me. They are so gruesome."

From her far side, the small voice of Quintus Faustus Americus, her son, piped up. "But that's what makes them so exciting, Mother."

Pulcra gazed on him coolly. "I was addressing your father, Faustus. Really, Quintus, for a boy of ten years, he has truly atrocious manners."

"Eleven, my dear," Quintus responded. "He'll be eleven on the Nones of September."

"Which makes it all the worse. He needs a proper teacher. There's geography, history, so many things, including manners, he should be taught."

"Eleven is a good enough time to begin formal education," Quintus countered. "A boy needs to be free to indulge his adventurous spirit until then, doesn't he, son?" he added fondly as he reached across his wife to tousle the youngster's yellow curls.

Quintus Faustus Americus had his mother's coloring, her gray eyes and pug nose as well. A thin, wiry boy, he had inherited his father's sadistic traits. He enjoyed tormenting small animals and treated all other children as inferiors. Gen. Gaius Septimus Glaubiae summed up the lad best, as being mean-spirited, filled with a deep-seated evil.

"Yes, Father. Oh, look!" Faustus blurted, pointing to a small, nail-bitten finger on a fallen man on the sand. "He's gone down already. I told you he was too old and frail. You owe me ten denarii."

"Done, my boy. Right after the games end," Quintus responded laughing.

Out in the arena, the oldest immigrant lay in a pool of blood, his life slowly ebbing, while the professional gladiator who had downed him with a simple, straight sword thrust with his *gladius* stood over him. He looked up at the box. Quintus gave him the sign to dispatch the unfortunate.

A short, sharp scream came from the old fellow when the *gladius* pierced his heart. To the left of the unfeeling gladiator, a sturdy young farmer, who had been bound for Oregon, smashed a surprising blow to the face of his opponent with the *caestus*. Blood flew in profusion. A chorus of boos came from the audience.

"I say, rather good!" Quintus cheered on the amateur. "Smack him another one."

Before the brave farmer could respond, his opponent's length of his chain with the spiked ball at the end lashed out and struck him solidly in the chest. Yanked off his feet by the effort to extract the spike point from the deep wound, the farmer fell face-first to the sand. His opponent closed in and stood above his victim while he swung the wicked instrument around over his head. The farmer rolled over, eyes wide with fright, and lashed out with his blade-encrusted fist. The tines dug into the partly protected calf muscle of the professional gladiator, who leaped back with a howl.

"He's going to die anyway, isn't he, Father?" The small hand of Faustus tugged at the edge of his father's toga.

"Yes, of course, they all are."

Gray eyes alight and dancing, Faustus clapped his hands. "Oh, good."

Two attendants rushed from the gladiator entrance portal to help the wounded professional off the sand. Another, armed like a Nubian, complete with zebra-print shield and long spear, took his place. He quickly finished off the second of the four pilgrims. With the farmer dead, that left only two. Faustus grew more excited with each feint and thrust of the four men before him. He stuffed his mouth with popped corn, a feat made difficult by the broad, wet smile that exposed small, white, even teeth, like those of a wolverine. A great shout came from the crowd as one surviving immigrant stumbled over the body of the first man slain and went to one knee.

"Oh, splendid!" Faustus squeaked as the gladiator in Thracian armor swiftly closed in on the off-balance amateur.

With cold deliberation, the Thracian swung his curved sword and cleanly decapitated the downed outsider. Faustus bounced up and down on his cushioned chair, his breathing roughened, as little gasps escaped his lips. His eyes grew glassy. He moaned softly as the headless corpse toppled sideways to flop on the sand. To his right, his mother gave him alarmed glances.

"Hasn't it been quite a good day at the games, my dear?" Quintus remarked idly to Pulcra.

"Yes, I suppose it has. Apparently Faustus thinks so."

Faustus licked his lips repeatedly now and groped for more popped corn while he fixed his lead-colored eyes on the death throes of the last captive. A low, soft moan escaped as the hapless man breathed his last.

Quintus spoke in low, confidential tones to his wife. "I only hope the men I sent will be successful. And, that they get back in time for the birthday games for Faustus. We will have the spectacle of spectacles when that living legend, Preacher, is on the sand. What a crowning event that would be for the boy's birthday!"

Preacher had other things on his mind at the time. Slipping unseen through the woods in late afternoon, he spied out the Tucker compound shortly before sundown. To grace it with the name of "compound," Preacher reasoned, had to be a gross exaggeration. It consisted of a low, slovenly cabin, the second story of which seemed to have been added as an afterthought. A rickety corral stood to one side, partly shaded by a huge old juniper. The mound and the recessed doorway of a root cellar occupied space on the opposite side. Right off, Preacher spotted a dozen brats.

They stair-stepped from a toddler of maybe two to a gangly youth of perhaps fifteen. The younger ones went about blissfully naked. The older ones were every bit as ill-clothed as had been Terry and Vickie. While Preacher observed, he began to note that all of them appeared to have some physical or mental defect. All except Terry and Vickie, who showed up in the last glimmer of twilight.

Perhaps they had a different poppa, Preacher speculated. Or another momma? A moment later, the situation became clearer when three adults showed themselves in the tree-shaded, bare, pounded ground in front of the cabin. The man and one woman looked enough alike to be twins, both with black hair and eyes, like most of the children. Preacher recalled the speculation on the part of Ruben Duffey.

That seemed to make more sense when he studied the other woman, whom he saw to be fair, with long, blond hair and pale blue eyes. To Preacher's consternation and as an assault on his sense of propriety, the man was openly affectionate to both women. He hugged them and bussed them heartily on their cheeks, held hands with the dark one while she gathered in the children.

Like most youngsters, the black-haired tribe frisked about some, holding out for only a few minutes more before surrendering to the indoors. The dusky woman cupped hands around her mouth and let out a raucous bellow.

"All right, that's enough. Inside this minute or no supper for anyone."

They scampered for the house with alacrity. All except Terry and Vickie, who dawdled along as though reluctant to face a meal in that house. Terry continuously scuffed a big toe against the firm ground. Preacher continued to watch until the adult trio disappeared inside. Disgusted by this *ménage à trois,* and apparently an incestuous one at that, he settled back to lay plans for how he would deal with them. Some of the alternatives he came up with seemed distinctly grim.

Deacon Phineas Abercrombie and Sister Amelia Witherspoon stood stock still, thoroughly astounded. The men who surrounded their three-wagon train, which comprised their "Mobile Church in the Wildwood," looked exactly like soldiers of Ancient Rome. Yet, how could that be? Here, in Wyoming Territory, in the year of our Lord 1848? One of them came forward into the flickering bonfire-lighted clearing from the surrounding woods.

He bore a large Imperial Eagle on a long, wooden rod; the laurel leaf wreath, which, like the eagle, appeared to be of pure gold, encircling below it the famous emblem of Rome— S.P.Q.R., *Senatus, Populusque, Romanus*—Deacon Abercrombie recalled this from his Latin studies. "The Senate and the Roman People." What madness could this be?

One, obviously their leader, stepped forward, haughty, fierce-eyed, every inch the domineering Roman centurion in his crested helmet, cuirass, kilt and greaves. "What are you barbarians doing in the realm of Nova Roma?"

New Rome? the stunned deacon echoed in thought. That accounted for it, then, his dizzied mind supplied. Still unsettled by this apparition, he spoke in a near babble.

"Why, we are not barbarians. We are Christian missionaries. We have come to spread the word of God to the heathen lands, to do the work of the Lord."

Cutting his eyes to a subordinate, the centurion commented, "Good Christians, eh? We'll get to see the lions again, eh, Sergeant?" His smile was decidedly unpleasant, Abercrombie thought.

His *contubernalis* (skipper) produced a wicked smirk.

"That'll be just jolly. I hope they save this fat windbag for last," he went on, with a nod to Abercrombie.

Astonished that he had no difficulty in understanding their Latin, Deacon Abercrombie flushed with crimson outrage at the depiction of himself. He was about to launch into an indignant protest when the centurion's next words stoppered his mouth.

"All right, round them up and get them in chains. First I want to ask a couple of questions." He turned to Abercrombie and spoke in perfect English, albeit heavily laden with a Southern accent. "We're looking for a man. He's been wounded, and probably traveling slow. Have any of y'all seen such a person?"

While Deacon Abercrombie struggled to frame a reply that included a protest, a startled yelp from his right silenced him. "Take your hands off me," Sister Amelia snapped. "I'll not abide any man to touch me, let alone a rude stranger."

A hard-faced legionnaire barked back at her. "Shut up, lady. The *contubernalis* says we put you in chains, that's what we're going to do."

"Why, the very idea! The nerve. How dare you treat us like this?"

"Sister, please," Abercrombie interrupted in an attempt to defuse the situation.

The soldier acted as though he had not heard a word. "Because we've got the weapons, Sister. Now, cooperate or suffer for it."

Quickly the twenty men and sixteen women were rounded up and thrust into chains. Few voiced protest. Several women began to pray aloud or to sing hymns. The crude legionnaires laughed among themselves and made nasty comments. Soon, the job had been completed. The centurion had as yet to get an answer to his first question. He bore in on Deacon Abercrombie.

"You seem to be in charge of all this. I want an answer, or it will go hard on y'all."

Abercrombie tried to compose himself. "What was the question?"

"Have you seen a wounded mountain man?"

"No."

"That's all? Just no?"

Deacon Abercrombie sighed in frustration. "No, none of us has seen such a person."

With eyes narrowed, the centurion put his face right in that of Abercrombie. "You sure y'all ain't hidin' somethin'? Not bein' entirely truthful?"

"Sir, I am a churchman. I do not lie."

The centurion pointed contemptuously at the Bible tucked under the deacon's left arm. "You ask me, that's all you do, is lie. Pack of nonsense between those leather covers. I'll ask one more question, then all of you back in your wagons or on horses. Have you, by chance, encountered a scruffy man goes by the name of Preacher?"

Several of the cowed missionaries shook their heads in the negative. Abercrombie drew himself up and glared defiantly at his interrogator. "Of that, I am absolutely certain. Had we encountered anyone with so outlandish a pretension in this wilderness, we would have remembered."

"Am I to take that to mean no?" the centurion asked with a sneer.

"Precisely. It is possible that this wounded man you are looking for saw us first and hid himself. So it may be that we have passed by him on his way, without knowing so. As to this Preacher you are speaking of, there's been no such person."

"So, if you are going to stick to that, you might as well load up. Maybe the curia's torturers can loosen some tongues."

"Where are you taking us? I demand to know," Abercrombie unwisely blustered.

"To New Rome, of course. Y'all are in our country without permission. The First Citizen will likely call you all Gallic spies. Whatever he decides, it's the coliseum for the lot of you."

At the news of this, wailings and lamentations rose among the faithful.

* * *

By ten o'clock that night, Preacher had it figured out. He waited until midnight, then glided out of his place of conceal-ment. Bent low, walking in moccasins for quiet, he crossed the clearing to the tumble-down cabin. A stench of neglected, spilled food and unwashed bodies leaped out to assault him. His nose wrinkled. The shambles of an outhouse behind the log structure gave evidence of being a total stranger to quicklime.

He had been upwind of the wretched hovel, Preacher re-called as he closed on the rickety front porch. He made not a sound as he crossed the warped, weathered gray boards to the front door. There Preacher paused while he reached for the latch string. Strangely, considering where the cabin was lo-cated, it hung outside as a welcoming.

Preacher eased it upward and winced at the slight scraping sound the bar made as it raised. When it came free, Preacher waited tensely, one hand on the butt of a Walker Colt. After half a hundred heartbeats, with no alarm shouted from inside, he eased the door inward. Another mistake in wild country. The hinges should provide added resistance against anyone trying to break in. Sucking in a breath, Preacher edged around the open portal.

He made not the slightest sound as he entered the smelly structure. He eased the door shut behind himself. A long wait to allow his eyes to adjust to the dimness within. Slowly, ob-jects began to define themselves: a counter along one wall, with crude cupboards above; a cast-iron stove, tilted rakishly because of a broken leg; a hearth and fireplace mantel; a large, leather-strung bed beyond a gauzy curtain. Satisfied, Preacher ghosted past the slumbering adults lying together in a tangle of naked arms and legs.

Carefully, he tested the rungs of a ladder that gave access to the loft where, he surmised, the children slept. He gingerly put weight on the first and thrust upward. No squeal betrayed him. Preacher took a second and a third step. Surprising for the slipshod construction in general, the ladder still did not give off a single betraying squeak. In due time, Preacher brought his head above the level of the elevated flooring.

Here and there in the starlit darkness he made out the huddled forms of sleeping children. Beyond their relaxed bodies, he found Terry and Vickie, asleep together as usual, fully clothed, their arms around each other. With that accomplished, he went back down to take care of the adults.

What a ruckus that caused! Perhaps Preacher had not chosen the wisest way of extracting brother and sister from the family bosom. What he picked to do was stand in the middle of the cabin floor, by a large table, and bellow his intentions to the parents.

"All right, folks. I want you to stay tight in that bed. Don't even twitch an eyeball. I've come to take those towheaded youngins outta here to someplace decent."

In the next instant, the women erupted in a hissing, spitting, nail-clawing cat-fight mode. Bare as the day her mother birthed her, the blond one hurled herself at Preacher with fingers arched into wicked talons. He deflected her with his raised left forearm, but not before she raked his cheek with sharp nails.

"You bastid, keep yer filthy paws off my babies!" she howled.

"They as much mine as yorn, Purity. T'same man fathered them as mine," the other wailed, closing in on Preacher's right.

Preacher stepped back and shoved the black-haired vixen away, toward the bed. Silas Tucker had not moved a hair. He sat in the middle of his harem bed with a bemused expression on his ugly face. He laughed at the startled look on Preacher's face.

"You done kicked a hornet's nest, mister," he declared through his mirth.

Preacher shook his head, determined not to be bested by a pair of fillies. "More'n likely *they* did."

They rushed him again and Preacher had to duck. A sizzling kick hurtled toward his groin. A hot rod of pain thrust into the outside of one thigh. This could prove more than he bargained for, the mountain man reckoned. Shouts from the loft joined in the pandemonium. Blond curls flying, the mother of Terry and Vickie charged in while Preacher held off the other woman.

Her fists pounded ineffectually off the broad, firm back of Preacher while she cursed and spat at him. He felt the wetness of her saliva on his neck, and it rankled some.

"Enough of that," he bellowed as he backhanded her in the upper chest.

She went tail over teakettle across the table. Preacher had time to gather only a short breath before the dark one bounced in the air and came at him with fists flying. He ducked, blocked what he could and took a stinger on the already black eye. It smarted more than he would admit. All of a sudden, the other woman had him around the ankles.

She held on for dear life. It deprived Preacher of any means of avoiding the wrath of the one throwing fists and feet at him. It began to look worse with every passing second. Then Silas Tucker roused himself enough to get into the fray. He came at Preacher low and mean, a long, wicked-bladed knife held in one hand.

7

Preacher swatted the blonde aside and cleared a space for a swift kick. His moccasin toe bit into the meaty portion of Silas Tucker's right forearm. The knife went flying. Preacher quickly hurled the furious black-haired gal full into Tucker's chest.

Tucker went flying with a yowl, which quickly turned into a bellow of pain when his bare rump made contact with the still-hot stove. He came off it mouthing a string of curses, and his hand groped blindly for a weapon. He found the short, hooked, cast-iron stove poker and launched himself at Preacher. Evidently the blond woman had learned her lesson. She hung back and satisfied her outrage by hurling metal cups, plates and other cookery items at the dodging figure of Preacher.

A white-speckled, blue granite cup clipped him as it zinged past Preacher's ear. He jumped to the opposite side, having his moccasin caught up in the tangle of legs and arms of the dark hoyden. Abruptly, he went down in a heap. Black curls swirled over his face as his wily opponent scrambled on top of him. She immediately began to pummel him with her fists.

"Git back, woman," Silas Tucker bellowed. He came at Preacher with the poker.

Faith Tucker rolled off Preacher in the wrong direction and at the wrong time. The descending poker caught her on the exposed point of her left shoulder. Her shriek of pain ended with a curse; then she added for emphasis, "Idjit, you done broke it."

Stunned, Silas looked upon his injured sister and dropped the metal rod as though it had been heated in the fire. Preacher used the brief interlude to spring to his feet. A large stewpot filled the entire range of his vision. He ducked and received only a slight graze across the top of his head. That bought valuable seconds for Silas Tucker.

He bolted to the corner of the cabin, by the fireplace. There his hands closed around the smooth, polished hickory handle of a double-bit axe. He hefted it once, grinned stupidly and advanced on Preacher's back, the deadly tool held high, ready to split the mountain man's skull. He learned how stupid he had been a moment later.

A shout—he thought it could have come from Terry— warned Preacher. He spun, took in the menace, now only four feet from him, and drew in one swift, sure motion. The hammer came back on his .44 Walker Colt and then dropped on the primer of a brass cartridge. Fire flashed in the cabin in time with the comforting buck of the six-gun in Preacher's hand. Smoke billowed, but not before Preacher saw the axe fly from Tucker's hands, and a spray of blood from the back of the man's shoulder showered both of his women.

They went berserk. Howling and screaming, they rushed to their wounded male, like females in a pride of lions. They completely ignored Preacher, who turned and headed for the loft. Pandemonium reigned above. Suddenly awakened, the children shrieked, screamed and wailed in confusion and fear. When he loomed up through the opening in the loft floor, Preacher rightly read a warning of fight in some of the older youngsters. Two of them came at him before he gained purchase on the flooring.

Preacher cuffed one of them aside and climbed off the ladder. He lightly felt a stinging blow to his side and yanked a naked, spluttering boy of ten or so off his feet. Preacher gave a disapproving cluck of tongue against teeth as he tossed the lad into three more who advanced on him.

"Enough!" he roared. The command had its effect.

Some of the smaller children clapped hands over their mouths and went round-eyed. Yet another brat challenged him. Growing amused, Preacher batted at the ineffectual blows in the manner of a man swatting mosquitos. His diversion lasted only a moment, until the sturdy boy of about thirteen snapped a kick at Preacher's groin. It connected before he could block, though without striking any vital targets. Preacher popped the youngster high on the cheek in reply and sat him down on his bare butt. The rest drew back in fear.

Preacher advanced toward the dormer alcove where Terry and Vickie had withdrawn. "C'mon, I'm takin' you outta this hell-hole," he commanded.

Accustomed to mistrusting all adults, Terry responded with defiance. "What if we don't want to go?"

Preacher cocked his head to one side. His expression clearly declared that he would not take a lot of that. "Do I have to hog-tie you, like before, an' drag you outta here? It can be easy or hard, your choice; either way, we gotta move fast. 'Cause them she-cats down there are like to recover from their weepin' an' wailin' over their head he-coon and come after me with a vengeance."

"One of them is our momma," Terry said as he continued his challenge.

A flint edge turned Preacher's eyes; and sarcasm, his words. "You got any idee which one?"

Terry had not expected that tack. "Why-why, the yeller-haired one, of course."

"If you expect to see her go unharmed, then you'd best move fast. There's knives and forks and things down there that can do a feller real harm. I don't intend to stand around an' let her poke any of them into me."

His head of steam deserted Terry, and his frail chest deflated under the raggedy shirt. "We'll go."

"Yes, Preacher, we'll go with you anytime," Vickie added, her cobalt eyes dancing in starlight.

"Now, that's more like it. 'Sides, you'll be better off where I'll be takin' you, better by far than livin' with this sordid riffraff."

Terry produced a pout. "She's still our maw."

Enough had come and gone for Preacher long ago. His face clouded, and his words rang in a hollow command. "Git down them stairs. Grab what belongin's is yours, especially any coats."

"Coats? You flang the only ones we had in the fire," Terry protested.

Nonplussed, Preacher could only shrug. "Rags. They was mostly rags," he defended his action. "Now, scoot!"

Oblivious to the deep chill, the youngsters scampered barefoot down the ladder. Preacher followed. The thirteen-year-old, still smarting from the punch Preacher had laid on him, shouted after. "Paw's gonna wrang your necks oncest he catches up to y'all."

Preacher turned his iron gaze over one shoulder. "You tell him to come on, as I reckon it'll be me does the wringin'."

On the ground floor of the cabin, the women still whooped and hollered over the wounded Silas Tucker. Silently, Preacher wished them the joy of it, then led the way to his horses.

"I don't *want* to sit still!" Terry Tucker sassed Preacher from atop the packsaddle at midmorning the next day. "It hurts my behind, ridin' like this."

"You spook that pack-critter an' I'll show you a hurt behind," Preacher warned.

Terry tried his repertoire of the cutest. "Why can't I ride with you?" he asked coyly.

"Cougar ain't used to carryin' double," Preacher grumbled.

"He can *learn*."

"Not now, he cain't, Terry. Not no-how," Preacher insisted. Right then, Cougar's ears twitched. The packhorse whuffled. Preacher reined in sharply and listened. His ears, then his nose caught the message. Injuns! Friendly, without a doubt. Else they would not have let the three whites ride in so close. Preacher nodded, raised his right arm and signed the symbol for peace. Then he waited.

Always perceptive, Terry spoke in a mere whisper. "What's wrong?"

Preacher's lips barely moved. "Cain't you smell it? They's Injuns out there."

Terry's eyes went wide and round. "They gonna scalp us?"

"I don't think so."

Fear and insecurity shivered through the boy's skinny frame. "You don't *think* so?"

"Take it easy, boy. No sense in gettin' them riled . . . if they ain't already."

Preacher signed again. This time a familiar figure walked his spotted pony out onto the trail. Preacher raised in the saddle and signed "friend."

"Ho! Ghost Walker, we meet again."

"Ho! Bold Pony, it is a good meeting."

"The hunting is plenty. We stay to fill our travois." He looked pointedly at the two towheads on the packhorse. "You found them, I see."

Preacher thought over the ordeal of last night, and the trials of this morning. The kids had taken to being bratty, as usual, right after breakfast. "Yep. More's the pity."

"You would tell me about it?" Amusement twinkled in the eyes of the Arapaho war chief as he rode in closer. He examined Preacher's face. "The parents were not so pleased with parting with their dear ones?"

Preacher grunted. "Sometimes your eyes are too keen, Bold Pony."

He went on to relate the visit to the Tucker house. The more colorful his description grew of the brief fight in the cabin, the more Bold Pony laughed and held his sides. Although unaware of why, the amusement of Bold Pony had an effect on the children. Before long, Terry and Vickie broke into fits of giggles with each revelation Preacher made. It put him in a scowling mood.

Preacher rounded on them to growl. "That's enough of that." He turned back in appeal to Bold Pony. "You see what I mean? These two have been a pain in the behind from the git-go." Then he told of their morning's fractiousness.

Bold Pony studied the predicament in which Preacher found himself. At last he answered cautiously, albeit with a hint of laughter in his words. "If my people did not believe that spanking a child is wrong, I'd suggest that you do just that."

Preacher soberly considered his friend's words. "Well," he announced at last, a gleam in his eyes, "these warts ain't exactly Arapaho. So, mayhap a willow switch would be just the thing."

Bold Pony nodded sagely. "I will leave you to your important work. May the sun always rise for you, Preacher."

"May the wind always be at your back, Bold Pony."

Without a backward glance, Bold Pony turned his mount and rode off silently. Preacher turned his attention to the youngsters, who had grown deathly pale. He dusted his hands together and kneed Cougar in the direction of a creek bed, where a long, narrow stand of weeping willows beckoned.

Terry read Preacher's intent in a flickering and blurted his appeal, thick with tears. "Oh, no, you ain't gonna do that. Please. You ain't gonna whup us?"

"You broke my only fire trestle, burnt the cornbread, dang near ran off the packhorse, an' shamed me by jibberin' like a pack o' monkeys in front of Bold Pony. Suppose you tell me just why I shouldn't?"

"'C-'cause Paw always whups up on us somethin' fierce."

Determined now, Preacher ignored the boy. At the creek bank, he dismounted and tied off both horses. Then he selected and cut a suitable willow switch. Stripped of its leaves, it made a satisfactory whir as he flexed it through the air. Face somber, Preacher walked over to the children.

"You first, Missy," he directed to Vickie.

Reluctantly, she came down from the packsaddle. Her eyes flooded as Preacher knelt and bent her over his knee. He up-ended the hem of her skirt and exposed a bare bottom. Swiftly, without any show of anger, he delivered four sound whacks. Vickie bit her lip to keep from crying out, but her whimpers tore at Preacher's heart.

Dimly, from memories best left buried, he dredged up images of the few times he'd been thrashed as a boy. Once begun, though, he could not stop in midstream, so's to speak. He set her on her feet and went for Terry.

"Don't touch me," Terry wailed. "I'll git'cha. I'll git'cha in your sleep," he threatened to no avail.

Preacher had him in the strong grip of one hand and hauled the slight lad off the packsaddle. The willow switch between the third and little fingers of the other hand, he quickly had the boy's britches down and his wriggling torso over an upraised knee. For only a moment did Preacher hesitate; then six fast, expertly delivered smacks left red spots, but raised not a welt. Returned to his upright position, instead of pulling up his trousers, the silently sobbing boy yanked on his shirt to expose his chest and back.

Angry, fresh red lines, knotted here and there with spots of infection, showed over the welter of earlier scars Preacher had seen in the cave. "See? You're no better than he is, Preacher." Then Terry broke into a gushing flow of tears. Vickie joined him.

Seeing the terrible punishment meted out by the animal who called himself the boy's father and hearing their pitiful sobs tugged at Preacher's heart. Impulsively, he reached out and hugged them to him. He held them tightly while their blubbering subsided.

"Nah—nah, that's all right, yonkers. You ain't hurt that bad this time. An' a feller's got to learn that he does wrong, he's gonna git punishment, swift and sure. It's what distinguishes us from the animals." Preacher stopped and jerked his head back, a surprised expression on his face. "Listen to me, speakin' words with more syllables than my tongue can tickle over. Next thing you know, I'll be takin' to Bible-thumpin'."

Out of their anguish came laughter. Preacher continued to press his case. "Understand, I want things to go right for you. I promised I'd find a home for the both of you, with someone who will love and care for the both of you. An' I'm gonna do it."

Sniffling, Terry and Vickie dried their eyes and padded barefoot back toward the packhorse. Vickie spoke first. "I promise not to give you a hard time anymore, Preacher. Really I won't."

"Me—me, too, Preacher," Terry croaked hoarsely. "It's hard. After so many years of bein' bad, it's—it's a *habit.*"

Preacher answered gruffly, his own throat constricted by a lump of memory. "See that you tend to your p's and q's an' we'll git along just fine."

He restored them to their perch atop the pack animal and mounted up. Preacher led the way out, much relieved, the children considerably subdued.

Preacher crouched by the hat-sized fire he had built in a protecting ring of stones. He looked up from the skillet of fatback and beans, savoring the aroma that rose. He had found some wild onions, added dried chili peppers, salt and a dab of sugar from his supplies, and water from the creek that flowed soundlessly a hundred yards away.

Only a fool, or a greenhorn flatlander, camped right up beside a noisy mountain creek that burbled and gurgled over rocks and made musical swirls as it rounded sandbars and bends. A whole party of scalp-hungry Blackfeet could sneak up on such a foolish person. Preacher had learned that before his voice changed. It had saved his hair on numerous occasions. He paused in his cooking duties.

"Terry, go fetch that foldin' bucket full of water for the horses."

"Why didn't we just camp by the crick?" Terry offered in a revival of his earlier attitude.

There you go, Preacher thought to himself. Flatlanders an' fools. He drew a breath, ready to deliver a blistering rejoinder, then mellowed. "Because it's foolish, even dangerous, to camp where the sound of water fills your ears and you can't hear anyone sneak up on you. Didn't I explain all that to you before?"

To Preacher's surprise, Terry flushed a rich scarlet. One big toe massaged the top of the other. He cut his eyes to the ground right in front of them. "I—reckon you did. I—I . . . forgot."

"Well an' good. You owned up to it, an' that's what counts."

Unaccustomed to praise for any reason, Terry glowed, his eyes alight and dancing, his cheeks pink for a far different reason. Preacher gave him scant time to rest on his laurels.

"Git on, now. Gonna be dark before long."

After her brother scurried off on his errand, Vickie came to Preacher. With all the natural wiles of a woman, she draped one forearm on his shoulder and bent toward him with an expression of earnest absorption. "When will we be at the trading post, Preacher?"

"Some time in the mornin', provided you two carry your end. We git up, eat, clean up, an' git. All before the horizon turns gray."

Vickie made a little girl face. "Why do we have to wake up so early? I like to sleep until the sun is up far enough to shine in the loft an' I can smell breakfast a-cookin'."

"There's no loft here, an' we be in a hurry," Preacher answered shortly.

"What's the hurry for?" Vickie asked in sincere ignorance.

Preacher studied her a moment. "You don't think your

poppa an' them herri-dans of his'n is gonna kick back and say, 'Ol' Preacher done stole our prize pupils. Ho-hum.'"

Vickie's eyes went wide. "You mean . . . they's a-comin' after us?"

"Count on it. Sure's there's stink on a skunk."

Twenty minutes had passed, with Terry not yet back from the creek, when Preacher's prediction proved true.

His teeth gritted against the constant pain in his shoulder, Silas Tucker had held steadfast to his determination to exact revenge upon the crazy man who had broken into their cabin and stolen his best earners. Why, then two could steal the gold from a man's teeth without him knowin' it. And the boy, even though Silas had no intention of letting him know it, was turning into a right capable killer.

With those two bringin' in the goods, Silas would soon have his women dressed in silks and himself in a woolen suit. Reg'lar nabobs they'd be. Then, along comes this mountain wild man and spoils it all. Silas' brow furrowed, and he flushed with mounting anger as he looked down into the small valley where Preacher and the children had made camp. They'd soon see, Silas decided. He turned to Faith and spoke in a whisper.

"Be sure not to hit them brats. I know you're a good shot, m'love. Allus was. That's why I want you to stay back up here and give cover fire, y'hear?"

"I know, Silas, I know. It's that Purity cain't shoot for beans."

Silas gave her a broad wink. "That's why she's comin' with me. I c'n sorta keep an eye on her." He paused and gave consideration to something that had been gnawing on him since Terry and Vickie had been stolen. "You know, I been thinkin' maybe I should git a couple more brats offen her. They's whip-smart, her git."

Faith hid the jealousy that nearly gagged her. "What's wrong with me?"

"We gotta face facts, woman. Those youngins of ourn

ain't travelin' with full packs. Somethin's sommat wrong with them."

"They're kin an' kin to our kin," Faith defended stubbornly.

Silas ground his teeth. "So be it, woman. Now you just get ready."

Preacher had poured himself a final cup of coffee when a bullet cracked sharply over his head. He lunged to the side and rolled to where he had rested his Hawken against the trunk of a grizzled old pine. The finely made weapon came into his hands with fluid ease. He turned back to the direction from which the shot had come.

His eyes took in a flash, bright enough in the twilight to be readily seen, and a puff of gray-white powder smoke. He sighted in the Hawken. The hammer had not struck the percussion cap when a fat lead ball smacked into the tree, two inches above his head, and Preacher flinched in a natural reaction. Bits of wood and bark stung as they cut the back of his neck. That caused his round to go wild. A hell of a shot, whoever it might be, Preacher considered.

"You youngins stay low. Hug the ground."

"It's Silas, come to git us," Terry announced, his voice quavering with his fear of the man.

Preacher mulled that over. "May be, but if so, he's gonna leave his bones here for the varmits."

"No," Vickie wailed. "No, he's gonna kill us all."

More shots came from closer in. Preacher dived for another position. But not before one ball cut a hot path across the top of his left shoulder. He came up in a kneeling position and took aim at a hint of movement among the aspens along the trail. The reloaded Hawken bucked and spat a .56 caliber ball into the treeline.

A grunt and muffled curse rewarded Preacher's effort. He put the rifle aside and drew one of the pair of new-minted .44 Walker Colts. Another shot came from uphill and forced

Preacher into a nest of rocks at the edge of the camp. Vickie yelped, and Terry uttered words that should never be in the mouth of a twelve-year-old. Preacher fired into the aspens and moved again.

Emboldened by Preacher's apparent retreat, Silas Tucker came into view. A red, wet stain glistened in the waning light of the sunset. He had taken Preacher's ball in the meaty flesh of his right side. Enough fat there, Preacher reckoned, to make certain nothing vital had been hit. Still, even a cornered rat had a lot of fight left in him. Silas peered short-sightedly around the clearing and located Terry, hunkered down on the grassy turf. Sudden rage at the boy's defiance blotted out his earlier evaluation of the youngster's worth. He raised a single-barrel pistol and took aim at the boy's slim back.

A hot slug from the .44 Colt in Preacher's hand shattered the radius of Tucker's right forearm a split second later. Impact caused his .60 caliber pistol to discharge skyward. Instinctively, he dove for a hiding place. Preacher started after him when another shot cracked from the aspens.

This could be a little harder than he had expected, the mountain man admitted to himself. He sure hated to kill a woman, but who else could Tucker have with him?

8

In rapid succession, three bullets sought a chunk of meat from Preacher's hide. He banged off two fast slugs at the hidden shooter and again moved to better cover. A fallen log seemed to offer the best advantage.

He had barely settled into position and begun to lament the lack of his rifle when a scurry of movement in the open caught his attention. On hands and knees, Terry scampered toward Preacher, with a Hawken, powder horn, ball pouch, and cap stick slung over his slender back.

"Git back, you little varmint!" Preacher shouted at him.

Terry kept coming. "You need these," he countered.

Well, damned if I don't, Preacher acknowledged to himself.

Terry reached the fallen tree in under five seconds. He paused as a ball smacked into the bark inches above his head. Then he adroitly flew over the rough surface of the trunk. At once, Preacher snatched the rifle from the boy, taking time only to pat the lad on his head in gratitude. A moment later Silas Tucker made his move.

"Git out there, woman," he bellowed as he charged, a pistol in each hand.

First one barked, then the other; lead cracked overhead and Terry scrunched lower behind the tree. The ramrod still in the barrel of the Hawken, Preacher set it aside and answered the two-person charge with his .44 Walker Colt. A freak change of direction on the part of Silas Tucker caused Preacher to blow the heel off the degenerate's right boot.

Preacher exchanged six-guns as Tucker and the woman bore down on him. Biting his lip, Preacher sighted in on the center of the woman's chest. She fired at him, missed by a long ways, and Preacher saw her golden hair streaming from under a bonnet. The mother of Terry and Vickie! Imperceptibly, Preacher changed the aiming point of his Walker Colt and triggered a round.

Hot lead tore a shallow crease along Purity Tucker's rib cage. She stumbled and sprawled headlong in the dirt. "Momma!" Vickie screamed.

Silas Tucker did not even miss a stride. Hobbling, he came on, determined to end it right there and then. Preacher was glad to oblige him. His .44 Colt bucked once, then again. Silas Tucker jolted to a stop, turned partly away from Preacher and looked down in amazement at the twin holes, which formed a figure eight in the center of his chest. He made a feeble attempt to raise his weapon again, then crumpled bonelessly into a heap on the ground, while his lifeblood pumped into his chest through a shattered aorta.

Made haunting by distance and the echo effect of the basin, a curse descended upon the living in the clearing. "You baaastarrrd!" A shot followed.

Calmly, Preacher completed the loading drill for his Hawken and hefted it to his shoulder. "You up above. You can give it up now. No harm be done to you if you do."

He waited for a reply. It gave Faith Tucker time to reload. A shower of bark slashed down on Preacher and Terry. Preacher grunted his reluctance away and took aim. He fired with cool precision. A weak wail that wound down to breathless silence answered his shot.

"D'ya git her?" Terry asked hopefully.

Preacher sighed heavily. "I reckon so, though I sure am sorry to have had to do that. Killin' a woman's not somethin' a man lives with easily."

"She treated us as mean as Silas did." To Preacher, Terry's

justification lacked conviction enough to vindicate what had been done. "What about our momma?" the boy asked.

Recalling the grazing wound he had given the woman, Preacher came to his boots. He swung a leg over the downed tree and cleared it with ease. Terry quickly followed. Rapid steps brought them to the side of the fallen woman. Preacher knelt and felt her wrist for a pulse. He found one, strong enough, if a bit rapid. She moaned, turned her head, and opened one eye.

"My babies?" she asked first off, surprising Preacher. "Are they all right?"

"Sure are, ma'am," Preacher assured her. "Terry's right here beside me."

"Silas would have killed them. Sure enough that black-haired bitch sister of his would have."

Preacher broke the news with the usual mountain man's lack of delicacy. "She won't be doin' no killin' anymore."

"She's dead?"

A straight face hid Preacher's feelings. "Yep. She was tryin' to take my head off with that rifle."

"She is—er—was a good shot."

"Shootin' downhill throws a body off some. Now, there's somethin' I need ask of you. In fact, I damn well insist you do it. Once I get you patched up, I want you to go back for the rest of the children and lead them to the trading post at Trout Creek Pass. If you have any love for your own two, you had best do as I say, and mend your ways. You're gonna have to do that, and give them the care and love they deserve."

"They have done some terrible things," Purity offered in the faint hope of sloughing off her responsibilities.

"I know that. But they's youngins an' were forced into the life they led. You're not and nuther am I. We got rules to live by, and for you to teach this pair. Let me get on about fixin' you up."

"What if I just leave here an' keep on goin'?" Purity sought yet for a way out.

Preacher cut his hard, gray gaze to her eyes. He remained silent long enough to cause Purity to flinch. "Well, consider this. If you have any idea of duckin' out, with or without those other youngsters, keep in mind that I will hunt you down and drag you in to the tradin' post, where they'll be obliged to put a rope around your neck."

Purity Tucker swallowed hard and nodded her understanding. With her children gathered around, Purity sat still while Preacher cleaned up the shallow gouge in her side, packed it with a poultice of sulphur, moss and lichens, and bandaged it. Then he lighted the fire and set out the makings for coffee.

"Come morning, you set out north; we're headed south." Purity started to raise her voice in protest. Preacher showed her the palm of one hand to silence her. "Nuff said. Now, do I have to tie you to a tree?"

Purity shook her head and settled down to sip coffee in silence. An hour later everyone lay down for a restless sleep.

Dawn seemed to come extra early. After one of Preacher's substantial breakfasts, Purity sent Terry to recover the horses used by her and the dead pair. Preacher admonished the boy to gather all of the weapons. When Terry returned, Preacher tightened the cinch on one animal and helped Purity to mount. Without even a goodbye to her children, she rode away to the north.

Terry turned imploring blue eyes on Preacher. "Think she will really come back?"

Preacher shrugged and snorted. "I wouldn't bet more'n a nickel on it."

With that he assisted the boy and his sister into the saddles of the newly acquired mounts, and the three rode off toward Trout Creek Pass.

Philadelphia Braddock looked up from the moccasin he was repairing on the front porch of the trading post at Trout Creek Pass. He worked with a bison bone awl and a curved, fish rib bone needle. He sewed the sinew thread in precise, neat stitches. He was putting on thick, smoke-cured, bullhide "traveling" soles. The soft, distant sound of approaching horses had attracted his attention. Philadelphia squinted his bright green eyes. The brown flecks in them danced in the tears this produced. He peered over the top of the hexagonal half-glasses perched on the bulb of his nose.

From the cut of him, that big feller in the lead could be Preacher, he reckoned. Philadelphia ignored a small twinge in his shoulder wound, which was mending nicely under the care of an unlicensed doctor, who had journeyed west, turned to trapping and later to hard drink. To his credit, the pill-roller abstained religiously whenever he had a patient who needed the best of his professional skills. Yep, he saw more clearly now. Couldn't be anyone else.

Philadelphia shook his long, auburn hair in eagerness, which made his over-large ears, with their long, floppy lobes, flutter like wings. He snorted his impatience as it seemed to take forever for Preacher and the smaller folk with him to descend the high grade to the northern saddle out of the pass. Did his eyes play tricks, or did those folk ride some ways behind Preacher?

No, he realized a minute later as Preacher drew near enough to make out his face. They were kidfolk. Preacher with a pair of brats? And whose, at that? Be they his? Philadelphia literally danced with urgency, yet he knew he would learn the answers soon enough. Preacher swung clear of the main trail and entered through the gateway of the palisade that surrounded the trading post compound. Already, his keen vision had identified Philadelphia, and he waved enthusiastically to his old friend.

"Whoo-weee! Preacher, as I live an' breathe," Philadelphia exploded, unable to contain himself.

When Preacher reined in and dismounted to tie off his big-chested roan stallion, Philadelphia rushed forward with a wild war whoop. Preacher spun and met him midway. Both had their arms extended and charged into a chest-banging embrace that raised a cloud of brown around them. At once they started a toe-stomping fandango that raised more dust. The longer they went on, the more violent their greeting became. Concern began to crease the high, smooth forehead of Terry Tucker. At last he could contain himself no longer.

"Hey! Hey, mister, go easy," he shouted at Philadelphia. "He's been wounded."

"Hell, that's never slowcd Preacher none, boy. Mind yer business an' we'll mind ourn."

All of the improved deportment he had learned in Preacher's company deserted Terry. He looped the reins around the saddle horn and jumped off the back of the horse acquired from the Tuckers. "That done it!" his squeaky voice declared. "Damn you, old man, I'm gonna kick you right in the balls!"

Terry charged forward, only to be plucked off his feet by Prcacher, who grabbed the boy by the tail of his shirt and the waist of his trousers. Terry squirmed and made ineffectual thrashing with his legs and arms. "Lemme go! Lemme go. I'll fix 'cm, Preacher."

Their hugging welcome ended by Terry's intervention, Philadelphia Braddock stepped back and turned those startling green eyes on the lad. He cocked his head to one side. "Who's your bodyguard, Preacher?"

"He's not a bodyguard," Preacher growled. "He's a bother."

Philadelphia gave Preacher a fish eye. "Since when you be travelin' with children?"

"Ain't the first, won't be the last time, nuther," Preacher rumbled.

For somc reason, Preacher felt loath to go into all the lurid details behind Terry and Vickie. Philadclphia would find out soon enough, and no call to embarrass the youngsters. He clapped Philadelphia on the shoulder and changed the subject.

"I got a powerful thirst, Philadelphia. Bc you buyin'?"

"I be. Best get these babies some milk." He made a face at the prospect. "An' a sugar stick to suck on; then we can settle down to some serious depletin' o' Duffey's supply of Monongahela whiskey."

Preacher lowered Terry to the ground and looked hard into the boy's eyes. "You gonna behave yourselves? Not gonna pull a stunt like last time?"

Terry shrugged skinny shoulders. "We ain't got nowheres to go."

"That mean you'll stay?" Philadelphia cocked an eyebrow at Terry's manner of speech.

"Yes."

"Yes, what?"

"Yes, sir."

"Fine. Now, go help Vickie down an' scoot inside. Ask Duffey for something to eat. C'mon, Philadelphia. Let's go wet our throats. By the by, I see you look a mite peaked. Been off your feed a little?"

"Not perzactly. It's a long story. One best told over a flagon of rye."

Once settled at a crude table in one corner of the saloon side of the trading post, Philadelphia related his tale of the strange city and the stranger men, how they dressed and acted and that they spoke in a funny, foreign tongue. When he had finished, they drank in silence for several long minutes while Preacher wondered at it. At last he made up his mind.

Slapping a big palm on the damp wooden tabletop, Preacher spoke plain and clear while he looked Philadelphia straight in the eye, his own orbs hot with invitation. "I reckon I needs to see these people. I want to learn all I can about them."

"Suits. I got my curiosities aroused, too."

"There's more. That city you told me about. Seems I've heard of it somewhere before. Something is nigglin' in the back of my brain pan, says I've seen such a place, or read about it. Buildings is all white, right?"

"Seen 'em with my own eyes," Philadelphia assured him.

"Hummm." Preacher drained his pewter flagon and hoisted it to signal for another round. Ruben Duffey complied with a will. When he departed, Preacher went on. "Thing that really rubs me where I cain't itch is all these folks, an' all those buildin's bein' out here in the first place, an' me not knowin' a thing about it."

Philadelphia tried to hide his own eagerness. "Well, I cain't say I blame you a bit for that."

"Tell you what, Philadelphia. When that shoulder wound you got from them downright unfriendly fellers heals, I'd be mightly beholden if you were to lead me to this strange city growin' in the wilderness."

For an instant, relief flashed in those brown-flecked, green eyes. "You got yourself a deal, Preacher, that you surely do."

Chariot wheels rattled noisily over the smooth, nicely set cobbles of the wide Via Iulius, which led to the foot of the Pontis Martius—the Hill of Mars—and the gladiator school of Justinius Bulbus that nestled in its shadow. Swelled with pride, young Quintus Faustus Americus held the reins as he stood beside his father. Although usually the task for slaves, driving the chariot had made the day into a golden one for the patrician boy. His bony chest swelled even more when he slowed the horses at the proper time and received a fond pat on the head from his father.

He halted the animals in good order and stopped the vehicle without incident, due to the hand brake, an improvement over the original design. Bulbus stood in the gateway to welcome them. Born Able Wade, Justinius Bulbus looked the ideal director of a school for gladiators. His thick, burly body, low brow, jutting jaw and hairy ears made a clear statement of his past as a brawler and a thug.

Cunning and ruthlessness lighted his pale blue eyes, rather than intelligence. When recruited out of the dockside slums of Boston by Marcus Quintus, Able Wade had been more than enthused by the proposition made to him. He had babbled on and on about various weapons and fighting styles of the ancient gladiators. It became clear to Quintus that Wade had likewise shared the benefits of a classical education. Only the lack of a keen intelligence, and his father's sudden loss of a vast fortune, such as that of the Reardons of Virginia, had ended that schooling abruptly and left Able in the lowest stratum of society. Quintus could not have cared less. So long as the newly named Justinius Bulbus could run a school to teach men exotic ways to slay their fellows, he would be amply rewarded. Quintus now returned the greeting salute of the master of games and dismounted from the chariot.

"You are just in time, First Citizen." Bulbus had had little difficulty becoming fluent in Latin, recalling snippets of it from his years in the finest schools. "We are about to begin the morning session. Come, join me in my box."

"With pleasure, good Justinius. You know my son, Quintus Faustus?"

"Of course—of course. A bright lad." Bulbus peered closely at his guest. "He certainly takes avid interest in the games."

"That he does. The games to honor his birthday are coming soon. I am sure you have prepared a magnificent program?"

"Oh, yes. You see, we have this new contingent of Christians. I'm sure the boy will fair pop a—ah—button at the spectacle I have planned."

Faustus brightened even more; his face writhed in expectation. "Christians, Father? How wonderful." He clapped his hands in emphasis.

Bulbus directed his important guests to the small, private box that overlooked the practice arena. Exactly one-third the size of the coliseum, it afforded space for only two pairs to fight at once, or for rehearsal of half of one of the "historicals" or farces at one time. The rest of the participants in the latter two presentations looked on from behind bars set into one wall of the arena. They studied the movements of their counterparts, then changed places and did the routine themselves. Final rehearsals would naturally be held in the coliseum. Bulbus made sweeping gestures to cushioned chairs in the front row, and father and son seated themselves.

Bulbus raised an arm. "All right, let it begin."

"Will Spartacus fight first?" Faustus asked the master of games.

Offended by this slighting of his star gladiator, Bulbus answered sharply. "Certainly not. Spartacus is my grand finale. Lesser-knowns are for opening the show. Today, and this will be a preview of your birthday games, young man," he confided, "Baccus Circus will open. He has taken to training well and shows real aptitude."

"He's a magnificent specimen." Quintus brought the subject back to Spartacus, who had appeared while Bulbus spoke to the boy, and was working out in a side cage that could be seen beyond the wall of the arena. He nodded to the huge black man.

"Our legionnaires found him wandering on the high plain east of here. No one in Nova Roma knows his real name. He's a runaway slave, of course. And, frankly, I don't care to know his identity. He is the best gladiator in Nova Roma, as I am sure you know. But, a slave is a slave, so Bulbus owns him. Spartacus likes his work.

"He's never been intractable or rebellious. That must also be true from before he came here." Quintus paused. "If you examine him closely, you'll find there's not a whip mark on him."

Bulbus was not to be put off a lecture on his favorite subject. "Timing is everything with the games. It is like the theater." He would have said more, but the shriek of wrought-iron hinges interrupted as the Porta Quadrila opened and two gladiators stalked out.

Big and burly, the first blinked at the sudden, bright sunlight. Thick muscles rippled in his shoulders and arms. He bore a spiked club and a small shield. His opponent, Baccus Circus, carried a round "target" shield and a twin-bladed dagger. Of nearly sword length, it made a formidable weapon.

They paced across the sand and saluted Bulbus and his distinguished guests.

"Begin," Bulbus commanded in a bored tone.

That this would not be a fight to the death soon became obvious. The middle-range fighter squared off with Baccus Circus, and they began a series of set-piece drills. They consisted of four or five varied attacks, at the end of which they engaged shields and weapons and rotated a quarter way around the arena. Both men soon glistened with sweat. Their smoothly shaven bodies sparkled in the sunlight. The speed of their drill increased with each engagement. Quintus, bored by so routine a performance, looked to his son.

Faustus stared intently at the battling men, jaw slack, lip parted, eyes glazed with excitement. His breath came harshly from a dry throat. Slowly, the pink tip of his tongue slid out and licked his lips. It was not, Quintus noted, a quenching gesture, rather one of unhealthy arousal for a boy so young. He quickly cut his eyes back to the contestants.

Their contest ended in the third quarter, when Baccus caught one of the spikes in the head of his opponent's club between the two blades of his weapon and disarmed the man. Quickly, Baccus stepped in and laid the flat of his dual knives against the throat of the other.

"Well done!" Bulbus shouted over his applause. "You are doing magnificently for a beginner, Baccus Circus." He turned to Faustus. "Now it is time to see some real blood flow, eh, lad?"

Faustus brightened. "Yes! Oh, yes . . . please.

Bulbus made a full arm gesture and called to his staff. "Bring in Spartacus. And . . . one of those teamsters from the freight wagons, I think."

Baccus Circus winced when he heard that. He hated the name given him. To himself, he would always remain Buck Sears. He hated what he had been forced to do. Most of all,

he hated it when a fellow teamster captured in the high plains
or the mountains was slaughtered needlessly to slake the
appetites of some crazy fool who believed he lived in ancient Rome.

Buck had been brought here six months ago, after his train
of freight wagons had been ambushed by men in the weirdest
outfits Buck had ever seen. When he heard them speaking a
foreign language, Buck at first thought the country had been
invaded by the Mexicans. Only two years past the big war
with Mexico, it seemed likely to him. Put into chains and
forced to walk with the other survivors and captives, his first
sight of New Rome stunned Buck.

This could not be. He didn't have a lot of book-learning,
only six years of grammar school. Yet, he had a haunting suspicion that he should recognize the sprawl of shining white
buildings and the seven hills they occupied. Rage almost
earned him the lash when the captives had been led to the
market, stripped, and sold like those unfortunate slaves in the
South. He and half a dozen others had been purchased by a
man whose function he did not then know.

Then he had been taken to the gladiator school. No
stranger to fighting, the idea did not bother Buck, until he
discovered that the contests were to the death. For all his
moral objections, eventually he became resigned to it. At
first, their training had been in English, with some Latin words
worked in as they grew familiar. Now he spoke Latin with all
the ease of those born in Nova Roma. Buck glanced up as
they neared the portal and passed through with the first sensation of regret he had known in a long time. Against his
better judgment, he quelled his reflections and remained at
the iron lattice to watch the slaughter of his brother teamster.

Spartacus gazed coolly at the sorry specimen standing
beside him. This wouldn't take long. The best Spartacus could
recall, this one had not been at the school more than a month.

What could he have learned in that time? Oh, well, the white boss says, "You do dis," you sho'nuf do it. He says, "Do dat." You do that. He shrugged it off and raised his arm.

"Ave Maestro! Morituri te salutamus."

"Give us a good show, Spartacus," Bulbus told the big black gladiator.

Now, that would be a hard one. Spartacus lowered his arm and prepared to step into position. Frightened to desperation, the shivering teamster did not stand on formalities. He struck swiftly and without warning. Only by the barest of margins did Spartacus elude death.

"Bis dat qui cito dat!" the spoiled little boy jeered down at Spartacus.

He gives twice who gives quickly, Spartacus thought angrily. That was supposed to apply to charity—snotty little brat. He made a quick lunge. His opponent dodged clumsily. Spartacus pressed in on him.

With wild slashes, the hapless teamster defended himself. Metal shrieked off metal, a spark flew. Then another. The clash of blades became a constant toll of chimes. In a surprisingly short time, the teamster's wrists began to weaken. Spartacus played with him like a cat with a mouse. Small cuts began to appear and stream blood from the chest, arms, and belly of the amateur. Eventually the big black man grew bored with his sport. Swiftly, with a confusingly intricate movement, Spartacus struck again.

The short, Etruscan sword went flying. For all his furious action, the teamster went pale. Spartacus loomed over him. Tasting defeat, his opponent lowered his shield and let his chin droop to his chest. Spartacus looked up at the box.

Before Bulbus could signify the fate of the teamster, Quintus interposed a request. "Since it is close to his eleventh birthday, and he will be *imperator* at the games in his honor, I'd like to make a present to Faustus at this time."

"Go ahead, Your Illustriousness."

"Faustus, you may have the honor of deciding the fate of this wretch."

Faustus gaped. "Thank you, Father." Then young Faustus leaned even farther over the arena and thrust out his arm, the fist closed, thumb extended. With an exalted expression of ecstasy, he made a quick, jerking movement and turned the thumb down.

9

By the third day after their return to Trout Creek Pass, Preacher had to admit he had all he could handle to keep up with Terry and Vickie. Much of it centered around behavior they considered entirely ordinary, yet that which most of society frowned upon, or saw as outright immoral. If ever he was to find a family to take in the youngsters—he had long since given up on the return of their mother—Preacher felt obligated to instruct them in manners and other socially acceptable conduct. To that end, he established an open-air classroom in a stand of fragrant pines.

Squirrels chittered and birds sang from above while the children sat on the low stumps of trees harvested to build the trading post. It was going the same way it had during the past morning and afternoon sessions. Terry and Vickie sat politely, still and attentive, their cherubic faces upturned to Preacher. One by one, Preacher dealt with their moral shortcomings, as he and his culture saw them. They listened, he felt sure of that. Then, in the most innocent of words, they dismissed entirely every manner of conduct that differed with the way they wanted to do things. This afternoon's session had finally gotten around to their sleeping habits.

"Now, over the past days, I've been tellin' you a lot about how decent people do things. Also about the sorta stuff the good folk would never do. Some of it, I'm sure you understood. What sticks in my craw is how you manage to make it sound out of the ordinary and your way to be better. To tell you straight out, that cain't be with what I want to talk about this afternoon. There comes a time—ah—when youngins reach a certain age—that decent folk just don't countenance them sleepin' together, if they be of opposite sorts."

"What do you mean?" Vickie asked, all sweetness and light.

"Take the two of you. Terry is twelve, you ten, Vickie. Decent boys and girls of those ages don't sleep together nekid, especially if they's brother and sister. They don't even sleep together in nightshirts. Or even like you sometimes on the trail, in all your clothes."

"Why not?" Terry prodded.

Preacher's face clouded. "We been over this before. You both told me you knew about animals an' stuff. How they get their young. An' that sort of thing went on a lot among that brood of kids with your folks. Well, if you an' Vickie continue to sleep like you do, other folks are gonna think it goes on betwixt you."

"But we *don't!*" they protested in chorus.

"I know that. But decent folks are gonna *think you* do."

Terry took on an expression of sullen defiance and challenge. "If they think those kinda thoughts, seems to me they cain't be too decent themselves."

Preacher's cheeks turned pink. "Now, there you go, boy. Deep in my heart I know I'm right, especial for brother an' sister. Yet, danged if I don't have to agree with you. Only dirty minds could dwell on those sort of notions."

Terry and Vickie gave him a "so there you are" expression. Preacher cut his eyes from one to the other, stomped the ground and turned away. Images of Indian children, all curled up together in furry buffalo robes, marched through his head. Over his shoulder he announced to them, "All right. Dang-blast it, all right. School's out for today. At this rate, I'll never make you fit to live among proper folk." He grumbled to himself as he walked off.

* * *

Preacher did not get off the hook that easily. Early the next morning, over a plate of fried fatback, beans and cornbread, he found his good mood spoiled by Anse Yoder, the factor of the trading post. A strapping, amiable Dane under most circumstances, Yoder had his visage screwed up into the best expression of disapproval and anger that his broad, pink face under a tousled mop of straight, blond hair could produce.

"Preacher, those little hellions of yours have gone too far. Hoot Soames got howlin' drunk last night. When he passed out, I put him to bed in the common room. Those devil's spawn snuck in there, and they dribbled molasses all over Hoot's face. Then they cut his pillow. He woke up this mornin' thinking he had been tarred and feathered."

Preacher's first response was to let go an uproarious belly laugh. He restrained himself and considered the situation over another cup of coffee. From what he had dragged out of Terry and Vickie, the children saw their former criminal activity as high adventure. It had taken some powerful talking for him to convince them to find another outlet for their charged spirits. He hadn't expected them to turn to stinging jokes on the customers at the trading post. He would definitely have to do something about it. That decided, Preacher prepared to relax, when Anse dropped the other boot.

"Just the other day it was Olin Kincade, near to killing himself trying to get out of the outhouse. Ya see, what those *schnorrers* of yours did was to rig some rattlesnake rattles under the bench in there, right by the opening. They had dem so that they made a purty real sound when a string got pulled. So, what happens? Olin went in to answer a call of nature. Those brats waited until he got settled all well an' good, then let go. Olin came up off that seat with a roar and nearly tore himself apart tryin' to get out. He forgot he had slid the latch bolt closed when he went in."

"Now, that's nothin' that ain't been done before," Preacher defended, all the while making a powerful attempt to hold in his laughter.

"That's grown men playing a gag on one of their fellows.

No, sir, I tell you, Preacher, I tell you true. You have to find a home for them and damned fast at that."

Grumbling to himself, Preacher finished his breakfast and looked up from his place. "All right, Anse, I'll do just that." With that he left to find Terry and Vickie.

"Nope. Sorry, but I heard about them two already. What I want is for them to be as far away from me and mine as anyone can get."

Preacher found the story the same wherever he went. Not a single household wanted anything to do with Terry and Vickie Tucker. After one silver-tongued effort to beguile a thickly set timber cutter, and father of four, the man rounded on him, double-bit axe in hands made hard by work.

"No, sir. I'd as leave have the devil hisself move in. Why that pair would pollute my youngins faster than a man can say 'Go.' Those Tuckers was nothin' but trash. Plain ol' hill trash from the west part o' Virginny. They just natural have the morals of an alley cat and the urges of a three-peckered billy goat. It's those mountains they growed up in, I think. Even the Injuns called them big medicine. The Cherokees, before they was removed from Carolina and Georgia, wouldn't set up a camp there. Only went for religion things. Whatever it is, it's done twisted those white folk that live there. Say what you might, Preacher. I just ain't gonna have them here."

After they rode off, Preacher's keen hearing hadn't any difficulty picking out the faint sound of sniffing. The children had dropped back slightly, so he turned to see what caused it. Tears filled the eyes of Terry and Vickie. Caught in an embarrassing moment, Terry took a quick swipe at his nose with the back of one hand.

"There ain't anyone wants us, is there, Preacher?" Vickie asked, her voice shaky with weeping.

Preacher roughly cleared his throat. "We ain't seen *everyone* yet."

"Don't matter," Terry fretted. "No one's gonna take us in."

Eyes squinted, Preacher challenged the boy's conviction. "I wouldn't be takin' any wagers on that, Terry." He sighed and looked back at the roof peak of the cabin they had just left. "Maybe we ain't gone far enough."

"But, you already said we'd come ten miles from the tradin' post."

Exasperated, Preacher snapped. "Right enough. Only maybe that ain't far enough, considerin' the reputation you Tuckers has hangin' on you." Then he softened his harsh words. "We'll look some other places."

After four more refusals over the next three days, Preacher had about talked himself into accepting Terry's cynical version of their predicament. He had even agreed with his doubting side that given another turndown, he would return to Trout Creek Pass and keep the kidlets with him, at least until he had time to journey to Bent's Fort and hopefully hand them off to some unsuspecting pilgrims.

What an awful thing to do to both sides, he thought charitably a few minutes later. He had crested a low saddle and saw beyond a tidily built, inviting-looking cabin of two stories, complete with isinglass windows that sparkled in the afternoon sun. Thin streams of smoke rose from two well-constructed chimneys at opposite wings of the building, one of them of real brick. A lodgepole rail fence surrounded it, and defined a generous kitchen garden to one side of the front. A corral of the same material featured high sides, and a sided lean-to for sheltering stock from summer's heat and spring's rain.

A half barn abutted it, no doubt the remaining portion dug into the hillside. Then, on another small knoll, with a huge, gnarled old oak shading the plot, he noted three small, fresh mounds of dirt behind a split-rail fence that guarded the final resting place of those who had departed. Preacher confounded the youngsters by removing his battered, floppy old hat and holding it over his heart as he rode past. At a hundred yards, he halted and hailed the house.

"Hello, the cabin!"

"Howdy, yourself," came the answer from the doorway to the barn, where a man appeared, a pitchfork in one hand.

"We be just the three of us. These youngins an' me are friendly, oncest you get to know us."

Their host squinted, then nodded. "I know you, right enough. Know of you anyway. You're Preacher, right?"

Terry groaned. "We might as well ride on," he said under his breath.

It didn't escape Preacher. "Now, hold on there, boy. Let him tell us that." To the stranger, he answered, "That I am."

"Ride on in, then. My wife's bound to have coffee on the stove. An' there's buttermilk or tea for these two," he added.

"My goodness, *tea,* as I live and breathe," Preacher said from the corner of his mouth. It brought a giggle from the children. "Mighty obliged, mister."

Down at the cozy, large cabin, Preacher learned that they were Cecil and Dorothy Hawkins. Two rug-crawlers clung to Dorothy's skirts and peeked shyly at the mountain man, their eyes widening when they saw Terry and Vickie. Tears sprang into Dorothy's eyes as she studied the towheaded youngsters.

"Are they . . . yours?" she asked in a low, grief-roughened voice.

"No, ma'am. They're not. You might say they is orphans. At least for sure on their pappy's side."

Cecil interrupted in an effort to spare his wife more sorrow. "You can tell us about it over some plum duff and coffee, Preacher."

"Obliged, Mr. Hawkins."

"Call me Cecil."

They entered the house, the children showing the nervous excitement common to the good smells they picked up. This Mrs. Hawkins must be the best cook in the whole world. Seated at a large, round oak table in the center of the main room of the cabin, Preacher felt himself relaxing—this was a house full of love. This was also a house that had experienced a recent tragedy. He longed to ask about it directly. Good manners prevented him from doing so.

"What brings you this way, Preacher?" Cecil asked as though their earlier conversation had not occurred.

Preacher took a big bite of the plum duff that had been set before him. "Well, like I said, Cecil, I'm lookin' for a home for these tadpoles." His hosts lowered their eyes. Preacher made a note of that. *Strike,* he thought in a cliche that had originated long ago in some army's surgical tent, *while the iron is hot.* "Did I say anything wrong?"

A long silence followed. At last, his eyes brimming with unshed tears, Cecil Hawkins answered him. "No, Preacher. Likely you said something right for the first time in a long time."

Always sensitive to the emotions of others, Preacher spoke softly. "How's that, Cecil?"

"We—we just lost our three oldest youngsters, Preacher. It was—was a fever that sort of sprang up all of a sudden. There ain't any doctors anywhere around here, not for a thousand miles. We didn't know what to do. We doped them with goose grease and sulphur, put cold cloths on their heads and chests. Nothin' did any good. It . . . took a long time. We buried the last only three days ago."

Sadness drew down the corners of Preacher's mouth. "I'm powerful sorry to hear that. The Almighty gives and He taketh away. It don't matter no-how what we wish things to be; the final outcome is in the hands of our Maker. I don't imagine, in your grief, you'd be willing to take on responsibility for two wild colts?"

Cecil and Dorothy cut their eyes, one to the other. A long, silent message seemed to pass between them. Cecil drew a long breath. "You say they are orphans?"

"Same as. I kilt their pappy, an' their momma has gone and deserted them."

"Are they well-behaved?" Dorothy asked.

Preacher took a deep breath, then let the words out in a

rush. "They could be, if you've a strong hand and a powerful will of your own."

Another silent conference occupied the Hawkinses. Cecil scooted back his chair and came to his boots. "You'll excuse us for a moment?"

"Certainly. Take your time."

Preacher drummed his fingers on the table while the pair left the cabin. Their muted voices came from outside. He could make nothing of what they said. At last, they returned. Expectation lighted Dorothy's face. Cecil cleared his throat, his hands doing nervous things with one another.

"We—ah—we talked it over, Preacher. Losin' those babies almost destroyed Dorothy. Our oldest was about an age with this boy. You're Terry, right?" Terry nodded, his face blank. "We know that—that you could never completely fill the place in our hearts that Tommy held, but would you . . . will you try?" He turned to Preacher again. "We want them to come live with us. We need their help and we believe they can help us. Our other two are so young, and Dorothy says she is in a family way again. With a new baby, she'll need someone to help with the chores. So, if it's all right with you, Preacher, and you children? We'd like to make you a part of our family."

Beaming, Preacher came to his boots. "Them is splendid words, Mr. Cecil Hawkins. I'm mighty happy for all of you. What do you say, Terry, Vickie?"

"Yes," Terry blurted. "I—I guess."

"Your two children are so cute, Mrs. Hawkins," Vickie made her thoughts known. "I'd love to help you with them, if I may."

"Of course, my dear." She opened her arms, and Vickie rushed into her embrace.

Preacher cleared his throat, finding it quite restricted. "Well, then, that's all settled. You two might as well stay here. Philadelphia an' I are headin' to the northwest to look into what is going on in the Ferris Range. I'll drop off your things on the way by."

"Oh, thank you, Preacher," Vickie squealed, rushing to hug him and turn up her face for a kiss.

"Thank you, thank you, thank you, Preacher," Terry squeaked. Then he pushed out his lower lip in a pout. "But I really would like to go along and see those strange men."

"Another time, boy. Not now. Well, I'd best be gettin' on my way. Thank you folks for bein' such good Christian souls." He cut his eyes to the ceiling. "I'm sure the Almighty will give you a fittin' reward." If he was aware of the irony, he didn't show it.

Filled with deep-rooted satisfaction, Preacher rode away some ten minutes later. Terry ran down the lane to catch up and leap up on Preacher's leg. The mountain man caught the boy, which freed Terry's arms to give Preacher a big hug.

"I'll never forget you, Preacher. Goodbye." The boy turned his head away to hide the rush of tears.

Preacher released the lad and brushed a knuckle at the corner of one eye. "Goodbye to you, Terry. Remember what I taught you about the things decent people expect of children."

And then he rode away.

Preacher counted the days on his fingers. He had been off on his quest for a week and a half by the time he saw the chimneys and rooftops of the trading post. He gigged Cougar into a fast trot. When he drew near, he recognized the stout figure of Philadelphia Braddock on the front porch. Philadelphia spotted him at the same time and bounded down the steps, his body visibly charged with energy. They met fifty yards from the double cabin that formed the trading post.

It instantly became obvious to Preacher that Philadelphia had made great strides in his healing. His face held its usual ruddy color, and he bounced around like a young puppy. His eyes twinkled with mischief as he questioned Preacher.

"I see you're alone. What happened, Preacher? Them two runned off again?"

"No. I found them a home. Let's go get the trail dust out of my throat and I'll tell one and all at the same time."

Inside the saloon, Preacher downed one pewter flagon of rye, signaled for another and waited for it to arrive. All the usual hangers-on crowded into the room. Their faces revealed how anxious they were for a good tale. Preacher soon obliged them.

"Yep, my quest ended in success," he declared the obvious. He went on to detail the search for a home, told of the Hawkins family and the evident pleasure Terry and Vickie had shown at being taken in by them. He concluded with an observation.

"Strange enough, they did not appear too happy about partin' with me. For all I drubbed their heads and switched their bottoms."

Ruben Duffey answered with sober sincerity. "Not so strange, Preacher, I'm thinkin'."

Preacher blushed. "What's done is done. Tomorrow Philadelphia an' me are off to the Ferris Range. I aim to get me a good look at these strange soldiers, or whatever they are."

"Need some company, Preacher?" a couple of the regulars shouted.

Preacher pursed his lips and gave it a moment's thought. "That's mighty nice of you, Clem. You, too, John. This first time, though, I reckon the less of us they see, the better. But stick around. Might be we'll want some help later on," he added prophetically.

Buck Sears sat on a stone bench in the dressing room of the public baths of New Rome. Gathered around were five of the new "gladiators." One man wore a hard, belligerent expression. He ground a fist into one palm when Buck told them that the penalty for refusing to fight or attempted escape was death in the arena. No matter how many a fellow fought and bested, he would die there on the sand.

"I don't wanna go back to those cells they keep us in.

Filthy, smelly, with rats and other critters runnin' around at night. I'm willin' to risk death to get out of here."

"Good. That's one of you."

"What are you getting at, Buck?" the pugnacious one demanded.

Buck studied him a long moment, while all five leaned toward him in anticipation. "I've found a way out of here. I need me some good men, ones with enough fire and fight in them to make an escape."

"But you just said yourself that the penalty for attempted escape is death," one pilgrim with a receding chin and pop-eyes protested.

Buck stared him down. "That's only *if you get caught.* I don't intend to. From what I hear, the trouble is in those big ol' black dogs this so-called Bulbus keeps. We try to break out of the school, they give the alarm, and any who doesn't get eat up are condemned to the arena."

"How'er you gonna get around that?"

Buck studied the mousey little fellow. "I'm tellin' that only to those willin' to go with me."

Pop-eyes averted, the captive gladiator turned away. "Well, I—I don't know. At least, we're still alive."

Anger flared in Buck's chest. "For how long? Sooner or later, we're all gonna be pitted against Spartacus. When that time comes, you'd better be ready to meet your Maker."

The angry one looked at his timid companion with contempt. "Count me in. I don't aim to be dog meat, an' I sure know I'm no match for Spartacus."

Buck cut his eyes to the others, hope shining in his face. "How about the rest of you?"

Slowly they turned away, shame-faced, and muttered feeble excuses. Disappointed, Buck stomped out through an archway to wait for the guards to escort them back to the gladiator school on the Field of Mars. A moment later, his only recruit joined him. He extended a hand.

"M'name's Fletcher. Jim Fletcher. When do you reckon on doing this?"

Buck gave him a relieved look. "Soon, friend Jim. Soon's we have enough to make it work."

Later that night, when the inmates of the school slumbered in deep exhaustion, the skinny pilgrim with the receding chin quietly left the small cell he occupied, being released by a discreet guard. Blinking in the bright light of oil lamps, he was brought into the presence of Justinius Bulbus. Bulbus studied him over fat, greasy fingers.

"You have some information for me?" he asked, licking meat juices off the tips.

Voice shaking, the informant replied softly, "Yes, I have."

Bulbus gestured to a tray piled high with steaming meat. "Have some roasted boar. It's really quite delicious. Besides, you need the meat to build you up."

In spite of the obvious intent behind the invitation, the betrayer indulged himself greedily while he informed Bulbus of what he had overheard at the baths. Bulbus listened carefully and considered the problem a while before making answer.

"You have been most helpful. Circus is a splendid gladiator. It would be a shame to lose him. Perhaps . . ." Bulbus paused, thinking. "Yes, perhaps a flogging, administered by Spartacus, would serve as an object lesson to all concerned." He turned to his chief trainer, who lounged on a couch at right angles to Bulbus.

"See to it, will you? Say, ten lashes. No lead tips on the flail, either. I don't want him marked up." Bulbus sighed heavily. "Ah, such a magnificent specimen. When his time comes, I want him to shine. See that it is done tomorrow morning, right after breakfast."

10

Philadelphia Braddock halted and turned in the saddle to look directly at Preacher. He gestured to a notch in the ridge ahead. "By jing, if it ain't been a week's time since we left Trout Crick. Over yonder is that strange city I told you about."

Preacher thought on it, as he had been doing over the past seven days. "I reckon if they have people out scoutin', we'd best hole up somewhere until dark, then move in close."

"Good idee, Preacher. But, first, don't you want to size it up in daylight?"

"Of course. If we stay inside the treeline, we can reach the back slope of the ridge unseen. We can pick a spot from there."

It went as Preacher expected. Near the pass that led through to the basin, his keen ears picked out the brassy notes of several bugles, yet they saw no sign of soldiers beyond the gap. On the opposite side, he found an entirely different, and amazing, situation.

Philadelphia had been right. Large, shiny white buildings now covered the slopes and tops of four of the seven hills. Construction, even at this distance, could be seen to go on at a feverish pace. Horsemen in scarlet cloaks and shiny helmets cantered around through the organized confusion. On the Campus Martius, formations of soldiers raised clouds of dust as they drilled with precision. Preacher studied the scene for a long while, then grunted his satisfaction.

"Over there." He pointed to a thick stand of slender pines,

as yet not fallen to the hunger of the axemen. "We can ease our way over there and be within range to look over that place by spyglass."

Philadelphia licked his lips. "Now, that shines. If I'd 'a had my smarts about me, I coulda done the same thing." For a moment he looked crestfallen. "Only m'spyglass is broke."

Preacher gave him a smile. "No time like the here an' now, I allus say."

Silently, and with the great skill of the mountain men, they worked their way to Preacher's suggested vantage point. They left their horses muzzled with feedbags to silence them, and crept through the undergrowth which crowded the stand of lodgepole pines. Preacher settled in, his Hawken rifle across his lap, and extracted a long, thick, bullhide tube from his possibles bag. From that, he slid a brass telescope.

He fitted the eyepiece in place and peered at the scene below. Men dressed in only sandals and diaperlike loincloths sweated in the warm afternoon sun. Many, Preacher noted, had scars from a heavily applied lash on their backs. Overseeing them were men in tunics and rough leather aprons. Here and there stood uniformed soldiers. Preacher blinked, and pursed his lips.

"Danged if they don't look just like them old-timey Romans. But, that cain't be. T'weren't any Romans got to the New World."

"That's what I thought," Philadelphia whispered back. "Then I reckoned my wound had got infected and I was seein' things. But, by gol, if you see 'em too, then they must be real."

"Only too real. We can't learn too much about them from here. We'll wait until night, then go down among them buildings and see what they're up to."

That suited Philadelphia fine. He settled back for a comfortable afternoon snooze. Preacher continued to study the oddly dressed men. He saw what he believed to be a chariot, pulled by a pair of sparkling white horses. Some big shot no doubt. Twenty men in uniform marched down a wide avenue toward the largest hill. They all carried long, slender spears. An hour shy of sundown, a shrill note sounded, as though from a reed flute, and the men quit working. They lined up and had chains fastened on their arms and legs. Then the men in tradesmen's aprons marched them away, out of Preacher's sight. Slaves, Preacher thought with disgust.

Preacher did not hold with slavery. Far from a frothing-mouthed abolitionist, he still did not think it right for one man to own another, like a horse, or pig, or cow. Quite a few Indians had slaves, mainly captive women or children from other tribes. Most times, once they had learned the ways of those who captured them, the children were adopted to fill the place of a child that had died, or the women married men affluent enough to afford two or more wives. Somehow, that didn't seem to Preacher to be so harsh a system. What was going on here, though, rankled.

"May an' have to do something about that," he whispered to himself.

Time edged toward sunset. Preacher stretched out the kinks in arms and legs and munched a strip of jerky. An hour after dark, he awakened Philadelphia. He bent close and spoke lower than the serenade of cicadas.

"Eat yourself a bit o' somethin' an' we'll move out in another half hour."

"I'll admit I ain't looking forward to this too much, though it does have my curiosity aroused."

"Not a big problem. Certain sure they ain't got senses half as sharp as an Injun. We've sure snuck into enough Cheyenne and Blackfoot camps to know how it's done."

"Even so," Philadelphia warned, "we could die here."

Silent as ghosts, Preacher and Philadelphia crept through the streets of New Rome. Every block brought new marvels. In moccasins, with rifles at the ready, pistols loaded, primed and waiting in their wide belts, they accosted marble statues; tall, alabaster columns of the same material supported high porticoes over stately porches. Philadelphia pointed a finger in amazement when they came upon a large, bronze brazier flaming with the eternal fire before the Temple of Vesta.

"Lookie there," Philadelphia whispered in awe. "I'll betcha someone is paid to keep that goin' all the time."

"More likely a slave," Preacher amended in a sour note, his mind on the shackling of the workmen at quitting time. "Cost less that way."

"Any way you look at it, somebody has to tend it. That must be some sort of church."

"More likely a pagan temple, if this is what we think it is."

"Better an' better." Philadelphia rubbed his hands in anticipation. "That's where they hold them orgies, huh?" He pronounced it or-*ghees*.

Preacher and his friend had no time to contemplate that vision. They rounded a corner in the forum and came face-to-face with the night watch. Armed with cudgels, flaming torches held above their heads, the city guards reacted instantly. With a shout of alarm, they dashed at the two surprised mountain men.

"Looks like folks know we're here," Philadelphia declared flatly as he flung away one of the watchmen.

Preacher saved the talking for later. Two burly sentries closed on him, their cudgels swinging with competence. When they raised them to strike, Preacher ducked low and stepped in under the weapons. Quickly he popped one with a right, the other with a left, under the chin. They rocked back on their heels. The chubbier of the two sat down abruptly, eyes wide with wonder. Preacher turned to finish the other one, when a cudgel caught him in the side.

He grunted out the pain and shock, then delivered a buttstroke from the half-moon brass butt plate of his Hawken that broke teeth and cracked the jawbone of his attacker. The clatter of fast-approaching sandals on the cobbles sounded like hail on a broad-leafed plant. A swift check of the immediate area told Preacher that between them they had accounted for four of the six. With a little luck, they still might make it.

Good fortune deserted the mountain men. A dozen more of the night watch rounded into the *Via Sacra* and pounded down on the Temple of Vesta. Preacher caught a blow from a closed fist in the side of his head that made lights flash and bells ring. A short sword flashed in the hand of one watchman, and Preacher forgot all about his determination not to use firearms.

The Hawken barked. Burning powder sparked in the wake of flame that erupted from the muzzle. Smoke rose in front of Preacher while his opponent twisted his mouth into an ugly gash, stumbled backward and clutched at his ravaged shoulder. Then the other guards arrived, and the great square of the forum became a welter of struggling human shapes. Many of the blows delivered by the sentries fell upon their fellows. Enough found their intended target to bring an end to the battle.

A ringing, thudding pain exploded in Preacher's head, and the Hawken slipped from numbed fingers. Shooting stars cut through the darkness that gathered in his head. He tried to turn, to put his back to that of Philadelphia, though he knew it to be already too late. Philadelphia had sunk to his knees, hands around his head to protect it, while the heavy blows of cudgels rained on his bent back. The next smash with the thick-ended nightstick made the darkness complete for Preacher.

Early the next morning, Preacher and Philadelphia awakened in a small, damp, slimy cell. The odor of human vomit hung heavily in the dank, still air. Preacher's head throbbed, and he located four separate goose-egg-sized lumps on it. The sour taste in his mouth told him who had vomited. Beside him, Philadelphia groaned.

"Where are we?"

Preacher answered glumly. "In the lockup. Damn, my head hurts."

"So's mine. Ah! Aaaah—aaah, my back, too. They tried to turn my kidneys into mush. I'll be piddlin' blood for a month."

"Be glad it ain't runnin' out your ears."

Philadelphia quickly forgot his own misery. "You hurt that bad, Preacher?"

"No. But no thanks to those fellers."

Footsteps tramped loudly in the corridor outside. A jingle of keys came to Preacher's ears. They sounded sharp and tinny through the buzzing in his head. A key turned noisily in the lock, and a low, narrow door banged open.

"Come out, you two," a voice commanded in clear English.

"Where are we going?" Philadelphia wanted to know.

"You've got a hearing before the First Citizen."

Preacher scowled. "I don't like the sound of that. If I recollect, I've heard that before. It escapes me what it means."

Outside the cell, each man was given a bowl of water and a crudely woven towel with which to freshen up. Then the indifferent turnkey passed over a lump of coarse bread and a clay flagon of sour wine. "Eat up, eat up," he snapped. "We don't have all day."

Preacher shot him a flinty gaze. "Maybe you don't."

Three uniformed soldiers joined the procession at ground level. In short minutes they found themselves once more in the open area of the forum. At this early hour few citizens filled the walkways and steps of the temples. They were directed to a building next to the Senate. Above the columns, inscribed on the portico of the Capitol, was the single word *"Curia."*

Preacher saw it and shrugged. "Looks like we get our day in court."

Inside, they were rudely shoved through a curtained archway into a brightly lighted room, a hole in the domed roof to allow smoke out and sunlight in. Before them, three men sat on a marble dais. The one in the middle had a wide purple band around the hem of a toga. The ones flanking him had two thin lines on theirs.

"Who brings charges against these men?" the burly man in the center demanded.

"The tribune of the watch, Your Excellency."

"What are those charges?"

A tall young man, his head swathed in bandages, stepped forward from a stool to one side. Preacher recognized him as one of those he had smacked with his rifle butt. "I, Didius Octavius Publianus, tribune of the *vigilii,* charge these criminals with trespassing in the domain of Nova Roma, of being enemies of the State, and spies for the Gauls."

Gauls? Preacher thought. How silly could someone get? He could not let that one lay. "Why, Your Worship, this whole thing is crazy. Downright redic'lous in fact. What Gauls? There ain't any Gauls anymore, an' this sure as hell ain't ancient Rome."

Quintus raised a restraining hand. "Ah, but it is, my talkative spy. It is Nova Roma, New Rome. Let me introduce myself. I am Marcus Quintus Americus, First Citizen of Rome. These are my fellow judges, Publius Gra—"

Before he could complete the introductions, Preacher exploded. "By damn, I remember now. First Citizen means dictator."

Quintus displayed a surprised, impressed expression. "Why, that's quite correct, my good fellow. Duly elected to that honored position by the Senate. You seem quite learned for such a rough and rude specimen of the frontier."

"Just because I've spent most of my days out here, don't mean I didn't get any learnin'. I studied history, includin' ancient Rome, at the University of the Shinin' Mountains."

"How odd. I've never heard of it."

Preacher eyed Quintus suspiciously. "Small wonder. From that accent, I'd say you got your book-learnin' way back east somewhere. Maybe Princeton? Or Harvard?"

Quintus widened his eyes at this astuteness. An amused twinkle lighted the gray orbs. "You amaze me. That's quite remarkable. Harvard it was. Class of Thirty-six. I would really like to take some time to talk with you about this university of yours." He sighed. "But, the duties of office, and your crimes, make that impossible. Tribune, are you ready to put on your case?"

"Yes, Your Excellency." Quickly the tribune outlined the encounter in the forum the previous night. His version markedly differed from Preacher's recollection. He made note to dispute them when his turn came. The opportunity came too quickly for him to marshal his arguments.

"Is there anything possible you can say in your defense?" Quintus leaned forward to ask condescendingly.

"Only that it ain't so. Not the way he tells it. We was just takin' a little stroll through your fine city, seein' the sights, so's to speak. We come around this corner and these fellers jumped us right off. We had no idea who they might be, so we had to fight back. I will admit he was right about how many we downed before it was over. Musta been a baker's dozen or more." He gingerly touched his head. "An' I must say they got in their licks, too. Well, no real harm done, an' no hard feelin's I say. Now, to that bein' an enemy of the state," Preacher went on.

"We ain't enemies of no state. Not at all. An' we come here on our own. We don't spy for anyone. At least not anymore, nohow. There was a couple of times we done some scoutin' for the Dragoons. I suppose some as would call that spyin'." Preacher put his hands behind his back and began to pace. "Like I said, there ain't any Gauls anymore, so that charge is out the window, too. Taken all in all, we'll just say we're sorry about bustin' up your watchmen here, and bid you a peaceable farewell."

"I think not!" The voice of Marcus Quintus cracked like a rifle shot. "My fellow judges and I will confer and render our verdict. Jailer, take them away."

Preacher and Philadelphia found themselves in a small, windowless room with a sobbing young girl. Curiosity prompted Preacher to ask her what had brought her here and caused her distress.

"I—I'm to be branded as a runaway," she wailed, her English rusty. "But I didn't really run off. I was caught by a terrible thunderstorm and had to stay over the night at the farm of Decius Trantor. It wasn't my fault. But the watch caught me before I could reach home and explain to my master."

"Why, that's hardly fair," Preacher commiserated. "What brought you here in the first place?"

"We—my family—were on our way with some others to the Northwest. Our wagons were attacked. I was—I was—they had their way with me, and then I was sold into slavery."

"Why, them black-hearted devils. How long you been here?"

"It seems forever. At least two years. I remember my last free birthday was my fourteenth. We had a party right on the trail. There was music from a violin and a squeeze-box." She put her head in her hands and began to sob wretchedly.

Preacher cut his eyes to Philadelphia. "When we get out of this fuss, we're gonna have to do somethin' about that."

"Yep," Philadelphia agreed readily. *"If* we get out."

Shortly before the noon meal, the guards came for Preacher and Philadelphia. Hustled into the trial room of the curia, they again faced Marcus Quintus and his fellow judges. Quintus looked at them sternly.

"It is the considered decision of this court that you are guilty as charged. You are to be scourged, then sold into slavery for life. Give your names to the clerk."

Preacher gave Philadelphia a quick wink first. "M'name's Arthur. I don't rightly know what my last handle happened to be. I been out here since a boy not yet in my teens."

Eyes suddenly aglow with interest, Quintus leaned down toward Preacher. "That's most interesting. Come now, do you also happen to answer to the name Preacher?"

Preacher hated deliberate lies. He swallowed his objection to untruthfulness and answered with a straight face. "I heard of him, of course. Why is it you ask?"

"I'm . . . most interested in this wildman Preacher. I've sent men after him, to have him fight in our arena, but none have returned."

"With good reason, too," Philadelphia answered sharply. "Preacher's the wildest, woolliest, ringtail he-coon in the High Lonesome. 'Less you send about a dozen or more, you'll never see hide nor hair of Preacher, other than he wants you to."

Anger tightened the skin around the eyes of Quintus so that they became flinty points. "You'll learn manners as a slave, or you'll be dead at a young age. Tribune, have the guards take these men off to be scourged." Quintus paused and sighed. "It is too bad you are not Preacher. What a glorious fight we would witness on the sand. See they are whipped quite soundly, but do not mark them. And notify Justinius Bulbus of these splendid fighting men we will have on the sale block."

11

"Everything is turned topsy-turvy in this dang city,"
Preacher lamented as their escort conducted them to the small
square off the forum, where a raised platform filled the center.

A crowd of men pressed close to the edges, faces turned
up, eyes fixed on the shapely young woman standing there
beside a burly fellow with a coiled whip over one shoulder.
He held a long reed pointer in one hand, and gestured grandly
as he called off what he clearly saw as selling points.

"She's broad-hipped and will deliver with ease. Notice
those smooth, straight shoulders, gentlemen. She can carry
heavy burdens. All in all, a treasure for a bargain price. Now
what am I bid?"

"Six," a voice called from the throng.

"What? Only six *sestercii?*"

"No. Six *denarii,"* came the answer, followed by laughter.

"Surely you jest? Why, I would gladly pay ten talents for
her myself."

"Then you buy her," the heckler taunted.

A more serious buyer bid himself in. "I bid four talents."

Brightening, the auctioneer located his bidder. "Now,
that's more like it. I have four, who'll give me five? Five-
gimme-five—five-five—yes! Now six." His chant rolled on
until he had worked the sale price to eleven talents. A lot of
gold for a young woman.

Her new owner claimed his prize and took her to the

cashier's table to pay his fee. The auctioneer motioned for the next sale lot. A muscular, bullet-headed assistant shoved forward two small boys. Their red hair, freckled faces, and dark brown eyes marked them as brothers.

"Lot number seven. Two house servants. They are brothers, aged nine and eleven. They were taken from a wagon train one month ago, and have mastered enough Latin to show they are quick learners. They will make ideal body servants for sons of gentlemen. Now, I'm going to open the bidding at ten *sestercii*, take your choice."

"They been cut?" a suspicious buyer demanded.

"No, sir. I'll guarantee that."

Not satisfied, the skeptical one pressed on. "A good look's the best guarantee I know of."

Sighing, the auctioneer tucked his pointer under one arm and reached for the white loincloths the boys wore as their only item of clothing. He gave hard yanks, which exposed them to all eyes, and humiliated the lads to their cores. Blushing all over, they stood with heads hung, tears running down their cheeks. "As I said, they have not been gelded."

"Why, that egg-suckin' dog," Preacher growled. "I'll fix him good when I get up there."

Philadelphia nodded to the javelin-wielding guards at the side of the platform. "More likely those bully boys would pin you with their pig stickers while that feller used his whip on you, Preacher."

Not one to waste breath on "if only," Preacher sighed heavily and accepted the inevitable. "It sure ain't the High Lonesome anymore. This sort of thing is downright shameful."

"Then maybe we oughta be thinkin' about takin' our leave," Philadelphia muttered silently.

"Now you're talkin', Philadelphia. We'll both work on that, keep our eyes open. First chance, we be gone."

"Count on it."

Their turn came sooner than either mountain man had expected. Not surprisingly, a burly man with a face mean enough to stop the charge of a bull bison purchased them.

"You'll make fine additions to my gladiator school," he told them as armed and armored men hustled Preacher and Philadelphia away.

Hoisting a gold-rimmed cup, Marcus Quintus called across the expanse of table to his principal guest, Gaius Septimus. "The two barbarians who were captured night before last will make excellent additions to the birthday games for Quintus Faustus, will they not?"

Septimus curled his lower lip in a deprecating sneer. "That sort of man is entirely too independent to make a good slave, let alone a gladiator. Do you not agree, Justinius?"

Bulbus, the third guest, glanced up from his intense study of a lovely young dancing woman. "Quite to the contrary, Septimus. They are quick and strong, and used to fighting for their lives. Once their spirit is—ah—molded to my liking, they become marvelous in the arena. Some are absolutely fearless."

"Yes, like Preacher, who I fear is still on the loose," Quintus snapped.

"Will I get to watch your new slaves die?" Faustus, at the fourth table, asked.

The two senators who had been invited hid their reaction to the boy's rudeness behind pudgy hands. Bulbus glanced idly at the youngster, who had been included at this all-male dinner party by his doting father. There was something . . . not at all right about the child, Bulbus thought, not for the first time. His reaction to the games was—odd. Were he a couple of years older, Bulbus considered, it might be ascribed to the erotic fires of puberty. For all his suspicions, he answered cordially enough. After all, the youth was the son and heir of the First Citizen.

"No, young Faustus. They show much too much promise to be dispatched so soon. Unless, of course, someone lands an unfortunate blow."

"Why is that?" Faustus asked, genuinely interested.

"Keeping a crippled gladiator is like having a pet elephant. The cost of feeding him is ruinous." Bulbus laughed at his own joke. "But, you are quite right, Marcus Quintus, these last two specimens are in superb condition. I will intensify their training so that they can appear at your son's birthday games."

Flattered by this, Quintus ignored the admonition of Bulbus about sparing them for future games. "Wonderful. It will surely be marvelous. They will die magnificently," he burbled on, his eyes fixed on some unseen distance.

In a numbing cadence, the bored voice of the drill master barked out the commands. "Strike left . . . strike right . . . strike left . . . strike right."

Another chanted to his victim of the moment, "Shield up! Parry! Strike target! Parry, dammit!

"Duck! Duck, you idiot!" quickly followed as the heavy wooden ball on the opposite arm of the practice frame swung around and clobbered the hapless former immigrant. His dreams of the Northwest had long been abandoned in the rigors of the gladiator school. He looked up pitifully as Preacher and another gladiator stomped by, trading sword blows with weighted wooden weapons. The metronomic throb of the drumbeat used to mark movements accelerated to a rapid roll and ceased.

At once, the student gladiators ceased and headed for the large fountain in the center of the training yard. Dripping with sweat, they plunged bare torsos in to the waist. Preacher found himself a place beside Philadelphia.

"To carry off that escape we talked about," he observed to Braddock, "we must first get out of this dang-blasted gladiator school. An' I don't allow as how I've figgered out a way to do that as yet, what with them big dogs."

"We'd best find it soon. We've been here the better part of a week now. I've got bruises where I didn't know a man could get them."

Standing to Philadelphia's right, Buck Sears listened with interest. Here was a pair who sounded like they still had some grit left. A quick check over his shoulder showed Buck that the trainers were occupied elsewhere. He decided to take a chance.

"Don't worry about that. I have it all figured out. And, believe me, it's the only way you can get out of the school." He paused to check on their overseers. "If you promise to take me along, I'll show you how."

Philadelphia gave him a gimlet eye. "Got it all figured out, huh?"

"Yep." A smug smile brightened by sudden relief bloomed on the face of the teamster. "I'll tell you all about it at the baths after tomorrow's training session."

"Mighty decent of you, Buck," Preacher said agreeably. "We'll be obliged for the help. An', sure, you can go along."

"That's a relief. I can't stand it in here much longer."

Preacher nodded and smiled back. "None of us can, son. Not a one."

Due to his lifestyle, Arthur proved to be a magnificent standout at gladiator training. In early afternoon the next day, a bemused Justinius Bulbus stood in his private box watching the ripple of muscles in the arms and shoulders of the big mountain man. He could not believe his good fortune. Bulbus had his doubts that the legendary barbarian, Preacher, who so preoccupied the thoughts of Marcus Quintus, could be much better.

Whatever the case, the master of games intended to match this one against Preacher when, or if, the famous denizen of the mountains was captured. Bulbus' shaggy eyebrows rose as he watched the big one batter down another of his trained gladiators. He raised an arm to halt the man scheduled to next face the powerful barbarian.

"Crassis, you take him," he instructed one of the trainers. With a big grin born of overconfidence, the heavily

muscled Crassis came forward; his small shield, strapped to
his forearm, was held up to protect his chest; his blunt sword
was poised. Bounding like a panther, Preacher surged out to
meet him. He struck the wooden shield with such force, it
split down the middle and broke the forearm behind it.

An expression of surprise flashed on the face of Crassis,
but was quickly replaced by a grimace of pain. Preacher
swung again and caught Crassis against the side of his head
with the flat of the blade. Rubber-legged, Crassis stumbled
away to drape himself over the lattice of iron strips that
formed the training ring. A ragged cheer went up from among
the captive would-be gladiators. Preacher looked around for
another opponent.

Bulbus quickly provided one. A bigger trainer, one who
taught the net and trident, came forward. "Julian, bag him
with your net and teach this upstart a lesson," Marcus Quintus
called from the cushioned chair upon which he sat, beside his
wife, Titiana Pulcra.

They had arrived unannounced and put the school into a
tizzy, not the least Bulbus, who wanted always to put on the
best of shows for his benefactor and patron. He had hastily
devised this test of strength for the enormously powerful
mountain man. It now seemed to have turned out ill-advised.
Even his trainers could not best the agile, resilient man.
Bulbus cut his eyes anxiously from husband to wife.

At least Pulcra appeared to be enjoying the exhibition. She
squirmed in her seat with each excellent blow by the mountain man. Now, while Bulbus covertly studied her, she crossed
her legs and began to swing one nicely turned ankle. A sure
sign a woman had a naughty itch to soothe, Bulbus thought
lasciviously.

"I'll have you down to size in no time," Julian taunted.
"Then I'll prick your hide to give you a good lesson."

Julian feinted to the right, dodged back to the left, spun a
full circle on his heel to gain momentum, then whipped out
his weighted net. Preacher ducked, picked up the edge of the
fan-shaped snare and did a wrist roll that collapsed it into a

long, folded filament. This he quickly climbed, mock sword in his teeth. When he reached the forearm of Julian, he let go with one hand and closed his fist around the hilt.

A swift swat to the temple and Julian went down, a stone dropped into a fathomless pool. And with hardly more than a ripple. Preacher came to his moccasined feet and turned toward the box. A steady flow of sweat blurred his vision and stung his eyes. It kept him from clearly seeing the occupants, though he rightly guessed one to be Bulbus and another Quintus.

Exasperated, Bulbus clapped his palms together. "I'll have an end to this at once! Two of you, have a go at him at the same time."

A pair from the training staff came forth. One wore a *caestus,* its usually sharp bronze talons blunted with India gum. The other bore a curved Persian sword. Preacher greeted them with a nasty grin.

Above him, Pulcra veritably writhed in her chair, her leg swinging ever faster, small beads of perspiration breaking out on her upper lip. Fascinated by this enthralling demonstration by the mountain barbarian, Marcus had eyes only for what went on in the arena.

Preacher went for the swordsman first, after a glance at the blurred figures in the box. He came in low, leading with his sword. The tactic thoroughly distracted his opponent, who raised his weapon to parry the blade with enough force to knock it from Preacher's hand and do a quick reverse that would have, had his own been sharp, disemboweled the hapless antagonist who so insulted their abilities. Only it did not work that way.

At the last second, Preacher let the tip of his sword drop, so that the edge of the other one slipped across the flat without making contact. Startled, the trainer stumbled off balance while Preacher drove straight in. He rammed the point of his weapon into the helpless man's gut. It drove the air from his lungs in a gush.

Preacher wasted no time on finishing him, and then spun

to confront his second threat. The armored fist lashed out at him and forced the mountain man to duck. Even with the sticky gum on the four triangular blades, they could inflict a terrible injury. Preacher avoided the *caestus* and hacked at the trainer's belly. Far quicker than the man with the sword, the trainer dodged the blow and tried to backhand Preacher in the head.

In a flash, Preacher went down at his knees and extended one leg. With a powerful push-off from one hand, he spun on his heel and swept the feet from under his opponent. A startled yelp came from twisted lips as the burly brawler left the ground and painfully landed on his rear. Preacher jumped to his moccasin soles and towered over the dazed man. He reversed his hold on the practice sword and rapped the trainer soundly at the base of his skull.

Preacher stepped back and let him fall. Then he placed one foot on the unconscious man's chest. Slowly he raised his eyes to the box.

"Blast and damn! Enough. You are through for the day, Arthur," Bulbus bellowed angrily. "You have won more than you have lost, so you get early baths, along with the other winners. Now, get out of here."

Beside him, Titiana Pulcra reached over and touched her husband's arm. "I'm going to leave now. The sun is too hot, and glaring. It has given me a headache."

"Very well, my dear. There is snow-chilled wine awaiting us at home."

She smiled sweetly. "I know I'll enjoy it."

Someone else had watched Preacher's performance—albeit with far less cupidity than Titiana Pulcra. Sister Amelia Witherspoon saved her feelings of desire for an image of Preacher as deliverer. When they had arrived in this horrid New Rome, they had been condemned to die in the arena, thrown to the lions.

Now, Sister Amelia was quite familiar with the heroic

stories of Christian martyrdom in the days of the mad Nero. Yet, deep in her heart, she knew that she was not ready to be fed upon by beasts for the sake of her faith if it could be reasonably avoided. She saw no conflict between her retreat from the martyr's role and the depth of her belief. Amelia had a healthy respect for life. And she wanted to escape from this horrid place like all get-out.

From the first time she saw this magnificent specimen of male prowess, Amelia just *knew* he was the answer to her prayers. Arthur would save them. Like her captors, Sister Amelia did not know that this brave, strong man was the legendary Preacher. She knew him only by the name those hated Romans called him. Now she felt all trembly at the sight of how swiftly and surely he had handled those men. How could she make her plight, and that of her brothers and sisters of the Mobile Church in the Wildwood, known to him? She hurried off to make her thoughts known to Sister Charity and to seek her advice.

Thick steam rose from the surface of the large pool in the *calderium* room of the *thermae publicus* of New Rome. Preacher gratefully sank his bruised hide and aching muscles into the hot depths. During his six days in the gladiator school, while he learned the ways of the strange new weapons, he had taken his share of punishment. He would ache for a while yet, he felt certain.

Taking a bath in the raw, in the presence of other men, had never bothered Preacher. He vaguely recalled weekly Saturday excursions from his early homelife in a single, large, wooden tub, and older brothers squirming around in it together with him. The first time he discovered that women, and children of both sexes, readily joined the men of New Rome in their baths, he had been quite disconcerted. Now he handled it with greater ease. He took care, though, to look the other way as best he could. He also made an effort to banish the blood-racing thoughts certain of the ladies engendered in his mind. All of which left him unprepared when a loud splash announced the presence of a shapely young woman who made a shallow dive into the hot pool.

She swam around him in circles, as graceful and as wriggly as an eel. At last, she let her legs descend and stood before him, the water up to her shoulders. Her long, blond hair hung wetly down her back. She smiled and touched a small, slender finger to his chest.

"You're that exciting new gladiator at the school of Bulbus," she stated coyly in English.

Tension added bluntness to Preacher's words. "Not by any choice of my own."

Teasingly, she moved her hand to his shoulder and draped it across the top. "You should be grateful. If you fight well, win a lot of battles, you could gain your freedom. You could even receive the *rudis.*"

"What's that?"

She puckered her mouth. "You really don't know? It's the wooden sword that is the symbol of your retirement from the arena. A free man, a citizen, and one who no longer has to fight. It's something to work for."

A sudden suspicion bloomed in Preacher's mind. "Are you allowed to talk to slaves?"

"I'm allowed to speak to anyone I choose. I'm Pricilia," she responded with no small heat. "Let's scrub down. I'll scrape you and you can scrape me. Then we can move on to the *tepidium.*"

Preacher found himself less reluctant than he had been when she had first appeared. After all, it had been a long time since any woman, especially one so young and attractive as this one, had shown interest in the rugged mountain man. It might be fun, he decided, shedding another inhibition, to partake. After all, she wouldn't bite. He screwed up a smile.

"If that's what you want, it's fine as frogs' hair with me."

"How quaint," she said through a titter.

After a thorough cleansing, the pair swam across the wide pool and climbed out. In the next room, the *tepidium,* they entered the luke-warm water eagerly. It made their skin tingle. Preacher had grown painfully aware of their nakedness while scraping her silken skin with a *stigilis,* the curved, bronze, knifelike implement used in the manner of a washcloth.

Now they frolicked like youngsters. Exactly like . . . Terry and Vickie, he thought suddenly. Soon the bright pinkness left their skin, and the water began to feel less refreshing. Pricilia tapped Preacher on the chest, her head canted to one side atop her long, graceful neck.

"Race you to the *frigidium.*"

"You're on!" said Preacher through a shout of laughter.

Now, that would be more like it, Preacher thought. Cold water being something he was most familiar with, he expected that a dip in it would calm the odd stirrings that teased his body. He crossed the pool with powerful strokes. Out and onto the warm tile floor. Through the curtained doorway.

Preacher beat her by half a length to plunge into the icy water that flowed directly into the pool from the stream outside. They splashed and swam for several minutes, until goose bumps appeared on Pricilia's shoulders and arms. She edged to the shallow end and drew herself out of the water to her waist on the marble-tiled steps. She threw her arms wide in a gesture of invitation.

"Come warm me, Arthur. I'm frozen."

After all his efforts to resist, Preacher found himself beguiled into dumb obedience. He crossed the frigid water in five long strokes and entered her embrace. After he had twined his strong arms around her, she drew his lips to hers.

In no time, they caused the icy liquid of the *frigidium* to reach a near-boil with the energy of their amorous romp.

12

Fully sated, Preacher lay on a bench, covered by a towel, when Pricilia made her departure. Entering as she left, Buck Sears and Philadelphia Braddock got a good look at her. One glance at their companion and they knew what must have gone on.

"You loon-witted he-goat!" Buck Sears blurted in shocked surprise. "You tryin' to get yourself killed before we can escape?"

Preacher sat upright, the sappy expression wiped from his face. "No? Why? What did I do that could cause that?"

Flabbergasted by Preacher's response, Buck worked his mouth for several moments before he could get any sound to come. "Don't you know who that was?"

Preacher blinked, suddenly suspicious of his recent amour. "Not for sure. She said her name was Pricilia. She was quite . . . friendly."

"I'll just bet she was. That happens to be Titiana Pulcra, the wife of Marcus Quintus Americus." He struck his forehead with the palm of one hand. "I wondered why those guards were not letting anyone enter the baths. If the Praetorian guard learns that we got by their watch at the door and saw— anything at all, they'll kill us along with you."

Preacher could not believe what he heard. Fooling around with another man's wife was definitely not a part of his code. Anger blended with self-disgust as he questioned Buck further. "Are you sure? D'you mean she's the dictator's woman—his wife?"

"I am only too sorry to say that I am sure," Buck lamented.

"Dang-bust it, I've been tricked. She done lied to me." His face turned dark red. "Me dossin' another man's wife. I'll never live it down. Though I don't reckon I should waste time tryin' to explain it to him. Only one thing for it now. We gotta go ahead with our plan to escape. Suppose you tell us how you got in mind for us to do that, Buck?"

Buck shrugged, then produced a smug smile. "It's plain as could be. In fact, it's right under your noses."

"What'er you gettin' at?" Philadelphia growled. He, too, felt his friend's chagrin.

"We all agreed we could not escape from the school. So that leaves having to be outside the school to make a break. And the only time we are outside is to get to the coliseum to fight or here to the baths."

"They told us we go to the arena by tunnel."

"That's right, Preacher, they said that," Philadelphia agreed.

"Then it has to be here. What about the guards?"

Buck gave a slow answer, his expression one of awe and bemusement. "You . . . are . . . *the* Preacher?"

"That I am, Buck. But there's no time to talk about that. How do we get out? What about the guards?"

Buck produced a sunny smile. "They are a sufficiently lazy lot. They're convinced there is only one way in and out of this place. I found out better, before I was sold to be a gladiator for hittin' my so-called master."

Preacher exploded with curiosity. "Go on—go on, tell us."

"I worked here at the baths. Part of my job was to clean out anything that got caught in the water system. The water comes in big tunnellike things. There is a way to get to them from behind a wall of the cold room. All we have to do is get to there, then walk and swim our way to freedom. Because, all the water that comes in has to go out."

"That shines. I like it. Don't stand there, show us the way."

"You mean right now, today?" Buck seemed uneasy.

"Do you want to wait around until that Marcus feller finds out I rode his filly?"

Buck grimaced at that graphic depiction. "All right. Come with me."

Preacher stopped him with a hand on one arm. "One thing, though. I don't figger to leave without my brace of Walker Colts."

Buck dismissed him. "We'll deal with that when the time comes. First thing is to get away from here and out of the far end of the entrance tunnel."

Preacher squared his shoulders and reached for his clothes. "I'm game. Let's go."

At first progress came easily. Ledges had been cut into the tunnel walls, a good two feet above the water that flowed with regularity into the *frigidium* pool, and beyond into those of the heated tanks. After some thirty paces, Preacher estimated that they had reached a place somewhere out near the middle of the forum. Only the single long, covered opening presented itself to them.

Preacher, Philadelphia, and Buck followed it beyond what must have been the southern edge of the forum. The walls grew wet and slick. Thick hanks of roots hung down above their heads. From his spyglass reconnoiter, Preacher recalled a garden, with bushes and hedges trimmed into the shapes of animals. That had to be what they passed under now.

Their pathway became narrower and closer to the water. The latter swirled by in oily blackness, its surface alone illuminated by the torch in Buck's hand. He had taken the lead, naturally enough, since it had been he who discovered this way out of Nova Roma. Preacher came next in line, with Philadelphia bringing up the rear. Little light reached the big-eared mountain man, and he stumbled occasionally, with a muffled curse for each time.

Philadelphia had about run out of cusswords when an even worse situation came to them. Buck halted his companions and gestured ahead with the torch. "We walk in the water from here. At about what I guesstimate to be a hunnard yards from the inlet, we have to swim for it."

"So nice, this route of yours," Preacher told him acidly.

Buck removed his slave's tunic and wrapped it atop his head, then stepped off into chest-deep water as he spoke. "Be glad there is any trail out of here, Preacher. These New Romans are damned thorough in everything they do."

One by one they followed him. Chill water swirled around them. Buck reasoned aloud that once out, so long as they moved through the city with an air of going about their usual business, their slave costumes would not be a danger to them. They could even get to within a hundred paces outside the walls.

"Then we cut and run," he added grimly.

Preacher eyed him sternly. "Now, that's why I want my Colt re-volvers an' Cougar. I can run a damn sight faster on a horse."

Buck lectured him in how to accomplish that. "There are storerooms in the house of the master of games for all that sort of captured things. Also a stable. Since it is built into the outside wall of the school, on the Via Martius, we should have no trouble getting there. It's the getting away that bothers me."

Preacher gave him a grunt and a knowing nod. "You let me an' my Walker Colts handle that."

Shaking his head in wonder, Buck spoke with awe. "You actually have a pair of those Texas guns?"

"Sure enough. An' a dang good Hawken. I left my fancy rifle at Trout Creek Pass." He nodded to Braddock. "Philadelphia's got him four of the nicest two-shooter pistols a feller could ever want. Sixty caliber they be. Ain't no spear-chucker can stand up again' our firepower for long."

"And I'll have my pick of what's in there, too," Buck added with a note of anticipation.

He led off once again and soon discovered that this late into summer, the water level had fallen enough that they did not have to swim at any point along the tunnel. Soon, a soft, gray glow emerged in the distance, around a bend. When Buck reached the turn, he paused a moment.

"Dang, I was afraid that might be," he spat.

"What's that?" Philadelphia asked.

"I worked the tunnels. All we ever dragged out was small bits of wood, a dead rat or two, some other animals caught in the water. Stood to reason they had a way of keeping bigger things out of the watercourse. See up ahead? There are bars across the opening to the river itself."

"Then we're stuck here?" Philadelphia demanded.

"Not necessarily," Preacher advised. "First let's get a look at them bars."

To Preacher's delight, they found them old, rusted and neglected. The current was stronger here and threatened to sweep them off their feet. Preacher gauged the weakest-appearing ones and took hold. He dug his feet into the sandy silt on the floor of the tunnel and heaved with all his might.

A bit of rust flaked off, nothing more. "You two, get in place to the sides. Each take a-holt of one of these and pull when I do," he instructed.

This time a faint groan could be heard above the rush of the water. The muscles in Preacher's bare shoulders bunched as he exerted even greater effort. Philadelphia braced himself and heaved again. Opposite him, Buck planted his feet against a smooth rock and strained against the resistance of the worn iron bars.

At first, nothing happened. Then a mighty shriek came from the grommets into which the rods had been fitted. Small chunks of stone and mortar rained down on the heads of the escapees, and the first bar popped free. Philadelphia flopped backward in the water.

"Consarn it," he yelped.

Preacher eased it into the hands of his friend and turned to put his full force on the iron rod in Buck's grasp. Together, they tore it loose with seeming ease. A gathering of driftwood floated through the opening in a lazy spin. Preacher studied the situation.

"Another one."

Facetiously, Philadelphia added, "Make it two more an' we can drive a wagon through there."

"All right," Preacher agreed readily. "Two it is. Your side seems weaker. We'll take those next in line."

"Awh, Preacher, one'll do," Philadelphia retracted his attempt at sarcasm.

Fate turned a jaundiced eye on the fleeing men. The next barrier held stubbornly in place, refusing to pop out of its header or footing. Buck and Philadelphia lined up on one side, Preacher on the other. He anchored himself on the neighboring bar and surged with his legs. In the back of his mind—as in those of the others—he held the thought that the alarm could be given, at any moment, of their being missing.

It added the necessary extra energy. With a grinding, cracking sound, the upright came free. They let it fall where it would. Quickly they waded through and up on the sloping bank of the river. Panting, Philadelphia wiped himself partly dry and put on his tunic. Preacher and Buck followed suit.

"I wish I had a wax tablet," Buck announced. At the look of curiosity from Preacher, he explained. "Anyone with a tablet of some kind is accepted as being at something official, and he's ignored. At least, that's the way I've seen it around here, and before in big cities, like St. Louie."

Preacher grinned and clapped him on one shoulder. "By jing, if you ain't got the right of it, Buck. Maybe we can—ah—borrow one somewhere on the way. Now, show us the way back to the school and that storehouse you talked about."

Buck cut directly across the burgeoning city of New Rome. He walked with the stride and head-up posture of an

important slave. Preacher and Philadelphia followed suit. Few
cast them a glance. At a market stall, Preacher paused. While
Philadelphia distracted the owner with talk about onions and
turnips, Preacher filched a wax tablet from a ledge inside the
display of vegetables. They quickly caught up with Buck, and
Preacher handed it to him.

"There you go," Preacher told him jokingly. "Now you can
be as important as you've a mind to."

Amazement glowed on Buck's face. "Where'd this . . . ?"

"No, don't ask."

"Thank you, Preacher, but stay close from now on."

On the far side of the forum, well away from the Via
Iulius, the street took on a twisty course around the base of
the Hill of Mars. Buck slowed and gestured the others close
for a quick word.

"If the alarm has been given, we'd best try to make for the
outside."

"And if it hasn't?" Preacher prompted.

"Then we get what we need and head for the high country."

Shut away in her private wing of the nearly completed
palace, Titiana Pulcra lay sprawled on her downy bed. Her
heart still fluttered from the intensity of her magnificent encounter with Arthur. Her body glowed. She hadn't felt *this*
good in a long time. What advantage was the life of the rich
and powerful if one's appetites could not be fully indulged at
will? That thought brought her mind to the disturbing topic
of her son's recent conduct.

She supposed all small boys took pleasure from tormenting insects and small animals. Her own brothers, in another
life, another world, had often gleefully tormented cats. That
violent aspect of the conduct of Quintus Faustus did not un-
settle her, although being on the cusp of eleven seemed
awfully old for such behavior. No, it was something else.

Since that time three weeks past, she had paid careful attention to his conduct at the games. Reflection on the hour

just past made all too vivid images of how he had responded to the nearly naked bodies and violent deaths of those who lost on the sand. In her memory, his gasps and quiet moans had sounded utterly too much like her own strident ones in the strong arms of Arthur. She stifled a thrill of horror. Surely Faustus could not be so—so *twisted*. She forced a change of subject.

Would she enjoy Arthur's presence soon again? Could she possibly risk it? Her husband was entirely too dense to ever suspect her. This wasn't the first time that a handsome gladiator slave had aroused her beyond caution. Pulcra was practical-minded enough to realize it would not be the last. Silently she offered a petition to the gods that Arthur prove a really good gladiator and last a long, long time. An anxious, if servile, scratching at the doorpost diverted her.

"What is it?" she demanded.

A clearly agitated slave entered, his forehead and upper lip bedewed with oily fear sweat. He advanced awkwardly. "A message for your husband, my lady."

"He is occupied elsewhere."

"May I ask where?"

"You may not. He is not to be disturbed." At least not until she had bathed. "You may give it to me."

"It's a matter of state, my lady."

Temper, mingled with sudden guilt, flared. "Dammit, must you be so obstinate? Give me the message."

Trembling now in fear of the arena, the slave stutteringly complied. "Three of the slave gladiators are missing, my lady."

Alarm stabbed at Pulcra. "Really? Their names?"

"Philadelphias, Baccus, and the champion of the day, Arturus."

Oh, God, Pulcra thought in pain. *I am alone. Utterly alone.* Duty demanded she rally herself. She girded her frazzled nerves. "Have the games master organize a search. I assume he has already conducted a roll call?"

"Yes, m'lady."

"Good. He's not the lack-wit I suspected him of being. Tell Bulbus to have the city searched first, top to bottom. Then the surrounding fields. They are not to be allowed to get away. More lives than theirs depend upon it."

She cast a quick glance into a mirror, evaluated her posture while reclining on her bed. Her pride swelled as she saw the steel she had in her when she needed it.

13

Ahead lay the entrance to the home of Justinius Bulbus. Two professional gladiators stood outside in light armor, with a pilum at the ready. Behind them, along the Via Iulius, Preacher, Philadelphia, and Buck heard the sounds of a search being organized. That told them they had been found out. They had to move fast. Preacher came up with a rudimentary plan.

"Wait here. I'll go up and get the attention of those two."

"How do you figger to do that?" Philadelphia inquired.

"By telling them what they expect to hear." With that he set off.

Preacher approached the two sentries with a blank, slave expression plastered on his face. "I have a message for your master," he announced.

"He is out."

"Where is he?"

"In the city. You need know nothing more."

"Yes, I do. Look, I have it right here. Do either of you read?" Preacher bent low, groping in a fold of his tunic.

Automatically the two guards leaned with him. When Preacher had them where he wanted them, he balled both fists and slammed them hard at that sensitive point under the jaw. Both men went down in a clash and clatter of bronze. Philadelphia and Buck came on the run.

"Quick, put on their gear and take their places."

Preacher went in like a wraith. He slid silently past the steward's office and followed Buck's directions down a long hall to a tall, thick, double door. An iron ring served as an opener. Preacher yanked on it, and it swung on well-oiled hinges. He went through and pulled the door to behind him. He found himself in a roofless courtyard. From one side he heard stable noises, and his nose identified it at the same time. Hugging the slim concealment afforded by the balcony overhang, he skirted the wall that enclosed the yard from the house. A two-piece door yielded easily.

Inside, he located Cougar and Philadelphia's mount, and the pack animal. He picked one for Buck, saddled all, and led them from the stalls. Outside, he took the animals at an angle across a tiled area where a fountain splashed musically. He ground reined them while he opened the portal that should lead to a treasure trove of belongings and weapons.

Buck's description proved to be right on the money. Preacher quickly found his .44 Walker Colts and Hawken rifle. Philadelphia's weapons came next. Dressed in buckskins again, Preacher fastened his wide, leather belt around his trim waist. He stuffed his knife and war hawk behind it, adjusted their position and added two .60 caliber pistols, then covered it all with his slave tunic.

Padding softly along the line of firearms, he selected a serviceable rifle and four pistols for Buck. Then he set about loading all. He doubled up on powder horns, boxes of percussion caps and conical bullets. He added sacks of parched corn, a big bag of jerky, another of coffee beans, flour, and a final of cornmeal. Salt and sugar concluded his shopping list.

Outside again, he packed away all his booty and started for what had to be the gateway that led outside. Its latch gave with a mild squeak; then the hinges squealed with noticeable protest. Preacher winced. At once, a wizened little clerk appeared through the doorway to the steward's office, a scroll clutched in one hand. His eyes widened and showed a lot of white when he saw the man in slave's clothing with four horses.

"What are you doing here?" he demanded in Latin. Preacher looked blank, and the clerk gestured toward the horses, changing to English. "What are you doing here with those animals?"

"Oh, I come to get them for the—ah—master of games," Preacher bent the truth slightly.

Emboldened by his freeman status and accustomed to having slaves cringe before him, the bean counter took two steps forward. "Not with all those weapons. You're—you're trying to escape, that's what you are doing."

Preacher gave him an expression of genuine regret. "Now you had to go and say too much for your own good, didn't you?"

Lightning fast, Preacher closed the remaining distance between them. His arm shot out, and he grabbed the surprised clerk by the throat. He throttled the frail little man into unconsciousness, then turned to leave.

"Not so fast," came a more authoritative voice behind the broad back of Preacher.

Preacher turned to find a man in the by-now familiar uniform of a centurion. He had his sword half drawn and advanced with a menacing tread. Preacher reached under his tunic and drew his Green River knife, with a blade almost as large as that of the *gladius* in the hand of the centurion.

"Well, shucks," Preacher said through gritted teeth.

No doubt, the Roman soldier had been well trained. He completed his draw and held the leaf-bladed short sword competently as he brushed past the sparkling fountain in the middle of the courtyard. His only weakness came from the fact he had rarely fought against another armed man, particularly one so well versed in the various means of killing his fellow creature.

With a soft, grunted challenge, the centurion launched his attack. Preacher parried the thrust easily enough and slid the keen edge of his Green River along the muscular forearm of the soldier. It laid open the back of his hand and the meaty portion at the elbow. The young officer cursed and jumped back. Preacher just jumped back. They squared off to face one another.

"You still have time to look the other way, Sonny," Preacher suggested.

"It's my duty to protect the home of my employer," he rejected Preacher's offer.

A little job on the side, eh? Preacher thought. They circled while Preacher evaluated what he knew of this man so far. At last he worked out something. "You cain't have been borned here, your English is too good. When were you captured?"

Strange emotions surged across the broad face of the centurion. "About—about six years ago. At least I think so. What is it to you?"

Preacher favored him with a comradely smile. "Then you ain't one of them Roman lunatics. Think of your past, man. Think of getting back there."

Loyalties warred on the face of the wanderer, who'd had his life turned upside down some six years ago. He had once had a wife and three children. Where were they now? Yet, he had won recognition and been rewarded by his captors, many of whom became his friends, or he now commanded. What was life supposed to be for him? Maybe he should ask *which* life? Past and present swirled in his mind, merged, and forged out his decision. With a shout, he launched himself at Preacher.

"Wrong choice, friend," Preacher told him sadly.

Nimbly, Preacher stepped outside the arc of the *gladius* in the centurion's hand. The tip of his own knife found the gap between the breast and the back plates of the officer's cuirass; the wide, sharp-edged metal quickly followed. Preacher wrenched sideways, twisted the blade, and freed it. Slack-legged, his opponent gasped out his final sigh and fell dead. Off to his left, Preacher heard the hurried scurry of sandaled feet. More trouble from that direction.

He turned to see a quickly retreating back. Time to hurry. He cleaned his knife and replaced it, then went to the horses. Swiftly he led them out of the compound and toward the front door to the residence of Bulbus. His two friends saw him coming and instantly abandoned their pretense of being guards. Philadelphia Braddock swung into his saddle with practiced ease. Grinning, he patted the stock of his favorite rifle.

"I see you found old Betsy. Now, we'd best take our leave of this place."

Jokingly, Preacher made himself appear in a casual mood. "What's your hurry, Philadelphia?"

Braddock frowned. "One of the servants of that Bublus feller come squallin' out the door, didn't look left nor right, just runned off down the street like ol' Nick hisself was after him. I reckoned you had a part in that, an' also that our escape is no longer a secret."

Laughing, Preacher patted Cougar on the neck. "Right you are. We'd best go while we still have a chance."

Buck nodded and started them along the *Via Iulius.*

It was utterly reprehensible, Deacon Phineas Abercrombie thought to himself for what must have been the hundredth time. It was so degrading, so demoralizing, to be herded together like this in a single, large cell. Not a hope of a moment's privacy. Men and women, whole families thrust cheek and jowl against one another. And that foul-smelling trench at the narrow end of the holding pen as their only place to relieve themselves. With not a curtain or blanket to conceal the most private of personal acts.

Voiding themselves right out in the open, like animals! Unspeakable. He could find no other word for it. He had complained at every opportunity. Only to be laughed at and told to turn his back if he did not wish to observe. It smelled so foul in here, so fetid, and dank. It had come to the point where he could no longer eat. Even if he tried, it came back up. Would they ever see the light of day again, or the light of freedom?

Somehow he doubted they would experience either. Sighing, he turned to hear the appeal of young Mrs. Yardley.

"Deacon, my boy, Johnny, he's got himself a case of the runs. Real bad. Says his belly aches somethin' fierce, and it is sore to the touch."

Deacon Abercrombie followed the woman to where a small boy of eight lay on filthy straw near the center of the herd of missionaries. The child whimpered when Abercrombie knelt beside him and lifted up his tattered shirt. At least no unusual swelling, the untrained man diagnosed. That could bode even worse if cholera got loose among them. Well, he would have to tell the Yardley woman something.

"I'm afraid you are right, Sister Yardley. See that he gets all the fluids you can find for him. Keep him covered, and all we can do beyond that is pray."

For a moment, anger flared hot and red in the eyes of Mrs. Yardley. "We've *been* praying, Deacon. All of us, day and night. As yet, it appears the Lord has not seen fit to hear us."

Abercrombie's eyes widened. He raised an admonitory, pudgy hand. "Careful, Sister, lest you stray into blasphemy. I will tell the others, and we will join in group prayer for your boy."

Chastened, Mrs. Yardley lowered her chin and spoke meekly. "Thank you, Deacon. Thank everyone for me. I'll try to find Johnny some water."

Pursuit began at the edge of the Forum of Augustus. Shouts came from the *vigilii* posted there, and they set off on foot after the mounted fugitives, leather straps slapping their scarlet kilts. People along the way, most in the grubby garb of "common citizens," pointed accusing fingers to direct the watchmen.

At least one thing served as an advantage to the fleeing men. All of those forced to accept life in New Rome had long ago learned that the clatter of horses' hooves in the city streets signaled to get out of the way. As in its historical counterpart, Marcus Quintus had found it necessary to erect vertical stone plinths across the avenues to slow the speed of young rakes in their chariots. That forced the horsemen to zig and zag, yet kept them well ahead of the policemen. Slowly, they even gained some. Then the main body of searchers joined the chase.

They came at right angles to the *vigilii,* effectively forcing Preacher and his companions to swerve onto another street that did not lead directly to a gate that gave access to the outside. Several of the newcomers rode horseback, and they pushed on ahead of the yelling men behind them. The gap began to narrow. That's when Preacher noted some of the details of the construction that went on all around.

A block ahead, a tall engineer's scaffold had been erected. It consisted of a beam that pivoted from a central point. Equipped with a counterweight, it allowed large blocks of stone to be lifted by ropes and lowered into place by means of pulleys. The mechanism was operated by a horizontal capstan, manned by sweating slaves. At present, Preacher noted, a huge, rectangular slab of marble hung suspended over the street. More slaves pulled frantically on ropes to swing the walking beam. Without hesitation, Preacher rode in among those around the capstan, their pursuers almost at the heels of his horse. Their mounts filled the center of the street.

Preacher pulled his war hawk from his belt and gave it a mighty swing. It severed the thick cable to the capstan with a single blow. The braided hemp parted with a musical twang. The pulleys responded instantly. With a loud shriek, they played out the loose rope and allowed the three-ton marble slab to descend in a rush on top of the mounted searchers.

Preacher could not resist a backward glance. The carnage was terrible. Only one horseman had escaped the bloody pudding that had been made of his companions. He sat slumped in his saddle, numbed by shock. Once more, the gap between fugitives and hunters widened. Preacher estimated another three blocks, once back on the Via Ostia, the main route to the gate and freedom.

He led the way around one corner, then a sharp turn to the right on the Via Sacra. With only a block remaining, Preacher

discovered that the word had gotten to the soldiers. The legion
cavalry had joined the search. They thundered forward to cut
off Preacher and his friends along the Via Ostia. Ahead, the
sentries labored to shut the heavy gates.

Preacher held back in the small plaza formed directly
inside the gate to empty a cylinder load from his .44 Walker
Colt. It slowed the cavalry considerably. Preacher exchanged
his marvelous six-guns and watched as Philadelphia, then
Buck, streamed through the narrowing gap in the gate. His
turn now. He spurred Cougar and bent low over the animal's
neck. They hit the opening at a full gallop. Preacher further
slowed its progress by blasting one guard into eternity with a
.44 ball.

Outside, the trio did not slacken their pace until they had
ridden beyond the last cultivated field. Gasping in excitement, Philadelphia slapped one thigh. "We got away. By jing,
we done it."

Preacher looked beyond him at the nearly closed gates.
"I'd not break my arm pattin' m'self on the back just yet.
Them gates is gonna slow the cavalry, but they're comin' after
us. You can be certain sure of that."

At the crest of the southern pass, Preacher called another
halt. He and his companions looked back. Far back among
the plowed fields they observed hurried movement along the
roadway. Preacher took out his telescope and extended it.
Peering through it, he made out the billowing scarlet cloak
and dancing plume of a centurion. Behind him, the mounted
troops of New Rome were strung out in a ragged formation
that more resembled men fleeing for their lives than determined hunters. He nodded, satisfied at the lead they had
created by the confusion at the gate.

"They won't be catchin' up any time soon. Well, boys,
what's your pleasure now?"

Philadelphia considered that a moment. "I say we hightail it to Trout Crick and gather up as many good ol' boys as we can. Then come back here and kick us some crazy Roman butt."

"Sounds good to me," Buck agreed. "But, I ain't a mountain man. Will they accept me goin' along on this?"

Preacher considered him with keen eyes. "If you kin hit what you shoot at, they'll welcome you like a long-lost brother. If you kin do that and not make noise goin' through the woods, they'll give you their sisters."

Buck turned him a straight face. "I know better than to walk on my heels. Spent some time with the Kiowa whilst I was freightin' on the Santa Fe. They taught me to walk on the edge of my foot, and I'm at home in moccasins."

Preacher and Philadelphia nodded solemnly. "You'll do. Only first, I think we ought to confuse them fellers a little before we leave these parts, don't you?"

Broad grins answered him. They set off, making no effort to conceal their tracks.

The stratagem worked. For only a moment the legion cavalry reined in where the escapees had halted. Then they set off at a rapid trot. Totally lacking in scouting skills, they made no effort to look ahead or to the sides. They stared only a few yards in front of their horses' heads, eyes fixed on the sign of those they sought. It didn't work.

The Roman soldiers soon found themselves in a box canyon. Confused and disoriented, they milled about at the face of the high wall that denied them further progress. Centurion Drago cut his eyes from one to another of his men. He was up for *primus pilus*—first spear, or adjutant to the legate—and dared not fail in this mission. Tradition in the Legio XIII Varras Triumphae said that the *primus pilus* was always elevated to command of the legion upon the retirement or death of the legate. He wasn't about to throw that away.

"Find how they slipped out of here without our seeing the trail," he commanded.

Thirty minutes later, a young cavalryman trotted up and

saluted. "We have found it, sir. They crossed over the stream and used the trees to screen them."

"Brilliant. A first-week recruit could figure that out. How many are they now?"

"Only two, sir."

On the heels of his remark came a solid, meaty smack, followed by a brief scream and the rolling crack of a rifle shot. Before Drago and his troops could recover, the centurion heard the rapid drum of departing hooves. Right then, Centurion Drago made an uncannily accurate observation to his men.

"Jupiter blast that man. First Citizen Americus may not know it, but I think he had this mountain man, Preacher, in his hands all the time."

Philadelphia looked up as Preacher ghosted in to the grove of aspen where he and Buck waited for the crafty mountain man. A broad grin spread when he saw the new layer of powder grime on Preacher's right hand. Preacher slid from the back of Cougar and dropped the reins. At once, the broad-chested stallion went to munching grass.

"There's one less of them."

"How far behind us are they?" asked the always practical Philadelphia.

"I'd reckon at least half an hour. Most likely more, their horses haven't had any rest, like ourn."

"The bad news is there is only one trail out of here, unless we want to spend our lead climbing one ridge after another. Well, back to the trail."

Preacher led the way. Two miles down the wilderness road they found another meander that circled a steep pinnacle and went beyond, with a side-chute that ended atop it. They rested up there, eyes fixed on the winding trail through the Ferris Range, while they munched strips of jerky and crunched kernels of parched corn. By the fat turnip watch in a pocket of Preacher's vest, forty minutes went by before the greatly subdued cavalry rode into view. At once they put away their eats and reached for rifles.

Preacher homed in on the third from the last man in the column. Philadelphia took the second; and Buck, the rear soldier. They fired almost as one. Swiftly, Preacher and Philadelphia began to reload. Below them, the trio of legionnaires jerked in their saddles and fell sideways off their horses. Shouts of dismay echoed upward to the ears of the shooters. Buck finished reloading last. Once more they took aim.

Three shots rippled along the canyon walls. Cries of alarm raised again, and Drago halted the column. A terrible mistake. It allowed the intrepid mountain men to reload and take three more from the backs of their mounts. Then Preacher was up and leading the way to their horses. Ten down, and they still had a quarter-hour lead.

Preacher led the cavalry of Legio XIII into four more blinds and successfully ambushed them, carving great gaps in the ranks. They had only settled down in another spot to pick off more, when the thunder of hooves alerted them to a danger they had not anticipated.

Fully fifty mounted troops, most foot soldiers unaccustomed to horseback, lumbered awkwardly toward their hiding place. Drago rallied his cavalry and charged with determination. No matter how well they fought, regardless of how many they killed, Preacher knew at once that they were doomed.

The Roman troops swarmed over them, took dreadful losses from the rifles, pistols and revolvers of the mountain men. Several received nasty knife wounds, and two had their skulls split by Preacher's tomahawk. At last, though, they prevailed. After suitable punishment for their prowess, the soldiers trussed them up and slung them over their saddles. Preacher, Philadelphia and Buck found themselves on their way back to Nova Roma.

* * *

Marcus Quintus Americus looked up sternly from the written report of Justis Claudius Drago. His brows knit, while anger ran rampant across his features. His words were formed carefully.

"Our laws are clear on this. Not only have you murdered twenty-seven members of our Thirteenth Legion, but you have escaped. The penalty for escape is death in the arena. My only regret is that you will not have long to regret your deeds and fear your ultimate death. My son's birthday is three days from today. There will be games, of course. You three will be the central attraction."

14

Excitement sent an electrical charge through the missionaries of the Mobile Church in the Wildwood. During all of their lengthy captivity they had never heard of anything so hopeful. Blue eyes shining, her long, golden curls a-bounce under the fringe of her modest, white-trimmed, gray bonnet, Sister Amelia Witherspoon hastened to take the latest news to her friend, Sister Carrie Struthers.

"It's a sign from God," Sister Amelia declared confidently. "If someone can escape from this dreadful place, then someone else can as well."

"But you said yourself that they were men," Carrie complained, her freckled face agitated below a wreath of auburn curls. "What can we possibly do, mere women?"

Amelia looked at her friend, blinked and answered sharply. "What can we do? We can put our foot down, that's what. Demand that the *men* in this company make some effort to effect our escape."

"Well, I'm not so sure . . . ," demure Carrie began, long, coppery lashes lowered over dark brown eyes.

Fists on hips, Amelia responded forcefully. *"I am sure!* The least they can do is try to get away from this insane community."

Deacon Phineas Abercrombie bustled over, his considerable girth inflated with righteous indignation. "Here now, what is this all about?" Amelia quickly told him. It did not sit well at all. He peered disapprovingly at her down his long nose. At last he spoke his mind. "I am sure you will agree. If it is God's will that we become martyrs, then so be it. Who are we to question Him?"

Stubborn, Amelia continued to press her point. "What sort of martyrdom is it to be killed by lunatics who believe this wretched place is some rebirth of Ancient Rome?"

Abercrombie dismissed that reasoning. "That is for the Lord to decide, Sister. I am afraid I must forbid you to discuss this topic with any others of our flock. Besides, I hear that the men who escaped have been recaptured. It is really all so futile," he concluded with a bored sigh.

Not one to be easily intimidated, Amelia Witherspoon flounced off to speak with others of their small congregation. In open defiance of the deacon, she urged them to join in making some sort of plan to effect an escape. Watching her from a distance, the deacon grew angry at the impertinent young woman. He made a casual, angled course to the bars at the front of their communal cell. There he made a covert signal to one of the guards.

A few minutes later, with Sister Amelia still urging at least resistance if not actual escape, a centurion arrived outside the iron gate to their prison. "Which one is Deacon Abercrombie?" he demanded.

"I am he," the deacon volunteered.

With a curt gesture, the centurion sent two burly guards into the holding pen, and they roughly dragged Deacon Abercrombie out into the stone corridor. Without another word, the centurion started off with his prisoner in the firm grips of the pair of thugs.

Buck Sears looked across the dining table in the gladiator quarters at his new friends. "We're going to be taken over to the coliseum tomorrow. There are to be rehearsals for the spectacles."

Preacher looked up, lines of concern etched in his forehead. "How do you rehearse being fed to the lions?"

"It's them Bible-thumpers, ain't it?" Philadelphia asked. "You're worried about them."

"There's women and children among them," Preacher explained.

"Fools for comin' out here, I say. An' to'd you just a short while ago."

Preacher sighed. "You're right, Philadelphia. On both counts. It's only with them bein' youngins, it's all so—so uncivilized bein' a cougar's light lunch."

"No matter. There ain't a thing we can do about it."

"Right again. Only keep your wits about you, and if an opportunity comes to . . . well, just be ready, hear?"

Philadelphia pulled on one large ear lobe. "Oh, yeah. For certain sure. I don't know what sort of weapon they might give me, but I sure would like to wet it in a little Roman blood."

Preacher forced a laugh he did not feel. "That's the spirit. How about you, friend Buck?"

Buck shrugged. He had been giving that question considerable thought since their recapture. "I'd rather be dead than forced to fight every time they have some sort of holiday."

Preacher rubbed dry, calloused palms together. "That's settled then. We'll look to give them a show like they've never seen before."

Philadelphia's sour expression belied his enthusiastic words. "Beats daylight outta sittin' around wonderin' which one o' them profess'nals is gonna do us in."

Bejeweled fingers aglitter, Marcus Quintus Americus caressed the gold wine cup he held, then set it aside as the centurion from the gladiator school entered with a portly, pompous-looking man with graying hair and the eyes of a prophet. The first citizen had dined sumptuously on roasted bison backribs, stuffed quail and an enormous fish. Recalling it made Quintus salivate. Then a flicker of annoyance shot across his face. Why could they never get the wine just right? It always tasted more like vinegar than a vintage selection. After a protracted three minutes, he raised his eyes and spoke.

"Yes, what is it?"

"He claims to have information for you, First Citizen."

Quintus studied the prisoner in silence, sipped from his wine goblet and motioned the captive forward. "Bring him forth, then."

Given a not-too-kindly shove, Deacon Abercrombie staggered forward. "I—I've come to you with a plot for an escape."

Quintus threw back his head and laughed loudly. "Did you now? Would it surprise you to learn that they were captured earlier today and returned to Nova Roma?"

Although quaking internally, Deacon Abercrombie stood his ground. "No. Not in the least. I am not referring to those three men. This has to do with some of my own flock. They are talking about overpowering some of your guards and making a break for it. A young woman, Sister Amelia Witherspoon, is behind it."

Quintus narrowed his eyes. "When is this to happen?"

"I . . . am not certain. Though I would imagine it would be when we are taken to the coliseum tomorrow."

Considering this, Quintus jabbed a ring-encrusted finger at Abercrombie. "And why is it that you have come to me?"

Abercrombie drew himself up, an otherworldly light illuminating his face. "I have reached the conclusion that it is our destiny to be martyred. Our Lord wishes to call us home."

Quintus despised these sanctimonious churchmen for their weakness. He could not keep the sarcasm out of his tone of voice. "How very convenient for your Lord that we have such efficient means to accomplish that. However, I am not clear as to why you slunk off to inform me of this. Hummm?"

For the first time, Abercrombie looked embarrassed. "I—I have come to the conclusion that while martyrdom might be a suitable end for many, and sacrifice for our Lord is always desirable, I—I simply feel that I have much more important work to accomplish during my time here. I have years of good works ahead of me. So, all—all I ask is that I be spared. My wife and I, that is."

Quintus feigned surprise. The jeweled rings on his fingers sparkled and sent off spears of brightness as he moved one hand to his chest in mock distress. "What is this? Do you mean to say you want special treatment?"

"Well . . . yes—yes, I suppose you could say that."

"Oh, you'll get special treatment, all right." Quintus produced a wolfish smile. "You will have the privilege of fighting your way to freedom. After all, the *rudis*—the—ah—wooden sword of retirement—is a cherished custom of the games. Think of it, my dear deacon. If you manage to fight and claw your way over the bloody, broken bodies of your fellow Christians, you will be a free man, a citizen of New Rome and able to do whatever you wish."

A low cry of anguish came from deep in Abercrombie's chest. His knees sagged, and the men who held him tightened their grip. Quintus gestured to the centurion.

"Take him back. No, take him right now to the coliseum. Put him in one of the small holding cells alone. It wouldn't do for him to have pangs of remorse and confess all to his followers." As the guards frog-marched a stricken Abercrombie out of the dining chamber, Quintus looked across the room to his son, reclining on a dinner couch. "By the gods, how I hate such craven villains. They haven't one drop of the sap of manliness."

Those words stung Phineas Abercrombie, although what followed utterly humiliated him. "Will he die in the arena, Father?" young Faustus asked.

"Oh, assuredly. He'll be the last to be chewed by the lions, because he will cower behind his people. And when he dies, it will not be with a roar, but rather a whimper."

* * *

Word came by way of the slave grapevine. Preacher, Philadelphia and Buck took the news with grim expressions. Someone among the passel of Bible-thumpers had started stirring them up with escape in mind. The time for this attempt would be the next morning.

"And confound it, there's two things wrong with this. First off, what I hear is, it is a female critter who done the stirrin' up *and* the plannin'. Whatever she come up with, you can be sure it won't work. That's for starters. Now, what's it you heard those guards sayin', Buck?"

Buck, the only one of them who spoke Latin, produced an expression of contempt and disgust. "It appears as how one among the gospel group tattled on them to this-here Marcus Quintus."

"You mean to that ol' he-coon of this whole place?" Preacher asked.

"The same. Thing is, what can we do about it? They're due to be thrown to the lions at the games two days from tomorrow."

"Yes," Philadelphia agreed. "That looks like the end for them."

Preacher took over. "Simple. There's little we can do about whatever they have in mind for tomorrow. What we have to concentrate on is to defeat our opponents in the arena, force our way out of there and take these soul-savers along with us."

Philadelphia gave him a blank face. "Oh, you make it all sound so easy, Preacher."

Early the next morning, two small boys splashed and laughed together in the *tepidarium* of the palace private baths. Without their clothing, one could not tell that the blond, curly haired lad wore the purple-striped tunic of a patrician, while the black-haired, shoe-button-eyed kid was his body servant. Master and slave had grown up together and formed a deep bond. Young Quintus Faustus confided all his really juicy secrets to little Casca.

Loyal Casca kept his silence about these revelations. In fact, he often shared in the more entertaining of them. Today, their early morning bathing was energized by their awareness of the looming excitement of the birthday games to be held for Faustus on the last day of September. The birthday boy was beside himself. He jumped and surged in the water, splashed his whole arm, flopped like a seal off the slick tile of the edge, and dived between his only friend's legs.

Casca did the same. Then they swam the length of the lukewarm pool and climbed out with their arms around the shoulders of one another. Light danced in Casca's eyes. "Is it for sure, Faustus? Your father is going to let you be *imperator?* All by yourself?"

"Certainly. I will be eleven, you know," he added solemnly.

"Yes. And I will be in two months."

"You're coming to the games with me. I have just decided. You can hand me ices, feed me grapes; we'll sit under the awning and you will have a parasol to shade us both."

"It sounds wonderful."

Faustus put nail-bitten fingers on his servant's shoulder. "It's the least I can do, considering you can't attend the birthday feast as a guest."

Casca produced a brief pout. "Yes. I know. And I understand. I really do."

For a moment Faustus looked like he might cry. "You're a true friend, Casca. You're the best friend any boy could ever have."

"You're my best friend, too, Faustus." His eyes twinkled as he tapped a finger on his friend's wet knee. "Will you— will you sneak me a bowl of your birthday custard?"

"Of course. This time it is a new kind of custard Mother learned about. It is called ice cream."

From an archway of a side entrance, someone cleared his throat in a deeper tone. Marcus Quintus stepped into the damp room, wearing only a towel over one shoulder. "There you are, son. I hoped I would find you here. You may go, Casca."

"See you in the *frigidium*," Casca called over one shoulder to Faustus. After the boy had padded barefoot toward the cold bath, Quintus sat on a bench beside his son.

"How does it feel? It's only two days away now. Are you really ready for it?"

"Yes, sir. I'm so excited. I wish it was this afternoon."

"It will keep. I wanted to urge you to remain stalwart. When you are the honoree master of games, you must retain your poise. Avoid any excessive show of emotion. Listen to Bulbus in regard to giving death to any of the professionals. And, do not flinch at assigning death to those who deserve it. You must show the people that you have the fortitude. Remember one thing. Your performance at the games will show that you either do or do not deserve the title *Princeps Romanus*."

Prince of Rome! How heady it sounded to Faustus. He got a faraway, glassy look in his eyes as he mentally reviewed past kills he had enjoyed in the arena. His nostrils flared and his breathing became harsh as he answered.

"Don't worry, Father. I *like* to see the blood flow."

Early the next morning, the guards roused the professional gladiators first, and they trooped through a wooden door to the tunnel that connected the school with the coliseum. They would have their breakfast there and spend the morning hours braiding up their hair and oiling their muscular bodies. This was done to prevent a handful of hair from being used against them, and to keep lesser fighters from holding on to them in a bear hug. Too much time and money had been spent on them to allow their defeat by an amateur.

Next, the lesser-trained gladiators were escorted by guards through the underground passage to identical, dank stone cells in the bowels of the large stadium. Preacher judged that an hour passed before the burly, well-armed warders came for him and his companions. As condemned men, they were kept separately from all other participants.

They had only reached the far end of the tunnel when the condemned missionaries got rousted out of their holding pen and directed into the tunnel. Angry shouts rose as Preacher, Philadelphia and Buck were roughly shoved into a cell. The sounds of a struggle came to their ears after the clang of the closing iron-slat door. It appeared the guards had been prepared for this resistance. The hollow, north-wind whistle and the crack of whips followed immediately, along with the cries of pain from those who received the lash. Meaty sounds of cudgels on backs and shoulders told Preacher and his friends of the swift end of the brief resistance. So much for their big escape.

Preacher spoke quietly to his companions. "At least some of them Bible-thumpers have got some sand. Maybe we can make use of that when we get out there."

Philadelphia did not agree. "More likely, they got what little spunk they had whupped out of them. Them laddies wield a mean whip," he added, as he remembered the scourging they had received after their recapture.

"With or without them, we're goin' over those walls and out of this place," Preacher declared hotly. "When they come back from practicin' that thing they're supposed to do before the lions, I intend to talk to a few of 'em."

Preacher had his opportunity shortly before the noon hour. The captives were driven back inside the lower levels of the arena and given a chance to slake their thirst. All of the regular gladiators had been released from their cells to be equipped for the practice fights. Preacher had been decked out in the flanged, peaked helmet, net and trident of a *riatarius*. For a while he strutted around the common room, in imitation of the professionals, until the wary guards grew lax. Then he sidled over to the bars of the cage that held the missionaries.

Quickly he outlined his intention to make an escape and reviewed the plans with several of the younger men. He concluded with a logical suggestion. "The more of us that makes the try, the better chance we have of getting away."

A middle-aged Bible-thumper stepped close. "It sounds like you have given this considerable thought. Only, we cannot be a part of it. We're nonviolent. Surely, the government has learned of this dreadful place. They will put a stop to it."

Preacher studied the man like he would a strange insect that had just crawled out of his shirt sleeve. "No man ever got free by whinin' about it until the government gave him freedom as a handout. Government don't give people freedom, they *take it* from them."

"You don't mean that. Our government—"

"Ain't no different in that respect from any other. That's why I spent most of my life out here."

With a self-righteous sniff, the pilgrim announced, "Our trust is with the Lord."

Preacher cocked his head to one side, a twinkle in his eyes. "Might be you need to look a little further into that Bible you're so fond of quotin'. Seems it's writ in there somewhere that the Lord helps them what helps themselves."

Without another word, Preacher turned on one heel of his fighting sandals and walked away. From a short distance off, Sister Amelia Witherspoon looked after him with a longing that was not the least bit sexual. She had been wondering about the whereabouts of Deacon Abercrombie when he had begun to talk with the men. What he said made her completely forget the deacon. She hungered for a man of courage like this one. Someone who would lead these timid souls to freedom. Sounded to her like this could be the one.

15

Two days went by swiftly. Preacher took Buck and Philadelphia aside for a final discussion on their plan to escape from the arena. His words were as grim as they were low.

"We cain't know when or how we'll do this. I figger we hoss one another up the inner wall and make a run through the onlookers. They won't be armed, and most of 'em will plain panic when we swarm in among them with weapons drippin' blood. That'll keep the guards away."

Overhead the coliseum was filled with noise as early spectators filled the rows of stone benches. Concessionaires could be heard hawking their wares. To Preacher it sounded like something they would do back East. A Fourth of July celebration or something.

"I think the best thing is to do it right off. Go after that brat kid of Marcus Quintus and use him as a shield," Buck opined.

Preacher slowly shook his head. "No, the guards will be watchin' right close at first, when we're fresh and all. If we can string it out until the gospel-spouters are brought in, we can probably get a half dozen or so to come along. We've all been in enough tussles to know when's the best time. Use your judgment, but keep an eye on me."

The long, valveless trumpets sounded, announcing the entry of the day's master of games. The crowd roared. Another fanfare, and then the other musicians joined in. Metal creaked and grated as the portcullis raised enough to let out a party of clowns. Preacher watched them with divided attention.

They did somersaults and cartwheels, ran into one another, took pratfalls and rolled in the sand. One, with an animal bladder filled with water, pounded on his companions until the thin skin broke and soaked the victim. The crowd howled in merriment. When the last buffoon scampered back inside the dark interior of the coliseum, the attendants went out to smooth off the killing ground. That accomplished, the trainers came to line up the whole company of gladiators and condemned prisoners.

A moment later, the trumpets sounded again, clear and crisp. The gate rumbled upward, and the lead fighters in the Company of the Dead stepped out onto the sand.

Young Quintus Faustus Americus entered the *imperator's* box with the first fanfare. Dressed in a snowy toga, with a broad purple hem stripe, he wore a circlet of gilded laurel leaves, with gold-strapped sandals. Followed by his body servant, Casca, he went directly to the center seat of the front row and raised his right arm. In his hand he held an ivory staff with a gold eagle on the top. He turned from side to side, as he had been instructed, and waved to the cheering crowd.

Some stomped their feet, others cheered and whistled. Led by the paid claque, they chanted his name in a wavelike roar. Eyes sparkling in pleasure, he nevertheless maintained his composure while he seated himself and stared serenely across the sand at the giant portal, behind which the gladiators and condemned prisoners waited. Casca popped a grape between the lips of Faustus. His father and mother joined him and took seats at either side. Bulbus came next, followed by a dozen patrician boys who had been invited by Faustus. When the box had been filled, Faustus rose and elevated the wand. The trumpets roared again. "The auguries are good! The gods are pleased. Let the games begin!" he called out in his squeaky boy's voice.

Casca handed Faustus a chilled cup of wine as the portcullis squealed open and out spilled the clowns. Their antics delighted the crowd. Their erratic tumbling absolutely captivated the birthday guests. Faustus laughed until the tears ran and he held his sides. Then he suddenly remembered the seriousness of his position today. He cast an uneasy glance at Casca, who winked at him; he then sobered and forced unwilling facial muscles into a placid expression. The *real* fun, he reminded himself, would come later.

When the clowns ended their performance, the trumpets blared again. The portcullis raised the full way, and the Company of the Dead marched forth. In the lead came the ranks of professionals, followed by those in training, and lastly the prisoners. A small smile of expectation flickered on the lips of Faustus. In perfect formation the participants in the games reached the base of the "emperors'" box. They raised their weapons in salute.

"Hail Caesar, we who are about to die salute thee!"

Faustus rose to speak the lines he had prepared. Leaning forward, he addressed them while Casca shaded him with a parasol. "Friends. Thank you for the spectacle you have prepared in honor of my birthday. I am sure that I will enjoy it. Now it is time to begin. Parade yourselves for my other friends to see, then bring on the first pairs."

It having been spoken in Latin, Preacher did not recognize a word. "Lotta jibber-jabber, you ask me," he whispered to Philadelphia.

Drums and wind instruments struck up, and the gladiators turned smartly to make a circuit of the arena. Behind them came the "accommodators" to smooth the sand. Although the air was cool on this last day of September, Preacher had worked up a sweat from the closeness of the coliseum and the heat of the sun by the time they returned to the cool interior of the underground cells.

At once, the clarions summoned the first two fighting

pairs. Four professionals stepped out onto the sand. They faced off, one-on-one, saluted one another and set to. A *riatarius* tested his skill against a gladiator dressed as a Samnite. The long, curved blade in the Samnite's hand danced a blue-white arabesque in the air. The trident man looped his net in a hypnotic pattern before the eyes of the swordsman. He prodded with his three-tined spear. Preacher and Philadelphia stood close to the iron lattice of the portcullis and watched intently.

Beyond the fighters, he saw Faustus lean forward raptly, his mouth sagging open, pink tongue flicking in and out. There was a grunt as the Samnite lunged with his sword. A moment later the crowd roared as the *riatarius* flicked out his net and snared his opponent's blade and right arm. The trident darted toward his exposed, bare belly.

Dancing on tiptoe, the Samnite turned to his right, away from the spear and free of the knotted lines of the net. A mighty shout came from the spectators. Lightning fast, the *riatarius* came after the retreating gladiator. The Samnite's sword slashed through the air and bit deeply into the wooden shaft of the spear.

"Gotta remember to keep from doin' that," Preacher said to himself.

"What's that?" Philadelphia asked.

"I was talkin' to myself. That feller almost got his spear chopped in half. Careless."

"There's a lot to learn for this kind of fighting," Philadelphia agreed.

On the sand, the net flared outward and fluttered down over the head and shoulders of the Samnite. At once, the *riatarius* ran around his helpless opponent and secured him in the snare. Then, with a powerful yank, he jerked the swordsman off his feet. He pounced on the supine body and raised his trident for the fatal blow. He hesitated at that point and looked up at the box.

Faustus, lights dancing in his eyes, leaned forward and shot out his arm. At the last moment, his father reached over and touched him lightly on his bare knee. Disappointment painted the boy's face momentarily. Then he turned his thumb upward. The mob shouted its approval.

When their bedlam subsided, a scream came from the lips of a gladiator with a spiked-ball flail. He had taken his eye off his opponent for a split second. That was all it had taken. With blurring speed, the gladiator with a *gladius* made a diagonal slash from the incautious fighter's right nipple to his left hip. Howls of approval and jeers for the wounded man.

"It's Brutus. Stupid Brutus."

"Brutus has never been any good." More insults came from the audience, though Preacher did not understand them.

"Finish him!" a woman's voice shrieked.

Brutus shuddered as he walked more into Preacher's view. Blood streamed down his torso in a shimmering curtain. He brought up his shield to cover his vulnerable body and began to swing his flail back and forth. The sword came at him again. Brutus blocked it with his shield and converted his sideways motion into a circular one. When the heavy, spiked ball reached a position directly behind its handle, he lashed it forward.

It struck with a clang on the small shield of his opponent. With a powerful yank, Brutus jerked the protective disc out of the other gladiator's grasp. At once he tried to free his weapon. That proved his undoing. The opposing gladiator came at him with a blizzard of varied attacks. It ended with a horizontal slash that opened the belly of Brutus an inch above his navel.

Brutus sucked air deeply and dropped the handle of his flail. He sat abruptly. His eyes grew wide, and he worked frantically to stuff his intestines back inside his body.

"That's dumb, Brutus," a critic directly over Preacher shouted.

Preacher looked over at the box along with the victorious gladiator. Panting in his excitement, Faustus wore the mask of a child demon as he eagerly thrust out his arm and turned his extended thumb downward. The swordsman quickly stepped over and struck the head from Brutus' shoulders. The crowd went wild.

Shoulder to shoulder, the three surviving gladiators marched to salute the young boy in whose honor this display of gore was being held. Then they returned to the gate, which rose to admit them. The trumpets blared and four more professionals came out. A quartet of confused, frightened men followed.

They saluted the *imperator* from the center of the sand and set to it with speed and energy. This round of combats lasted only a short time and the blood flowed freely. Two of the half-trained fighters died within a minute, dispatched by the downturned thumb of Quintus Faustus. The survivors strutted back to the holding pens. Another fanfare brought out the clowns.

Only these were not the same frisky children who had performed first. They appeared to be dazed, uncertain of where they were, or what their purpose might be. Handlers quickly goaded them into fighting one another. Some were armed with tubes of sewn skin, filled with sand, others with air-filled bladders. Another group carried straw-stuffed objects that Preacher could only guess at being animal parts. He watched them with a growing frown as they began to flail away at their companions.

Philadelphia approached him and nodded toward the grotesque performers. "I hear around that those poor folk are captives who have been tormented into states of craziness. They're supposed to whoop it up out there for a while; then comes the really bad part."

"What's that?" Preacher asked him.

"Wait, an' you'll see."

"Sounds grim. Might be you an' Buck can get more cooperation out of those Bible-thumpers. Why don't you go in among them and give them a little backbone?"

"Suits. I'll get Buck." Philadelphia turned away and

went to find the teamster. Preacher soon saw them talking earnestly among the missionaries. He looked away, back at the sand, when gales of laughter filled the arena.

"'Pears to me that it's them that's watchin' an' laughin' that's got the sick minds," he grumbled to himself.

The sorrowful clowns had milked their antics for all the laughs they could generate. At a signal from the real master of the games, Bulbus, small gates opened around the arena. Out rushed huge, ferocious, starved mastiff dogs. Screams of terror came from the pitiful, demented clowns as the dogs fell on them. The audience loved it. Preacher made a face of disgust as he looked beyond the slaughter to the small boy in the marble box.

Faustus squirmed in a frenzy of excitement. It made Preacher's stomach churn.

"I tell you, friend, if you don't decide to fight back, you'll get what them poor fellers out there are gettin'. It don't feel nice gettin' ripped apart by a cougar," Preacher told three intently listening young missionaries. "Believe me, I know. I done got mauled by one some years back. If I didn't have a big knife an' a war hawk with me, he'd a-been dinin' on my innards before noon."

One of his audience swallowed hard and made a gagging sound. "If I have something to fight with, I'll fight," he declared shakily. To the angry glare from the son of Deacon Abercrombie, he added, "I have a wife and two children to protect."

"A child has the right to decide for himself," Phineas Abercrombie replied snippily.

Defiance crackled in the words of the young father. "If a child cannot make decisions about property, or his schooling, or anything else, Brother Phineas, I say he cannot properly decide to die for the greater glory of the Lord."

"Careful Brother Fauts, you are close to blasphemy."

Fury born of his protectiveness exploded. *"Damn* your blasphemy! I'll fight, and you would, too, if you had any stones."

Philadelphia left them to further pursuit of that possibility when a burly handler gestured to him with his coiled whip. Buck, too, had been gathered in. Their warders took them to where Preacher stood. Three of the toughest professionals joined them a moment later.

"You will fight in pairs. You condemned men, if you win this match, you will be paired with another gladiator until you are killed. So, fight your best and give the people a good show."

When the last of the demented victims succumbed to the ravenous jaws of the mastiffs, the accommodators cleared the arena. Hawkers moved through the aisles, selling wine, popped corn, slices of melon and other fruit. Others cut shaved-thin slices off roasted joints of meat and built sandwiches. The spectators ate and drank and talked through their laughter as they recalled their favorite kill by the vicious dogs. It all made Preacher want to drive the three tines of his trident into their guts and twist while they shrieked in agony.

With the clean-up completed, the clarions brayed again, and the six fighters stepped out onto the sand. They advanced in two ranks, with Preacher, Philadelphia and Buck behind the professionals. At the center, they halted and saluted the boy *imperator.* Faustus rose and addressed them, his voice husky with barely suppressed emotion.

"You three who defied the authority of New Rome will die here today. And I will take great pleasure in watching your blood soak into the sand. So, do not slack. Give us a good fight, so we can thrill in your agony." He pointed his ivory wand at Preacher. "Especially you, my magnificent specimen. I expect great things from you. Now, let the fighting begin."

Trumpets shivered the air. All six fighters squared off. Preacher knew he had to make this quick. He began to circle his opponent, the net held loosely in his left hand. He feinted tentatively with the trident. Suddenly, the gladiator opposite him burst forth with a frenzy of furious blows.

Tall, lean, and muscular, Vindix bore in on Preacher with a smooth network of thrusts and slashes. He smiled grimly as Preacher gave ground. He batted the trident aside and pressed forward with a springy right leg. Blinding hot pain erupted in his thigh as Preacher recovered from the beating and drove two of the three tines of his weapon deeply into the flesh of an exposed thigh.

A fraction of a second later, he hurled the net, ensnaring Vindix. With a stout yank, Preacher hauled the gladiator off his sandals. He drew the small dagger from his belt and knelt beside the fallen fighter.

"I'll make this quick, to spare you pain."

Vindix smiled through his agony. "That's what I intended for you. No need for us to provide entertainment for that sick, twisted child."

Preacher looked up at the boy, to see an expression of fury on the soft features. "You were too fast. That's not fair. Spare him," Faustus' squeaky voice commanded.

Preacher replaced his dagger and offered a hand to Vindix to help him come upright. The crowd cheered. Vindix was a favorite. Preacher spoke softly to him. "You live to fight another day."

Vindix gave him a grim smile, face contorted with pain. "More's the pity." He limped away, to be replaced by another gladiator. This one bore the spiked mace. He came after Preacher in a rush.

Philadelphia had been matched with a squat, brawny brute who took particular pleasure in maiming his opponents before finally finishing them off. Despite the lingering discomfort of his old wound, Philadelphia Braddock danced lightly away from the *gladius* that darted before his eyes.

Sweat began to trickle down from his temples. He concentrated on the eyes of Asperis and the tip of his sword.

So quickly that Philadelphia almost missed it, Asperis widened his eyes in anticipation of a slash that would sever the mountain man's left arm, leaving him without a shield. With a swift jerk, Philadelphia raised the round metal protector, and the iron blade in his opponent's hand rang loudly against it. Philadelphia swung his right leg forward and pivoted, to smash his armored *caestus* into the point of the left shoulder of Asperis. The triangular blades bit deeply, and blood flowed in a gush when Philadelphia withdrew his *caestus*. He shifted his weight and kicked Asperis in the belly.

Numbed and bleeding profusely from the shoulder, Asperis doubled over, and Philadelphia clubbed him with the armored fist. Unfortunately it left him vulnerable for a moment, during which Asperis drove the tip of his sword into the meaty portion of Philadelphia's side. Fire flashed through the muscles of Philadelphia's torso. Biting his lower lip, he hauled back and rammed the spikes of his *caestus* into the side of Asperis' head. The gladiator went down in a flash.

A low groan came from deep in his chest, and Asperis began to twitch his arms and legs. Philadelphia knew what he had done and wasted no time checking with the pouty-faced brat for the signal to finish Asperis. Behind him, the portcullis clanged again, and another contender entered the arena. Philadelphia turned to see that it would be a *riatarius*.

"More trouble," he grunted.

Buck Sears faced a gladiator done up as a Nubian warrior, complete with zebra-painted shield, towering headdress and assagai spear. Braided elephant-tail hair and feather anklets circled his legs above bare feet. They rippled hypnotically as he bounced and jounced up and down in an advance punctuated by sharp cries from a mouth ringed by a wide smear of black grease paint.

Buck took this all in and lowered the tip of his sword to the sand. He threw back his head and laughed. "Now, ain't you just the silliest damn critter I've ever seen."

The gyrations abruptly ceased. "Huh?"

"I said you look like a fool," Buck called out.

Howling in outrage, the imitation Nubian charged with his spear held over his shoulder in one of the classical positions employed by the Zulu and the Masai, whom the ancient Romans lumped together as "Nubians."

Buck lunged out of the way of the advance. He swung the flat of his blade and smashed it into the ribs of his opponent. Laughter rose from the stands. Buck began to enjoy himself. Before the Nubian could turn, Buck booted him in the seat of his pants. He stumbled and lowered his shield. Buck thrust with his sword and cut a line along the gladiator's forehead right below the gaudy headdress. A sheet of blood poured out. The mob loved it.

Even that evil-minded brat had started to giggle and clap his hands, Buck noted. He quickly found out he had paid too much attention to such matters. Solis had recovered himself and came at Buck driven by fury. He battered and hacked at the shield Buck carried. Buck's strength wavered momentarily, and Solis seized the advantage. Setting his feet, he slammed his own shield into Buck's face.

Buck's knees buckled, and he dropped onto the left one. Blackness swam before his eyes. He shook his head in an effort to clear it while he fended off the plunging assagai. With a desperate effort, he brought his *gladius* around and drove it through the fire-hardened zebra-print shield. The tip sliced three inches into sweaty flesh. Solis grunted, gasped and loosed a thin wail. Buck pulled back and regained his feet.

Above him, all around the coliseum the throng went wild. They stomped their feet and pelted the sand with greasy strips of paper that had held sandwiches and popped corn. Some threw cushions they had brought along for comfort on the stone benches of the common bleachers. A gray pallor had washed over the face of Solis. He blinked back fear, sweat and blood and tried to focus on his opponent.

Sucking in large draughts of air, Buck found Solis easily enough. His shield arm sagged; the knob-hilled assagai hung in an unresponsive hand. Pink froth bubbled on his pain-distorted lips. Balefully, Buck advanced on him. Deep inside, he did not want to do this. Then he remembered he was supposed to solicit a decision from the *imperator.*

He turned his head upward. Faustus seemed to be on the edge of ecstasy. He rapidly licked his lips and stared fixedly at the bleeding wound in the chest of Solis. At last he regrasped what was expected of him. Solis was a professional. Faustus spared him.

Two arena helpers escorted him out. Another gladiator took his place. The six men—three sapped and worn from their earlier battles, the other trio fresh—faced the box and saluted.

"Awh, hell, we've gotta go through this all over again," Buck muttered. He squared off with the others, and the attacks came immediately.

16

Through the open squares formed by the iron gate to their holding pen, Sister Amelia Witherspoon looked on. At first she viewed the grisly spectacle in horror. Then, as the mountain men and their teamster ally bested one professional gladiator after another, her perusal changed to amorous fascination with Preacher. He had to be the bravest, strongest man ever born.

A shiver of delight ran through her slender body, hidden under the prim, gray dress and her bonnet. If what he did before her very eyes were not so absolutely terrible, she might suspect that she was becoming enamored of him. Possibly even falling in love. *Stuff and nonsense,* she told herself. Cries of trepidation came from others among the missionaries. One of the young men convinced to put up some resistance by Philadelphia spoke quietly beside Sister Amelia.

"Is any of them going to be around to lead the way to freedom?"

An unusual light sparkled in Amelia's eyes. "I'm sure that one will. Arturus. He has finished off three gladiators so far. Spared the lives of two. He is a true champion."

With an indulgent chuckle, the young man nodded toward Preacher. "'Arturus' is it? That may be what these crazy folk call him, but the one named Philadelphia told me he is really the mountain man we were questioned about, Preacher."

Amelia's eyes widened. "I knew it! I knew he had to be the best there is. Oh, Preacher, fight for us," she offered up prayerfully.

Out on the sand, it appeared as though Preacher had heard her appeal and responded accordingly. He swung his net, snared another gladiator, and hurtled the hapless fighter toward the deadly tines of the trident. A moment before the barbed spikes entered vulnerable flesh, a high, thin voice barked from above and behind Preacher.

"Hold!" Preacher released his victim. "He has fought well," Faustus continued. "He is free to retire. You will face yet another, more worthy opponent," he told Preacher. "At once."

Looks like the folks in the imperial box have got impatient. Not gonna wait for all of us to finish our fights, Preacher thought to himself as the gate ground open and a huge fellow lumbered out. Taller by a head than Preacher, he was armed with a *caestus* and a twin-bladed dagger. He immediately went for Preacher with a roar.

He swung the *caestus* with practiced ease, and the spectators greeted him by name. "Dicius! Dicius! Dicius!"

Like an elephant attacking a toad, he loomed over Preacher and contemptuously swept aside the net when it hissed toward him. He stepped in and engaged the trident with the dual-bladed knife, gave a mighty twist and yanked it from Preacher's grasp. Preacher tried with the net again and missed as Dicius danced away. Then the muscular gladiator came at Preacher again.

He bounded forward, jinked to his right, tempting another throw of the net. Preacher obliged him. The tar-stiffened, knotted snare fanned out and lofted over the head of Dicius. Before it could descend, Dicius leaped to his left and struck a powerful blow with the *caestus*.

Fortunately for Preacher, the punch landed askew, to glance off the side of Preacher's head. One of the blades cut a ragged line in the hair above one ear. Stunned, Preacher sank to one knee. Dimly he heard the shrill scream as Amelia cried out.

Philadelphia Braddock looked up at the sound of that anguished wail. He saw Dicius poised with his *caestus* raised above his head to deliver a fatal blow. For the moment Philadelphia ignored his own tormentor to grasp his sword in front of the hilt and hurl it like a lance. It flashed in the afternoon sunlight as it sped to the target.

Paralyzed by enormous misery, Dicius emitted a faint moan as the *gladius* pierced his side and sliced through the soft organs in his belly. He rocked from heel to toe for a moment, and the *caestus* dropped without force to land on Preacher's shoulder. Shaking clear of his momentary blackout, Preacher scrambled to retrieve his trident.

He stood over Dicius, who feebly tried to cut the hamstring of Preacher's left leg. With a powerful thrust, Preacher drove the middle tine through his opponent's throat. He looked up with a nod and a smile for Philadelphia.

"I reckon they aim to kill us for certain sure. No reason we have to play by their rules," Preacher told his friend as he abandoned his trident. Then he bent, retrieved the *gladius* and tossed it back to Philadelphia.

So astonished by the swift action that he failed to press his attack, the gladiator contesting Philadelphia only then broke his frozen pose. He came on strong, yet the mountain man managed to elude his darting weapon. Philadelphia gave ground slowly, eyes alert for an opening. While he did, Preacher retrieved the spiked mace of an earlier opponent and looked to the portcullis, where his next enemy would appear.

It turned out to be Spartacus. At the sight of this, Faustus bounced up and down on his chair, thrilled by the prospect. Preacher did not greet it quite so enthusiastically. He gave a tentative swing of the spiked ball at the end of its chain and advanced on the huge escaped slave. A moment later, Philadelphia got too busy to watch.

With catlike grace, the gladiator advanced on an oblique angle to Philadelphia. He prodded at him with the tip of his *pilum.* The slender spear had been equipped with a soft lead collar at the base of the tip to prevent it from being withdrawn from a wound. Altogether a nasty weapon. Philadelphia gave it due respect. His opponent's advance forced him toward where Buck had just dispatched his latest enemy. Weakened by his recent wounds, Philadelphia could not maintain his balance when he backed into the supine body of the dead gladiator.

His knee buckled and he stumbled. At that critical moment, the professional thrust the javelin toward him. Only at the last possible moment, Philadelphia covered himself with his shield, turned the *pilum,* and regained his balance. He hacked at an exposed knee, and the blades bit into flesh at the bottom of the gladiator's thigh. That let Philadelphia recover completely.

Ignoring the threat of the javelin, he pushed in on his opponent. At that moment, Philadelphia would have given anything for a good tomahawk. The short sword would have to do, he decided. At least until he could equip himself with something better. At first he made good progress, his antagonist hobbled by his wound; then Philadelphia planted his foot in a pool of blood while attempting a thrust to the chest.

His feet went out from under him, and he plopped onto the ground. Hoots and jeers rose from the onlookers. Eyes alight with renewed hope, the gladiator moved in on Philadelphia.

Eager to win Spartacus as an ally, rather than having to kill him, Preacher raised his left hand in a cautionary gesture; the net hung limp in his grasp. "It don't have to end here, Spartacus," he prompted.

"Don't talk that talk to me, white man," Spartacus growled truculently.

Preacher ignored him. "I mean it. You can get out of here, too."

Spartacus would have none of it. He came at Preacher with a huge cudgel, a single, long spike protruding through the side of the thick tip. It swished through the air as Preacher jumped backward. Muscles rippled under the oiled black skin as Spartacus planted another big foot on the sand and advanced again.

Preacher whipped the air with his flail. The spiked ball smashed into the boss of the shield on Spartacus' left arm. It made a resounding, thunder-clap sound. Instead of retreating, Spartacus stepped in. The men found themselves chest to chest. The muscles in Preacher's left arm and shoulder strained to hold the powerful arm that supported the cudgel.

To the onlookers they appeared to be dancing as they shuffled their feet to find better purchase. Some began to clap rhythmically. Cries of "Fight! Fight!" rang in the tiers. Preacher spoke quiet reason to Spartacus.

"Even though slavery is the law of the land, it don't amount to a hill of bison dung out here. If you join us in winnin' free, an' takin' them helpless missionaries with us, I'll personally guarantee that you can make a new life for yourself in the High Lonesome, an' live a free man."

Spartacus curled his lips in a sneer and snarled his reply while he cuffed Preacher with a backhand blow with the cudgel. "What do I want that for? I'm due to earn the *rudis* soon. That'll make me a wealthy man, an' free. Why should I risk all of that for a passel of white folk who prob'ly owned slaves before they got captured?"

Preacher gave it another try. "They're Bible-thumpers. Mission folk. Their kind don't hold slaves."

"Knowed me a preacher-man down South. He owned hisself three house slaves. I'll be a big man around here after I kill you an' retire."

Unable to obtain dominance above, Preacher used an old Indian trick. He shifted his weight to one leg, shot the other forward and hooked his heel behind the ankle of Spartacus.

With a swift yank forward, he toppled the big black gladiator off his feet. At the last second, Preacher rolled away as

Spartacus crashed to the ground. Impact forced grunted words from Spartacus' mouth.

"You're good, I give you that. Who are you, anyhow, Arturus?"

Preacher decided to gamble it all. He turned his flinty gaze straight into the eyes of his opponent. "They call me Preacher."

An expression of respect, flavored with awe, filled the gladiator's face. "Fore Jesus, I didn't know."

They had come to their knees now. The force of their impact with hard-packed sand had knocked the flail from Preacher's hand. He saw the trident only a scant foot from his grasp. Spartacus hefted the club and licked his lips.

"I'll be the richest man around if I finish you," Spartacus declared.

"If. I'd think on that were I you."

Spartacus found that to somehow be funny. He threw back his head to laugh, and Preacher quickly unfurled his net and flung it over the kneeling man. Spartacus flung it off like a mere cobweb. Though not before Preacher could snatch up his trident. Opposite him, Spartacus bounded to the soles of his high-laced sandals. Preacher seemed to react slowly, gathering his net.

With the quickness that made him famous, Spartacus charged. The cudgel led the way. Preacher deflected it with the shaft of his trident and prodded at the chest of his opponent. Spartacus laughed mirthlessly and came on. Forced to give ground, Preacher brought his heel down on the haft of a dropped weapon. Instantly, he stumbled and tottered off to one side.

Spartacus seized the moment. "You gon' die, Preacherman."

Preacher recovered himself as the deadly club swished past his left ear. The heft of the lethal object slammed painfully into the top of his shoulder. Already directed to its target, the trident cut a ragged gash in the lean side of Spartacus. Dizzied by repeated injury, Preacher missed an opportunity to end it.

Pain made his next cast erratic. The net slid from the oiled skin of his opponent and fluttered to the ground. Goaded by the press of time, Preacher hastily gathered it. A blur of movement told him Spartacus had anticipated the miss. The black man bore down on him and forced another retreat.

Feeling the effects of blood loss, Preacher stumbled again. Seized by a frenzy, the crowd howled and stomped their feet. Spartacus acted at once on the tiny break given him. Overconfident now, he stepped in for the kill, only to have Preacher let loose the net again, this time tightly furled. Using a technique he had learned from the instructors, he sent it out like a sinuous snake to coil around Spartacus' ankles.

Immediately he recovered his balance. Preacher ran swiftly around the black gladiator and bound his legs together. Then, a hefty yank took Spartacus off his feet. In a staggered rush, Preacher closed with him and held the trident poised to drive two tines into the man's thick neck. Slowly, reluctantly, he looked up at the imperial box.

Quintus Faustus had bounded to his sandals moments earlier. He jumped up and down in agitation, his face white, eyes wild, his small, red mouth twisted grotesquely. His breathing came rapidly, and he showed obvious signs of arousal. He cut his pale blue eyes to Preacher's hot, gray orbs as he stuck out his arm.

Slowly, almost lasciviously, he turned his thumb down.

"Last chance," Preacher told Spartacus.

With considerable regret and hesitancy, Spartacus nodded in the affirmative. Preacher relaxed the position of his weapon. Above him, the shrill voice of Faustus held an edge of hysteria.

"Kill him! Kill him!" he wailed.

Calmly, ignoring the willful child, Preacher reached down and unbound the legs of Spartacus, raised him to his feet and disarmed him. Then he turned to the box.

"He yielded," he said simply.

Face clouded with tantrum warning flags, Faustus shoved out his lower lip in a spiteful, pink pout. "I don't care. It's my games, and my birthday, and I want to see men die."

Preacher replied with calm restraint. "I will not kill a man who yields to me."

White froth formed in the corners of Faustus' mouth. He dropped his wand of authority into the cushion on his chair and made small fists of his slim, long-fingered hands. His sallow face flushed scarlet as he stamped one foot like a girl.

"I want him dead! Now! Now! Now!" he shrieked.

To his surprise, Preacher looked on as Marcus Quintus rose from his chair and spoke into his son's ear. At the first words, the boy went rigid, and he shook with the intensity of his childish fury. The more Quintus spoke, the lower the shoulders of Faustus drooped. At last, his tower of rage was reduced to a pitiful bleat.

"But, Father."

"Do it!" His father hissed loud enough to be heard by the men on the sand.

In a show of bad grace, the boy gave a reluctant nod of agreement. He picked up his wand and raised it above his head. The trumpets blared. By then it had become unnecessary. The spectators perched on the edges of their seats in silent expectation. Faustus pointed to the surviving gladiators, one by one.

"Come forward," he intoned.

Preacher, Spartacus, Philadelphia, and Buck did as commanded. They were the only ones. Faustus shook with his barely suppressed outrage, and he stammered as he addressed the four fighting men. He again pointed at each one with the staff of office.

"Since you three are under sentence of death for attempted escape, and you, Spartacus, have made a cowardly surrender and are already a dead man in our eyes, you shall all be thrown in with the Christians and lions. Let the games proceed."

17

Preacher faced the frightened missionaries in the large holding pen. Arms folded across his chest—a gesture of strength and determination he had picked up from the Indians, rather than one of weakness—he addressed them in a low, hard voice.

"I am only going to say this once. The only way out of here is to fight. There will be plenty of weapons about the arena. I seen 'em puttin' out swords and some spears. They won't be as good a quality as what the gladiators have, but you can kill with them."

"To kill another man is to damn your soul for eternity," Phineas Abercrombie blustered. "Not a one of us will do that."

Preacher cocked his head to one side and eyed Abercrombie with a cold eye. "I was thinkin' on them mountain lions. They're fixin' to eat you before you have a chance to turn a sword on a man. You'd best be willin' an' able to stop them before you go worryin' about facin' a man."

Raising a stubborn chin, Phineas answered stubbornly. "If it comes to that, we'll be martyred with a hymn on our lips."

"Where's your pappy, Sonny? Best be hidin' behind his skirts," Preacher grunted, then turned to the others, ignoring the pompous Abercrombie. "Your best bet is to fight back-to-back, four of you together. Protect your wimmin an' children inside the squares. That way no lion can come at you unexpected. When the last one is finished off, that's when we go for the walls. Help one another up an' over and then we make a dash for it."

Encouraged by Preacher's positive outlook, Sister Amelia Witherspoon came forward. "Do you think we really have a chance?"

"If you do what me an' my friends say, you have a lot better chance than followin' this feller here who seems hellbent on dyin' for no reason. Seems to me he's a few straws shy of a haystack. For the rest of you, I reckon you know what to do when the time comes."

"What if we do kill the lions, only to be faced by men?"

Preacher gave them a nasty smile. "Well, there ain't many of them left. Or didn't you watch us out there? But, by damn, if that's the case, you kill them, too. It's the only way."

Blaring notes sounded the final fanfare.

Out on the sand, the missionaries stood in blinking confusion. Boos and insults greeted Preacher and his fellows. Ignoring them, the four fighting men quickly armed themselves. Catcalls and jeers rang down on the terror-stricken Gospel-shouters. Tentatively, Sister Witherspoon began a hymn.

That brought gales of raucous laughter. More mocking retorts came from the audience. One bloodthirsty spectator pointed at Amelia. "Hey, that one's good-looking. Wonder how she'd be in . . ."

"Why aren't they in the buff, like usual?" inquired another.

"Where's that fat one I saw brought in?"

A smaller, low gate swung open, and one of the handlers gave a mighty shove to the back of Deacon Abercrombie. He stumbled out onto the sand, bare to the waist. His pale, bleached-looking skin and flabby condition produced a windstorm of scornful sniggers. His wife ran to him, tears bright in her eyes, face a-flame with embarrassment.

"Cover yourself with my shawl."

Shame encrimsoned the deacon's face. "You might not want to be kind to me, my dear. I—I betrayed you all to that monster Quintus. I only wanted freedom for you and I. I fear I may have prevented your one good chance to escape."

She draped the shawl over his shoulders and patted him consolingly. "There is a strange man, one of the gladiators, who says we still have a way to get out of here."

"Where is he?" Abercrombie asked eagerly.

"Over—over there." Agatha Abercrombie pointed to Preacher.

Phineas Abercrombie scowled. "The troublemaker. I'd not put much stock in him, my dear."

And then they let out the lions.

At once, Deacon Abercrombie began to edge toward Preacher. The spectators cheered and shouted. They rose and clapped their hands in a wavelike motion around the tiers of seats. At first, the cougars seemed as confused and blinded by light as their intended victims. They padded about without direction, sniffed the air and uttered menacing growls. Tension built while the short-sighted critters sought to locate their prey. Two met head-on and traded swats and snarls. Three of the Mobile Church in the Wildwood's women uttered shrill screams.

One big, anvil-headed beast raised up from sniffing and turned baleful yellow eyes toward the sound. The women screamed all the more. One of the men broke and began to run to the far side of the arena from the deadly animals. At once the golden-orbed puma changed into a study in liquid motion. Flawlessly he streaked through the frightened missionaries, most of whom had remained stock still.

It rapidly closed the ground and launched itself at the back of the running Bible-thumper. Long, curved claws ripped mercilessly into tender flesh and raked along the back of the helpless man. His screams of agony set off a new explosion of yelling, stomping and applauding among the onlookers. At once, Deacon Abercrombie's flock came to life and scrambled as one to put distance between themselves and the ravenous animals.

* * *

Preacher turned with all the fluid ease of the deadly cat and hacked through its spine, above the shoulders, with a single blow from the *gladius* he held. It died at the same time as the missionary it had attacked. Instantly, Preacher turned to face another of the beasts bent upon attacking him.

"Dang it," he roared as he split open the nose of the offending puma, "do like I said!"

With Philadelphia on his right, Buck on the left, and Spartacus behind, the four fought off three more cougars. First two, then six more of the missionaries got the idea from this efficient means of downing the snarling bundles of lightning-fast fury. They quickly armed themselves and formed defensive squares. Only Deacon Abercrombie remained alone and exposed. One big cat soon discovered this. While his wife screamed with terror and the deacon made squawking noises, the cougar pounced.

"Stop! I command you in the name of the Lord," Abercrombie found voice to thunder. Then he was shrieking out his life. The sand soon pooled with red. A woman among the missionaries screamed when a mountain lion dragged her out of one formation.

Only a short distance away, Preacher took two fast steps forward and plunged the leaf-bladed *gladius* to the hilt in the animal's chest. It released the woman, shivered mightily, arched its back, and fell dead as Preacher drew out the sword. Fickle as always, the crowd went wild.

Now the spectators cheered the beleaguered missionaries. They had thought to be amused by the pitifully useless antics of the condemned wretches, only to find objects of admiration in the sudden courage displayed by desperate people. Preacher took note of it and spoke to his companions.

"Imagine that. All of a sudden they're on our side. Reckon that'll jerk the jaw of that bloody-minded boy-brat."

Buck answered through a grunt of effort as he split the

skull of yet another cougar. "He likes to see blood run, right enough. But I don't think it's that of his prize cats. That one's sick in the head. You can tell by the look in his eyes."

"Best save our breath for fightin'," Preacher advised. "Let's get these folk on the move, form up close together, in two lines. Less target for the cougars that way."

One of the tawny creatures leaped into the air for a high attack. Preacher squatted and split open its belly with his *gladius*. "What good will that do?" Spartacus grumbled as he drove a *pilum* into the chest of a raging puma.

Preacher answered quickly. "We can move around the sand like the hands on a clock. Finish off what's left in no time."

At the shouted urges of the mountain men, the desperate missionaries began to form into two lines, back-to-back. Over his shoulder, Preacher called to those behind him. "Can you walk backwards an' still fight them critters?' When they assured him they could, he issued a loud, if imprecise, command. "Then let's git to it."

The crowd howled in glee as the enraged cougars died one at a time. When only a single pair remained, those on the sand could not hear a word said by anyone beside them. All around them, the last of the big cats could smell the odor of their dead companions. Fangs dripping the foam of their fury, they flung themselves at the wall of human flesh that inexorably forced them to move. A scream emboldened them as an inexperienced missionary went down, his chest and belly clawed open. The cougar that had felled him did not get to savor its victory.

Even before the line had formed, Amelia Witherspoon had taken up a *pilum* and had speared one of the cats. Now she sank the javelin into the side of the blood-slobbering beast that had disemboweled Brother Frazier. The creature screamed like a woman, arched its back and lashed out uselessly with weakened paws. Amelia hung on to the shaft and felt the power of the animal vibrate through her arms. The hind feet left the ground, and she had to let go quickly to keep from being dragged down onto the dying cat.

"Good girl," Preacher said, though no one could hear him over the roar of the mob in the stands. "I knew she had some pluck."

An instant later, he had to defend his life against the last of the beasts. It hurtled at his part of the line with a mighty, bowel-watering roar. Preacher buried his *gladius* in its chest, though not before it had its forelegs wrapped around him and the claws bit agonizingly into his back. Then, half a dozen swords, javelins, and tridents sank into the golden coat to drive the last of life from the animal. Pressure eased in Preacher's back, and he felt the gentle touch of Philadelphia as his friend pried the claws from him.

"It's all done."

"I doubt that, Philadelphia."

Once assured that no more mountain lions lurked to spring upon them, the surviving force turned as one to face the blighted little boy who ran the games. Preacher saw through the haze of pain, and the sting of sweat in his eyes, that Faustus' face had been twisted into a mask of evil. With a sudden-born smile of such sweetness as to melt the hardest heart, the boy made a signal with his imperial baton.

First came the cleaning crew. They hauled off the carcasses of the dead cougars, spread fresh sand over the pools of blood, then exited. It gave everyone time to catch their breath. It also allowed the timid among the missionaries to exercise their imaginations on what might come next. Preacher, Philadelphia, Buck, and Spartacus considered the same thing, though not colored by fear and trepidation.

"I reckon that little monster is going to throw something else at us," Philadelphia opined. "Why ain't we moving?"

"He'll have to do something. He's got his neck stuck a whole ways out sayin' how we would all die," Preacher agreed. "Whatever it is will maybe give us a better opening." Preacher turned to the black gladiator. "What do you figger, Spartacus? And—ah—it'd be kinda nice to know your real name."

Spartacus flashed a white smile. "It's no better'n the one they hung on me. It's—you won't laugh?—Cornelius."

Preacher fought the quirk of a smile. "Then Spartacus it is."

"Obliged. I expect as hows that li'l bastard will send in the whole rest of the gladiators. They'll finish these weaklings fast. Then it'll be up to us."

"Not if I can come up with something better," Preacher promised.

"It had best be good," Buck put in his bit.

Above them, the trumpets brayed. The portcullis raised to admit the twenty remaining trained gladiators. Their weapons were of the serious type. No gaudy costumes or colorful shields. They carried workmanlike swords, flails, javelins, and two had bows. They advanced, their arms at rest, to salute the box. That's when providence handed Preacher a large portion of good fortune.

"I gotta make this fast. All of you sheep listen up. Whatever we do, you do. And that starts now! Run at them," Preacher shouted as he set off at a fast trot toward the unprepared gladiators.

With their weapons aimed more or less at the advancing gladiators, the missionaries followed in the wake of Preacher and his companions. Preacher let out a caterwaul as the unexpected charge closed with the newcomers. It froze them for a vital moment. Preacher smashed one to his knees with the flat of his blade, and shoved through to stab another in the gut. Beside him, the arms of his friends churned in deadly rhythm.

Philadelphia drove a *pilum* into the gut of a burly gladiator who had leaped aside to swing his spiked ball at Preacher. When the tip entered his flesh, he dropped his weapon and doubled over on the shaft of the spear. He clutched it with trembling fingers as he sank to his knees. Philadelphia left the *pilum* in his victim, snatched up the flail and shoved on into the melee of struggling gladiators. The audience lost their

minds while the four courageous fighters hacked and slashed
their way through the ranks and came out on the other side.

At once, Preacher led the way to the gate, which had not
as yet begun to close. He darted under the pointed ends of the
portcullis and downed a guard with a sword thrust. Beside
him, Buck Sears killed the guard at the windlass that controlled the wooden-framed iron barrier and quickly grabbed
hold to secure it.

Behind him came Philadelphia and Spartacus. They made
short work of the three astonished handlers who stood gawk-
ing at the furious battle. Then they turned back to hold the
opening for the missionaries.

Hewing like gleaners in a wheat field, the Mobile Church
in the Wildwood's members smashed through the ranks of
gladiators. They streamed by ones and twos toward the open
gateway. Preacher noticed that the handsome young woman
with the spear fought with the ferocity of the men. While he
registered this, she poked the iron tip of the *pilum* into the eye
of a huge man with a long sword. He fell screaming. The
iron-slat gate held motionless while they dashed under its
pointed ends.

When the last one cleared the barrier, Buck let it go. It
crashed down with a resounding roar. Buck quickly slashed
the rope that supported it. Led by Preacher and Philadelphia,
the missionaries rushed down the stone corridor, into the
bowels of the coliseum. Amelia Witherspoon had dropped
her *pilum* and clung to Preacher all the way.

"Where are we going?" she panted in question.

Preacher nodded to the tunnel entrance. "To the home of
the master of games."

"But, why? Isn't that dangerous?"

"Not so much as *not* doing it. For one thing, I'm not leaving here without my horses and my shootin' gear. I've got me
a pair of Walker Colts I've grown right fond of."

"Walkers? I've not heard of that breed before."

"They ain't my horses, Missy, they's shootin' irons."

"Oh! . . . *OH!*" she squeaked.

Preacher chuckled. Then he thought he had better explain it to these featherheads so they'd know. He slowed his pace, halted them midway in the tunnel and spoke in a low, earnest voice that still echoed off the walls.

"Listen up, folks. This ain't over yet. We're goin' to the storehouse at the games master's house. You can get better weapons, an' you'll need them, and horses to make a quick getaway."

"You mean there'll be more fighting?" Agatha Abercrombie asked in a trembling voice.

"Sure's skunks stink, ma'am. There's the better part of two legions out there."

"Oh, dear, dear, maybe we should not have done this," she wailed.

"You could have always gotten et up by the lions, like your husband," Preacher told her coldly.

"You cruel, cruel man," she chastised.

"I'm cruel? What about that devil's spawn brat who ordered all that? I got no more time for you. Keep movin', folks."

Entering the storeroom at the house of Justinius Bulbus from the gladiator school proved easier than the frontal approach. The two guards at the far end of the tunnel had gone down like one man when Preacher and Spartacus unexpectedly appeared. With them out of the way, Preacher had called upon the great strength of Spartacus to help him breach the iron gate.

It gave with a noisy screech, and the refugee missionaries stumbled through. Being empty, the school had an eerie quality to it. Buck Sears led the way to the passageway that issued into Bulbus' residence. Preacher took the point with long strides past the colorful tile murals that lined the hallway. The subjects being gladiators in various forms of killing and maiming, he paid them scant attention. He signaled for a halt when he reached the far end.

A wooden-barred gate closed off the passage. Preacher

gave it a try, and it swung open on well-oiled hinges. He found himself again in the courtyard with its tinkling fountain. This time, the steward happened to be out picking posies for his master's table. He saw Preacher and let out a yelp that could have been heard at the Temple of Vesta, had there not been such an uproar from the coliseum. It did serve to summon three burly sentries.

They soon showed that they did not lack the courage to engage the gladiators who boiled out of the passageway to the school. For all their willingness to fight, they did not last long. Their leader, an off-duty *contubernalis* from *Legio II, Britannicus,* took on Preacher—much to his regret as it turned out.

By far not a skilled swordsman, Preacher had nevertheless learned tricks in the gladiator school that were foreign to this stolid soldier. The sergeant lost his sword hand in his first precipitous rush. Preacher nimbly sidestepped him and chopped downward with his *gladius.* The hand, and the weapon it held, appeared to leap from the end of the legionnaire's arm. Desperately he clutched the blood-spouting stump with his other hand while he sucked air in a muted whoosh. With the shield lowered, Preacher got a shot at an exposed neck. A swift cut ended the life of the sergeant. Preacher looked to his left.

Spartacus held one of the guards over his head, straightened out like a man asleep on his back. The startled yelp that came from him broke the illusion of slumber. His scream ended with a loud crack when Spartacus hurled him against the lip of the stone fountain. At once, the huge black gladiator strode across the courtyard to where Buck held half a dozen more sentries at bay in the doorway of the guardroom. Preacher looked the other way to check on Philadelphia Braddock.

To Preacher's right, Philadelphia let go a bear growl and smashed the shoulder of the last guard. Stunned, the man went to one knee, his shield up to protect his head. Laughing, Philadelphia swept the soldier's supporting leg out from under him and crowned him solidly on the top of the head with a heavy cudgel.

"Spartacus, stay there with Buck. We'll bring you weapons, food and a horse."

"Sho'nuf, Preacher." Spartacus grinned and rippled the muscles of his shoulders and arms.

In the arms store, the more aggressive among the young missionaries acted like kids in a vacant candy store. Preacher three times had to caution one or another about taking too many rifles."Takes too long to reload. Tires your horse, too. Take four or six pistols instead."

He quickly found his favorites and loaded them all. He turned to the suddenly belligerent pilgrims and instructed, "Load up every one you take. We'll be needin' 'em to get out of this place."

That prediction proved only too true the moment they reached the street. Two *contaburniae*—twenty soldiers— trotted their way in formation down the Via Iulius. Shields up, their piliae aligned perfectly, the legionnaires advanced, only their shins and grim faces visible. In his insane state as Marcus Quintus Americus, Alexander Reardon had made only one mistake. He had insisted on accuracy in arms and armor, and the Romans had fought long before gunpowder came into being.

Preacher knocked the sergeant of the first rank off his feet with a .56 ball from his Hawken, then laid the smoking rifle across his lap. He let fly with one of his .44 Walker Colts. In rapid succession, three more soldiers fell. His friends, Preacher noticed, accounted for themselves rather well also.

Philadelphia dumped two in the second rank and went for another pistol. A legionnaire yelped, and blood flew from a scalp wound as the .36 caliber squirrel rifle in the hands of Amelia Witherspoon barked to Preacher's right rear. He decided the time had come to depart this place. Setting spurs to Cougar's flanks, he led the charge on the dismounted men.

Their advance became a rout. Shot through the shield and chest, one soldier staggered to the side to lean on the wall of the gladiator school. He died before the last of the escapees rode out of sight. Panic broke out in the streets. Women screamed and men shouted in angry tones, until they saw the thoroughly armed band that thundered down on them. Then they gave way rapidly.

In seemingly no time, the fugitives reached a gate. Preacher took aim and shot down the guard who wrestled to draw closed the thick, heavy barrier. Then he shouted good advice.

"C'mon, folks, don't dally. We've lots of miles to put between us and them."

18

Confusion and surprise turned to panic when the order to shut the gates was taken too literally by the stadium staff. Spectators swarmed into the aisles, only to find the entrances to the coliseum barred against them. They began to push and shove, then to fight among themselves. In the imperial box, his face a flaming scarlet in childish fury, Quintus Faustus shrieked impotent demands and threats. Robbed of his bloody climax, he lost what tenuous hold he had on his reason.

Marcus Quintus saw the trembling boy with slobber and foam flying from his lips and rose to confront his son. He put a hand on Faustus' shoulder and squeezed gently. Frenetically, Faustus jerked away from his touch. Exasperated and embarrassed beyond endurance, Quintus lost his grip for a moment. He swiftly raised an arm and delivered a solid backhand slap. A red spot appeared on the pallid skin of his cheek, and Faustus bugged his eyes.

"Control yourself," his father snapped.

Faustus sat down abruptly and buried his head in his toga. His thin shoulders shook violently as he bawled like a baby. Marcus Quintus knew at once that he must take command. He raised cupped hands to the sides of his mouth and shouted over the tumult.

"Open the *vomitoriae!* Clear these people out of here." In stentorian tones, he brayed for his army commanders. "Bring Legate Varras. I want his cavalry after that vermin at once. Bring me Legate Glaubiae! Start a search of the city. Do it now!"

Varras appeared beside Quintus and saluted. "Get out of here, use the private tunnel. Organize your cavalry and get after those people," Quintus screamed at him. Varras saluted again and departed hastily.

Gaius Septimus Glaubiae came next, his face flushed with the effort of climbing the steep steps to the box. Quintus raised his arm casually to return his salute. He leaned slightly forward and screamed in his general's face. "I want the legions organized at once. Outfit them for a long time in the field. They are to search for the escaped prisoners. I want them back. All of them."

"Do you believe they have gotten out of the city?" Glaubiae asked.

Quintus' eyes narrowed. "They will have by the time order can be restored."

Then he began to scream at the panicked crowd. He was still screaming orders when the escaping prisoners swarmed out the southern gate.

Preacher led the fleeing prisoners at a fast pace down the Via Ostia, named for the port to the west of ancient Rome. Why the madman who had created this place had picked that name for the road to the south, Preacher did not know. He doubted that this Marcus Quintus feller knew either. Two miles beyond the corrupt city, he slowed the pace to a quick walk. Elation slowly swept over all but one of the missionaries, he grumblingly noted as they began to chatter among themselves.

"We've lost everything," wailed Agatha Abercrombie. "Our wagons, our portable organ, even the pulpit."

"Be thankful we got out of that place alive," Sister Amelia Witherspoon told her coldly.

That pleased Preacher mightily. That li'l gal had some pluck. She was learning fast. For the first time Preacher looked at her in another way than as a nuisance. Pretty little thing, he mused. Clean her up a little, get some clean clothes on her. . . . He suddenly had to cover his mouth to hide a broad grin and suppress a hearty guffaw that bubbled in his throat as they continued their exchange.

"Excuse me? I am unaccustomed to accepting such criticism from anyone. Especially from my inferiors."

Sarcasm dripped from Amelia's words. "Oh, that's quite obvious. Only I don't see myself as your inferior. I didn't see *you* raise a hand to defend yourself, let alone anyone else back there."

Outrage painted Agatha's face. "How dare you!" She looked around herself for some support, only to see a laughing Preacher. His shoulders shook with his mirth. She redirected her anger. "This is all your fault, you heathen barbarian!" she lashed out.

Nodding, Preacher choked back his hilarity. "Yep. It sure is. An' right proud of it, I am. Weren't but five of you folks got harmed. Might be if you'd lent a hand some of them would be with us now. As fer this fine young woman, she carried her share of the load, fought bravely and did for a couple of cougars, two gladiators an' a soldier. On my tally sheet, that puts her head and shoulders your better, ma'am. Danged if it don't." Preacher's eyes widened, and he screwed up his mouth as though to spit out a wad of chew tobacco. "By damn, there I go speechifyin' like a politician. I'd best put a lid on my word bucket."

He held his peace until the cavalcade crested the saddle notch and halted on the far side. By then he had worked out what needed to be done. He called them together in the shade of a tall old pine that soughed softly in a fresh breeze. "Everybody rest some; drink a little water and eat something." Then Preacher began enlightening them on something that had been bothering him for a long while.

"The way I see it, our best chance lies with splittin' up. That way it thins out them that comes after us. Now, there's somethin' we need to decide on. I declare, that place is the foulest nest of snakes I've ever runned across. Ain't gonna change much, from what I guess. So, this nasty business has to be ended right and proper. To do that, we have to have help." He pointed to Philadelphia and Buck.

"I want you to set off to find any old woolly-eared fellers that's nestin' out there somewhere. Philadelphia, you take the west trails; Buck, you head east. I'll cut down to the southwest, find Bold Pony an' his Arapahos. A couple of those prisoners who died at the hands of Quintus' gladiators were from his band, I learned. That gives him a stake in fixin' this tainted meat. Spartacus, you done good to join us. I want you to stick with these pilgrims. Teach them more about how to fight for when the time comes they need to. Take the big trail south to Trout Creek Pass; it's well marked. We'll all rendezvous there and lay plans."

"Preacher, how do I get any of these mountain men to join us?" Buck asked.

"You tell 'em you're askin' in my name. An' I'll send along a note to that effect. Most of these boys can make out writin' good enough, an' those what can't do know my name an' my Ghost Wolf sign."

"I—I want to stay with you, Preacher," Amelia Witherspoon spoke up.

"Why, the brazenness of that—" Agatha Abercrombie began, to be cut off by a hard look from Preacher.

He shook his head as he spoke to Amelia. "No, it'll be too dangerous."

Undeterred by this logic, she continued to press her issue. "What could be more dangerous than what we just faced?"

To his surprise, Preacher did not have any quick reply for that. He mulled it over a moment. "I can't answer that, Missy. Danged if you don't argue like one o' them Philadelphia lawyers." He shot a glance at his fellow mountain man. "No offense, old friend. But, the answer is the same, Miss Amelia.

Where I'm going, the Injuns mightily favor a long lock of yeller hair on their scalp poles."

"Bu—but you're friends with them; I've heard Philadelphia say so."

Preacher smiled to soften his demeanor. "We're friends when they're in the mood for it. Otherwise, they'd lift my hair, too. This time I've got a reason for them to keep right cordial. It wouldn't do, though, to provoke them before I get out my message."

Preacher turned to the rest of them, the subject closed for his part. "So, we'll all rendezvous at the tradin' post. I'll bring in the Arapaho last to prevent a panic."

Preacher took a narrow trail to the southwest when he departed from the others. Leading his packhorse, he made much better time than Spartacus and the missionaries. He was far out on the Great Divide Basin when sundown caught up with him. He made a hasty cold camp and settled in for the night. He doubted he would see anything of the soldiers from New Rome, yet he did not want a fire to betray his presence. No, he'd not see the legions of New Rome again, not until he wanted to. Far off, in the rolling hills behind him, he heard the musical call of a timber wolf.

"Hang in there, ol' feller. We's a pair, we be," he said softly to his distant brother.

That night, Preacher slept well under a blanket of stars that frosted the night as a harbinger of the coming winter.

Marcus Quintus Americus hurled a gold-rimmed wine cup across the room to splinter on the plinth of a bust of Augustus Caesar. Thin, red wine washed over it and stained the first Roman emperor purple. Shocked, Legate Varras of the cavalry watched as the liquid pooled on the marble floor.

"Are you totally incompetent? How can you come to me with a report like this?"

Varras answered mildly. "Because it is my duty, and it is the truth. Beyond the territory of New Rome, we found no trace of them. A large body of the fleeing prisoners rode south on the main trail for some while; then their tracks faded out."

He did not know of the drags that Spartacus had rigged on the last horses in the column, which spread out from side to side on the trail and obliterated every trace of their passage. It was an old trick Spartacus had learned on the Underground Railroad. It would not have fooled a Blackfoot, Cheyenne or a Sioux, but it did confound the inexperienced trackers of the cavalry legion. Quintus fumed a long, silent moment, then turned partly away from Varras. His voice dropped from its previous furious bellow.

"How could four barbarians and that lot of pitiful Christians defeat professional gladiators and outwit my well-trained soldiers to make good this escape?"

Varras was smart enough to remain silent. His first sword centurion stood rigidly at his side, helmet tucked under one arm like his commander. He cut his eyes to Varras and grimaced. Quintus collected himself after his rhetorical question.

"Well, they'll not get away with it. I want you to get out there by an hour after sundown. Best possible speed. Catch up to those vermin, kill only those you must, and bring back the rest. Take what supplies you need and don't leave any area unsearched. Now, leave me. I must talk with the commanders of the other legions."

Glaubiae and Bruno entered together. Quintus eyed them coldly, arms folded over the front of his toga. When they both grew uneasy enough, he poured wine around and handed each general a cup.

"Your health, gentlemen. I must compliment you on the thoroughness of your search of our city. Unlike that incompetent ass, Varras, who lost all trace of the fugitives, you did come up with three escaped slaves. That they were not involved with those from the coliseum is not important. Given that those condemned prisoners had already ridden out of the gates, you did the best you could. Now, I have to ask more of you. I am not convinced that we have seen the last of those miscreants. Here is what I want you to do."

He began to pace the floor as he spoke. "I want you to establish watch towers completely around the rim of this basin. Staff them with enough men to be alert around the clock. Also set up heliographs and signal fires. Have horses so a messenger can reach the city well ahead of whoever comes back." His pacing grew faster. "Set your engineers to manufacturing ballistas, catapults and arbalests."

"You are certain they will attack us?" Gaius Septimus asked.

"Of course," Quintus snapped. "I have learned only this morning that there are enough of these barbarian mountain men with savage allies to form a force that will outnumber us. The important thing is not to let the Senate and the people know that. If we are prepared, if we have advance warning, the quality of the legions and the power of some—ah— weapons I have provided will assure our victory."

That caught the interest of both generals. "What weapons are these?"

Quintus answered guardedly. "Some firearms. Also a few cannons that will far out-perform our other artillery." A wicked smile illuminated his face.

Septimus and Bruno caught up his enthusiasm. "How many firearms? What sort of cannon?" Septimus urged.

Thinking on it, Quintus answered evasively. "Enough to tip the scale."

Bruno wasn't buying into it. "And when do we train men to use them?"

Quintus surprised him with his answer. "We start this afternoon. Now, get out of here, get orders published for what is needed, and get to work."

* * *

Buck Sears had traveled the trails of Texas, driven teams on the Santa Fe Trail, and most recently, had rented his talents to those seeking to take goods overland to the Northwest Territory. It made him fairly savvy about movement where Indians were a factor, and how to repair wagons when the nearest wheelwright or coach shop lay five hundred miles behind. It had not taught him how to find mountain men when sent to round up any who remained in the ranges of the Rocky Mountains. In fact, it was they who found him, more or less.

"You there, stumblin' around in the bush," a voice called out as Buck floundered around in an attempt to find the trail he had been following, which had abruptly disappeared a quarter of an hour earlier. The unknown voice called again.

"If you be friendly, sing out an' let us know who you might be."

"Hello. The name's Sears. Buck Sears. I'm a freight wagon teamster."

A low chuckle answered Buck, then words made soft by amusement. "You're sure an' hell a long ways from any wagon route. C'mon in, set a spell, an' have some coffee."

That completely amazed Buck. "You—uh—you've got a *camp* out here?"

"Shore enough do. Head yourself due north an' you'll run into it."

Buck blundered through the brush, leading his mount, until he came to a small clearing surrounded by ash and juniper trees. Three men sat around a stone-guarded, hat-sized fire over which a coffeepot steamed. Buck ground reined his horse and came forward.

"Well, here I am. Buck Sears."

The one who had called out to him spoke first. "M'name's Abel Williams, but folks most call me Squinty. This here's Jack Lonesome and that other feller is Three-Finger. Git yourself around some Arbuckles," he invited, with a gesture toward the blue granite pot.

"Obliged," Buck responded.

Settled on a mat of aspen leaves, Buck sipped the strongest coffee he had ever tasted, worried for the lining of his stomach, and exchanged incidentals with the three mountain men for several minutes. Then, when Squinty Williams hinted delicately at what business brought Buck into the mountains, he unveiled his story of New Rome.

They listened in amazement, doubt written plainly on their faces. Buck noted this and concluded his personal story to get to the heart of the situation. "The thing is, six years after I was taken by these lunatics, two of you mountain men were captured; Philadelphia Braddock and Preacher."

"Naw. Couldn't be," Jack Lonesome rebutted. "No amount of fellers runnin' around in skirts could best Preacher."

"All the same, it's true," Buck insisted. "He said I might run into some—ah—resistance. Sent along this note." He dug into his shirt pocket and produced the scrap of paper upon which Preacher had scribbled his appeal.

Squinty took it and peered intently at it. At last he nodded. "That's his name, right enough. An' his Ghost Wolf mark. What's it say, Jack?"

Jack Lonesome took the message and read it aloud. *This is to advise any fellers contacted by Buck Sears that we has us a large problem needs solvin' right fast. Buck will explain it to you an' I ask you to come fast to Trout Creek Pass and lend a hand. Yours for old times, Preacher.*

Squinty cocked his head to one side. "Well, I'll be damned. You got our help, Buck. Tell us about this place again; then we'll make use of the rest of this day gettin' out of here."

Buck related the final days in New Rome and what Preacher and Philadelphia were up to at the moment. All three mountain men thought on it; then Squinty came to his boots. "We know where half a dozen of our friends are fixin' to hang out for the winter. We'll go get them and then head for this rendezvous with Preacher. I ain't never seen me a man in a skirt before, but I reckon we can sure put the fear of God in a bunch of 'em."

On his fourth day away from New Rome, Philadelphia Braddock ambled into a camp in the Medicine Bow range occupied by Blue Nose Herkimer. There he also found Four-Eyes Finney, a wild Irish brawler turned mountain man; Karl "Bloody Hand" Kreuger; Nate Youngblood; and, surprisingly to him, Frenchie Dupre. After a few bear hugs, some foot stomping, and a lot of genial cussing, Philadelphia filled them in on what had been happening in the Ferris Range. Bloody Hand Kreuger did not believe it.

"Pferd Scheist! That's all it is, horse shit. I was through there back a ways, and I never saw anything like that."

"How long ago was that, Karl?" Philadelphia asked, using the German mountain man's given name because he knew Bloody Hand did not like it.

Bloody Hand thought on it a moment. "Ten . . . maybe twelve years ago."

"A lot can happen in that time. An' it surely did. That's about the time this crazy feller, calls himself Marcus Quintus Americus, came out here. Boys, I've been there, saw the buildings, took baths in a fancy buildin', and fought for my life in a place where folks come an' watch ya die for the fun of it. Preacher was there with me, like I said. Now, fellers, what'll it be? Are you goin' to join us in doin' away with this place of corruption or not?"

An old and dear friend of Preacher, Frenchie Dupre rose and dusted off the seat of his trousers. "I am ready, *mon ami.* These people sound to be *tres* evil. If Preacher needs our help, I say we give it to him."

"You can count on me," Nate Youngblood agreed.

"I'm with you, Philadelphia," Blue Nose Herkimer added.

Four-Eyes Finney tugged at a thick forelock of sandy hair. "Sure an' it sounds like a fine donnybrook. Count me in."

Although the Kraut mountain man had a long list of grievances against Preacher, Karl Kreuger sighed heavily and nodded in acceptance. "I'll go. What the hell, Preacher is one of us, and no fancy Roman is gonna put down a mountain man."

Philadelphia could not hide his happy smile. "By jing, that shines. Ya can all head out at first light; it's a ways to Trout Crick Pass. I'm leavin' now to see if I can scare up some other fellers."

19

Preacher found Bold Pony and his band settled down in their winter camp in a tidy little valley. He was welcomed with stately courtesy. Then Bold Pony noticed Preacher's injuries. He sent at once for the medicine man.

"I coulda taken care of that for myself," Preacher protested without sincerity. The poultices the shaman put on his cuts and bruises felt cool and soothing. And the Arapaho medicine man could get to the claw marks on his back better than he had been able to.

"Not while you are in my camp, friend," Bold Pony responded. "You will speak of how you received these injuries at the council fire tonight?"

"Yes. I sort of hunted you down for that exact reason. There's some mighty bad people out there that need a lesson taught them."

"We eat first. And drink coffee."

After filling himself with elk stew, Preacher sat back and belched loudly, rubbed his belly to show how much he had enjoyed it, and allowed as how he was ready to talk to the council. They gathered around a modest fire in the center of the village. Bold Pony spoke first, as was his right, then formally introduced the man well known to them. Preacher rose and addressed the council while Bold Pony translated.

He told them of New Rome and what had happened there. "Until some dozen years ago, only the Crows and the

Blackfeet roamed through the Ferris Range," he began. He went on to describe the city that had grown there, of the cruelty of the people who lived in it. When he came to the games, Bold Pony used the Arapaho words for "savage" and "barbarian." That amused Preacher. Although he knew the Arapaho tongue well enough to pass the time of day, Preacher wanted to be sure the whole sordid story of New Rome came across clearly. It appeared to him that Bold Pony was doing that right enough.

Angry mutters rose when he described the Arapaho warriors who had been enslaved and killed, and added, "We sang their death songs after the gladiators finished with them." He concluded his account with the escape and an appeal for help in destroying this menace. Buffalo Whip, an aged former peace chief, rose to speak against the Arapaho involvement. "We do not know these people. They have done us no harm. Those men you told about are not of this band. It is not for us to avenge them. It is not wise to take the war trail against people who do not have anger toward us." He rambled on awhile, then repeated the admonition to avoid war.

Preacher rose again. "Thing is, they've got anger toward everyone. They call us barbarians, an' you folks, too. A feller who had been there six years told me they plan on fighting everyone out here. An' he tells the truth."

Another older councilman stood to argue against joining in Preacher's fight. A third followed him. Preacher considered that it wasn't going well. Then came the turn of some of the younger men. Yellow Hawk took his place in front of the assembly.

"There are too many white men out here now. Most are like our friend, Preacher. These men have bad hearts. They hurt women and children. I say we fight them."

Badger Tail agreed. Buffalo Whip spoke again. Two more of the fiery, youthful warriors responded, urging that a war party be organized. The debate raged on into the night. The fire burned low, and young boys, apprentice warriors, built it up again. At last, Bold Pony put a hand on Preacher's shoulder.

"You might as well take some sleep, old friend," he advised. "This will take a while."

Preacher nodded and came to his boots. Stifling a yawn, he ankled off to the lodge where he would spend the night.

Birds twittered in the trees outside the Arapaho camp while the eastern sky turned pink. Preacher emerged from a buffalo-hide lodge as the velvet dome above magically turned blue overhead. He wore a huge, relaxed smile on his leathery face. He tucked his buckskin hunting shirt into the top of his trousers and paused. He turned back to wave a sappy goodbye to the occupant, one thoughtfully provided by Bold Pony, and received a very feminine giggle in reply.

After his morning needs had been taken care of, he sat down with Bold Pony to a bowl of mush that sported shreds of squirrel meat. They ate contentedly. Then Bold Pony nodded toward the center of camp, where the debaters had already begun to assemble.

"You must have other visits to make, Ghost Wolf. You may as well tend to them now. This will be a long time deciding. Go to the trading post and wait for us. We will be along, if we are coming, within two days.

In New Rome preparations for war went on at a fevered pace. The two bold legions—actually their strength compared more realistically with two understrength platoons—conducted mock battles on the Field of Mars. The Campus Martius swarmed with armed and armored troops, their faces grim and set in concentration. Centurions raised their swords in signal, and the sergeants of the *contaburniae* bellowed the command to lock shields and prepare to form the tortoise. The centurions lowered their weapons rapidly.

"Form . . . up!" the leather-lunged sergeants commanded.

At once, the soldiers in the middle of the squares raised their shields overhead, shielding themselves and the outer two ranks as well. Each *pilum* pointed outward, a hedgehog of defense. A shower of blunted arrows moaned hauntingly to the top of their arcs and descended on the shields. They clattered noisily as the brass-bossed, hardened hides shed them. At another command, the ten squads disengaged their shields and faced the same direction.

"Forward at the quick time," came the order.

At once the soldiers stepped off at a rapid pace, their javelins slanted forward. Twenty paces along the base course, the commands came again. With more assurance the formation evolved into the famous tortoise. Standing in his white chariot, its basket supports set off in gold, Marcus Quintus Americus looked on with satisfaction. His heart thundered with excitement. Elsewhere, those men who had proven to be passable marksmen drilled with the rifles. What a shock that would be when those mountain rabble returned. Gaius Septimus rode up on a white charger. The stallion snorted at the scent of its fellows drawing the chariot. Wet droplets of slobber stained the sleeve of the military tunic worn by Marcus Quintus.

"A couple more run-throughs and my legion will be ready for a cavalry charge."

"Excellent. They are learning faster than I expected, and I'm pleased."

"Here's the bad news. Some of your spies have ferreted out the information that the condemned man, Arturus, was in fact Preacher."

Color flared on Quintus' face. "By all the gods! All that while I had my hands on Preacher and did not know it? How could that have happened?"

Septimus looked embarrassed. "I suspected it when I saw him fight at the school. Yet, I had nothing to prove it."

"Who verified his identity?" Quintus demanded.

"Bulbus for one. He overheard one of the other gladiators call him that."

Quintus scowled. "The fool. He should have reported it. We could have kept him in a cell alone, and fought him differently. None of what happened would have been possible."

"And we wouldn't be running around like chickens with our heads cut off trying to prepare for war," Septimus muttered to himself.

"What was that?"

"Nothing, Quintus. I have to get back to my *primus pilus.*" His need to meet with his first spear—his adjutant—was a convenient excuse to avoid the wrath of Quintus.

Half an hour later, a messenger came from Glaubiae to say that his troops were ready for the cavalry. He sent the man on to another part of the Field of Mars, where the mounted troops had been practicing. With whoops of glee, they whirled into attack formation and rumbled across the turf toward the defensive squares of the Thirteenth Legion. A shower of javelins hurtled toward them.

Quickly the spear carriers resupplied the hurlers, and the squares bristled like aroused porcupines. By design, the spears landed short, albeit not *too* short. Marcus Quintus was tickled pink. Not a waver. Not a man broke formation. Those Celtic fools called the plains barbarians the finest light cavalry in the world. Let them come up against the tactics of the legions and see what happens to them. The cavalry whirled and made another approach.

Again the rain of javelins broke their charge. Suddenly the tortoises broke apart and the legionnaires counterattacked, the keen edges of their *gladiae* striking blue-white ribbons from the autumn sun. They descended on the stalled cavalry and began to break into man-to-man duels. Dust became a blinding curtain, from which only sparks from upraised swords could be seen. Quintus knew that Septimus and his officers would be judging the effectiveness of both forces and was not surprised when a *buccina* sounded to end the battle.

Proud of their ability, Varras, the cavalry *legio,* trotted his men forward to salute the First Citizen. Marcus Quintus was beaming with satisfaction, thrilled with how well this mismatched rabble had welded themselves into a disciplined army. That pleasure ended quickly when he recognized his eleven-year-old son, in full armor, in the front rank of cavalry, face begrimed, sweat trickling from under his helmet. It instantly struck him that the boy had been fighting among all the others.

Riveted by that thought, he advanced to the next obvious revelation. *He could have been killed!* For all their well-conducted performance, the legionnaires were only partly trained. One could have gotten carried away, gone farther than orders allowed. And Faustus could be lying on the ground, bleeding, or headless. It chilled his blood and brought an imperceptible shudder to his burly frame. Before he could control himself and rethink the situation, he burst out with a bellow.

"Quintus Faustus, get out of there!"

Faustus could not believe what he had heard "But, Father, I . . ."

Imperiously, Quintus pointed to the driver's position in his chariot. "Get off that horse, come over here, and get in this chariot."

"But, Father, Varras said it was all right, that I would be safe."

Blood boiling, Quintus narrowed his eyes. "There is no such thing as 'safe' in a battle. Even in practice, mistakes happen."

Faustus' voice rose to a near whine. "Father, *please!* I'm not a baby anymore."

"Come here now!"

Faustus swung a bare leg over the neck of his mount and hung from the saddle, to drop to the ground. He walked stiff-legged across the space that separated him from the chariot. With each step his face turned from white to a deeper red. His lower lip slid out in a pout until he discovered it; then he sucked it in and bit it with small, even teeth. The first tears slid down his cheeks as he reached one large wheel of the two-person vehicle. The driver stepped to the ground, and Quintus snapped at him.

"Bring that horse and come with me," he commanded. To a thoroughly frightened Varras, he growled, "I'll see you later at the palace, Varras."

He said not a word while he drove straight to the palace. There he started to lecture Faustus, who bolted and ran off sobbing, to cry his heart out. Still disgruntled by how he had handled the situation, Quintus found little sympathy from his wife.

Titiana Pulcra stared unbelievingly at her husband. Small, slim hands on her hips, she stamped one slender, sandaled foot. "How could you, Quintus? To humiliate the boy in front of all those soldiers like that is unconscionable. It could have a terrible effect on my son. It could even make him into a sissy."

Burning with his own demons, Quintus turned deaf ears to his wife's protests. This impending war would be the ruin of him yet. *Goddamn you, Preacher!* he thought furiously.

Vickie reached across the darkened room and lightly touched her brother on the arm. "Terry, Preacher's comin' back," she whispered.

"Who told you that?" Terry asked crossly.

"Nobody. I just . . . *know.*"

"You an' your knowin' things," Terry heaped in scorn. "It's like you sayin' he was in real big danger. A body can't know those sort of things."

Vickie defended herself staunchly. "Well, I can. I sort of . . . feel things. Preacher's been hurt, too. I know that, so there."

"How'd he get hurt, smarty?"

Tears threatened in Vickie's words. "Oh, Terry, I can't tell you that. I don't know how I know these things."

Terry pondered that a moment. "What do you suppose we should do?"

The tears leaked through this time. "Don't ask me. That's for you to figger out."

Pausing a long moment in the dark night, Terry turned that over in his head. "Why don't we go to meet him?"

"We don't know where he's coming from," Vickie objected.

"Yes, we do. He went north from here when he left us our new clothes. We'll just go north."

"Really? Do you think it will work?"

"We won't know unless we try. And we can't tell anyone."

"When do we go?"

"Tomorrow."

Sister Amelia Witherspoon stood in the center of camp. Another two days to reach this trading post. She remembered one they had come upon along the North Platte River. Low-slung buildings, with crude thatch roofs, smelly and dirty inside, hardly more than a poor excuse for a saloon. It reeked of stale beer, spilled whiskey, greasy food and human sweat. She had almost gagged when she entered.

If they had not needed supplies so desperately, she would have prevailed upon the new Deacon Abercrombie to pass this pestilential place by. Thought of their former leader, and how he had died, brought a pang to her heart and a lump to her throat. She swallowed hard, hoping she would not break into tears, because she also recalled that he had betrayed them when the first attempt had been made to escape. And that brought her to Preacher.

Oh, how handsome he had looked when he left them on the trail. She remembered him as a shining knight in buck-skin on that day he rode off from them, for all his disreputable appearance. She wondered how he would look when he had washed off all that blood, dirt, grease and powder grime, and had a chance to shave. She would find out when he reached the trading post and rejoined them. She could hardly wait.

A sharp report of a pistol from across the campsite drew her away from her favorite subject. Laughter followed.

"Brother Lewis, you're supposed to take that thing out of the holster before you pull the trigger."

A thoroughly shaken, crimson-faced young missionary stood with a group of those who had elected to continue to fight. Smoke ringed his knees, and Amelia saw the splintered leather at the bottom of the holster fastened at his waist. Poor Lewis Biggs, she thought. He had always been so clumsy. Only now he could get seriously injured, or even killed, for it. If only Preacher were here to teach them.

That brought back images of the lean mountain man. His eyes normally held a far-off look, as though he saw things a thousand yards away. She really knew so little about him. Though she had heard plenty of wild stories from Spartacus, her practical side found little of it credible. Like wrestling with a bear and killing the beast with a knife. Or leading a wagon train of women from Missouri to the Northwest Territory. No one man, no matter how able and clever, could do that alone.

Which got her to wondering how Preacher had resisted the charms of so many unattached ladies. With a shiver of delight, she thought how much she would like it if Preacher succumbed to her charms. Her missionary zeal abandoned, Amelia imagined those strong arms around her, holding her tight, his full lips pressed to hers. She wondered how her somewhat bony, angular body would be fitted to his hard, muscular frame. Oh, when would they reach the trading post? When would Preacher join them?

20

Trout Creek Pass looked mighty good to Preacher when he reached the trading post there three days later. One-Eye Avery Tookes spotted him first and let out a whoop. That brought his partner Bart Weller, Bloody Hand Kreuger, Squinty Williams, Blue Nose Herkimer and Frenchie Dupre. The others were out hunting game for the table. The back slaps, shoulder punches, elbow rib gouges, to say nothing of the general jumping up and down and stomping the ground, went on for a good fifteen minutes.

"We heard you was lookin' for fellers to join a real, ring-tailed mixup, Preacher," One-Eye Avery Tookes declared when the welcoming calmed some and the participants had repaired to the inside of the saloon.

"That I am, Ave." Preacher allowed. "Philadelphia an' me got ourselves in one hell of a fix up north in the Ferris Range."

Three of the mountain men rounded up mugs and dispensed whiskey and foaming flagons of beer while the others pressed close around. Frenchie Dupre spoke for them all.

"We learned some of it from Philadelphia, Preacher, but we would like to hear it from you."

Preacher studied on it a moment, downed half a mug of beer to soothe the trail dust from his craw, then launched into the story of New Rome. "Seems there's this feller, 'bout three beaver shy of a lodge, who's took it in his mind that he's the emperor of Rome. Built him a right accurate copy of the ancient town in this big valley in the Ferris Range." He went on to describe the highlights of the stay he and Philadelphia had endured.

Several times, one or another of the mountain men would interrupt with a question. Through it all, only Karl "Bloody Hand" Kreuger maintained a skeptical expression. When Preacher concluded, he spoke slowly, through a thick German accent.

"Dot don't zound right. Vhy haff vun of us not seen dis place in dcr twelf years you zay it has been there?"

Preacher gave him the benefit of a one-eyed squint. "How many pelts have you taken in the past dozen years, Bloody Hand?" he asked mildly. "For that matter, how many of us has been in the Ferris Range in the same time?"

Shaken heads answered him. It urged Preacher to push on a little further. "You all know the fur trade is dead as last year's squirrel stew. There ain't a one of us what has made a living entire off of takin' beaver. Shoot, there ain't even enough beaver for us to harvest them like we used to." He paused to pour off the last of the beer. "Monongahela rye, Duffey," he called to the barkeep. Then he turned back to Bloody Hand Kreuger.

"Now, you listen to me, Bloody Hand. I seened all that with my own eyes. So'd Philadelphia and that young 'prentice, Buck Sears. An' that reminds me. If Buck ain't got him a handle hung on him already, I reckon to call him Long Spear."

That brought hoots of laughter. Blue Nose Herkimer asked through his chortles, "Is that for what I think it is, Preacher?"

Preacher pulled a face of mock disappointment in his fellow men. "No. It ain't. It's because hc done some fierce fightin' with one of them *pilum* things the Roman soldiers use in their army." He downed a respectable swallow of whiskey, smacked his lips and continued. "Buck ain't near as good as some of us, but he's got sand, and he carries his own weight an' then some. He learns quick. And we need every gun we can get for this fight with the crazy Romans."

"Vhy vould anyone lif dot vay?" Kreuger pressed, disbelief plain in his small pig eyes.

Preacher cocked his head to one side, sipped more rye. "Y'know, that's a question I asked myself a good many times. Don't seem that anyone a-tall, with any brains worth countin', would put up with the loco things this feller calls hisself Marcus Quintus Americus expects of 'em. They dress in these outlandish clothes, all robes and nightshirt-lookin' things, and wear sandals, too, like them brown-robed friars come through the Big Empty back in thirty-one, weren't it? Why, their soldiers even wear skirts."

That proved too much for Bloody Hand Kreuger. "I told Philadelphia that dis vas horse shit, *und* dot's vhat it iss. *Pferd Scheist!* No zoldiers vear zkirts."

Preacher's dark gray eyes turned to flint. "You callin' me a liar, Bloody Hand?"

Kreuger, who had already decided it was a good time to take Preacher to task, barked a single word. "*Fawohl!*"

Preacher downed the last of his Pennsylvania whiskey and dusted dry palms together. "Well, then, let's get to the dance."

"Outside! Take it outside," a nervous Ruben Duffey shouted from behind the bar.

"More'n glad to oblige, Duffey," Preacher told him amiably.

He started to rise, then shifted his weight and lashed out his booted foot in one swift movement. The dusty sole caught the chair in which Kreuger sat at the center lip of the seat and spilled it over backward. Preacher got on him at once. He grabbed the confused and startled German by the back of his wide belt and scruff of shirt collar and made a speedy little run toward the front door. Kreuger dangled in Preacher's powerful arms, feet clear of the floor.

With appropriate violence, the batwings flew outward when Kreuger's head collided with them. Preacher took quick aim and hurled his human cargo into the street. The Kraut mountain man landed in a puddle of mud and horse droppings at the tie rail. Immediately Kreuger let the world, and Preacher in particular, know his opinion of being so used.

"Verdammen unehrliche Geburt!"

"Oh, now, Bloody Hand, you know better than to call Preacher a damned bastard," Frenchie Dupre observed dryly from the porch of the trading post saloon.

A few chuckles went the rounds; then the fight turned serious. Kreuger came to his boots shedding road apples and urine-made mud. Before he could locate his enemy, Preacher walked up from behind him and gave him a powerful shove that sent Kreuger back into the quagmire.

Hoots of laughter ran among the mountain men. Kreuger's face went so darkly red as to look black. On hands and knees he crawled toward the dry, hard-packed ground. Unwilling to lose an important good shot in so critical a battle as the one he visualized upcoming, Preacher determined to go easy on Kreuger. He knew the cause of some of the bad blood between them, yet had not seen the man in some while and could only guess at what other grievances and faults the German had assigned to him. On the other hand, Kreuger sincerely believed this to be the time to tumble Preacher from his high perch, to show him to be no more than any other man. Through the red haze of his fury, he spotted his foe.

Springing quickly to his boots, Kreuger swung a looping left that connected with the point of Preacher's shoulder. Preacher shed it easily, then whanged a hard fist that mushed Kreuger's mouth. Blood flew in a nimbus that haloed Kreuger's head. The huge, bullet-headed German absorbed the force of Preacher's blow and took a chance kick at the mountain legend's groin.

Preacher saw it coming and danced aside. He whooped and jumped in the air, waggling one open hand under his chin at Bloody Hand. Kreuger stared at Preacher uncomprehendingly. On the way down, Preacher enlightened the Kraut as to the purpose of his childish taunt. His target sufficiently distracted, he swiftly jabbed two of those extended fingers toward the man's eyes.

Kreuger recoiled so violently that he tottered off balance. Preacher's boot toes lightly touched when he launched a one-two combination at the midsection of Karl Kreuger. Dust puffed from the buckskin shirt Kreuger wore as the piston fists connected in a rapid tattoo. Grunting, he rocked on back. He went over his center and plopped to the ground on his rump. Anxious to end this before harming even this uncertain an asset, Preacher swiftly stepped in on Kreuger.

Only too far!

A well-aimed kick from Kreuger landed deeply in Preacher's groin. Sheer agony radiated outward from Preacher's throbbing crotch. When the yawning pit of blackness receded from his mind, Preacher recovered himself in time to clap his open palms against the sides of Kreuger's head. So much for going easy, he thought grimly.

Their fight turned deadly serious. Not that Preacher would willingly go so far as to kill Kreuger, so long as the German mountain man would let him avoid it. Howling in pain, Kreuger dived forward and wrapped his arms around Preacher's legs. Digging in with a shoulder, he drove Preacher off his boots. Preacher landed heavily. Dust rose around him as he tried to suck in air.

Kreuger did not give him the chance to fully recover. He climbed Preacher's legs, grunting and growling as he went. Savagely, he bit Preacher in the thigh. Then his forward progress got halted abruptly with a sledgehammer fist. Preacher drove it down on his opponent's crown with all the force in him. A shower of colored lights went off in Kreuger's head. Preacher heaved mightily and sent his antagonist flying. Wincing to hold back a cry of agony, Preacher came upright and stepped over to Kreuger.

"Give it up, Bloody Hand. This ain't fittin'. We got us a whole wagon load of trouble out there we need to be facin' together."

"You go to hell, Preacher."

Their fight might have gone on longer had not the long-expected arrival of the missionaries put a quicker end to it.

They streamed in through the stockade gate as Kreuger sputtered out his defiance. In the lead, Spartacus halted them abruptly with a raised hand.

"No need mixin' up in that, folks. Preacher, he got ever'thin' in hand."

And indeed it appeared he had. After Kreuger's outburst, Preacher shoved the German forward while he pile-drivered a big right to the broad forehead below an unruly shock of wheat straw hair. The birdies sang loudly between Kreuger's ears. Groggily he tried to get his feet under him. Preacher shook him like a rag doll.

Kreuger pawed at Preacher's arm. Preacher punched him again. Kreuger went rigid, and his eyes rolled up in their sockets. He sighed wearily, and his legs twitched a few seconds before he went still and limp.

Amelia Witherspoon looked on in mingled admiration and horror. She reached out a hand now to touch Spartacus lightly on the arm. "That man? He isn't dead, is he?"

"New, Missy Sister Amelia. I figger Preacher to be a more careful man than that. I also reckon he be mighty glad to see you again."

Amelia flushed. A hand flew to her mouth. "Do—do you think so?"

"Pert' near a certain thing," Spartacus answered with confidence as the downed man recovered consciousness.

Kreuger started to roundly curse Preacher, and Amelia covered her ears with her hands. Her eyes went wide when Preacher treated the swearing man like one would a foul-mouthed boy. The sound of Preacher's backhand slap cracked through the chill, high mountain air.

"Lighten up, Bloody Hand, or you'll be sleepin' with a pitchfork in your hands tonight."

"Go diddle yourzelf, you zon of a—" The hand returned with more punishment.

"I'm gonna leave it at this, Kreuger. Someone dump a bucket of water over this sorehead. It'll cool him off."

Preacher turned to walk away, only to stop in surprise. "Well, I'll be. You folks been there long?"

"Long enough," Amelia Witherspoon responded snappishly, only to stop and blush in confusion as she realized how in conflict were her spinsterish words of criticism and the emotions in her heart.

Preacher cut his eyes to a spot on the ground somewhere between them. "I apologize for what you had to witness. That man's got him a mean on like a boil. You folks got here without any trouble?"

"We did," she responded, then gushed out her true feelings, "and I'm so glad you're here."

It became Preacher's turn to be embarrassed. "Aw, that's kind of you to say, but I ain't nothin' special."

Crimson glowed in Amelia's cheeks. "I think you are," she gushed out.

She reached out a hand, and to her surprised relief, Preacher took it. Without another word, the lean, powerful mountain man led her away into the woods behind the trading post.

"I'm cold."

Terry looked at his sister, seated across the small fire from him. "So am I."

"It will be winter soon," Vickie added meaningfully.

"I know that. We've just got to find Preacher."

Vickie offered an unwelcome suggestion. "We could always go back?"

"No, we can't. We stole and lied to those folks. It wouldn't be fittin'."

"They'd understand, Terry. I'm cold and hungry and so tired. Why haven't we found Preacher yet?"

Frustration at his failure goaded Terry. "I don't know. Leave it alone, will you?" He thought it over awhile, forced himself past pride and stubbornness. "I tell you what. We'll wait it out two more days, keep going north. If we don't find Preacher by then, we . . . we can start back."

"But I want to go back now. I'm scared out here, Terry."

Terry sighed off a heavy burden for a twelve-year-old. "All right. I'll take you back. At least until we're in sight of the house. Then I'm headed for the tradin' post."

Over the next day, some ten long-legged, rangy men clustered in the trading post compound. Well accustomed to the rigors of the High Lonesome, they had heard the call for aid for a fellow and dropped what they worked upon and headed to the small settlement. To Preacher's surprised relief, that swelled their number to thirty-five. Now, if only the Arapaho came in, they stood a chance, he reasoned. Amelia Witherspoon provided him pleasant distraction from the preparations for war.

They sat under a huge juniper, redolent with the scent of resin and ripe berries. There had not yet been a sharp frost, so the small, round balls, which served as the base flavor in what the English called geneva, had not turned their characteristic dark blue. Amelia had brought a picnic basket, and they lunched on cold fried chicken and boiled turnips. When the last crumbs of a pie had been devoured, she got to the heart of her purpose in being there.

"I know that those people are simply awful, sinful and terribly vicious. But isn't it up to our army to do something about them?"

Preacher snorted. "I ain't seen a soldier-boy in nigh onto a year an' more. They keeps to their little block-house forts and ride the Santa Fe Trail to protect what folks back east call commerce. Now that Santa Fe, an' all New Mexico, is American, business is boomin'. That's what the politicians will want the soldiers to guard. I hear there's even talk of openin' a stagecoach line. *Civilization,*" he spat. "It gums up ever'thin' wherever it goes."

Amelia smiled and patted him on the arm. "I'm not so sure. People are . . . so much more tranquil in the East."

"Controlled, you mean. I've been there. It's like one great big prison. A feller can't carry a shootin' iron down the street without being gawked at, or even arrested in some places. Folks that live like that ain't free."

"But they are safe, and protected."

Preacher looked long and hard at her. "Miss Amelia, I don't mean to pry, or to offend, but that makes me wonder. If that be the case, then why in tarnation did you folk come out here?"

Amelia tried to find the right tone of answer and failed. Instead, she laughed and leaned a shoulder against Preacher. "You have me there, Preacher. I could say it was our calling. Or that adventure beckoned. Truth to tell, I suppose it was to be away from the strictures of society." She frowned and returned to her original theme. "Though, when I think of the price to be paid, the terrible things that happened to Deacon Abercrombie and the others, all the blood spilled—and more to come. It makes me question the purpose behind fighting those sick people out there."

Preacher's voice took on an edge. "Because we're the only ones to do it, Miss Amelia. An' it dang-sure needs doing." He bent in the silence that followed to help her pick up the picnic leavings.

Back at the trading post, Karl Kreuger nursed his bruises and aches and avoided eye contact with Preacher. He would go along, he allowed. "Because I giff my vord."

The next day, three more mountain men straggled into the gathering. That called for another whooping, foot-stomping, powerful drinking welcome. The assorted company had hardly settled down when a lone Arapaho warrior appeared at the gate to the compound. Preacher went out to greet him.

"Yellow Hawk, it is good to see you."

Yellow Hawk returned Preacher's sign of greeting and made the one for peace. "It is good to see you, Ghost Wolf. We have come. There are six hands of warriors from the village of Bold Pony and four hands from the village of the people who lost their braves to the Ro-mans."

Fifty warriors, Preacher tallied. Better than he had hoped for. He nodded his acceptance. "We number nearly as many. More will be picked up on the trail. An' maybe some of my Cheyenne friends would like to get in on this."

Yellow Hawk made a face. All was not love and roses between the Arapaho and the Cheyenne. Yet, they had fought together before and perhaps would again. He signed acceptance. Preacher read the thoughts of Yellow Hawk on his stern visage. No matter. They would get along or not. The Cheyenne could always fight alongside the mountain men.

"Bring 'em on in. You can make camp outside the stockade. We leave tomorrow at first light."

A bit after mid-afternoon the next day, Preacher came upon a complication that left his jaw sagging a moment before he let go a low, controlled roar. "What in hell are you doin' here, boy?"

Saucy as ever, Terry Tucker stood at the side of the road, face beaming, while he waved at the man he so admired. "I want to go with you, Preacher."

Preacher's eyes narrowed. "We've been over this before. Where's your sister?"

"I took her back, then come to find you."

"Back? That mean the both of you runned off?"

"Yes, sir. We tried to find you north of here. Saw a lot of fellers dressed like you, but you didn't come along. Vickie got scared and tired and so I took her back. I can come along, can't I?"

"No. Not only no, but hell no."

Terry looked as though he might cry. "I want to join the

fight. I can do it, you know that. I—I'm grateful to you for helping Vickie an' me escape a life of crime, and I want to make amends. I can do odd jobs around the camp, care for the horses, that sort of thing."

What a quandary. Preacher removed his old, slouch hat and scratched the crown of his head with a thick fingernail. "I swear I don't know what to do with you. It's more than dangerous where we're going. I've been there onecst an' it ain't no pony ride. Still . . ." he faded off, considering the alternatives. "I can't spare a man to return you. Nor can I trust you to go on your own, given your stubborn outlook. So, I reckon you'll have to come along."

Terry's face came alive, and he gave a little jump of joy. "Really? Oh, Preacher, thank you."

Preacher bent toward the boy. "You'll not be thankin' me five days from now when we run into them Romans. Now, you cain't walk all the way. We got to scare up a horse for you."

With the same coy expression, an impish light in his clear, blue eyes, Terry asked the identical question he had put to Preacher before. "Why can't I ride with you?"

Laughing, Preacher reached for the boy. "I suppose we can make an exception this one time. At least until I can scare up another mount." He swung the boy aboard Cougar, noting that the improved victuals had added to Terry's weight.

Messengers arrived at the palace from the watch towers on a regular schedule. The one that was just shown in to Marcus Quintus brought worrisome news.

"Reporting from Watch Tower Three, First Citizen. We have observed increased movement by the red savages to the east. All appear to be men, heavily armed and moving to the south."

Quintus scowled. That did not sound good at all. "Do you have a count of them?"

"Yes, sir. They number approximately thirty-six."

"Not an exact figure?" Quintus goaded.

Independent service in an isolated command had loosened the reins of discipline for the messenger. "We weren't about to send someone out to parlay with them and count heads, sir."

Anger flared for a moment in Quintus; then he regained control. "No. Of course not. Standing orders remain not to provoke the savages. I wonder where they are heading?"

21

Some ten miles out into the Great Divide Basin, Preacher's small army came upon the advance scouts of the Cheyenne party seeking them. Some grumbling ran through the Arapaho warriors at this, though the two war party leaders, Yellow Hawk and Blind Beaver, kept their men in check. Crow Killer, leader of the Cheyenne, had been a small boy when Preacher first met him. That had been over twenty years ago. He still had the sunny disposition and good sense of humor of his childhood, and greeted Preacher warmly.

"I thought you to be with the Great Spirit by now, Preacher."

"You ain't no spring chicken yourself," Preacher growled good-naturedly.

Crow Killer made a face. "Have you grown as mean as you have old?"

"Dang right. An' fit to wrassel a griz." Preacher let go a big guffaw. "How'er ya doin', Crow Killer?"

"I have a wife now, and three children."

Preacher blinked and cocked his head to one side. "Is that a fact? You had no more than thirteen summers the last time I saw you."

"It has been a long time, Ghost Walker. I have twice that number of summers now."

"An' three youngins. You got started early."

Crow Killer cracked a white smile. "I went on the war trail

first time the summer after you hunted buffalo with our village. I took a wife five summers later."

Grinning, Preacher shook his head knowingly. "Ah, but it is the winters that count in catchin' babies, right?"

Grinning, the Cheyenne motioned his men into the column. "We scout for you, Preacher?"

"Yes, that would be good."

Crow Killer's next words surprised Preacher. "We saw these people you go to fight."

"Did you now? When was this?"

"Three suns ago. We rode past their valley of shining lodges. They make ready to take the war trail. Aha! We have known of it for some time. We did not know how evil these men are, so we left them alone. I will grow much honor fighting at your side."

"The honor is mine," Preacher responded modestly. "What can you tell me from what you saw?"

Crow Killer considered it. "They have built some platforms, like burial racks, put up on the ridge around their basin."

"Watch towers. Reckon they saw you?"

"Oh, yes. We did not try to hide."

Preacher chuckled at that. "That must have given ol' Marcus Quintus a tizzy."

"Who? I do not know that name."

"The he-coon that runs that strange place. Injuns make him nervous."

Crow Killer scanned the ranks of Arapaho and his own Cheyenne. "Then he will soon be very nervous."

Laughing together, they rode on. An hour before sundown, the column pulled into a circle, the Arapaho and Cheyenne on the outer two rings, and settled in for the night. Two of the Cheyenne scouts had taken a small elk, and the savory odor of roasting meat filled the air inside the campsite. Most of the mountain men had brought along ample supplies of stoneware jugs full of whiskey, and the mood became festive. Not so for

Preacher and the more experienced among them, nor for the Indian leaders.

"We can't let any of them Arapaho or Cheyenne get a hand on that likker. We'd have us one hell of a war on our hands if they did. Keep a good watch," Preacher advised the war leaders, Philadelphia, and Frenchie Dupre.

Early the next morning, Terry Tucker rode beside Preacher. Blind Beaver noted this and rode over. "You have a son now, also, Preacher?"

Preacher looked surprised, then embarrassed. "No. Not likely. It—it's just something that growed to me." For all his denial, Preacher gave Terry a wink.

Blind Beaver beamed. "I have two. One is five summers, the other one. The other is a girl. And she is beautiful."

"I'm sure she is." Preacher gave Blind Beaver a hard, direct look. "When we make camp tonight, we will hold council. I want to paint a word picture of how we will attack these bad men."

Grunting in agreement, Blind Beaver made his thoughts known. "It is good. Are they truly Moon Children?"

Preacher considered it. "I don't think so. Ol' Marcus Quintus might be a lot tetched, but he's sane enough to know right from wrong. So do the others. I figger it this way. They're just lettin' themselves go. The pleasures evil can offer can be mighty temptin'."

"Most true, *mon ami*," Frenchie Dupre agreed from the other side.

"Tell me about this boy," Blind Beaver urged Preacher.

Preacher reached out and ruffled Terry's white hair. "He's a stray. Attached himself to me a while back an' I found a home for him and his sister. Now he's run off to help me in this fight."

"You are young for your first war party," Blind Beaver told Terry in Arapaho, with Preacher translating.

"I'm twelve," Terry responded sharply, with only a hint of his usual defiance.

"When I had twelve summers, I still used a boy's bow and hunted rabbits."

"It was meant as a compliment," Preacher added to his translation.

Terry surprised Preacher yet again with his depth of diplomacy. "I'd really rather be."

"You are brave. You will do well," Blind Beaver told the boy. Then, to Preacher he added, "I will go forward, see what has been found."

What the Cheyenne scouts had found would astonish all of them.

Only the day before, one century of Varras' cavalry (actually only fifty-seven men, not one hundred) had at last discovered the tracks left by the fleeing missionaries. They followed it to the southeast now, hungering for contact. Shouted jests as to what they would do to the survivors flew through the air, flung from their mouths by a quick canter. Their concentration so centered on the anticipated targets, they failed to take note of an eagle feather that seemed to flutter incongruously from the center of a large sage bush.

A close study of that out-of-place object would have informed them that the tip had been dyed red. So had the white goose fletchings on the arrows the watcher carried, the shafts of which bore two red bands of paint and one yellow. The watcher's cousins, the Sioux, called them *Sahiela*—which translates loosely into English as "they-come-red"—and the white men called them Cheyenne.

Red Hand had been scouting ahead for hours, and had only swung directly back onto the trail a short while ago. He lived, as did all his brothers, by "Indian time" which took no notice of seconds, minutes, or hours, only of day and night, before high sun and after, of suns (days) and moons (months). So he had no exact idea how long he had ridden forward before his keen hearing picked up the rumble of many mounted men. Alerted, he guided his pony off the trail and dismounted.

His experience quickly led him to the large clump of sage, and he concealed himself there. A hundred heartbeats later, these strange men rode into view. Were they contraries? What odd clothing. That bright red cloth could be seen for miles. And only four hands of them carried bows. What sort of warriors were they? He waited until they had ridden far beyond his hiding place. Then he came out of the brush, gathered dry sticks, and clumps of green grass.

Quickly Red Hand built a small fire. When it went well, he weighted two corners of a blanket with stones, threw the greenery on the blaze and covered it with the square of cloth. He counted heartbeats, then quickly raised the blanket. A large ball of smoke formed and drifted lazily upward. He waited, fed the fire, then repeated the process twice. Crow Killer would soon know.

Crow Killer returned to the mixed column of mountain men and Indians at a gallop. His pony snorted and stamped hooves in excitement at the run when the Cheyenne war leader reined in. He had plenty to tell.

"You weren't gone long," Preacher dryly observed.

"You saw the smokes?"

Preacher nodded.

"There are many. I watched them. Two of my scouts are behind them, to give warning if more come."

Preacher nodded again and spat a blade of grass from his mouth. "That is wise. I'd leave have half our men behind them, catch 'em in a box. How many?"

"Five two-hands and a hand more and two."

Pursing his lips, Preacher thought on that. "Sure it's the Romans?"

"Yes. All on ponies."

Preacher planned quickly. "Chances one or two will get

away from the fight that's sure to come. Wouldn't do for them to know us boys was out here. I hate to turn down a battle with those devils first off, but it's best if they think it's only Injuns. Bold Pony has some good men with the rifle. How about you?"

"I have three hands who are good at it."

"Fine, fifteen more rifles will sure help. I'll get the Arapaho ready, and you set up your warriors. Have 'em try to pot the leaders first off. This ain't for honor, it's for revenge."

Crow Killer's face indicated he didn't think much of that, though he readily agreed. "That is how it will be done."

"Good. Remember, no individual challenges or fights until the leaders are knocked out of the saddle."

After explaining his plan to Bold Pony, Preacher set about convincing the throng of mountain men. "I know this won't sit well with a lot of you. But we've got to keep our intentions hidden from any of the Romans who get away."

Karl Kreuger seized on that. "Vhat are you talking about?"

"There's about fifty-five, sixty Roman cavalry on their way. The Injuns are gonna take them on. Chances are some will get away. They can't take it back to New Rome that we have this large a force. Plain an' simple. We hide over that ridge behind us until the thing is done. No exceptions."

"Who appointed you general?" Kreuger growled.

"I did," Preacher answered simply. "Now, we'd best be moving. Them boys in the red capotes is not far away."

Preacher watched the Roman cavalry approach through his long, brass spyglass. First to appear over the ridge that masked off the swale they had so recently occupied came the horsehair-plumed helmets and tossing heads of the mounts. The men showed next. They rode at a canter, uphill. Stupid, Preacher thought.

When the Romans reached the bottom of the reverse slope, the centurion in charge raised his hand in the universal signal to halt. Changing his field of view, Preacher saw the reason why. A dozen Cheyenne warriors had risen out of the tall grass, as though sprang new from the earth itself. They held drawn bows, the arrowheads angled high, to reach for the enemy. *Clever,* Preacher thought.

Sounding like nothing more than the cry of a shrike, the centurion issued his command, echoed by the sergeants. Swords hissed out of scabbards and made pillars of brightness in the sunlight. Another birdlike command and the sergeants separated their squads from the square formation they had traveled in so far. It also identified all of the leaders to the patient Cheyenne. *Idiotic,* Preacher thought.

From hidden locations on the flanks, puffs of smoke rose from the grass. There followed a fraction of a second, and the four sergeants went off their horses, dead before they struck the ground. The crack of discharging rifles followed Preacher's ears. The centurion wavered in his saddle, shot through the breastplate. *Brilliant,* Preacher thought.

Left in confusion, the soldiers milled about, their horses made fractious by the smell of blood. Then they were given something to concentrate upon. The meadow came alive with Cheyenne and Arapaho warriors. Their horses snorted as they rolled upright and came to their hooves. Another volley sounded from the hidden marksmen. Arrows flew from the twelve on foot. Swiftly the Indians mounted their ponies. Before the cavalry soldiers realized it, they found themselves the target of a whooping, hooting, lance-waving Indian charge. *Magnificent,* Preacher thought.

Since the advent of the horse, standard tactics for most plains tribes consisted of swift, powerful charges to ring the wagons of white settlers, or an enemy village, then close the diameter with a gradual inward spiral. Or of individual challenges and man-to-man, vicious hand-to-hand combat. Indians, Preacher had ample reason to know, rarely fought in organized, disciplined ranks. Almost anything could end the fighting: victory, or a perception of bad medicine, or omens like an owl flying in daylight, to a sudden chill wind. Pity the poor pilgrims coming after him, Preacher thought, if this fight today changed all that.

It didn't appear that it would, Preacher acknowledged as he watched, telescope at his side now, while the cavalry formation disintegrated through attrition and the Arapaho and Cheyenne braves picked out individuals to challenge. One by one, the kilted fighting men of New Rome met death at the hands of the Indians. Only seven of them managed to keep their wits long enough to make an escape. One of those lost his chance to a long-range rifle shot. Their commander fared even worse.

Frightfully wounded, he much preferred the peace of the grave to the torture and torment that capture meant. He had heard the stories, of course, and chose the only sensible alternative. He removed his cuirass, reversed his *gladius* and pressed the pommel to the ground, then fell on his sword.

Blind Beaver appeared at Preacher's side. "In the end, he was a woman," he stated scornfully of the centurion. Preacher thought that made a good sum-up of the entire battle, which had not lasted fifteen minutes by his big Hambleton turnip watch.

During the next two days, seventeen more denizens of the High Lonesome wandered in. The word had spread far and wide. Duke Morrison was among them, as were Bunny Tilitson and Haymaker Norris. The Duke approached Preacher during the nooning rest.

"Are you serious about these—"

Preacher cut him off. "Yeah, yeah, them Romans is real enough. D'ya check the trophies our Arapaho an' Cheyenne allies collected off the cavalry?"

"No, but I'll have me a look."

Eyeing the younger mountain man, Preacher reached a conclusion. "Duke, yu'rt purty nigh expert at slippin' an' slidin' around after dark, ain'tcha?"

Modesty commanded that Duke eye the ground beyond

Preacher's shoulder. "I've done my share of dark-time stalkin'. You don't intend on *sneakin'* up on these Romans, do you?"

"Yep. On some of 'em at least. Now that you're here, it comes to mind that we ought to do somethin' about these outposts I hear the Romans done put up. Best done at night."

Duke nodded. "You're right on that, Preacher. When do we have a go at it?"

"Reckon you an' me an' a couple of Bold Pony's boys ought to pull out early tomorrow, get a day or so ahead of the rest. Then we can have a look around and see what can be done."

A broad grin spread the full lips of the big man. "I say that shines. Count me in."

Shortly before nightfall, two days later, Preacher and Duke Morrison crested the notch that separated them from the New Rome basin by but another valley and ridge. Careful to remain behind a screen of trees, they made a detailed study of the saw-tooth line across the way. After a seemingly long two minutes, Preacher lowered his spyglass. He pointed at a shadowy object partially obscured by tree limbs.

"A watch tower, right enough. I reckon they'll be spread around so's to overlap a slight bit of the view from one to another. I counted six men. Most likely there's some snoozin', an' a couple who act as messengers."

"I saw another tower," Duke revealed. "It looked to have the arms of one of those whatchamacallits—you know, a signal thing."

"A heliograph, or something like it, eh?"

"Yeah. That's it."

"That way they don't waste time sendin' a message, at least in daytime. The thing for us to do tonight is hit enough of these things to make bein' here plain uncomfortable. We want to get these boys all bollixed up. Seein' things that ain't there, firing off reports and alarms to call out the soldiers at all hours."

Duke clucked his tongue. "That won't make the troops very happy."

"Nope. An' it will make them careless. You 'member from bein' a kid the story about the boy who cried wolf? Well, by the time our outfit gets here, that's what the regular soldiers will be thinkin' about these fellers on the ridge. Then maybe we pop up . . ." Preacher went on to outline his plan.

They picked a spot on the far side and settled in among the pines to rest until the best time of night. Preacher and Duke gnawed on strips of jerky and cold biscuits to fill the empty space in their bellies, then caught a few hours of sleep.

Elijah Morton had quickly become bored with this duty. They could hang a Roman name on him, make him learn Latin, but he knew who he was, or at least who he'd once been. Elijah Morton had been a small-time highwayman who preyed on isolated trading posts along the North Platte. At least until the urge to move farther west, brought on by an increased presence of mounted federal troops, had brought him into the Ferris Range some two years ago. He had been captured and quickly volunteered to join a legion.

Often after that, he had regretted his decision. Not nearly so much as he would this night.

Elijah did not see the dark figures ghosting through the trees toward the watch tower. He had watch and had grown bored with staring into black nothing. Opposite him, Graccus peered toward the distant platform where two others did the same dull task. He sensed at the same time as Elijah the vibration of a footfall on the ladder leading upward. Could it be their relief?

Not likely, Graccus discovered a split second before bright lights exploded inside his head, to bring excruciating pain for a brief moment, when Duke buried his war hawk in the top of his head. Preacher swarmed over Elijah at the same moment.

His forearm pressed tightly against the throat of his victim, which effectively cut off any sound. Preacher leaned close, smelled garlic, onions and rancid, unwashed body, and whispered in one ear.

"You want to live, keep quiet and do as you are told."

The head nodded feebly. Preacher went on. "How many are there up here?"

"Two," Elijah mouthed. Sudden pain erupted under his left ear, and he felt the prick of a knife point.

"Don't lie to me. I counted six men earlier." Preacher eased the pressure to allow for a reply.

"Four are sleeping. There's the messenger down below. Didn't you . . .?"

"He's tied up," Preacher answered with part of the truth.

Preacher and Duke had closed on the unsuspecting messenger, to find out he was a mere boy, hardly older than fourteen or fifteen. Preacher clapped a big hand over the lad's mouth and yanked him off his feet. They had quickly tied him up, carted him away from the tower and strung him up, head down, in a tree. He prodded again.

"What time is your relief?"

"I don't know. In another hour, maybe."

"What's your name?"

"Elijah Morton."

"You don't have a Roman name, Elijah?"

"Yeah. It's Virgo. I hate it."

"All right, Elijah, if you want to live, you'll answer everything, and then you'll be tied up and gagged. We won't kill you."

"I'll do what I can."

"Good. What's going on in New Rome?"

Elijah talked freely about the preparations for war. He detailed the training exercises of the legions and spoke of the firearms. That came as a nasty surprise to Preacher. They would have to hit at night, spike those cannons and move right into the city. Somehow the idea did not sit well with him.

"Anything else?"

"Oh, sure. The watch towers were built, and we've been in them ever since. Once a week we are supposed to be rotated back to our legion. So far that hasn't happened, and we're gettin' fed up with it."

"Now, that's right interestin'. Well, we're gonna leave those other boys to snooze, lock 'em in that room over there and wait to see what comes of that. I'm gonna turn you loose now. Don't fight me, turn around and put your hands behind your back."

"I hate this place. Can't I come with you?"

"Nope. We've got more of this kinda thing to do. But if you want to ride away from it when you get loose, head due south. When you come to some folks, ask for Philadelphia Braddock."

"I knew some Braddocks back home."

"Where's that?"

"Philadelphia," Elijah answered simply.

Preacher considered that a moment. "Now ain't that interestin'? Turn around."

Elijah complied in silence. After trussing him up, Preacher lowered Elijah to the platform floor. Then he and Duke eased over to the shelter that housed the slumbering sentries. Preacher located a loose piece of wood and used it to wedge the door tightly shut. With that accomplished, they stole off into the night to visit yet another tower.

They completed their jaunt uneasily close to first light. A soft, silver-gray glow hung along the eastern ridge when they rejoined the Cheyennes. Both of them had big grins and six fresh scalps tied to their belts.

"That ain't gonna do them Romans any good when they think about spendin' time out here. Might be we can raise a little more ruckus tomorrow night."

22

A considerable uproar followed Preacher's excursion. The fourteen deaths were attributed to the red savages, and any who had been spared by Preacher and Duke kept their own counsel. It worked so well, Preacher decided, that they would try it on two or three of the other towers the next night. In order to avoid the patrols that had been sent out at first light to search for the perpetrators, he, Duke and the Cheyenne had withdrawn beyond the second ridge out of the city.

"Heck of a thing," Preacher announced when they returned after nightfall. "Looks like our funnin' with them has backfired on us." He referred to the neat rows of cooking fires that spread around the meadow outside the walled city.

"What's that?" Duke Morrison asked.

Preacher gave a short, sharp grunt. "That's the legions. They've taken to the field. Changes our plans somewhat. But that can wait until the rest git here. Now's the time to shake them up a bit more."

Things had changed on the final rim also. Two sentries guarded the base of the first tower Preacher and Duke approached. It took them only slightly greater stealth to close on the alert guards than it had the unsuspecting messengers of the previous night. From the moment he had learned that the towers operated independently, Preacher had been working on fateful decisions for those who occupied the ones they would visit tonight.

No more sparing of lives. To create the maximum of fear and terror, all would die. It didn't make a problem for the Cheyennes, albeit he and Duke went to it grimly, taking no pleasure from the task. The two guards died swiftly and without a sound. The slumbering messenger awakened in time to see the blade of a war hawk descending toward his head. His scream died along with himself. The moccasins of the two mountain men made only the softest of whispers as they ascended the ladder to the platform.

One of the watchmen, more attentive than his partner, sensed more than heard the silent approach. He turned, his hand going to the heft of his *gladius*. Preacher bounded up onto the boards of the platform and turned off the source of such commands with his tomahawk. The blade sank to the hilt in the soldier's forehead. Before he could wrench it free, Duke joined him and finished off the other sentry.

Preacher spoke softly. "There's two more in there, most likely."

Duke nodded, and they moved cat-footed to the door. Duke pointed to his chest and then the closed portal, indicating he would go through first. Preacher dipped his chin a fraction of an inch and yanked open the crudely made panel. Duke went through with Preacher at his heels. The scuffing motions of their moccasins awakened a light sleeper. Duke's big Hudson's Bay Company knife sank into the unfortunate legionnaire's chest and trashed his heart.

He died with a soft sigh. Preacher swung to split the skull of the dead man's companion, only to find his wrist in a grasp like iron. The big man grunted, but did not cry out. The coppery tang of blood in the air told him there would be no one to hear. He tried to rear up, but Preacher's weight bore down on him and pinned him to the straw mattress. Preacher used his free hand to draw his Green River knife and plunge it into soft tissue below the rib cage. He was aware of the amazing rubbery tension of skin for a brief moment, before the tip sank into muscle and angled upward.

The soldier convulsed as the blade pierced his diaphragm and sped on to his heart. His tremors became more violent, and then he went rigid and lay still. Preacher took a deep breath.

"Time to get movin'," he told Duke.

Cassius Varo stared into the night. Had he seen slight movement in Tower Seven? If so, it could only be the men on watch, he told himself. Bored by long, fruitless hours of this static activity, he paced the two sides of the plank square for which he was responsible. Time went by so slowly. Varo's eyelids had started to droop when a sudden, very wet *thok!* came from below.

Suddenly alert, he touched his partner on one shoulder, then leaned over the railing to call softly to the guards on the ground. "Titus, Vindix, what's going on?"

His answer came in the form of a broad-head arrow that drove into his forehead. His single, violent convulsion sent him crashing over the rail. By then, Preacher had ascended the ladder and had only to swing smoothly to smash the brains from the other sentry with his war hawk.

Duke quickly joined him, and they finished off the sleeping pair without even a stir. Outside, Preacher nodded to the tall, black bulk of another tower, standing out against the starlight. "Two down, one more to go."

At mid-morning the next day, the mountain-man-and-Indian army arrived beyond the third ridge from New Rome. Preacher and Duke greeted them and called for a parlay of all leaders. Bold Pony, Blind Beaver and Philadelphia attended. Terry Tucker hovered at Preacher's elbow. Most of the former fur trappers stood around in a loose circle. Their long lives of independence gave them license to eavesdrop, or so they believed. Having done it enough times himself, Preacher made no further notice of them.

He got right down to business. "Things have changed. We shook 'em up a little an' they put their legions out in the field. They's camped all around the city. So we'll not be scalin' any walls right off. Put your men to makin' ladders fer it, anyway. We'll need 'em after we deal with the soldiers, I reckon."

"How do we do that?" Philadelphia inquired.

Preacher gave him a smile. "I thought you'd never ask. First thing is we've got to draw them out. I see you brought along a couple dozen more than we had at our last camp together. That's good."

"We're more than a hunderd an' fifty strong now, Preacher," Philadelphia announced. "An' that could git bigger by tomorrow."

"Even better. Cold camp tonight. We don't want our Roman friends knowin' we're here. I know it'll be hard not gettin' in some drummin' an' singin', Bold Pony, Blind Beaver, but you've both done some war trail sneaks before, I'm sure. We can all dance up a storm oncest this is over." The war leaders nodded solemnly. "Now here's how we get them to come to us. First off we have to get rid of all those watch towers they've built. Then, the morning after that's done, we show up in a double line on the last ridge. That'll make us ringtailers and the Cheyenne."

"Vhat about the Arapaho?" Karl Kreuger asked nastily from the sidelines. "You goin' soft on dem vor a purpose."

"Nope. Not at all. Matter of fact, they've got the hardest part of all. Before we show ourselves to the Romans, they've got to sneak down into that valley durin' the night . . ." Preacher went on to describe where the Arapaho warriors would go and what they would be doing.

"Sounds complicated," Philadelphia Braddock observed.

"It ain't. Not if ever'one does what he's supposed to. If all of us keeps our place and not act on our own, we can have this over before nightfall."

"You said they had cannons," a voice came from a mountain man Preacher did not know.

"Those we take care of the same time we empty the watch towers. Which reminds me. Duke an' me learned a whole lot about how they are run. After the soldiers are tooken care of, we leave two men in each tower to make the morning signal. Then those boys can join the rest of us. As far as the cannons go, I found these little things in one of the towers we hit last night. Must be used for holdin' somethin' together. Thing is, they'll serve our purpose." Preacher unwound from his squat on the ground and went to his saddlebags.

From them he took a buckskin bag about six inches long. From it, he removed three dull, grayish objects. They had been flattened on one end, and the opposite one tapered to a fine point. He raised his arm to show them around.

"While the towers are being silenced, Duke an' me and a couple others will slip in among the Romans and spike the touch holes of those big guns."

That didn't sound too good to Philadelphia. "Won't they hear you doin' that?"

Preacher gave him a confident smile. "Not if we use padded wooden mallets. A couple of pops on each, then break them off. Those tired soldier-boys will think it's just horses stompin' in the night."

"If you say so," Philadelphia relented, still unconvinced.

"I want to go with you, Preacher," Terry pleaded.

"No. You'll stay on the ridge with them towers. An' that's final."

"When do we get all this started?" another mountain man asked.

Preacher swept his arm in an inclusive gesture. "We'll git us a little rest now. Then, when it is good and dark tonight, it all begins. Them Romans will never know what hit them."

Prudence, as much as good luck, guarded Preacher and the five mountain men with him as they glided across the tall grass of the central meadow. For some reason, he had noted, the cannons had been left outside the temporary palisades of the nightly encampments of each cohort. He had no way of knowing that the cause was ignorance and laziness—twelve-pound Napoleons weighed over a ton, and were hard to move around.

The generals had decided where they would fight the enemy when he came, and so the long guns had been laid to provide the maximum effect. There they would stay. Coincidentally, that put three cannons on each flank of the supposed Roman main line of resistance. Well and good, Preacher figured. Shortly before sundown, Haymaker Norris, who claimed to have put his trapping aside for two years to serve in the Mexican War as an artilleryman, instructed the sabotage party in the proper way to spike a cannon. Along with the mountain men who were to take out the watch towers, they set out on foot at midnight.

Leaving a cold camp, their night vision was not affected in the least. Those who used tobacco chewed on sweetened leaf or, like Preacher, chomped on the butt of an unlighted cigar. They moved with astonishing speed and silence. No one spoke; not a loose item of equipment or clothing clattered or rattled. Not even a clink came from the Roman plumb bobs—for that's what the lead spikes were identified as by Four-Eyes Finney, who had been an apprentice carpenter before he ran away to the Big Empty. It seemed no time until they had crested the first of three ridges that separated them from New Rome. Preacher called a short halt there to catch their wind. Funny, neither he nor any of them had needed to do that in the past, even packing around some respectable wounds.

He eased over to each of the men with him and repeated whispered advice.

"We'd best be givin' some time for those boys up ahead to do their dirty work."

"Another ridge to cross," Four-Eyes Finney reminded him.

"Then we'd best be gettin' there," Preacher declared as he

set off along the trail. The others followed at once without having to be told.

When Preacher and his companions reached the watch tower beside the main southern trail, not a living person remained there. The other force of mountain men had done their work well and vanished into the night to their next objective. Preacher again ordered they take a breather. They had made it this far without another stop, which pleased him. Now the hard part would begin.

"We'll take the cannons on the right flank first. That's our left," he added for the benefit of Blue Nose Herkimer.

"I know that," Blue Nose whispered back in mock irritation.

"You do *now,*" Preacher responded through a low chuckle.

They began their descent five minutes later. Avoiding the roadway in order not to be seen, the mountain men angled across the basin, through the tall grass nearly invisible even to one another. Preacher's long, meticulous survey of the valley paid off. He had a fairly accurate map of the terrain in his head. It took not the least effort to direct the spiking party to a wide, deep ravine that cut diagonally across to the Roman right flank.

At five minutes after three in the morning, they arrived at their objective. The perfect hour, when the circadian rhythm of human life ebbed lowest. It was the time of deepest sleep, when dreams formed and the body became sodden with relaxation. Working two to each gun, the mountain men placed the spikes, then rapped on them with padded mallets. The soft thuds that accompanied each blow did indeed sound like the stomp of a hoof. Preacher had insisted that they not strike together or too rapidly.

His precaution paid unexpected dividends. When the last spike had been broken off, they entered a small gully on hands and knees. Preacher's keen hearing picked up soft voices speaking in English from the main gate to the camp as they passed it.

"Lazy cavalry. Picketed their horses outside the camp," came a scornful remark.

"All right with me," the other sentry answered. "I don't like the smell of horse crap at breakfast."

A soft chuckle rose for a moment. "Considering what they feed us, how can you tell the difference?"

Like soldiers anywhere, Preacher thought as he crawled away.

They reached the second trio of cannons without incident. Preacher squared off on the flattened top of a lead plumb bob and gave it a whack. Ice shot down his spine a second later when an inquiring voice came from behind the palisade.

"What'cha doin' out there with horses?"

Preacher thought fast. He'd have to make some response. Fortunately the question had been in English. "Early patrol. The generals are getting nervous." He could speak as correctly as any man when he chose to do so.

"You horse soldiers have it made," came an envious response.

"Don't we though?" Preacher hoped the man would shut up with that. He did not like the idea of chatting away with the enemy when there were so many so close.

"Good luck," served as words of dismissal. Preacher let go a soft sigh of relief.

Plop! came from another cannon touch hole. Then again. Then it was Preacher's turn. He took a swat, then glanced nervously at the stockade. Two more followed his. He suddenly realized he was sweating bullets. Much of this could take years off a life. He tugged at the spike to check its set, then hit it on the shaft. It bent but did not break off. Damn. He did not dare risk another. Preacher raised his hand to signal the others, and they stole off into the darkness, their task completed.

Preacher's small party, and those who had attacked the watch towers around the rim, waited out the rest of the night on the intermediate ridge. Their horses would be brought up to them. Elated, and relieved that they had encountered no difficulties in the night's activities, Preacher chose to spend his wait on a good snooze. He reckoned as how he would need every bit of alertness and stamina he could recover during the day to come. An hour before dawn, the main force arrived. Preacher roused himself to speak with the leaders.

"Yellow Hawk, I want you and your warriors to take your place where I told you about now. Have 'em keep low and be danged quiet. They must stay complete out of sight until I give the signal."

Preacher had brought along six fat, greasy, paper-wrapped sticks of blasting powder from the trading post. He had caps and fuse for them in his saddlebag. Some would be used to distract and confuse the enemy, or to blow down the gates to the city. The first one would be to signal the Arapaho to attack.

"Have them take plenty water gourds, too. Wouldn't do for 'em to get too thirsty to fight proper."

Yellow Hawk nodded his understanding. "You have fought many more battles than I, Ghost Wolf. It is good to have wise counsel. Only one thing worries me. That we are not to fight in the open, pick our enemy and count coup before we slay him and go for another. We have never fought this way before."

"Let's hope you never have to again," Preacher said fervently, recalling his earlier thoughts on the subject. "But this time it is important. The way the Romans fight makes it so. Now, if you please, go on and put the braves in the right places."

Preacher turned his attention to the others. "Philadelphia, you'll lead our boys in this fracas. I'll be quarterin' the field between you an' the Cheyenne. It's gonna be pure hell to keep them dog soldiers from breakin' ranks and countin' coup before we can spring the trap. So I'll mostly be with them."

"Think they'll listen to you?" Philadelphia asked with an eye on the patient Indians who remained with their mountain men allies.

"They'd better, if they want to stay alive. In the right

hands, them javelins have might near the range of a Cheyenne arrow. They ain't like a head-heavy flint lance point. Timin'. Everything in this counts on timin'. We're outnumbered, sure's hell. But if we do this right, there won't be enough Roman soldiers left to form one of those . . . what do you call them ten-man outfits?"

"Contaburnium," Buck Sears supplied.

"Yeah. That's the one."

Buck scratched his head. "You seem so sure of this, Preacher. Did you learn it from some army feller?"

"I'll tell you about it later, Buck. Right now, I want to go convince Blind Beaver to keep a lid on his men." Before he could do that, he had one more task to complete. He squatted before Terry and put a big, hard hand on one slim shoulder.

"You do right like I said. Stay here on this ridge tomorrow. Don't move a muscle."

Shortly after the sun rose two fingers over the eastern rim of the valley, the mountain-man-and-Indian army crested the ridge to the south. Not a signal went out to announce their arrival. Below, in the camps of the legions, the soldiers went about their morning fatigue duties of taking down the stockade and tents. The approaching host had ridden halfway down the reverse slope when someone first noticed them.

Brassy blasts on the long, straight, valveless trumpets sent the men hastily to their weapons. Tent mates helped one another into their breastplates and greaves. Bawling NCOs brought order to the ranks, which formed in the traditional Roman squares. By then, the bandsmen had been assembled.

While the invaders walked their horses onto the floor of the meadow, the *buccinae* hooted and the *clarinae* tooted, while the *timpanii* throbbed and rumbled in fine martial style. Lastly, the legates of the legions appeared, dashing on their powerful chargers, the cavalry legion of Varras swinging into the traditional position in the order of battle. They took their reports from their adjutants and began to exhort the legionnaires to do their utmost in battle. The enemy rode inexorably closer.

At about two thousand yards, their double line began to change shape. The flanks, two ranks deep, curved inward, while the middle, consisting of three ranks, hung back slightly. When they had molded in a bison-horn formation, they halted. All of this brisk human activity had frightened the small animals and birds to flight or silence. When the invaders halted, an eerie silence enveloped both sides. Curious eyes studied the "barbarians."

Equally curious eyes took in the boxlike formations of the legions from the other side. Squinty Williams nudged Philadelphia in the ribs. "What they all bunched up like that for? They're just askin' for a shower of Cheyenne arrows."

"We'll find out soon enough, I reckon, Squinty," Braddock replied. "Accordin' to Preacher, the old-timey Romans were real mean fighters. Whupped ever'body they went against."

"Wull, they didn't never come against us fellers, I bet."

Philadelphia stifled the laugh that rose in his chest. "No, Squinty, they didn't."

Abruptly the drums opposite them began to throb. Bull-roar voices bellowed orders. In full regalia, complete with cavalry and band, the Roman legions began to march forward like a single man, rather than nearly nine hundred.

Marcus Quintus Americus gazed over the ranks of his brave legions. Pride swelled his heart. They were ready. They surely were honed as fine as any soldiers could be. They had about a thousand *stadia* to cover, and then the cannons would open up. The legions had heard them fired enough not to falter when they blasted away. And then the cohorts would pick up the pace to a trot, pilae slanted forward at eye level to these unprotected barbarians.

Riflemen would open up at the same time. This should be over soon enough that he could be back in the palace for a soothing bath and a light lunch. How tedious these matters could be. It would bloody the legions, which they would need. Knowledge of New Rome had undoubtedly become widespread outside the valley. Secrecy could not be maintained forever, he knew. Yet, he had hoped to keep the true enemy ignorant of his power and intentions for a while longer. A sudden shout came from ahead of him at the left-hand battery. It was repeated by stentorians until he could make meaning of the sounds.

"The cannon have been spiked! The cannon are useless!"

Those fateful words chilled Quintus. Everything hinged on the artillery. He looked about him in serious despair. He had to act. He must do something, and it had to be right.

23

It wouldn't do to start off with all this fanfare and then retreat in the face of a determined, if small, hostile force. There could not be more than a hundred and fifty of them, Marcus Quintus made a quick, inaccurate tally. *Be decisive.* The words mocked him. Yet, he must do something. Marcus Quintus turned to the trumpeter beside him.

"Sound for the legates," he commanded.

With a nod, the signalman put the mouthpiece of his instrument, one which had been coiled to compact it, to his lips and blew. It produced a mellower note than the straight trumpets. At once, Glaubiae, Bruno and Varras turned the heads of their mounts and cantered to the center. They saluted formally.

Quintus spoke brusquely, not meeting their eyes. "I am sure you heard the disastrous news. Somehow those barbarians had the wit to infiltrate our encampment and spike the cannons. That places the burden of victory more directly upon your soldiers. We will advance within range of our archers and pilae. The cavalry is to divide and take positions to sweep those thin flanks back on the main body."

"First Citizen," Varras spoke urgently. "I recommend against splitting my force."

"Why not?" Now Quintus glared directly into the black eyes of Varras. "Given a good shower of arrows and javelins, these unarmored louts will break ranks and flee. You will be able to slaughter them at your leisure."

"Need I remind you that they all have guns? Even most of the red savages."

Quintus found that a subject for contempt. "Savages cannot hit what they shoot at. See that it is done as I have said. I will take the center in my chariot."

He dismounted and climbed to the platform of the gold-chased chariot. There he drew a silver inlay *gladius* and held it at the ready. Disgruntled, yet keeping their tongues silent, the legates of the three legions of New Rome rode back to their commands. There they conveyed the orders of their supreme commander, and the cavalry departed for the flanks of the mountain men's formation.

When they reached the desired location, Quintus raised his sword and ordered his troops forward. The band began again, and the soldiers stepped out with a steady, measured tread. They came right on until a distance of only fifty yards separated them from the invaders. Not unlike an exercise on the drill field, the commands barked from centurions to sergeants to the men. Javelins hissed through the air while arrows arched above and moaned their eerie song.

"Now ain't that obligin' of them to come in so close?" Philadelphia Braddock drawled.

Preacher agreed with him. "Sure enough is. Steady on, boys," he added as the Romans halted, their formation still perfect.

Then came the commands to fire. The projectiles seethed through the air. Unlike the static squares of the Roman soldiers, the mountain men and Cheyenne allies were free to move at will. Which they did by jumping their horses forward enough to be missed by the missiles. A split second after recovering from the movement, they fired a ragged volley.

Bullets punched right through bull-hide shields. Even the brass ornaments on them yielded to .56 caliber lead balls.

Preacher had taken aim at a fancy dude in a glittery uniform who seemed to be in command. His slug shattered the breast-bone of Yancy Taggart and ended the career of General Gaius Septimus Glaubiae. The gaudy uniform became a heap of lifeless clothing at the feet of the *primus pilus* of the Thirteenth Legion. At such short range, not a one of the mountain men and Indians could miss. One hundred fifty-seven Roman soldiers went down in that first volley.

Marcus Quintus Americus stared on in horror as he saw his senior general slain with casual indifference. Another flight of arrows and javelins answered the fire, only to be avoided while men rapidly reloaded. The air turned blue with powder smoke once again.

Preacher made quick note that the discipline of the troops they faced had begun to falter. With a little luck, he might not even need to use the Arapahos. He drew a .44 Walker Colt, and the mountain men around him went to pistols also. The more rapid fire had a withering effect on the legions.

It had even more on the fancy-dressed fellow in the two-wheeled cart, Preacher realized as that one—it must be that Marcus Quintus—shouted an order. Another shower of arrows and then the Romans began to withdraw, marching backward, long rows of leveled javelins pointed at the men whom they left in command of the field.

"Well, if that don't just beat all," Preacher declared wonderingly. "Don't know what to make of that."

"Me neither," Philadelphia remarked. "A feller gets himself all worked up for a fight like they did, it usual lasts a spell. They sure's the devil had us outnumbered."

"They may be back. Best pull back a ways and stand fast. I mark that Quintus feller to be a tricky bastard."

While the archers let fly another deadly flock and the soldiers hurled their slender javelins, Marcus Quintus Americus looked around him in confusion. Another ragged volley came from fifty yards off. Why weren't his own riflemen firing?

For a moment, it plagued him; then he recalled that he had assigned them to cover the cavalry, which as yet had not engaged the enemy. Another thought struck him.

He would have to get a replacement for Gaius Septimus. His first spear had all the imagination and initiative of a stone post. Who could it be? Rufus Longinus of the Second? Yes. He had almost as much knowledge of military matters as Glaubiae had possessed. Bruno could get himself a new *primus pilus*. But this was hardly the place to hand out promotions. He turned to right and left, bawling out the most bitter order ever given by a commander.

"Fall back on the camp. Make it in good order and keep an eye on the enemy."

Trumpets sounding, the order was relayed by the adjutants of each legion, one in temporary command of his. Slowly the tramp of thick-soled military sandals sounded, and the century squares became a retrograde movement. Dust began to rise in thick clouds. Not enough, though, to mask, let alone protect, potential targets.

Although puzzled by the retreat, the mountain men and Indians kept up a steady fire into the dwindling ranks of the legions until they maneuvered out of range. Quintus ordered his chariot to turn and get around the formations of troops. He wanted to be calmed and refreshed when he met with his generals to promote one man and offer advice. Tomorrow would be a far better day, he convinced himself. Besides, the omens had not been all that promising at the morning sacrifice.

Four-Eyes Finney seemed mightily pleased with himself. "He who hits and runs away . . . ," he quoted.

"Is a yellow-bellied cur," Jack Lonesome added his own version to the end.

"Naw, that ain't it, Lonesome," Four-Eyes corrected. "It's about livin' to fight another day."

"Why'd they run? Why didn't we just finish them here an' now?" the grizzled mountain man pressed his point.

"Tell you what, Jack," Preacher began diplomatically. "We got 'em whittled down some, and it's for certain sure those cannons don't work. But there's at least five of them for each one of us. What say we pull back to the base of the ridge and settle in. They'll do somethin' 'fore long."

Preacher turned out to be right on that. An hour later, three officers, one with a white flag, rode out from the Roman camp. With them came a number of soldiers and a line of wagons. The one with the truce flag advanced to where the mountain men lolled on the ground, eating and sharing some scarce whiskey.

"Which one of you is the general in charge?"

Preacher came to his boots and tucked the stick of jerky he had been gnawing on in a shirt pocket. "I reckon that would be me. But I ain't no gen'ral."

"What do you call yourself?"

"Folks around these parts call me Preacher."

"By Jupiter and all the gods," the young Varras blurted. "Gaius told us you were the one we saw fight in the arena." His tone turned rueful, and his expression became wry. "No one but you could have made good on that escape." He saw that his flattery had no effect on Preacher. That decided him to come to the point.

"We came to ask permission to recover our dead and wounded."

"He'p yourselves. We've got no quarrel with them."

"But you do with us?"

"Somethin' like that. There's those among us who don't take kindly to having our friends made into slaves and forced to fight to the death."

The trio of officers exchanged glances. The one in the middle, with the flag of truce, looked back at Preacher. "What's wrong with that? It's a good way for a barbarian to make a living." They all laughed.

Preacher instantly developed a thunderous expression. "You keep that up an' you'll be joinin' those you came to get."

Varras' protest came at once. "Bu-but we're under a flag of truce."

Preacher reached up and yanked the white flag from the astonished general's hands. "Funny, I don't see a damn thing."

Youngest and the most nervous of the junior officers, the one on his left spoke in a soft, quiet voice. "Legate Varras, I think he's serious."

"At least *you've* got it right, Sonny," Preacher snapped.

Touching a lightly trembling finger to his lips, the youthful general pushed his point. "Let's—uh—get on with it, shouldn't we?"

To their stiff backs, Preacher said, "You can come back for this rag when you're done." To the others he spoke in a low tone. "We're gonna have to do somethin' about that rudeness."

By the time the dead and wounded had been retrieved from the field, darkness hovered on the ridge to the east. Westward, magenta and gold washed over the pale blue of the sky. Preacher had men busy making objects from the thorns taken from the underbrush and rawhide strips. While they worked, he went among them, explaining what would happen.

"When it gits good and dark, we're gonna take these things out and scatter them in front of those little movable forts of theirs. Really sew the ground with them. Then some of us is gonna pay a visit to the big city."

"How do ve get past dose soldiers?" Bloody Hand Kreuger asked in a surly tone.

"*Ve* don't. You'll be with the others spreading these here caltrops. Horses don't like 'em much and men don't either. Messes up their walkin' right smart. I'll pick those goin', and everyone eat a good meal. We'll start out at midnight."

True to his word, Preacher led an expedition out from their camp at midnight. He and eleven others would penetrate into the city and cause what havoc they could contrive. Another party, under charge of Philadelphia Braddock, set off to scatter the deadly four-point caltrops in the tall grass outside the Roman camps. Preacher's picks had smeared soot and grease on their faces, and all wore dark clothing.

They had a variety of flopped hats and animal-skin caps to break up the regularity of the shape of their heads. All carried pistols and knives, a few tomahawks. Rifles would only hamper them. At Preacher's direction, fire pit trestles had been heated and one end of each bent into a hook. Ropes had been attached and knots tied along their length. Preacher had remained secretive about the purpose of these.

When they reached the walls, the fires burned low behind the palisades and everything lay in silence. Preacher wrapped his hook in cloth and shook out a length of rope. He gave it a steady swing, moving his hand and arm faster with each circle. At last he let it go and it sailed upward. It struck a foot short with a soft thump. When it dropped back, Preacher tried again. Once more he failed.

"This one'll do 'er," he assured the others in a whisper.

It didn't.

At last, on the fifth toss, the hook sailed over the wall and stuck fast when Preacher pulled on the rope. Quickly the others with hooks began to throw them at the battlement. When the sixth one caught, Preacher leaned back and went up his hand over hand, feet braced against the outside of the rampart. More men quickly followed until all twelve had scaled the barrier.

"We're here, now what?" Squinty Williams asked.

"I'd say a visit to the baths," Preacher offered.

"Me?" Squinty squeaked out. "I've done took my summer bath."

"I was thinking of breaking a few things in there and flooding the streets," Preacher responded. "You won't even have to take off those ripe-smellin' moccasins, Squinty."

"Don't you be doin' that to me, Preacher. I'll have to swim for it if you break that place apart."

"Not if you run fast enough. Now, let's go."

The twelve-man party made it to the baths without the *vigilii* spotting them. Inside, they subdued the night watchman and spread out through the series of pool rooms. Buck Sears led the way to the confluence of the underground waterways. There they plied crowbars and mauls to break the plaster away and penetrate the brick walls.

In no time after that, they were walking ankle deep in swift-flowing water. It spread through the baths and headed for the front door. Enough done here, Preacher thought. He directed them to split up into pairs and go do mischief.

"Keep a sharp eye for those watchmen," he cautioned. He and Squinty headed for the central square, the forum.

"What are we going to do there?"

Preacher chuckled as he explained. "We're gonna wake up some ladies and scare them out of their nightshirts."

Squinty cocked his head, then shook it. "You actual thinkin' about dallyin' with some wimmin in a place as dangerous as this?"

"Nooo. Just scare the Vestal Virgins a mite. Stir up some hullabaloo."

Portia Andromeda awakened to something that she had not believed possible. A man in the cloisters of the Temple of Vesta! Not only a man, but a brute-ugly one at that. He had a hairy face, gaps in his teeth, which were too dark to be healthy, eyes too close together and squinched up. The shock of it robbed her of immediate speech.

"What are you gawkin' at, you ugly old prune?" a raspy voice asked her.

By the gods, are those animal skins he is wearing? Portia asked herself. In all of her years in service to Vesta, she had never seen such a creature. As senior priestess, she must maintain her composure, her brain reminded her.

"Get out of this cell," she demanded coldly, finding her voice at last.

A shriek came from another cell down the hallway. Had the barbarian army defeated the legions and entered the city? No. That was too preposterous to believe.

"How about a little kiss first, Sister?"

And then, Portia herself screamed. It seemed to come up from her toes to ululate through wide-stretched lips that trembled from more than the force of her wail. When she again opened her eyes, the man had disappeared.

"Where we headed now?" Squinty asked Preacher after they left the cloisters in shrieking feminine confusion.

"To the gladiator school," Preacher told him simply.

"You joshin' me, ain'tcha?"

"Nope. I told Buck and the others to meet us there."

"What do you want to go there for?"

"Simple, Squinty. There's bound to be about fifty highly trained fighting men locked up in there. We're gonna let them out. If they wants to join us, they'll be welcome."

"I can see that. We need more on our side, right enough. Only, what if they want to stay right there and are willing to fight to do it?"

"We can leave those locked up. Down that street there, the Via Julius."

Fires had drawn all of the watch away from seeking those who had started them. The twelve mountain men reached the gladiator school within five minutes of one another. Preacher advised speed.

"We've got to do this quick-like. Go in, free the ones want to come with us, and get out. Then it's for the walls."

Two guards at the entrance to the cells died swiftly, downed by .44 bullets from one of Preacher's Walker Colts. A quick twist of key in lock and the men beyond began to yell in confusion and some in rekindled hope. Preacher and his band moved rapidly along the corridor, snapping back the wooden bolts that held the cell doors. Forty-seven wanted to join in the fight against New Rome.

"There's all sorts of firearms in a storage room I'll show you in the house of Bulbus." They cheered him loudly as Preacher and Buck set out to lead the way.

All of the noise in the streets had awakened Bulbus. He looked wistfully at the trim posterior of the young slave girl in his bed, gave the bare buttocks a pat and climbed from his bed-clothes. Once fully dressed, he headed for the atrium. He got there at the same time the mountain men swarmed into the central courtyard garden.

Swords and javelins proved no hindrance to the blazing pistols of the wild and woolly men of the High Lonesome. They brought down the five guards in as many seconds and surged toward the stores. Suddenly angry beyond any vestige of fear, Bulbus went for them with a *gladius* flashing in his pudgy hand. Preacher turned in time to see the blade poised to strike his head from his shoulders.

Having practiced long ago to speedily unlimber a six-gun, he filled his hand in a blur of controlled movement. The hammer came back and he squeezed the trigger. The small brass cap went off flawlessly, and the powder charge instantly followed. The .44 ball smacked into the thick middle of the master of games. A second ball went higher, through his heart, and flattened against his spine. Bulbus dropped the sword and staggered toward the fountain.

With a mighty cry, which sounded of regret more than pain, he pitched over the lip of the basin and splashed face-first into the water. Preacher watched Bulbus' right foot jerk spasmodically for a second and then turned to the men.

"Right through there. Pick the best, there's plenty of it. An' bring along all the powder, shot and caps you can haul. We have to beat these Roman mongrels to the wall."

* * *

Preacher soon found that they had lost the race to the parapets. Helmeted soldiers lined the southern and western ones. He veered his much larger band into a darkened street and plunged along it toward the east wall.

Only a dozen men topped that bastion, Preacher discovered when they reached it. Easy as anything. He picked out five of the ex-gladiators who had taken helmets from the fallen guards and sent them up the stone steps.

"Tell 'em you've been drafted to help defend the city," he instructed.

Halfway up the stairway, the "relief" force had attracted the attention of all but one of the soldiers. That was when thirty shots cracked in sharp echoes off the walls of buildings and the stone barrier. Thirty balls sieved the defenders, who pitched headfirst off the parapet or lay where they had fallen. Preacher led the way up after the decoys.

At the top he found a determined sergeant holding the two former gladiators at bay with a *gladius*. Preacher looked at the other man for a second, then clucked his tongue as he fired a fatal shot to the forehead of the sergeant. Then he studied their surroundings.

"Too bad we didn't get back to our ropes. We'll have to go back down and get out through that little bitty gate."

Several looked at Preacher as though he were mad. "We can't make it," one protested.

"I say we can. Now, git movin'."

With trusted mountain men to serve as rear guard, Preacher started the freed gladiators through the low, narrow gate toward the outside. He cautioned them to remain quiet and stay close to the base of the wall. They might not know about the movable forts of the Romans. Nearly half of the escapees had disappeared into the tunnellike passage through the thick base of the stone rampart when others discovered their presence.

Some sixteen of the *vigilii* rounded the corner nearest the portal and stopped abruptly. These watchmen carried javelins in addition to their swords, Preacher noted at once. Made edgy by the sudden uproar within their city, and so far unable to account for it, the men of the watch reacted quickly. They all rocked back, and each hurled a *pilum*.

One whistled past the left ear of Preacher, even as he drew his left-hand Walker Colt. He eared back the hammer the moment the weapon came clear of the holster and quickly aligned the sights. The big .44 bucked in his hand, and one of the watchmen cried out in pain. Other pistols fired a moment later. Eight of the watchmen had gone down in the first exchange. Preacher aimed at another and fired again.

In such an unfair contest, there could be no doubt of the outcome. The remaining eight died in a hail of bullets. Unfortunately, it served to announce the presence of the invaders to those on the walls. Hard sandal soles scuffed on the stones of the parapet as other sentries called to one another and closed in on the knot of men at the gate below.

"The main gate! Open the gate! Barbarians in the city," one leather-lunged soldier bellowed.

While legionnaires poured in through the slowly opening portals, Preacher urged all speed and left New Rome at last. Behind him, the sky glowed orange from the fires in the buildings and gardens of New Rome. Alarmed shouts rose to the stars. Women and children were trampled by panicked citizens and the confused legions who hunted for a phantom enemy. Now all they need do was get past the legion camps and safely back to the ridge. Yeah, that was all.

24

Once again, daylight found the legions drawn up outside the bastions of New Rome. With blaring brass and throbbing drums, they formed their battle squares and began a slow, stately advance toward the distant collection of what Marcus Quintus Americus referred to as rabble and gutter-born barbarians. Like before, those he held in such disdain spread out in a long, double line and came forward. Following their strategy of the previous day, they deployed into a bison-horn formation. Only this time they were nearly fifty stronger. That had caused some dispute, and not a little discontent, among the generals.

All was not well in New Rome, they maintained. The turmoil of the past night had left deep marks on many. The senior Vestal Virgin and the Chief Priests of Jupiter and Mars had argued against resuming the battle so soon. The dawn auguries had foretold misfortune, they explained. One of the doves had been missing a heart, and the sheep had a large tumor on its liver. Furious at the insult handed him by the barbarians within his own walls, Marcus Quintus Americus scoffed at the omens for the first time since he had begun his childhood sacrifices at age ten.

Since then, he had completely forgotten his identity as Alexander Reardon. Like his son, he had been fascinated by blood as a child, and had taken an exhilarating, sensual pleasure in tormenting, killing, and examining the entrails of small animals. Now, enraged by the humiliation he felt, he turned his back on that and ordered the legions forward. Although still deprived of his cannons, the process of clearing the touch holes long and tedious, and requiring precision, he went forth with high expectations. The forces of New Rome still outnumbered the enemy by better than five to one. He sent the infantry against the center of the enemy line, now three ranks deep.

Riflemen opened fire first. He had included a number of them with the infantry this time. Poorly trained at best, they had little effect beyond causing a few of the scruffily dressed barbarians to duck with exaggerated motions, which elicited raucous laughter from their fellows. The steady tramp-tramp of sandals made a hypnotic rhythm as the infantry continued to advance. This would be easy! The legions would roll over this ragtag collection like a giant wave, Quintus thought to himself. He had instructed his generals to have the men take as many prisoners as possible. The games that would follow would be quite amusing.

"When they git to a hundred yards, open up on them," Preacher ordered in a calm voice.

Obediently, the mountain men raised their rifles and took aim. The pretty boys in the band would get the worst of it, Preacher considered, pleased that there were noticeably fewer of them today. When the heads of the musicians rested in the buckhorn rear sights of the long guns of the mountain men, a ragged volley erupted along the line. The first rank knelt to reload while the second immediately fired over their heads.

Down went a third of the band and one centurion behind them. The range had closed to seventy-five yards. Another crash of weapons from the third rank. By then the first rank had reloaded and discharged their rifles from the kneeling position. With each man who dropped in the front rank of the advancing cohorts, another took his place from behind. At fifty yards, there was no longer a band, and the last volley barked from the rifles. From here on it would take too long to reload.

At fifty yards, the first flight of arrows hissed from the Roman squares. Three men among the ex-gladiators went down with slight wounds. Two in the front file, intent on readying their pistols, died for their incaution, transfixed by Roman arrows. The flat reports of handguns filled the air. The Roman enemy kept coming.

With all ranks firing and the flanking "horns" of the formation engaged also, the legions began to falter and slow. Preacher bellowed loudly to his army.

"Hold fast. Just a little longer now. An' watch out for them spears."

A flight of javelins seethed through the blue morning to rattle and quiver when they struck only grassy turf. Another flock of deadly, feathered shafts took flight. To be answered by the roar of a hundred pistols. Cheyenne shafts answered them. More javelins arched in the sky and moaned through their descent. The shield wall of the Romans had closed to within twenty feet. Spear tips darted like the tongue of a rattler, probed all before them. Another bark of pistols brought down thirty soldiers.

Preacher emptied one Colt six-gun and drew the other. Soon now. He eased up the stick of blasting powder from behind his belt and made sure it would come free easily. Three legionnaires brought down as many among the ex-gladiators. They launched a final cluster of spears and drew their swords.

Suddenly the Cheyenne wavered and began to give ground. Soon the entire middle did the same. Menaced by the darting blades of the legionnaires, they appeared to have entirely lost their nerve.

Marcus Quintus saw it at once. He pointed out the faltering lines to Rufus Longinus at his side. "See? The savages flee in disorder from my magnificent legionnaires," he smugly brayed. "They won't last long now."

Inexorably the Roman center was drawn deeper inside the tips of the "horns," something which held not the least significance for Marcus Quintus. His chest swelled with pride as he saw for the first time a litter of barbarian and Indian bodies on the ground, rather than only his soldiers. Aware now that the one commanding his enemies was the living legend, Preacher, Marcus Quintus took extreme pleasure from watching the destruction of the invaders. He turned to Longinus again.

"Send a messenger to Varras. Have his cavalry sweep the field obliquely. They are to try to get around behind the enemy and prevent any escapes."

"As you wish, First Citizen." Privately, Rufus did not like this the least bit. The evolution of the battle plan had a hauntingly all too familiar appearance. Something they had studied at West Point, he recalled, back in another lifetime, but not the name of the engagement or its outcome.

Stubbornly, the three ranks, minus the Indians, continued to hold, though now bowed in slightly. Then the cavalry began their charge. They had ridden only a few lengths, enough to be within the limits of the "horns," when the buckskin-clad Preacher raised his arm and arched his body sharply. He hurled an object with all his strength.

It exploded a foot off the ground and disintegrated four legionnaires. A dozen more received injuries. Then, before the horrified eyes of Varras, the Arapaho, who had been hidden in a deep ravine to the left rear of the battle formations, rose up and fell upon the horsemen and the backs of the advancing cohorts.

Preacher timed the throw perfectly. With scant seconds left of the fuse, he hurled the blasting powder with all his might. "Let 'er rip!" he shouted to those around him.

With the roar of the explosion fresh in their ears, the

mountain men steadied their line, and as the Arapaho seemed to materialize out of the very ground, the Cheyenne turned back to face the enemy. They laughed and hooted to show their complete lack of intimidation. It had a disastrous effect on the Romans. So did another stick of blasting powder that landed in the midst of a battle square.

Bodies flew through the air, and parts sailed higher. Dust cloaked everything, and the screams of men dying to their rear demoralized the front ranks. The tight, disciplined Roman formations dissolved into swirling masses of men, desperately engaged in hand-to-hand fighting.

A terrible slaughter began. On a low hill nearby, young Terry Tucker danced from foot to foot in anxiety. The night before, he had won his contest with Preacher to be allowed closer to the battle. He had not seen *anything* from the tower on the ridge. Even here, the dust had grown so thick he could no longer distinguish Preacher from the other fighters.

The conflict lasted for hours as the Arapaho and Cheyenne took revenge for their murdered brothers. Reduced to tomahawks and big, wide-bladed fighting knives, the mountain men hewed through the struggling legionnaires with deadly accuracy. The scent of blood thickened the air in a cloying, coppery miasma. Unremittingly, the numbers diminished for the Romans. Preacher's men were able to fall back and take time to reload pistols. Their addition to the fray took a brutal toll.

At last, the bedraggled survivors among the legions broke off and fled the field for the imagined safety of New Rome. Preacher called out to halt pursuit.

"Hold back now! We gotta get organized. Then we go after them. I want a tally of how many we have fit to fight."

Subordinate leaders, appointed by Preacher, and the war chiefs of Arapaho and Cheyenne made quick head counts. It turned out that only forty had been killed—less than the number who had joined from the gladiator school. Another sixty had been wounded, ranging from serious to cuts and scrapes. It left Preacher mightily pleased.

Blue Nose Herkimer swaggered up to Preacher, who was cleaning his revolvers and Hawken rifle with little Terry Tucker standing proudly at his side. Herkimer had a big smile plastered on his face. He clapped Preacher on one shoulder. "That was sure something, I declare. Never seed the like. How come those fellers was so dumb as to fall for it?"

Preacher thought on that a moment. "They failed to scout the battlefield. And, I reckon they never had much use for old fights fought a long ways off."

"How's that?" Herkimer asked. "An' more to the point, how'd *you* know what to do an' that it would work?"

An enigmatic smile bloomed on Preacher's face. "A little reading I did a while back," Preacher informed him. "About a feller named Hannibal and the Battle of Cannae."

With his forces rallied now, Preacher went about laying siege to Nova Roma. The palisades of pointed-tip lodgepole pine saplings came down first, then the gaudy tents of the officers and plain ones of the enlisted men. From the bastions, the defeated Roman legions looked on in numb disbelief. How had it happened? How *could* it happen?

More than one asked that of his comrades. Meanwhile, given the distance between the camps and the city, they could retaliate against their primitive enemy only by hurling a few stones and large darts from ballistae and arbalests. Preacher had even considered it safe enough to allow Terry Tucker to join him. With night coming on, the destruction was completed. Fires were kindled and the invaders enjoyed sumptuous hot meals from the supplies of the officers of the legions. At least, the demoralized legionnaires consoled themselves, there would be no more fighting this day.

Early the next morning, their respite ended. Under cover of the most expert marksmen among the mountain men, Preacher rode to the large southern gates and buried the last four sticks of blasting powder under one pivotal corner. He tamped it down firmly, and wedged a big, flat piece of limestone between the ground and the wooden portal. Then he lighted the fuse and swung atop Cougar to race away without a scratch.

Moments later, the explosion shook the ground and threw gouts of dirt higher than the walls. When the smoke and dust cleared, the gate panel hung drunkenly on its upper hinge, canted sharply inward. The scaling ladders would not be needed. A superstitious mutter rose among the Indians. A couple of mountain men made the sign of the cross.

"Awesome," Squinty Williams breathed softly.

Preacher was not done yet. "Let's go!" he shouted, waving a Walker Colt in the sign for an attack.

With a roaring shout, mingled with war whoops, the small army rushed the gate. Boiling water poured down on the assault force until sharpshooters picked off the soldiers who dumped it. Rocks rained down, along with a shower of arrows and javelins. Men fell screaming, yet nothing slowed them.

Mountain men swarmed through the opening and spread out in the streets. They left the legionnaires behind them for the Arapaho and Cheyenne to deal with. Those able warriors did so with grim efficiency. Far better trained, since childhood, they kept three arrows in the air to each one fired by the Romans. Those arrows hit their targets, tumbling legionnaires from the walls in a continuous spill. Shouts and the screams of the dying became a constant bedlam.

In a swirl, the battle turned into house-to-house fighting as the legionnaires abandoned the exposed positions on the wall and rallied in small numbers to resist the invaders. Leading a dozen stalwarts, Preacher made for the half-finished Imperial Palace. From the forum he had seen the distinctive figure of Marcus Quintus Americus disappear in that direction.

Twenty well-armed soldiers held them at bay half a block from the front of the marble structure. Their rifles cracked in irregular volleys. Preacher and the others spread out and returned fire. Two of the guards died. Another one screamed hideously when he discharged an inadvertently triple-loaded rifle. Three times the normal powder load ripped the breech plug from its threads and drove it into his mouth. It mushed his lips, shattered teeth, and embedded itself in the back of his head.

His scream changed to a gurgle that ended as he died. That broke the nerve of two others, who rose from behind the low wall and ran toward the building. Three quick shots dropped them. A deeply appreciated lull followed.

"I'm goin' around back. I got a feelin' that feller Quintus has got a lot of rabbit in him."

Preacher had the right of it about Marcus Quintus Americus. While the legionnaires fought and died outside to buy him time, the First Citizen of New Rome hastily stuffed large panniers full of gold bars and shouted for servants to hurry in packing his clothes. His wife, Titiana Pulcra, stood in one corner of the treasure room and dithered.

"Why are you doing this, Marcus?"

"Shut up, woman, and help me."

Shocked at his tone, Pulcra gathered her past store of grievances and responded hotly. "Alexander Reardon, don't you dare speak to me like that."

Shocked at that, Quintus paused with one ingot in each hand. His voice held an artificially calm tone. "I don't believe this, Pulcra. You have always obeyed me. Please do so now."

Pulcra began to weep. "It's all coming apart, isn't it? We are destroyed, I feel it in my heart." With a soul-wrenching sob she ran from the room.

Taken aback, Quintus stared after her, then recovered. "Faustus, come in here," he yelled. "Quintus Faustus, come to your father."

Woefully lacking in training, the two guards at the rear of the palace fired at the same time. It had been easy for Preacher to trick them into doing so. He had simply jumped into sight at the edge of a marble column, shouted and popped a round into the air. At once they brought up the rifles they carried and cut loose. By that time, Preacher had disappeared behind the pillar. Not even his great experience as a fighting man could prevent him from wincing when the fat balls smacked into the opposite side of the stone plinth. Then he came out with a 44 Colt blazing.

Down went one soldier, who had bent over his weapon to reload. The other died a second later. Preacher advanced when a voice came from behind him.

"Want some company?"

Buck Sears and Philadelphia Braddock grinned broadly as they approached. They found trouble the moment they entered the column-supported hallway. More *gladius*-waving soldiers awaited them. With hoarse shouts, the fighting men of New Rome came at the invaders.

"Dang," Preacher quipped. "What is it with these fellers who don't bring the right tools to a gunfight?"

He shot one in the chest, cocked his Walker Colt, and put his second .44 ball through the hand holding another *gladius*. The iron blade rang noisily when it hit the stone floor. Time to change. His second Colt brought down a third who moaned and rolled on the floor, clutching his belly.

Beside Preacher, Philadelphia took aim at a sergeant who lunged at him with a *pilum*. The javelin went wild as the mountain man discharged both barrels of his pistol at once. Slammed backward, the sergeant grew a shocked expression, his eyes wide, mouth round, while he clattered against a wall in numb shock and darkness settled over him.

Wisely, those remaining fled. Preacher sent a shot after them and hastily reloaded his pistols. That accomplished, they started toward the central core of the building.

A trembling messenger stood before Marcus Quintus Americus. Helmet tucked in the crook of his left arm, his face smeared with blood, dirt, and sweat, he panted out his litany of doom. "General Varras and what was left of the cavalry have been surrounded and destroyed by the red savages. General—er—Legate Longinus has fallen in street fighting near the forum. You already know about Legate Glaubiae."

Trembling from the effort to restrain himself, Quintus spoke with heavy sarcasm. "Is there any good news to tell me?"

"N-no, First Citizen. I mean, we continue to fight, and the enemy is taking losses . . ." his voice trailed off.

Bitterness colored the words of Quintus. "Only not so many as we, eh?" In a moment of clarity and sanity, he added in a tone of sorrow, "I am afraid the only advice I have is for you to find your way out of the palace and get as far from Nova Roma as you can."

Relieved not to have been summarily executed as the bearer of bad news, the young centurion nodded his agreement, saluted, then turned to make his departure. That was when Preacher, Philadelphia and Buck stormed into the room.

Preacher let out a roar when he recognized Marcus Quintus. His first shot went wild, but sent the centurion with the First Citizen to the floor in an ungainly sprawl. To his regret, the young officer had already learned that a *gladius* had little use against firearms. He hugged the marble floor, feigning death, until a boot toe dug painfully into his ribs. He grunted in discomfort and rolled over, intending to hack at a leg with his sword, only to find himself staring down the barrel of the oddest weapon he had ever seen.

It had a round part with holes in it that revolved when its owner pulled back on the spur at the rear. Beyond the extended hand and arm, a powder-begrimed face grinned at him.

"The Mezkins has got a sayin', feller," Preacher told him. "It's addyose."

And the centurion learned one final fascinating fact about the strange weapon. Flame spat from its mouth a moment before excruciating agony and utter blackness washed over him and the back of his head flew off. He never heard the bang. Preacher checked on his companions and found them otherwise occupied, each engaging four guards who had rushed into the treasury room at the sound of the Walker Colt. Grinning now, Preacher turned to Marcus Quintus.

"Looks like you're mine," he declared. "Reckon that's sort of fittin', you bein' the bull elk of this place."

"Quite fitting indeed. You really are Preacher, aren't you?"

"Yep. That's what folks call me."

"Then prepare to die like a man."

To the utter surprise of Quintus, Preacher threw back his head and laughed. "I don't allow as how it's gonna be me does the dyin'," he brayed.

Quintus snatched up his *gladius* from the table where he had laid it and charged Preacher. The mountain man held his ground until the distance between them closed to ten feet. Then he raised his arm and squeezed the trigger of his .44 Colt.

Nothing happened. Only a loud click. In the heat and speed of battle, Preacher had forgotten to count the number of rounds he had fired since last reloading. He jumped aside as Quintus made a mighty swing with his sword, and drew his second Colt. The heft of it in his hand told him that it, too, had been fired dry. Quintus came on, and Preacher nimbly jumped over a table, putting it between himself and the Roman tyrant.

"That will not do you any good," Quintus spoke in precise English.

It gave Preacher time to draw his tomahawk. Over the years, the old war hawk had stood him well. He hoped it would again. Quintus lunged over the small table. Preacher batted the leaf-shaped blade of the *gladius* away with the iron head of his war axe. Quintus developed an expression of surprised appreciation. A truly worthy opponent. He maneuvered to get past the barrier that kept him at a disadvantage.

Preacher countered it. A sharp scream punctuated by a gurgling gasp told of another legionnaire on his way to his

Maker. Preacher did not break his concentration as Quintus reached a low commode beside a desk. His left hand darted out and snatched up the bowl of pine nuts resting there. With a bellow intended to freeze his opponent, he hurled the confection at Preacher. Quintus followed it.

A spray of roasted pine nuts hit Preacher in the face. Quintus made a horizontal slash with his *gladius* that cut through the buckskin shirt and opened a fairly deep line across Preacher's pectoral muscles. Blood flowed in a curtain. Quintus had little time to savor his brief victory.

Ignoring the pain and accompanying weakness, Preacher swung his tomahawk, and the keen edge bit into flesh in Quintus' left shoulder. The Roman grunted and staggered precariously close to the edge of the table. In the last moments, he righted himself and leaped to the larger counter where the gold reserves had rested earlier. Fire throbbed in his deltoid muscle as the blade of the war hawk tore free. Quintus made another pass at Preacher as he gained the storage shelf.

Preacher batted the *gladius* aside with the flat of the 'hawk and did a fast, two-step shuffle forward. When Quintus brought his arm up for an overhand stroke, Preacher aimed for the Roman's exposed knee. The tomahawk bit deeply, with a loud *plock!* that turned heads in other parts of the room. Face squinched in overwhelming pain and mouth open in a soundless howl, Quintus dropped to his good knee. With a kneecap split, his *gladius* became as useless as his other leg.

He abandoned it for the double-edged dagger on the belt at his waist as Preacher came at him again. Bright steel flashed in the air, and Quintus made a fortunate cut on the right forearm of his opponent. Preacher was forced to drop his tomahawk as blood streamed from a severed vein. Only then did Quintus remember the small .50 caliber coach pistol he had concealed in the folds of his battle cloak. He reached for it eagerly.

"Preacher, here," Philadelphia Braddock shouted when the deadly little pistol appeared in Quintus' hand.

Preacher caught the double-barreled pistol Philadelphia had tossed left-handed and fired it the same way.

"No!" Quintus shouted in useless denial as first one, then a second .60 caliber ball smashed into his body. His eyes went wide as they sought to capture some of the fading light in the room. His body would no longer obey his commands. Slowly he sagged down, his death rattle loud in the silence.

A sudden disturbance at one entranceway drew the attention of the mountain men from the dying man. *"Father!"* young Quintus Faustus shrieked as he dashed through the archway, a dagger held high.

He hurled himself at Preacher, intent on burying the slim blade in the man's heart. Seemingly from nowhere, little Terry Tucker darted into the room at an oblique angle to Preacher and flung himself between the man and the Roman boy.

His exposed chest took the full brunt of the blow aimed by Faustus, though not before he triggered a round from a small pistol he held. The ball blew the brains out of Quintus Faustus before Terry collapsed into the arms of the man he admired above all others.

"I—I got him, didn't I?" Terry gasped. Then, at Preacher's wooden nod, he slumped into unconsciousness.

Blood dripped from his fingertips as Preacher gently brushed the hair from Terry's face as he cradled the lad in his arm. "Awh, Terry, Terry-boy, didn't I tell you to stay clear of the fightin'? But you saved my life, certain sure. Today . . ." The words would not come. Preacher swallowed hard. "Today you became a real man. One I'd be proud to call friend. Go with God, Terry Tucker."

Terry must have heard him, for a small smile froze on his peaceful face as he quietly died.

Preacher took a deep breath and allowed himself no further time to grieve for the boy who had saved him. He brushed a knuckle at the moisture that stole stealthily from his eyes, cleared his throat, and came to his boots.

"What now, Preacher?" asked Philadelphia, reluctant to intrude on the mountain man's sorrow.

"I'd be obliged if you would bind this arm and my chest, Philadelphia. An' you, Buck, round up the rest. Tell them to clean up this abomination, pull down the buildings, and burn everything. Free any slaves, and any who want can he'p them down to Bent's Fort and a chance to return to a normal life."

"What about you, Preacher?" Philadelphia and Buck asked together.

"Me? Why, I'm off for my winter home. Got myself a nice, blond bed warmer a-waitin'."

"What?" a startled Philadelphia demanded. "You mean that frisky young gal what took up arms and fought her way out of the arena with us?"

Preacher sighed through a spreading grin. "Yeah, that's right. The once-upon-a-time Bible-thumper."

Connect with

Visit us online at
KensingtonBooks.com
to read more from your favorite authors, see books
by series, view reading group guides, and more.

for sneak peeks, chances to win books and prize packs,
and to share your thoughts with other readers.

facebook.com/kensingtonpublishing
twitter.com/kensingtonbooks

Tell us what you think!

To share your thoughts, submit a review,
or sign up for our eNewsletters, please visit:
KensingtonBooks.com/TellUs.